P9-CFG-804

Trading Up

Trading Up

CANDACE BUSHNELL

HYPERION NEW YORK

This book is a work of fiction; names, characters, and incidents are either products of the author's imagination or are used fictitiously. Any resemblance to actual events or persons, living or dead, is entirely coincidental.

Copyright © 2003 Candace Bushnell

All rights reserved. No part of this book may be used or reproduced in any manner whatsoever without the written permission of the Publisher. Printed in the United States of America. For information address: Hyperion, 77 West 66th Street, New York, New York 10023-6298.

Library of Congress Cataloging-in-Publication Data

Bushnell, Candace.
   Trading up : a novel / Candace Bushnell.
   p. cm.
   ISBN: 0-7868-6818-X
   1. Models (Persons)—Fiction. 2. Hamptons (N.Y.)—Fiction. 3. New York (N.Y.)—Fiction. 4. Young women—Fiction. I. Title.

PS3552.U8229T73 2003
813'.54—dc21

2003044963

Hyperion books are available for special promotions and premiums. For details contact Hyperion Special Markets, 77 West 66th Street, 11th floor, New York, New York 10023-6298, or call 212-456-0133.

FIRST EDITION

10 9 8 7 6 5 4 3 2 1

For my beautiful mother, Camille

And for my grandmothers:

Elsie Salonia, who was always
a big reader

The late Lucy and Lena

And my new grandmother, Jane

ACKNOWLEDGMENTS

And special thanks to the darling Anne Shearman for her title

Trading Up

Book one

IT WAS THE beginning of the summer in the year 2000, and in New York City, where the streets seemed to sparkle with the gold dust filtered down from a billion trades in a boomtown economy, it was business as usual. The world had passed into the new millennium peacefully, the president had again avoided impeachment, and Y2K had fizzled like an ancient bottle of French champagne. The city shone in all its magnificent, vulgar, and ruthless glory.

At that particular moment, the talk of the town was Peter Cannon, an entertainment lawyer who had bilked several celebrity clients out of an estimated $35 million. In the months and years that would follow, there would be more scandals, billions of dollars lost, and the general ripping off of the American public. But in the meantime, "the Peter Cannon affair" had involved enough bold-faced names to at least temporarily satisfy gossip-hungry New Yorkers. Everyone who was anyone either knew Peter or knew someone he had thrillingly cheated—and after all, they asked themselves, shouldn't his clients have known better?

One of the victims was a thirty-one-year-old rock musician named Digger. Digger was one of those one-name wonders who, like so many great artists, had modest beginnings coupled with slightly freakish looks. He hailed from Des Moines, Iowa, had dirty blond hair and frighteningly white translucent skin through which one could see blue veins, and was given to wearing porkpie hats, which were his trademark.

On the Friday afternoon of Memorial Day weekend, he was calmly sitting by the pool at his $100,000 summer rental in Sagaponack in the Hamptons, smoking a filterless cigarette and watching his wife, Patty, who was heatedly talking on the phone.

Digger stubbed out his cigarette in a pot of chrysanthemums (there was a small pile of cigarette butts in the pot that would later be removed by the gardener), and leaned back on a teak chaise longue. It was quite a beautiful day and he really couldn't understand what all the fuss over Peter Cannon was about. Being the sort of person who considered his purpose in life to be that of a higher nature than the grubby pursuit of filthy lucre, Digger had no real concept of the value of money. His manager estimated he had lost close to a million dollars, but to Digger, a million dollars was a shadowy abstract concept that could only be understood in terms of music. He figured he could earn back the million dollars by writing one hit song, but on that pleasant afternoon, ensconced in the lazy luxury of a Hamptons day, he seemed to be alone in his laissez-faire attitude.

His beloved wife, Patty, was in a stew, and for the past half hour had been blathering away on the phone to her sister, Janey Wilcox, a famous Victoria's Secret model.

As he gazed across the gunite pool to the gazebo where Patty sat hunched over the telephone, taking in her pleasing, slightly zaftig figure clad in a white one-piece bathing suit, she glanced up and their eyes met in mutual understanding. Patty stood up and began walking toward him, and as usual he was struck by the simplicity of her all-American beauty: the reddish blond hair that hung halfway down her back, the cute snub nose smattered with freckles, and her round blue eyes. Her older sister, Janey, was considered "a great beauty," but Digger had never seen it that way. Although Janey and Patty shared the same snub nose, Janey's face was too crafty and feral to attract him—and besides, he thought that Janey, with her screwed-up values about status and money, her flippant, arrogant airs, and her obsession with herself was, quite simply, a narcissistic asshole.

And now Patty stood before him, holding out the phone. "Janey wants to talk to you," she said. He pulled back his lips in a grimace, revealing small, unevenly spaced yellow teeth, and took the phone from Patty's hand.

"What's up?" he asked.

"Oh Digger." Janey's musical, slightly accented voice that always put him on edge came tinkling down the line. "I'm so sorry. I always knew Peter was going to do something really, really stupid. I should have warned you."

"How would you know?" Digger asked, picking a piece of tobacco out of his teeth.

"Well I dated him a few years ago," she said. "But only for a couple of weeks. He called everyone a fucking Polack . . ."

Digger said nothing. His real last name was Wachanski, and he wondered if Janey had intended the insult. "So . . . ?" he asked.

"So I always knew he was a creep. Darling, I'm so upset. What are you going to do?"

Digger looked at Patty and grinned. "Well, I figure if he needs my money that badly he can keep it."

There was a gasp on the other end of the line and then a small silence, followed by Janey's melodic laugh. "How terribly, terribly . . . Buddhist of you," she said, unable to keep a slight sneering tone out of her voice. And then, not knowing what else to say, she added, "I suppose I'll be seeing you at Mimi Kilroy's tonight."

"Mimi who?" Digger asked, adopting the same bored tone of voice he employed when someone asked him about Britney Spears. He knew exactly who Mimi Kilroy was, but, as she came from that segment of society that, like so many of his generation, he reviled—i.e., WASP Republican—he had no intention of giving Janey this satisfaction.

"Mimi Kilroy," Janey said, with mock patience. "Senator Kilroy's daughter . . ."

"Oh, right," Digger said. But he was no longer paying attention. Patty had sat down next to him and, shifting his weight, he wrapped a skinny leg around her waist. She turned her face toward his and touched his shoulder, and as usual he felt an overwhelming desire for her. "Gotta go," he said, clicking the OFF button on the phone. He pulled Patty on top of him and began kissing her face. He was deeply and romantically in love with his wife in a completely uncynical manner, and as far as he was concerned, that was all that mattered. Peter and Janey could go fuck themselves, he thought; and they probably would.

Well, really, Janey Wilcox thought. If Digger cared so little about money, why shouldn't he give some to her?

She peered through the windshield of her silver Porsche Boxster convertible at the endless stream of cars jammed up in front of her on the Long Island Expressway. It was so passé to be stuck in traffic on the way out to the Hamptons, especially if you were a supermodel. If *she* had an extra million, she thought, the first thing she'd do would be to take the seaplane out to the Hamptons, and then she'd get an assistant who would drive her car out for her, just like all of the rich men she knew. But that was the problem with New York: No matter how successful you thought you were, there was always someone who was richer, more successful, more famous . . . the idea of it was sometimes enough to make you want to give up. But the sight of the gleaming silver hood of her car revived her a little, and she reminded herself that at this point in her life there was no reason to give up—and every reason to press on. With a little self-control and discipline, she might finally get everything she'd always wanted.

Her pink Chanel sunglasses had slipped down her nose and she pushed them up, feeling a little thrill of satisfaction at owning the must-have accessory of the summer. Janey was one of those people for whom the superficial comfortingly masks an inner void, and yet if anyone had called her shallow she would have been genuinely shocked. Janey Wilcox was a particular type of beautiful woman, who, acknowledged only for her looks, is convinced that she has great reserves of untapped talents. Hidden under her glossy, nearly perfect exterior was, she believed, some sort of genius who would someday make a significant contribution to the world, most likely artistic as opposed to commercial. The fact that there was no evidence to support this hope didn't dissuade her, and, indeed, she believed herself equal to anyone. If she were to meet Tolstoy, for instance, she was quite sure that he would immediately embrace her as a kindred spirit.

The traffic had slowed to twenty miles an hour, and Janey drummed her left hand on the steering wheel, her eighteen-karat-gold Bulgari watch flashing in the sun. Her fingers were long and slender—a fortune teller had once said that her hands were "artistic"—marred only by stubby fingertips with nails bitten to the quick. In the past nine months, ever since she'd been picked, Cinderella-like, to star in the new Victoria's Secret campaign, every makeup artist in town had pleaded with her to stop biting her nails, but it was an old childhood habit she couldn't break. The physical pain she inflicted on herself was a perverse way of controlling the emotional pain the world had inflicted on her.

And now, the frustration of sitting in traffic while imagining the seaplane flying overhead bearing the smarter members of the New York social set nearly drew her fingers to her mouth, but for once, she hesitated. She didn't really need to bite her nails—after all, she was finally on top of the world herself. Just a year ago, at thirty-two, she'd been practically washed up—her acting and modeling career had ground to a halt and she was so broke she'd had to borrow money from her rich lovers to pay her rent. And then there had been those shameful three weeks when she was so desperate she'd actually considered becoming a real estate agent and had even taken four classes. But hadn't fate stepped in and saved her, and hadn't she known it would all along? And glancing at herself in the rearview mirror, she reminded herself that she was far too beautiful to fail.

Her car phone rang and she pressed the green button, thinking that it must be her agent, Tommy. A year ago, Tommy wouldn't even return her calls, but ever since she'd landed the Victoria's Secret campaign and had her face plastered on billboards and featured in every magazine in America, Tommy was her new best friend, checking in with her several times a day and keeping her apprised of the latest gossip. Indeed, it had been Tommy who had informed her that morning that Peter Cannon had been arrested in his office yesterday, and they'd had a delicious chat dissecting Peter's character flaws, the main one being that Peter had lost his head working with celebrities and had somehow fancied that he'd become a celebrity himself. New York might have been the land of reinvention, but everybody knew there was an unbreachable line between "celebrities" and "service people," and lawyers, for all their education and expertise, are still "service people." Peter's story was now circulating as a cautionary tale: When one tried to circumvent the natural laws of celebrity and fame, the result was likely to be arrest and a possible jail sentence.

But instead of Tommy's sycophantic "Hi gorgeous," a woman's voice with a clipped English accent inquired, "Janey Wilcox, please."

"This is Janey," Janey said, knowing immediately that the person calling was the assistant to someone in the entertainment industry, as it had recently become *de rigueur* in that field to employ an English assistant.

"I have Mr. Comstock Dibble on the phone. Can you take the call?" And before Janey could respond, Comstock himself came on the line.

"Janey," he said gruffly, as if he intended to get right to the point. Janey hadn't seen or heard from Comstock Dibble for nearly a year, and the sound of his voice brought back a host of unpleasant associations. Comstock Dibble had been her lover the summer before, and Janey had actually fancied herself *in* love with him—until he suddenly became engaged to Mauve Binchely, a tall, reedy socialite. His rejection of her in favor of another woman (and one who wasn't, Janey thought, even remotely pretty) had been made all the more bitter by the fact that this was a scenario that had repeated itself many times in the past. While men were perfectly happy to date her, when it came to the ultimate union of marriage, they always seemed to spurn her in favor of a more "suitable" candidate.

On the other hand, Comstock Dibble, the head of Parador Pictures, was one of the most powerful men in the movie business, and it was entirely possible that he was calling to offer her a part in his next film. So, although she longed to teach him a lesson—even if that lesson was simply that she wasn't impressed by him anymore—she knew it would be wiser to tread lightly. That was what surviving in New York was all about—putting aside your personal feelings in favor of the possibility of advancing your position. And so, in a voice that was cold (but not nearly as cold as she would have liked), Janey said, "Yes, Comstock?"

His next words, however, sent a jolt of fear through her body. "Janey," he said. "You know that you and I have always been friends."

It wasn't that his statement was so patently untrue—they weren't, by any normal person's standards, "friends"—but that the phrase "you and I have always been friends" was a code employed by powerful New Yorkers to signal the beginning of a potentially unpleasant discussion. It usually meant that some injury had been committed against the first party, with the implication being that since both parties were members of the same, exclusive New York society, they would try to reason it out first, before resorting to lawyers or gossip columnists. But in a second, fear was replaced by indignation as Janey wondered what possible injury she could have caused Comstock Dibble. *She* was the dumpee, not he, and as far as she was concerned, he owed her. Still, it would be far better for him to show his hand first, and getting a hold of herself, she said flirtatiously, "Are we friends, Comstock? Gosh. I haven't heard from you in nearly a year. I thought maybe you were calling to offer me a part in your next movie."

"I didn't know you were an actress, Janey."

This was a jab. Comstock knew perfectly well that she'd starred in that action-adventure film eight years ago, but she didn't take the bait. "There are a lot of things you don't know about me now, Comstock," she said playfully, adding, "because you haven't called."

She knew he was under no obligation to call her, but she also knew that there was no better way to needle a man than to make him feel guilty about fucking you and not calling for months afterward.

"I'm calling *now*," he said.

"So when am I going to see you?" she asked.

"That's what I'm calling about."

"Don't tell me that you and Mauve broke up . . ."

"Mauve's a sweetheart," he said, somehow implying that Janey wasn't. This was another insult, and Janey said snidely, "Why shouldn't she be? I mean, what has she ever had to do but inherit millions of dollars . . ." To which Comstock replied in a warning tone of voice, "Janey . . ."

"Well, come on, Comstock. You know it's true," Janey said, falling back into the easy banter she'd used so successfully with him last summer. There was a part of her that hated him for rejecting her, and another part that loved being on intimate terms with one of the powerful men who ran New York. "After all," she continued smoothly, "it's easy to be nice when you've never had to work for your money . . ."

Comstock sighed as if she were completely hopeless and said, "Don't be jealous."

"I'm *not* jealous," Janey squealed. There was nothing she hated more than having her deficiencies pointed out to her. "Why on earth would I be jealous of Mauve Binchely?" Mauve was, in Janey's estimation, practically ancient for a woman— nearly forty-five—and had only one good feature: her hair, which was dark and wavy and hung halfway down her back.

But Comstock had obviously grown bored with the direction of this conversation, because he suddenly repeated, "Janey, you and I have always been friends," and added, "so I know you're not going to make trouble for me."

"Why would I make trouble?" Janey asked.

"Now, come on, Janey," Comstock said, in a low, conspiratorial growl. "You know you're a dangerous woman."

Janey's initial reaction was to be pleased with this sally—in her more egotistical moments she did fancy herself a dangerous woman who might someday take over the world—but she suspected there was a veiled threat behind Comstock's words. Last year, when she'd been broke, people had whispered behind her back that she was a whore. This year, now that she was finally successful and making it on her own, they were whispering that she was a dangerous woman. But that was New York. In a sultry voice that belied her growing consternation, she said, "If you want to be friends, Comstock, you're doing a pretty bad job of it."

He laughed, but in the next second his tone became menacing. "You know better than to fuck with me . . . ," he said, and for a moment, Janey wondered if he was going to explode in one of his legendary outbursts. Comstock Dibble, while acknowledged as a genius in the movie business, was equally known for his irrational displays of temper—he often called women "cunts"—after which he usually sent flowers. There were at least a dozen powerful men like him in New York, who could be charming one minute and rabid the next, but as long as Comstock remained the head of Parador Pictures, and as long as Parador continued to be the media's darling, Comstock would not suffer for it, and that was New York, too.

A less confident girl might have been frightened, but Janey Wilcox wasn't that kind of girl—she'd always prided herself on not being intimidated by powerful men. And so, in a voice full of wide-eyed innocence, she said, "Are you *threatening* me, Comstock?" as he spurted out, "I know you're going to Mimi Kilroy's tonight."

Janey was so surprised she started to laugh. "Really, Comstock," she said. "Don't you have better things to do than to call me about a . . . *party?*"

"As a matter of fact, I do," he said, adopting their familiar tone of bantering. "And that's why I'm so pissed off about this. Goddammit, Janey. Why can't you just stay home?"

"Why can't you?" Janey asked.

"Mauve is Mimi's best friend."

"So?" Janey said coldly.

"Listen, Janey," Comstock said. "I'm just trying to give you a friendly warning. It's better for both of us if no one knows we know each other."

Janey was unable to resist reminding Comstock of their former relationship. "No, Comstock," she said with a laugh. "It's better for *you* if no one knows you fucked me last summer."

And then Comstock finally did lose his temper. "Will you shut up and listen?" he shouted. Adding, "You fucking cunt!"

His scream was so loud that Janey was convinced he could be heard through her cell phone by people in the neighboring cars on the Long Island Expressway. And if he thought he could talk to her like that, he was sorely mistaken. She wasn't that desperate little girl he'd fucked over last summer, and she meant him to know it. "Now *you* listen, Comstock," she said with a frigid calmness. "All you're saying is that I was good enough to fuck last summer, and this summer I'm not good enough to know you. Well, let me tell you something. I don't operate that way."

"We all know how you operate, Janey," he said ominously.

"The difference between you and me is that I'm not ashamed of anything I've done in the past," Janey said. This wasn't entirely true, but she had to admit that it sounded good.

Comstock, however, wasn't impressed. "Just keep the fuck away from me," he said. "I'm warning you. This could be a disaster for both of us."

And with that, he hung up.

Goddamned Comstock, Janey thought, as she pressed down on the brake. The traffic had come to a standstill and she leaned her head to the side, frowning at the line of cars.

This was supposed to be her triumphant summer, she thought angrily. Her new commercial, in which she pretended to sing and play a white electric guitar while wearing nothing more than a white silk bra and panties, had begun airing three days ago to great fanfare—and now that she was a famous supermodel, she knew this was the summer to strike. She planned to cultivate the movers and shakers who populated the Hamptons every summer; her dream was to have a "salon" where artists, filmmakers, and writers would gather to discuss intellectual topics. If pressed, she would have to admit that eventually, she wanted to direct . . . But most of all, she was assuming her new supermodel status would mean she didn't have to deal with assholes like Comstock Dibble anymore, and would enable her to get a much better man. Naturally, she wanted to be in love, but behind every great match, wasn't there a touch of cynicism? And there was nothing the public loved more than the alliance of two famous people . . .

But suddenly, Comstock's phone call made her question all that, and for a moment she wondered nervously if she had, indeed, come as far as she'd imagined. All her life, it seemed, she'd been forced to sleep with rich men in order to survive— short, paunchy, bald men with hair in their ears and funguses on their toes, men with gaps in their teeth and fur on their backs, men with penises that never quite got erect, men, in short, whom no self-respecting woman would ever have sex with save for the fact that the man had money. She'd vowed that this summer would be different. But that one comment of Comstock's—"we all know how you operate, Janey"—suddenly made her unsure . . .

She gripped the steering wheel, and as she did so, her eyes fell on her bitten nails. She quickly slid one hand between her legs so she wouldn't have to think about her fingers, and tried to reassure herself that what Comstock had said wasn't important. After all, he was probably angry that she'd become a famous supermodel and he had let her go . . . But his words were a niggling reminder of everything that was wrong with New York: A man could sleep with as many women as he liked, but when it came to sex, there were still quite a few people in society who clung to the old-fashioned notion that a woman shouldn't have too many partners. Oh, a woman could certainly have some sex—indeed, it was expected. But there seemed to be some unspoken limit as to the number of men a woman could bed, and having passed that limit, a woman was no longer considered "marriageable."

And it was so unfair! Janey thought furiously. She certainly did seem to have more sex with more men than most of the women she knew, and she knew that, behind her back, people had whispered that *she* was a slut. But what nobody understood was that every time she *did* have sex with a man, even if it only entailed giving him a blow job in the bathroom of a restaurant, she was doing it because she thought that maybe he *was* "the one."

Or that was what she always told herself, anyway.

Her phone rang again, and she grabbed it, wondering if it was Comstock calling back to apologize.

"Janey?" asked a slightly familiar woman's voice. The accent was cultured and East Coast, and then, as if the speaker had finally contacted a long lost friend, she cried out, "Mimi Kilroy here. Darling, how *are* you?"

For a second, Janey was too surprised to speak. Mimi was certainly not a good friend; indeed, their acquaintance consisted of little more than bumping into each other at parties over the years. But Janey was immediately thrilled. Mimi Kilroy was at the very top of the social heap in New York—her father was a famous senator who, it was rumored, might be appointed to Finance Commissioner if the Republicans won the new election—and it was whispered that Mimi, who had been on the scene since the age of fifteen when she started going to Studio 54, secretly ran New York society. In the past ten years, Janey had barely spoken more than three words to Mimi—until this moment, Mimi had always made it a point to ignore her or to pretend that she didn't know who Janey was—but nevertheless, Janey wasn't particularly surprised that Mimi was calling. After all, as soon as you made it in New York, people who had never acknowledged you before suddenly wanted to become your best friend.

And so, in a voice that implied that she and Mimi were, indeed, old friends, and that Mimi had never once cut her at parties, she purred, "Hello, Mimi. You must be going crazy getting ready for your party tonight." Then she sat back against the seat and, glancing at herself in the rearview mirror, smiled in satisfaction.

Oh, it was morally wrong, of course, to suddenly pretend to be Mimi's friend—just because Mimi suddenly seemed to want to be hers. But Janey was never one to stand on ceremony, especially when a situation might potentially work to her benefit, and in the next second, Mimi exclaimed with a touch of guilt, "I hardly lift a finger. The caterers and party planners do it all . . . I only have to taste the hors d'oeuvres!"

Janey was suddenly uncomfortable. She'd given exactly two parties in her life, both disasters (she had a miserly quality and each time the alcohol had run out), and the fact that Mimi was famous for her parties *and* was able to hire caterers and party planners only seemed to highlight the gulf between them. Faced with a reminder of her lesser status, Janey's usual reaction would have been a snide comment. But this time she caught herself, and instead of remarking sarcastically, "Can't you find someone to do *that*?" she merely laughed politely.

"Darling," Mimi said, "I just wanted to make sure that you're coming to the party tonight. There's someone special I want to introduce you to. His name is Selden Rose, and he's just moved here from California . . . Do you know him? He's the new head of MovieTime, the cable channel . . . You're probably like me, you don't watch TV, but apparently it's a very important job . . . *And* he's gorgeous and forty-five, divorced, no kids thank God, so he's relatively fresh . . . but most of all, darling, he's terribly, terribly . . . real. Yes, I think that's the word for it. He's *real*. Not a bit like us," Mimi said, with a knowing laugh. "Of course, I don't expect you to fall in love with him, but he's an old friend of George's and hardly knows anyone, and it would be so sweet if you were just a tiny bit nice to him . . ."

"I'd *love* to meet him," Janey said warmly. "He sounds divine . . ."

"Oh darling, he is," Mimi said. "And naturally I never forget anyone who's done me a favor . . ."

The conversation went on like this for a few more seconds, and then Mimi hung up with a salutation of "Big kiss, darling." And suddenly, Janey was on top of the world again. Selden Rose didn't sound particularly promising—from Mimi's description, he might even be another Comstock Dibble—but the fact that Mimi had called to fix her up with him reassured her that she had come as far as she'd thought. And wouldn't that be a slap in the face to Comstock Dibble, and a way of showing him that he mustn't mess with her. She didn't know what Mimi meant, exactly, about being "sweet" to Selden Rose (if she expected Janey to give him a blow job in the bathroom, she could forget about it), but she would certainly pay him some attention, and when Comstock saw that she'd made it into Mimi's inner circle, it would drive him crazy . . .

The traffic came to yet another halt just before Exit 70, and feeling a renewed sense of her personal power, Janey took the opportunity to flip open the large lighted mirror in the car's sun visor. Her reflection never failed to satisfy her, and leaning forward, she marveled at her own beauty.

Her hair, long, thick, and blond, was like cream; the shape of her face nearly perfect with its high forehead and small, neat chin. Her eyes were blue and turned up ever so slightly at the outer corners, promising a certain mysterious intelligence, while her full lips (recently made even fuller by injections from her dermatologist) implied a certain childlike innocence. Indeed, the only technical flaw was her nose, which had a slightly bulbous, turned-up tip, and yet, without this nose she would have been a cold, classical beauty. Because of it, her beauty became accessible, giving the common man the impression that he could have her if only he could manage to meet her.

She was, indeed, so engrossed in her appearance that she didn't notice that the traffic had finally begun to move until a few sharp horn blasts from the car behind her broke her reverie. Annoyed and slightly embarrassed, she looked into the rearview mirror and saw that the offending driver was a stunningly handsome young man sitting behind the wheel of a hunter green Ferrari. Janey was immediately filled with envy—she'd always loved that Ferrari—but her resentment turned into pure jealousy when she saw who the passenger was: Pippi Maus.

Pippi and her younger sister, Nancy Maus, comprised the Maus acting sisters from Charleston, South Carolina. They had faces like little mice but possessed enviable figures of the type so rarely found in nature: They were skinny girls with naturally huge breasts. Notoriously talentless, in Janey's mind they represented "everything that was wrong with the world"; still, they had managed to carve out careers by playing quirky characters in independent films. Janey couldn't imagine how, or why, Pippi was on her way out to the Hamptons—from Janey's point of view Pippi wasn't the sort of person who belonged there—but even more mysterious was what she was doing with such an amazingly gorgeous guy. Even stuffed into the little Ferrari seat she could tell that he was tall—maybe even 6'4"—with the lean body, full lips, and chiseled face of a male model. Perhaps he was gay— Pippi, after all, was the kind of girl who probably only hung out with gay men—but Janey suspected from the macho way he had leaned on his horn that he was not.

And then, adding insult to injury, the Ferrari made a sudden sideways move and pulled onto the shoulder. In a second, it was passing her as if she were no more significant than a bug. Pippi squealed with delight as Janey glared at the driver. His eyes met hers, and for a second, Janey was completely taken aback. His shocked expression was that of a man who has suddenly seen an angel . . .

But then the green car disappeared around the bend in the exit, and Janey was left feeling, once again, that somehow she'd been left behind. If she couldn't take the seaplane to the Hamptons, then she ought to be in a car like that, with a guy like that . . . Nibbling absentmindedly at an imaginary hangnail, she consoled herself with the fact that she was sure the driver had instantly fallen in love with her—and that he might be exactly the sort of man she was looking for. And expertly sliding the clutch into third gear, she mused about how much fun it would be to take him away from Pippi Maus.

TWO

MIMI KILROY'S MEMORIAL Day weekend party was legendary and strictly A list; and as it was covered by every newspaper and magazine in town, it was impossible to pretend that it didn't exist—which was the only option if you weren't invited. Janey had never been asked before, and every summer it had been a thorn in her side to know that one hundred of the coolest, most talented, and most important people in New York had been invited, and that she was most specifically *not* among them. No matter how hard she tried, no matter how many times she said in a scoffing tone of voice, "It's only a stupid party, *please*," she could never get over the distinct feeling that Mimi had cruelly and deliberately passed her over.

And this feeling was not mediated by logic—after all, Mimi didn't really *know* her. Nevertheless, in years past, Janey had done everything possible to finagle her way into the party, from giving a blow job to a man she hardly knew in the hope that he would take her as his guest, to reconnoitering the beach behind Mimi's house to see if she could sneak in the back. But the real blow had come four years ago, when she was dating Peter Cannon and *he* had been invited to Mimi's party. "Why would she invite *you?*" she'd asked in disbelief, and he'd just looked at her and said snidely, "Why *wouldn't* she invite me?"

"Because," Janey said stubbornly. She longed to say, "Because you're a nobody," but she didn't, because how would it make her look that she was dating a nobody? And besides, she wanted him to take her to the party.

Peter wasn't averse to taking her (every now and again, Janey noticed, he was capable of behaving like a human being), but Mimi prevented him. He RSVPed for two, then Mimi's assistant had called and asked for the name of his guest.

"Janey Wilcox," he'd said.

She called back two hours later. "I'm sorry," she said, "but *who* is your guest?"

"Janey Wilcox."

"Yes, but who *is* she?"

"She's a *girl*," he'd said.

"But who is she? What does she *do*?"

"She's a sort of . . . *model*?" Peter said.

"I'll have to get back to you."

Janey had yelled at him: "Why didn't you tell her that I was an *actress*?"

"I dunno," Peter said. "Because you really haven't been one for five years?"

"That's because I'm waiting for the right part," Janey screamed.

Then the assistant had called back. "I'm *so* sorry," she said, "but I talked to Mimi, and it turns out we're overbooked this year. No one is allowed to bring a guest."

This was a lie, and they all knew it.

At that moment, Janey's feelings about Mimi crystallized into hate. She didn't really know Mimi, but she hated her anyway—the way one might hate a movie star or a politician: She hated what she represented.

Unlike most people, Janey thought bitterly, Mimi had never wanted for anything. She'd never had to struggle; she'd never had to worry about how she was going to pay her rent. Technically, she'd had "careers" (as a model for Ralph Lauren, a VJ for VH1, a jewelry designer, and, most recently, an importer of pashminas, which she sold to her friends), but in Janey's mind, Mimi had never really *done* anything, and was nothing more than a useless socialite who was always swaddled in designer clothes and whose photograph appeared in the party pages of various magazines each month.

But for Janey, the bitterest pill concerned Mimi's appearance: She was tall and skinny, with that kind of thin, naturally blond hair that always looks stringy; nevertheless, everyone always insisted that she was "a beauty." Janey couldn't believe it. If Mimi weren't rich, if she didn't come from such a prominent family, there wouldn't have been one guy in New York who would have given her the time of day. In short, Mimi was a blazing advertisement for the unfairness of life: If it weren't for an accident of birth, she would be *nothing*.

Mimi's mother was Tabitha Mason, a fifties movie star who came from a prominent Philadelphia family. Her father was Robert Kilroy of the California Kilroys; at the time of their marriage in 1955, he was the second youngest senator to be elected in history. When their first child, Sandy, a boy, was born in 1956, Tabitha gave up Hollywood to raise her family; two years later she gave birth to a baby girl, Camille, whom everyone called Mimi.

As a child, Janey knew everything about Mimi—from her favorite color (pink), to the name of her pony (Blaze), on whose back Mimi had won a shelf full of trophies and blue ribbons. Janey knew all this, because all through the sixties and into the early seventies, women's magazines like *Good Housekeeping* and *Ladies' Home Journal* featured stories about the glamorous Kilroy family; indeed, "The Kilroy Family Thanksgiving" was a yearly staple on which the less glamorous denizens of America could rely as solidly as cranberry sauce. And there was Mimi herself, year after year, in a pink dress with a lacy white pinafore and pink patent-leather Mary Janes, her hair done up in pigtails or fastened into a ponytail with a shiny ribbon; and later on, Mimi in her first long "hostess" gown, her stringy hair pulled back and topped with one of those large, fake buns that were so popular in the early seventies. In these photographs, Mimi always appeared slightly gaunt, with large blue eyes that seemed to pop out of her head, but her expression was also slightly defiant, as if she knew how ridiculous it all was and frankly had better things to do with her time.

And little six-year-old Janey Wilcox, with her pudgy face and thick, mousy brown hair, would study those photographs and wonder why she hadn't been born Mimi Kilroy! Somehow, this Mimi Kilroy person had ended up with what should have been Janey's life.

But time passed and things happened, and Janey forgot all about Mimi Kilroy—until she arrived in New York in the late eighties.

Janey was barely twenty years old and had just returned after modeling in Europe for the summer. She was immediately taken up by an investment banker named Petie—he was probably in his early thirties but to Janey he seemed ancient. He wore his dark hair slicked back from his forehead, his eyes were too close together, and he had the soft, delicate hands of a little girl, but he was easy to manipulate. One night he took her to an exclusive, private party at the Grolier Club; he hadn't been invited himself but as he was one of the big investors in the club, they had to let him in.

The party was for the bad-boy Southern writer Redmon Richardly, and the crowd, raucous and drunk, had a self-satisfied air, as if there were no better people in New York and no better place to be. Right away, Janey could see that Petie, who was wearing a heavy English-style pinstriped suit, didn't really belong there; he had an oily smoothness that Janey had interpreted as being urbane, but taken out of his element and placed in this crowd, she suddenly saw that he was nothing more than a sleazy money guy.

"Let's go," she whispered.

He looked at her like she was insane. "Huh?" he said, and taking her hand, pulled her upstairs to the bar.

There was a girl at the bar surrounded by several men; as Petie ordered drinks, her eyes flickered and she jumped up from her barstool. Janey hadn't seen a photograph of Mimi Kilroy for years, but she instinctually knew it *was* Mimi Kilroy, and she took a step back in awe.

She would always remember exactly how Mimi looked, for her elegant, deceptively expensive style was one Janey had been trying to copy ever since. She was wearing a crisp white shirt with large cuffs pushed halfway up her forearms and fastened with a pair of men's heavy gold cuff links; the shirt was loosely tucked into a pair of fawn-colored fine suede pants. A man's gold Rolex watch jangled on her wrist like a bracelet; on her right hand was a large oval sapphire ring. She wafted money like expensive perfume.

Mimi came up behind Petie and put her hands over his eyes. Petie jumped and turned around, grabbing her hands. She looked at him soulfully and said, "Hello, darling."

She was one of those women who are much better looking in person than in photographs, as if what made her special was far too rare and elusive to be captured on film. Indeed, in years to come, Janey would muse that this might have explained why Mimi, for all her quality, never really made it beyond the borders of her small, circumscribed world—what she had couldn't be transported and delivered to the masses. Still holding Petie's hand, she leaned in and said, "There's something I need to discuss with you in the bathroom," and suddenly an expression of annoyed resignation crossed Petie's face, as if he understood that he was once again about to be used.

"In a minute," he said, and turning away from her, he took Janey's arm and pulled her closer. "Do you know Janey Wilcox?" he asked.

Mimi held out a slim hand, and without interest said, "Nice to see you." As her gaze slid back to Petie's face, Janey was struck by the sound of her voice—she hadn't known what to expect, but she'd never heard a voice like that, so rich and refined, and seeming to contain a range of subtle meanings. "Janey's new in town," Petie said. "She's a model."

Mimi looked at Janey coldly and, with a little laugh, said, "Who isn't?"

Then Janey, out of an innocent desire to make an impact on her idol, found herself saying, "I used to see your picture in magazines . . . when I was a kid . . ."

And in the uncomfortable silence that followed, all Janey could think about was how her voice had come out in an annoying squeak.

Mimi looked at her as if summing her up, and then, deciding that what she saw was of no importance, said, "Really? I have absolutely no idea what you're talking about . . ." And giving Petie a meaningful look, turned away.

For a moment, Janey stood staring after her in shock: She knew she'd been thoroughly and rudely dismissed, but she couldn't understand why. Petie, seeing her expression, said, "Don't worry about it. Everyone knows Mimi hates other women, especially if they're younger and prettier than she is . . . You'll get used to it," he said with a laugh as he handed Janey her drink.

Janey took a sip but her eyes never left Mimi. She was destroyed but fascinated—by the way she moved her arms, by the way she tilted her head; as she opened her mouth to speak, Janey imagined she heard Mimi's voice again, and she was transfixed, wondering what Mimi might be saying.

But she never got the opportunity to find out, because even though she would run into Mimi again and again over the next ten years, each time Mimi's eyes would look over Janey's shoulder, and her cold, rich voice would declare, "Nice to see you again"—the greeting New Yorkers used when they had no idea if they'd met before. The message, Janey understood, was clear: She and Mimi might be in the same room, but Janey was as far from Mimi's world as she'd been as a six-year-old kid, staring at Mimi's photograph in *Good Housekeeping*.

But eventually, Janey began to notice a subtle change in Mimi's attitude. Whereas before Mimi had merely been noncommittal, in the past five years her "nice to see you again" began to take on a tone that bordered on open dislike. Janey suspected that this was because she'd slept with many of the same men Mimi had slept with, and Mimi was jealous.

Janey figured that she and Mimi had at least ten lovers in common, including Redmon Richardly and the screenwriter Bill Westacott. It continued to gall her that while everybody knew Mimi was a wild party girl who slept with whomever she pleased, nobody ever called Mimi a slut or looked askance at her behavior. It proved yet another truth about New York society: A rich girl could sleep with a hundred men and people would call her bohemian, while a poor girl who did the same thing was labeled a gold digger or a whore.

But all that had changed the day Janey became a Victoria's Secret model. It was as if, after all those long years in New York, she'd suddenly emerged in full color. People suddenly *got* her, they understood who she was and what she was doing. And then the coveted invitation to Mimi's party had arrived.

Exactly one month ago to the day, a heavy cream envelope had been messengered to Janey's apartment in New York. She lived in the same walk-up building on East Sixty-seventh Street that she'd moved into ten years before, and she mused that she was lucky she was home at the time, because if she hadn't been, there was no doorman to receive the missive, and then what would have happened?

On the envelope was written only her name, "Miss Janey Wilcox," with no address—implying that an address might be tacky—and even before she opened the envelope, she knew what it contained.

Carefully sliding her finger under the flap, so that the envelope would remain in pristine condition (these were the kinds of things she liked to save), she removed the simple ecru card inside. Written on the upper-left-hand corner in the English style, her name was written out in calligraphy, and printed below were the words: "Mimi Kilroy and George Paxton, at home, Friday, May twenty-seventh." And in that moment, Janey's deep hatred of Mimi evaporated. It was difficult to sustain hatred, especially when it was bathed in the warm light of attention and acknowledgment. And Janey had reflected that while New York could certainly be superficial, it was a glorious sort of superficial, especially if you were on the inside.

Three years ago, at the age of thirty-nine, Mimi Kilroy had finally settled down and married George Paxton, the billionaire.

Five years earlier, George Paxton, who supposedly hailed from outside of Boston, which could mean anywhere really, had suddenly popped up on the social scene in New York. It was practically a rule in New York society that every few years, a billionaire would appear as if from nowhere, usually in the form of a middle-aged man who had suddenly made a fortune and was in the throes of a midlife crisis. Having slaved for years to make money, he was now in the position to finally enjoy his life, and the very first thing to go was always the first wife. Such was the story of George Paxton.

His first two years in New York followed the usual lines: He was feted and petted, and continually fixed up on blind dates, because there is nothing more exciting to society than a newly single man flush with a fortune he isn't exactly sure how to spend. And after he'd had two years of dating the finest single women the Upper East Side could offer—women with fake breasts and no breasts, women with bodies perfected by Pilates, women with caramel-colored hair and sable coats, women who sat on boards and ran their own companies, women who were lawyers and doctors and real estate agents, women who were divorced from other rich men; and after he'd had his cock sucked and pushed into vaginas and anuses, been tied up and held down, had his nipples squeezed and his balls shaved and suffered the perpetual worry about getting (and keeping) a hard-on—then, and only then, was he introduced to Mimi Kilroy.

Mimi wasn't the sort of "gal" George Paxton ever thought he'd end up marrying—she was like a high-strung racehorse, and George was a basic kind of guy—but after two years of feeling like a publicly traded stock, Mimi was, as he put it, "a breath of fresh air." She didn't take any of "it" too seriously, and besides, George had always prided himself on his ability to recognize a "good deal." Not that George was the kind of man people imagined Mimi would marry. They'd expected a brilliant marriage—to a movie star or a handsome politician or even to one of the lesser English princes—and George was as nondescript as they came. Still, it was terribly clever to land a billionaire, and a middle-aged paunch could always be disguised under an expensive Italian suit. And if anyone knew how to spend George's money it was Mimi, and that would be fun for everyone.

One of the very first things Mimi had done was to organize the purchase of the old Wannamaker estate in East Hampton. For years, this sandstone house, considered a white elephant with its fifteen bedrooms, indoor pool, and imported Italian frescoes, had stood vacant, the folly of Chester Wannamaker, who had built up a fortune in department stores in the early and middle part of the 1900s, and then had lost it all in the late 1970s when he tried to expand. The bank foreclosed on the house and the price was $8 million, but time, sand, and salt water had ravaged the mansion, and it was estimated that restoring the house would cost twice the purchasing price. It was exactly the sort of project Mimi loved, and in April, the restoration was finished, complete with a landing pad for George's helicopter.

And now, all afternoon and into the early evening of the Memorial Day bash, this helicopter had been busily employed in ferrying high-profile guests from Manhattan to the house. At 7 P.M., as Janey turned the Porsche onto Georgica Pond Lane, the Sikorsky Black Hawk VH60 swooped out of the sky and disappeared behind the hedges next to the house. Janey wondered whom it contained and what kind of status was required to score not only an invitation to Mimi's party but a lift on the helicopter as well, and she vowed that next year, she would be on that helicopter.

Nevertheless, it was still a thrill to present her invitation to the very nice man who stood at the foot of the polished granite stairs leading up to the house. "Your card, please," he asked, and Janey opened her purse, which was small and beaded and all the rage because the designer had made only ten and had given one to her, and handed him her invitation.

"Welcome, Miss Wilcox," the man said. "I'm sorry. I should have recognized you."

"No problem," Janey said graciously. She lifted the hem of her long yellow Oscar de la Renta dress that she'd borrowed for the occasion and tripped lightly up the stairs, noting the flowering apple trees and inhaling the sweet fragrance of the blossoms. There were jugglers in between the trees, tossing golden apples, and at the top of the steps, a string quartet. The heavy wooden doors to the house were thrown open, and Janey entered breathlessly to the sweeping wail of a violin.

Mimi stood resplendent in a white Tuleh gown at the end of a marble foyer, and, with a jolt of pleasure, Janey saw that she was talking to Rupert Jackson, the

English movie star. Mimi turned and waved, and Janey approached, unable to prevent herself from thinking about what a great couple she and Rupert Jackson would make.

"Janey, darling," Mimi said, coming forward to take her hands and kiss her on both cheeks. Her wrists were encircled in diamond bracelets; there were diamond earclips on her ears. Like so many New York women, Mimi had aged hardly a bit in the ten years or more that Janey had known her, and Janey wondered what she'd had done.

"What *beautiful* bracelets," Janey remarked.

"Oh darling, they're *nothing*," Mimi said.

"Don't you love the way rich people always act like a million dollars is nothing?" Rupert said.

"Darling, you know Janey Wilcox, don't you?" Mimi asked.

"No, but I think I'd better," Rupert said. There are two different types of actors, Janey thought—those who aren't anything like their characters and those who are exactly like them, and Rupert Jackson was definitely the latter. He was as handsome in person as he was in his movies; he had the same crinkly smile and that forelock of brown hair that flopped over his forehead, and he said, "I've seen your photograph everywhere, and I've always wondered what that girl would be like in real life. You must promise to discuss your underwear with me later."

Janey laughed out loud, and Mimi said playfully, "Now Rupert, Janey *is* the most beautiful woman at the party, but you're practically engaged, and besides, I've already picked out someone else for her."

"I'm terribly hurt," Rupert said. "Who is this lucky man?"

"Selden Rose," Mimi said. "The new head of MovieTime. He just arrived by helicopter . . . He got stuck on the Long Island Expressway and we had to send the helicopter to rescue him."

"Really? How extraordinary. What sort of man has to be rescued from the Long Island Expressway?" Rupert asked, and with an expression of mock horror on his face, he turned to Janey and winked. Janey had to agree with him—she had yet to meet this Selden Rose, but already he didn't sound promising.

"Don't listen to a word he says," Mimi said. "Selden's an old friend of George's—but don't worry, he's not nearly as dull. I can never figure out exactly what George does, you see, other than the fact that he seems to own everything."

Janey and Rupert laughed dutifully, and out of the corner of her eye she saw Comstock Dibble enter the house with his fiancée, Mauve Binchely. This was good—Comstock wouldn't dare misbehave toward her in front of Mimi. But Mimi was facing away from him and had yet to note his appearance.

"Sometimes I tell George that he owns *me*," Mimi continued gaily, "and he loves it." She had a way of making everything sound like a secret, and leaning toward Janey and touching her arm, she said, "Don't ever get married, Janey, or at least not before you absolutely have to. It's too boring. But Selden *is* different—he's supposed to be brilliant—in any case, I've heard he actually reads books. George doesn't read a thing, of course, unless it has dollar signs on it. I think he was a literature major at Harvard."

Janey could feel Comstock's eyes boring into her back. Tilting her head to the side and emitting a tinkling peal of laughter—a gesture she had copied from Mimi years ago—she said, "George?"

"Oh, no, *Selden*," Mimi said. "George did go to Harvard, but sometimes I swear you would never know it . . . just look at him!" She indicated an unremarkable man of medium height, who was holding a lit cigar in one hand while furtively shoving a shrimp cocktail into his mouth with the other. "George!" Mimi called to him from across the room. George looked up guiltily, and taking the proffered napkin from the uniformed waitress who was holding a tray, wiped his mouth and strolled over. Seeing him dressed in cream-colored trousers and a navy blue blazer with gold buttons, Janey had to agree that what everybody said about him was true: His appearance was so dull and ordinary that you wondered if you would recognize him the next time you met him. Even his eyes looked like they'd been inserted into his head on an assembly line.

"Darling," Mimi said, exhaling a long sigh. "You know you shouldn't smoke and eat at the same time . . . What would Mother say?"

"Luckily, Mother is dead, so I doubt she'd say anything," George responded.

"Husbands are just like children," Mimi said. "It's something people always tell you, but you never believe it until you get married. George, have you met Janey Wilcox?"

George wiped his hand on his napkin and held out five stubby fingers. "Don't know you but I know all about you," he said. And then, without preamble, asked, "What's it like knowing that half of America has seen you in your underwear?"

"George!" Mimi exclaimed.

"I was about to ask that very question," Rupert said.

"Maybe you should try it," Janey said.

"I'm afraid I'd become more of a laughingstock than I already am," Rupert said. And Mimi said, "George, I swear darling, if you weren't so rich, I'd divorce you."

And then Mimi turned and saw Comstock and Mauve. Janey caught Comstock's eye and he quickly looked away.

The inevitable moment of meeting was diverted, however, when Mimi said, "Rupert, darling, come and say hello to Mauve, will you? She's got a terrible crush on you, but I promise to spare you at dinner." Turning to George she said, "And as for you, darling, if you're going to be rude to our guests, can you at least make yourself useful? Janey needs a drink." And bearing Rupert away, she left Janey with George.

As he led her into an ornately decorated living room, he began babbling about the renovation, but Janey soon found herself losing attention. She was taken with her own thoughts, those being that Mimi and George's marriage was exactly the sort of union she'd been trying to avoid her whole life. This wasn't entirely truthful, as, so far, *any* man—rich or poor—had yet to express an interest in marrying her. But right now, being forced to listen to George go on and on about the costs of the different kinds of paneling in the room, it seemed like a blessing, and she wondered why the fabulous Mimi Kilroy had succumbed to marrying George Paxton. It wasn't that he was *so* awful—summing him up, Janey could see that he had a glimmer of humor—but that he was so completely out of his element. Nor did this bode well for the "brilliant" Selden Rose: It certainly didn't recommend him much if George was his good friend.

As George went on and on—she believed he was talking about the packing methods for shipping furniture from Europe to America, a topic on which she did not, and never would, have an interest—she spotted Pippi Maus by the French doors leading to the terrace, and was immediately reminded of the delicious young man she'd seen her with in the car. At the moment, he was nowhere to be found, but that didn't mean he wasn't at the party. Using the excuse of needing some fresh air, Janey strolled toward Pippi, and then, when she was nearly on top of her, pretended to suddenly see her. Arranging her expression into one of pleasant surprise, she said, "Pippi?"

Pippi looked up at her with that expression that is typical of all famous people: a mixture of eagerness at being recognized, coupled with a fear of being ambushed by an overeager fan. Janey nearly snorted with derision—in her mind, Pippi wasn't famous enough for that look, but she held out her hand and said, "Janey Wilcox."

"Oh," Pippi said. Janey could tell that Pippi had no idea who she was, which was all the more annoying as under normal circumstances, Janey wouldn't have wasted her time with a chit like Pippi—after all, there was nothing Pippi could do for her. But at the moment, she was dying to find out at least the name of Pippi's afternoon companion, so she said, "You remember? We met . . . oh God, I can't even remember where we met . . ."

"I can't even remember what day it is most of the time," Pippi agreed, nodding her head.

"I think you passed me on the Long Island Expressway this afternoon."

Pippi opened her mouth in recognition, as if finally able to place who Janey was. "I'm sure we did," she said. "We passed almost everyone. Did you see me? I was in a green Ferrari."

Janey ignored the obviousness of her remark and said, "I *love* that car."

"So do I," Pippi said. "I wish it was mine, but I can't afford it."

"Is it your boyfriend's?"

"Oh no. I mean, it is his car, but he isn't my boyfriend. Not yet, I mean . . . He's a *polo player*," she said breathlessly, as if that explained everything.

Janey nodded wisely, knowing that poor little Pippi, with her mousy face and eyes that were spaced too closely together, hardly had a chance, and in a voice dripping with sympathy said, "You should have brought him to the party."

"I wanted to, but I *couldn't*," Pippi said in agony. "He had to have dinner with some old guy . . . Harold something . . . ?"

"Harold Vane?" Janey said, trying to hold her excitement in check. Harold Vane was yet another of her former lovers, and a good friend—she must remember to call Harold tomorrow and find out all about this mysterious polo player.

"What's his name?" she asked casually.

"I can't remember. Harold . . . ?"

"Oh, I *know* Harold," Janey said, with a superior laugh. "I meant the polo player."

"Zizi?" Pippi asked. And then the light of understanding appeared to dawn on her. "That's what everyone calls him anyway. But I haven't found out if he has a last name or not . . ."

"Really," Janey said, smiling vaguely. Pippi was so dumb, she thought, and now, having achieved her aim, she wanted to escape. Turning, she saw a savior in the form of Rupert Jackson.

He was obviously looking for her, because he came right over, and in a scolding tone of voice declared, "Miss Wilcox, you've been very naughty. I've just discovered that you know this scoundrel, Peter Cannon. Is it true you actually dated the man?"

Janey would have preferred that Rupert hadn't been acquainted with this information, but it was impossible to keep secrets in New York, and in a second, her dismay was quickly replaced with the pleasurable knowledge that Rupert Jackson must certainly be interested.

"Oh really," she said airily. "I only dated him the same way I date every man. For a minute."

"You *are* naughty," Rupert said, shrieking with delight. His voice attracted the attention of nearly everyone in the room, and he said, "You must tell Uncle Rupert all about it." And then, in full view of the party, her took her arm and led her away to a remote corner of the terrace.

The party had swelled and grown, and cries of "Isn't it a perfect evening?" rang out across the terrace, as if the guests themselves had arranged for the weather and not Mother Nature.

But who wouldn't have wanted to take credit for such an evening? The night air was a temperate seventy-two degrees, there was a full moon and just the slightest hint of a breeze off the Atlantic Ocean. The soft wind mingled with the strains of music from the steel band, picking up the bell-like peals and sprinkling them over the party like so much fairy dust. Flowering fruit trees in pots, their branches trimmed to resemble lollipops, were spaced at even intervals along a bright white balustrade, and framed between two of these trees now stood Janey Wilcox.

Having moved away from the crowd for a moment, Janey situated herself to her best advantage, in a three-quarter pose facing the ocean. Her hands rested on the balustrade, and she leaned over slightly, pushing out her chest and arching her back, so that her breasts were more prominently displayed. She tilted her head back a bit and closed her eyes, breathing in the night air and knowing as she did so that she was creating the impression of a lovely young woman who was lost in thought.

But in reality, her mind was awhirl. It was, she decided, already a thrillingly successful evening for her: There was that long and promising conversation with Rupert Jackson, and then Mimi had introduced her to the new editor in chief of *Harper's Bazaar,* who hinted that she might use Janey for a cover. In all her years as a model, Janey had never rated the cover of a magazine, and she marveled at the capriciousness of life, about how, when one good thing happened to you, other good things seemed to follow.

And then there was Mimi herself. Janey wondered why she'd mistrusted her for so many years—like most people, Mimi was perfectly nice once you got to know her. It crossed Janey's mind that perhaps the fault had been on her side—maybe Mimi had simply suspected that Janey didn't like *her.* But that was the wonderful thing about New York: Years of bad blood could be wiped out with a single gesture of friendliness, the unspoken understanding being that no one ever need acknowledge the previously awkward relationship.

She took a sip of champagne, and stared out over the ocean. Separating herself from the crowd was an old party trick of hers, and one that she used deliberately to allow an interested man to approach without fear. Keeping her gaze on the ocean, she wondered idly what sort of fish she would hook, when suddenly, she heard a familiar and not entirely welcome voice cry out, "Well, if it isn't Janey Wilcox. In the flesh."

It was Bill Westacott, the screenwriter.

"Jesus, Janey," he said, coming toward her. "I can hardly walk down the street in New York without seeing your goddamned picture somewhere. What the hell is going on?"

This should have been gratifying, but coming from Bill it was merely exasperating, reminding her of the many times in the past when Bill had annoyed her. Taking on his subtly snide tone, she said, "Bill! What are *you* doing here?" as if she were surprised at his being invited, and he said, "Why shouldn't I be here?"

Janey gave a superior laugh, and said, "There's no reason why you shouldn't be here, I'm just surprised, that's all." Moving closer and lowering her voice, she said, "I thought you didn't *like* Mimi Kilroy."

Bill refused to take the bait. "Come on, Janey," he said. "I may have had some issues with her over the years, but Mimi is one of my oldest friends."

"Oh yes," Janey said, giving him a sarcastic smile. "I forgot."

"And I seem to recall that *you're* the one who has a problem with her," Bill continued heedlessly. "'She's ugly and old, and I can't believe people still pay attention to her,' were, I believe, your exact words."

Janey took a step away. "I never said that," she hissed, trying to take refuge behind a potted fruit tree. Why was it always like this with Bill? Somehow, he always managed to spin the conversation around so that everything was her fault, and it wasn't fair.

"You did say it," he said. "But I'm not going to hold it against you. I've lived in New York long enough to understand how these things work. Now you're the belle of the ball—why shouldn't you be Mimi Kilroy's new best friend?"

"I'm hardly her best friend," Janey said with annoyance.

"You will be," Bill said casually. "You never miss an opportunity to get ahead." And fixing her with a piercing look, he added, "And Mimi never misses an opportunity to seduce the latest star . . ."

"Oh please, Bill," Janey said, the note of disgust in her voice conveying the impression that she wasn't going to dignify this with a response.

Bill wasn't deterred. "So what did Rupert Jackson want?" he asked with an amused grin.

So that was it! she thought. There it was: The old jealousy. Bill, who was married to a crazy woman and had two kids, had been her lover two summers in a row. He would never leave his wife, but with typical male egotism, couldn't stand her having other boyfriends, either. Last summer, Bill had nearly gone insane when he'd found out she was seeing Comstock Dibble, and sensing an opportunity to goad him, she said seductively, "What do you *think* he wants?"

Instead of a jealous reaction, however, Bill laughed out loud. "I don't know, but it's probably not what *you* think he wants."

"Oh really?" she asked, raising her eyebrows in disbelief.

"I'm just stating the obvious," Bill said, with a triumphant grin. "Rupert Jackson is gay. Everybody in Hollywood knows it. The fiancée is a beard."

Janey gasped and then turned on him in a rage. "I can't believe you're this bitter,

Bill. Just because your career is going nowhere . . ." She was about to continue, but he cut her off.

"In the first place, I just sold a screenplay to Universal. So my career is going great, thank you very much," he said evenly. "And in the second, why can't you stop being so defensive? Not everybody is out to get you all the time . . . As a matter of fact, I was just trying to give you a friendly warning. A little tip to prevent you from making a fool of yourself over Rupert Jackson, the way you did over Comstock Dibble last summer. As I recall, I was the one who told you he was engaged . . ."

"Married. You said he was married," Janey said.

"What's the difference? The point is, he was with someone else . . ."

Well, she knew that, she thought, but stated so plainly, his words were like a little shock, reminding her of the unpleasant conversation she'd had with Comstock that afternoon. But she didn't want Bill to see that he'd nailed her, and staring boldly into his face, she said pointedly, "So what, Bill? Haven't you noticed that most of the men I've been with have been involved with someone else?"

And then, as if sensing her unease and going in for the kill, Bill asked casually, "By the way, whatever happened to that screenplay you were writing for him?"

This was such an obviously nasty dig that for a moment, all Janey could think about was *why* Bill was being so mean. She'd always thought of Bill as being fucked up, but never inherently unkind. The surface of New York's social interactions was as smooth and shiny as a sheet of ice, but underneath were water moccasins and snapping turtles—and while she knew of men who automatically became jealous of anyone else's success, including a woman's, she never thought Bill would fall into that category. For a moment, she soothed herself by feeling sorry for Bill, sorry that he'd become so pathetic. And then, shrugging off his comment as if it were of no importance, she said evenly, "What do you mean?"

He crossed his arms and leaned toward her aggressively. "I thought the big plan last summer was to become a famous Hollywood screenwriter. Didn't you tell me that Comstock paid you to write a screenplay?"

"As a matter of fact, he did," Janey said, shrugging her shoulders as if she couldn't understand what he was getting at.

"So did you finish it? Are they going to make it into a big Hollywood movie with you as the star?"

"Oh yes," she laughed, trying to make a joke of it. But inside, she was reeling. In the heady success of the last few months she'd managed to forget all about the fact that Comstock had paid her $30,000 to write a screenplay last summer—and while she had written thirty pages, she'd never been able to finish it. She couldn't stand the idea that she had failed, especially at something that she'd always proclaimed was easy, and last summer, in an attempt to put Bill in his place, she'd boasted endlessly about how well her screenplay was going and how great it was going to be. And now she was in the embarrassing position of having to defend herself to him.

"Well?" he demanded.

"Well what?"

"Did you even finish it?" he asked in a superior tone of voice, as if he knew she hadn't.

"I'm almost finished with the second draft." This was a complete lie, but she couldn't help it. All along, Bill had told her that she wouldn't be able to write it, and now there was no way she was going to give him the satisfaction of having been correct.

"Really?" he said, as if he didn't believe her. "You'll have to let me read it."

"Oh, I *will*," she said.

They looked at each other, locked in a stalemate—after all, Bill couldn't prove that she hadn't written the screenplay—and Janey took a step forward as if to signal that the conversation was over. But then she had another shock: Coming toward them and completely unaware of their presence was Comstock Dibble himself, deep in conversation on his cell phone. In a few seconds, he would reach the balustrade and be a mere three feet away, and Janey knew that Bill was just vicious enough to mention her screenplay to him.

And what would Comstock say? She looked around for an escape, but she was trapped—wedged between a flowering fruit tree and the balustrade, she could either knock Bill over or jump over the railing.

Bill caught the look of distress on her face and turned around to see what was bothering her. Comstock still had no idea they were there. His face was red with anger, and he was covered in his usual coating of thick sweat. In a raised voice, he said, "If they think they can pull this kind of crap on me, they've got another thing coming . . . I'll fuck with their kids, for Christ's sake." Snapping his cell phone shut, he suddenly turned and saw them.

His eyes narrowed and his lips pulled back into a vicious grin, revealing two front teeth separated by a large gap; Janey had a secret theory that his mother drank when she was pregnant and that Comstock Dibble, who wasn't more than five feet, six inches tall, had suffered from fetal alcohol syndrome. And then, in mounting confusion, she saw that his smile wasn't for her, but for Bill, and that he wasn't even going to acknowledge her.

"Westacott," Comstock said, holding out his hand. "My buddies at Universal tell me you did a great job with that screenplay."

Bill suddenly morphed into the Hollywood professional, folding his arms and standing with his legs spread apart, so that he no longer towered over Comstock.

"They've just given it the green light," Bill said. "Rupert Jackson's agreed to star . . ."

"Really?" Comstock said. "I love Rupert and he's a fine actor, but you'll have a hard time getting him out of bed before eleven . . ."

"I've heard that," Bill said. And then Janey, unable to contain herself any longer, said defiantly, "I've just had a long talk with him, and I think he's a doll . . ."

As soon as the words came out of her mouth, she realized how stupid they sounded, but she didn't care. She wasn't going to stand there, being ignored, and she looked from one man to the other with an expression on her face as if daring them to challenge her.

Bill looked at her with mild surprise, but Comstock regarded her blankly, as if he had never seen her before and had no idea she actually talked. "Well . . . ?" she said, faltering. And then Bill, unable to keep the amusement out of his voice, said, "Comstock, you know the lovely and talented Janey Wilcox, don't you?"

"I've never had the pleasure," he said. His words were mild enough, but the expression on his face said, If you fuck with me, I'll break your kneecaps.

He held out his hand and Janey, shaking with anger, took it. How dare he do this to her, and especially in front of Bill, who *knew* that they'd had an affair. She was still in the process of forming a retort when Comstock's cell phone rang, and turning away as if there were nothing going on beyond the usual burdens of being a high-powered movie producer, he said to Bill, "Sorry, the office. They never leave you alone, no matter where you are."

"Time difference," Bill said. "Try Australia."

"I *have*," Comstock said, and holding the cell phone up to his ear, he barked, "Yeah?" into it and began strolling away.

All Janey could think was that Comstock was getting away scot free, and she took a step toward him, intending to give him a piece of her mind. But Bill stopped her; as she expected, as soon as Comstock was out of earshot, he began making fun of her. "Didn't you have sex with him?" he asked mockingly. "What the hell did you do to him—bite his penis?"

A dozen nasty responses flittered through her mind, but Janey caught his expression and hesitated. He was taking too much pleasure in her obvious distress, and instinct told her that an angry display was exactly what he was hoping for. Lowering her head and pouting like a wounded child, she stared up at him through long dark lashes.

Faced with this display of female submissiveness, Bill's protective male instincts kicked in, and he gently put his arm around her shoulders. "Come on, Wilcox," he said. "I was just kidding, and everyone knows Comstock is an asshole. There's no point in bothering with men like that unless you have to, and besides, you're too good to have sex with such a disgusting little fart anyway . . ."

"I'm not upset," she insisted. And then, suddenly feeling that Bill was the one person who could understand, she blurted out, "I only slept with him because I thought it would be good for business!"

Bill's face registered surprise at her unexpected candor, and he laughed. "I can't say I agree with you," he said. "But that's probably the most honest thing you've said in years."

Janey glared at him, suddenly realizing she'd been caught. After all, she'd officially convinced herself that she was in love with Comstock, and she'd probably told Bill the same thing. "If you're implying that I'm a liar . . . ," she said.

"Oh, I'm not implying anything. I'm stating it as fact," Bill said. "You are a liar, and worst of all, you lie to yourself . . ."

"My goodness. You two look like you're embroiled in a lovers' quarrel," Mimi said, coming up behind them.

Janey gave Bill a dirty look, furious that they'd been caught unawares in such an obviously intimate conversation. Bill was dangerous; in the future she'd have to be careful not to let him back her into a corner—after all, she'd let him do it before and every time they'd ended up in bed. But Bill wasn't fazed: He casually stuck his hands in his pockets and, leaning back against the railing, said, "Janey and I are old friends. We always fight like brother and sister."

Mimi gave Janey a sympathetic look. "And that, I'm afraid, is Bill's definition of friendship," she said. "He's been fighting with me since we were in the sandbox together as kids."

"That's only because you wouldn't let me play with your shovels," Bill said.

"You were a bully then, and you haven't changed a bit," Mimi retorted. "In any case, I've come to tell you that we're sitting down to dinner . . . Janey, you're next to Selden Rose . . ."

At the name Selden Rose, Bill suddenly smirked. "Janey will eat him for breakfast," he said.

"Oh, Bill. Stop it," Mimi said, giving him a warning look. And then, with a glance that indicated that Janey should follow her, she said, "I don't know what's wrong with Bill. He seems to get more and more bitter every year. Do you think he has money problems?"

Janey had no idea, as she'd only known Bill for two years, and he had always been this way. But there was no reason to tell Mimi this, so she said, "I think Bill just hates women, period."

Mimi stopped and looked at her in surprise. "You know, I think you're absolutely right."

"I'm sure it has a lot to do with his wife," Janey said, giving Mimi a meaningful look.

Mimi smiled and, in a conspiratorial gesture, took Janey's arm. "I'm sure it does," she whispered. "Poor Helen. She used to be such a nice girl . . ."

And as they entered the dining room together, the sting of that embarrassing encounter with Comstock and Bill began to fade. After all, for tonight anyway there was no one more important in the room than Mimi Kilroy—and Mimi was treating her as if she were one of her very best girlfriends. And her pleasure was complete when Mimi indicated a place in the center of the room and said, "We're right here, Janey. I hope you don't mind, but I've seated you at my table."

THREE DAYS LATER, at just after one o'clock in the afternoon, Patty Wilcox was sitting on a bench outside the Ralph Lauren store in East Hampton, waiting for her sister, Janey, to show up.

Patty wondered why, when she knew Janey would be late, she had rushed to leave the house so that she would be at the store at precisely one o'clock, which was the time they'd agreed to meet. It wasn't, she thought, looking fruitlessly down the street, because she thought Janey might actually be on time. But rather that when Janey spoke, Patty jumped. Theirs was a typical big sister–little sister relationship, and there were times when Patty was just a little bit afraid of Janey . . .

That morning, at eleven o'clock, Janey had called her up, and in her usual cheery voice, which implied that everything in *her* life was just fantastic, thank you very much, asked Patty if she wanted to go shopping that afternoon.

"I don't know," Patty said hesitantly. "I'm not sure it's appropriate."

Janey's laugh indicated that Patty was being ridiculous. "You don't have to *buy* anything."

"It's not that," Patty said. "I'm just not sure if I should be seen out shopping right now."

"It's not like you have photographers following you around, Patty. I mean, no one's going to know who *you* are."

No, Patty thought, but they *would* know who Janey was, and although Patty had no evidence of this, it crossed her mind that Janey was entirely capable of calling up one of the gossip columnists and telling them that Digger's wife, who had been bilked out of a million dollars by Peter Cannon, was out shopping at Ralph

Lauren. And then, as she always did when she thought bad things about Janey, Patty felt guilty, and the guilty part of her found itself agreeing to meet Janey at one o'clock. And now, hungry and slightly annoyed, Patty looked around and thought about getting an ice cream cone.

But then she realized she couldn't do that either, because if Janey walked up and saw Patty eating an ice cream cone, she would give her "the look." And on that particular day, with all the other stuff she was coping with, Patty didn't need to be made aware of her shortcomings. Far better to go hungry than to be reminded—by Janey—of the fact that she probably *did* need to lose five or ten pounds.

Of course, Digger wouldn't agree. Staring up the street toward the movie theater (*Bag o' Bones*, one of Comstock's films, was playing), she thought about how Digger was always telling her to stand up to her sister. But she wasn't particularly thrilled with Digger at the moment, and besides, Digger didn't know Janey as well as she did. Digger was the only person she'd ever met who seemed to be mysteriously immune to Janey's charms—and while she had to admit that if that weren't one of the reasons she had married him, it was certainly one of the things that had made her like him, it also meant that Digger could never understand the way she really felt about Janey. The truth was that while she was sometimes afraid *of* Janey, she was also equally afraid *for* her.

There was something very seductive about her, but it was a dangerous sort of seduction, because inevitably Janey had a way of damaging anyone who became involved with her. It was a fact of which Janey appeared to be blissfully unaware, and there were times when Patty couldn't help wishing that something bad would happen to Janey and she would learn her lesson, although she wasn't exactly sure what that lesson should be. And then she would feel guilty, because Janey was her sister, and you shouldn't feel that way about a sibling.

But even as a child, Janey hadn't been what was considered normal, Patty thought, standing up and peering down the street in vain. There had always been a supreme indifference about Janey: Every summer at the country club, while the other kids were swimming and playing tennis, Janey, who was fat and not athletic and didn't like being seen in a bathing suit (now *that* was ironic), would sit at a picnic table in the woods, playing cards. Other kids tried to be friends with her, but Janey would dismiss them with a cutting remark.

And so it wasn't really surprising that the whole family had been relieved when Janey had been accepted into the Ford modeling agency at sixteen. That first summer, Janey had been gone for three months, and Patty remembered it as the best summer of her life—she'd won the twelve-and-under state championship in swimming—and for once, no one in their family was fighting. And then the following summer, Janey had supposedly gone away for good. But eventually that seemed to go all wrong as well, although nobody in the family ever talked about it or said why, including Janey. All Patty knew was that she would never forget the end of that second summer, when Janey was eighteen and had come back from the South of France as different as if she'd gone to another planet and returned an alien. She had Louis Vuitton suitcases and designer clothes from France and Italy, she had handbags from Chanel and shoes from Manolo Blahnik, and in the afternoons, she would show Patty her things and tell her how much they had cost. Patty remembered that one handbag alone had cost $2,000, and when she looked scared, Janey had told her—in that new voice she'd developed with the fake European accent—that life wasn't worth living if you couldn't have the best it had to offer.

Patty returned to the bench with a sigh. Being a Monday afternoon in June, the main street in East Hampton wasn't particularly crowded, but Patty was beginning to feel uncomfortable. A Mercedes passed, and then a Range Rover and a Lexus; it seemed that nobody in the Hamptons had a car that cost less than $100,000. She reminded herself that her own Mercedes was equally expensive, but that did little to prevent her from feeling like an interloper who, try as she might, never really felt like she belonged in this scene. It was just like the Mercedes, which Digger had paid for, and therefore wasn't really hers.

Maybe the problem was that it was all a little *too* perfect, she thought; with the meticulously maintained antique houses that lined the beginning of Main Street, eventually blending into the pristine white buildings that housed expensive shops. Or maybe it was just that the whole place screamed money: The windows of the real estate office behind her featured poster-size aerial photographs of $10 million estates, while the lingerie store next door charged $150 for a pair of cotton underpants. Or maybe it was the reality that being in the Hamptons wasn't really getting away from New York, and at any moment one might run into an unwelcome acquaintance.

And that, of course, is exactly what happened. Patty's thoughts were interrupted by a disembodied high-pitched staccato voice, screaming into a cell phone: "But I told you not to let him in! The client is furious!" and in a moment, the somewhat stumpy figure of Roditzy Deardrum emerged from behind a tree.

Roditzy was one of those public relations girls whose photograph had recently appeared on the cover of *New York* magazine; she was exactly Patty's age—twenty-eight—and, thanks to her mother's money, headed her own PR company called Ditzy Productions. Roditzy would later end up in a French jail due to a freak boating accident in the South of France, in which several of her friends would lose arms and legs during an Ecstasy fest arranged by Roditzy herself, but at the moment, nothing bad had happened to her and she was considered the party queen of New York, the girl who was responsible for arranging the most outrageous events and producing the best guests. Her last event had been some ridiculous extravaganza involving dogs dressed up in one-of-a-kind designer dog clothes, and she had managed to convince several unwitting movie stars to attend. Patty knew that if Roditzy spotted her, she was a goner, but in a second it was too late because she heard Roditzy say, "Okay, I've just seen Patty Wilcox so I have to go," and then Roditzy was upon her.

"Pa-a-a-a-tty!" she screamed, causing passersby to swivel their heads. "How a-a-a-a-re you?"

"I'm doing fine," Patty said, as Roditzy did the kiss-kiss thing on both cheeks.

"I haven't seen you for a-a-a-a-ges," Roditzy said. "What are you doing now?"

This was just the question Patty was hoping to avoid, but as it was now inevitable, she said, "Nothing."

"Nothing?" Roditzy asked, as if unable to comprehend such an answer.

"That's right. Nothing," Patty said. "I'm a housewife now."

Roditzy's expression indicated the very opposite, but she said, "Ohmigod. That is sooooo retro. Cool."

Patty crossed her arms and nodded, but inside she was convinced Roditzy was looking at her like she was some kind of freak.

"So, like, what do you do all day?" Roditzy asked.

"Oh, stuff . . . ," Patty said. She certainly wasn't going to tell Roditzy that for the last year she'd been trying to get pregnant but hadn't been able to, that she longed to have a child more than anything because she loved her husband with a crying ache that seemed to dictate that they had to deepen their relationship by producing a child—because what could a girl like Roditzy understand about the magical mystery of being young, in love, and heartbreakingly committed to a man?

Roditzy leaned in, attempting to create a bond of intimacy that didn't exist between them, and lowering her voice, asked, "How *is* Digger? I mean, with the stuff about . . ."

"Peter Cannon?" Patty said, stiffening. "He's fine."

"Good," Roditzy said. "I don't understand what happened to Peter Cannon, do you? I mean, everybody thought he was such a great guy. He was best friends with everybody . . . Remember those wild parties at his loft? I mean, if we'd only known that he was paying for that Cristal Champagne with our money . . ."

"Whatever," Patty said.

"Whatever," Roditzy agreed. And then demanded, "Are you guys around next weekend? I need you to come to this party I'm having for . . ."

"Digger's going on tour," Patty said firmly, cutting her off. "He'll be gone for two months."

"Well, then, *you* have to come," Roditzy insisted. "I'll have one of my assistants send a car. That way, you can party without having to worry about driving home."

Roditzy fixed her with the bright stare of someone who won't take no for an answer, and Patty was unable to protest. "Great!" Roditzy said, and then, with the air of someone who has important places to go and many people to see, she snapped open her cell phone and marched into Ralph Lauren.

Patty collapsed weakly onto the bench, suddenly acutely aware of the fact that with Digger away on tour, that was another two months when she wouldn't be able to get pregnant. And on top of it all, now she would be forced to go to some party she had no interest in attending—why was it that everyone in New York was always demanding your presence at something or other?—and it was all Janey's fault for being late. If Janey had been on time for once, she probably would never have run into Roditzy.

But now, here came Janey at last, roaring up Route 27 in her Porsche Boxster. You could hear her coming a mile away because she drove that car like it was a race-horse—she shifted the gears so you could hear the engine turning over, and she did it on purpose, so people would look up and see her. She always wanted everyone to see her now, and that made Patty worried. Because in the past, people hadn't always said the nicest things about Janey . . .

The car pulled up in front of Patty, and with a great flourish, Janey got out and slammed the door. She was wearing a red Prada halter top and white jeans (white jeans had just come into style, but Janey had been wearing them forever), and with a completely natural smile that wasn't at all like the phony, slutty smirk she wore on her billboard, waved to Patty. And in that moment, Patty crumpled inside as she always did and took back every bad thought she'd ever had about Janey: After all, how could anyone as beautiful as Janey be as evil as she'd imagined?

And then it was even worse, because with a chirpy "Hi Sis," Janey took her arm (much in the way Mimi had taken Janey's arm a few nights before) and said, "Listen, I didn't want to tell you this on the phone because I knew you'd say no, but I want to buy you something at Ralph and then take you to lunch at Nick and Toni's"—one of the most exclusive restaurants in the Hamptons—and Patty felt like a heel all over again.

"Do you mind if we skip the shopping?" Patty asked, wanting to avoid another chance encounter with Roditzy Deardrum. "I'm starving."

"Of course not," Janey said. And then, fixing her sister with a gimlet eye, she asked, "By the way, how's Digger?" Her tone was nonchalant, but her eyes seemed to pierce right into Patty's brain as if she could see the truth, and for a moment, Patty had that terrible feeling she'd been having lately, as if she were drowning.

"Well, he's . . . ," she said lamely, and Janey nodded wisely. But with that simple assent, Patty felt that Janey understood everything. And as they walked up the street to Nick & Toni's, Patty reflected that the really good thing about Janey was that she made you feel like you could tell her all of the terrible, deep, dark thoughts you had in your head, and that she would understand.

At the age of eighteen, Janey came to think of herself as the sort of person who could draw out confidences, and had quickly understood that getting information was power. It wasn't always the information itself that was important (which was the mistake that most people made), but the act of being told things: It formed a bond between her and the confessor—a sort of unspoken pact of friendship, which she could draw on later to get what she needed.

And now, seated at a table in the front section of Nick & Toni's, her face was arranged in the soft lines of commiseration appropriate to these kinds of situations, and although she appeared to be concentrating, another part of her brain was attuned to the door. At any moment, she expected Mimi Kilroy to arrive, which would require the employment of a different set of her considerable social skills.

Earlier that morning, Janey had telephoned Mimi's house under the pretense of thanking her for the party. Mimi wasn't there, and Janey, by telling the housemaid who answered the phone that she was a "very good friend of Mimi's," managed to extract the information that after her riding class, Mimi was expected to lunch at Nick & Toni's. At that moment, Janey decided that she, too, would be lunching at Nick & Toni's. The only hitch was that she couldn't eat at Nick & Toni's by herself, and doing a quick mental tally of potential lunch dates, decided on Patty.

She didn't have a moment's hesitation about using her sister to further her own ends; after all, it wasn't like she didn't genuinely adore her. She'd always loved Patty, of course, in the automatic way people do in families, but it was only in the past two years that she'd begun to like her. And that was, she insisted, only because she didn't *know* Patty before—they'd never moved in the same circles until Patty had become a producer for VH1 and had met Digger and, last year, married him. Since then, Janey had come to appreciate Patty's simplicity and kindness, and her refreshing lack of ambition: Three months after marrying Digger she'd given up her job in order to run their lives and hopefully raise their as yet unborn children. Of course, Janey also understood the value of having a sister who was married to a rock star. Although she didn't inherently *like* Digger, she would have to admit that if Patty had married a plumber instead (the way Janey had once pictured she might), the two sisters wouldn't have been nearly as close.

And indeed, with their blond heads bent together in familial intimacy, there couldn't have been a prettier picture of sisterly affection. Of this, Janey was happily aware—it was exactly the image she wished Mimi to see, knowing that it would cast her in a broader, more human light. And so, wrenching her thoughts away from her own selfish advancement, Janey forced herself to concentrate on Patty, who was struggling with a white linen napkin that had been folded into a complicated origami swan.

"Patty?" she said.

"Yes?" Patty asked.

"How are you? *Really?*"

"Well," Patty said, having tamed the napkin and spread it on her lap, "I'm okay. I saw Roditzy Deardrum going into Ralph Lauren."

"How *is* Roditzy? I actually like her, you know? I think she's *fine*," Janey said.

"You *do?*" Patty said. "I think she's awful."

"She *is* a little obnoxious," Janey agreed, "but at the end of the day, all she's trying to do is to make it just like everybody else. She's always nice to *me* . . ."

"Of course she's nice to *you* . . ."

"Isn't she nice to you?"

"She's trying to force me to go to this party on Saturday night."

"What's wrong with that?" Janey signaled to the waiter. "You probably *should* get out more."

"But *why?*"

"Why not?"

"What's the point?"

"Maybe there isn't one. Maybe it's just about people going out and seeing their friends."

"But most of those people don't even *like* each other."

"How do you *know* that? People aren't perfect, you know? They're limited. Maybe they like each other as much as they *can* . . ."

"That's not enough for me . . ."

"Oh Patty. What's *wrong?*"

"I mean," Patty said, "why is everyone always trying so hard to be these *people* . . . to prove that they're important? When I saw Roditzy, I thought, I know what her problem is. She has low self-esteem."

Janey smiled. "Is this a Digger thing?"

"No," Patty said, slightly insulted. "*Think* about it. Why is she always running around, making so much noise on her cell phone like a big, squeaky mouse? For that matter, you and I probably have low self-esteem. Have you ever wondered why we're never really happy?"

Janey considered this. It *was* true. She never was *really* happy. She always had the slight feeling of having been cheated by life in some way, although in exactly *what* way she couldn't name.

"You see?" Patty said. "It's because of something Mom and Dad did to us when we were kids. They never really encouraged us to do anything. Have you noticed that they never once told us that we could succeed? That we could make anything of our lives?"

"They encouraged *you*, Patty," Janey said.

She sat back in her chair. She was beginning to get annoyed. Patty was one of those lucky people who managed to get whatever they wanted in life without trying. When they were kids, Patty had been the cosseted youngest child, adored by both her mother *and* father—Patty seemed to have a special way of talking to each parent, while Janey couldn't connect with her father at all, and had only a combative relationship with her mother—and on top of it, Patty had actually been considered the pretty one in the family. She'd even been a cheerleader, and although she'd never made particularly good grades, somehow she'd been accepted into Boston University. It passed through Janey's mind that maybe Patty had slept with an admissions officer to get in (which is what, she had to admit, *she* would have done), but you could tell just by looking at Patty that she was one of those women who had never sacrificed her moral values to get ahead. And then she'd met Digger and fallen in love. Janey had never really been in love herself, at least not in the way that Patty was, but she still held it in the highest regard, and still believed that if you had true love, you had everything. The problem, of course, was finding it, and she said, with slight exasperation, "Patty, you have *every reason* to be happy."

Patty looked down at her napkin, shifting her reddish blond hair over her shoulder—*It would be so much better if she would only lighten it a bit,* Janey thought—and asked, "Have you ever been pregnant?"

What a question! Janey thought, and took a moment to answer. "Well," she said jokingly, "I've *told* people I was pregnant . . ."

"But really, Janey . . ."

"Not that I *know* about . . ."

"Well, I've been trying to get pregnant for the last year, and I haven't," Patty said.

And at this very moment, Mimi Kilroy arrived.

Janey had been anticipating her entrance for what now seemed like hours, but instead of behaving in the usual manner, which would have been to look up and greet Mimi with a wave, she forced herself to appear as if she were completely absorbed in her conversation with Patty. "But Patty," she said. "You know that doesn't matter. Everyone knows that it's normal for it to take a year . . . Have you seen a doctor?" But her thoughts were completely directed toward Mimi.

Driving home from Mimi's house on Friday night, Janey had had an epiphany: She'd never had many female friends, but she suddenly saw the value of having a female friend like Mimi—and she realized that Mimi's friendship might be more useful than most of the relationships she'd forged with powerful men. People never questioned a friendship between two women, while they were always suspicious of a friendship between a man and a woman, especially if the man was rich and the woman was beautiful. On the other hand, Mimi was as powerful and as influential as most of the men she knew (indeed, most of these men even seemed to be afraid of her); if she could turn Mimi's interest in her into an actual relationship, she had a feeling that she could go far. With Mimi's approbation, every door would be open to her . . .

The only problem was that, at first, Janey wasn't exactly sure how to go about winning Mimi's friendship. It wasn't simply that everyone wanted to be friends with Mimi, and that Mimi, like most popular New Yorkers, didn't really need any new friends, but that Janey had never developed those easy skills that lead to instant friendships with other women. As a child, she'd been betrayed by a group of little girls who made fun of her and teased her mercilessly for having a crush on an older boy; as an adult, she'd done her share of getting even by stealing men out from under other women's noses. As a result, her relationships with women were always uneasy: Janey didn't trust them, and they (often rightly) didn't trust her. But Janey's instincts never betrayed her, and just the other night she had realized that seduction isn't always about sex, and that she might pursue Mimi the same way she would pursue a man.

The first step in her plan was to throw herself in Mimi's path, hence the shang-haiing of her sister, Patty, to lunch. It must appear as if it were mere coincidence that she and Patty were eating at Nick & Toni's, but more importantly, as with a man, Janey knew she couldn't appear too eager. She wanted Mimi to come to her and not the other way around, and, with this in mind, she'd insisted on a table in front, near the door. Unless Mimi were blind, it would be almost impossible for her not to spot Janey, and then the dictates of social behavior would take their natural course, and Mimi would be forced to at least say hello.

And so, appearing to concentrate on Patty while watching Mimi out of the corner of her eye, Janey arranged her face into its most sympathetic expression and asked, "What do you think you should do?"

Patty, who was completely oblivious to Mimi's arrival and to Janey's hidden agenda, said desperately, "I don't *know*. Sometimes I'm afraid I'll turn into one of those crazy women who steal someone else's baby . . ."

And before Janey could respond, Mimi suddenly saw her and in a low, creamy voice, cooed, "Janey, darling. Is that you?"

Janey turned around, feigning surprise. Mimi had come straight from her riding lesson, and was dressed in a crisp white short-sleeved shirt, white jodhpurs, and tightly fitted custom-made riding boots; an Hermès Birkin bag was slung over her shoulder, out of which peeked the tail end of a small, braided leather whip. In general, it was considered déclassé to trip around East Hampton in your riding togs, a recent affectation of visiting showbiz people and the nouveaux riches. But as Mimi was so obviously old school, and, as Janey noted with a touch of envy, probably the only woman in the world who could still look devastatingly slim in a pair of white riding pants, she could get away with it.

"Mimi," Janey said, rising gracefully from her chair and holding out her hand. If Mimi kissed her, that would be a good sign, but as Mimi was older and more established, it was up to her to initiate this gesture. And indeed, after taking Janey's hand, she leaned forward to allow Janey to brush each cheek with her lips in the customary manner.

"This is such a coincidence," Janey said. "I just called your house to thank you for the party."

"It was a good one, wasn't it?" Mimi said. She must be at least forty, Janey thought, but she still had that boyish quality to her face that was *so* appealing. "Rupert was absolutely crazy about you, and George told me three times how beautiful he thought you were . . . I finally told him that maybe he should divorce me and marry you. And Selden seemed *very* interested. You two seemed to be having quite an intense talk at dinner."

This wasn't, Janey thought, entirely accurate, as "disagreement" was probably a more appropriate word, but this was hardly the time to reveal her true feelings about Selden Rose. "I thought he was *so* interesting," Janey said with conviction, and Mimi looked pleased. "Did you?" she asked, but as Janey really didn't, she turned to her sister and said, "Do you know Patty? My sister?"

Mimi held out her hand. "I certainly know your husband. Everyone's always talking about how talented he is—they say he's going to be the next Mick Jagger . . ."

He's not anything like Mick Jagger! Patty wanted to shout, but instead found herself saying, "Thank you," primly. It was certainly ironic that Mimi was pretending to know Digger, and to like him, as he most definitely didn't like her. But in the next moment, and in typical New York fashion, her sister and Mimi seemed to have forgotten all about her, because Mimi turned to Janey, and in a faux-scolding kind of voice, like Janey had actually done something wrong, said, "Janey, you didn't tell me you were out here during the week."

"Oh, I *am*," Janey said. "For the whole summer."

"Well then, we *have* to get together," Mimi said. "It's so dull out here during the week. George is out only on weekends, but his sons are here, and I think it's rot-ten for kids to be left with a nanny all the time . . . And Mauve is out here too. You know Mauve, don't you?"

"Oh yes," Janey said, nodding. This wasn't technically true, as Janey had been introduced to Mauve only once or twice, but in this situation "know" meant nothing more than the fact that she and Mauve were aware of each other's existence.

"Poor Mauve," Mimi said in a stage whisper, shaking her head in a manner that made Janey suspect everyone had been saying "poor Mauve" for years. "Marrying Comstock Dibble. I keep telling her that she doesn't have to do it, but she won't listen. She says she's in love with him—and what nobody understands is that they really are two peas in a pod. Mauve's got a terrible temper . . . they can't even decide when to get married."

Patty looked from Mimi to Janey with growing disgust. She wasn't so much of a rube that she didn't know that Mimi and Mauve were supposedly best friends, so why was Mimi talking about her friend like that? But naturally, Janey was completely ignoring this fact—she had that intense, catlike expression on her face that could make you think you were the most interesting person in the world—and in the next moment, she said breathlessly, "Maybe it won't happen."

"Oh, it will," Mimi said. "And then it will be a disaster . . . In any case, you must promise to call me tomorrow . . . I love Mauve, but I don't need to have lunch with her every day . . . By the way, do you ride?"

Janey hesitated for just a moment before she said yes.

"That's excellent," Mimi said. "We'll go for a hack and talk about Selden . . . I'm really very excited about this. I just may have found Selden a wife!" And Janey, caught up in the glory of the moment, emitted her trademark tinkling peal of laughter.

Moments later, after the horsey-faced Mauve Binchely had arrived (she had a sour expression on her face, which Patty guessed might have been permanent), and Mimi and Mauve had gone off to their table, Janey finally sat back down. She looked like she'd just won a gold medal, and Patty wondered what it was about Mimi that made her so interesting to Janey.

As she picked up her fork (their salads had arrived while she and Mimi were talking), all Janey could think about was how that little scene with Mimi had come off much better than she'd hoped—unbelievably so, in fact—and how even though you could never tell when people like Mimi Kilroy were being genuine, she'd certainly been insistent about meeting up. And what a coup that was: It was one thing to be invited to a party of a hundred people, but a completely different thing to be asked to spend time with Mimi alone. Indeed, she was so consumed with her own triumph, that when she looked up and caught Patty's eye, she was actually expecting her to share in her moment of glory.

But the expression on Patty's face quickly brought her back to earth. Patty's look seemed to be implying that somehow Janey had betrayed her, and Janey was reminded once again that even though Patty was married to a rock star, she actually wasn't very worldly. Last year, Patty had enjoyed a small flurry of media attention when she'd married Digger, but she hadn't really enjoyed it, and had withdrawn as soon as she could, claiming that she thought the whole thing was "fake." And for a second, Janey saw herself and Mimi as Patty might have—as two glamorous, silly, superficial women flinging compliments at each other that they didn't really mean—and realized Patty was half right. But ultimately, Patty's perception was too simple: Patty was too immature to understand the value of hyperbole, and how it might smooth the waters for more interesting sights below.

"Now Patty," she began, but Patty cut her off.

"How could you do that?" she asked.

"Do what?" Janey asked, all innocence.

"In the first place, you've never even been on a horse . . ."

"Oh that," Janey said dismissively. "All we're going to do is walk . . . I mean, really, Patty. How hard can it be to sit on a horse?" Janey's eyes had narrowed to the point where her irises appeared to be cold blue stones, and Patty knew that Janey hated nothing more than to have her motives questioned.

"But you lied," Patty whispered.

"Really, Patty." Janey put down her fork in resignation. "You have to stop taking everything so . . . *literally*. Why shouldn't I go riding with Mimi Kilroy? Am I really so awful that I shouldn't have a new friend?"

Patty's mouth turned down and her shoulders drooped in defeat. Once again, it seemed, Janey had somehow gotten to the emotional heart of the situation, and even though Patty knew that something wasn't right, she couldn't argue with Janey's logic—after all, who was she to tell her sister who she should or shouldn't be friends with? But still, why did that friend have to be Mimi Kilroy? Why couldn't it be a normal person?

"Come on, Patty," Janey said firmly. "Mimi is nice. And besides, you're probably just upset about that comment she made about Digger. How is she supposed to know that you can't get . . . ?"

"Janey!"

And Janey, remembering the admiration in Mimi's voice when she mentioned Digger, was reminded once again of how potentially fruitful Patty and Digger's alliance was, and what a shame it would be if something happened to destroy it. "Now Patty," she said, reaching across the table to squeeze Patty's hand. "You have to be calm about this. I'm sure there's a simple answer. Have you ever considered the fact that maybe Digger smokes too much pot?"

A look of realization and relief passed across Patty's face and Janey smiled in acknowledgment, pleased that she'd been able to help Patty.

And in the back corner of Nick & Toni's, Mauve Binchely's eyes kept wandering back to Janey. And Mauve thought, *Janey Wilcox is beautiful, one has to grant her that*, but she comforted herself with the fact that it was a cheap kind of beauty. "Really, Mimi," Mauve said. "How can you even speak to her? She's so common, and she has that reputation. They say she's slept with everyone. Including Peter Cannon."

"Who?" Mimi demanded. And following Mauve's eyes, she exclaimed, "Janey Wilcox?" And then she laughed. "You know I don't care about reputations, Mauve. If I did, the first person *I* wouldn't speak to would be Comstock Dibble!"

•   •   •

New Yorkers sliced everything into tiny categories, and then, like diamond sorters, examined and graded each particle. And this was most true of the Hamptons.

The thirty-mile span from the towns of Southampton to East Hampton is considered most desirable; within that category the area "south of the highway" is superior to "north of the highway," the highway being the two-lane road known as Route 27. From there, a hundred nuances could be employed to determine what makes one acre more favorable than another, from proximity to the ocean to the professions of one's neighbors. Janey was acutely aware of these tiny distinctions, but there was one area in which she'd always disagreed with the general consensus: Secretly, she preferred the area north of the highway to that to the south. She loved the vast expanses of farmland and the familiar winding back roads, which she'd discovered the first time she'd come out to the Hamptons ten years ago. Driving these roads had always been her escape, the difference being that in the past, which really wasn't more than a year ago, she'd had to drive them in a car borrowed from whichever man she was sleeping with at the time. And now, downshifting to third gear and taking the sharp turn by a farm stand at a good forty miles an hour, she took great relish in the fact that she was finally in her own car.

Leaving her sister and Mimi in East Hampton, she had decided that it was a perfect day for a late-afternoon drive. There was a straightaway from Sag Main Road to Scuttle Hole Road, and Janey slid the stick shift into fourth gear and accelerated to seventy. Her hair, secured in a ponytail, blew madly behind her; she loved the feeling of freedom speed gave her, and at that moment, she reflected that she could never go fast enough. But then she had to slow down to make the turn that led to the Two Trees horse farm.

Smoothing back her hair, she eased the car down to twenty miles an hour (she swore she could hear the engine crying against such restraint), and scanned the mown field where several cars were parked. Sure enough, parked at the end on an

arrogant angle, so no other cars could park next to it, was Harold Vane's black
Maserati. She recognized it immediately, because three years before she'd been
Harold's girlfriend for the whole summer, and had spent far too much time in that
car being driven around by Harold. Harold was too jumpy to be a good driver, but
when Janey had pointed this out to him, he'd looked at her in alarm and had ground
the gears, so she never mentioned it again.

She steered the Boxster along a dirt track, thinking that dear, darling Harold,
with his shiny bald head and his ever-shiny shoes, was really *quite* a show-off. But
as he was so charming and kind (he'd loaned Janey money last summer when she
was broke), it was difficult to fault him for anything.

And now, Janey thought, checking her face in the mirrored sun visor and
leisurely applying her trademark Pussy Pink lipstick, he had taken up polo! It was
extraordinary, really, especially as Harold, who was little and neurotic (he was over
fifty, but couldn't keep still), was the last person she could imagine on a horse. But
Janey had a "feeling" that polo was going to be very big this summer, and Harold
was one of those people who loved being on the leading edge of the next stylish
thing. And as he had supposedly made a killing in the stock market in the past two
years, why shouldn't he spend his leisure time as he pleased, no matter how ridiculous it might make him look?

In the distance, tiny riders on tiny horses raced up and down a green velvet
field, but they were too far away to make out their identities. Janey began strolling
toward them, thinking about how pleased (and surprised) Harold would be to see
her, and immediately found that there was a small impediment: It had rained in the
past two days, and her three-inch, spike-heeled Dolce & Gabbana sandals were
sinking into the earth, giving her an ungainly gait. This would never do, so she
stumbled the few feet back to her car to take off her shoes.

As she bent over to unfasten the strap, she had the uncomfortable feeling that
someone was watching her. She hated being caught unawares—had, indeed, always
hated being in situations in which she couldn't control the impression she might
create—and she jerked her head up. Sure enough, not only was she being watched,
she was being watched by the very person she had secretly come to impress: Zizi.

Now, this was unfortunate, she thought. He was leaning against a Range Rover
with his arms folded across his chest (where on earth had he come from, Janey
thought, the field had been deserted when she'd driven in), and on his face was an
unmistakable smirk of amusement, as if he *knew* she had come specifically to find
him. And the worst thing about it, she thought, as she checked her balance against
the car, was that he was every bit as good-looking as she'd thought he would be
when he had passed her on the highway in his Ferrari. No, cancel that: He was

better-looking. He had that dangerous sort of male beauty on which a woman might stupidly and readily throw away her pride, and he knew it.

For a second, she considered getting into her car and driving away (now *that* would confuse him), but then he started walking toward her. She quickly looked down at her feet, wondering if he was going to stop and talk to her, but instead, he strode by (he was a good five inches taller than she was, and she was 5'10"), and as he passed, he said playfully, "You need boots."

"Boots?" she scoffed. "What for?"

"The mud," he called over his shoulder.

And that was it.

She had a nearly uncontrollable urge to run after him, which was probably what he expected her to do (which was what she imagined *he* expected *all* women would want to do), as she stood awkwardly with one naked, exposed foot poised over the grass.

And then he stopped and turned.

"Well?" he asked.

"Well what?" she said.

"Can I help you?"

"I'm looking for Harold Vane," she said, as if to emphasize the fact that she was not looking for him.

"Ah, *el patrón*. I will take you to him," he said, giving her an intense look that implied there might be a larger meaning behind his words. He walked back to the Range Rover, opened the door, and removed a pair of rubber boots.

"Here," he said with a smirk.

He held out the boots to her and their fingers touched. A jolt of electricity passed between them. The shock left Janey dizzy and slightly disoriented, as if she'd lost all sense of the horizon, while other details came into sharp relief: a gray crack on the tip of one black rubber boot, the gritty texture of the rough grass beneath her foot, and, burned into her brain, the strange creamy green color of his eyes, which reminded her of the warm Caribbean Sea through which one can clearly see shells and small bright fish against an oatmeal-colored bed of sand. Had he felt it too, she wondered wildly, or was it all in her imagination? And if not, what did it mean?

And then he was striding across the field with the confidence of a young god, as she clomped awkwardly after him, trying to keep up. She couldn't take her eyes off him (who could have?), and as he turned and smiled, she saw that he had that air of deliberate kindness combined with a world-weary aloofness that is the mark of a person whose beauty has set him apart from the rest of humanity. "You are a fan of the polo?" he asked, and she answered with uncharacteristic honesty, "No. I don't care a thing about it."

She raised her eyebrows as if daring him to disapprove, but there was less aggression and more frank girlishness in this move than she would have normally employed with a man with whom she felt on uncertain footing, and he rewarded her with an appreciative laugh. She answered with a laugh of her own, uncontrived, and marveled at how her layers of bullshit seemed to have fallen away, revealing her pure being. And then their eyes met in shining conspiracy.

"This is really turning out to be a good day," she said.

A thundering of hooves distracted them, and from the far end of the polo field a pack of horses and riders came galloping in their direction and passed by to the goalpost at the opposite end; lagging behind was a lone rider whose form might best be described as a sack of potatoes loosely strapped to a saddle. The sack seemed to veer dangerously in all directions at once; as it came closer Janey could make out the human form of Harold Vane.

Suddenly, the pack at the other end of the field turned and began galloping toward him; Harold's startled expression indicated that he knew a collision was inevitable. Abandoning all pretense of riding ability, he threw himself upon the mercy of his horse, which, he no doubt assumed, probably did not want to be trampled either, and literally wrapped his arms around her neck. The horse, an old mare named Biscuit who had recently been brought out of retirement for the express purpose of safely squiring Harold on her back, immediately understood what to do. Chomping down on the bit so that no amount of pulling on Harold's part could deter her, she determinedly set off for the barn at a brisk trot.

At that point, Harold Vane's only concern was staying on Biscuit for the mile-long trek to the barn, at which point a groom or stable boy would come running out with an annoying air of repressed disapproval; but suddenly his eye was caught by the pleasing lines of a beautiful woman, and a second later he realized that that woman was none other than Janey Wilcox. What the hell was she doing here? he wondered. And then he saw, with consternation, that she was standing close—too close—to his star polo player. They weren't touching (*yet*, he thought), but nevertheless were posed in an attitude of intimacy, with her face tilted up toward his and his eyes looking down upon her, and, he thought, he would be goddamned if he allowed his only ten-goaler to get caught up with Janey. He would definitely have a little chat with Zizi and nip this thing in the bud, and he told himself that he was only doing it for the sake of the team—he intended to win, and he needed Zizi's full concentration.

And Zizi would have to listen to him, he thought, clinging to Biscuit's neck with the crablike patience of a rich man who is always confident of succeeding.

After all, he was the boss, the man who was shelling out half a million dollars a month for the team, and the Argentinean polo players were intensely loyal to the wishes of their *patrón*. And so, he decided, he really had no need to be overly worried about Janey Wilcox. He reminded himself that he had had her and rejected her, and that Janey was one of those women who are great at getting men but lousy at keeping them.

But, as the sight of the barn thankfully appeared from behind a copse of trees, there was one truth to which his male vanity would never admit, and that was envy. Yes, he had rejected Janey Wilcox, but that didn't necessarily mean that he wanted another man to have her. And especially not a man who was twenty years younger, a hundred times better-looking, and, most of all, a good twelve inches taller.

He is exactly what I want, Janey thought, driving home in her car. When it came to basic human emotions, such as love, hate, envy, joy, and triumph, Janey was neither sophisticated nor poetic, but she felt what she felt with the force of a genuine truth— and she decided that she was as in love with Zizi as she'd ever been with anybody.

In any case, she thought, coming out onto Route 27 from Hayrack Road (on purpose—the slow traffic would give her time to think), she was not going to go for Selden Rose, especially not now, after those magical few minutes with Zizi. And now, with the Boxster throatily purring along in the thick traffic, and the warm weight of summer beginning to make itself felt, the memory of her encounter with Selden Rose at Mimi's party three nights ago filled her with a triumphant sense of amusement.

Her first impression of Selden Rose was that in looks, anyway, he was acceptable: He was tall and dark, and while obviously over forty, his face still had some of the fat of youth. But as he shook her hand, giving her a vague, tight smile, she saw that he had the off-putting attitude of a man who knows that he is a catch and doesn't mean to let anyone forget it.

And so, with a tiny air of resignation, she took her seat next to him. As she sat down, he deliberately turned away, and she experienced the distinct disappointment that her dress had been wasted on him.

He was in the middle of leading their half of the table in conversation. "The problem with people right now," he said, with the confidence of a man who assumes that his opinions will always be taken seriously, "is that without war, there isn't any moral purpose . . . People have become soft and amoral because they've been allowed to forget about the reality of death . . . We've become inured to it. Nowadays, death takes place behind closed doors . . . nobody ever *sees* death anymore . . ."

And Janey, who really could not take this conversation too seriously, said, "'Inured'? That's an awfully big word for East Hampton."

He turned to her—and about time, she thought—and without a trace of sarcasm in his voice, as if he really did think she was a dummy, said, "Oh. Would you like me to explain its meaning?"

"What? And spoil the pleasure of having to look it up in the dictionary? I think not," Janey said, as she pointedly took a sip of champagne, which was a dry vintage Laurent-Perrier—the one that came in the pretty flowered bottle.

"Oh, well, suit yourself," he said, as if he had no idea what to make of her, and Janey decided he had none of the subtle social graces at all, probably because he was from LA. And then she deliberately turned to the man on her left and he to the woman on his right.

The man to Janey's left was the Republican senator from New York, an easygoing yet powerful man in his sixties named Mike Matthews. By discussing the benefits of the new, cleaned-up New York, Janey managed to keep the conversation going through the appetizer—a luxurious serving of beluga caviar mounded on top of three tiny cold potatoes—but when the plates were cleared away, there was a lull in the conversation and she was drawn back to Selden. He certainly seemed to have no end of stupid opinions, Janey noted, as she overheard him talking about the differences between men and women with the elegant middle-aged woman to his right. This particular type of conversation was inevitable, Janey thought, given that Selden was single—it was always only a matter of time before someone asked a single man *why* he was unattached—and, as if on cue, Selden said, "The truth is that—*biologically*—men choose women based on their looks." And then had the nerve to add triumphantly, "And that's the one thing feminism will never be able to change."

The middle-aged woman smiled indulgently while Janey let out a ringing laugh of derision, causing him to turn back to her.

Janey smiled. His timing, she thought, couldn't have been better; she'd been waiting for a moment just like this one. A few days ago, when she'd been in Book-Hampton, she'd picked up a new neofeminist tome titled *Beauty: How Men's Expectations Have Ruined Women's Lives,* and in her usual manner, had flipped through it, absorbing a few salient facts that she might later use at dinner parties. "As a matter of fact," she said pleasantly, "you're wrong. Before the 1900s—before the industrial revolution and the redistribution of wealth and the advent of the gold digger—men usually chose women based on the woman's income and position or her ability to bear children or her ability to work. A man's choice of a mate didn't have anything to do with looks . . ."

"Oh please," he said dismissively, as if he'd been interrupted by an annoying child. He took a sip of water (Jesus, did he even *drink*? Janey wondered), and said, "What about Helen of Troy?" as if this proved everything.

Janey *knew* he would bring up Helen of Troy—the book had warned that men like him always did. "What about her?" she shrugged. "What about the English, who choose their wives based on family background and character?"

"Are you saying that's better?" he asked, with the sarcasm of a man who isn't used to being contradicted.

"I'm not saying it's better *or* worse," Janey said, sweeping her hair over her shoulder. "All *I'm* saying is that you shouldn't make generalizations about the entire male population based on your own immature desires." And then she sat back in her chair, her heart thumping in her chest, and for a moment, she was afraid that maybe she'd gone too far . . .

But she had certainly put *him* in his place, she thought gleefully, taking the turn onto Ocean Road, and for the rest of the dinner, she had deliberately disagreed with everything he said, so that he was forced to talk to her even though she could tell he didn't want to. And then, as soon as dinner was over, they had both risen at the same time and walked off in opposite directions, and when she passed him later on her way to the bathroom, she had merely given him a polite nod, as if she hardly knew who he was.

And that, she decided, as she turned into the driveway of her house, was exactly what she planned to do the next time she ran into him.

FOUR

IT WAS THE middle of June and the first weekend of the polo season in Bridge-hampton, and the temperature stood at an unusually sweltering ninety degrees.

Under a large, white tent, Janey Wilcox sat on a gilded folding chair, fanning herself with a copy of *Hamptons* magazine. Her hair was pulled back into a chignon, and she was practically naked in a gold tank top and tiny pink shorts, but her bare skin provided no relief against the heat, and rivulets of sweat kept running down her neck and into her cleavage. Two days before, a strange, hot wind had begun blowing in from the north, whipping the sand across the beaches and covering everything in a fine layer of pollen and dust. Beach-going was impossible—indeed, even being outside was uncomfortable—but still the summer social season forged on, and the Hamptons people smiled and had their pictures taken, and talked about the parties they'd been to the night before with valiant enthusiasm.

On Saturday afternoon, the place to be was the Polo, although it was implicitly understood that the game was of little interest to anyone. Actually watching the polo was what you did when you wanted to get away from the swirling, glamorous crowd inside the VIP tent; nevertheless, for the past twenty minutes, Janey and Mimi had been blithely defying social convention by sitting in the VIP seats at the edge of the field, sipping champagne. Mimi was holding a pair of binoculars to her face, and as she removed them, she leaned over to Janey and, pointing to Zizi, said, "Now that young man is absolutely gorgeous. I believe he's the only thing that makes this game worth watching."

Janey giggled and took the binoculars, pretending that she was noticing Zizi for the first time, while thinking that Mimi's way of occasionally talking like an old woman must be yet another one of the strange affectations of the very rich, which she had discovered two days ago, when Janey had called her up and asked if she wanted to go to the Polo.

"Darling," Mimi said, as if she were pulling herself out of the grave, "do you know how many polo matches I've attended in my life?" And for a moment, Janey had been afraid she was going to decline. But in the next second she said in a school-girl voice, "But one must do what has to be done, so of course I'll go with you."

It would have all been perfect, except that on Friday Mimi called up and said that Selden was going to be out this weekend, and did she mind if he joined them at the Polo? There was nothing to do but pretend she couldn't think of anything better, when in actuality, she couldn't have imagined anything worse. And then Mimi had suggested they meet for lunch beforehand, without Selden, so they could talk about him. Selden was the last thing she wanted to discuss, especially when all she could think about in the man department was Zizi. But as she and Mimi really didn't know each other well, Selden was a good jumping-off point from which to move on to more interesting gambits, specifically conversations about all the other people they did know in common, such as Comstock Dibble.

Janey was sufficiently versed in social politics to know that, until she knew Mimi better and could fathom her motivations, it would be a terrible mistake to reveal the truth about her affair with Comstock Dibble; however, she wasn't above a vague inference that at some point, Comstock had come on to her, and everybody knew that when it came to women, he couldn't be trusted. Comstock Dibble was on her mind, due to the very disturbing letter she'd received that morning. The letter had been forwarded from New York City with the rest of her mail; it had probably originally been mailed just before Memorial Day. It was from Comstock Dibble, suggesting that they had some business to conclude about her "screenplay," but as far as Janey was concerned, the business between them was finished, and the mis-sive was nothing more than a pathetic attempt on the part of Comstock Dibble to scare her—although why he was persisting in his fright campaign, Janey couldn't imagine. In any case, she meant Comstock to know that she couldn't be threatened, and she thought the best way to achieve that end was to pretend that she didn't know a thing about it and, even if she did, couldn't have cared less.

And so, continuing with the theme of the day, which seemed to be "mild sub-terfuge," she squinted fiercely into the binoculars, and followed Zizi's sublime form as he lifted his arm and swung his mallet with a ferocity that sent the polo ball skid-ding to the opposite end of the field. It was too soon to reveal her true feelings about him, and so she asked innocently, "Who is he?"

"He must be that polo player Pippi was going on about," Mimi said. "She seemed to think he was interested in her."

"But if he's so interested, where is she?"

"She had an audition."

"Oh, I'm sure he's one of those men who makes *all* women think he's interested," Janey said, thinking that this rule applied to every woman but herself. Studying Zizi's face through the lenses of the binoculars, she recalled every word of their conversation, and decided that it had felt far too real and genuine to be his usual flirtation.

"It doesn't matter anyway," Mimi said. "One can't marry a polo player."

"Why not?" Janey asked fiercely.

Mimi laughed. "In the first place, they haven't any money. And in the second, they travel all the time"—she held out her hand for the binoculars—"so it's like being married to a juggler in the circus . . . Well, maybe not quite. He looks like he'd be an awfully good fuck."

Janey immediately rose to his defense. "I'll bet he isn't like that," she said. "He looks like he has a *soul*."

"If he does," Mimi said, handing her back the binoculars, "it won't last long in the East End." She appeared to have lost interest in Zizi, because she began looking around. "I'm worried about Selden."

I'm not, Janey wanted to say, but instead asked casually, "When was he supposed to get here?"

"Three o'clock," Mimi said. "And it's nearly a quarter to four. I hope he didn't get lost again. You don't see him anywhere, do you?"

Reluctantly, Janey tore her eyes away from the polo field, making a pretense of scanning the crowd behind them through the binoculars. Mimi went on absentmindedly: "George is crazy about Selden. He thinks he's going to be a huge deal . . . not that Selden isn't already, but George says he wouldn't be surprised if Selden had a G5 in a couple of years."

"Real-ly?" Janey said. "But you know I don't care about money."

"Janey Wilcox!" Mimi exclaimed. "I hardly know you, but if you tell me you don't care about money, you'll be lying. And I can't be friends with a liar!" This was delivered in an eerily juvenile tone, and Janey suspected that it was the tone taken by rich teenage girls in boarding school. She couldn't tell if Mimi was kidding or serious, and she felt the vast differences between them.

She wanted to be conciliatory, so she said, "I guess every woman cares about money . . ."

"They do," Mimi said. "It's no use pretending one doesn't, because there's nothing worse than having to support a man . . . And you can't be put off by the way Selden looks. Really successful men don't usually look like much of anything."

"I actually thought he was . . . handsome," Janey said, nearly choking on the word. And then, to cover up her distaste, she added, "But Mimi, I told you before, I honestly don't think he liked me."

"Now, darling," Mimi said, "I know men, and believe me, Selden is interested. You wouldn't believe how excited he got when I told him I was going to the polo with you."

"Maybe he changed his mind," Janey murmured, training the binoculars on the entrance to the polo—a narrow track clogged with cars that ran between two fences. "There's still a long line of cars to get in," she said. "That's one of the problems with this place. They can never figure out the parking."

As she scanned the line of cars, her eye was caught by a rare 1948 Jaguar XK 120 with a six-cylinder engine. The car was so extraordinary (the first two hundred were crafted by hand), Janey had seen only one in her life—at a classic car show at the old Bridgehampton racetrack. She had even considered trying to have sex with the owner in order to get closer to the car, but it turned out he wasn't there. And now, wondering who would be rich enough—and sophisticated enough—to own such a car, she focused the binoculars on the driver's head.

There was, she thought, something disturbingly familiar about the driver's hair, and with a jolt she saw that Selden Rose's face was attached. She wondered what Selden Rose was doing in a car like that—a car that was far too cool for him—and she turned to Mimi. "I just saw Selden Rose. He should be here any minute," she said with a sigh, thinking it was one of the more unfortunate rules of life that it was always the jerky guys who had the best cars. And with a touch of resignation, she turned her attention back to the field.

Selden Rose had a headful of thick nappy hair that looked like it never grew and therefore never required cutting or maintenance. His big boyish grin exposed fluoride-hardened teeth that were not perfectly straightened by sixties orthodontia; he was from outside Chicago and appeared to be as sweet as pie. After meeting him just two or three times, one might take him as merely a strict company man who was working his way up the ladder of a big corporation, but he was much more than that: He was one of a handful of men who had succeeded to the very top, and in reality was as tooth-achingly ambitious as a mouthful of saccharine. As the head of MovieTime, there were only one or two spots above him, and he meant to succeed there, sooner as opposed to later. His goal was to run all of Splatch Verner.

MovieTime was a division of Splatch Verner, a media conglomerate that considered itself bigger and more important than any government and whose business practices were completely American. In other words, on the surface "the company" appeared to take care of its employees, providing them with benefits and stock options; it was politically correct, spouting its commitment to multiculturalism and a guarantee against sexual harassment (information circulated through regular e-mails); but below the surface it was business as usual, run by men who tacitly agreed that their work was the closest thing to going to war without going to war. In the past fifteen years, Splatch Verner had bought up magazine and movie companies, cable stations, publishing houses, Internet servers, telephone and satellite providers, and advertising agencies. The company made entertainment and marketed it and distributed it; it was into branding, and as long as the public bought its product and bought it en masse, no one need question its true motives, which were to make money at all costs. The men who succeeded up the ladder at Splatch Verner understood it was "company policy" to squash anyone who opposed them like a bug; the individual had no chance against them, there would never be a David and Goliath story, and the higher-ups sometimes joked that anyone who threatened them would "never eat lunch in this world again."

Selden Rose, being the exemplar Splatch Verner man, was decorative in neither clothes nor manner; the one area in which he meant to express himself was in his choice of his second wife.

Many of his counterparts, who were heads of other divisions and, like him, in their mid-forties, had recently taken second wives, trading in their first wives (who were mostly attractive, a year or two younger, and serious, like Selden's first wife, who was a lawyer) for more exciting women who were ten or fifteen years younger. The head of advertising had married a prima ballerina with the American Ballet Theatre, a small, dark-haired girl who was wide-eyed and mysteriously mute; the head of cable was married to a White Russian pianist who claimed to be a direct descendant of the Romanovs. Other second wives included a Chinese Internet genius who had attended Harvard, a Republican political pundit with her own show on CNN, and a fashion designer. Janey Wilcox would not only add to this list, she would surpass it, making him the envy of the company. He was already beginning to label her in his mind "model . . . and international beauty."

Selden Rose parked his car on the grass and got out, adjusting his prescription Ray-Ban sunglasses. Normally he would have put the top on and locked up the car, but he was feeling unusually cavalier. He'd been quite happy to discover at dinner on Friday night that Janey Wilcox was not as stupid as he'd feared she might be—or as stupid as people told him she was—and underneath what he categorized as her "bitter" exterior, he thought he saw depths of kindness. Like many men who lack real experience, and therefore understanding, of women, he found it impossible to imagine that a beautiful woman could actually be a bitch, nor could he accept the idea that she might not like him. Instead, he ascribed Janey's sharp remarks to an understandably defensive nature, as those of an essentially sweet girl who has been battered and abused by men not as "good" as himself. He suspected that Janey Wilcox had never really been loved, and that she had never been in a "healthy" relationship (and in this, at least, he was right), and in Janey he sensed a woman who needed rescuing.

Selden Rose liked to think of himself as the knight-in-shining-armor type, and as he strolled toward the tent and the VIP rope strung across the entrance, he reflected that he certainly hadn't shown himself in his best light at Mimi's party. But that was mostly due to nerves, and it excited him to realize that a woman could still make him nervous. In the two years since he'd been divorced, Selden had been with beautiful women, but they tended to be of the LA-bimbo type, who wore their beauty like a suit they'd purchased that afternoon. But Janey Wilcox was different: She *inhabited* her beauty with a kind of genius.

Today, he would be careful to make the right impression, he thought, as he gave his name to a young woman holding a clipboard. The edict at Splatch Verner was to spot brilliance and snap it up before the other guys could discover it, and he was sure the same principle applied to Janey. It didn't bother him that no other man had seen her light before, but it was an axiom that once something was recognized by *someone,* others were never far behind. And so his strategy would be to strike and act quickly, and before the summer was over he was determined to have secured his prize.

The girl with the clipboard checked off his name and lifted the velvet rope without interest; on the short path to the tent, there was a cluster of seven or eight photographers, whom Selden planned to slip by. But stopped just in front of him, looking both pleased at and resigned to the photographers' attention, was Comstock Dibble. He was standing with his arm wrapped stiffly around the waist of a tall, dark-haired woman whose smile revealed a good half inch of gum; Selden recognized her as Comstock's fiancée, whom he had met at the party. It amused him that Comstock was supposedly engaged to a woman like Mauve Binchely, who was probably older than Comstock, and it made him half think that Comstock was losing his edge.

And that wouldn't be surprising, Selden thought. Comstock Dibble was one of those—thankfully, now rare—maverick types who had succeeded where he shouldn't have, and therefore felt entitled to act on his own. That was fine twenty or thirty years ago, but these days, when there were billions of dollars to be made, Comstock was considered a wild card whose temper was undisciplined; people were beginning to whisper that he couldn't be trusted. Selden had never been particularly fond of Comstock and suspected that he would be reined in—one way or another— soon. But they *were* in the same business and had known each other for years, and so, giving Comstock a casual slap on the back and holding out his hand, he said genially, "Comstock."

Comstock turned, his small red-rimmed eyes revealing that he expected an unwelcome intrusion. Selden couldn't tell if he was happy to see him or not; he guessed not.

"Selden Rose," Comstock said. And then, after a beat, "What are you doing here?"

"Same thing you are, I guess," Selden said. "Watching the ponies."

"Is that what this is about," Comstock said, as if to put Selden in his place with insider cynicism.

"That's what I've heard," Selden replied.

"So you've decided to do the Hamptons scene," Comstock said, barely able to disguise his displeasure.

"Excuse me," one of the photographers said. "Can we get a picture of the two of you?"

"No thanks," Selden said, with a wave. He turned to Comstock Dibble and, adopting the same insider tone Comstock had used on him, said, "Some of us would rather be recognized by our peers than by the public."

The remark was delivered in a joking, offhand manner, but it hit its mark, and Comstock glared. The fact was, Comstock's mother liked to show off his photographs to her friends—it made her proud and they all thought he was the equivalent of Prince Charles and she the Queen Mum. But that was something a privileged asshole like Selden Rose could never understand.

For a moment, he stood staring after Selden as he disappeared into the sweaty throng, until an insistent tug from Mauve on his shirt sleeve brought him back to earth. He gave the photographers a look that said *enough*. He had never liked Selden Rose, but at that moment, his enmity crystallized into a hard, glittering rock of hatred.

So many secrets, Mimi thought later that afternoon, looking around the table. Well, she had a few of her own. The only one who wasn't hiding his feelings was Selden; he was pursuing Janey with a courtly charm, pouring her glasses of champagne and trying to get her to talk about her modeling career.

The group consisted of herself, Janey, Selden, Mauve, and Comstock. They had inevitably gathered at a corner table under the tent, considered a prized location due to the breeze. There was a plastic bucket containing a bottle of Veuve Clicquot on the table, along with a plate of tea sandwiches catered by the ridiculously expensive Loaves and Fishes (*Thieves and Bitches,* Mimi thought—she liked jokes like that), but nobody seemed to be having a particularly good time. The atmosphere was as heavy as the oppressive heat and there was misery in the air. Nevertheless, Mimi was enjoying the spectacle.

Comstock and Janey were ignoring each other with the kind of studiousness that makes one think there was more to their relationship than they were letting on. Three times already, Mimi had seen Janey giving Comstock an angry, questioning look, and each time, Comstock had deliberately turned his head away. Mauve seemed to have caught it as well, because she was now grilling Janey about her relationship with Peter Cannon. Mauve had seen Peter at a party the night before, and was outraged that he would dare to appear in public. Selden was pretending to be interested in the conversation, but it was clear he wished Mauve would shut up so he could talk to Janey. And Janey, probably for the sole reason that she didn't like Mauve, was vigorously defending Peter Cannon's right to go out in public.

"Nobody has any shame these days, eh, Comstock," Selden said. There seemed to be a pointed barb in the comment.

"Shame never got anyone anywhere," Comstock grunted.

There was a deadly lull in the conversation. Janey took a sip of champagne and looked toward the field, where Zizi's team was accepting a silver cup. "I didn't know you were such a big polo fan," Selden said to her.

"There are a lot of things you don't know about me," she replied curtly. Mimi wished Janey would be just a little bit kinder to Selden. Selden was essentially a nice guy and he had everything; he was one of those men with whom one had to look beneath the surface. He wasn't glamorous, but he had too much pride and confidence to acknowledge that it might matter. And for him, of course, it didn't.

Comstock, however, was an entirely different story. He had the strangest body—a huge barrel chest combined with short, skinny stick legs—and every time she saw him, Mimi couldn't help wondering if his dick matched his upper or lower half. This afternoon, he had squeezed himself into a skin-tight black Prada shirt with a zipper up the front and he was wearing heavy black Prada sandals. He was sweating profusely, mopping his face with a linen handkerchief, but then again, he was always sweating, as if the very act of living were an exertion.

But that didn't stop him from lighting up a cigar.

"So, Comstock," Mimi said. "You haven't told me what you're working on."

"Movie with Wendy Piccolo," he said.

"Who is she again?" Mimi asked. "Oh, I remember. That little girl with the great body."

"I don't know anything about her body," Comstock said, glancing toward Mauve. He sat back in his chair and smoked, as if the conversation were closed. Like most mogul types, he couldn't be bothered to make an effort unless there was something in it for him, Mimi thought.

"Well," she said, giving him a look as if he were no more significant than a houseboy, "I think we should be going."

Janey looked up. "Let's stay," she said. She had already decided that there was no way she was going to leave without talking to Zizi again. "I want to congratulate Harold."

"I forgot Harold Vane was running this team," Mimi said.

"I guess I'll stay too," Selden said. "Meet the owner."

"I think he's called the *patrón*," Janey said, more sharply than she needed to.

"Didn't you use to date Harold?" Mauve asked.

"I did," Janey said. "I think he's adorable."

"He grew up in New York," Mimi said.

"On Fifth Avenue," Janey confirmed.

"Funny we didn't know him," Mauve said.

"Why would you?" Janey said. "Do you know everyone who grew up on Fifth Avenue?"

"He went to Harvard, I recognize the name," Selden said, jumping in.

"Well, then, he's definitely a loser," Comstock said. "No one who went to Harvard ever amounted to anything."

"Listen to him," Mimi said. "Selden went to Harvard."

"Apparently it's a negative in some circles," Selden said.

"Well, as we're all going to stay, we need more champagne," Mimi said, lifting the bottle from its bucket and pouring the last drops into her glass.

The party picked up the moment Harold Vane and Zizi came over and sat down, but the harmonious energies one tries to achieve at a table were still missing. Being the consummate hostess, Mimi could never help but notice these things, and she saw with some annoyance that Janey had managed to get Zizi on one side and Harold on the other, so that Selden was now stuck between Mauve and Harold. That was too bad for Selden, but Mimi could understand Janey's actions: Zizi was so attractive it was impossible for a woman to be in his proximity and not desire sex. Mimi studied Zizi's face more closely. He didn't have a bad angle; the more you looked at him, the better-looking he became, so that one was left with the feeling that he wasn't actually human but a creature fashioned by God for a more perfect planet. Janey, of course, was stunning herself, but that still didn't make the pairing right.

Disguising her feelings, Mimi smiled and looked around the table. Harold was talking to Selden about business, while Janey was trying to keep Zizi's attention by insinuating that he was a rube because he had grown up on a farm in Argentina. Despite her beauty, Janey had a chip on her shoulder when it came to men, and she had that technique of being aggressive with a man in order to engage his interest.

Unfortunately, Mimi thought, taking a sip of champagne, she was employing this technique on the wrong man. In the way one breed of dog instinctually recognizes another, Mimi saw instantly that Zizi had old-fashioned European values and would only find Janey's aggression baffling (indeed, he was already beginning to look around the table as if in search of rescue), and the person on whom Janey should have been employing her wiles was Selden.

Zizi suddenly turned to Mimi and smiled, and a look of mutual understanding passed between them. Mimi liked Janey; she had that warm feeling toward her that women have when they know they're going to become friends. Nevertheless, if they were to be friends, Janey must learn that she couldn't take whatever man she wanted, especially if Mimi was there. She would have to learn to defer. And so, employing a tried and true technique of her own, she said to Zizi, "Did you play in Palm Beach this year?" She knew she was the only person at the table who knew anything about polo, and therefore, by engaging Zizi in his favorite topic, was able to completely monopolize his attention.

FIVE

JANEY WILCOX WAS the kind of woman other women considered a bitch, but whom dogs and children mysteriously loved. Sitting in the bleachers at the twenty-third annual Fourth of July Huggy Bear Celebrity Baseball Tournament (so named for reasons no one could now recall), she was flanked on either side by two little boys. The two boys, aged six and eight, couldn't have been more different—one was painfully thin and the other extremely fat—yet they were not only brothers, but the issue of none other than George Paxton and his first wife, Marlene.

The younger boy, Jack, was clutching Janey's hand with the sort of open and unabashed fervor that is found only in small children who have yet to discover cynicism, while the older boy, George Jr. ("Georgie Girl" to the cruel children at his school), was busily studying the scoreboard with the mathematical curiosity of an actuary. Digger was up at bat. "If he hits a home run, they've got a fifty-three percent chance of winning," Georgie said, with great confidence. He was a nearly miniature version of his father, right down to his propensity for heft and crumbly toenails—the result of a stubborn nail virus. "On the other hand," he continued, "if he doesn't get a hit, they have a twenty-four percent chance of losing."

"Is that so?" Janey said, peering across the baseball diamond to home plate, where Digger, who was dressed in a wife-beater T-shirt, clam-digger-length khakis, and a canvas fishing hat of the style normally worn by old men in Florida (which was obviously his idea of a baseball uniform, Janey thought), was taking a few practice swings on the bat.

"Do you think he *will* give us an autograph?" Jack asked nervously, wiggling a loose tooth with his finger. His teeth were a source of consternation for him—they always seemed to be falling out these days, and even though everyone said they would grow back, he wasn't sure. "What if we ask him for an autograph and he says no?"

"Let's ask Patty, just to make sure," Janey said kindly. She leaned across to Patty, who was seated on the other side of Jack, and said, "Jack's afraid Digger won't give him an autograph."

Patty tore her eyes away from Digger—when she was around him at these kinds of events, she always feared for his safety, afraid that a photographer wouldn't really be a photographer but some kind of crazed fan who was out to get him—and rumpled Jack's hair. "If he doesn't give you an autograph, you come right to me," she said. Both Janey and Patty were extremely nice to children, having, as young teenagers, earned money in the time-honored tradition of baby-sitting, but in the Hamptons, where child care was mostly left to professionals, not every young woman was as kind.

From the bleacher above them, Roditzy Deardrum regarded this little scene with a disgust that was coupled with jealousy. She prided herself on "knowing everyone"—the celebrities and the spectators, both of whom could attend only by invitation—and could have seated herself with anyone, yet she had decided to grace Janey and Patty with her presence. Granted, her actions *were* partly motivated by a desire to claim a closer acquaintance with Digger. Nevertheless, she hadn't expected to be upstaged by . . . *children.*

And the worst thing about them, Roditzy thought, was that they didn't even fit the basic requirement for children—or anyway, for children one brought out in public—and that was cuteness. The little one shook like a Chihuahua, while the bigger one was, well, just so *big*! Roditzy hadn't been around many children, but she had no idea they came in so large a size these days. The kid had a beer belly the size of a middle-aged man's—shouldn't he be off at a spa or something, losing weight and being fed a restricted diet of lettuce and wheat-grass juice? Giving Georgie a dirty look, she leaned over him and, picking up the thread of their earlier conversation, said to Janey, "Well, he's definitely going to jail."

"Who?" Janey asked, having ceased to pay attention to her minutes before.

"Peter Cannon!" Roditzy said. "My father's a lawyer and he says they've just been waiting to get him on something . . . Of course, he didn't pay his taxes, either."

Patty sighed audibly and rolled her eyes at Janey. Janey ignored her. Not wanting to be unpleasant to Roditzy, whom she considered "useful," Janey said to Roditzy, "What I can't understand is why so many movie stars trusted him."

"Ha. Movie stars are not exactly known for being the sharpest tools in the shed," Roditzy said. "And besides, he got them all early on in their careers. Before they made money," she said, with a glance toward Patty.

"How much longer are people going to talk about this?" Patty demanded.

"Oh, until the next scandal comes along. Then they'll forget all about it," Roditzy said knowingly.

Back on the field, a formerly A-list movie star named Jason Bean threw a speed ball at Digger, who was now up at home plate. According to the gossip columns, Jason Bean had descended to C list when he tried to run for public office. It wasn't his politics that were the problem, but his lack of imagination—he'd gotten the idea to become a politician from the fact that he had played one in a movie. Digger took a swing at the ball and missed, while several photographers took his picture.

"Isn't there anything that isn't documented by the paparazzi?" Patty asked.

"Patty, it's for *charity*," Janey said.

"Who is that *girl*?" Roditzy, who had the attention span of a gnat, asked. "She's been staring at Patty for, like, half an hour."

"What girl?"

"That girl," Roditzy said, nodding toward the edge of the crowd. A young, dark-haired woman, dressed in a denim halter top, denim miniskirt, and cheap black spike-heeled shoes, was staring in their direction; when they looked at her, she quickly turned away.

"I have no idea," Patty said.

"She's so Jersey!" Roditzy said, outraged. "I mean, how the hell did she get in? The Hamptons are *really* going downhill!"

Janey laughed, noting with irony that some people had said the same thing of Roditzy, and, glancing into the crowd, her eyes narrowed and her stomach gave a sickening lurch, the way it always did when she unexpectedly caught sight of Zizi. Sure enough, in a scenario that had now become annoyingly familiar, he was with Mimi, and they appeared to be caught up in an amusingly intimate conversation. Janey would have been suspicious, but Mimi had a tendency to be superficially intimate with everyone, and Janey couldn't imagine that Zizi found Mimi attractive, especially as she was at least fifteen years older than he. Besides, all they ever seemed to talk about was horses. Nevertheless, this brought its own frustrations: As Janey had already declared her complete lack of interest in the beasts, it was impossible to insert herself into their conversations without appearing like she was desperately vying for Zizi's attention.

"Can we go to the Maidstone after this?" Georgie asked eagerly. "I've got a new card trick I want to show you."

"Oh, Georgie, how sweet," Janey said, watching as Zizi and Mimi made their way toward the bleachers. "But I can't today. Maybe Mimi will take you."

At the name Mimi, Jack's face drooped like a spaniel's, and Georgie looked down, concentrating on the tip of his sneaker. There wasn't much love lost between

Mimi and George's boys: Mimi thought Jack was "too clingy" and with Georgie it was worse—she could barely bring herself to look at him, and whenever he entered the room, she would make an excuse to send him out with the maid.

Janey had befriended the boys because she knew all too well what it was like to be a child and an outsider, to be constantly uncertain of what was going to happen to you. But lately the boys seemed to have fallen a little too much under her care. At first, she'd been thrilled when Mimi had invited her to accompany them to the Maidstone Country Club, which was the most exclusive club in the Hamptons, but in the past two weeks, on more than one occasion, Mimi had disappeared for an hour or more, leaving Janey to entertain the boys by herself. Each time Mimi had returned claiming that there was an emergency at the house, but Janey wondered why, with a live-in staff of four, there was so much at home that needed Mimi's personal attention.

And now, with the queasiness that often accompanies an unwelcome insight, Janey wondered if that "crisis" was Zizi. But that, she thought, trying to reassure herself, was impossible. Nevertheless, there was Zizi below her, helping Mimi up onto the first bleacher, his kind, handsome face concentrated in delight at something Mimi was saying. Why didn't he look at *her* like that anymore, Janey thought with frustration, remembering that that was exactly how he *had* looked at her the first time they'd met. But since then, every time he saw her, he treated her with a vague, jovial heartiness, as if he were the high school football star and she one of a legion of giggly, mousy girls who were in love with him. Of course, his behavior only fanned the flames of her desire, and she felt as if she were reduced to a puddle when she was around him.

She would get him, she thought, if only she could figure out how! In the past few weeks, Zizi had quickly become a star on the Hamptons social scene—with his looks and charisma, he was naturally invited everywhere—and his desirability had only increased due to his refusal to, as yet, fall prey to any woman's charms. He could have easily run through a bevy of beauties by now, but the fact that he hadn't, and that he always showed up alone, seemed to indicate that he was a man who was serious about finding the right woman—and true love.

And what she wouldn't give for that kind of love, Janey thought, staring intently at his long back, with those broad shoulders that tapered down to a beautifully narrow waist. Why, she would easily give up all this, she would travel with him, they could live in Argentina—she wouldn't even mind if they were *poor*.

She felt a blinding flash of jealousy as Mimi put her hand in his and let him pull her up onto the second bleacher. For a second, Mimi wobbled on a loose board, and Zizi grabbed her arm to steady her. They laughed and Janey wondered for the hundredth time what it was that Mimi had that she didn't. Money, certainly, and social status—undoubtedly Zizi was impressed with the idea that Mimi was "America's Princess." She tore at a hangnail with her teeth in irritation, reminded, once again, that no matter what she might do, she could never change the fact that she came from an ordinary, middle-class family. But still, *she* was in the spotlight, not Mimi; *she* was the one who was on TV and in magazines and on billboards, and if that wasn't enough to capture a man's interest, she didn't know what was. Meanwhile, Mimi was really nothing more than a society hostess . . . and on top of it, she was married!

But maybe that was the key, Janey thought, rearranging her hair under a baseball cap as she watched Zizi and Mimi with lowered eyes. Maybe the fact that Mimi *was* unavailable made Zizi feel safe. In the eyes of the Hamptons social set, it appeared that Zizi was Mimi's protégé, whom she had taken up and was now squiring around like a pampered pooch, to be petted and fed bits of lobster from the table. For that matter, one might say that Mimi had taken her up as well. Surely Mimi could see that there would be nothing more perfect than if Janey and Zizi were to become an item, and yet, she'd been no help in that department at all.

Digger took another swing at the ball and missed, as next to Janey, the two boys groaned in disappointment. Well, Janey thought. She was certainly familiar with the type of man who was only interested when he thought a woman wasn't, and if that's what it took to get Zizi, she was perfectly capable of making herself unavailable. She would start dating someone—anyone—maybe even, she thought with a bitter laugh, that damn Selden Rose!

Selden . . . Ever since that first polo game, when she'd gone for a ride with him afterward in his car (she could have resisted him, but not that car), he'd been following her around like a puppy. It was a shame, really, because for a minute or two, when she first got into the car, marveling at its beauty, she had actually considered him a possibility. The car indicated that he had position and money and taste . . . But then he'd gone on and on about the details of the car—how he'd tracked down the original leather-makers for the seats and the special chrome they'd used on the spokes—and after fifteen minutes, her eyes had glazed over in boredom. Being Selden, though, he hadn't seemed to notice, nor had his interest flagged, despite her constant refusals to go on an actual date with him. She knew she had only to crook her little finger and he would come running, and watching Mimi and Zizi take a seat in the bleachers in front of her, she decided that that was exactly what she just might do.

Mimi and Zizi turned and waved, and little Jack looked up, his eyes widening in fear. There were tons of people who came to his father's house every weekend, and he and his brother, Georgie, couldn't be bothered to remember them, but he did remember the polo player. He'd come to the house twice when only Mimi was there, and each time had threatened to put Jack on a horse, saying they'd make a little jockey out of him yet—as if that were something anyone would ever want to do. Sensing Jack's discomfort, Janey tore her eyes away from Zizi and pulled Jack close to her. She was undecided about having children herself (if she were to have them, she would definitely have nannies, unlike Patty, who seemed to think there was some kind of moral superiority in taking care of your own children), but there was one point about children on which she was clear: She knew that, for the right kind of man, there is no more compelling image than that of a young woman in affectionate congress with children.

Digger finally got a hit and the crowd erupted in loud cheers.

"Okay, so they now have a twenty-seven percent chance of winning," Georgie said solemnly.

"What do you think, Jack?" Janey asked.

"I dunno. I don't like math," Jack said.

"You know what? Neither do I," Janey said. She smiled and ruffled his hair, and as he buried his face in her arm, she prayed fervently that Zizi was watching.

Unfortunately, as so often happens when humans try to direct Cupid's arrow, the missile hit the wrong mark, and it was Selden Rose instead of Zizi who was struck down.

Minutes before, as Selden Rose parked his car at the end of a long line of cars parked on an obscure back street in East Hampton, he had vowed that this would be the very last time he would degrade himself by attending a Hamptons event. (He had gotten lost again, it was impossible to get decent directions out of anyone in the Hamptons; they gave vague instructions like "It's behind the A&P," assuming, of course, one knew where the A&P was in the first place.) As he followed the line of cars back to its source (he still wasn't exactly sure where the baseball diamond was), he reflected on the overall pointlessness of his summer so far. Nearly every minute of every weekend had been taken up with some party or event or opening (from stores to movies to pathetic displays of art), and each one of these happenings was deemed "the" place to be, as if being there bestowed a special identity on the attendees. But the people at these parties were always the same, and after one had seen the same people at six different events over the weekend, the conversations became painfully banal, and Selden had now decided that these Hamptons people were like rich children sent to expensive summer camp, where they were constantly in need of silly distractions.

He joined the small crowd that was making its way across what appeared to be the playing fields of a high school, thinking that while he didn't have an inherent objection to socializing, he preferred to spend his time in a constructive way. In Los Angeles, manners were crude or nonexistent, but at least "socializing" consisted of the driving forward of deals and relationships, while here, its only point appeared to lie in the phenomenon of being "seen," as if implying that if one weren't, one would disappear. It was a soulless pursuit, and often, as he stood at these events, holding a glass of cheap champagne and nodding absentmindedly, he wondered if any of these people longed for beauty and nature, for a connection that went deeper than the coincidence that they all happened to be thrown together in the same little world. And now, giving his name once again to another faceless young woman in black with a clipboard and headset, he suddenly wished that he'd followed his instincts and taken out his boat instead.

And he would have, he thought with anger toward himself, if it weren't for that damn Janey Wilcox. For the past month he had stupidly and foolishly contrived to be at every event she was, thinking that if she saw him enough and got to know him, she'd see his inherent value. But she had rejected him at every turn, scoffing at his invitations to dinner with a disdainful, "Really Selden, dinner on a Saturday night in the Hamptons in June? I've got four parties to go to," and he was finally beginning to accept the fact that she wasn't interested and never would be. For a month now, he had fervently believed that if he could only get her away from this world, the real Janey Wilcox would blossom, for he thought he had seen in her the same intellectual love of beauty and art that he himself possessed. She could talk extensively (and surprisingly intelligently, given the fact that she had never attended college) about literature and movies and paintings, but he now guessed that her conversation wasn't the result of deep passion, but a mere party trick, employed to gain the attention she craved to further her place in society.

As he made his way along the fence behind home plate, he decided that he was through wasting his time with her. New York was filled with hundreds of accomplished, beautiful young women, and he was an eligible single man; if he couldn't have Janey Wilcox, certainly he could find someone else as good if not better. But then the satisfying *thwack* of a ball striking wood brought him out of his reverie, and he followed its trajectory.

The ball rose high in the air over third base, and suddenly, as his eye was caught by the sight of Janey sitting between George Paxton's two boys, all of his resolve went out the window. It was if she'd been captured unawares in some secret snapshot, for her face had an unusual softness he'd never seen before. The child was snuggled next to her breast (and how he longed to be there himself); her expression held the radiant kindness of a Madonna. His heart leapt and the world regained its equilibrium, for he saw that he had been right about her all along. He must save her from herself; she was wasting herself on this path of frivolity and superficiality, and it was his duty to lead her to a higher and more meaningful plane. He pictured her bent over their own children (and their children would certainly be more appealing than George's), and then, as if fate were confirming his plans, she glanced up and caught his eye, and a soft, knowing look seemed to pass between them.

In any case, she waved—and Selden thought her hand as graceful as the fluttering wing of a butterfly.

Jack Paxton was going to get sick. He never should have shoved that hot dog, nearly whole, down his throat, but Georgie had dared him, and Jack hadn't had a choice. And now, standing in the parking lot on the perimeter of the cluster of adults, Jack felt his stomach turn over with the inevitability that signals an impending puke. His biggest fear in life was of having puke come out of his nose, as it had when he was three years old—indeed, his earliest memory of his father was of getting sick and then saying, "Daddy, puke came out of my nose," and his father saying, "I know, son—" and right after that, his father had left home.

Jack felt the blood drain from his face. The game was over, but as usual, it was taking forever for the adults to leave. "There's a cocktail party on Flying Point Road," Roditzy Deardrum was saying. She was like a small, yappy dog, running around the legs of the adults and jumping up for attention. "I don't know," Patty said vaguely. She glanced up at Digger, smelling the sweat on him and thinking about sex. She wanted to lose herself in his finely sculpted body (he was 6'4" and weighed 180 pounds) and his strange, otherworldly eyes, which were widely spaced and shaped like marquise-cut diamonds. She knew he was thinking about sex, too, because his arm tightened around her waist and, cocking his head toward hers, he gave her a wink.

Janey saw the exchange between Patty and Digger, and, standing in the parking lot in the dull, afternoon heat, torn between her longings for Zizi and her desire to punish him by paying attention to Selden, she was suddenly struck by that quiet display of secret, unshakable intimacy between a man and a woman. She had always thought of love as a vague, formless feeling, but in that small moment, as the glamorous crowd made its way toward their cars, she suddenly saw that love had a definite shape, a firm form that could be expressed in actions and gestures. She wanted what her sister had, and looking around at the three men—Digger, Zizi, and Selden—saw how insignificant Selden looked next to the tall, young energies of Digger and Zizi. Selden was trying to catch her eye, trying to move her away from the group, but she was suddenly sure that she would never feel that way about him, and that it was hopeless to try. And knowing this, she knew that she could never take up with Selden, no matter how fruitfully it might serve her purposes.

"I'm going to show Janey my new pilot," Selden said.

Janey glanced at him in horror. She didn't like the way he spoke so firmly, as if there were something decided between the two of them. There was a tension in the group of time running out and she looked at Mimi and then Zizi, sensing that both she and Mimi wanted to go wherever Zizi was going. But Mimi had the children.

"You can't take Janey," Roditzy said to Selden. She was one of those people who only ever thinks about her own agenda. "Sophia Loren's son is going to be at the cocktail party."

"I have to *go*," Zizi said. He was tanned and his teeth were hard and white; he looked like a young, shining god with his aura of self-contained independence that was so irresistible to women.

"We're with you," Digger said. Again, that secret look passed between Patty and Digger, filling Janey with an envious ache. If she could just get away from Selden, she might be able to follow Zizi, or at least find out where he was headed.

"We're going," young Georgie said to Jack. He had been anxiously observing the group from the outside, trying to keep abreast of their movements, for he had a feeling that Mimi was perfectly capable of forgetting all about them and leaving them behind. A strangled cry came from the other side of a car, and Georgie looked around to see Jack standing unsteadily, his eyes tearing and his face a rather unnatural shade of green. But as Mimi was kissing everyone good-bye—in a minute or two she would probably take off without them—he whispered impatiently, "Hurry up!"

Jack made a valiant effort at pulling himself together. Clutching the autographed baseball Digger had given him (at least the adults hadn't lied about that), he stumbled into the middle of the group. "I think there's something wrong with that kid . . . ," Roditzy Deardrum said warningly, just before Jack's stomach turned over with a painful heave. Squeezing the treasured baseball between his knees, he bent over and opened his mouth as the hot dog inched searingly up his throat and, with one final wrench of his stomach, deposited itself nearly whole on the tip of Roditzy Deardrum's shoe.

• • •

Seated in the cool, marbled interior of the Wanamaker mansion, Janey shook the ice cubes in her glass with undisguised annoyance and said, "He's only a child, George." Normally, the opulence of her surroundings would have soothed her—she was now in and out of Mimi's house with such regularity that it had almost begun to feel like her own—but the day had taken on a jangled, disordered feeling that for once couldn't be mediated by a rich setting.

"I suppose it wasn't his fault," Mimi said. She was moving restlessly around the vast living room, as if she couldn't decide whether or not to sit, or even if she wanted to be in the room at all. Mimi had insisted that Janey come back to the house to help her with the kids, and Janey had agreed, partly because it meant she wouldn't have to go to Selden's and partly because she had made it a policy never to turn down an invitation to Mimi's. But as soon as she entered the house she realized she'd made a mistake—the marble hall with its gilt mirrors and Roman busts suddenly seemed overdone, and her relationship with Mimi felt oppressive, as if she were drowning in somebody else's life. Looking down into her ice water, she wondered why she'd let herself become lieutenant to Mimi's captain, and she longed to be anywhere else—anywhere where she might once again be the star of her own life. "You can't let children sit out in the hot sun, Mimi," she said sharply, and as soon as the words were out of her mouth, she realized she was angry, and that Mimi's behavior toward Zizi was the reason. She *would* talk to Mimi about Zizi, she thought, catching Mimi's eye in the large mirror that hung over the fireplace; she couldn't let it go any longer. If George would only *leave* . . .

Mimi's expression looked decidedly guilty, but being Mimi, she simply changed the subject. "George, you *will* be nice to Comstock when he and Mauve come for dinner, won't you?" she asked.

George rolled his eyes, looked at Janey, and winked. He seemed to find his wife endlessly amusing, if not terribly serious, and Janey knew that he loved goading her. "That depends on what you mean by 'nice,'" George said. "As long as you don't expect me to *sleep* with him . . ."

"Oh, George!" Mimi said, as George let out a burst of high-pitched laughter. George also, Janey noted dryly, seemed to find himself endlessly amusing. He turned to Janey for confirmation of this fact, and Janey gave him a wan smile.

"So you don't like Comstock," she said.

"The truth is, I can't stand him," George said, watching Mimi. "But Mimi insists on having him over."

"I don't insist," Mimi said. "It's one of those social things. He's Mauve's fiancé, so he can't be avoided."

George's thick eyelids suddenly closed halfway, giving his eyes a hooded look and focusing his normally bland expression. "You're entering into dangerous waters, Mimi," he said warningly.

Mimi spun around. "Oh, come on, George. Just because he's the only man who ever beat you in a deal . . ."

"If he had beaten me, it would have been fine," George said coldly. "He cheated me fair and square. And then to have the man in the house . . ."

"It was a long time ago," Mimi said.

"So was Auschwitz," George shot back.

Mimi drew herself up. She could be terrifyingly arrogant when she thought she'd been challenged, and so cold and dismissive she made you feel like she might never talk to you again. It was an effective technique, and one that Janey was trying to copy, but Janey wondered why she was being so insistent on picking a fight with George.

"George Paxton," Mimi said, rolling her vowels in a voice that was meant to intimidate, "that isn't how we do things in polite society. We don't let business interfere with friendship. If we did, no one would speak. Besides, I'm sure that one day you'll have a chance to do in Comstock, and then you two will be best friends."

George raised his eyebrows and, as if not the least bit affected by her speech, said, "A friend's a person you can do business with, Mimi."

"Yes, but I wouldn't want to be friends with any of your business associates. I think I'd die of boredom," Mimi said with finality.

They stared at each other in a stalemate, and Janey heard a phone ringing somewhere in the recesses of the house, and a maid answering, "Paxton residence."

Janey took the opportunity to try to escape. "I think I should be—"

"Oh no, Janey," Mimi said, turning to her with a frightening smile. "I want to talk to you."

A maid in a gray and white uniform entered the room. "It's for you, Mrs. Paxton."

"Thank you, Gerda," Mimi said gracefully. "I'll be right back. George, don't let Janey leave."

"And that was a command," George said, as Mimi exited the room.

Janey sighed and sat back in the white silk armchair. George was right—when Mimi spoke that way, there was no arguing with her, and with some annoyance Janey mused that it was an affectation of those who were born rich to assume that everyone—especially those who weren't rich—would do their bidding. But her mind was mostly focused on Zizi. Was his elusiveness a game, or was it possible that he really wasn't interested?

But then George stood up and, crossing the room, took a seat on the edge of the couch nearest her.

Janey raised her eyebrows at him as if to question what he was doing. She wasn't comfortable being alone with him—when Mimi was around, he was fine, but on the one or two occasions when Mimi had been upstairs and Janey had been forced into conversation with him, he had given her the impression that she had only to say the word and he would sleep with her, as if that were anything she'd ever want to do. It wasn't what he said in particular, but rather his undisguised leering glances as his eyes slipped toward her breasts. On the other hand, she knew how to handle men like George Paxton—she'd been doing it all her life. Not bothering to cover up her boredom, she said, "How have you been, George?"

"I hear you've been seeing a lot of my friend Selden," he said. George always tried to bring the conversation around to sex, as if talking about it would somehow result in its action.

"You probably see him as much as I do," Janey countered.

"So he hasn't hooked you yet," George said knowingly.

"I don't know why you think he ever will."

"Oh, Selden's an old hound dog," George said, taking a sip of his scotch and crossing a thick ankle over the opposite knee, as if to display his penis. "He usually gets what he wants." He leaned back on the couch, peering across the room at a painting of Harlequins by the artist David Salle. "It's pretty funny if you knew what he was like before. Hell, all he did in high school was drop acid and play tennis. Can't believe he's gotten to where he is today. He must have spent half of his life stoned."

Janey laughed unbelievingly. "Selden Rose dropped acid?"

"In between screwing cheerleaders," George said, lifting his glass to his lips. "The big joke was . . . how'd *he* ever get into Harvard?"

Janey didn't bother to answer. She began to rise, murmuring, "I think I'll go find Mimi . . ."

"Hold on," George said, suddenly reaching out and grabbing her wrist. Janey gave him a sharp look and he quickly tried to cover up his gesture with a hearty laugh. "You know there's no point in that—it won't make her get off the phone any faster," he said. "Besides, I hardly ever get to talk to you . . . alone," he added, his eyes inevitably straying to her chest.

"Anyway," he continued, "I want to hear about your work."

"My work?" Janey scoffed. "George, I'm a model. And besides, I have the summer off." Her tone was sarcastic, but George's line of questioning suddenly made her feel guilty. She hadn't meant to fritter half the summer away. She had intended to read the great books, maybe to have even finished that screenplay (thank God she hadn't heard from Comstock about that again); in any case, she'd been planning to somehow advance her career. But, once again, time had gotten away from her, and she'd become caught up in the superficialities of life . . .

As if reading her thoughts, George said, "I've been studying that TV commercial of yours, and I've decided you've got talent. Real talent. And I'm someone who's made money on that kind of horse sense."

"Really George?" she said, giving him a disdainful laugh. She looked at him, trying to assess whether he was serious or simply engaging in a ploy to get her into bed. But still, she couldn't help being flattered—as she always was, whenever someone recognized her for something other than her beauty.

"Well," she said slowly, dangling her fingers over the arm of the chair, "I've been thinking that I might make a good producer." In reality, she'd never thought about it before, but the idea suddenly popped into her head and she liked the way it sounded—it gave her weight.

"Like Selden," George said, rubbing his thigh.

"Not *exactly* like Selden," Janey said. She had no idea what she was talking about, but she was beginning to enjoy herself. "I'd produce small movies that I really cared about, that *said* something to the American public . . ."

"And you think there could be money in that?" George asked. His face had lost its dull quality—Janey was convinced his eyes were gleaming with interest.

"Why not?" she said. "After all, the only guarantee of making money is if you do something that's good—that the American public thinks it needs."

"I've been thinking about getting into the movie business myself . . . ," George began, but was suddenly interrupted by the brisk staccato of Mimi's heels on the marble floor.

"Well, you wouldn't believe who that was," she said, bursting into the room. "Roditzy Deardrum. She wants someone to give her money to replace her shoe!"

The name Roditzy Deardrum brought back the events of the afternoon, and Janey frowned, more determined than ever to talk to Mimi about Zizi. "I really should *go*," she said, thinking that this was the only way to get Mimi alone.

"You'll say good-bye to the children, won't you?" Mimi said, becoming the concerned stepmother.

"Of course," Janey said. She stood up, leaning over George to give him the requisite kiss on the cheek. "Don't forget about our little talk," he whispered. "If you have any ideas, call me."

Mimi appeared to be in a state of high excitement as she led Janey up the wide, front stairs. "Let's not go in to the children yet," she said. "I have to tell you something." Janey followed her down the long corridor to the master bedroom suite, and as they passed a series of framed, hand-painted Currier & Ives prints of racehorses, she was convinced that that "something" had to do with Zizi. The air hung heavy with his unspoken name; with girlish imagination she irrationally imagined that Zizi had told Mimi he was secretly in love with her and had asked Mimi to act as his messenger . . .

From a large inner chamber containing the great canopied bed that Mimi shared with George, French doors led out to a deck with a green striped awning. A white wicker table was laid with preparations for tea—a blue and white china teapot and a plate containing cucumber and salmon tea sandwiches—for it was one of Mimi's edicts as a world-renowned hostess that guests should always find something delightful to eat at any time of the day. Mimi sat down at the table, and with long, slim fingers, picked up the teapot and began pouring hot water over a silver tea holder into a cup, but her actions seemed more driven by habit than out of any desire for sustenance. Her eyes shone with a kind of evil delight, as if she'd done something wicked and was proud of it, and in a particularly intimate voice, as if

Janey were the dearest person in the world to her, she said, "Darling, I'm afraid I've done something *terrible* . . ."

Janey strolled to the railing and looked out to the sea. It was that hushed, tender time of day when evening has begun to fall and yet the beach is still alluringly warm, and with a quickly beating heart, she turned back to Mimi. She meant to finally be straightforward about her feelings for Zizi, and without preamble, she began, "I know you're really good friends with Zizi . . . ," but then the startled, guilty expression on Mimi's face caught her off guard.

"Oh Janey, promise you won't be angry," Mimi cried. "I meant to tell you before, but I had no idea what was going to happen, and I didn't want to get you involved. But you, of all people, should understand . . ."

Janey suddenly felt the same acute queasiness she'd experienced earlier in the afternoon, and sensing the answer, nevertheless found herself asking the question, "Understand what?"

Mimi looked at her in confusion. "But I thought you had guessed . . . I figured you had to know . . . Zizi and I are having an affair. We have been, for the past three weeks."

The confirmation of this fact hit Janey like a blow, and for a moment, she couldn't speak. But then she heard the crashing of the waves on the beach below, and saw Mimi sitting before her, glowing with excitement and fear. A response was expected of her, and tossing her hair over her shoulder, she emitted a cold laugh and said, "Of course I knew. After all, it's pretty obvious."

"Is it?" Mimi asked in horror.

"It is to me, anyway," Janey said. And again, she laughed coldly. "But then, I know you so *well*," she said, gladly allowing a note of irony to creep into her voice. The fact was, she didn't know Mimi *at all*—and certainly had no idea she could be so treacherous.

"Janey!" Mimi said with astonishment. "You're angry."

She *was* angry—indeed, she was furious—but she would rot in hell before she would let Mimi get another thing over on her. "Don't be silly," she said evenly. And to further cover up her feelings, she asked, "When did it start? At the polo?" Thinking what a fool she'd been to ask Mimi to that game. And Mimi, who was completely caught up in the drama of her romance, gave her a look of relief.

"I thought he was gorgeous, just like everyone else," she said. "But I had no idea he was interested until you left that afternoon with Selden . . . to ride in his car. And then Zizi and I arranged to go horseback riding the next day . . . that's why I never asked *you* . . . and then he followed me into the stall and we kissed . . ."

Janey leaned over the railing. For a moment, she thought she was going to be sick! Why, oh why, had she allowed Selden to talk her into going for a spin in his car after the match? With that one stupid decision, she had inadvertently thrown Mimi and Zizi together, but how could she ever have guessed that Zizi would be interested in *Mimi*? And with the viciousness of the romantically wounded, she blamed Zizi. He was a gigolo . . . the very worst sort of opportunist who preyed on rich, married women . . . He was probably already asking her for money . . . Really, she was lucky she'd had nothing to do with him. Somehow, she managed to rearrange her face into a look of piteous concern. "But Mimi," she said. "Do you really think it's a good idea . . ."

"Oh no," Mimi cried. "It's a very bad idea. But it's too late. You see how wonderful he is . . . Of course, I'm crazy in love with him . . ." Her hands tore unconsciously at the tea sandwiches. "And the worst thing about it is that he *says* he's in love with me, too."

This was another blow. Janey could entertain the idea that Zizi was sleeping with Mimi for ulterior motives, but never that he was in love with her. "What about George?" she hissed.

The question seemed to bring Mimi back to earth. She swept the pieces of crumbled sandwich into a napkin, and said, "What *about* George?"

"You *are* married to him."

Mimi turned on her. There was a challenging expression in her eyes, as if Janey had suddenly become the enemy. "So what?" she said, with a slight shrug of her shoulders. "Frankly, I'm surprised you're being so provincial. I never expected you, of all people, to be bourgeois about an affair."

There was a sudden chill in the air. Neither woman spoke; their friendship had come to a crossroads. Janey could either endorse the affair and remain friends, or she could disapprove and lose everything.

In the deadly silence, Mimi dropped two cubes of sugar into her teacup, and for a moment, Janey hated her. When it came to sexual conquests, she had never lost a man to another woman before, and yet, Mimi wasn't "just another woman." She would always take whatever she wanted, because she was rich and she always had done so; she wore her birthright as easily as fashionable women wear designer dresses. She would continue with Zizi either way, and she wouldn't care what Janey thought—she would simply drop her. And once again, there would be whispers, and Janey would be back to feeling like she was on the outside, struggling to get in . . .

No, she thought with cold calculation. She had worked too hard at this friendship with Mimi to let a stupid man ruin it. Mimi's affair would work to her advantage—it would bind them together. And so, taking a few steps forward, she said, "I was only thinking about you, Mimi. I just don't want you to get caught."

The atmosphere suddenly cleared. In the nature of female friendship, it is customary to avoid confrontation, and once a conciliatory gesture is made, the rules dictate that it must be returned. "Oh no, Janey. I didn't mean that at all," Mimi said. "It was just that, for a moment, I thought maybe *you* were interested in Zizi . . ."

Both women laughed, and as the maid, Gerda, appeared in the doorway to clear away the tea, she was struck by the seeming perfection of the scene. The green-and-white striped awning flapped gently in the breeze, and underneath, the two fine ladies—blond and tan and pretty—were posed in sharp relief against the background of the blue sea. They were leaning toward each other, sharing a private joke; Gerda thought that they must be talking about men . . .

And in the next second, she was proven correct, as she overheard Janey saying: "Don't be ridiculous, darling. As a matter of fact, I've decided to start seeing Selden Rose."

Book two

ON SEPTEMBER 10, 2000, the *New York Times* announced that Jane (known as Janey) Wilcox, thirty-three, a Victoria's Secret lingerie model, was married four days before to Selden Rose, forty-five, the CEO of MovieTime, in a small, private ceremony in Montradonia, Italy.

It also made mention of the fact that Peter Cannon had gone to jail, with a companion piece about how white-collar jails were not the country clubs they used to be, and how tax evaders, financial swindlers, and insider traders were in for a surprise, the least of which was the bad food.

Meanwhile, the business section trumpeted the failure of three dot-com startups, while a young financial journalist named Melvin Metzer wrote, "If you listen carefully, you can hear the faint beat of tom-toms coming from Wall Street warning of economic disaster"—a line that somehow slipped past three editors and resulted in several letters complaining about the Indian reference, as Indians had once lived on Wall Street until the early Dutch settlers built a wall to keep them out.

But for most New Yorkers it was just another brilliant Monday morning in the second week of September. That day, Comstock Dibble was thinking about buying a $10 million apartment on Park Avenue, thereby ratcheting himself up another rung on the social ladder, but as usual, it was a sweaty process. Standing in the lobby of 795 Park Avenue, a building that, he had been assured over and over again by both the real estate agent, Brenda Lish, and his fiancée, Mauve, was one of the best in New York, his face glistened and beads of perspiration formed in his sparse hairline. Nevertheless, his eyes darted around the lobby with pleasure. Over the weekend, his accountants had warned him that for the first time in three years, Parador

Pictures was going to show a mid-year loss. But on Thursday night he was being honored by the mayor of New York for his humanitarian contributions to the city, and by the weekend, he hoped to be well into a deal that could easily net him $50 million or more. Recently, he'd been thinking about expanding his horizons—yes, he loved movies, but eventually one had to admit that it was a business for kids— and wouldn't he make an excellent politician? He wiped his brow with a linen handkerchief, and as Brenda Lish continued her endless prattle, he smiled.

"I don't have to tell *you* about this lobby," she said, turning to Mauve. "It was designed by Stanford White and it's been meticulously maintained—everything is original. If you tried to sell this lobby at Sotheby's, I think it would be worth some-thing like twenty-five million dollars."

The walls were of paneled mahogany; a large marble fireplace formed the cen-terpiece, and on its mantel stood a vase with a three-foot-high spray of flowers. Uniformed doormen wearing white gloves drifted silently through the lobby like ghosts; the atmosphere was one of timeless discretion and luxury, as if all of the events of the past eighty years had left this little oasis of class untouched.

"Comstock, what do you think?" Brenda Lish asked.

Comstock looked at her—she must be in her mid-forties but somehow man-aged to be both schoolmarmish and girlish at the same time—and what, he won-dered, was with that flowered dress she was wearing?

"What I think is . . . ," he said slowly, "I'm not buying the lobby."

At this, Mauve rolled her eyes, but Brenda laughed as if he'd said something extremely funny. If he had any awareness of how he appeared in this setting—of how his boorish manner was made only more glaring against the backdrop of these surroundings—he didn't show it. Nor did Brenda Lish acknowledge it. Brenda was from an old New York family, from the time when that actually meant something, and her grandmother had lived in this building. Fifty years ago, a man like Com-stock Dibble wouldn't have been admitted, but he might have had enough sense and pride not to want to live in a building like this one anyway. But those days were gone, along with the Lish fortune; it had all disappeared by the mid-1980s. At which point Brenda, who had the quiet modesty and sensible practicality of her Puritan ancestors, became a real estate agent, using her insider knowledge of the best buildings in New York to build up a clientele who was willing, and able, to spend millions and millions of dollars on the right apartment. She didn't personally approve of men like Comstock Dibble, but while he was cruder than most of the arrogant, tasteless men with their trophy wives who had changed the face of society in the eighties, he wasn't completely out of the mold. He had a name, he had money, he was being honored by the mayor (which would help with the board in considering him an upstanding citizen—indeed, he had already mentioned that he would get a letter of recommendation from His Honor), and he was marrying Mauve Binchely. That would help with the board, too.

"Should we step outside?" she asked, and the three wandered out into the bright sunshine.

"Now Mauve, I don't have to tell *you* this," Brenda said. "But you know apartments in this building don't come up very often . . . The last one was three years ago, so if you're interested, I would make an offer right away, of at least the asking price . . ."

Mauve sniffed the air as if detecting a foul odor, and said, "I'm worried about the noise."

"Noise?" Comstock said. He suddenly seemed to be on the edge of a temper tantrum, and Brenda, who heard a great deal about people through her line of work, wondered if she was about to witness his legendary loss of self-control.

"You should be used to the noise by now. You *already* live on Park Avenue," he said, turning to Mauve accusingly, as if she'd just stolen something from a store.

"So what?" Mauve said. "I heard a loud noise."

"That was probably Brenda talking, you twit," he snapped.

"I *heard* a car horn," Mauve said, not responding to the insult. It was one of the things he liked about her—she had a hide as tough as an old alligator's.

"Well, the windows are double-glazed, but you could certainly have them triple-glazed, for probably . . . fifty thousand dollars?" Brenda said. She suddenly remembered a story she'd heard about Comstock Dibble, about how he had put nipple clamps on some woman and attached strings to them and then fucked her up the butt, riding her like a horse. And apparently, the woman had liked it.

"You know I can't tolerate noise," Mauve said primly. "Brenda, you remember, even when we were girls, I used to scream every time I heard a siren."

"And I can't tolerate you right now," Comstock said. "Where the hell is my car?"

He was, of course, standing right in front of it—a black Mercedes with tinted windows and bulletproof glass. "Good-bye Brenda," he said, glaring at Mauve. "*I* will call you."

"Anytime," Brenda said, with a little wave.

"He's hideous, isn't he?" Mauve said.

"Hideous" was too kind a word for it, Brenda thought, but she said, "Oh yes."

"But I can't help it. I love him," Mauve said.

Brenda wanted to laugh. Unlike most of her contemporaries, she didn't feel sorry for "poor Mauve"; rather, she saw her impending alliance with Comstock as a sort of divine retribution. Brenda and Mauve had been at Brearley together as girls, and Comstock was absolutely right—Mauve was, and had always been, a twit. She really had screamed every time a siren went by, and once she had even wet her pants. They probably would have kicked her out of Brearley, but her parents had too much money and were somehow related—like only about a hundred other people in the city—to the Vanderbilts.

"If you love him, that's all that counts," Brenda said.

"Oh, I *know*," Mauve said. She removed a gold compact from a blue snakeskin Fendi bag and dabbed at her long, pointy nose with powder. "I really *should* be going, dear. Fashion Week starts today."

"It was great to see you again, dear," Brenda said, leaning forward for the two requisite air kisses. "You look exactly the same as you did twenty years ago."

"So do you," Mauve said. "You know, I'd forgotten how wonderful those old Laura Ashley dresses are. Maybe they'll make a comeback."

"Everything does, eventually," Brenda said. She smiled as she watched Mauve teeter down Park Avenue. She didn't mind that Mauve had made a dig at her Laura Ashley dress; Brenda herself was the first person to admit that she was hopelessly old-fashioned. But still, she made more than $2 million in commissions a year, and as someone who had seen the mighty fall again and again, the last thing she was going to do was waste her money on designer frocks.

How foolish these rich people were! she thought, as she raised her hand to hail a cab. As if wearing designer clothes could give Mauve Binchely a personality. She settled into the back of the cab and gave the address of her next appointment. She was feeling gleeful—despite Mauve's protests, she knew Comstock Dibble would buy the apartment, or would attempt to, anyway. The apartment he was interested in, 9B, was a four-thousand-square-foot "classic eight," with a living room, dining room, study, three bedrooms, and a maid's room, but she suspected he would have bought an apartment the size of a shoebox if it were the only thing available. It wasn't just that 795 Park was one of the best buildings in the city, but that Victor Matrick, the crazy CEO of all of Splatch Verner, lived in the building, and, apparently, where Victor lived, Comstock must live as well. The entire time she'd been showing them the apartment Comstock had asked endless questions about Victor Matrick's apartment—its location in relation to 9B and its size, and even who had done the interior decoration. It was all so typical and pathetic, Brenda thought, the way these rich, powerful men, who should have been above it all, nearly always made decisions based on their petty little egos.

Just a couple of blocks south, on Fifth Avenue and Seventieth Street, Mimi Kilroy entered the tiny elevator that opened into her and George's apartment, and greeted the elevator man, who pressed the button for the lobby so that she wouldn't have to exert herself. Two doormen were stationed in the lobby; as she passed, nodding, one

of them hurried to the heavy brass door that led to the street and held it open for
her to pass.

"I don't think the car is here, Mrs. Paxton," he said, with great concern, as if the
idea of her walking caused him physical pain.

"I'm not taking the car today, Jésus. I'm riding in that. Isn't it marvelous?" She
indicated a strange contraption parked at the curb, which consisted of a rickshaw
attached to a bicycle. On it sat a wiry young man wearing a baseball cap.

"That looks dangerous, Mrs. Paxton," Jésus said, and Mimi laughed. "You
know nothing ever happens to *me*," she said.

Stepping outside, her spirits soared at the day. Fifth Avenue was one of the
most wonderful places in the world and it was always the same, year after year—it
was one of the few things in life you could really count on. And then she thought
about how interesting that was, that a street could give you more comfort than family or friends, but she'd found in life that it was important to take little bits of happiness from wherever they sprang, because so often the things that people told you
would make you happy didn't.

She stepped into the fancy rickshaw, decoratively painted yellow to attract the
eye of the tourists for whom these conveyances had been invented. She crossed her
legs, smoothing down the skirt of her fine tweed shift; her feet were clad in beige
suede boots—impossibly impractical and ridiculously expensive, but that was the
point. The driver nodded at her and set off into the traffic, and as they gently
swayed down Fifth Avenue, she took her emotional temperature.

She was, she decided, happy that day. She was forty-two, and recently her days
had either one of two casts: depressed or ridiculously giddy. When she was giddy,
she felt like an eighteen-year-old girl again, like it wasn't too late and she could still
do anything, like start an all-girl rock band and learn to play the electric guitar and
sing on a stage in front of thousands of people. When she was depressed, she felt
old, she felt like she hadn't done anything in her life, she felt that soon she would be
completely undesirable and no one would ever want to have sex with her again. She
would go through menopause and her vagina would dry up—as it was, it was sometimes embarrassingly difficult to become lubricated, especially with George. But
George hadn't demanded sex from her much in the past year. She guessed that he
might be getting it elsewhere like most of the husbands she knew, but she didn't
mind, as long as he was discreet.

A few years ago, such thoughts would have been anathema to her. Her father
had been a cheater (for all she knew, he still was), and she had seen a grimy film of
bitterness and misery develop beneath the surface of her mother's otherwise buoyant personality. When Mimi was a teenager, she hated her mother for never object-

ing to the mysterious nights her father spent away from home, but her mother made it clear that it was a topic not to be discussed, with the comment, "I will never criticize your father, dear." That comment had haunted her for years; she sometimes wondered if it was what had made her so rebellious in her twenties and early thirties, refusing to settle down, to marry, to "do something." And yet, as a *concept,* she admired the sacrifice her mother had made. She had often wondered if it was something she could do, and she suddenly realized, with an inward laugh, that it was exactly what she *had* done with George. She had put her personal preferences aside for what she had believed would be the greater good.

But the greater good for whom? she wondered, as they passed the stunning white marble mansion that had once been a millionaire's private home in the 1920s but was now the Frick Museum. Her actions had been for herself, of course; after all, George was a very rich man, and it had always been expected that she would marry a rich man, if only for the purpose of adding to the Kilroy fortune. But she had also known that she'd be an excellent wife for George, that she would enhance him. The realization and eventual acceptance that this was to be her purpose in life had not come easily, and for years she had chafed at the idea like a young stallion that refuses to take the bit. As a child, she had always thought that she would be something—a star—an Olympic rider or even a jockey, an actress, a journalist, but her attempts at these professions had always been met with tacit disapproval by her family, and although their objections were never articulated, they were felt as strongly as a pair of handcuffs. She mustn't be too much in the public eye, where she might fail or be ridiculed by critics (well, she had been ridiculed by critics when she'd appeared in an off-Broadway play at twenty-two); she mustn't embarrass the family and, most of all, her father. The unspoken message was always: Why should she do anything since she didn't have to? Wasn't it enough to be gracious and charming, to look beautiful and be beautifully dressed? And so, she wondered, what the hell was she doing having an affair with Zizi?

She was having a midlife crisis. Nobody ever told women what was going to happen to them emotionally when they got into their forties. First, there was a wonderful sense of peace. You understood that you couldn't control everything, that not everything that happened had something to do with you, and there were so many things that you once thought mattered but suddenly realized they didn't. And yet you still felt young, you could still read the menu in a restaurant at night. But then came an emotionally sickening thud, when you wondered what was the point of life, what was the point of *your* life, especially. You suddenly wanted meaning, you wanted connection, you wanted love, and you saw that those things had somehow been worn away; you were an automaton, going through the motions, doing the things you'd always done, but you weren't excited by them anymore, you saw the underlying *pointlessness* of it all. There were nights when she went to bed and wished that morning would never come. But it did come, always.

Of course, neither George nor anyone else knew about her feelings. She would never speak of them. Her mother had always said that there was nothing more unattractive than a rich girl who complains about her life. She knew she was lucky. She knew she was better off than nearly everyone else in the world. She tried to remind herself of it every day, she tried to spread a tiny bit of joy around, but sometimes it just didn't work.

And then she'd met Zizi. She knew Janey was interested in him and that he was curious about her, but she'd quickly put that to rest. That little Harold Vane had warned him off her anyway. Janey somehow had a bad reputation, there were murky rumors of her being a whore, of taking money from men, but Mimi didn't necessarily believe them. Janey's flaw was that she didn't quite have the élan to captivate a man like Zizi, whose father, unbeknownst to Janey and everyone else, was actually a German count. His family had moved to Argentina before Zizi was born, and Zizi, being the second son and therefore not in line to inherit either money or the title, had turned to polo.

Zizi was the man she would have married had she not married George, and had Zizi been fifteen years older. This was one of life's cruel tricks, impossible to solve until it played itself out and revealed its true meaning. She couldn't leave George (dealing with the resultant scandal was unimaginable to her), but for the moment, she couldn't deny herself Zizi either. He was probably the last beautiful young man she would ever have sex with for the rest of her life.

The traffic had slowed at Sixty-fifth Street, and the rickshaw cyclist took the opportunity to turn back to his passenger and smile. "I'm Jason, by the way."

"My name is Mimi," Mimi said. She leaned forward to hold out her hand, both out of conditioning and in an attempt to cover up the formality with which she'd said her name. "Do you live here, Jason?" she asked.

"I'm staying with a friend in Brooklyn," he said, and she immediately imagined a dilapidated row house—she'd only been through Brooklyn on her way to the airport, when the driver took that route to avoid traffic.

"I see," she said.

"Only for the summer," Jason said. "I'm from Iowa. I do this in the summer to make money to pay for school."

"Well," Mimi said. "I admire your enterprise."

She smiled and, glancing to the left, saw that they were passing the large sandstone building where she had grown up. Her family had had an entire floor—ten thousand square feet—with two live-in Irish maids. Looking up, she saw her old bedroom window, and was suddenly reminded of her childhood. Central Park Zoo was right across the street, and when she was little, she'd hear the lions roaring at night . . . And for the first time in years, she remembered that she liked to think that her father was with the lions on the nights when he didn't come home.

The lions were long gone, having been rescued from the zoo years ago by animal rights activists. But there *were* peregrine falcons in the park now, feasting on pigeons and squirrels and rats, and the occasional small dog—indeed, an old woman's Chihuahua had been snatched by one of these very falcons on East Sixty-third Street when she was walking it early in the morning two days before. The incident had made the second page of the *New York Times;* it was suspected that a pair of falcons were nesting under an ornately sculpted eave in the Lowell Hotel.

Two floors below, in a large suite that consisted of a foyer, sitting room, two bedrooms, three bathrooms, and a working fireplace, a recently conjoined human pair were preparing for their own forays into the city. Selden Rose pushed a pair of gold cuff links through the buttonholes of his crisply starched white shirt as his wife, Janey, applied a thin line of brown liquid liner to her eyelid.

Selden was in the second bedroom, humming to himself. So far, everything had worked out beautifully, and he congratulated himself for having the foresight to have rented a two-bedroom suite those many months before when he'd first moved to New York. It meant he and Janey could now comfortably remain in the hotel while they looked for an apartment. The maids had moved his clothing into the closets in the second bedroom and his secretary had arranged for Janey's belongings to be moved into the first bedroom while they were away in Tuscany. It had been a wonderful trip, he reflected; they had seen at least ten churches and many little museums, and they had gotten along beautifully, save for that third-to-the-last day when Janey had freaked out in the square of the walled town of Puntadellesia. They were drinking tiny cups of the local dark Italian coffee, having just taken photographs of each other in front of a large stone archway, below which spread a valley of patchwork quilt farms in seemingly every color of blue, yellow, and green. "When you see that kind of view, you understand where the Catholics came up with the idea of heaven," he said, and when she nodded laconically, he figured that her lack of enthusiasm was simply due to the heat.

"How about a lemonade? Or an Italian ice?" he'd asked. And when she didn't respond, only stared at him with those large blue eyes that were the color of sapphires, he took out his map of Tuscany and unfolded it on the round green metal table. "I thought we'd have dinner at the villa again tonight," he said. "After all, there's no point in going out when we've got a cook, and then we can drive to Montrachet in the morning. There are supposed to be some beautiful paintings from the sixteenth century in the museum—the Met's been trying to get them for years but they won't let them leave the country, much less the *countryside* . . ."

He thought that, as usual, she would enjoy his little joke, but instead he noticed that there was a peculiar look in her eyes, and suddenly, she hurled her coffee cup onto the cobblestones, where, amazingly, it bounced.

"Can't you understand?" she screamed. "I don't give a *fuck* about your sixteenth-century paintings."

For a moment, they simply stared at each other in shock, both taken aback by the force of her vitriol.

"But I thought . . ."

"You don't *think*, Selden. You just *do* . . . whatever *you* want . . . and you expect me to like it." And then she burst into tears.

The square was filled with old people—women dressed in black with scarves over their heads and men playing chess—and they all looked over, wondering what the commotion was about. He caught a few snatches of Italian, and their words, coupled with their angry looks, told him that they were wondering why "the man" was "abusing" the "beautiful American girl."

He threw five thousand lira onto the table and grabbed her arm. "Come on," he said.

"I'm not going. I'm hot and I'm tired . . . Why can't we go to Portofino or Capri, where we might at least know some people. I'm sick of all these old Italians, I'm sick of museums and dirty churches . . . Can't you see how fucking *dirty* it is here?"

"Hurry up," he snapped. "Unless you want to deal with the police."

She had let him lead her to the car, and once she was inside and they had begun the slow, winding descent from the town, her tears subsided. "What's the problem?" he asked. "Is it that time of the month?"

"No, it isn't that time of the month," she snapped. "I'm sick of driving. I'm sick of pasta. And I'm sick to death of paintings."

"But we discussed it," he said helplessly. "You said you loved Caravaggio . . ."

"We haven't seen any Caravaggio . . ."

"We will then. We'll go to Rome . . ."

She started weeping again, silently, the tears rolling down her cheeks.

He pulled over to the side of the road. She was his jewel; he couldn't stand to see her hurt. He put his arms around her and pulled her head onto his shoulder. "What is it, baby?" he asked gently. "Please don't cry. What do you want to do?"

"I want to go to Capri," she said. "Or at least Milan. I want to go shopping. And the prices are so cheap there . . ."

"It's too late to go to Capri, but we'll go to Milan tomorrow, I promise," he said, thinking, with a pang of regret, that it was a shame to leave the villa three days early when it had cost him $20,000 a week. But he was sensible enough to realize that now was not the time to think about money. "We'll go to Milan," he assured her, "and we'll stay in a suite at the Four Seasons . . ."

And then, when they were happily ensconced in the $1,500-a-night bridal suite, and she was unpacking endless bags of clothing that he'd purchased (at a discount—thank God all the clerks had recognized her), he'd pointed out that if she was unhappy about something, all she had to do was *tell* him how she felt and he would understand . . .

Now, back in New York and about to begin his first day at work as a newly married man, he reflected that these little adjustments were to be expected at the beginning of a marriage, and probably even more so in this particular marriage. Considering the fact that he and Janey had known each other only a little more than three months, they were doing amazingly well, he thought, fixing his tie in front of the dressing-room mirror. And there was that mind-blowing orgasm she'd given him that morning, and, remembering it, he suddenly missed her, even though she was only in the next room.

He snapped his gold Bulgari watch around his thin wrist and went through the living room and into the master bedroom.

She was in the bathroom, carefully applying makeup in front of a round magnifying mirror. Her eyes smiled at him through the reflection, and he came up behind her, lifting her hair and tenderly kissing the back of her neck.

"Hello, darling," she said.

"Hello, Mrs. Rose," he said. "Now what is it that you have to do all day?"

"Going to fashion shows. With Mimi. We've got to choose our clothing for next season," she said playfully.

"I think *you* should be modeling the clothes."

"Mmmm," she said, closing one eyelid to apply mauve shadow. "It's a ton of work . . . a big pain . . . and all the girls they use now are young and flat-chested—they don't want to have to pay them . . . Are you sorry you missed the Emmys?" she suddenly asked. "I saw in the paper that Johnny Block's movie won . . ."

"The Emmys happen every year. Our honeymoon is a once in a lifetime event."

"Yes," she said. "I suppose it is . . . In any case, there's always the Golden Globes. And the Oscars . . ."

"Oh, those are miles away," he said pleasantly, not wanting to tell her that the CEO of MovieTime was always expected to escort one of their actresses. "I've been thinking," he said, changing the subject as he took a seat on the edge of the Jacuzzi tub. "Why don't we stay home tonight? It's our first night back, and we could order room service . . . caviar and steak with béarnaise sauce . . ."

For a second, he thought he caught that same peculiar look in her eye that he'd first seen in Tuscany, but then she said regretfully, "Oh, Selden. You know we can't. Tonight's the first night of Fashion Week, and we've got Calvin Klein's show to go to and his dinner afterward, and then the big Visionnaire party . . . You don't have to go, but if I don't go, people will think it's weird."

"And that," he said, standing, "is something I will never understand."

"Oh, but you will, darling," she said, smiling up at him. "And then we've got the Armani party on Wednesday and the opening of the new Prada boutique—down-town—and on Thursday, the mayor's awards—we definitely can't get out of that one because the head of Victoria's Secret wants us to sit at his table . . ."

Selden wanted to get out of all of it, but his wife's eyes were so bright with excitement he didn't have the heart to disappoint her. "Where do you want me to meet you tonight?"

"At the tents in Bryant Park. Seven o'clock—if you're fifteen minutes late it doesn't matter, the shows never start until half an hour after they say they will. Just go inside—they promised to give you a first-row seat next to me . . ."

She suddenly turned and threw her arms around him. "Be good, darling," she said. "I'm going to miss you so much today. I don't think I'll be able to stand it until seven o'clock."

"In that case, I won't be late," he said, regretfully tearing himself away.

A few minutes later, he was down on the street and getting into the back of the black Lincoln Town Car that ferried him to and from work every day. He settled back against the leather seat and picked up the car phone, dialing his office.

His secretary answered. "It's me," he said. "Any calls?"

"Gordon White *just* called," she said. "Should I get him back?"

In a few seconds, Gordon White, his associate at MovieTime, was on the line. "Selden," he said, his oily voice oozing sexual innuendo. "How was the honeymoon?"

"Brilliant," Selden said.

"Did you see the Emmys?" Gordon asked.

"Johnny Block won. That's excellent for us."

"But he didn't thank MovieTime."

Selden frowned and suddenly became a different person. "Have business affairs take a look at his contract," he said, looking out the window as the car crawled past the Sherry-Netherland Hotel on Fifth Avenue. "There's probably a loophole. See if you can figure out a way to take away his credit."

• • •

He's gone! Janey thought. And suddenly felt relief.

She could breathe.

She put down her makeup brush and flopped onto the bed. It wasn't that she didn't love Selden Rose—there were moments, hours, even whole days, when she felt madly in love with him. But there were also other moments, hours, and days when she felt she didn't love him at all, when she looked at him and felt *frightened* that she'd made the biggest mistake of her life. And it was impossible to know which feeling was right, because everybody said that being scared was normal, a natural part of the process of getting married.

As she lay on the bed, she recalled the feelings that had led up to their marriage. That fateful moment when Mimi had told her she was seeing Zizi had reminded Janey of the harsh reality of love and romance, of the fact that a woman's choice of partner is always limited to men who want her, not vice versa. And as she drove home from Mimi's that afternoon, she decided that she wouldn't be left behind again. And so, as millions of women have done through the ages, she made herself fall in love with the man who was in love with her.

It wasn't easy at first, and for the first two weekends, when she'd allowed him to squire her around the Hamptons and had even held his hand, every part of her had resisted; she could barely bring herself to kiss him. His kisses were small and hard, like an old man's; the idea of having sex with him repulsed her. But still, he persisted, and she watched and waited, searching for the good in him, hoping the moment would come when he would suddenly be able to break down her defenses . . .

And Mimi's enthusiasm helped carry her forward. There is nothing a married woman loves more than the possibility of pulling the unconverted into the fold, and day after day, she made her arguments in support of Selden: He was the kind of single man who didn't come along very often; women were already lining up to date him. He might not be the man Janey had always imagined she would marry, but the man you *did* marry never was. Janey had already dated every man in New York and nothing had worked out. And Selden was crazy about her—everyone who saw them together remarked upon it—and it was always better to have a husband who was more in love with you than you were with him (if one could stomach such an arrangement, Janey thought).

And then, at last, the moment did come when she fell for him.

They'd been seeing each other for about three weeks when he suggested a trip to Block Island on his boat. At first, she hadn't wanted to go at all (what, or more accurately, *who*, was on Block Island?), but Mimi had pointed out that it might be helpful to see Selden in a different light. And it was true: Away from the hustle and competition of the Hamptons, Selden had literally appeared to grow . . .

His boat was wonderfully glamorous—an antique wooden thirty-foot Chris-

Craft with red seats. As soon as they stepped onto the boat, Selden's personality changed; he suddenly became the captain, piloting the boat with a joyful expertise. For the first time, his attention wasn't on her but on what he was doing, and the creation of that space made room for her own feelings to grow. Standing next to him at the wheel, she drank beer with him and laughed about the silly people they knew in common, like Mauve Binchely. And when she stripped down to a tiny pink bikini and he slipped his arm around her waist, she realized that, for one of the few times in her life, she felt comfortable with a man. Unlike most of the men she'd been with, he wasn't swollen with his own ego . . .

They arrived on Block Island salty and windblown, and spent the afternoon bicycling around the island, picnicking on a rocky beach strewn with driftwood and seagull bones. They told each other their stories, and that night, when they stayed at the big old hotel overlooking the harbor, it was easy to fall into bed with him, and his kisses weren't hard at all. Afterward, she had studied his face. He had a strong jaw and good features, and while none of it quite added up to handsomeness (there was something in the placement of his mouth and teeth that could border on goofiness), she saw that his was the sort of face that would grow to handsomeness through the eyes of affection.

And she made up her mind to go for him.

But despite her resolve, there had still been moments leading up to the marriage when she was so panicked that at times she felt numb, she couldn't speak, she felt like she was drowning. And then she'd had dreams that she was getting married, and when she got to the altar, *the wrong man* was waiting there. And on those days, when she felt panicked, all she could see were Selden's flaws.

On the bad days, the days when she felt she didn't love him, everything else was blotted out. On their second day in Tuscany, Selden had worn dark socks with sandals. When she'd seen him in that getup, she realized there was no way she could be with him, and that whole afternoon, when they'd "explored the countryside" (which seemed to be one of his favorite pastimes), the beautiful yellow hills dotted with hayricks were invisible to her—all she could picture were those navy blue socks (they seemed to be new, but still, there was a thread sticking out of the toe on the left one), encased in the heavy brown leather sandals. The sandals were Prada, but even designer shoes couldn't save a man with inherently bad taste, and all afternoon she agonized over it. Should she call off the wedding? But to cancel a wedding over a sartorial error implied a level of shallowness to which even she could not descend. Should she tell him to take off the socks? But she was afraid if she did, her voice would be filled with such disgust it might release a whole litany of complaints about him. So she did nothing and said nothing, enduring an almost nauseating despair, like that of a prisoner on her way to the guillotine.

Finally, when they had finished their tour and had spotted the landmark—a lone sandstone tower on the top of a hill—that pointed the way to the dirt road that led to their villa, he noticed her distress.

"You're so quiet," he said.

She could only nod in terror.

"Are you frightened?"

"Aren't you?" she asked timidly.

"Of course I'm a little scared," he said. He took his eyes off the dirt track to look at her and reached over to squeeze her hand. In that white Tuscan sun, his brown eyes had flecks of gold in them. "But more than anything, I know we're going to be great together. We're going to be happy. We're going to have everything we've always wanted . . . and I can't wait to give it to you, baby. I love you so much . . ."

It was the same argument he'd made when he'd asked her to marry him, one week after that jaunt to Block Island. They were to be married in five days, and if he'd shown one chink of hesitation or fear or anger, she might have found a way to get out of it.

But he didn't. Not for nothing was he a CEO at Splatch Verner.

And, she thought, lying on the bed in the suite at the Lowell Hotel and gazing at her engagement ring (*that* was a fun afternoon—they'd purchased the ring at Harry Winston the day before they left for Tuscany on their wedding journey), on the day of her wedding, she hadn't been frightened. She'd been giddy with excitement and so had he—they'd made love as soon as they'd woken up and then had begun drinking champagne, bottle after bottle of Cristal, which Selden had had flown over specially from Paris. They had swum in the long, black pool, luxuriating in the warm water, unable to get over the fact that in a couple of hours, they'd be married. Then they'd gotten dressed together. She wore a white Grecian-style Valentino gown that was off the rack (but still $6,000); he an off-white Ralph Lauren suit with a pink shirt. When she looked at him, she wondered what she'd been thinking before because, suddenly, he was the most beautiful man in the world to her and she thought, crazily, that everyone else had to see it, too.

And then their four guests arrived. They still laughed proudly about that—at how they'd had only four guests, and those guests only because they also happened to be vacationing in Tuscany at the time. They were Harold Vane and his latest girlfriend, Mariah, who was Janey's age and the publisher of a new magazine about shopping, who kept telling Janey how lucky she was, and Ross Jared and his wife, Constance, whom Selden knew from Splatch Verner. Ross was the CEO of the Internet division and his wife was the ballet dancer. She was about the size of a pea, Janey thought, dark-haired and about five foot two and probably less than a hundred pounds. She hardly said a word but seemed to get very drunk, because later on in the day she ran across the lawn, leaping like a fairy.

The ceremony took place in the large courtyard; Selden, again, had miraculously found someone to festoon it with flowers. A Catholic priest performed the bans (Selden had an Italian grandmother somewhere in his past and said he felt an affinity for the religion) and the ceremony had been in Italian and Janey hadn't understood one word, except for the parts where she said her name, and then, "I do."

Afterward, someone put on the Grateful Dead and the Allman Brothers, and they danced madly. "This is the way to do it, baby," Harold Vane kept saying, over and over again. "This is the most fun wedding I've ever been to in my life."

And Janey had thought that the fear was gone for good.

But it wasn't. And since their marriage, there were times when she found herself *despising* her husband with a level of hatred she'd never felt for any man before. She was stuck with him and his flaws, like the way it seemed to take him forever to get out of the house, because he always had to check for his keys and wallet three times, and the way he would stop in the middle of the street to talk on his cell phone, making her stand there for sometimes five minutes or more, and when she opened her mouth to protest he would rudely hold up his hand. Or that belly he was developing and his flat, sagging ass, and his penis—it was a perfectly normal size, but why couldn't it have been just a little bit *bigger*? And the problem was that he had taken away her possibilities. When she was thinking these black thoughts, she wondered why she hadn't aimed *higher*.

Her imagined dissatisfaction stemmed from the idea that without his job, Selden Rose was really nothing more than a nice guy from Chicago. He wasn't inherently glamorous, he didn't possess a creative talent that had lifted him above the masses. He didn't come from a particularly distinguished family (even though his father, she knew, had been a lawyer and his mother worked at a newspaper)—he wasn't even a "killer," like Comstock Dibble or George Paxton. In short, he was an average American guy from an upper-middle-class family. And while there was nothing inherently wrong with that, it was her background, too—the very background she'd been trying to escape ever since she was a teenager.

Until she got married, she had always fantasized that when she did marry, it would be to some kind of European royalty, or a movie star, or a successful painter or novelist. She had seen herself with someone exceptional, someone who, in every minute of their life, stood out from the morass of humanity. And by marrying Selden Rose, she had denied herself that opportunity forever.

Well, maybe not forever. Selden had told her, again and again, that there was no way to predict whether a marriage would work out, no way to predict what would happen in the future. It didn't matter if a couple had known each other for five years or five minutes before they married, the important thing was to take a chance, to make the commitment. And then to live each day as it came.

The phone rang—two short bursts, indicating a call from the front desk—and she picked it up, knowing it would be the concierge, announcing Mimi's arrival. What a little fool she was being, she thought, jumping off the bed. The suite was strewn with her spoils from Milan—dresses and shoes and handbags and even gloves—and Selden had been so sweet, and so excited, to pay for it all. Naturally, like most men, he'd made a bit of a show about the prices, shaking his head over a sheer sleeveless and backless turtleneck that folded up into a five-by-five square that was no thicker than a quarter inch ("five hundred dollars for a little piece of fabric that wouldn't cover a baby's bottom?" he'd exclaimed), but she could tell by the glint in his eyes that he was enjoying dressing his beautiful young wife. And it did give her pleasure to give him pleasure . . .

If only he would leave her alone every once in a while! she thought, digging through an open suitcase to find the turtleneck. He was always on her, watching her, as if he were fascinated to see what she might do next. Just that morning, after she'd given him a blow job (at least it was easy to please him in that department) and they were sitting at the table drinking coffee and reading the paper, he had suddenly put down his cup, and she realized, as she was in the middle of turning a page, that he was staring at her fingers. She caught his eye, giving him a sharp look, and he gave a little embarrassed laugh, and his mouth formed into that goofy smile that always made her stomach sink in despair. If only she could train him not to smile like that! "Your hands just look so beautiful, turning the page," he said, reaching over to capture her hand in his two hands. He bent his head and looked up at her, opening one hand to reveal hers, as if it were a little bird, and then he leaned down and kissed it.

What could she do? She didn't want to be unkind, but she could feel tears of frustration forming in the corners of her eyes. "Oh, Selden," she snapped. "My fingernails are disgusting . . ."

The bell rang and she hurried to the door, throwing it open. "Hello, married lady," Mimi said. "Am I happy to see you."

"Isn't it wonderful?" Janey said, as they exchanged kisses. Her misgivings about Selden disappeared as she suddenly thought, *I'm equal to you now . . .*

Aloud she said, "Come in. It's a mess of course, we just got back last night and the maids haven't had a chance to clean up . . ."

"Don't hurry on my account," Mimi said, entering the living room. "They wouldn't dare start without me, considering how much I buy from Oscar . . . It's so funny, you and Selden living here as a married couple. You know, the Lowell is where all the men stay when they're getting divorced from their wives."

"Oh, I *know*," Janey said. She had made several visits to the Lowell herself over the years.

The two women exchanged an amused look of mutual understanding. There was between them not the bond of genuine old friendship, perhaps, but something nearly as strong: The natural affinity that two beautiful women have for one another that comes from having had similar experiences in life.

And a few minutes later, they were chatting excitedly as the rickshaw carried them down Fifth Avenue to Forty-second Street, where the fashion shows were staged under large white circus tents. Heads turned, and the awareness that they were being remarked upon only added to the animation of their conversation. As they pulled up to the entrance, the throng of photographers looked up in curiosity and raised their cameras.

"Here comes trouble," one remarked.

"Who are they?"

"Janey Wilcox, Victoria's Secret model. Mimi Kilroy, socialite," someone hissed.

"It girls."

"Except they've been around forever."

"Aging It girls."

"Janey! Mimi! Over here," they shouted.

"Hey Janey, how's married life?"

"We want to see the ring!" someone said.

"The ring! The ring!"

Janey held out her left hand.

Mimi put her arm around her waist and drew her closer. "So how is Selden, really?" she asked. "Are you madly in love?"

"He said the cutest thing on the plane coming back," Janey said. "He took my hand, and with dead seriousness said, 'Janey, we're going to rule New York.'"

They smiled for the cameras.

SEVEN

THREE DAYS LATER, on Thursday morning, Patty Wilcox got up, went to the bathroom, and got her period.

Damn, damn, damn, she thought. But what else was she expecting? Digger had been on tour for nearly the whole summer, and she'd seen him only once in the last two weeks, but for some stupid reason she'd been hoping that she would get pregnant. It was ridiculous—she was only twenty-eight years old and they'd been trying for a year and now she was really beginning to think that there was something wrong with her. It should have happened already. Especially since everything else in her life had gone according to plan—but that was only because she worked so hard to make everything right.

She inserted a tampon, and as she did so, she remembered about the puppy. The last time Digger had been home, she'd said, "You know, I think if I don't get pregnant next month, or even if I do, we should get a puppy. We can call it Triscuit. Little Triscuit. Isn't that cute?"

And he'd nodded, his mouth full of pizza. "Triscuit. I like it."

"It won't be a big dog," she'd said, standing over him and stroking his hair, so his head bent back and those startling green eyes gazed up into hers. "But it has to have lots of personality. Like, it shouldn't mind if we dress it up and take it to the Halloween parade."

He had put his arms around her neck and pulled her onto his lap. They had started kissing like teenagers, and after a couple of minutes, she'd said, "You sure do like to make out a lot."

"I know," he'd said. "I guess I forgot to grow up." They had looked at each other and laughed. This exchange was one of their favorite private jokes, which began on their third date when Digger had come to her apartment and pounced on her, and wouldn't let her go for at least an hour. It was on that night, two years ago, when they'd both realized how serious their relationship was going to be.

"So you like the idea of the dog," she'd said.

"I do," he'd said, rubbing his cheek against hers. "I love you so much."

"I love you so much, too," she'd said. "If anything happened to you, I'd have to die so I could go to heaven to find you again."

"How do you know I'd be in heaven?" he'd asked.

"Oh, you would be. I *know*," she'd said.

So today was the day she was going to get the dog, she thought, pulling up her underpants. Well, it was something to look forward to anyway. Lately she'd been feeling insignificant. She wanted to make a contribution, but she feared the world wouldn't let her and she didn't know what she wanted to do anyway.

She put on a pair of low hip-hugger combat pants and a T-shirt she'd ordered from the Abercrombie & Fitch catalog. She usually dressed like this, in the democratic uniform of her generation, affordable to almost everyone and universally available. Then she got into the elevator and went down to the lobby and nodded at Kenny, a tiny man with newsprint-stained fingers. Kenny manned the newsstand and always brightened when he saw Digger, because Digger bought a pack of cigarettes from him every day when he was in town, even though he smoked only occasionally, just to give the guy some business.

"Hi, Kenny," she said. Kenny was sitting on a metal folding chair next to the newsstand, where he seemed to perch for most of the day.

"Your husband coming home soon?" Kenny asked.

"Next week," she sighed. "I can hardly stand it."

Kenny nodded sympathetically, as if he had firsthand knowledge of all the troubles a human being might suffer in the world.

Then she passed Sarouk, the sad-looking Middle Eastern doorman who was more of a security guard than an actual doorman—even if you were struggling with packages or bags of groceries, he wouldn't leave his desk, but he would smile kindly, as if he, too, understood the difficulties of being middle class in New York, which meant carrying your own bags. "Hello, Sarouk," she said as she went out onto the street.

The building they lived in, 15 Fifth Avenue, was a yellowish, crumbly old structure that had once been the Washington Square Hotel. You could still see traces of grandeur in the ornate gilded frescoes on the ceiling in the lobby, and in the grand marble entrance on Fifth Avenue with its gold scalloped awning. But no one ever used that entrance, as if it were fruitless to pretend that the building was still elegant. The walls in the hallways were stuccoed a sickly shade of green, and hundreds and hundreds of people lived in the building, mostly in tiny one- or two-roomed warrens with kitchens built into the ends of their living rooms. But Patty loved the building anyway. She loved the funny old ladies who had been living there forever, who still paid rent (probably about $400 a month for a one-bedroom apartment), and flaunted themselves in a variety of interesting getups. One had neon-purple-painted toenails and always carried a funny little dog that looked like a stuffed lion whose fur has been rubbed away by too much affection; another wore tank tops and hip-hugger pants and high heels with impunity, as if daring anyone to comment on the hanks of flesh that hung boldly from the top of her back and her upper arms.

The building was very bohemian, its denizens a mix of rich young show-business people like herself and Digger, who lived in the big gothic penthouse apartments at the top of the building, and hardworking middle-class types, who lived in the studios and one-bedrooms. They were either young people with a bit of glamour who seemed to be on their way up, or middle-aged people in their forties and fifties and sixties (Patty imagined that they were mostly single), who had accepted the fact that this was it, they weren't going to make it big after all and the next significant thing that would happen to them was probably cancer. Some of them seemed beaten down by life, by the endless routines of meaningless jobs, and their clothes were always black and slightly misshapen and dirty, as if they'd been in mourning for a long time. But others seemed to have some bigger purpose in life, like the fifty-year-old woman who worked for the Animal Rescue Fund, who was brisk and cheery and determinedly friendly. Her apartment was across from the elevator, and whenever it opened on her floor, Patty would hear lively conversation coming from behind her door. And somehow, this always reminded her that there was good in life . . .

She was lucky and she knew it, she thought, as she stepped out into the sunshine. She would probably never have to worry about what would happen to her when she got old, but that was so far in the future it felt like it would never happen. There were two young women standing near the entrance in what appeared to be a state of confusion, but Patty didn't think anything about it—there was a bus stop in front of the building and a PATH station for the train to New Jersey nearby, so there were always people around who looked like they didn't know where they were going. She began walking up Fifth Avenue and turned down Ninth Street, thinking about her life. Ever since she'd stopped working, she'd been having disturbing thoughts about the kind of woman she really was.

Recently, she'd been examining the fact that she didn't have to work because Digger was rich. The reality was beautiful, but she couldn't make peace with the idea of it. Of course, she could have avoided this mental perplexity by keeping her job, but then she would have had to reckon with a different dilemma, because she'd become soured on her work. For at least a year before she'd quit, she hadn't been able to prevent herself from seeing the truth: That producing documentaries about rock stars for VH1 was all about an inflated sense of self-importance on the part of everyone involved, including herself. It was possible to continue only by applying mental blinders that forced her to focus on the endless minutiae required to get the job done, and then she had to believe that getting the job done was of national importance. The system disgusted her and so she had finished with it, but that didn't, she knew, make her an admirable person, just a privileged one. After all, almost everyone had to work their whole lives under the same conditions, hating their jobs but not having a choice about whether to have them or not. And so a part of her felt like a fraud for quitting.

And now, by not working and letting Digger support her, another part wondered if, morally, she was a whore.

Ever since she was a little girl, she'd instinctually been repulsed by the idea of the "traditional marriage." She wondered why the rest of the world was not disgusted by a woman's obviously cynical exchange of sex, housework, and child-raising for a roof over her head and food on her table. The fact was, the only way you could find true love was if you didn't need financial support from a man. Otherwise, you made compromises and concessions; you had sex with a man you didn't genuinely find attractive. You could convince yourself that it was okay, but really, Patty thought, it was all nothing more than an acceptable form of prostitution.

And now, here she was, having become exactly what she'd always despised.

Sixth Avenue was a teeming mass of humanity. A group of pimply boys slouched down the sidewalk, their baggy jeans hanging below the cracks in their asses. Old ladies wheeled shopping carts; a young woman marched by, shouting into her cell phone, "I'm glad you finally had the guts to tell me. This has been affecting our friendship for three years . . . !" In front of Balducci's, the gourmet food shop for the well-heeled where she and Digger joked that everything in the store was $6, including eggs, a young homeless man sat wrapped in a blanket, looking pathetic and clutching a beagle in his arms. The man couldn't have been more than twenty-five, and a sign next to him explained that he was trying to collect $40 for a bus ride to Pennsylvania, but so far, in the past year that Patty and Digger had lived on the block, he seemed to have no intention of going anywhere.

On this particular morning, he was talking to a young woman who was folding up a blanket. "I've been on the street since 1997," Patty overheard him saying proudly. "The homeless are coming back. The mayor's going to be out soon, and then we'll take back the streets."

Patty wondered how he managed to stay on the streets at all, since it was the mayor's policy to collect up all the homeless people every night and stick them in shelters; some people even said they were bused out of the city. She took $20 out of her wallet and handed it to him, which was something she did nearly every week, out of guilt. She knew he probably didn't deserve it, but she had so much money and he obviously had so little, what difference did it make?

He looked up. "Ah, my guardian angel," he said. "How are you today?"

"I'm good," Patty said. "I'm going to get a puppy."

The light changed. As she crossed the street, Patty thought that she was able to tolerate herself only because of love. Not the love that she had for herself, which didn't seem to be much these days, but the love that she had for Digger. Between them, they had the kind of rare, miraculous feeling that people call "true love"— that pure form of affection that makes it possible to actually believe those words in the marriage vow, "For better or worse, for richer or poorer, in sickness and in health." True love, Patty thought, was the opposite of feeling like you had an empty place inside you; instead, you felt full, as if you'd eaten the most perfectly satisfying meal in the world . . .

On the other side of Sixth Avenue, two girls, heavy-set and dark-browed, dressed in black with thick-soled shoes (they were probably college students at NYU, Patty thought), stood in front of a table waving coat hangers. "Kill the Republicans now," one shouted at passersby. "A Republican vote is a vote for the Middle Ages."

"Down with Bush," the other one shouted.

"Hey," said the first girl, as Patty tried to walk by. "Are you Republican or Democrat?"

"What do you think?" Patty asked.

"The Republicans want to take away your right to an abortion."

"I don't want an abortion."

"Are you for women or against women?" the girl asked suspiciously.

"For . . . ," Patty said awkwardly.

The girl shoved a clipboard under Patty's nose. "Then register to vote Democratic."

A little farther down, on Christopher Street, was the pet store. Four puppies were rolling around in cedar shavings—a little brindled bulldog with huge brown eyes saw Patty and leapt at the glass. That's the one, Patty thought, and went inside.

She felt a little bad about buying a puppy from a pet store—everyone said you shouldn't. The puppies might be sick or badly formed and they were raised on pet farms, where cruel owners made the females have one litter after another, and then, when they were used up, killed them and fed them to the other dogs. But it wasn't the puppies' fault, Patty thought, and, if she didn't buy one, God only knew what would happen to them. So she went in.

"I'd like to buy a puppy," she said to the salesgirl.

"Do you know what kind?"

"I think the little stripey one. With the big eyes."

"She's a French bulldog," the girl said, opening up the back of the Plexiglas box and pulling out the wriggling puppy. "Actually, she's from Russia. But the breed is very rare. They're hard to get here. We only got her because her coloring's a little bit off."

"Oh, I don't care about her coloring," Patty said, taking the puppy into her arms.

A few minutes later, she emerged from the store with a collar and leash, and little Triscuit in a soft-sided dog carrier. She reached the corner, and unable to contain herself any longer, bent down to take Triscuit out of the carrier. She leapt out like a missile, firmly attaching her teeth to Patty's nose. Patty laughed—the puppy's teeth were tiny and not terribly sharp—and as she did so, she heard a young woman's voice demand, "Patty Wilcox, right?"

She looked up, and at first she thought the two women before her must be girls she'd met at some party, whose names she couldn't remember. There was something familiar about the dark-haired one, and then Patty remembered with a shock that she was the same girl who'd been staring at her during that baseball tournament in July in the Hamptons. And then she realized that the girls had been standing outside of her building when she came out, and that they must have followed her. But why?

"You *are* Patty Wilcox," the other one said. She was bigger than the dark-haired girl, taller, with red hair that was obviously dyed. The shorter one with the dark hair was, Patty saw, actually pretty, and in a flash Patty knew that they were that particular type of girl who comes from Brooklyn or New Jersey, who inevitably takes the short hop across the river to Manhattan to make it. And the dark-haired one, whose breasts were pushed up and shoved out of a tight-fitting sheer flowered shirt (you could see the lacy bra underneath), was obviously planning to use her looks to see where they might take her.

"I'm sorry," Patty said, "but I don't think I know you."

"You don't know us, but we know you," the red-haired one said. She appeared to be in charge of the situation, while the dark-haired one had a look on her face that seemed to indicate she thought Patty was beneath her. "It's about Digger," she said.

Oh, Patty thought, with some relief. They were fans, then. Two slightly crazy fans who had somehow found out where they lived and wanted to meet Digger. It happened sometimes, and the best thing to do was to be as polite and friendly as possible and then get away quickly. "If you want Digger, you should contact his record company. Ask to speak to someone in the publicity department . . ."

The two women exchanged looks. There was something ominous in their demeanor, and Patty suddenly felt afraid.

"We don't want publicity," the dark-haired one said.

"But you know there's going to be publicity anyway," the redhead said. "The *Star*'s already called . . ."

"I'm sorry," Patty said. "I have an appointment. I have to go . . ." The puppy was wriggling in her arms; it was as slippery as a little seal with its huge belly and tiny legs.

The red-haired girl took a step toward her. "We think you're going to want to hear what we have to say. Marielle here took the day off from work."

"I'm sorry," Patty said. "But I can't help you."

"Oh, we don't want your help," the girl named Marielle said.

"Marielle's going to be a big star. Like J. Lo," the redhead said.

"I'm just trying to do the right thing. Sandy and I talked it over, and we figured the right thing was to tell you first," Marielle said.

"Tell me what?" Patty cried.

"You'd better get used to the idea that you're going to have to share your husband," Sandy said. "Because Marielle here is going to have Digger's baby."

• • •

"Have you talked to your sister lately?" Selden asked casually, by way of making conversation.

"She's hasn't been answering her phone," Janey said. "Maybe she went to Europe to meet Digger."

It was Thursday evening, the night of the mayor's Humanitarian Awards for Fashion. Janey was sitting in the bedroom at the small dressing table having her makeup done by a pretty Asian girl, while a stylist laid out three dresses on the bed. In the midst of this small commotion, Janey's eyes crinkled up at Selden with affection; she was enjoying the new feeling of getting ready for a big evening out with her husband.

"I suppose you'll hear from her sooner or later," Selden said, self-consciously looking through his drawers for his black bow tie. He was slightly uncomfortable about getting dressed in the middle of such extensive female preparations.

"Oh, Barbara," Janey said to the stylist. "I think I'm going to wear the blue Luca Luca with the fur. Black is so over, don't you think? I've decided it's the color for assistants who don't have any money, because black goes with everything else that's black. Whereas, if you wear colors, it's trickier, you really have to know what you're doing with your wardrobe . . ."

"That is so true," the makeup artist said.

"I thought black wasn't a color," Selden said. He leaned over to give his wife a kiss, but she turned her head away, so that his kiss ended up on her hair. "Darling, please," she said. "My makeup . . ."

"Does that mean I can't kiss you all night?" he asked.

"No," the makeup artist said bluntly. "You can't."

"My husband doesn't quite understand about going out in New York yet," Janey said.

Selden thought he'd better go into the living room and fix himself a drink.

He put three ice cubes in a glass and poured a finger and a half of vodka on top. He wasn't sure if he could take another one of these evenings and it was only Thursday. He counted—this was the eighth party they'd gone to already that week, although Janey had pointed out that tonight was an easy night because it was the only party they had to attend. And it wasn't just the parties he was weary of, but the endless preparations—hours of hair and makeup, trips to and from the designers to borrow dresses, people calling to arrange for cars, messengers coming in and out. And it seemed to him that the goal was often nothing more than a photograph in Sunday's *New York Post* or the society page of *Vogue* magazine. Selden couldn't see the point, but he didn't want to spoil Janey's fun. When she was out on the town, there was a glow about her that she hadn't had in Tuscany, and from the other room he heard the pleasurable peals of her laughter . . .

"Your husband is adorable," he heard the stylist say, and then Janey's response, "Isn't he? I got a good one, didn't I?"

He sighed. Ever since they had returned from their honeymoon, she'd been attacking New York with the zeal of a mountain climber determined to reach the highest summit, with him, it seemed, relegated to a Sherpa in cummerbund and black tie. But he told himself that it couldn't last for long; she'd grow tired of all the socializing and then she'd settle down and get pregnant and they'd have children. They'd talked about getting an apartment right away on Park Avenue or Fifth, but he was beginning to think it might be a better idea to wait and buy a house in the suburbs, in Greenwich or Katonah—after all, *he* didn't have to live in the city, and he couldn't imagine raising their children there anyway . . .

In the next moment, however, his thoughts were interrupted by Janey's triumphant, "Well?" and he turned around to see her looking resplendent in a simple off-the-shoulder gown. Her skin was still a tawny shade of gold from the summer, and the blue of the gown picked up the blue in her eyes, so they appeared to shine out of her face like sapphires; her hair was partially upswept with long curls hanging down the back of her neck in a seventies style—which, Selden remembered, Janey had told him was back. And suddenly all was forgiven.

"You look absolutely beautiful," he murmured to her, suddenly pleased that they were, indeed, going out. Who he was and what his place was in the world came home to him; he was a hugely successful man with a gorgeous wife—he was what every man wanted to be, and he had everything he'd always imagined for himself.

In the elevator going down to the lobby, he took her hand and pressed up against her, being careful this time not to smudge her makeup, but he still felt her stiffen next to him. "You look *beautiful*," he said again.

"Oh, darling," she sighed. "Thank you." There was a mirror in the elevator and she glanced in it with unself-conscious pleasure, arching one eyebrow. Then her hand went to her neck. "I should have some jewelry though," she said.

"You don't need jewelry," he whispered, implying that she was beautiful enough without it.

"Oh, but I do," she said, deliberately ignoring the insinuation. "I could have borrowed something from Harry Winston, but lots of times they send a guard, and I thought that wouldn't be much fun for you."

"It wouldn't," he laughed. "It's bad enough sharing you with all of New York as it is . . ."

For a brief second, he thought that she rolled her eyes, but then the elevator doors opened and she became the laughing, loving wife, taking his hand as they walked to the waiting limousine. As she settled into the backseat, she said, "I've been thinking I should get an assistant. Barbara couldn't believe I didn't have one. She says everyone has a P.A. And I know Mimi has one . . ."

"Who's Barbara?" he asked.

"Selden! The stylist. She works with everyone, dresses all the movie stars when they come to town . . ."

"How much would it cost?" he asked.

"Oh, I don't know," she shrugged, as if money were not a concern. "Maybe two hundred dollars a day."

Two hundred dollars a day! he thought. That was $4,000 a month—nearly as much as his secretary was paid. Naturally, he wanted her to have everything she wanted, and it wasn't the money per se that was the problem but his middle-class upbringing, which told him that since she did work, and it was business, she should pay for the assistant herself.

He had already discovered that his wife had an aversion to spending her own money, but nevertheless he ventured, "Of course, you can do whatever you want with your own money . . ."

"But I thought she'd work for both of us," Janey said, turning to him with surprise. "She could do all kinds of things, like take your shirts to the dry cleaner . . . You do need clean shirts, don't you?"

He had always taken care of his own shirts, but was suddenly touched by her wifely concerns for him. Taking her hand and stroking the underside of her palm, he said, "If that's all it's about, we can talk about it."

But in a second, she appeared to have forgotten all about the conversation, and snatching her hand away, quickly began touching up her lipstick, for they had arrived at their destination.

An hour later, Selden Rose sat staring bleary-eyed at a plate filled with some kind of fish, his boredom beginning to border on irritation. Seated on his right was Janna Glancy, the editor in chief of *Vogue*. After they'd exchanged a few cursory comments, it had become immediately apparent that they had nothing in common, and Ms. Glancy, who was wearing sunglasses, had turned her back to him and was now in an animated discussion with the man to her right, a famous shoe designer. Meanwhile, he'd discovered that the young woman on his left literally *couldn't* speak—English anyway—and from what he'd been able to gather from the few snatches of Spanish that he recognized from school, she'd just arrived from a farm in Brazil to be in the new Victoria's Secret campaign. Two seats away sat Mauve Binchely, whom he at least knew a little and who could certainly speak English, but the configuration of the large round table made it almost impossible to have a conversation with anyone other than the people sitting next to you.

And so he sat sipping ice water, pretending to take in his surroundings. The "room" was really a large, cavernous space on East Forty-second Street across from Grand Central Station, which Selden guessed at one time might have been a bank. It was filled with round tables of ten, and an effort had been made to make it look festive: There were leopard-print tablecloths topped by centerpieces of black and white flowers; the men were in black tie and the women were dressed in splendid gowns—for the obvious purpose of outdoing one another. And yet, despite the glamorous surface, as the evening dragged on there was an increasing weariness to the whole affair, as if the guests, hoping for something different, had been reminded once again that they'd attended a few too many of these parties already, and that in the end, nothing ever changed.

The exception, he thought, was his wife. Watching her from across the table, he marveled at the fact that as the evening progressed, she seemed to grow more and more animated. Her face glowed and her smile was warm and clearly inviting: A parade of beautiful people kept stopping by her seat to congratulate her on her recent marriage—at which point she would gesture and wave to Selden. And now, picking listlessly at his fish, he reminded himself that although he'd known Janey was "social," he was only beginning to understand what that really meant. And he certainly hadn't expected such a response when they'd first arrived and had walked down the red carpet . . .

He'd done his share of Hollywood events, but as he'd never been the subject of photographs himself, he hadn't paid much attention. But as soon as their limo had pulled up in front of the tent, they'd been met by the ubiquitous girl in black, who explained that she was their escort for the evening and would "take care" of them, then she'd shouted into her headset that Janey Wilcox was there, and in a second, they seemed to be engulfed in a blinding white blaze of flashbulbs. The photographers were screaming her name, asking her to look to the left, to the right, to take a step forward or back, and for a second he'd thought, *Wait a minute.* This was not what he'd bargained for . . . if he'd wanted *this*, he would have married a movie star.

But she was holding his hand, and leaning into him for a kiss—her makeup didn't seem to be an issue in front of the paparazzi. Then they were asking her for photographs by herself, and for a moment, he stood there alone, feeling redundant. But thankfully the young woman in black had rescued him and led him away.

Janey wasn't finished, however, and the photographs and interviews went on for at least twenty minutes. But when he finally thought that Janey had been released, that they could have a drink and talk to each other for a minute, they were herded off to a VIP area, where more photographers had asked to take Janey's picture, and he was left once again feeling like the odd man out.

And then they had been escorted to their table. Which was no mean feat because of the crowd, every member of whom Janey seemed to "know" in some way or another. They were like a bunch of children who had just returned to school after summer vacation. "Hey Janey! How was your summer?"

"Fabulous, darling. I got married."

"Janey darling! Love your dress."

"Thank you, darling. It's Luca Luca. My new favorite Italian."

"Come on, baby, let's sit down," he said at one point, trying to pull her away from a short, cheery gay man.

"Oh, don't worry about it," she said. "No one sits down until the last minute anyway. And Oliver is just telling me about his trip to Capri, which is where *we* should have gone on our honeymoon . . ."

And so on.

They were, apparently, seated at one of the best tables, although what made their table better than the others was unclear to Selden, unless it was due to the presence of Comstock Dibble, who was one of the evening's honorees. Janey had been surprised, and, he thought, secretly pleased, to find that she was seated next to him; Selden was merely annoyed. "Let's switch the place cards," he suggested.

"Selden! We can't. You know that husbands and wives aren't supposed to sit next to each other, and besides, someone always notices when you switch place cards and then it ends up on Page Six." And then she'd smiled and allowed him the briefest kiss on the lips.

Comstock and Mauve had arrived at the table just before the first course was served. Comstock was shining and hearty, like a man who has just come in from the cold and knows he has good whiskey and a Cuban cigar waiting. This was his territory and he knew it. "Damn bore these things, eh, Rose?" he asked, as if he and Selden were old friends.

"You got that right."

"Wait until the old lady drags you to three in one night."

"I think the old lady has better things to do."

Comstock said nothing, just raised his eyebrows in an expression that implied Selden had a lot to learn, and, spotting someone he knew over Selden's shoulder, slid away.

The fact was, Selden thought, pushing the fish around on his plate, that what Comstock Dibble did, thought, or said would have been of no importance to him whatsoever, if he hadn't been seated next to his wife.

Ever since they'd sat down next to each other, Selden was convinced that Comstock had been flirting with Janey. If he hadn't known better, he might have even guessed that at one time they'd had something between them. There was an unmistakable familiarity in the way Comstock kept tilting his head toward hers and speaking to her out of the side of his mouth, and in the slightly smirking manner in which she received his comments, as if she'd heard them before. But everybody knew about Comstock's reputation with women—the amazing thing was that given his looks, he managed to get any women to pay attention to him at all . . .

From the other side of the table, Comstock Dibble leaned over and said to Janey, "Your husband hasn't taken his eyes off us. I think he's jealous."

"Jealous! Oh, Comstock, don't be ridiculous. He's madly in love with me, that's all."

"But are you in love with him?"

"Of course I am," Janey said, finishing her third glass of champagne. She'd had quite a lot to drink, but didn't feel drunk. "God, you're nasty, Comstock."

"You know I'm nasty, but so are you. Maybe we could be nasty together again."

Janey laughed. "What would Mauve think?"

"Mauve wouldn't know."

"I don't do that sort of thing anymore. I'm married, remember?"

"You don't now, but you will again. You'll see," Comstock said.

Janey knew she should have found him insulting, but she couldn't be bothered. The fact was, she was relieved. He'd been rude to her all summer, but apparently whatever had been bothering him wasn't on his mind tonight, and he'd made no mention of the two letters he'd sent her. Of course, he was riding high, as puffed up in his tuxedo as a penguin, and everyone was talking about how wonderful he was thanks to his recognition by the mayor. But she was riding high, too, and while her honeymoon had been a bore, her triumphant return to the city as a woman married to a powerful man in the entertainment business had made it all worthwhile. Giving Comstock a suggestive smile, she said, "You know, we really *should* try to be friends."

Comstock's answering smile was like that of a lion about to eat his prey—one could practically see the saliva dripping off his teeth. "Yes," he said, "I think we should do that."

"What on earth were you talking to Comstock Dibble about?" Selden asked in the limo on the way home.

Janey shrugged. "Movies, what else. I was telling him that he should make Edith Wharton's *The Custom of the Country* into a movie. It's never been done before and he'd be good at it."

"And did he take your advice?"

"Why shouldn't he? It's a good idea," she said, leaning her head back against the seat. "I thought that was a fantastic evening, didn't you?"

"Sure," Selden said. He looked out the window at the lit-up stores on Madison Avenue. "I had no idea you and Comstock were such good friends."

"We're not," Janey said. "But naturally I've met him over the years . . ."

"It's amazing that a man like that would get a humanitarian award."

"Well, he does shoot a lot of movies in the city," Janey said, reaching out to take his hand.

"But that doesn't make him a humanitarian."

"God, Selden," she said. "Everyone knows those things are fake anyway. No one expects them to be *real*." And turning to him with glittering eyes, she delivered her blow: "If you think about it, it's really no different from the Emmy Awards. Everyone knows that they're political as well."

He opened his mouth to protest, but then thought better of it. He had to admit that she wasn't entirely wrong, and so they rode the rest of the way in silence.

The concierge hailed them in the lobby of the Lowell Hotel. "Mr. Rose, I have a package for you," he said, handing over a bundle of mail. Selden looked at the labels—they were all addressed to Janey, forwarded to her new address.

"Your mail," he said, giving her the package.

"Thank you, Neil," Janey said to the concierge. "I've been waiting for this."

In the elevator, she made a point of flipping through her mail, glancing at him

every now and again with a cold smile that indicated she was not going to acknowledge his bad mood. He'd already learned that this was a trick of hers, but it still
had the effect of making him feel like a bad little boy who has fallen out of favor
with his beloved mommy, and he knew he wouldn't be able to withstand this treat-
ment for long. When they were in the apartment, he said, "I'm going to go to bed,"
but she merely gave him that cold, curious smile, and sitting down at the writing
desk in front of the fireplace, she said, "I'm going to open my mail. I'll be in in a few
minutes."

He took off his jacket and threw it on the chair, then removed his pants and
bow tie. He went into the bathroom and brushed his teeth, then he looked at the
empty bed and went into the living room.

She had lit the Duracell log that lay in the fireplace, and she sat, opening an
envelope with a silver letter opener. The warm glow from the fire had turned her
skin a burnished copper; her white-blond hair gleamed against her back. What a
fool he was to fight with her over nothing, he thought, and he went to her and
brushed her hair aside, kissing the back of her neck.

"Hello, darling," she said.

"You must think I'm crazy," he said.

"I just can't think of what you're upset about. I do everything in my power to
make you look good . . ."

"Oh, I know, my darling," he said, moving around so that he was standing
before her. He leaned over and took her hand. "I just couldn't stand the way Comstock Dibble was looking at you. I kept thinking crazy things, like maybe you'd slept
with him or were going to. And all I could think was that if you *had* slept with him,
or if you *did,* I would never be able to look at you again, much less be married to
you . . ." He broke off. "I know I'm an idiot, darling. You'll have to forgive me."

He chuckled, but for a second, he thought he saw an expression of guilt cross
her face. But then the corners of her eyes crinkled up into kindly amusement.
"Comstock Dibble," she twittered. "Oh, Selden, he's the last person in the world
you have to worry about. I find him disgusting. And frankly, I'm a little insulted that
you *would* think I'd slept with him." Her voice was full of confident amusement, but
inside, she was annoyed. If he felt that strongly about it, she would have to be vigilant in making sure that he never found out the truth.

He pulled her to her feet and embraced her, smoothing her hair. "I can't help it.
I'm a jealous husband. Will you come to bed now?"

She kissed him back for a moment, but then pulled away. "In a minute," she
said. "I really do have to go through this mail—it's full of invitations and there
might be some things we want to go to." And, catching the expression on his face,
she added playfully, "You see? If we had an assistant, I wouldn't have to do this."

"Point taken," he said, responding in kind. "I'm going to watch the news to find out if anything important has happened in the world while you plan our social calendar."

"Let me know if anything's been blown up," she called back gaily, as he went into the bedroom.

She sighed, running her hands through her hair as she removed the bobby pins that had kept it up all evening. As her hair fell to her shoulders, she heard the sound of thunder and the subsequent heavy pattering of rain on the rooftops and street, and was drawn to the window. She probably would have eventually told Selden about Comstock, she sighed, especially if Comstock had continued sending her letters. But having lost the opportunity, she couldn't tell Selden now. In any case, she certainly wouldn't pursue a friendship with Comstock, at least not for a while. She wasn't crazy about lying to her husband, but, on the other hand, lying to men was often an issue of survival, and besides, what Selden didn't know would never hurt him . . .

Looking down onto the dark, glistening street, her eye was caught by a lone figure on the other side of the pavement, hunched up against the rain as she desperately tried to hail a cab. On closer inspection, Janey saw that it was a young girl and pretty, wearing a black party dress and high-heeled shoes. But she *would* be pretty being in this neighborhood—she'd probably been at a swanky party filled with arrogant rich men who traded pretty young girls like baseball cards. And suddenly, Janey was swept back in time, to herself just a few years ago when she was that girl, going to parties in the hope of meeting a savior and praying that she had enough cab money to get home if she didn't. And as the girl raised her face as if to ask, "Why me, God?" the rain ran down her cheeks and hair, down her legs and into her shoes. And Janey felt the girl's distress, felt the sensation of her shoes filling with water, knowing that they were ruined and that she'd spent her last $200 on them because they were designer and on sale . . .

With a look of resignation, the girl took one last glance back at the street, realizing that she wasn't going to get a cab and would have to walk home. Janey wanted to open the window and cry out, "Come inside! Come up here where it's warm and dry," but it was a foolish thought, especially with her husband waiting impatiently in the next room. And if she were somehow able to invite the girl up, Selden would probably assume it was for sex, for a threesome, and for all she knew, the girl might do it in exchange for the chance to get out of the rain. She'd probably already learned that sex was a small price to pay for a nice bed with clean sheets and a bathroom that wasn't filled with cockroaches . . .

Janey leaned her forehead against the window, watching as the girl moved quickly down the street, her head bowed against the rain. She was probably already regretting her evening, Janey thought. Pretty girls were a category unto themselves, she thought, and sometimes it was better not to be pretty. Pretty girls were always told that their looks would make them special, that good looks meant that something marvelous was waiting just around the corner, but so often that marvelous thing was only a pair of sodden shoes you couldn't afford to begin with. Reluctantly, she tore herself away from the window, knowing that at heart she *was* that girl, the only difference being that somehow she was now a success, and married to a rich movie producer . . .

Well, she supposed she had paid for it, Janey thought idly, sitting back down at the desk and picking up a letter that had been lying halfway into the pile. But suddenly, her thoughts took a fresh turn when she saw the return address with "Parador Pictures" embossed above. With a rising sense of panic, she turned the letter over and saw that there was no stamp and that it was addressed to her at the Lowell Hotel, meaning that it had probably been hand-delivered that afternoon.

With a trembling hand, she slit the envelope open and unfolded the letter.

It was just like the others, except that this one was official, from Comstock's lawyers, demanding that she pay back the $30,000 he'd given her for writing a screenplay that she had supposedly never delivered. Shock and rage came over her, and all she could think was, How dare he? He owed her that money after he had fucked her and fucked her over. So that was why he'd been so friendly all evening— he'd actually thought that he could charm her into getting his way, and that she wouldn't have the nerve to stand up to him . . .

"It's getting awfully lonely in there," Selden said, coming up behind her, and she jumped.

She turned around, struggling to compose her face. "Why, what's wrong?" he asked. "You look like someone just bit you."

"Oh, it's nothing," she said, emitting a small laugh. For a moment she hesitated. Should she tell Selden about the letter? But then she'd have to tell him about her history with Comstock Dibble, and she couldn't do that, not *now* . . . "It's only a letter from a charity," she lied. "Asking if I would be the chairman of their committee . . . *if* I could donate ten thousand dollars. *Really*," she went on, "can you imagine? It ought to be enough that they want to use your name, but then to ask for money on top of it . . . as if *I* had ten thousand dollars to give away anyway . . ."

"Is that all?" Selden asked, giving her an indulgent smile.

"Stupid, isn't it?" she said, crumpling the letter and throwing it onto the fire.

EIGHT

"IS THAT ALL?" the cashier asked.

She was enormously fat. Tiny little eyes peered at Janey suspiciously, as if straining to see through the adipose that threatened to engulf them; an enormous hank of flab, the size of a paddle, hung from her upper arm.

"Yes, that's it," Janey said, sliding the magazine toward her.

Janey looked around surreptitiously. God, this store was dirty. And filled with sad-looking people. There were only two cashiers, who were taking their time, and at least twenty people were waiting to pay for their purchases, but the weird thing was that the people on line weren't complaining. They didn't even look impatient, as if they were too beaten down to protest and had become resigned to the fact that a good portion of their life would consist of waiting to pay for a candy bar and a large plastic bottle of soda.

"That's a dollar thirty-nine," the cashier said, glancing away.

"I'm sorry . . . what?" Janey asked.

"A dollar thirty-nine," the cashier said, looking at her like she was an idiot.

Janey riffled nervously through her bag, searching for change. What on earth cost a dollar thirty-nine these days? she thought. It was such a small, inconvenient sum it really ought to be free. And then the cashier really looked at her, her face blossoming with recognition.

"Hey," she said. "Don't I know you?"

Janey froze. She had no idea how to respond to this question. Should she say "no" in a haughty voice, grab her magazine, and run, or should she explain that she was Janey Wilcox, Victoria's Secret model, and that the girl had probably seen her on TV?

"Oh, *I* know," the cashier said. "You're that *underwear* model."

Janey reached for her magazine. "Yes," she said, nodding and forcing herself to smile.

"Hey, Washington," the cashier said, calling to the girl on her right. "This here's that Victoria's Secret model."

"Oh yeah?" The other cashier eyed Janey up and down. "How come they don't got no fat girls as models? I'm sexy."

"Skinny white bitch," she heard one of the customers mutter under his breath.

She felt herself redden, but willed herself not to respond to the insult. Hurrying out of the store, she emerged from the Duane Reade drugstore onto Second Avenue shaken and breathless.

What the hell was happening in the world? she thought, looking around for her car. Who *were* these people? Were they so mixed up that they thought being skinny was bad? And she wasn't even that skinny! Any one of these days she was probably going to have to have liposuction . . . She saw her car a few yards up the street and hurried toward it, opening the door and hurling herself into the comforting black leather interior.

The driver, an Indian man named Rashneesh, looked at her in the rearview mirror.

"Where now, miss?"

"The Four Seasons," she gasped. "The restaurant. On East Fifty-second Street. Not the hotel."

Her heart still pounding in response to the random hostility of being called a skinny white bitch, she picked up the magazine and began fanning herself with it. What the hell had she ever done to deserve such arbitrary aggression? But that was the way the world was these days, filled with angry, grasping people, all of whom felt they deserved something more, simply because they had been born—and why did they all seem to want to be lingerie models?

And now there was this! she thought, unfolding the magazine. "STAR" was printed in big white letters across the top; underneath was a photograph of Gwyneth Paltrow looking miserable. "Gwyneth's Secret Oscar Heartache," the caption read. And at the very top, above Gwyneth, was a tiny photograph of Digger, sweaty and holding a guitar, with a banner that said: "Rock Star's Secret Love Child."

She didn't want to read it but she had to. Just two hours ago, while she'd been finishing up the Victoria's Secret catalog shoot, Patty had called her, and in a low, quiet voice said, "It's in *Star* magazine." Then she'd hung up.

"Does anybody have *Star* magazine?" Janey shouted.

"Why?" the photographer asked.

"My sister's in it," she said.

"How exciting!" the makeup artist said. He was from Costa Rica. "It is my life-long *dream* to be in *Star* magazine . . ."

"Isn't that one of those magazines where they go through people's trash?" the photographer's assistant asked.

"I would *love* it if someone went through my trash. They would find so many interesting things . . ."

"Like what? Condoms?"

"Used condoms are *not* interesting," Janey said firmly, as if the subject were closed.

Well, this was her life now, she thought, flipping quickly through the pages. Her sister was in *Star* magazine.

The story took up one page near the beginning of the magazine. There was a big picture of Digger in the middle, with a smaller picture of a dark-haired girl in a black getup that resembled a dominatrix outfit, and then an even smaller picture of Patty on the street, bending over a tiny brown-and-black dog that was squatting on the sidewalk. Patty's hair was disheveled and she was wearing blue Nike sweatpants, the kind that unsnapped on the sides, and she looked like she had just gotten out of bed, which, Janey figured, she probably had. But what was with that dog? And then she remembered that somewhere in the jumble of this whole mess, Patty had bought a puppy. She began reading:

> Sultry singer Marielle Dubrosey spent a night of lovemaking with Digger . . . and now she's having his baby!
>
> The twenty-two-year-old up-and-coming stunner met Digger back-stage at a gig in Minneapolis, and the two ended up spending the night together.
>
> "As soon as Digger laid eyes on Marielle, you could see the sparks flying between them," a friend of Marielle's told *Star*. "He couldn't keep his hands off her. He kept kissing her and touching her breasts."

Well, Janey thought. That certainly sounded like Digger. He couldn't keep his hands off Patty either.

> Digger then whisked Marielle off to his room, where they spent a night of gorgeous lovemaking . . . No one saw either of them until four the next afternoon.

And now gorgeous Marielle is pregnant!

There's only one problem, though. Digger is *already* married—to twenty-eight-year-old former VH1 producer Patty Wilcox!

Patty is the statuesque [Well, that's hardly true, Janey thought] stunner who captured Digger's heart two years ago when they met at a VH1 shoot. "Patty and Digger are truly in love," a source says. "Patty won't give him up without a fight."

"I don't care," says Marielle, who plans to have the baby, due in May. "I don't want to hurt his wife, but Digger is a wonderful person and a beautiful lover. He's talented and kind. My night with him is one evening I'll never forget!"

Janey threw the magazine onto the seat. What an outrageous piece of trash. Why had Digger been so stupid? And to go after such an obvious tart—she'd probably planned the whole thing. She'd created a trap, and Digger had fallen right into it. Now he would have to pay. But it wasn't Digger who was paying, it was Patty. He had ruined Patty's life . . . she'd probably never recover from this.

But then she found her hand snaking back toward the magazine. The hand, seeming to act of its own accord, began turning the pages back to the story.

She picked it up and studied Patty's photograph. As she did so, a terrible thought occurred to her. She was actually a tiny bit . . . *envious.*

How disgusting! How could she even think that way? But she *was* jealous, she thought. *She* wanted to be in *Star* magazine. Not the way Patty was, of course. But still, it would definitely help her career if she *was* in there somewhere, on the fashion pages, for instance. All of the women on those pages were actresses and more famous than she, but she was certainly more beautiful, and at least as interesting . . .

She leaned back against the seat, suddenly overwhelmed by the unfairness of life. Every day was a fight just to keep your place in the world. For the past two days, shooting the cover of the Victoria's Secret catalog, she had struggled to be a model of patience, trying to be nice to everyone, and trying not to complain when the lights blew out or the hairstylist couldn't get that stray strand of hair on the top of her head to stay down or the clothing stylist kept rearranging the pads in her bra—all the while, Janey thought, deliberately poking at her breasts. It was so *dull* being a model now—that was what no one understood—and what she really got paid for was sitting around and not losing her mind . . . And it was all for—*what?* A photograph that people would look at and hiss, "Skinny white bitch, skinny white bitch . . ."

The car slowly drove past the entrance to the Four Seasons, which was blocked by several black town cars like her own. Looking up, she suddenly screamed, "Stop!" at the driver.

"But Miss," he said, turning around. "I cannot stop in the middle of the street. The mayor made all these new rules. If I stop in the street, it's a four-hundred-and-fifty-dollar ticket!"

"I don't care," Janey snapped. Jesus, every time you got into a car or a taxi these days, the driver complained about some potential new driving fine the mayor was trying to slap on them, as if it were *her* fault. "I don't want to have to walk," she said. She opened the door and jumped out, but not before telling the driver to wait. "And make sure you're at the front of the entrance when I come out," she said, slamming the door.

She strolled through the revolving door of the restaurant, where she was met by an obsequious woman who begged to take her coat even though she wasn't wearing one. And suddenly, she was reminded of how terrible it was to be rude to service people, and was glad that Mimi hadn't been there to see it. But still, considering the circumstances of her day, it made her feel much better.

Patty was sitting by herself in the middle of an enormous brown leather banquette. Her hair was wrapped up in a yellow bandanna, gangsta-style—Janey was surprised that they'd let her into the Four Seasons at all—and even from across the room, Janey could see that she'd lost weight. Over a week had passed since that Marielle person had approached Patty on the street, but for the first five days, she had told no one, not even Digger. Instead, she had locked herself in her apartment, refusing to answer the phone or the door.

After two days of begging by phone (Digger was away, on tour in Europe with his band), Digger had finally gotten the super to unlock the door and look for Patty; the super had supposedly found her in bed with gummy bears stuck in her hair, as this was all she'd had to eat in the house. ("Oh, Patty. Gummy bears?" Janey had said. And Patty had replied that they were Digger's favorite food . . .)

Mimi had been kind enough to accompany Janey to Patty's apartment three days ago, after Janey had gotten a call from her mother who'd gotten a call from Digger (Why couldn't Digger have just called her himself? Janey thought, but it was probably because he knew she would have ripped his head off), to tell her mother that Patty was "upset" about "something" and that someone should check on her. His hands were tied because he was in Amsterdam, but he had cancelled a couple of concerts to return to New York the next day.

"Did he sound stoned?" Janey asked her mother.

And her mother, who was French by birth and liked to pretend she was a grand lady, snapped, "What is this 'stoned'? I do not know 'stoned.'"

"If he was high on marijuana, Mother, he might be making the whole thing up," Janey sighed.

But apparently, he wasn't.

Janey and Mimi had gone down to Patty's apartment, and had managed to extract a garbled story of Digger's infidelity. Then Mimi had given Patty a sleeping pill and had left her with a handful of Xanaxes to take when she woke up.

"She could have been *dead*," Janey said grimly.

"I *know*," Mimi replied.

And now, Janey leaned over the table to give her sister a kiss. "Hi darling," she said brightly. "How are you?"

"Fine," Patty said dully.

"Have you been taking the pills?" Janey asked. "Don't take more than three a day . . ."

"I won't," Patty said. "How come you're wearing so much makeup?"

"I had a shoot today," Janey said, as if speaking to a small child. "For Victoria's Secret."

"How was it?" Patty asked.

"Oh, you know," Janey sighed. "Boring."

Patty cracked the briefest smile. "Now, Patty darling," Janey continued. "I hope you don't mind, but Mimi's coming to lunch as well."

"I don't mind," Patty said. "I don't mind anything."

"Good," Janey said, unfolding her napkin and putting it on her lap. "You know, Mimi's very good with scandal. She's had a lot of experience. She's been in *Star* magazine twice . . ."

"She has?" Patty asked. "For what?"

"Oh, for dating movie stars. She was actually on the cover once, for going out with Prince Charles."

"All lies," Mimi said, sliding into the banquette on the other side of Patty. She leaned across the table to Janey, and, speaking over Patty as if she were a deaf old man, asked, "How's she doing today?"

"Better, I think," Janey said.

"Have you found out anything more about Digger?"

"Not yet."

"Good, then I haven't missed anything."

The waiter arrived at their table. "I'll have a glass of champagne and some caviar," Janey said.

"Caviar?" Patty asked.

"You have some, too. It'll make you feel better," Janey said.

"Give her the caviar," Mimi said to the waiter. "In fact, bring caviar for three . . . No, I'm hungry. Better bring caviar for five . . ."

"Caviar for five, ma'am, very good," the waiter said.

"And a bottle of Veuve Clicquot?" Mimi said, looking at Janey.

Janey shrugged. She'd never been crazy about champagne, but Mimi was, and in the past three months, she'd developed a taste for it. "I think Veuve's fine during the day."

"Who's paying?" Patty asked.

"Digger, darling," Mimi said, patting her hand. "That's one of the first things you need to learn. When a man cheats, he pays. And big."

The waiter returned to the table with the bottle of champagne and an ice bucket. "Three glasses?" he asked doubtfully, looking at Patty. "I think just two," Janey said. "Champagne might be too much for her . . ."

"Now Patty, darling," Mimi said, "what did he say?"

"He said he didn't do it," Patty said, looking from Janey to Mimi.

Janey and Mimi exchanged looks. "Of course he's going to say that," Janey said. "But what was his excuse?"

"He says that she came after him. There was a party in his room, but he didn't sleep there. He took Winky's key—that's the drummer—and slept in his room, and Winky slept with . . . with . . ."

"The slut?" Mimi said, nodding. "And I suppose this Winky corroborates the story. God, what a scumbag, passing the buck on to someone else."

"He says she's doing it to get publicity. For her *career*," Patty said, looking at Janey.

"Now listen, darling," Janey said. "You know what you have to do, don't you?"

"No," Patty said. "I don't know what to do. My whole world has fallen apart."

"These kinds of things happen from time to time," Mimi said.

"You have to leave him," Janey said.

"But I can't leave him," Patty said.

"Once a man starts cheating, he usually keeps it up," Mimi said warningly.

"Who knows how many girls he slept with *before* this one," Janey added.

"But he says he didn't . . . ," Patty protested weakly.

"Come on, Patty. Of course he's going to deny it. I'm sure he still loves you and realizes he's made a big mistake. But the girl is pregnant! *Pregnant!* She's having the baby you should have had," Janey said, sitting back triumphantly.

"God, that's harsh, Janey," Mimi said, taking a sip of champagne.

"She's got to face the truth," Janey said. "It's the only way."

"But what if it *isn't* his?" Patty said. Under normal circumstances, she would have been horrified that Janey was bringing up her infertility problems in front of Mimi. But ever since she'd started taking those lovely little pills Mimi had given her, these kinds of things didn't matter . . .

"Even if it isn't, he's got to *go*," Janey said. "What if he pulls this kind of stunt again?" It was one thing, Janey thought, if a man treated *her* badly. But it was quite another thing for her sister to have to suffer . . .

About an hour later, Patty escorted Janey and Mimi to their cars. They were both more than a little drunk, and Patty realized that once again, even though she was the one with the problem, somehow, Janey had managed to snag the spotlight. She *should* have been angry . . . but she wasn't. Again, it was those pills Mimi had given her . . . What did they call them? *Dolls.* Those sweet little dolls were making everything okay . . .

"Now Patty," Janey said sternly. "I'll go with Mimi in her car and you take my car."

"I can take a taxi," Patty said.

"Absolutely not, darling," Mimi said. "One never goes commercial when one can go private."

"Victoria's Secret sent it, so don't worry, it's free," Janey said.

She went up to the driver, who was sitting inside the car, talking on his cell phone. "Do you mind taking my sister home?" she asked. He looked put out, and she remembered her little outburst earlier. She should give him a small tip, she thought, and opening her wallet, she debated whether to give him $5 or $10.

In the end, she decided five was sufficient.

The driver looked from the bill to Janey. He shook his head ever so slightly. "Thank you," Janey said.

"No, thank *you*," he said sarcastically.

"Poor thing," Mimi said, as the car pulled away from the curb.

"She's the last person I *ever* thought this would happen to," Janey said. "I always thought they were really, *really* in love." She shook her head. "It just goes to show you that you can't trust *any* man . . ."

"It's terrible, isn't it?" Mimi said. "Muhammad," she called to her driver, "don't you find that the temptations of the world are stronger than true love?"

"Oh yes, ma'am," the driver said, nodding. "It's very, very sad."

Mimi reached over and touched Janey's hand. "In any case, I'm so happy to see *you*, darling. We always have such a good time."

"We do," Janey said.

"Were we too hard on her?" Mimi asked. And then, clapping her hand over her mouth, she said, "I almost forgot to tell you. Mauve says Comstock is buying an apartment in 795 Park. For ten million dollars!"

"You're kidding," Janey said with the appropriate amount of astonishment.

"Darling," Mimi said slyly, changing the subject. "Do you still have *your* apartment?"

"The one on East Sixty-seventh Street?" Janey asked.

"Do you think Zizi could stay there?"

The name "Zizi" made Janey wince slightly, like a nerve that suddenly flares up in a tooth. Mimi rarely brought up Zizi's name, and for a while, Janey had been hoping that the affair had fizzled. But if Mimi was trying to find him a place, it obviously hadn't, and the knowledge set Janey's teeth on edge. She still couldn't understand why Zizi had chosen Mimi over her. She didn't really want Zizi staying in her apartment—simply because she didn't want to make it easier for Mimi to see him. But to out and out refuse would be a breach of her friendship with Mimi. "I don't mind," Janey said vaguely, "but I *was* thinking about renting it."

"Oh, Zizi can pay," Mimi said.

Janey had no choice then. "It's fine," she said.

"Are you going out tonight?" Mimi asked. Now that the arrangement was settled, she didn't want to dwell on it. She still suspected that Janey had wanted Zizi for herself, and was slightly sore about it.

Janey rolled her eyes. "We have to go to Greenwich. *Connecticut*. For some Splatch Verner dinner."

"How . . . *awful*," Mimi said.

"I have to meet all the other Splatch Verner wives."

"You'll look fantastic darling, and they'll all be jealous."

The car stopped at Sixty-third Street and Madison, and Janey got out. "Goodbye, darling," she said.

"Good-bye," Mimi said. "Call me tomorrow and tell me all about it."

"I *will*," Janey said.

The car pulled away, and Janey looked around. It was all so civilized here—really, it was a *relief*.

As she strolled up the street to the Lowell Hotel, she passed a chic little French bistro with a green awning, under which sat a few attractive European men, dressed in the Eurotrash uniform of jeans, Italian loafers, and expensive sport coats. The proprietor, Christian, a man of medium build with a face like a movie star, was standing outside smoking; when he saw Janey his face lit up and he threw open his arms.

"Ah, here she is!" he exclaimed. "We never see you any more now that you're married."

He took her left hand, and with a clownish pantomime, said, "Let me see the ring! Ah, very, very nice," he said, looking at her with respect.

"My husband is wonderful," Janey said.

"Ah, but he is the lucky one," Christian said, waving his cigarette in the air. "You must never forget that!"

Janey moved away, smiling. It was the end of September, but still warm, a perfect seventy degrees. Somehow, she had managed to do better than everyone, she thought smugly. Her situation was certainly better than Patty's, who had a cheating husband, and Mimi's, whose husband was so awful, she had to get sex elsewhere . . . Meanwhile, her own husband was madly in love with her, and she didn't mind having sex with him in the least. And entering the lobby of the Lowell Hotel with a confident step, she felt that she was finally sure of her footing . . .

But her illusion of safety was shattered nearly immediately. "Mrs. Rose," the concierge whispered, "there's a man here who's been waiting to see you." She could tell by the expression on his face that this person was not the type that was welcomed by the Lowell Hotel. Turning around, she saw a man with a lumpy, misshapen face occupying one of the two armchairs set in a small alcove; as she took a step toward him, he stood up.

"Janey Wilcox?" he asked. He was wearing a beige polyester leisure suit with stitching up the front and along the lapels; it crossed Janey's mind that he had "dressed up" for the occasion.

She suddenly felt afraid. "Yes?" she asked, feigning impatience.

"I have a letter for you. You need to sign for it."

She was immediately suspicious. "Who's it from?" she demanded.

"Parador Pictures."

Her eyes narrowed as she tried to think of some way to refuse the letter. "What if I won't sign?" she demanded.

"You can do whatever you like," the man said. "But if you don't sign, I'll be here tomorrow. And the next day . . ."

Janey glanced over her shoulder. The concierge and the bellboy were watching the exchange out of the corners of their eyes; if she made a fuss it would become a topic of conversation, and eventually someone would mention it to Selden. Taking the pen from the man's hand, she quickly signed her name and grabbed the letter, shoving it into her bag.

"Is everything all right, Mrs. Rose?" the concierge asked.

"It's fine," Janey said, smiling.

But it wasn't fine, she thought, going up in the elevator and then walking down the hall to the suite. She turned the key in the lock and stormed into the room, throwing her bag onto a chair. Then she ripped open the envelope and quickly scanned the contents. It was just like the others, demanding that she pay Parador $30,000 . . . How dare Comstock keep demanding money from her? Especially when he was buying a $10 million apartment . . .

Technically, she supposed, she did have the money in her savings account. But that money was all the money she had in the world, and she'd opened it fifteen years ago, when she returned from that first summer of "modeling" in Europe. Since then, she had scrimped and saved, carefully putting money away every time she received a check—for she knew her future was uncertain, and someday, she might need every penny of that money in order to survive. It wasn't fair that Comstock Dibble, who was rich, should take one dollar from her, and besides, hadn't she earned that money? She had tried to write the screenplay, and Comstock had had his way sexually with her as well . . .

She paced back and forth across the living room. She had to think! She must do *something* . . . she must put an end to this once and for all. Even if she did give Comstock the $30,000, there was no guarantee that it would be over—he was perfectly capable of dreaming up some other transgression with which to persecute her. *If only she were a man,* she thought. Men like Comstock Dibble were members of their own little club; the unspoken agreement was that they never messed with anyone who had equally expensive lawyers. She sat down in the chair in front of the writing desk, drumming her fingers on the leather inlay. There were some situations in life that a woman couldn't take care of on her own—to go up against Comstock herself would be foolish. In the past, she had used men to take care of her problems for her, and she was an old hand at the nuances involved in the manipulation; it was only a question of finding the right man for the job.

The phone began ringing, but she ignored it. She needed help from a man as rich and powerful as Comstock, if not more so; Selden was now out of the question, and Harold Vane had loaned her too much money in the past (which she still, technically, "owed" him as well) to be willing to help her out again. It would have to be some man who didn't know about her past troubles, who would believe she was being taken advantage of. But that shouldn't be difficult, because she was being taken advantage of!

The problem was that, generally, men did these kinds of favors in exchange for sex, or the promise of sex. But she couldn't offer that now, now that she was married. She closed her eyes and raised her fists to her forehead . . . her hands were tied, and what difference would it make anyway; if Selden found out, even just about the money, he'd be sure to ask questions, and then he would find out that she and Comstock had had an affair—for a whole summer! She should have told Selden the truth about Comstock when she'd had the chance, but he'd made it so difficult, and now, it was too late. If only she could find someone who hated Comstock as much as she did . . . and lowering her fists, she looked around the room for inspiration.

Her eyes alighted on a row of invitations placed on the mantelpiece, and in a fury, she stood up. She couldn't go back to her old life: going to party after party in the hope of meeting "someone," sucking up to people she could barely stand, giving blow jobs to men who would pretend they didn't know her when they saw her next;

and underneath it all, the constant worry about money, and the niggling fear about what would happen to her in the future—what would happen when her beauty diminished and she had nothing to offer . . .

With a cry of despair, she swept the invitations off the mantelpiece. A heavy white folded card with raised lettering landed at her feet: It was the invitation to the Winter Gala for the New York City Ballet. Mimi was the head of the committee and she'd already asked Janey to sit with her and George . . .

George! she thought. And looking at the invitations littered over the carpet, she immediately felt ashamed, like a small child who has ruined her favorite toy in a fit of temper.

Picking up the invitations one by one, she carefully replaced them on the mantelpiece. And then, when everything was back in place, she picked up the phone and called George.

Half an hour later, a black Mercedes SUV pulled up in front of a discreet entrance to a building on Park Avenue and Sixty-ninth Street. The SUV had tinted, bullet-proof windows, a television, and an Internet connection; in the past year the SUV had replaced the limousine as the vehicle of choice for high-profile moguls. Its major selling point was that in an emergency, it could be used as a mobile office, allowing the mogul to do business while being spirited away from the angry masses who were clamoring for food because the scanners at the supermarkets had become disabled— which was one of the many popular Y2K predictions about what would happen when the clock struck 12:01 on January 1, 2000. But like most apocalyptic prophe-cies, Y2K had come and gone without a peep, with no interruption to the flow of goods and services. But the super-luxury SUV continued to be all the rage.

This particular car was owned by George Paxton; the driver, Mr. Pike, was a Sikh who wore a turban. Like George's other driver, Muhammad, Mr. Pike was trained in the martial arts, but George liked to joke with people that Mr. Pike kept a sword stashed in his head wrap, a physical impossibility, which most people never-theless believed. Dressed in the traditional Indian garb of an embroidered silk tunic, cummerbund, and matching trousers, Mr. Pike got out of the car and held open the back door. The only problem with the SUV was that it was impossible to enter or exit gracefully, and so, after a moment of awkwardly shuffling his feet in order to determine which leg should emerge first, George Paxton hopped out of the vehicle.

Wearing a perfectly tailored suit, he was as glossy as a black beetle. As he was expecting, Janey Wilcox was waiting by the entrance, clutching her bag to her chest with the secretive, fearful attitude of a person hiding plutonium; when she saw him, she immediately swung her arm down and tossed her hair over her shoulder in an attempt to look casual.

She was so beautiful, George thought.

Extending a beetlelike arm, at the end of which was fastened a large, eighteen-karat-gold Bulgari watch, he said, "Welcome. Come in. Let me show you around the place."

He pushed a small, gold buzzer located next to a heavy wooden door that appeared to have no handle; in a moment the door was opened by a tall, cadaverous man dressed in a gray morning suit with tails. "Good evening, Mr. Paxton," the man said, bowing his head.

"Good evening, Buswell," George chirped. "Mr. Buswell, this is Janey Wilcox, a friend of my wife's. I'm showing her the apartment on the sly, so keep it under your hat."

"Very good, Mr. Paxton."

She followed him willingly through the tiny lobby, painted sky blue with white, scalloped moldings, but balked slightly at the elevator. "George, I . . . ," she began. He held up one hand, sliding the brass gate open with the other. "Plenty of time for that later," he said, motioning for her to get in. The elevator was no larger than four feet square, and squeezing themselves into the corners, George said, "The only problem with these places are the elevators. They built them back when elevators were a brand-new invention, and no one quite trusted them—an elevator used to be considered a luxury rather than a necessity."

The elevator slowly squeaked upward, and she smiled at him, but he caught a flicker of panic in her eyes. She probably thought he was going to demand sex from her, but he guessed that by the time their encounter was over, the reverse would be true. "George, where *are* you taking me?" she asked, with enough humor in her voice to prevent the question from sounding offensive. And softening his eyes in order to indicate that she had nothing to fear from him (which she didn't, at that point), he leaned toward her and said, "It's a surprise. I know you like beautiful things, and I thought you might enjoy seeing this."

"But what is it?" she cried, as the elevator stopped and the door opened. George stepped out into an inlaid marble foyer with shining walnut walls; the antique wood being so expensive it was almost never used as paneling. "It's an apartment," he said.

"An apartment?" she asked, looking around with a mixture of awe and annoyance. The apartment was completely empty, the former occupants having moved out the year before, but even bereft of furniture, it was impressive. The rotunda ceiling was twelve feet high, painted with clouds and cherubs and edged in gilt; as Janey tilted her head back, George noted the youthful smoothness of her neck, and the beautiful flow of her breastbone into her chest.

"Ah, but it's not just *any* apartment," he said, leading her into the largest of the three front parlors. "It's the biggest, grandest apartment in New York City, and the most expensive. Twenty thousand square feet, thirty rooms, twelve bedrooms—all for the asking price of thirty million dollars."

"George!" she said, astounded.

He looked at her appraisingly; in the face of such riches, she seemed to have temporarily forgotten about the mysterious trouble that had driven her to call him and beg to see him immediately. "But you already *have* an apartment," she said accusingly, as if no one should be allowed more than one.

"That I do," he nodded. "But you're lucky if an apartment like this comes on the market and you happen to have the money to buy it. I do. You know who used to live here?"

"No," Janey said, shaking her head.

"Maury Finchberg. Remember him? In the mid-eighties, he was the richest man in New York City."

"Everyone said he was awful!" Janey exclaimed.

"He did look a bit like a tortoise," George said, taking a seat on one of the radiators. He was enjoying himself immensely, loving her amazement as she slowly turned around on the floor in front of him, but then, when you were enormously rich, as he was, you almost always had a good time.

"What are you going to do with it?" she asked.

"I'm going to give it to Mimi as a surprise Christmas present." He sat back, taking in her look of shock—and, as he suspected he would see, jealousy—but what woman wouldn't be jealous? "Janey," he said, folding an ankle over his knee, "have you ever wondered why a man becomes rich?"

"That's easy," she said, with the scoffing manner of a child who thinks she's been asked a dumb question. "For sex."

"Yes, that's what all women think," George said, smiling. "But you're not giving us rich men enough credit. The truth is, some of us actually do it to do good."

"Oh, George," she said, spinning on him with playful aggression. "What good have you ever done?"

"Aha!" he said. "Like most people, you disdain the rich man. Even though you happen to be married to one."

"Selden isn't nearly as rich as you are," she said.

"But don't you think that, after a certain point, it doesn't matter?" he asked.

"But it does, obviously," she said. "Selden couldn't afford an apartment like this."

"I was thinking about donating it to the city to be a school," he said. "But sadly enough, those kinds of huge, charitable donations have a way of backfiring on you—the public doesn't get the satisfaction of thinking you're evil because you're rich—and your business associates think you're soft in the head. Just before he lost his money, Maury Finchberg donated huge chunks of it to revamp the subway system . . . the next thing he knew, the IRS was on top of him and his company was dismantled in a hostile takeover."

"I see," Janey said thoughtfully. Frowning slightly, she turned and walked slowly to the window, giving him the benefit of viewing her profile and figure to its best advantage. At the window, she turned, and her eyes sparkled at him flirtatiously. "You're not anything like the way I thought you were, George," she said softly.

He wasn't surprised; he was not, he knew, good at parties or in large public gatherings, being a man who revealed his private self only to those who were closest to him. But her comment showed him that, despite herself, she was falling under his spell—in any minute she might start coming on to him.

She was, he thought, too fine a specimen to turn down for sex, and he had already decided that if the opportunity presented itself, he would go for it— although out of respect for Selden, he would never make the first move. The reality was that he would probably never have to: He hadn't become a billionaire several times over without some knowledge of human nature, and he was all too familiar with the behavior of women suddenly confronted with a man who has a great deal of money; at times he even believed their reactions were biological. The only women who could resist a man with money were young and idealistic, who had no idea of the struggles ahead of them; or the truly talented, creative types, who possessed something bigger than money; or the occasional rich woman, who had no need for it. But the most desperate were the so-called career women—they were either playing at working until they found a rich man, or they were really working, in which case they understood the drawbacks of hard labor and were tired and wanted a break. In either case, both types were the most sexually rapacious—by the end of the first date they were usually offering at least a blow job, out of the mistaken belief that this would somehow prove to him that they liked him for *him*, and weren't playing games by holding back on sex. And that, he thought, rubbing his face as he gazed at Janey, was exactly what he'd appreciated about Mimi—she'd never pretended that she actually liked *him*. From the beginning, she'd explained that she found him a complete boor and would tolerate him only as long as he remained rich.

But Janey Wilcox was, he thought, another type. Where Selden Rose saw an innocent, he perceived an operator. He didn't blame Selden for marrying her—Selden was still clambering up the woodpile, trying to get ahead, and like most clever men he understood the value of having the right wife—he only hoped that Janey would cause him no pain, as Selden had had plenty of that from his first wife. And so, smiling warmly in response to her comment, he said, "You're not like what I imagined either."

He leaned back against the window, enjoying the sight of her obvious pleasure, and thinking that he was only partially lying. The fact was, she was exactly what he thought she would be, the exception being that underneath her cold and slightly studied sophisticated exterior, she had a childish side. That side, he suspected, could be either warm and loving, or cruel and demanding, depending on its level of comfort; if pushed, he guessed that her id would seek satisfaction no matter what the cost, even if it meant her own self-destruction.

Holding out his hand, he said, "Let me see this letter that's got you all riled up."

A ripple of some emotion—anger? frustration?—crossed her face, and reaching into her bag, she removed the letter and handed it to him with disgust. "It's all so embarrassing," she said, but he held up his hand to silence her, and as she hovered over him, began silently reading. "Dear Ms. Wilcox," the letter began.

As of June 15, 2000, we have been attempting to speak with you regarding the matter of the untitled screenplay for Parador Pictures. This is now our fourth attempt to contact you.

It has come to our attention that you have a verbal agreement with Comstock Dibble for the delivery of an original, untitled screenplay. In consideration of said screenplay (hereby known as "Untitled Screenplay"), our records indicate that you received a check for $30,000 on May 23, 1999. According to the bylaws of the Writers Guild of America, a verbal agreement coupled with an exchange of payment shall be considered equal to, but not in excess of, and governed by, the standard Writers Guild union agreements for an Untitled Screenplay, in consideration of which the Writers Guild standards for delivery of Untitled Screenplay and payments shall apply.

Writers Guild standards specifically call for the delivery of an Untitled Screenplay within 90 (ninety) days from the date of the contract or the date of payment, whichever shall come first. If the Untitled Screenplay is not delivered within 90 (ninety) days, the contract shall be considered null and void, and the Writer in breach of said contract. In such case, Writer must remunerate to Studio (Parador Pictures) all of the monies received by Writer within 30 (thirty) days of the date of breach of contract.

According to our records, you have not delivered said Untitled Screenplay, nor have you made any attempt to do so. As eighteen months have passed from your receipt of the payment for an Untitled Screenplay, we must therefore ask that you return all the monies paid to you, specifically in a check written out to Parador Pictures for the amount of $30,000.

If you have any questions, or if you have, in fact, delivered an Untitled Screenplay, or if there has been some misunderstanding on this issue, please feel free to contact us.

Yours Sincerely . . .

George smiled to himself, folding up the letter and placing it behind him on the windowsill. There was obviously much more to the story than the letter itself revealed, and studying Janey's face, he wondered how much of the truth she would tell him. "Well," he said. "What does Selden think?"

"Selden?" she said, unable to keep a note of exasperation out of her voice. She checked herself; she was clearly gearing herself up to put on a show. Lowering her eyes and looking up at him like a child who knows she's done wrong, she said, "As a matter of fact, I haven't been able to *tell* Selden . . ."

"So you'd tell me, but not your husband," he said.

She sat down next to him on the radiator, forcing him to move to the edge. "If Selden found out . . . ," she began, then quickly looked away.

"But Selden knows all about these kinds of contracts," George said reasonably. "He's probably sent out one or two of them himself."

"That's just the problem," she said, prettily covering her face with her hands. "If Selden found out . . . ," she said again, placing her body in an attitude that practically screamed for him to comfort her.

George's dull brown eyes gleamed with interest. "Ah, I get it," he said. "It's not really about business."

"That's right," she said with relief. She lowered her hands and looked frankly into his eyes. "The only problem is . . . Can I trust you, George? You have to promise not to tell anyone . . . not even Selden."

"Cross my heart," George said reassuringly.

"I was really stupid," she said, gazing off into the middle distance. "I didn't have any money and I didn't know what I was getting into . . . and Comstock Dibble took advantage of me!"

For a moment, he was taken aback—he'd had no idea she'd been involved with Comstock Dibble—but on the other hand, it made sense; people did say she'd been with everyone. Masking his surprise, he said, "Go on."

"I met him at a party," she continued. "It was a while ago, and, well, let's just say that I was a little bit down on my luck. Comstock came on to me . . ."

"As he always does with every woman," George said sympathetically.

"And he was very persistent," Janey said, nodding. "I did like him at the time, and I wasn't seeing anyone . . . and I *thought* he wasn't either."

"And you didn't think about his reputation?" George asked, raising his eyebrows.

"I take people as I see them, George. I never pay attention to their 'reputations,'" Janey said, her voice taking on a slightly injured tone. "So when he told me he loved me, I believed him."

"He told you all that . . ."

"And more," she cried. "He said he wanted to . . . marry me."

On that point, George thought, he was sure she was lying. Nevertheless, he asked, "And what did you say?"

"Well, I told him it was impossible, of course. I'd only just met him. And little did I know . . ."

"That all the while he was engaged to someone else."

"That's right," Janey said, looking away as if the memory wounded her.

George nearly laughed, but he had made it a policy never to be cruel unless he had to be. Instead he asked, with as much dispassion as he could muster, "So did you sleep with him?"

"George!" she said, pretending to be shocked.

His face hardened. "You want me to help you, Janey. So I've got to know the truth about the situation."

"Of course I did," Janey said, giving him such a seductively bold glance, he thought she might unzip his pants and go down on him. "I had no reason not to. I thought we were dating exclusively. I thought he was serious about me. And then, well, he must have started feeling insecure. There's nothing worse than a man who feels insecure . . ."

"Especially Comstock Dibble," George said.

"He offered to help me," Janey said. "It was his idea that I should write a screenplay, and then he . . . gave me thirty thousand dollars to rent a house for the summer." She suddenly put her hand over her mouth and leaned forward as if she were about to be sick. "I just realized how terrible that sounds. You must think . . ."

George leaned against the wall, nodding his head wisely. "Thirty thousand dollars is a lot of money, no matter how you look at it."

"But I was totally innocent!" Janey protested. "I had no idea . . . I genuinely thought he wanted to help me."

"And did you write the screenplay?" George asked smoothly.

"That's not really the point," Janey protested. She was willing to show George the letter, but the screenplay opened up a whole different can of worms. "The problem was that I broke it off, at my sister's wedding, when I found out he was engaged. And frankly, I didn't think of it again until I got the letter." Janey lowered her voice so George had to lean forward to hear her. "You're a rich, powerful man, George. You don't know what it's like to be a single woman. These kinds of things happen all the time, and you have no one to defend you. All I could do was shrug my shoulders and go on."

"I see," George said.

"He can't stand the fact that I've gotten married. And I'm happy," Janey continued. "The other night, when I saw him at the mayor's Humanitarian Awards, he actually came right out and said he wanted to start sleeping with me again. Naturally, I laughed in his face, but then I started getting these letters!"

"So *you* think he's blackmailing you?"

"He *is* blackmailing me," Janey said. And as soon as the words came out of her mouth, she became convinced they were true. "I wouldn't mind fighting him myself," she said, tracing a pattern with her finger on her pant leg, "because I know I'm right. But if I do, it's bound to come out in the press, and think about how that would look for Selden."

"Sure," George said, nodding his head. "It makes his wife look like a whore."

Janey gasped—until that moment, she hadn't really considered how the situation might look to others, only how inconvenient it was to herself. And suddenly, as if on cue, her eyes opened wide and she turned to George with an expression of shock as two tears dribbled down her face.

George didn't know what to think. He suspected she was weeping crocodile tears, but found himself somewhat moved by her performance.

"Here's the thing, Janey," he said. "No matter what Comstock's motivations really are, the fact is that he's probably completely within his rights sending you that letter, and the best way to get rid of him is to just pay him back the money. Pretend it's a loan he made you . . ."

Her face blanched and she held her stomach, as if the thought were too sickening for her to entertain. She took a deep breath and stood up. "That would be fine . . . for *you*," she said accusingly. "But the fact is, I haven't got the money."

"Come on," George said smoothly. "You must have the money. You're a famous model. You must have thirty thousand dollars lying around . . ."

"I don't have money 'lying around,'" she said coldly. "Models don't make as much money as everyone thinks. My agency takes twenty-five percent, and after that, the government takes half. I'm lucky if I take home a hundred fifty thousand a year . . . And in case you've forgotten, that's barely enough to cover rent in New York."

"You do have Selden," he said mildly.

"I think it's cheesy for a woman to be completely reliant on her husband," Janey said, giving him a pointed look.

Oh Jesus, he thought, running his hand over his hair. If she had that kind of pride, she would never give back the money. And as she made a show of picking up the letter and slipping it into her bag, he was torn between wanting to help her and wishing he could wash his hands of the situation.

"If it's a question of thirty thousand dollars . . . ," he said.

She spun around. "I'm not going to take money from my husband's best friend," she sneered, struck by the irony that in the past, she certainly would have.

But this wasn't about money, she told herself now, it was about principles. She was sick and tired of being messed with by the Comstock Dibbles of the world. "Besides," she asked, "don't you see that if I do pay him there's nothing to prevent him from making up some other claim against me in the future?" And she began walking toward the door.

"Here's the problem," he called after her.

"Yes?" she asked. She stopped, but didn't bother to turn around.

"It's one thing if *I* have a problem with Comstock Dibble," he explained. "But it's a completely different kettle of fish getting involved in someone else's problem . . . If I called him on the phone, he'd probably tell me to fuck off."

She turned her body halfway around, looking at him over her shoulder. "I totally understand," she said coldly. "I'd like it if you'd do me one small favor, though—if you don't mind, could you pretend that we never had this conversation?"

George suddenly laughed. She *wasn't* exactly how he'd imagined after all—she certainly had more guts than he would have given her credit for. Standing up and taking a step toward her, he said, "Admit it, then. The truth is you just want to give that little fucker a kick in the balls."

Their eyes met in mutual understanding. "That's right," she said, inclining her head.

"You should have said that from the beginning," George said roughly.

"I would have," she replied, "but you didn't give me the chance."

"It's settled then," he said, sticking his hand in his pocket and feeling around for his keys—a gesture that implied he was ready to go. "I'll have my lawyers tell his lawyers to call off the dogs."

For a moment, neither of them said anything; in another second, he was convinced that she would fall into his arms, which might be a problem because he was beginning to think that he liked her more than he was prepared to. He began walking toward the elevator and she fell in beside him, their footsteps echoing in the empty apartment.

"I can't imagine what it would be like to live in a place like this," she commented, looking around her.

"Mimi's probably one of the few women in the world who can handle it," he said. "Not that you couldn't . . ."

"Oh, *I* don't know anything about houses or decorating," she protested modestly. "All I know how to do is show off a bra."

If her intent was to make him think about her breasts, she had certainly succeeded, he thought, as they got into the elevator. Trying to change the topic, he said, "Can I ask you to do me some little favor?" meaning to ask her to keep the secret of the apartment from Mimi. But she apparently thought he was asking for sex, because she moved closer (in the tiny space in the elevator, they were nearly touching anyway) and, turning her head so that her mouth was practically in his ear, said, "Of course I'll do you a favor, George. I'll always be grateful to you . . . All you have to do is ask."

And then the elevator door opened and they spilled out into the lobby.

Buswell held the door open to the street. "Goodnight, Mr. Paxton," he said.

"Goodnight, Buswell. I'll be back next week," George said.

"Well then," George said, when they were out on the sidewalk. He held out his hand, but Janey pulled him forward, offering up her cheek for a kiss. As he moved forward to touch his lips to her face, she tilted her head to the side, so that the kiss landed—he was sure intentionally—next to her mouth.

"Good-bye, George," she said gaily. And as she walked off, turning back once to wave at him, George had the not-unpleasant realization that he'd just been thoroughly and completely manipulated.

• • •

"I'm not sure you want to wear that to a dinner party in Greenwich," Selden said.

"What? *This?*" Janey said, looking down at her dress with calculated innocence. "What's wrong with it?" she asked, leaning forward in the mirror as she tilted her head to the side, clipping a large, gold hoop onto her earlobe.

"It's just a little . . . ," Selden said helplessly, faltering in the face of sartorial description.

"A little *what?*" Janey asked. "It's terribly chic."

"Isn't it the kind of dress you would wear to a nightclub?" Selden asked.

"I guess I could," Janey said, frowning. "But the fact is I've been saving it for a special occasion."

"I see," Selden said, shaking his head as he exited the bathroom. He didn't want to get into a fight with his wife about a dress; on the other hand, he didn't want his wife going to a corporate dinner in Greenwich looking like a Russian hooker.

"Maybe you could cover it up with something. Like a sweater?" he asked.

"Oh, Selden. Don't be ridiculous," she said, coming out of the bathroom as she adjusted the hoop on her ear. "Do you know how stupid a sweater would look over this dress? It would give your friends the impression I was ashamed to wear it."

I wish you were, Selden thought, and then immediately felt guilty.

The dress in question was a white plastic vintage mini dress, which Janey had snagged from the designer Michael Kors a few days before. The dress had been designed in the mid-eighties, and there were only five in existence—it was a showpiece really, intended for eventual display in a couture exhibition. But Janey had seen it and had to have it, and against the mild protestations of poor, sweet Michael, had tried it on. The effect was startling—it was as if the dress had been made for her—and naturally, Michael had had no choice but to "lend" it to her, in her mind, permanently.

It was, she thought, gazing at herself admiringly in the full-length mirror on the wardrobe, the perfect weapon with which to batter the other Splatch Verner wives; by wearing it, no one would be able to forget that she was the famously glamorous Janey Wilcox, Victoria's Secret model. The husbands would drool while the women would gnash their teeth, and there wouldn't be a damn thing they could do about it.

If only Selden weren't so uptight, she thought, opening the wardrobe to search for a pair of boots. On the other hand, it *was* amusing . . . Finding the boots underneath a large pile of shoe boxes, she thought about how easy it was to shock him, and how it gave her such pleasure, for it meant she was in the driver's seat and had control over him.

"What do you think about these?" she asked, holding up a pair of white, patent-leather boots with silver Gucci buckles across the instep. Without waiting for a reply, she sat down on the bed, zipping the boots up the sides of her calves. "I bought them in 1994 . . . I thought they were so expensive back then—they were eight hundred dollars and I had no money—but now I'm happy I bought them . . . They're collectors' items, you know?"

"Are they?" Selden said. He didn't know what to say, as he'd never had much interest in clothing and that seemed to be all she talked about these days.

She stood up, displaying the complete outfit. With the addition of the patent-leather boots, she really did look like a Sixth Avenue hooker, Selden thought, with mounting irritation. This was the one evening he'd been looking forward to—he wanted to show off his wife and show her the kind of lifestyle they might have—and once again, she'd somehow managed to inadvertently ruin it. He wished she would wear something a little more normal, something sweet . . . Why did she always put her desires before his? There was a willfulness about her behavior, as if she knew but didn't care about how her actions might affect him.

Unable to express his thoughts, however, he merely said, "How much did the dress cost?" It was a legitimate question—he'd just paid off his American Express bill and had almost been sick at the amount of money she'd spent in Milan on clothes—nearly $40,000. It was impossible, he thought, that anyone could need that much clothing, and here she had gone and bought another dress.

"Why you *silly*," she said, playfully chiding him. "If that's all you're worried about . . . It was free, as a matter of fact. The designer gave it to me."

"Oh," was all he said, thinking that once again, she'd somehow managed to make him look foolish. He had to get out of this mood, he thought. And glancing at his watch, he said, "We should be going . . . the car's downstairs waiting."

At that moment, she must have suddenly understood that he wasn't pleased with her, because taking a step forward and cocking her head up at him in a submissive manner, she said, "Why Selden, what's the matter?" And then changing her tack, asked, "Don't you want me to look sexy?" in an arch, teasing voice.

"Yes, but . . . ," he began, thinking that this might be an opening in which he could convince her to change her outfit without tears, but she suddenly knelt down and, with the skilled fingers of an expert, unzipped his pants.

Janey attacked her task with gusto. Ever since she'd left George, she'd been in a buoyant mood. She suddenly realized how much the threat of exposure by Comstock Dibble had been weighing on her; now freed, she saw that life could go on as it should . . .

With a sigh that sounded like pleasure, Selden placed his hands on her head, hoping that the act would be finished quickly so they could make it to the dinner on time. A minute ticked by and he groaned involuntarily: What a fool he was! Nearly every man in America would give his right arm to be in his position—in possession of a wife who was not only an object of desire, but an eager and willing practitioner of sex, who gave satisfaction without being asked.

Mark Macadu and his wife, Dodo Blanchette Macadu, lived in a large, recently built monstrosity known derisively as a McMansion. The house, located on a pricey spit of land that jutted out into Long Island Sound, was built along the lines of what the architect imagined a "Colonial mansion" might look like, if, indeed, such a house had ever existed in history. It had white clapboards and four columns that rose from a stepped, flagstone entryway; inside were four fireplaces, six bedrooms, a conservatory (really, an attached greenhouse containing a couple of overstuffed armchairs), and, at the back of the house, the pièce de résistance: a five-hundred-square-foot state-of-the-art kitchen.

In the middle of this kitchen, surrounded by a mess of bowls, cooking utensils, copper pots, two Cuisinarts, spilled red wine, and a trail of flour that led, mysteriously, from the back door to the sink, Dodo Blanchette stood in front of a large butcher-block island, preparing dinner. Dodo attacked every aspect of her life with the zeal of a determined businesswoman, was a great believer in "improving her skills," and was a recent graduate of a two-week cooking course at the Culinary Institute of America. She had specialized in "veal"—and in turning any kitchen into a disaster area.

Standing nearby, with an expression of both horror and admiration on her face, was Sally Stumack, a teenager who lived next door. Sally was a tall girl who somehow managed to appear both gawky and heavy-set at the same time; her hair was long, blond, and frizzy, and she wore glasses with the defiant air of a young girl who is determined not to enter the beauty Olympics. The ever-enterprising Dodo "hired" Sally to help her out at dinner parties, Sally's best point being that she was meek and Dodo could boss her around.

"Sally, can you get me the whisk?" Dodo demanded. She was making tiny pancakes on which she planned to fold up pieces of smoked salmon topped with salmon roe to serve as the first course. "Where is it?" Sally asked, scurrying around the kitchen like a large, ungainly mouse.

"In the sink?" Dodo asked. She poured some milk into a bowl, where it splashed out and landed on the Victoria's Secret catalog, open to a page of Janey modeling a gold bathing suit. Dodo picked up the catalog and shook the drops of milk into the bowl. "I can't believe Selden Rose is bringing a Victoria's Secret model," she snapped, for the fiftieth time that day.

"But isn't she his wife?" Sally squeaked. She had just found the whisk in the garbage can and was surreptitiously washing it off. For the past hour, Dodo had been going on and on about Janey Wilcox, and Sally wished she would stop—for her part, she'd never met a Victoria's Secret model and was looking forward to it.

"The problem is," Dodo said, taking the whisk from Sally, "this Victoria's Secret model is going to throw off the whole balance of power. Every man, including my husband, is going to be drooling over her, and I told him if he even so much as looks in her direction, he won't get a blow job for a month. Men are like dogs, you know," she said. "They respond to positive and negative reinforcement."

"I don't know what you're worried about," Sally said. "You're just as beautiful as she is."

"That's exactly what I told Mark," Dodo said. She stirred furiously for a moment, and then glanced back at the large, round clock above the porcelain double sink. "Sweetie, can you take over for a moment? I've got to go upstairs and change." She wiped her hands on the front of the apron she was wearing, and hurried out of the room.

"But I don't know what to do," Sally cried.

"Just stir," Dodo shouted.

Passing through the dining room, she stopped to stare at her reflection. Ruffling her hair, she said aloud, "You look great!" Although Dodo was, on the surface, a young woman of great confidence, she was not, by any means, a beauty—her squarish face had a masculine quality, and her skin was pale and freckled—but she was so convinced of her own attractiveness that eventually others began to wonder if they were missing something.

In the entrance hall, she met her husband, Mark, who was just coming in. Mark Macadu had a full head of dark curly hair, and had been able to maintain his physique until he was forty, at which point he had gone to fat, dumped his first wife, and, four years later, married Dodo. Mark was dynamic and sensible; everybody thought he was "a really nice guy"; and there were times when he prayed that his wife wasn't insane.

"Hel-lo," he said, throwing the *New York Post* onto a side table.

"Hiya big boy," Dodo said, which was a bit of a stretch, as Mark was only 5'5". "I'll be right down—Sally's in the kitchen."

She cantered up the stairs and along a carpeted hallway to the master bedroom at the end of the hall. Once inside, she closed the heavy oak door and turned the key in the lock. She grabbed her purse and began riffling through a jumble of old receipts, phone numbers written on napkins, nail glue, four tubes of lipstick, dirty tissues, eyebrow tweezers, pressed powder, two leaking pens, a wallet bursting at the seams, four one-hundred-dollar bills, a black mascara wand, and a hairbrush full of broken bleached-blond strands. In frustration, she dumped the whole mess on the bed, and pawing through it, finally found what she was looking for: a tiny plastic bag filled with white powder.

Inserting her little finger into the bag, she removed a mound of powder on the tip of a long, acrylic fingernail. Like Janey, Dodo was a secret nail-biter, but she would be damned if anyone knew it and had a standing appointment once a week for the application and varnishing of her fake nails. She closed one nostril and inhaled, then, closing the other nostril, repeated the process. Leaving the mess on the bed, she put the plastic bag in her lingerie drawer, then went into the bathroom to check her nose.

Dodo Blanchette considered herself a thoroughly modern young woman. She was thirty-three, and, in her mind, extremely successful; she was unabashedly ambitious, joyfully competitive, and called herself a neofeminist; she believed in women helping other women (hence her hiring of Sally), she was always thinking about how to get ahead in her career, how to take over the world, and how to get her name in the papers. She had tons of girlfriends, and her favorite expression was "Women rule!," which she accompanied with a high five. Like many young women of her generation, she had no qualms about using sex to get ahead, and had invariably fucked all of her bosses, which was how she'd met Mark.

But the problem was that it was all so exhausting! As the lifestyle reporter for the local CBS affiliate (she covered everything from movie premieres to the best place to get a fake tan to kittens that fell out of apartment windows), she rose every morning at 6 A.M. to go to the gym, then she and Mark took a car at 7:30 for the hourlong ride to the city, during which she read four newspapers, then she had to research her story, then she had her hair and makeup done, then she usually went "on location," then she went back to the studio to edit her piece, and then she was *on TV,* and then she had to keep up with her friends, which often included endless cocktails at trendy bars, *then* she had to go out to dinner, consuming several glasses of white wine, *or* she had to return home to make dinner for Mark and whomever else they'd invited to their house who might be beneficial to their careers.

She was a big believer in hard work, and in doing a thing well if one was going to do it at all, and she often said that more things happened in her life in one week than happened in most people's lives in a year. But on top of all that, she had to look good, she had to be skinny, and therefore she was constantly engaged in the struggle to lose ten pounds.

Dodo was, by nature, a rather hefty, athletic girl who had played soccer as a teenager, and had even been All-American at Tufts University. She had large pendulous breasts, which she stuffed into push-up bras and with which men had been fascinated her entire life, but that wasn't enough, and she'd already had liposuction from her waist down to her knees twice. When she was twenty-two and an intern at the *New York Times,* she had discovered both cocaine and the power of her breasts: After six months she was fired, ostensibly because she could never get to work before eleven o'clock, but secretly because she was sleeping with her boss who was married—when his wife found out, she forced him to fire Dodo. Since then, Dodo had kept her cocaine habit under control, but she had never been able to master her sexual addiction to powerful men. She was subconsciously influenced by the depictions of beautiful women in advertising and strove to be like them, while at the same time she was horrified by the power bimbos could wield over men. *Beauty: How Men's Expectations Have Ruined Women's Lives* was one of her favorite books, and she was always quoting lines from it, such as "man's recent obsession with female beauty is at least party responsible for the erosion of the family," at dinner parties. Nevertheless, she still couldn't resist the idea of a powerful man being obsessed with her and her beauty . . .

Standing in front of the bathroom mirror, she began applying red lipstick; then she leaned forward and studied her lips in the mirror, pushing up her top lip with her finger. If she had a few collagen injections, she would look every bit as beautiful as Janey Wilcox, she thought, and then wondered what she was worrying about. Janey Wilcox was sure to be a complete bimbo, and the truth was, in *their* circle, it didn't matter how beautiful a woman was—if she wasn't accomplished, if she couldn't talk about business and politics, if she didn't really *do* anything, then the men usually lost interest and ignored her.

But even if you *could* do all those things, it wasn't a guarantee that a man would pay constant attention to you, Dodo thought bitterly. In the last six months, she'd sensed a dropping off in her husband's level of interest in her: He used to watch her broadcast every day at five, but lately, when she'd questioned him about it, he admitted that he'd missed her, using the excuse that he'd "forgotten." She'd had to point out to him, in no uncertain terms, that your wife was not something you "forgot," like your keys. In the past, her fits of high dudgeon had always supplied the needed results, but lately, when she went "off," he merely rolled his eyes and went into the other room to watch TV. So it was really his own fault that she had recently ended up in the arms of his best friend, Paul Lovelady.

Paul Lovelady and his wife, Carolina, who was a concert pianist and who claimed to be some kind of Russian princess (which Dodo didn't believe), were coming to dinner; all afternoon, in between worrying about Janey Wilcox, Dodo had wondered if Paul would make some kind of move on her. In the past month, she and Paul had slept together twice—both times on the weekend, when Mark was at the gym and Carolina had had a rehearsal at Lincoln Center; she and Paul now spent about an hour a day on the phone. Paul told her that she was "brilliant" and "beautiful," and even though Carolina was technically one of her best friends, Dodo didn't feel guilty. She had long ago decided that guilt was a useless emotion, and her feeling about married men was simple: If a wife couldn't prevent her husband from cheating, it wasn't *her* problem.

She dotted her lips with gloss and smacked them together, and, exiting the bathroom, heard the siren song of the little plastic package of cocaine calling to her. She did two more quick hits, just to pick her up a little and get her through what was sure to be a long evening, vowing that it was all she would do . . . until tomorrow.

And downstairs, Mark Macadu entered the kitchen with a touch of trepidation, sniffing the air for signs of disaster. In three years of marriage to Dodo, he had learned to expect anything—on several occasions he'd walked into the kitchen and found something aflame—and while he was scared to death of the house burning down, Dodo was never the least bit concerned; she said kitchen fires were a way of life if you were a certified chef, like herself. He didn't think that two weeks of cooking classes made a person a certified chef, but Dodo insisted that it was true, and he'd found that it was often easier to agree with her than not, even if it meant agreeing to a lie.

But on this particular evening, all was calm. The kitchen was a mess, of course, but it always was, and there was sweet little (*big?*) Sally from next door, stirring something in a bowl, and the fragrant scent of roasting lamb coming from the oven.

"Hi, Mr. Macadu," Sally said.

"Now Sally," Mark said, crossing to the refrigerator for a bottle of white wine, "you can call me Mark. I'm not your father . . ."

"I know, Mr. Macadu," she said.

They had this exchange every time they saw each other, and picking up a special black Rabbit corkscrew, he smiled to himself, thinking about how nice and civilized the suburbs were compared to the city.

• • •

Carolina and Paul Lovelady arrived exactly at seven-thirty. Carolina leaned over to Dodo for a kiss and asked, "Is she here yet?" and when Dodo shook her head, she leaned over to her other ear and whispered, "Do you have anything?"

"In my lingerie drawer," Dodo whispered back. In the past two years, Dodo and Carolina had become great friends, mostly due to their shared love of cocaine, a secret that they guarded assiduously from their husbands.

Seeing the two women whispering, and suddenly fearful that Dodo had told Carolina about their little affair, Paul said, "What are you two girls whispering about now?" and rolled his eyes at Mark.

"Nothing," Dodo said. "We were just talking about the Victoria's Secret model."

"Paul's been thinking about her all day," Carolina said. "He won't admit it, but I can always tell *exactly* what he's thinking. Can't I, *dear*?" she asked, patting him on the cheek.

Paul experienced another jolt of panic, suddenly wishing that he had never slept with Dodo to begin with. He had thought it was nothing more than a friendly neighborhood fuck, but after the second time, she'd begun calling him every day at work. He was going to have to put an end to it, starting tonight, but then he caught a glimpse of her tits, and he changed his mind. She was wearing a suit jacket with only a bra underneath; her breasts strained out from between the lapels and he could see the lacy blue of her bra—the same bra she'd been wearing the first time they'd had sex. He immediately remembered the feel of those full, comforting breasts, and he decided that one more time with her wouldn't hurt anyone—especially as his wife was not nearly so well endowed. Carolina was elegant, to be sure, but he'd stopped finding her sexy after about a year of marriage.

Aloud, he said, "Hey, I'm a red-blooded American male. I can't help myself . . ."

And Dodo responded, "As long as you keep your pecker in your pants," and gave him a meaningful look.

"I'm going to the bathroom," Carolina said, disappearing up the stairs.

Ross and Constance Jared arrived a few minutes later. Constance was, as usual Dodo thought, strangely dressed, in a blue ruffled shirt and velveteen skirt that went below her knees, as if she was still trying to give the impression that she was a virginal teenager, which she had been when she'd first joined the American Ballet Theatre. Carolina thought Constance was weird, but Dodo always defended her—she was a perfectly nice, sweet girl, she always said, who was a little mixed up because her feet had been squished into toe shoes all her life. But mostly, Dodo liked Constance because she never talked, and therefore never robbed Dodo of attention.

The three couples went into the living room, where bowls of nuts and olives, and a platter containing soft French cheeses, had been laid out. For fifteen minutes, the men talked about office politics while Dodo and Carolina analyzed the personality of one of Dodo's colleagues, a new young female recruit who, Dodo swore, had been giving her dirty looks. Then the doorbell rang, and after a momentary lapse in conversation, everyone studiously went back to their discussions.

Sally opened the door. Once the first guests had arrived, Dodo always "let" her answer the door as a "favor," telling her that it would improve her hostessing skills, but it usually only made Sally feel like a servant. Tonight, however, was different, and she didn't mind playing butler at all—she would be the very first person to clap eyes on this Janey Wilcox character, and she was excited about it.

Dodo had mentioned that Janey was probably a killer bitch, and while Sally had come across several killer bitches in her private school, she had yet to meet an adult version. Nor had she ever seen a model in real life. Dodo told her that she wouldn't look anything near as good as her photographs, but Sally wasn't sure. In any case, she certainly wasn't prepared for the vision that met her eyes when she opened the door, and taking a step back in awe, she nearly tripped on the Oriental rug.

Sally knew *she* was tall—she was sixteen and nearly 5'10"—but Janey appeared to be a creature of Amazon-like proportions. Sally had never seen anyone with such a perfect figure—she didn't know a human being could actually look like that. And then Janey spoke, her voice pouring over Sally like cream. And what she said was:

"Are your parents home?"

"Oh!" Sally said, fumbling with the door handle. "They're not *my* parents . . . I mean, I live next door . . . ," she said helplessly.

"That's nice," Janey said, looking around her with what Sally was convinced was amused disdain. There was a large painting of Dodo in the entrance hall, wearing pearls and a peignoir—the painting had been done from a photograph and wasn't very good—and as Janey's eyes alighted on the painting, a brief smile touched her lips, and Sally was suddenly embarrassed for Dodo.

"Everyone's in the living room," she said breathlessly, watching Janey and Selden as they strolled into the next room. Then she scurried gleefully back to the kitchen. Janey Wilcox was every bit as beautiful as her photographs, and Dodo was going to be furious. The only disappointing thing about Janey was her husband, she thought, sneaking a small glass of white wine, which she knew the Macadus, who were big drinkers, would never notice. Someone who looked like Janey should be with a movie star, she thought. Not with some ordinary guy who seemed just like her father and Mr. Macadu, and every other man in the neighborhood.

"Mark!" Selden said loudly, entering the living room.

Mark looked up—in fact, they all did—and then they all quickly looked away, with the exception of Mark, who came striding forward, his hands outstretched. He clasped Selden's hand in both of his, and then they clapped each other on the back.

"This is my wife, Janey," Selden said.

Mark smiled, being careful not to appear too friendly, and shook Janey's hand.

All of the men were trying to look anywhere except at Janey, Dodo thought with annoyance, which only made it all the more obvious that they wanted to gape at her. Janey was, Dodo thought, exactly what all men wanted—a trashy, sexy, dumb-looking girl—and taking her time, she rose from the couch and crossed the room.

"Hello. You must be Janey," she said.

"Yes. And you are . . . ?"

"Dodo Blanchette. Mark's wife," Dodo said coldly, fuming that Selden hadn't apprised Janey of at least her name. But then again, she thought, maybe he *had*, and Janey was simply too stupid to remember it. "Did you have any trouble finding our humble little abode?" she asked.

"Actually, the driver got lost," Janey said.

"Sorry about that," Mark Macadu said. "Dodo's never been very good with directions . . . she couldn't find her way out of a paper bag."

Dodo shot Mark a dirty look. She couldn't decide who she wished more dead: her husband . . . or Janey Wilcox.

"I'd like to make a toast," Dodo said, tapping her water glass with her knife. She stood up unsteadily, holding her red-wine glass aloft at a dangerous angle—she'd already had quite a lot to drink and more cocaine than she'd planned—and she was feeling quite high. "To the newest member of our little family. Janey Wilcox, welcome."

"Hear, hear."

Janey took a sip of her wine and sat back in her chair, forcing herself to smile. She would never be a member of this little family, she thought, no matter how hard she tried. She was like a foreigner who didn't speak their language, and, looking around the table, she felt completely and utterly alone.

That Dodo was insane, she thought. Before dinner, Dodo had insisted on taking Janey on a tour of the house, during which she kept emphasizing how they could have lived in the city, but $5 million bought more space in Greenwich . . . and then she had taken Janey into the bedroom and offered her cocaine, which Janey had refused. Nevertheless, Dodo had trapped her in the bathroom for a good fifteen minutes, blathering about her technique for avoiding pregnancy, which was to take an ovulation test and to avoid sex on the days she was fertile. "Can you imagine *me* with a child?" she kept asking. "But that's all they want, these men. They want us for sex and breeding—as if I don't work hard enough as it is! I have to take care of this house, and Mark, and God knows *he* doesn't do anything . . ."

And then there was Carolina. Carolina had the kind of long, aristocratic face that would have been considered the height of beauty two hundred years ago. But under the surface, she had the angry, watchful air of a woman who knows her husband is cheating, but has yet to find the hard evidence. Which shouldn't have been difficult, Janey thought, since Dodo was all over Carolina's husband, Paul, whispering jokes in his ear and pressing her leg up against his . . .

And finally there was poor little Constance. She was so skinny Janey thought she might faint from lack of food, and everybody was ignoring her, as if she were a large doll that someone had brought to the table and seated on a chair.

And they were all so smug and sure of themselves.

"I still say the Republicans will ruin the economy," Ross said heatedly to Selden.

"Come on, Ross, that's crap and you know it," Selden said. "The economy charts its own course—whether the president is Republican or Democratic is irrelevant . . ."

"As the only person in this group who actually works on TV, I say the stock market is going to recover," Dodo said.

"Ross, dear, you've completely forgotten about Reagan," Carolina said.

Janey picked at her lamb and said nothing. The lamb was far too rare for her tastes, and she wondered if uncooked lamb could give you food poisoning.

"Do you have money in the stock market?" Ross suddenly asked her.

"A little," Janey responded.

"Janey probably has a business manager who handles her money. Isn't that how models do it? So you don't really have to know anything about the stock market yourself," Dodo said.

"Actually, a lot of models handle their own money," Janey said.

"I was talking to this guy the other day who's somehow involved in the modeling industry, and he told me that the secret about a lot of the top models is that they're smart," Paul said. "They have to be in order to succeed."

"Come on, Paul," Carolina snapped. "Smart in comparison to *what*?" And in the dead silence that followed, she quickly added, "I don't mean *you*, Janey."

And then someone quickly changed the subject to the mountain-climbing trip they'd all taken in India last year.

Janey found it impossible to concentrate on the conversation. She hated sports and she'd never been to India; glancing surreptitiously at her watch, she saw that it was only nine-thirty. What a strange group they were, she thought. If you didn't know who was married to whom, you would never have been able to match them up correctly, for there didn't seem to be any real deep, underlying affection between the members of each couple. They were like adolescents, playing at being adults . . .

"What should we do this year?" Carolina asked.

"I still think we should fly the Ferraris out to Montana and race," Michael said. "You've got a Ferrari, don't you Rose?"

"I've got something better," Selden said. "A Jaguar XK 120."

"How fast can it go?"

Selden shrugged. "A hundred, a hundred and twenty?"

"We'll leave you in the dust," Dodo said.

"Why Montana?" Janey suddenly asked, attempting to insert herself into the conversation.

"Because there's no speed limit?" Carolina said, in a voice that was just subtly rude enough to escape the notice of the men.

"Are you *just* a model, Janey?" Dodo asked. And then, looking around the table as if she might have made a faux pas, she said quickly, "It's just that so many top models do *other* things as well, don't they? I mean, that elegant girl, the one with the stunningly beautiful face . . . what's her name?" she asked, turning to Carolina.

"You mean Christy Turlington," Carolina said. "She has her own company and clothing line—I think she even does yoga videos . . ."

"That's right, Janey," Paul said, giving her a drunken leer. "Tell us all about *you*."

They were all staring at her. Janey felt a rising sense of panic—she was almost dizzy. She suddenly felt like she was suffocating; she couldn't *feel* herself; even her outfit, which would normally have given her a sense of identity, seemed to be failing her . . . If she said nothing, they would all think she was an idiot, and she'd be damned if she gave them *that* satisfaction . . .

Taking a sip from her wineglass, she said smoothly, "Actually, I'm a movie producer."

"You *are*?" Dodo said, impressed.

"What are you working on?" Carolina said, taking a cigarette out of her bag.

"Oh Carolina, don't smoke," Paul said.

"Fuck you," Carolina said, and lit up.

"I wrote a screenplay last summer," Janey said, finding, as usual, that once she began to lie, the lie got easier and easier. "And right now I'm in the process of getting it made."

She took another sip of wine, not daring to look at Selden. She could see, out of the corner of her eye, that his face wore an expression of shock, as if he couldn't believe she would tell such a fib. But what else was she supposed to do?

"What's it about?" Carolina asked.

"It's about a model, and how everyone tries to use her," Janey said.

"An old story," Selden said dismissively.

"Selden's mad because I didn't tell him about it," Janey said to Carolina and Dodo. Turning to Selden, she added, "I didn't tell you, darling, because I wanted it to be a surprise. How *else* did you think I was spending my afternoons . . . ?"

This brought a round of laughter. "You didn't think she was spending her afternoons *shopping,* did you?" Dodo asked.

"I can never figure out *what* you women do," Selden replied. And quickly changing the subject, he said to Ross, "What's happening with the Old Man?" "The Old Man" being the code name they used for Victor Matrick, the aging CEO of Splatch Verner.

"Slowly going insane," Ross said.

"Word is, he bought a plane," Mark said.

"Plane?" Paul sneered. "What are you talking about? It's a jumbo jet. A 727 . . ."

"Does anybody have any idea where these profits are really going?" Selden asked.

Leaning across him, Dodo whispered to Janey, "You know, *I* used to be a model."

"Is that so?" Janey asked, feigning interest.

"You were a model for two months," Carolina sneered. "I did it for a whole year."

"Hello? You're wrong?" Dodo said. "I was a Tropicana bathing-suit model for two years . . ."

"In any case, it was awful," Carolina said.

"I don't know how you do it," Dodo said. "It's so boring. And then every photographer wants to sleep with you . . ."

"You're right," Janey said. "It *is* awful. But it's weird, you know?" she said, sipping her wine. "Because nearly every pretty girl I've ever met has either tried it or wants to."

"Well," Janey said pointedly, as they got into the car. "That little *neighborhood girl* was nice."

"They were *all* nice. They're great people," Selden said.

Janey sat back against the seat in a huff. She was suddenly angry, although she wasn't sure why, and felt a fight coming on.

"Constance is always sweet," she said, "but I wonder if there's something wrong with her. Do you think she has an eating disorder?"

"She's actually interesting if you take the time to talk to her," Selden said.

"Ah. Well," Janey said. She looked out the window, wondering if they would be able to make it home before the fight erupted; if they could, it might be avoided.

Taking her reply as a retreat, he said, "Mark's wife, Dodo, is a lot of fun."

"She's fun all right," Janey said vaguely. "But she's not a very good cook. Do you think raw lamb can make you sick?"

"She's very successful—one of the most successful young women in broadcasting," Selden said. He looked at Janey, wondering what was wrong with her. His first wife, Sheila, had always had a lot of girlfriends, and she'd excelled at making friends with the wives of his business associates. "The truth is, Janey, you hardly gave those women a chance," he said, loosening his tie.

Janey turned to him with astonishment. "Me?" she asked, thinking how stupid men were. "They hated me from the beginning. Didn't you see that Dodo's face when I walked in? And did you hear what they were saying about models . . . ?"

"Well, maybe you shouldn't have worn that dress!" Selden retorted. There—he had said it. He probably shouldn't have, but at least he'd finally gotten it off his chest . . .

She shook her head in disgust. "Your business associates seemed to like it," she said pointedly.

Now that was too much, he thought. Why were they always fighting? Every time he tried to have a civilized discussion with her, it turned into some stupid battle of wills. This was exactly the way she had been, that first night he'd met her. And while he'd always thought their exchange that evening had been nothing more than the exciting, antagonistic banter that led to sex, he was beginning to wonder if perhaps that enmity was representative of a real difference in values and morals. And then she had *lied* about being a producer . . .

"I think we need to have a discussion," he said.

"Do you?" she asked. "About what? You can't expect me to sit there and take their insults without defending myself . . ."

"Fine," he said. "I can't do anything about the way they feel. But why did you tell them that you were producing movies, for God's sake?"

"Why *shouldn't* I have told them?" she asked, her eyes blazing.

"Because it's a *lie*," he nearly shouted.

As usual, when he lost his temper with her, she gained the upper hand.

Crossing her arms, she said, "I won't be scolded like a child. Not even by you, Selden Rose."

Now he was on the defensive. "Okay. I'm not scolding. I just want to know why. You're my wife, goddammit . . ."

"So you expect me to tell you everything?" she asked, deftly drawing him away from the point of the discussion.

By now, he knew *this* trick of hers, at least. "Janey," he said. "You are *not* a producer. And what was that nonsense about a screenplay?"

The screenplay! How had she come so close to spilling her secret? In an offensive move, she said quickly, "Maybe I haven't produced—or written—anything *yet*. But you should know it's something I plan to pursue, very, *very* seriously in the future. So if you have a problem with it, we'd better deal with it now."

For a moment, he was torn between wanting to shake her like a child—to shake the truth out of her—and a crazy desire to laugh. The *fact* was, she had no idea how to be a producer, no clue as to what it took to get a movie made—after a couple of days playing at being a producer, she would likely give it up and go back to shopping. And so he said:

"Suit yourself then."

"Thank you," she said. She stuck her finger in her mouth and looked away. Until that moment, she'd had no intention of pursuing this producing scheme; she would have dropped it if Selden had let it go. But she began to see that it might be a good idea; Dodo's and Carolina's reactions had showed her that it would give her the respect she craved. Of course, she hadn't meant to lie, but now that she had decided to do it, it wasn't a lie at all, no matter what Selden thought . . .

She glanced out the window. They were on the highway now, speeding back to the city, passing gas stations and billboards, and ticky-tacky houses—how depressing it would be to *live* here, she thought, suddenly relieved that the evening was over. "Listen," she said, touching his hand in a conciliatory gesture, "let's not fight, okay? Especially over a bunch of people I'll probably never see again . . ."

Selden drew his hand away in annoyance. Was it possible that there was *no* understanding between them? "Of course you'll see them again," he said. "Especially if we move to Greenwich. You'll see them all the time . . ."

"Move to Greenwich?" she cried in horror.

"Yes," he said, with mock patience. "That was always the plan."

"Was it?" she said, in a panic. She couldn't remember their discussing Greenwich before, except in the context of visiting his friends. If they moved to Greenwich, she would *die,* she thought, she'd be nothing more than a housewife—she might even end up like Dodo . . .

"Mark says there's a great house for sale just down the street from them, right on the water. We could keep the boat there. Remember how much fun we had last summer on the boat?"

She glanced at him; his face was impassive, and there was a hardness in his eyes, as if daring her to challenge him again. But her womanly instincts told her that now was not the time for another fight, and so she yielded.

"Yes," she said vaguely. "That *would* be fun."

He immediately relaxed and, thinking that the crisis had passed, took her hand. "I'm not sure if the property has a dock, but we can certainly build one, and the house is big enough for everything we need. We can even build a gym if you want one . . ."

Exercising was her least favorite pastime, but she murmured, "That could be nice . . ."

"I'll call Mark tomorrow then, and get the name of the real estate agent."

She yawned, feigning sleepiness. Moving in next to him, she put her head on his shoulder; in a moment, he began stroking her hair.

She closed her eyes, although she wasn't tired. Her mind was awhirl, trying to work out various escape routes, and she suddenly realized that marrying Selden Rose might have been a huge mistake. Inevitably, her thoughts turned to George and his apartment. She had said that she couldn't live in a place like that, but now that she'd viewed life in Greenwich, she saw that she'd been fooling herself. Suddenly, there was nothing she desired *more* than to live in the grandest apartment in New York City—and if she'd had any sense, she would have gone after George long ago and married him, instead.

George, she thought with a start. George—with all of his power and money— now *that* was the kind of man she should be with.

NINE

THE TWENTY-FOOT CHRISTMAS star hung staunchly over the intersection of Fifth Avenue and Fifty-seventh Street, the lampposts were garlanded with wreaths, and the department store windows featured mannequins done up in all manner of holiday finery. December in the year 2000 was bitterly cold—averaging a mere twenty-five degrees—but the shops and restaurants were filled with patrons determined to spend as much money as possible, for the fashion magazines had declared that fur was back and excess was in—from plastic watches adorned with real diamonds to $5,000 red crocodile boots. The stomach was heralded as the new erogenous zone and was on display even in the chill of winter, and for a certain fee, a plastic surgeon in California would reshape a woman's vagina into a more youthful design.

"As if what God gave us wasn't good enough!" Pippi Maus declared with indignation, as she spun through the revolving door of Cipriani's restaurant out onto the sidewalk. Pippi was tipsy; she was, Janey noted with satisfying disapproval, always at least *slightly* drunk, although on this particular afternoon, so was Janey.

"Is that so?" Janey remarked, thinking that Pippi's vagina was probably the only part of her body that was still real.

"Mimi doesn't understand," Pippi said. "Things supposedly happen down there when you get older."

"Meaning what?" Mimi demanded.

"You know. The lips. They . . . stretch," Pippi said, screaming with laughter as she grabbed Janey's arm. "Which means mine must be as wide as the Grand Canyon, considering all the men I've slept with."

"Oh, Pippi. That is the most absurd thing I've ever heard," Mimi said, pulling on her gloves. "Now you've got me completely freaked out. What if—someone—looks down there and thinks that *I'm* old?"

"Are you talking about Zizi?" Pippi asked, covering her mouth as if she suddenly realized that she'd inadvertently let the cat out of the bag. "But of course he thinks you're old," she said. Her tact was about equal to her gait, which was awkward and clomping, as if she'd never quite mastered the art of wearing high heels. Her unsteady walk, combined with her loud voice and the very fact that she was Pippi Maus, the actress, was beginning to attract attention on the street.

"Come on, Pippi," Janey said, trying to smooth things over. "You don't want to end up in the gossip columns again, do you?"

"I'm always in the gossip columns," Pippi declared. "And I can state for a fact that they always lie."

"Should we walk or take the car?" Mimi asked.

"The car," Janey said firmly, assessing Pippi's condition. She "loved" Pippi, "adored" her, and even agreed with Mimi that Pippi was "hysterical." But secretly she resented the fact that spending time with Pippi so often involved acting like a baby-sitter. Pippi gave in to all her impulses: She drank and took cocaine, and was given to wandering off—disappearing into a bathroom with a man she'd just met at a party or passing out under a table. Then everybody had to look for Pippi, and, having found her, minister to her emotional hysterias. She was as likely to be sobbing over some imagined slight as plotting a vicious revenge toward someone who had done her wrong. Janey would have gladly done without her at all, but as she was so often in Mimi's company these days, she was unavoidable.

"Anyway, Mimi," Pippi continued—when she was drunk or high, she became aggressive, and would keep hammering away at a point long after everyone else had lost interest—"You *are* twenty years older than he is, and have you ever been with a man who was twenty years older than *you* and *not* thought that he was disgustingly old?"

"Yes," Janey said.

"But you like older men," Pippi said, as if Janey didn't count; and Janey said defensively, "Selden isn't old."

"He's at least fifteen years older, if you're not lying about your age . . ."

"Pippi!" Mimi said warningly, signaling to her car.

"Hey," Pippi shrugged. "I lie about *my* age, not that I'm going to tell you guys the truth . . ."

"I know the truth," Mimi said. "Remember darling, I've known you since you were ten years old . . ."

The black Mercedes slid up to the curb and Muhammad stepped out and opened the back door. "Thank you, Muhammad," Mimi said pointedly. The three women got in, and the car crawled into the crush of holiday traffic on Fifth Avenue. The ten-block ride would probably take a good fifteen minutes, but it was so glamorous, Janey thought, to be traveling in a chauffeured Mercedes, to be rich and swathed in fur coats, to be laughing and slightly drunk after a champagne lunch at one of the city's most exclusive restaurants, to be beautiful and to have beautiful and famous friends, and to be on her way to a jewelry auction at Christie's. She touched the window with her gloved finger, smiling at the perfection of it all. She had made the cover of the Victoria's Secret Christmas catalog, wearing a diamond-encrusted bra and panty set, which had been delivered by an armored guard to the photography studio. And later, the guard had stood no farther than three feet away from her when she modeled the bra at the press conference. But the coup de grâce was the cover of *Maxim* magazine, on which she appeared in a black leather outfit that was little more than a few well-placed straps dotted with silver studs. The combination of the two covers—the good, angelic girl vs. the bad one—had generated an enormous amount of publicity; nearly every entertainment show had covered the story.

In the car next to her, Pippi began shifting uncomfortably, searching through her bag for a cigarette. "How is Selden, anyway?" she asked.

"We're doing wonderfully," Janey said firmly. This wasn't completely true, but she wasn't going to complain about Selden to Pippi. And ever since she'd appeared on the two covers, she and Selden seemed to have reached some kind of truce in their relationship, and Selden had hardly brought up Greenwich at all. Janey suspected that the excitement of seeing his wife on two magazine covers, and knowing that millions of men desired her, was probably behind Selden's change in attitude, but she didn't want to delve too deeply. Lately, Selden had been as compliant as a puppy, as willing to please as he had been when they'd first married, and when he occasionally did mention moving, she would sigh despondently and say, "I'd love to, but I'm so busy, what can I do?"

Mimi, however, was a different story. "Janey, did you call Brenda Lish yet? I promise you, if your marriage ends it's going to be because you and Selden went crazy living in that hotel."

Janey's laugh tinkled as brightly as a small bell. "Selden's hardly ever home anyway. And besides, he never notices his surroundings."

Pippi took a deep drag on her cigarette, and Janey, with some annoyance, pressed the button to open the window a crack. Cold air rushed in as Pippi said, "Well, he certainly seemed to be noticing Wendy Piccolo at Dingo's the other night, but I don't get it. She's so tiny you wouldn't think anyone would even see her."

Janey's lips were still curled into a smile, but her eyes were challenging. "What are you trying to say, Pippi?" she asked. "That Selden is having an affair?"

"Of course he isn't," Mimi said firmly. "He's only been married for three months. But if you don't find a place of your own . . ."

"I know lots of men who slept with someone else the night before their wedding," Pippi pressed on. "I even know a guy who stashed his mistress at the hotel next door when he was on his honeymoon."

"That's because the only people you know are actors," Janey said.

"*I'm* an actor," Pippi snapped, rising to defend her profession. Janey laughed, amused at her arrogance; no matter how much time they spent together in Mimi's company, they would never really be friends. There was too much competition on Pippi's side, which Janey found pathetic, especially as she didn't consider herself and Pippi in the same league. "Her nose is just so . . . *pointy*," Janey trilled to Mimi one afternoon. And Mimi said, "Oh, I know, but men find her sexy." Janey, saying nothing, had smiled wisely—the only reason men found Pippi sexy was because she was so available for sex.

"Selden isn't the type to have an affair anyway," Mimi said firmly. "Believe me, Janey will have an affair before he does."

For a moment, the reality of Mimi's own affair with Zizi hung unspoken in the air, and then Janey said lightly, "I couldn't imagine having an affair on Selden. But I suppose I'm lucky. I married a man I'm truly in love with."

This wasn't, she knew, exactly the truth, for there were too many moments when he irritated her to fool herself about her feelings for him. But she'd said the line so many times—to reporters at press conferences and on the red carpet line, and to the people who congratulated her at parties—that by now it had become rote.

"Well, I didn't!" Mimi said boldly, as if trying to convince herself that it wasn't important.

"Come on, darling, you *do* love him," Janey said.

"Love, but not *in* love," Mimi said. She added briskly, "Let's not talk about George."

"Okay," Pippi squeaked. "Let's talk about Zizi. What are you going to buy him for Christmas?"

"A watch," Mimi said. "All he ever talks about now is how much he wants a decent watch. And it's true. If you're a man in this town and every other man has a fifteen-thousand-dollar watch, you do feel left out."

The cruel streak in Janey wanted to giggle derisively, but she stopped herself by turning her face to the window and lifting her gloved knuckles to her lips. In the three months since Zizi had moved to New York, he had changed for the worse. Janey had seen the scenario happen a million times: In the Hamptons, Zizi had appeared to be the master of correct behavior; he was always gracious and he didn't fool around. But there weren't as many temptations in the Hamptons as there were in the city, and in short order, Zizi had become notoriously well known on the club circuit, often partying until four in morning, and had developed a reputation for being a rogue. His looks made him irresistible to women—it was rumored that several tried their luck with him each night—and Patty had even told her that any girl who scored became a member of some secret "Zizi club."

If only Mimi would listen! Janey thought, with frustration. Time and again, she'd tried to hint to Mimi that Zizi wasn't what he seemed, but Mimi merely seemed to take her suggestions as evidence that Janey was jealous. Which couldn't have been farther from the truth: Every time Janey heard about one of his escapades, or saw him out with some bright young thing, she was relieved she had rejected him, which was how she told herself that things had happened with him. Mimi still paid his rent though, and Janey guessed that given Zizi's love of money, he would eventually meet a wealthy, eligible young girl whose family riches would entice him into marriage, and Mimi into insanity—Janey could almost imagine the perfectly mannered Mimi Kilroy foaming at the mouth . . .

As they passed Tiffany, where a line of eager tourists clamored to get inside, Janey chewed on the tip of her glove. She'd always prided herself on her ability to analyze a man's true intentions and on the fact that she never lied to herself about what a man really wanted, and there was a part of her that had no patience for women like Mimi, who willfully deluded themselves about a man's real intentions. But now her friendship with Mimi demanded that she obscure the truth about Zizi as well, and she wondered what would happen when she could no longer lie . . .

"And what about Uncle George?" Pippi asked. Janey winced; she hated Pippi's inappropriate familiarity with people, but Mimi hardly noticed. "Oh, I'll buy him a pair of cuff links, I guess," she said. "Something old and rare, maybe a platinum pair from Asprey's; in any case, he'll be happy as long as they're one of a kind and nobody else has them."

"Oh, I think George has excellent taste," Janey said. Mimi gave a great whoop of laughter, and reached across Pippi to touch Janey's hand. "Don't tell me you've got a crush on my husband, Janey, although I can't think of a more perfect solution. If you want him, you're welcome to him, although I can't imagine what anyone would do with *two* husbands . . . You'll definitely have to learn to decorate, darling!"

Mimi continued laughing and even Pippi joined in, and as the car pulled up to the curb and the three women got out, Janey felt her face redden. Ever since that afternoon at the apartment, George had been in the back of her mind—and when they ran into each other at dinners and parties, she was convinced that there was "something" between them, although naturally, as there were always other people around, nothing whatsoever had happened.

"The truth is, I think George is a sweetheart," Janey said primly.

Mimi laughed again. "He's the best, darling, there really is no question of that. And I *do* adore him . . ."

But as they entered the auction house, Janey wondered how George would feel about those cuff links, in comparison to what he was going to give Mimi.

Two hours later at Christie's auction house, Janey stood at the cashier's desk, paying for a $50,000 black pearl necklace with Selden's American Express card. She was still giddy with the excitement of having bid for the pearls and won, and in a bold hand scrawled "Janey Wilcox Rose" on the bottom of the credit card slip, deliberately avoiding looking at the total. With tax, it would be about $54,000, and though the auction house offered to send the pearls out of state in order to avoid the sales tax, Janey had just laughed and said that if Selden could afford $50,000, he could afford the tax.

"Oh, but that's where you're wrong," Mimi said, scolding. "Men don't mind spending money if it's going to do something for them, but they hate spending money unnecessarily."

"Just give him a blow job," Pippi advised, "and he'll forget all about it." She waved and clomped off to a cab, her fox-fur coat swinging open to reveal heavy breasts straining against the thin fabric of a green cashmere sweater.

Taking Janey's arm as they strolled to the curb, Mimi said, "You can't pay attention to Pippi. She's a sweet girl but she *is* jealous. Especially now that you're doing so well, and her career is going nowhere. She nearly went crazy over that *Maxim* cover."

"Exactly what *did* she say?" Janey asked.

"The usual. Just that she didn't understand why they'd picked you for the cover of *Maxim* and not her."

"But she hasn't even been in a real movie for three years," Janey protested. "And the last one went straight to video."

"That doesn't matter. She still thinks she's as famous as she was ten years ago. And being her friend, we allow her to think so."

"I think she could be dangerous," Janey said stubbornly, but Mimi laughed. "Pippi? She's too dumb to be dangerous, although I wouldn't leave her alone with those pearls you just bought. She has a tendency to get mixed up over what belongs to her and what belongs to other people."

Janey laughed and instinctively touched the choker of black pearls that in the thrill of ownership she had decided to wear home, wondering again why Mimi would choose to be friends with someone like Pippi. As if reading the question in her eyes, Mimi said quickly, "Oh, I know Pippi's a pain and on the very edge of crazy, but I grew up with her and she's like a little sister to me. Her godmother was my mother's best friend, and since little Pippi and her sister never really had a family, she spent practically every holiday with us. And besides, it's not like we don't all have our *own* flaws—I know I do, and at my age, I'd rather be forgiven for them. Something happens when you turn forty. You actually see the benefit in being kind to people."

Janey gave a little titter that she used to mask her embarrassment at being caught out, and said, "I didn't mean . . ."

"Oh no. Of course not," Mimi said. "It's just that we can be nice to Pippi because we understand where she's coming from. She's tired, desperate, and scared, and on top of it, she has no money and no man to take care of her; no wonder she feels mean."

"You're right, of course," Janey said. Mimi smiled and squeezed Janey's arm. "I've got to fly—I promised to pick up George's children at the airport. But I'll see you later?"

Janey nodded, watching Mimi as she hurried to her car. She had so many small, elegant movements, like the way she tapped once with a finger on the window of the car to signal the driver and the way she tilted her head as she waited for him to open the door. As she was about to slide onto the seat, she paused, gathering up the folds of her fur coat. "If Selden gives you any trouble about the pearls," she called out, "tell him I *forced* you to buy them!"

"I will," Janey called back. For a moment, she watched the car disappear into the traffic, and then she turned up Madison Avenue. Slipping her hands into the pockets of her white mink coat, she was blissfully aware of the frosty December air and the quiet gray sky above, and of that particular expectant hush in the air, signaling snow. An easy joyousness marked the faces of the people passing on the sidewalk, as if, with the prospect of snow, the holiday season had truly begun.

Janey had always considered the first snowfall of the season a special day, when anything could happen, and she again touched the pearls at her neck. It was good luck, she thought, to have bought the pearls on the same day as the first snowfall, but in a moment, her good mood was marred by what was sure to be Selden's inevitable reaction. He had plenty of money—by means of subtle questioning she'd gathered that he *had* to be worth at least $30 million—but when it came to spending it, he had a decidedly middle-class attitude. His favorite expression was "Are you sure you *really* need that?," which he employed every time he discovered one of her new purchases. Finally, in frustration, she'd responded, "Are you sure you *really* need a five-hundred-thousand-dollar vintage car?" To which he'd replied coldly: "If you're talking about the Jag, it's a work of art. And I'd never sell it."

Well, that was exactly what she would tell him about the pearls, she decided: They were a work of art, too! But still, it was all so unfair, she thought, pushing her way through the holiday crowds. Especially considering the fact that Mimi had

spent so much more money than she had: In addition to a $20,000 gold watch for
Zizi, she'd bought a $150,000 diamond necklace for herself, which she had declared
she must have as soon as they'd walked in and spotted it dangling against blue velvet in a locked glass case.

How Janey had *wished* she were married to George instead then, as she stood
next to Mimi agonizing over the pearls. How wonderful it must be to be able to buy
whatever you wanted, to never have to feel like you had to go without . . .

"You never see pearls like this anymore," Mimi had said, motioning to the
attendant to take them out of the case. The pearls were a creamy pewter, and eleven
millimeters in diameter—just large enough to be impressive without looking like
they must be fake. "Not new ones, anyway," Mimi continued, holding the pearls up
to her neck. "These are completely natural—it would have taken years and years to
collect them, especially as they're all the same size. I've always thought that black
pearls were so elegant. You can wear them with anything . . . My grandmother had
a strand that she wore when she was presented in court to Queen Elizabeth . . ."
For a moment, Janey had been afraid that Mimi was going to buy the pearls as well
as the diamond necklace, and she suddenly decided that she *had* to have them.

"They *are* beautiful," she said, holding out her hand to take the pearls from
Mimi. She put them around her own neck, admiring the way the gray pearls were set
off against her creamy skin, and thinking how much better they looked against her
youthful neck as opposed to Mimi's . . . They weren't nearly as nice as Mimi's necklace, of course, but they would do, and aloud she declared, "I'm going to take them."

"Good," Mimi said. "If you can get them for less than fifty thousand dollars,
they're a real bargain . . ."

And so, sitting in the third row of the stuffy auction room, and cutting a sharp
figure in a lace-and-velvet blouse paired with a fine, tight tweed skirt and suede
boots, Janey had raised her paddle again and again, bidding against a nattily dressed
gay man, whom Mimi insisted was probably bidding for the wife of some new billionaire, because new money wouldn't have had the taste to realize the value of the
pearls. Caught up in the fearful excitement of bidding, as the price grew closer and
closer to $50,000, Janey didn't sense the irony of being new money herself and reck-
lessly spending her new husband's new money; all she thought about was how
refined she would look with the black pearls clasped about her neck, and how she
would make love to Selden wearing only the pearls if she had to . . .

"Sold! To the beautiful blond lady," the auctioneer had finally called out—and
Janey had nearly collapsed with the thrill of victory. A gleeful voice in her head told
her that she'd struggled for so long, she deserved to spend money like this, and she
had no reason to feel guilty—after all, there were women like Mimi who did it all
the time . . .

And now, as she strolled up Fiftieth Street, the triumph of securing those pearls for herself was like a rich, metallic taste in her mouth, the taste of money . . . and there was poor Pippi, unable to buy a thing. Admiring the wire reindeer strung with small white lights that decorated the mall on Park Avenue, she suddenly felt ashamed at her attempt to flay Pippi Maus. She *must* try to be more like Mimi, she thought: If she could be more like Mimi, with her calmness, her warmth, and her ability to stand off from other people and assess their motives without getting them all mixed up with her own insecurities, she might be able to handle people better. In a second, though, her admiration for Mimi was touched by the old jealousy: On the other hand, if *she'd* grown up with all of Mimi's advantages in a life where nothing bad had ever happened, it would be easy to be kinder, but she brushed it away. She had no reason to be envious of Mimi now, and besides, Mimi was the only friend she'd ever had whom she'd truly admired.

She reached the corner of Fifty-seventh Street. Looking down the block, she spotted the comforting Burberry plaid on an awning and decided to nip into the store. She'd pick Selden up a little something—maybe a wallet or a key chain. If she came home bearing a small gift, it might divert him from her purchase of the pearls, especially since she never bought him anything.

This reminded her of Zizi, and what Mimi had bought for him, and walking down the block, she thought smugly: Poor Mimi! Janey could never imagine "keeping" a man in any guise—even the thought of having to pay for a man's dinner made her queasy. A few years back, when she was in her late twenties, she'd stupidly allowed herself to go on a "date" with an extremely good-looking aspiring actor, whose biggest claim to fame was that he had appeared in the latest Woody Allen movie. It was a Saturday night, and he had taken her to one of those awful hamburger restaurants on Third Avenue, where they'd had to wait in line for forty-five minutes for a table; then, when the bill came, he'd opened his wallet and embarrassedly declared that he had no money—if she paid, he had said, he promised to pay her back tomorrow. Janey was broke then herself—she had $40 in her wallet meant to last for the next two days—and as she paid the check, she felt like she'd never sunk so low: Not only was *she* a loser, she was dating one as well.

But the story got worse: In an attempt to be gentlemanly (perhaps to "make up" for his lack of cash), he had insisted on walking her home, and then on escorting her up the stairs and into her apartment. Once inside, his personality changed. He tried to kiss her, and when she pushed him away, he shouted at her, calling her a "rich bitch" who thought she was better than other people. That much was true, she remembered thinking at the time—she certainly did think she was better than him. And then, in a sort of pathetic cliché, he tried to date rape her, but his penis was small and he never managed to get a hard-on, and finally, in a fit of rage, he left—

but not before giving her a slap across the face that was so hard it knocked her to the floor.

For the next couple of hours, Janey had stayed in bed with an ice pack on her cheek—she would have been freaked out about her face, but she hadn't had a modeling job in weeks, and didn't have another one scheduled for another two weeks. It was too pitiful, really, to bother to call the police; being a single girl without a regular job, without anyone in her life to even notice her comings and goings, she knew these kinds of things could happen at any time, and that she was responsible for her own protection. But mostly, she was mad about the $40. Paying for his dinner meant that if she wanted to eat the next day, she would have to call up one of her male "friends" and ask to be taken to dinner; if she was really lucky, she might be able to get out of sex by begging off that she was tired . . .

She reached Burberry, where a smiling uniformed guard held open the heavy glass door with a "Good afternoon, miss." As soon as she entered the store, she was reminded of how much she loved shopping in designer stores, where everyone was so cheery and helpful . . . The interior of the store was warm and beige, somehow managing to convey the comfy feeling of being wrapped up in a soft blanket, and looking around for the accessories counter, her eye was caught by a pair of high-heeled, knee-high boots in the Burberry plaid. She was suddenly overcome by a pleasurable excitement that was nearly sexual, and striding over to the boots and picking one up in her hand, she declared out loud: "I *have* to have these!"

A handsome young salesman was immediately at her side; in a voice that contained a wink, he said, "Can I help you, Ms. Wilcox?"

"Oh, yes," she said, her excitement rising at being recognized. "I'm praying that you have these in my size—size nine. If you don't have them, I don't know what I'll do . . ."

The salesman disappeared in search of the boots, and Janey sat down on a beige leather couch, having completely forgotten about Selden. In a few minutes, she was relieved to see the salesman returning with a box, but then she was nearly crushed when he said, "This is the last pair, and I'm afraid they're size eight and a half . . ."

"Don't worry about it, I'll make them fit," she said, removing her shoes.

"I could call around to our other stores," the salesman said. "I think the Los Angeles store might still have a nine . . ."

"But I want them *now*," Janey said decisively. "If I have to wait to get them, it'll spoil the fun."

"I completely agree," the salesman said, nodding.

She unzipped the back of the boot and forced her foot in—there was a little bit of a pinch that she would probably regret after an hour of wearing them—but they might stretch, and she was determined to have them. Wedging her foot into the other boot, she stood up, sashaying across the carpet to a mirror, aware that other people in the store were admiring her and perhaps even coveting her boots . . .

As always when she stood before a mirror wearing something new, she had a fantasy about herself. She imagined she was wearing the boots in some exotic locale (perhaps with palm trees and stark white buildings), crossing the street with an expression of determination and fear on her face . . . She was in danger and alone . . . with a gun in her handbag . . .

And suddenly, in her left ear, she heard a male voice purr, "There is nothing sexier than a woman in boots that are too small." And spinning around, she was annoyed to find that the speaker was Zizi, wearing an expensive chocolate-brown suede coat, and looking just as gorgeous as she'd remembered him from the summer before. What the hell was he doing in Burberry, she thought. But of course—he was obviously buying himself things on Mimi's credit card. With a toss of her head, she snapped, "They're not too small. They fit perfectly . . ."

"I thought I saw an expression of pain in your eyes," he said, giving her an amused smirk.

"That's only because . . ." she said, thinking about her fantasy. Why did he always seem to catch her out in an embarrassing situation?

"Congratulations," he said. "I hear you're married now."

"Oh yes," she said, coldly, walking back to the couch and sitting down. For some bizarre reason he followed her and, as if he had nothing better to do and they were old friends, sat down next to her. "I'm truly happy," she said, "my husband is great . . ."

"Yes, I remember him. Selden Rose. He seemed like a nice guy."

"He *is* a nice guy," Janey said, suddenly irritated by the fact that calling Selden "a nice guy" seemed to somehow diminish him.

"You look well," Zizi said. He stared at her as if he were assessing a piece of horseflesh, and Janey felt herself tingle under his gaze. How was it possible that his mere presence managed to conjure up all the feelings she'd had for him the summer before, and with a slightly trembling hand, she unzipped the boots, distressingly conscious of her feet—she had corns—in their beige panty hose.

"Why wouldn't I be well?" she said, motioning to the salesman. "I'll take these," she said, and then, leaning forward, reminded him in a whisper that she had a thirty percent discount.

She gave Zizi a bold look, daring him to give her grief about the discount, which she got in nearly every designer store as a courtesy for being in the fashion business and for potentially being photographed in the clothes. But he didn't say anything, and she said pointedly: "*You* seem to be having a good time. I keep reading about you in the gossip columns."

He laughed—it was like a Greek statue suddenly coming to life, Janey thought—and replied, "You're one to talk. I see your name everywhere."

"Yes, but . . . ," she began, torn between being pleased that he'd been keeping up with her and wanting to tell him off. What could she say—that she knew he was fooling around on Mimi? But she wasn't even supposed to know about the affair, and given his dismissal of her the summer before, she knew that accusing him of sleeping with other women would only make her sound bitter.

The salesman returned with her boots and her credit card; as she signed the slip she realized that she'd completely forgotten about Selden's present. That would have to wait, she thought, glancing at Zizi—she told herself that right now, all she wanted to do was to get out of the store and get away from him. She was suddenly furious that he'd rebuffed her advances, and standing up, she wondered what his problem was. Perhaps, in his warped Argentinean sensibility, he hadn't found her "good enough." Holding out her hand she said coolly, "It was nice to see you, Zizi."

"Oh, come on," he said, rising slowly as if he had all the time in the world. "I thought you and I were friends."

That was a damn insult, she thought, but if she showed her feelings, he would know that she cared. Tilting her face up to him she said smoothly, "Of course we're friends, Zizi . . ." And in that moment, she suddenly knew what she had to do.

It was an evil plan, but it would show Mimi once and for all the true nature of Zizi's character, she thought, as she opened her purse and rummaged around for her favorite lip color, Pussy Pink. Walking to the mirror, she puckered her lips seductively; catching Zizi's eye, she gave him a questioning look. Sure enough, as she'd known he would, he answered her with a wink.

This was all the information she needed then, she thought grimly, winding down the lipstick with an expert twist. He'd ignored her all summer, but now, away from Mimi's watchful eye, he was practically making a pass at her!

Poor Mimi! she thought again. Like most women, she probably didn't understand how untrustworthy men could be, but Janey knew. All her life, she'd been fighting off advances from men who were "in love" with other women, who were married, who had children, and this harsh truth had shaped her ideas about relationships—was it any wonder she was cynical? Look at what had happened to poor Patty, she thought. Turning to smile at Zizi, she was determined that the same thing wouldn't happen to Mimi; as a friend, she owed it to Mimi to show her the truth.

If she could prove to Mimi that Zizi was unworthy, she would be saving her a lot of future heartache. Besides, she didn't necessarily *have* to sleep with him, she thought, eying his slim physique, and then letting her gaze slide down to his crotch, which was encased in a tight pair of worn blue jeans. But if things *did* get that far, the fact that Zizi would sleep with her best friend might snap Mimi to her senses and cause her to drop Zizi once and for all.

Taking a step toward him, she said casually, "I never see you anymore, Zizi. Are you enjoying my apartment?"

"The apartment is very nice . . ."

"How I miss that sweet little apartment," Janey said, with a sigh. "I have so many memories of the place . . ."

This should have been his cue to ask her over, but instead, he took her bag and, walking her to the door, said, "Which way are you going? Can I get you a cab?"

For a moment, she was taken aback by the ease with which he was letting her go, and she suddenly thought that maybe she'd miscalculated. But she would probably never have another opportunity like this—with Mimi safely on her way to the airport and Selden at work—and biting her lip, she said, "I haven't decided. Where are you going?"

"I'm going to walk home. I love to walk in New York City."

"Do you?" she said, with surprise. "I do, too." There was, in fact, nothing she liked less, having spent most of her early years in New York having to walk because she couldn't afford taxis and was frightened of the subway. But if she had to walk in order to get him to seduce her, she would. "I'm going that way, too," she said. "We can walk together."

They set off up Madison Avenue. He was so tall, and good-looking, and, catching their reflection in a shop window, she was struck by what a perfect couple they made. If she were with Zizi instead of Selden, she thought, how much more glamorous her life would be, for there was nothing the public loved more than a beautiful young couple. They would be invited everywhere, and would probably become part of the young, international jet set, going to parties at Elton John's castle in England and on Valentino's yacht in the South of France . . .

Then she suddenly remembered that he had no money and, laughing to herself, was struck by the fact that all her fantasies about him were just that—fantasies. If they were together, they would probably be living in her apartment, squeezed into four hundred square feet like two mice stuck in a shoe box. *She* would be the one buying him clothes and spending her precious money on $20,000 gold watches, although if he were with her, she thought, glancing up at him out of the corner of her eye, she would make sure he didn't have the opportunity to cheat . . . And suddenly, she was struck afresh by the offensiveness of his behavior: At the very least, he should have the decency to act like a woman, and be faithful to the person who was supporting him . . .

As usual, the conversation between them seemed to have dried up. If she was going to get him into bed, she was obviously going to have to make more of an effort. Matching her step to his, she asked sarcastically, "Exactly what do you do in New York, Zizi? Besides going to clubs, that is. After all, there aren't any horses here . . ."

"I'm about to start traveling for the *patrón*," he said. And then, in a joking voice that contained a trace of sexual innuendo, asked, "Will you miss me?"

This was reassuring, Janey thought; he was clearly one of those men who liked to think that every woman had him on her mind. "Oh yes," she said, nodding her head and taking up his tone. "I'll miss you terribly."

"Good," he said. "Then I will be sure to return to New York."

Ha! she thought. Was he really so stupid that he actually believed she would think he would come back to New York for *her*? Why, they hardly knew each other. But apparently, he couldn't help himself . . .

"Well, whenever you come back, Zizi, you know I'll be waiting," she said. Her tone was bantering, but the look in her eyes suggested that she knew there was something between them—at any moment, she was sure he would make a pass . . .

But instead, he frowned, and looking straight ahead as if there were something that interested him in the distance, he picked up the pace. After a momentary silence, he asked, "Where do you live now?"

"Oh. In a hotel," she said, trying to keep the disappointment out of her voice. "On Sixty-third Street."

"Here we are then," he said courteously. "I suppose this is where I leave you."

She looked up in annoyance and saw that they had indeed reached her corner; across the street was the familiar Roberto Cavalli store, with its mannequins dressed in sumptuous silk and fur dresses; next to her was the newsstand where she bought her magazines. She had to stall for time, and there was no way she could invite him up to her place. Walking to the newsstand, she called over her shoulder, "Do you mind? I just want to get a paper . . ."

She mustn't let him get away, she thought; and yet, the way he was shifting his feet seemed to indicate that he was longing to escape from her. Of course, he would *have* to act like that; to pretend that he wasn't interested . . . After all, she was Mimi's best friend. He was like most men, then: He would pretend to himself that it wasn't his fault; that what had happened was out of his control; therefore, all he needed was an excuse. Pretending to look for a magazine, her eye fell on the *Star*, which was hanging from a clip attached to a string. The banner across the top read: "Rock Star's Wife Breaking Up the Band," and it was yet another installment of the Digger and Patty debacle, which the *Star* had picked up and now followed weekly like an ongoing soap opera. Janey had already read the story, which was about how Patty had gone to meet Digger on tour (true) and was watching him like a hawk, not allowing him to hang out with the other band members (probably not true), but she suddenly saw that she had her solution. Emitting a small scream of shock, she snatched the magazine from the clip. For a second, she felt a tiny bit guilty about using her sister's misfortune to further her own means, but then she justified it by thinking that it was only fitting to use a cheater to catch a cheater.

Her maneuver had its desired effect, and in a second, Zizi was by her side, with his arm around her shoulder as he asked what the matter was. She turned away, and in a voice that was near tears, said, "It's too awful . . . too embarrassing to talk about . . ."

"Hey. Are you going to pay for that?" the proprietor asked.

"If it's so terrible, perhaps you shouldn't read it," Zizi said, pulling her away.

"Oh no. I have to," Janey said, staring up at him with wide eyes. "It's about my sister. My poor, sweet sister, who never did anything wrong . . ."

Zizi's face was filled with concern; without taking his eyes off her he measured out the required change. "Are you okay?" he asked, taking her arm and bending his head down to hers.

She shook her head. "I . . . I think I might faint. I really feel like I should sit down . . ."

"I'll take you to your hotel. It must be right near here . . ."

"Oh no. I *couldn't*," she said forcefully. "It's very stuffy and proper . . . They'll all wonder what's wrong, and then they'll read *this* . . . And then Selden and I might be asked to leave . . ."

"Because of a story in a paper? I doubt that," he said. "What is this paper anyway?"

He was trying to be reassuring, Janey thought, but really, he was just being stupid. Why was it taking him so long to get with the program? Clutching his arm to steady herself, she said, "I'll explain it all later . . . I just need to go somewhere to think . . ."

"I'm sure there's a coffee shop up the street," he said, patting her gloved hand.

"I need someplace quiet . . . where there are no other people around," she said, placing her free hand over his. Looking up at him with plaintive eyes, she asked: "Would you mind if we went back to your apartment? That is, if you're not expecting anyone . . ."

Ten minutes later, she was following Zizi up the dirty narrow stairs that led to her old apartment—a small one-bedroom on the third floor of an ancient brownstone on East Sixty-seventh Street. As she stared at his muscular bottom, she marveled at how well those tried and true methods of female manipulation worked on men, especially, she thought, on a man like Zizi, who wasn't, in her opinion, particularly smart. She knew that nowadays, most women felt they were above using feminine wiles, but Janey had no such scruples, especially when the deployment of these tactics made it almost pathetically easy to get what she wanted. Without thinking about it, Zizi had hailed a taxi and bundled her into it, and during the short cab ride, she'd sat with her leg touching his, as she'd explained what had happened to Patty. He was incensed; striding up the stairs in front of her, he was moving with the purpose of a man on a mission. And then, on the second-floor landing, he suddenly turned around and she almost bumped into him.

His handsome face was slightly twisted in pain, as if the effort of thinking were almost too much for him. "But how do you know?" he asked.

"Know what?" Janey said.

"That he *is* guilty. How do you know that Digger isn't telling the truth? That maybe this girl is lying . . ."

Oh God, Janey thought. She hoped he wasn't going to bang on about Patty and Digger all afternoon; if he did, it might make it really difficult to get him into bed. "Well, Patty certainly seems to believe him," she said, brushing past him in the hope that he would follow her—she had a feeling if she didn't keep him moving, they might get stuck talking in the stairwell—"but then again, she's in love with him."

"But maybe it's something between them," he said, frowning. "It's a private thing, between a couple . . ."

She glanced back at him in annoyance. Was he trying to make a reference to his relationship with Mimi? And giving him an injured look, as if she were personally hurt by his comment, she said, "But that's just the problem. It isn't private. And if the girl isn't lying . . . Well, nobody can know the truth until the baby is born." Turning her head away, she added, "And there's poor Patty. All she ever wanted to do was to get pregnant and have Digger's child . . ."

"Ah yes, that's true," he said dreamily, as if he were thinking of someone else. "For a woman, having a child is the most beautiful thing . . ."

Ugh, Janey thought—there was nothing more off-putting than a man who believed that a woman's sole purpose in life was to breed, but she said, "Oh yes. The *most* beautiful."

They reached the door to the apartment, and turning the key in the lock, he pushed open the door and motioned for her to go through. For a moment, she was startled by how small the place was, and how dismal, and for a second she couldn't believe how long she'd lived there.

Viewed optimistically, it was the starter apartment of a young person who spent as little time at home as possible, and who wasn't terribly successful financially. The living room was a narrow chute with a window at the end, overlooking Sixty-seventh Street; the entire apartment had once been one large room, but had been chopped into two rooms with a galley kitchen and a tiny bathroom that contained a molded plastic shower instead of a tub. There was a shallow fireplace in the living room, but it didn't work and the mantelpiece was constructed of plywood with fake plastic brick tiles glued to the wood—a legacy of the former occupant. Janey had always meant to replace it with a marble mantelpiece, but she'd never had the money when she was living there, and now that she was renting it out, there didn't seem to be any point.

"Do you feel better now? Being back in your old home?" Zizi asked, sliding the fur coat from her shoulders.

"Oh yes. So much better," Janey said.

"I'll make you some tea."

"I'd prefer vodka," Janey said. "A splash of vodka on ice would be nice, with a little twist of lemon if you have it?"

He looked at her curiously, but said nothing; removing his coat and hanging it up in the closet, he went into the kitchen.

Janey moved some papers off the couch and sat down, crossing her legs. The couch was the only decent piece of furniture—it was covered in an expensive red velvet fabric and was a castoff of Harold Vane's. Janey couldn't tolerate disorder and had always kept the apartment tidy, but glancing around now, she saw that it was filled with a sort of boy-mess—the dirty accumulations of a young man who doesn't clean and refuses to put things away. An ashtray filled with old cigarette butts sat on top of the television, the detritus of a long evening spent with a friend; three muddy rubber riding boots were in the corner; a coat and shirt hung over a chair; in front of the window was a folding card table, on which sat a dirty coffee cup. Peeking into the bedroom, Janey saw that the bedclothes were in disarray: a pillow, stripped of its cover, lay on the floor, and the dresser was heaped with clothing. She wondered how Mimi could even come here, and she shuddered to think that this might have been her life . . .

But still, *he* was awfully attractive, she thought, watching him move around the tiny kitchen. He was wearing a black cashmere turtleneck sweater, with the kind of fine, narrow fit that showed off the lines of his chest and was probably designer—Prada or Dolce & Gabbana—when you were young and beautiful like Zizi, Janey thought, a black turtleneck and jeans could take you anywhere.

"There's no lemon," he called from the kitchen.

"I didn't think there would be," Janey responded.

He came into the living room, carrying a tumbler filled with ice and vodka, and as she took it from him, Janey noticed his hands. They were large and smooth—a model's hands, without the knotty joints one often found on slim fingers—and she suddenly wondered what it would be like to have those hands on her breasts.

He sat down on the couch next to her, watching as she took a sip of her drink. "You're feeling better, yes?" he asked. His voice was kind enough, but underneath, Janey sensed a desire to be rid of her, and she wondered why.

"A little," she said, sipping her drink and looking up at him; his answering gaze was slightly perplexed, as if he couldn't quite figure out how she'd ended up sitting on his couch. "Can you excuse me for a moment?" she asked, standing up and going into the bathroom.

She checked her appearance in the mirror, and then looked around. The sink probably hadn't been cleaned for months—there was brown soap scum around the faucet and dried toothpaste in the basin; a can of shaving cream with a missing top sat on a glass shelf, next to a toothbrush with bristles worn down to the nub and a hairbrush filled with blond hairs and lint. She picked up the hairbrush, thinking about the kind of man who had so little regard for cleanliness, and so little self-consciousness, but Zizi was a type of man she wasn't used to. He was younger and poorer, and, she thought, spotting a mildewing towel thrown over the top of the shower door, more natural—the essential male nature still ran strong in him. Most of the men she had been with were groomed and housetrained, like a carefully bred species of civilized dog. The richer they were, the cleaner they became; evidence of the messy and personal was removed (by maids) and their style of lovemaking was goal-oriented and neat. Replacing the hairbrush on the glass shelf, she imagined what Zizi would be like—raw and unfettered and energetic, that his hands and his mouth would be all over her and that he would be dirty enough to stick his tongue inside her and spread her cheeks and lick her asshole . . .

There was a tentative knock on the door. "Is everything okay?" she heard Zizi ask. Looking around in a panic, she spotted *Maxim* magazine on the floor in the tiny space between the toilet and the wall and, bending down to pick it up, she said, "I'll be right out."

It was the December issue, the one with her on the cover, and seeing her own photograph with the narrowed, come-hither eyes and her hips jutting out toward the camera (her waist, hips, and thighs had all been airbrushed and her torso slightly stretched in order to make her appear longer), she suddenly had an idea. She would give him the thrill of his life; she would make the imaginary object of desire real. The power of it made her giddy with excitement. It would be fun and sexy, an experience neither one of them would ever forget. As she removed her blouse and skirt with impatient fingers, she remembered that there were other men for whom she'd performed this same act, in this same bathroom in this very apartment, and how much she enjoyed it. She slid off her panty hose, thinking that it had been a while since she'd indulged herself sexually—the last time had been months ago, in the spring, when she'd gotten slightly drunk ("relaxed" was a better word for it), and had displayed herself across the mantelpiece in the home of a restaurateur; she'd made him lick her pussy from below.

Still, she hadn't had much sex of the type she imagined she might actually enjoy, and the bland kisses and caresses of most men typically left her cold. She experienced a strange disconnection from her body to her brain, and often felt nothing—but the lack of feeling was made up for by the sense of power she gained in arousing a man's sexual passions. She felt she could control men with sex, and the *power* was her turn-on. She loved to see a man losing control under her touch; at times it was so overwhelming, she would have a fantasy of reaching forward and placing her hands around the man's neck, of strangling him and seeing the shock in his eyes; there were moments during the administration of a blow job when she wondered gleefully if the man had any idea how easy it would be to grab a knife and stab him. And there were times when she very occasionally wondered if she would ever lose control . . . but she wouldn't. She never did.

She heard the phone ringing in the kitchen, and Zizi's sharp, slightly accented, "Allo?" Checking her appearance in the mirror again, she wondered if it might be Mimi. But that wouldn't matter. Even if Zizi told her that she was there, they both had a perfectly logical explanation, and this was still, technically, her apartment; there was no reason why she shouldn't make the occasional visit. Of course, she wouldn't tell Mimi right away about Zizi's indiscretion—she would save it for the right moment, when Mimi was already upset with him, thereby hammering home the final nail in the coffin of their breakup. Or, she thought, idly running her hands over her chest and stomach, she might not tell her at all. Her little moment with Zizi might be something she would want to repeat, and consequently must be kept a secret.

"Yes. No problem. I'll meet you in half an hour," she heard Zizi say, and giving herself one more glance in the mirror, she was happy that she was wearing good lingerie that day—a white, lacy push-up demi bra and matching thong panties; on her feet were lavender high-heeled sandals, since it was now considered the height of fashion to wear sandals in the winter, as it implied that you were rich enough not to have to walk. The pearls gleamed around her neck like burnished pewter, and for a moment, she thought of Selden. But *no,* she just wouldn't *think* about Selden right now . . .

She heard Zizi hang up the phone, and then, pulling open the bathroom door with a flourish, she stood with one hand on her hip and the other resting on the doorjamb. In the same sultry voice she used in her Victoria's Secret commercials, she cooed, "I don't think you're going *anywhere.*"

He was standing in the kitchen, filling a glass with water from the tap, and his shock was so great he nearly dropped the glass in the sink. At first, his look was one of confusion, and Janey expected that in the next second, it would change to knowing anticipation. But instead, he took a step backward and, balancing the glass unsteadily on the edge of the sink, asked in horror, "What are you doing?"

"What do you think I'm doing?" she trilled, taking a step toward him. In a second, they were both trapped in the tiny kitchen and he was backed up against the wall; she slid her hand behind his neck and pulled his face down for a kiss.

His lips were stiff and unyielding, but that was probably only due to the surprise of seeing her nearly naked and available. Keeping her back straight, she bent her knees, sliding her hands down his chest as she gracefully sank to a squatting position—looking up at his face, she saw that his expression hadn't altered from a sort of disbelieving shock, and she was anticipating how his face would change when she got her hands on his penis. She snapped open the top button of his jeans, and for a second, her fingers were poised above the zipper, as if in delicious anticipation of pulling the little teeth apart. And in that second, his mouth opened and he emitted a mighty roar.

He might have meant to say "no," but the sound was more guttural than that—it was more the cry of an animal defending its turf. Reaching down, he somehow got her underneath the arms and hurled her backward; she fell sharply onto her butt and toppled sideways, but before she could get up, he was racing toward her like a linebacker, and scooping her up into his arms he rushed toward the couch. Thinking he was overcome with pent-up desire, she wrapped her arms around his neck, and as he tried to throw her onto the couch, she tightened her grip, so that he had no choice but to fall on top of her. Locked in this deathly embrace, she wrapped one leg around him and began nuzzling his neck, as he struggled to break free. Finally, he grabbed her hands and pinned them over her head, sitting on top of her and shouting, "What the *hell* are you doing?"

They were both panting. Janey couldn't speak—she was overwhelmed by the physical feeling of him on top of her. It was violent and luscious; she was already remembering the soft buttery texture of his skin. Her normally latent sexual desire was aroused—it felt as new as if she were a teenager. Twisting beneath him, her only thought was that he must kiss her. She wanted him to take her, no matter what the consequences . . .

He studied her face for a moment, and then, in disgust, shoved her hands away and stood up. "Is that . . . what you do to men?" he demanded, with a sweep of his arm. His upper lip was curled in anger, revealing hard white teeth with pointy incisors. Janey looked at him, wishing that he hadn't broken the moment of passion, but pleased that she'd caused such a reaction. Sitting up, she reached out her hand. "Come on, darling," she said.

He shook his head at her and stalked to the bathroom; he returned carrying her clothes. "Get dressed," he hissed.

She laughed and rolled onto her back. She knew she must look delicious lying on the couch in only her tiny lingerie; giving visual pleasure like this was one of her few sources of self-esteem, and she was still confident of getting him to have sex with her. "What if I don't feel like it?" she asked, languidly tracing a circle in the air with her finger. "After all, it *is* my apartment. I suppose I can do what I like in it . . ."

"Get dressed!" he said, tossing her clothes on top of her.

The indignity of having her clothes flung at her was like a cold slap, shocking her out of her reverie. She grabbed her skirt and hurled it back at him, but she missed and it fluttered weakly to the floor near his feet. She was willing to take everything he had dished out so far, in the name of dangerous sex, but this was an insult. "How dare you?" she cried, jumping to her feet. She flew at him, driven by a sudden, violent emotion, longing to hit him, to smack him across the face. He stepped to the side, grabbing her wrist and twisting it behind her back, and then pushed her away from him.

She stumbled forward, grabbing on to the mantelpiece, where, she saw, he had placed a photograph of an exotic, dark-haired woman, most likely his mother. "What the hell is your problem?" she shouted, wiping her mouth.

"What is *your* problem?" he asked furiously, as if he were the injured party. "How can I make it more obvious that I *don't* want to have sex with you?"

She was so surprised by his answer that at first it barely registered. His lack of interest was not a possibility, she thought, unless he was gay. "That's ridiculous," she said boldly, finding her emotional footing again. "Everyone wants to have sex with me."

For a moment, he looked at her pityingly, as if he didn't find her sexy at all; under his gaze, she felt her confidence drain. "Yes," he said softly. "That's the problem."

He bent over to pick up her skirt; as he did so, she was suddenly full of fear. She wasn't sure what he meant, but his words had the effect of draining the blood from her face. "You wanted to sleep with me . . . this summer," she gasped.

"No." He shook his head, handing her the skirt. "Please," he said. "Get dressed. Don't make this more embarrassing for yourself . . ."

Between them, the skirt hung from his hand like a flag; it was a symbol of her failure and she could not take it from him. She thought he was unbelievably arrogant. She hated him and desired him at once. She felt she must win, she felt driven to come away from this experience with something, no matter what the cost to herself. "You *did* want to sleep with me this summer. Why won't you admit it?" she demanded.

For a second he looked at her fearfully, measuring her anger and her level of craziness. Without taking his eyes off her, he laid the skirt on the couch. "If you don't want to get dressed, I won't force you," he said. "But I'm going out. I have an appointment I must keep."

"With Mimi?" she spat.

"With Harold Vane," he said. "We have the matter of some horses to discuss."

"Horses!" she sneered, followed by a cruel laugh. "So that's it. You prefer horses to women . . ."

"Sometimes," he said, looking her up and down. Then he passed by her and went into the bedroom.

Some small rational corner of her brain told her to gather up the threads of dignity she still had left, to get dressed and to go. But she had reached that irrational emotional point where the only place left to go is down; she would disgrace herself, she would make the womanly sacrifice of her pride and self-respect in the misguided idea that this would somehow make him love her. Years ago, when she was in her early twenties, she'd dated a wealthy young man who had dropped her with no explanation after they ran into his parents at a restaurant, and in a fury, she had filled his Jeep with mud when she'd spotted it parked outside the Conscience Point Inn, a club in the Hamptons. He'd called her insane, of course, but she wanted him to explain his behavior. She'd heard rumors that he'd heard something unsavory about her past, and the not knowing made her crazy, made her want to punish him . . .

And now, watching Zizi move about in the tiny bedroom, she was filled with the same fury. How dare he walk away unscathed? She marched into the bedroom, coming up behind him—he was changing his shirt and his bare, lean, muscled back was in front of her. "I want to know *why!*" she shouted. He turned, grabbing a button-down shirt from on top of the bed and sliding it over his arms.

"That is stupid," he said.

She slapped his arm. "Why did you choose Mimi over me?"

"It wasn't a choice," he said evenly, pushing past her. She followed him through the living room. "Tell me!" she cried. "I won't leave until you tell me."

"There is nothing to tell," he said, with the typical frustrating male obstinacy that drives women crazy. He went to the front closet and removed a tie, then he went into the bathroom to fasten it in front of the mirror.

"What does she have that I don't have?" Janey screamed, flailing at him with her hands.

He had reached that point where she was no longer of interest to him. She had gone too far, but this kind of thing happened to him with women all the time. She was broken now, sobbing in the corner of the bathroom, turning her wet, swollen face up to him and asking, "Why, why, why?"—but for him she was like a dirty wet rag tossed on the floor. He stepped by her and took a cashmere sports jacket from the closet. He put it on, and then slipped a long tweed coat over it. He picked up his gloves from the mantelpiece and when he turned around, she was standing in front of the door with arms and legs akimbo, blocking his exit.

"I won't let you leave until you tell me why!" she screamed hysterically.

He sighed. Why did women always make these scenes? He didn't want to be unkind, but when he treated her like a human being she took it as a sign that he was in love with her. He had been slightly interested in her at the beginning of the summer—for one minute, because she made such a show of herself it was impossible not to look at her and wonder. But he had been informed as to her nature, and he didn't want a woman like that. In a neutral voice, he said, "I will ask you to move away from the door."

"And I will ask you to tell me *why*," she said, defiantly, starting all over again.

He grabbed her by the waist and pulled her away from the door. She tried to grab on to him, so he had to shove her to the side. She took a couple of steps to try to steady herself, and in that moment, he took the opportunity to yank open the door and propel himself into the hallway, slamming the door behind him.

For a moment, he stood taking a breath as he ran his hands through his hair. Then he started down the steps. She wouldn't come after him now, he thought, dressed only in her bra and panties—even she couldn't be that crazy. When he saw her next, she would probably ignore him out of embarrassment over her behavior; he would never tell anyone about the incident and, he guessed, neither would she—it was too shameful and made her look like a fool, and it would ruin her reputation to present herself as a failed seductress. And so, while the matter might never be forgotten, it wouldn't be spoken of, and he was safe, he thought.

But then he heard someone clattering down the stairs behind him. He turned, shocked that she'd been able to get dressed so quickly, and the sight of her sickened him. Her hair stuck out in disarray and she hadn't bothered to button her blouse; her face was grotesquely swollen and her red-rimmed eyes were glazed with anger. This was the real Janey Wilcox, he thought—a shrieking harridan whose true nature obliterated her superficial beauty. His first instinct was to run—but then fury took over. He wasn't an animal who could be forced to provide sex on demand, nor was he under an obligation to provide sex to the multitudes of women who "fell in love" with him because he was beautiful. "Do you want to know why I won't sleep with you?" he shouted. The fact that he was going to answer her took her aback, and she stopped three steps above him.

"Why?" she asked, putting her hands on her hips.

"Because you're a *whore*," he spat. "And I don't sleep with whores."

She took a step forward as if to slap him, but he turned quickly, racing down the stairs as she tripped after him. "You're a fool!" she screamed. "That's a real joke . . . Everybody knows that Mimi is the biggest whore in town . . . She's only with George Paxton because of his money . . ." Finally reaching the entry door, Zizi twisted open the bolt and stepped outside. He looked up and down the street in search of a taxi, and in that second she was upon him.

"Don't think you can get away with this," she hissed. "I'm going to tell Mimi that you tried to seduce me . . . I wonder how you'll feel when your meal ticket dries up. You're the only real whore in this situation . . ."

Adjusting his gloves, he said coldly, "I didn't hate you until that remark." And as he took a step back, a woman's voice said tentatively, "Janey? Janey Wilcox?"

She didn't take her eyes off his face, but immediately underwent a transformation. Her face relaxed and she smoothed one hand over her hair, clasping the top of her fur coat together with the other. With a maniacal smile, she turned and said, "Yes?"

Zizi's only impression of the woman was that she was the sort of blandly pretty blond woman one saw constantly on the streets of the Upper East Side; she could have been anyone, really. The woman was looking at Janey with an expression of eager surprise that slid into perplexity at the realization that Janey hadn't recognized her.

"It's Dodo. Dodo Blanchette . . . ?"

"Ohmigod, *Dodo,*" Janey said.

"I'm not interrupting anything, am I?" Dodo said, looking from Janey to Zizi with an insinuating smirk.

"I have to be going," Zizi said sharply. Seeing his escape, he turned and walked quickly up the street.

Both women watched him from behind. He possessed an indefinable elegance that made him look as if he were too good for her old street of run-down brownstones, and thinking about him that way made Janey want to cry again. She couldn't figure out what had happened or why—all she knew was that she felt a terrible sense of loss, as if something essential had been taken from her, and she was depleted.

"What a *dish,*" Dodo said, as if Zizi were literally something she'd like to eat. "He's gorgeous. If I didn't know better, I would have thought you two were having a *lovers' quarrel!*"

Dodo was one of those nosy kinds of women who was always trying to get information, Janey thought. Her brows were tweezed down to thin rows of hairs that marched over her eyes like a line of ants; her bleached hair was broken off at the ends. But for a moment, Janey was tempted to tell Dodo the whole pathetic story. She had a feeling that Dodo would be sympathetic—until she ran home and told the Splatch Verner crew about Selden Rose's wife. Turning away, Janey realized that, while she longed to speak about it, there was no one she could tell. She had no real best friend, no confidante whom she could trust.

"Oh, Zizi?" she said, in a voice that was too unsteady and too high. "He's my tenant. I was just collecting the rent check."

Dodo appeared disappointed by this information, but she didn't press it. "By the way," she said, "we've decided to go heli-rafting in the Grand Canyon in March and we're hoping you and Selden can come."

Janey was forced into several more minutes of pointless chitchat with Dodo, who was on her way to get a pedicure, and as she finally made her escape, it began snowing. She suddenly became aware of her feet, which were freezing, and the absurdity of wearing sandals in winter . . . She knew she should find a taxi but she was confused . . . she had to get herself together before she could go home, but she wasn't exactly sure how.

Finally, she ducked into a narrow black marble doorway and took out her cell phone. A terrible sense of guilt made her want to call Mimi, to hear her voice—if Mimi behaved normally (and why wouldn't she?), it would be like the whole incident with Zizi had never happened. But it *had* happened, and going over it in her mind—the way he had thrown her to the floor and called her a whore—she cringed with a shame that was like physical pain. He had hurt her—cruelly and deliberately, she thought—he was violent and dangerous. For a moment she hesitated—*should* she tell Mimi?—but then shame became anger, and she dialed her number.

She could tell that the Paxton household was in a state of confusion by Mimi's hurried, "Hello?" She'd just returned from picking the boys up at the airport and they had brought their dog, which had peed on the carpet. "The boys keep asking about you, darling," she said. "Jack keeps wondering when he's going to see you . . . You will come and visit them, won't you?"

"Yes, of course," Janey said, leaning against the wall. She passed her hand over her eyes; she thought she might become sick. She wished she *were* in Mimi's warm, elegant house, which was homier than the one in East Hampton, drinking hot chocolate and playing with the boys . . .

"What did Selden say about the pearls?" Mimi asked, and then shouted to the dog: "Sadie, go to your room! Jack, please take Sadie upstairs . . ."

"He hasn't seen them yet."

"Oh?" Mimi said, distracted. "What did you do?"

"I went shopping. At Burberry . . ." and as soon as she said it, she realized that she'd left her boots at Zizi's. It would give her an excuse to go back there, to settle the score with him. Thinking about it now, she felt that there was something dark and unfinished between them. He had to be punished. He had to suffer for rejecting her, he had to feel the sting of her anger . . .

"Is everything okay?" Mimi asked. "You sound funny . . ."

"Well . . . ," Janey began. She stepped out of the doorway and onto the sidewalk. She was back on Madison Avenue. She passed the Prada store and saw that there was a dress she wanted in the window. She stopped, realizing that Mimi's question was her opening, but suddenly knowing that she didn't have the guts to tell Mimi the whole sordid story.

"Did something happen? With Selden?" Mimi asked distractedly.

"No, Selden's *fine*," Janey said. "It's just that . . ." She didn't know where to begin. Zizi now had secret knowledge of her—would he share it with Mimi? she thought wildly. How often did they see each other anyway, she wondered, thinking if only there were a way to prevent them from getting together . . .

"Is it Patty?"

"Yes," Janey said, with relief. She suddenly saw the solution to her problem. "Patty and Digger are coming back next week . . . I just talked to her and it isn't going well, so I think she's going to need to stay in my apartment for a while."

"Oh. I see." Mimi's voice became less friendly.

"I'm sorry about it, but there isn't anything I can do," Janey said firmly, her confidence increasing. "She's had such a bad time . . ."

"It *is* your apartment, Janey," Mimi said. "Obviously, if you need it, Zizi will have to find someplace else. Although how he's going to find a place the week before Christmas . . ."

"Maybe he can go to East Hampton. He *could* stay in your guest house," Janey said, wondering why she hadn't thought of this lie before. It was going to make it all so *inconvenient* for Zizi, and when Mimi told him he had to move out, he would know why and he would feel her power over him . . .

"Don't worry about it, darling. We'll figure out something." Mimi was suddenly warm again, and for a moment, Janey felt guilty. But then she thought, Why should she? Mimi was rich . . . if she wanted to fuck him so badly, she could put him up in a hotel—if she could find a hotel during the Christmas season. And feeling much better, Janey said, "I just wanted to let you know. Good-bye, darling. Give the boys a big kiss for me."

She closed her phone, thinking triumphantly about how clever her plan was. With George's boys around, Mimi and Zizi might not be able to see each other at all, and then Zizi would have to move out, and then George and Mimi would go to Aspen for two weeks for Christmas. She was safe, she thought: She would pretend that the incident had never occurred, the way she'd pretended so many things in her life had not happened, and everything would go on as before. Then she caught sight of her reflection: She was a fright. Her hair, wet from the snow, was sticking to her head; her skin was mottled. She couldn't let Selden see her like this—he was always studying her and would know that *something* had happened—as it was, he might already be at home, wondering where she was . . .

She ducked into a fancy coffee shop. It was one of those places where they charged customers $10 for a cheeseburger, but the bathroom was clean. She combed her hair and pulled it back into a chignon, fastening it with the bobby pins she always kept in her purse for emergencies such as this, and then she began working on her face. As she dabbed at her skin with pressed powder, her eyes fell on the pearls. With a sigh of resignation, she remembered that she was going to have to do the same seduction number on Selden that she'd tried to do on Zizi—but that Selden certainly wouldn't turn her down.

TEN

THE SPLATCH VERNER building was a large, black, newly constructed marble slab that squatted unceremoniously on the northern corner of Columbus Circle. Five years earlier, Victor Matrick had had the brilliant idea of consolidating all the Splatch Verner companies under one roof, in order to promote synergy, and while the building had been completed on time two years ago, somehow they'd never quite gotten around to finishing the landscaping. The outdoor area was still under construction—to enter the building one had to walk through a maze of plywood walls and scaffolding—and from a distance the building appeared to rise from wooden shanties.

The building was forty-five stories high with eight elevators and a commissary for the regular employees on the third floor. On the forty-second floor was an executive dining room, and on the very top floor, where Victor Matrick had his offices, which included a bedroom and a bathroom with a shower and a Jacuzzi, was an executive-executive dining room, with its own private kitchen and chef, where Victor Matrick had entertained the president of the United States on three occasions.

Selden Rose's office was on the fortieth floor and overlooked Central Park and midtown—from his window he could see the Empire State Building and, on a clear day, the World Trade Center. His office was thirty feet by sixty feet—larger than many New Yorkers' apartments—and contained a heavy mahogany antique desk that he'd splurged on twenty years ago, when he was just starting out, and which had followed him from one job to another as he'd worked his way up the corporate ladder. The office had two doors: One led through to his secretary's office, and another, "secret" one that was always locked went directly out into the hallway, in case the occupant needed to make a furtive escape.

Selden Rose prided himself on being a hard worker, but at five o'clock that day he was standing in front of his window, looking out on the snow that was beginning to fall on Central Park. He kept patting the top of his nappy head, as if to reassure himself that all his hair was still there. His mind was not on his work, which was, in itself, a source of consternation, but on his wife. For he had just taken a call from American Express informing him that $50,000 had been charged to his credit card that afternoon from a well-known auction house. His first thought was that, somehow, the credit card he'd given Janey had been stolen, but then the "nice" woman at American Express explained that the only reason they were checking was because the purchase had been made by Mrs. Selden Rose, and they wanted to make sure that he was, indeed, married.

Goddamn her, he thought. Fifty thousand dollars was a good chunk of a down payment on a house; it was a pool or landscaping; it was a child's private school education (for at least a couple of years, anyway); it was a nanny's salary. At first he'd thought that Janey simply didn't understand about money, but now he was beginning to suspect that she willfully refused to comprehend his situation. Technically, and by nearly anyone's standards, he *was* rich, but he was a salaried man, and most of his wealth was in stock options, which wasn't exactly money in the bank. Nor had that November dip in the stock market helped . . .

He'd tried, too obliquely perhaps, to explain all this to Janey on one of the rare nights when it was just the two of them having dinner at a restaurant, but she had only stared at him blankly, nodding her beautiful head—and then she had seen "someone she knew" and the topic had been forgotten. He should have made her listen—and not have been afraid of her displeasure. But as always, in money matters, she somehow made him uncomfortable: Instead of making him feel like they were partners, she acted (although she never came out and said it) like she expected him to be an endless source of cash, and if he wasn't, she was going to move on. There was always between them an unspoken tension that she might someday leave him, that he wasn't quite good enough, which had the effect of making him want to prove her wrong. And now he was stuck with a $50,000 charge on his American Express card, and he didn't know what to do.

He could pay it, of course, but the bottom line was that it was *his* money, and he ought to be able to decide how he wanted to spend it. And so he went around and around: He could make her return whatever it was she had purchased, but then there would be a scene, and like most men he would rather cut off a finger than have to endure crying and screaming. Or he could simply not mention it, and take back the credit card. But how would he get the card from her? If he asked her for it, again, there would be a scene. He could sneak it out of her wallet, and when she noticed it was missing (which she would, in about a minute), he could say he'd decided to take it back and leave her to figure out why. Or he could do nothing. Which, he thought, with a horrible feeling, was probably what he *would* do.

But that still didn't alleviate *his* feelings, which were that he felt ripped off, robbed, and betrayed. Looking out the window at the wan flakes of snow fluttering slowly from the gray sky, he suddenly wished he'd never met her and that he could be rid of her once and for all. He had a disturbing desire to jump out the window, which was immediately followed by the thought that maybe she would meet with an accident and die, and then he wouldn't have to deal with her and her spending ever again.

His thoughts were interrupted by a leisurely, "Hey Rose," and Gordon White came into the room. Gordon was his second-in-command and privately liked to describe himself as "Rose's loyal henchman," but Selden knew he had been hoping to be promoted to the position Selden now occupied, and would rat him out if ever given the opportunity.

"Gordon," Selden said, as Gordon took a seat in one of the leather club chairs in front of the desk, sitting sideways with his legs draped over the arm like a teenager. Gordon was, in Selden's mind, a typical New York male, meaning that, at the age of forty-one, he was like a big, overgrown adolescent who had never had a serious relationship in his life. The only difference between a real teenager and a man like Gordon, Selden thought, was that Gordon had his own money, his own apartment, and his own Porsche, and no one to yell at him when he came home at two in the morning. On the other hand, he thought, looking at Gordon, who was wearing an expensive Italian black wool suit, maybe the only difference was the *clothes* . . .

"So I hear that Parador deal might be falling apart," Gordon said casually, picking at something in his teeth.

"What's the problem?" Selden asked, distractedly. The name Parador made him think of Comstock Dibble, and that made him think about Janey again.

"There's something funny with the books," Gordon said.

"There's always something funny with the books in the movie business," Selden said dismissively.

"Okay, something *strange*," Gordon said insistently. "I don't know what it is yet, but there's a rumor your friend George might be interested. Supposedly he senses a fire sale."

"That's what George does."

"I hear Comstock's desperate to sell. Before the market goes down again."

"Everyone says the market will recover," Selden said.

"It better," Gordon said, brushing a piece of lint off his trouser leg. "I've got to buy a house in the Hamptons this year."

"Planning on doing some landscaping?" Selden asked, and Gordon laughed. The joke around Splatch Verner was that the dip in the market was the reason the landscaping hadn't been completed on the building.

The buzzer on his phone sounded and Selden picked it up.

"A Mr. Nick Vole is here to see you," his secretary, June, said.

"Send him in," Selden replied.

Gordon stood up, made his hand into a gun shape, and pointed it at Selden. "Hey, don't forget what we talked about, Rose. If your wife has any friends . . ."

My wife doesn't have any friends, Selden thought.

Gordon White left and "the Vole," as Selden had already begun to think of him, entered the room.

His first thought was that the Vole was exactly what he'd expected him to be— he was nearly a cliché. He looked to be in his late forties but could have been as old as fifty-five, with a dyed black handlebar mustache and thinning hair that hung nearly to his shoulders. He was dressed in jeans and a cheap brown leather jacket, but he held himself like a man who knows he's in good shape and can still win a fight, which wasn't surprising, Selden thought, as he billed himself as being a former member of the Special Forces.

He was carrying a manila envelope, which he shifted under his left arm in order to shake hands.

"Selden Rose, right?" he asked. His voice was gruff and unrefined, but Selden had been expecting that, too.

"That's right," Selden said, shaking hands. He motioned to one of the club chairs. "Will you take a seat?"

"Don't mind if I take a load off," the Vole said, sitting down. "Selden's a strange name," he said, taking in the size of the office. His eyes were brown with heavy lids—he wasn't a man who would be easily fooled, Selden thought.

"It's an old family name," Selden said. "Do you mind if we get down to it?"

"It's your dime," the Vole said. "In any case, you're probably going to be happy." He slid the manila envelope across the desk, and Selden had the distinct sensation of suddenly being in a movie—possibly a bad one.

"Oh? Why's that?" Selden asked, raising his eyebrows as he undid the clasp on the envelope.

"Well," the Vole said, sitting back in the chair and folding his hands, "she's got a legal husband, for one."

"Aha," Selden said, removing the contents from the envelope and spreading them out on his desk. There were several black-and-white photographs of Marielle

Dubrosey with an emaciated, evil-looking young man with black eyes and white, pockmarked skin; they were standing on the porch of a dilapidated row house, probably in Brooklyn, and from the expressions on their faces, they appeared to be fighting. Selden held up the photograph with a questioning look.

"That's her legal husband," the Vole said. "Guy named Tim Dubrosey—he works at the Fulton Fish Market . . ."

"When you say 'legal' . . . ?" Selden asked.

"She's passing him off as her brother. At least, that's what she told the landlord where they live."

"Her brother?" Selden said. "They don't look a thing alike."

"Since when was that ever a requirement?" the Vole asked with a shrug. He stared at Selden from under his hooded lids, thinking that, as usual, rich people didn't know anything about the world.

Selden went back to studying the photographs. A dark, grainy picture featured Marielle, her stomach beginning to show a bit, in a tiny G-string and pasties, giving a man a lap dance in a grimy club; the expression on her face was completely blank, as if she were trying desperately to divorce herself from the proceedings, and Selden suddenly felt sorry for her. "My God," he said. "Is she a stripper on top of it?"

"She does the occasional lap dance, but it's all to finance the singing career," the Vole said. "The idea is she's going to be the next Jennifer Lopez and Timmy-boy there is going to be her manager . . . I guess he got sick of the smell of fish."

"So the whole thing's a scam," Selden said. "What is it they want? Money?"

"They want what everyone wants. Fame and fortune. They watch *Entertainment Tonight,* and they think, Why shouldn't that be me, walking down the red carpet?" the Vole said.

Selden patted the top of his head absentmindedly. "That's the problem, isn't it?" he mused aloud. "Everyone wants to be famous, everyone wants to be rich, but no one wants to work for it."

"Sort of like the stock market," the Vole said. He tapped one thumb on top of the other, wondering how much Selden Rose made a year—one million, two million?

The buzzer on the phone went again. "Yes?" Selden asked.

"It's Craig Edgers. He wants to know if you're still on for drinks at your hotel tonight," June said.

"Tell him yes," Selden said.

The Vole stood up. "I've given you a written report, but none of it means that what she's claiming isn't true. She *was* at your brother-in-law's hotel that night, and she did meet him. The thing you've got to understand about women like this is that they have a way of getting pregnant when they need to . . . and of having the right man be the father."

Selden frowned. "Or, in this case, the wrong man."

"Everyone's got to pay the piper," the Vole said.

"How much do I owe you?" Selden asked.

The Vole took a glance around the office again. "Five thousand dollars."

He was being ripped off, Selden thought, as he took out his checkbook, but again, there wasn't a damn thing he could do about it.

Selden Rose scuttled along the plywood ramp that led to Broadway. Puddles were already forming on the sides from the snow and he didn't particularly want to get his shoes wet. On the street, he stopped and took stock of his surroundings. On the surface, everything appeared normal: There was his town car, for instance, parked in its usual spot on the corner of Sixty-second Street, with his regular driver, Peter, sitting behind the wheel drinking a Starbucks coffee; but Selden sensed menace in the air. A police car, siren wailing, wove through the traffic on Broadway while a scruffy young woman in a long black coat glared at him for no reason. The buildings on Broadway looked gray and lifeless, almost Soviet. And suddenly he remembered a day like this one, nearly thirty years ago when he'd been twenty-one and had been sent by his mother to rescue his younger brother from a cult.

As a kid, he'd had fantasies of himself as a comic book hero. He alone was the one who could steal the serum to save his mother's life. In third grade, he had defended his kid brother in a schoolyard brawl, punching a fat bully named Horace Wiley in the stomach—he'd been scared to death, but miraculously, the kid had actually gone down and started crying (they'd called it "blubbering" in those days). He was sent to the principal's office and his mother had to pick him up, but she kept hugging him and trying to kiss him and called him her little Superman, and from then on, that was the tenor of his role in the family—he was the golden son, a serious, shining boy who could always be depended upon to do the right thing and to defend the honor of the family.

This family myth was partly responsible, he knew, for driving him to succeed even as a child—to get the best grades (he was number one in his public school class) and to get into Harvard. His younger brother, Wheaton, faced with such daunting competition, naturally fell apart—when he was fifteen, he was caught selling a joint to a couple of thirteen-year-old girls. His mother always said that Wheaton's problem was that he didn't think he could be as good as Selden, and therefore Selden had to be especially kind to him, but like most young people with raw ambition and a taste for achievement, Selden had very little tolerance for Wheaton's weaknesses, which he considered ingrained personality flaws.

So he wasn't surprised when he received a frantic phone call from his mother in early December of his junior year at Harvard. Wheaton had managed to get into the University of Florida, but no one had heard from him for two months. And then one of his mother's friends, a battle-ax of a woman named Mary Schekel, had taken her yearly trip to New York to watch the lighting of the Christmas tree in Rockefeller Center, and had seen Wheaton on Fifth Avenue (!) in front of Tiffany (!), begging with a small band of Hare Krishnas (!). And he was one of them. He had a shaved head and was wearing an orange robe over a red hooded sweatshirt, and when he asked Mary Schekel for money (he obviously didn't recognize her), she had screamed and said, "Wheaton Rose! You should be ashamed of yourself!" and then Wheaton had run away, followed by the other Hare Krishnas. And Mrs. Schekel had almost had a heart attack.

Selden was in the middle of studying for finals, but it was understood that "this family business" took precedence over everything else, including, possibly, his future. Family was the most important thing in life, and whatever his true feelings might have been, Selden never questioned that he "loved" his mother and father and that he "loved" his brother. To not care about family was heresy; family members were the first people for whom one developed the sympathetic emotions that made you a human being. And so, feeling every bit the grim avenger, he boarded the Amtrak train to New York City on a cold morning in December.

He'd stayed at the Christopher Hotel on Columbus Circle, which Mrs. Schekel had recommended, its selling point being its proximity to Lincoln Center. Looking up the street now as he strode to his car with the manila envelope tucked under his arm, he saw that the hotel was still there and even shabbier now, if such a thing was possible. Dirty green-and-white striped awnings hung in near shreds from the windows, and a neon sign spelled out the name of the hotel. He had thought the neon sign rather grand back then, but now it looked tawdry, like an aging showgirl who refuses to leave the stage.

He reached his car and knocked on the window. Peter looked up but didn't bother to get out of the car, and Selden let himself in.

"What's the weather forecast, Peter?" Selden asked, as he always did, by way of making conversation.

"It's going to snow all night, Mr. Rose. But only a couple of inches. You know what that means."

"Slush in the morning," Selden said. It had been snowing the day that he'd come down to New York from Cambridge, but it had been a heavy snow. It was a Friday, and for some reason, the train was full; he'd had to stand in between the cars. One of the doors hadn't closed properly, and for the entire five-hour journey, snow blew in through the crack. He had stood freezing, with his hands in his pockets, thinking about the task ahead of him. There were eight million people in New York, but he had had that mysterious, almost supernatural power of youth that can will things to happen; it had been impossible to conceive that he might fail.

And then, miraculously, on his second day in New York, he had seen his brother walking up the street with another Krishna. Wheaton had looked frail and his brown eyes had seemed to stick out of his head, and he was still wearing the dirty red hooded sweatshirt. But it hadn't taken much convincing to get him to come with him to the Christopher Hotel, and then the next morning, they had boarded a plane for home and once again he was the hero . . .

He had imagined that he would remember the incident for the rest of his life, but somewhere, in the passage of time, he *had* forgotten about it. Almost completely. He hadn't thought about it for years and years—looking out the window at the traffic stalled between Fifth and Madison Avenues, he couldn't even remember the last time he *had* thought about it. Was it ten years ago . . . or fifteen? His brother was now a lawyer in Chicago, married to his second wife. Did he remember it? Did he think about it from time to time, and wonder at what a fool he was? Or had it completely disappeared from his mind as well? And leaning back in the seat, Selden thought about how astonishing it was, how whole sections of one's life could disappear from memory, as if they'd never happened at all.

And if one didn't remember them, had they really happened? And if they had, what was the point? He thought about what he was like twenty-five years ago— more cynical and angry, and more judgmental (when he finished college and went out to LA, his father had once embarrassed him by saying he had no sympathy for people and should learn some), and so convinced that everything was significant. Life felt big back then, everything that happened felt important. But new things came along and the old faded away. Time and nature devoured everything. Even the hand of death couldn't stay the unraveling of memory, like when someone he vaguely knew died and three days later he would realize that he had forgotten about them as completely as if they'd never been born.

Ten years from now, he wondered, would he remember this moment? This instant right now, sitting in the car, stuck in traffic with a red Santa Claus standing on the corner, ringing his Salvation Army bell? Would he remember that he was angry with his wife for spending $50,000 or that he'd hired a private detective to investigate a paternity claim against his wife's sister's husband? He wouldn't, and suddenly he felt his life disappearing before his eyes. In twenty years, he would retire, and chances were that he wouldn't even have memories to sustain him . . .

He grabbed the manila envelope, overcome by a desire to hold on to something solid. He might not have memories, but in that moment, he would have life, and if he had life, he could be important. He could do things—hell, he was doing things all the time, he was juggling issues and solving problems, which was why his brain had no space left for memories.

He withdrew the photograph of Marielle at the strip club and studied it. Women had babies all the time, but this, he thought, was a travesty. If the child *was* Digger's, he would have his head, he thought angrily. He had assigned himself the role of head of the family, and had acted as a go-between for Patty and Digger, counseling Patty to join Digger on tour and then getting his secretary to make her travel arrangements so she wouldn't have extra stress. Janey had been against it, but Selden felt that he and Patty had a special understanding, and Patty had listened to him. And now this information would be a sort of gift to Patty, proof that she shouldn't give up on her marriage. Though he himself was divorced, Selden still believed in the sanctity of marriage, in its ability to challenge the human being to grow to greater levels of love and understanding; and when he reached the Lowell Hotel and exited his car, he was feeling very much the hero again.

His first instinct was to tell his wife. As he turned the key in the lock and entered the foyer, he waited for her usual trilling "Sel-*den*?" But there was no sound from the interior of the hotel suite, and, feeling slightly miffed and let down, he went into the living room.

He tossed the manila envelope onto the writing desk and removed a cigarette from a small silver box on the mantelpiece. As he sank onto the chintz sofa, he suddenly realized he was bored without her. She had her flaws, and their marriage, as yet, certainly wasn't perfect. But Janey herself was interesting, and he was never quite certain what she would do next.

Sometimes when he came in, he'd find her in the shower, sleepily soaping her magnificent body, and he knew that she had been napping or lying in bed and had jumped in the shower when she'd heard him come in, in order to hide her laziness. He also knew that she thought she was fooling him with her ruse, but it seemed like such a funny thing to be embarrassed about that he never had the heart to catch her out. And if she wasn't in the shower, she would usually call out to him from the living room, where he would often find her with one of the classic books in her hand, and Mozart or Beethoven on the stereo. It was another of her obvious attempts to impress him with what she wasn't yet or what she wanted to be, or thought *he* wanted her to be, but he found it charming that she wanted to make an effort for him, even if her efforts were mostly pretense.

Marrying Janey would either turn out to be a gorgeous mistake or a beautiful triumph, he thought, but for the moment, he had to admit that he was still in the honeymoon phase of his second marriage. There were things about her that annoyed him, but there was still plenty to find amusing: From her shockingly beautiful face that was just on the wrong side of classic, to her frenetic attempts to please him in bed, to her unabashed delight in her new status. He had to admit that it *did* satisfy his ego to be able to provide her with a happiness in life that, he imagined, had always eluded her—until she had met him.

He stood up, suddenly in need of movement. The fact was, he thought, rather pleased with himself as he walked to the window, there weren't many men who could "handle" a woman like Janey Wilcox, and, he imagined, she had suffered unfairly for it. She had what he liked to think of as an idiot savant's unerring judgment when it came to human beings, combined with a courtesan's skill of manipulation. To him, her manipulations were enchantingly obvious, but he imagined that for most men, consumed with their egos and places in the world, they were not. Even the most sophisticated man could easily be swayed by her outward charms, but confusion and anger usually set in after a short period of time, when the man understood that those charms were simply part of a greater scheme.

But other men, he thought, glancing down at the snow, which was beginning to fall steadily, were not his problem. Indeed, he could even think that he was *their* problem, for he was the one who had carried off the prize . . .

He looked at his watch—it was past six-thirty. He wondered, with a touch of amusement, if some misadventure had delayed her, and then he was struck by the thought that perhaps she was afraid to come home, afraid that he would be angry about the $50,000. Well, he wasn't angry about it anymore, and now he was beginning to worry. Craig Edgers would be arriving at any minute, and he wanted her to be there . . .

He dialed her number, but her cell phone went immediately to voice mail, and he suddenly felt guilty. Was it possible that some instinct told her that he was planning to use her a little, and had caused her to stay away? He knew that her sometimes inappropriately high regard for herself would take high-handed offense at being regarded as an object, to be trotted out like a dumb racehorse. But on this particular evening, her potential displeasure was overridden by his selfish desire to show her off a little in front of his old friend.

Craig Edgers had been Selden's roommate during their last two years at Harvard, and even though they'd pretty much lost touch in the past few years, Selden wasn't surprised when Craig had called him the week before, ostensibly "wanting to catch up." Craig had read about his move to MovieTime in the business section of the newspaper, and about his marriage in the gossip columns, and he'd confessed that he'd always wanted to meet a Victoria's Secret model. Selden couldn't resist the idea of showing off Janey to Craig, and had invited him and his wife for a drink. But Craig had immediately said that he'd prefer to come without his wife, Lorraine, which, Selden understood, would allow him to gawk openly at Janey without fear of retribution. Nevertheless, he thought, it was an indication of his *own* collusion in the subterfuge that he had deliberately "forgotten" to mention to Janey that his old college roommate would be dropping by.

Sitting on the couch, he noticed that a book lay sprawled open facedown on the coffee table, like a woman abandoned after sex. The book was an expensive hardcover edition of Plato's *Republic;* next to it was the pink, girlish highlighter Janey used to underline passages that stirred her mysterious emotions. In a protective gesture, he picked up the book and folded the highlighter inside it. Normally, he wouldn't have minded if she'd left the book out for days, but its prominent display on the coffee table coupled with the telltale pink highlighter was just the sort of obvious stab at intellectual pretension that Craig would pinpoint and deride mercilessly.

Selden looked around for a place to hide the book, and chose the drawer in the little writing table. The drawer was filled with papers—scraps of notepads with phone numbers and doodles, bills, empty envelopes, and a couple of official-looking letters—but he squished the book on top and shoved the drawer closed. With the book out of sight, he felt better, knowing that if Janey tried to engage Craig on an intellectual level, Craig wouldn't hesitate to destroy her, stripping away her ideas with the precision of a surgeon's knife.

Craig Edgers was one of those men whose only satisfaction in life came from his unshakable belief that he was vastly superior in intellect to the rest of the population. All he had ever wanted to be was a "great novelist"; even as a student, he'd possessed a bitter envy toward everyone else's work, which seemed to be the burden of the "unrecognized genius." He'd been poisonous after graduation, when Selden had moved to LA and immediately landed a job finding material for a famous producer. In his first week, Selden had discovered the book *Discarded Land,* which became a multimillion-dollar movie, securing Selden's place in the entertainment business and earning him his first $100,000; meanwhile, Craig had moved to New York and taken a low-paying job as a fact checker for *The New Yorker.* In the intervening years, Selden's star had continued to rise, while Craig had struggled. Despite publishing numerous essays and writing three novels—and being considered "a promising literary talent" in the small circles in which such things mattered—Craig's work had gone largely unnoticed.

But all that had changed in the last three months, when Craig had published his great tome, *The Embarrassments,* in September. The book had immediately jumped to number one on the *New York Times* best-seller list, and Craig was being lauded as the next Tolstoy. He was on talk shows and panels, and his picture was everywhere—although Selden suspected it was an old photograph, probably taken years ago when Craig was still in his thirties.

The buzzer sounded and Selden told the doorman to send Craig upstairs. He stood by the door in curious anticipation—this would be, he thought, the first time he had seen Craig as a success, and he wondered how it might have affected him. In a moment there was a knock, and Craig came in, reeking of cold air and cigarettes. He was, Selden thought, greeting him with a bear hug, as badly dressed as ever, but he was now about thirty pounds overweight.

Craig wandered casually into the living room, taking a look around.

"Jeez, Rose," he said, with an underlying sneer that after twenty years of struggling for recognition had probably become a permanent part of his verbal repertoire, "I thought you were a big deal now. I didn't expect to find you living in a hotel."

"And I thought the whole point of becoming a successful novelist was to be able to dress like you weren't an unsuccessful one," Selden said.

"Yeah, well, you always had the touch, Rose, I didn't," Craig said, plopping onto the couch and struggling out of a worn, tweed overcoat. "There's a goddamned blizzard out there."

"What can I get you?" Selden asked. "Vodka okay?"

"Lorraine will smell it on my breath, but what the hell. Did you ever think you'd end up marrying your mother?"

Selden laughed. "I had one mother; that was enough."

"Hence the ten-years-younger supermodel, huh?"

"That's right," Selden said evenly, thinking it was too early in the evening to let Craig get his goat.

"Sure," Craig said, scratching his hair, which, Selden saw, needed a wash. "By the way," he asked, "do you ever hear from Sheila?"

Selden stiffened. "She remarried on the day the divorce papers came through." He went into the kitchen and poured vodka over two glasses of ice, thinking the last thing he wanted to talk about was Sheila and the reasons for the demise of their marriage. "Hey Edgers," he called out. "Now that you're finally successful, aren't you afraid of losing your edge?" He walked back into the living room, handed Craig a glass, and raised his own in a toast. "You know, money and fame have a way of making you forget how awful the world really is . . ."

"Tell me about it," Craig said mournfully. "I spend half my day trying to remind people how much they're supposed to hate me, because they're all so fucking stupid and I'm so fucking smart. But everyone agrees with me now, except for Lorraine. Every day she tells me that even though my book has been on the best-seller list for three months, I'm still an asshole."

"Some things never change," Selden said.

Craig buried his nose in his drink, and when he came up for air, said, "I've got to hand it to you, Rose. I know I shocked the shit out of people when I wrote a best-seller, but I think your marriage trumps it."

Selden smiled, taking a seat in the armchair. "I've always been one step ahead of you, Edgers."

"It's driving everyone crazy," Craig said. The alcohol was warming him up to his subject, and he continued: "They're all talking about it. The men are jealous as hell, and the women are going crazy. They think if Selden Rose can marry a super-model, so can *their* husbands—and the men agree. I've even found myself looking at Lorraine these days, wondering what it would be like to . . ."

Selden laughed and took a large sip of his drink. Craig, he thought, was even more odious than he was in college, for he now had the veneer of a dirty old man about him. "Don't kid yourself," he said, with a false smile, wondering how quickly he could get rid of him. "You sound like every other slob out there in America: You see these girls on TV, and you think that access is the only reason you're not with one . . . It's like a three-hundred-pound man thinking he can ride a racehorse."

"Don't give me any ideas," Craig said bitterly.

"Besides," Selden continued, leaning back in his chair and crossing his legs, "I thought you and Lorraine were doing great. All your interviews refer to your happy six-year marriage . . ."

"We're fine," Craig conceded. "As fine as two people who were once madly in love can be. But seriously, who doesn't think about being with someone else? And especially about being with the girl in the ad. It's the driving force behind the obsession of the consumer-oriented male: woman as product."

"I'm sure Lorraine wouldn't agree," Selden said, thinking about Craig's wife. Lorraine was a short, energetic woman with frizzy blond hair who was militant about controlling all aspects of her life, including which way the toilet paper rolled.

"Only because she couldn't *be* a product," Craig snorted.

"Well," Selden said, unable to disagree with this assessment. "Thank God, *you* can."

"I'm resisting," Craig said, his voice laden with sarcasm, as Selden suddenly remembered reading recently that Craig had had offers to buy his book for a movie, but was so far holding out. "I still have some artistic integrity left. Unlike you," he said. He removed a pack of cigarettes from the tweed overcoat and placed them on the table, as if he intended to stay for a while. "But it seems we've both become clichés: I'm a best-selling author who's trying to hang on to his artistic integrity, and you're a Hollywood mogul married to a blond bimbo."

Selden was stung. He knew that Craig's idea of humor was to make the aggressive, cutting remark, but this, he felt, was going too far. It was one thing to insult *him,* he thought, but another to insult his wife. Banging his glass down on the coffee table with a derisive laugh, he said, "I'll admit that *you're* not quite as bright as Janey, but she's at least as intelligent as Lorraine."

"But is she as complicated?" Craig asked, pointing his finger at Selden in triumph, clearly enjoying the effect of his words. "Lorraine might not be a beauty, but at least she has something going on in her head. I mean, you see these girls and you think, 'I'd like to sleep with that, but I don't want to have breakfast with it in the morning.'"

"A more jealous sentiment has never been better expressed . . ."

"Give me a break, Rose . . ."

"And there comes a time in every man's life when he begins to understand the value of sweetness . . ."

"Come on," Craig nearly shouted. "You sound like a perverted old English don. All I want to know is, do you have anything to talk about? What *do* you talk about? Or is it completely dull, except for sex . . . ?"

"Dull?" Selden asked. "*Sheila* was dull." And he gave Craig a look that implied he thought Lorraine was dull as well.

At that moment he heard the key turn in the lock and the door open and shut. And then there was the sound of Janey's trilling "Sel-*den* . . . ?" as she entered the foyer. Selden sat up proudly, suddenly reminded of how pleasant her beautifully round, musical voice was, and wondered if Craig had noticed it as well. "My wife's home," he said, glancing over at him. Craig was staring straight ahead, like a child who is determined "not to look," and as he raised his glass to his mouth, Selden saw that his hand was shaking ever so slightly. Why, he's as nervous as a schoolboy, Selden thought triumphantly, as he called out, "We're in the living room . . ."

She suddenly appeared in the doorway, silhouetted in the bright light from the table lamps, and, with the riveting self-consciousness of an actress entering a room in a play, she paused for a moment, and then slowly removed her fur coat, revealing her perfectly curved figure. He noted with pleasure that she was dressed expensively, with that particular style that's both sexy and ladylike, and she took a step into the room, her lips pushed out into a question. "We . . . ?" she asked.

"A friend of mine from college."

"Oh!" she said. She looked taken aback; he knew her well enough to see that she wasn't quite herself. Her energy seemed scattered; there was a nervousness about her and a chill, almost as if she were undecided about being there. Her face was slightly puffy, and he wondered if she'd been crying. And then she took another step into the room and he thought he spied the cause: The thick strand of gray-black pearls that glowed around her neck. So that was what she'd spent his money on! Even from a distance he could see that they were magnificent, probably worth the price. The poor thing must have been scared to death to tell him, and that's why she'd been crying . . .

He stood up as she hurried across the room to him. "I'm so sorry," she said, turning her face up for a kiss. "I've had the most ridiculous day. I thought I had a pimple so I went to the dermatologist, and actually agreed to let him do a light peel. Can you believe that?" She kissed him on the lips, lightly stroking his hair, and then turned to address Craig. "I know it sounds silly, but that's what it's like being a model. You become obsessed with the tiniest little flaw—and then you have nothing else to talk about. It's no wonder people think models are dumb!" And holding out her hand, she said, "I'm Janey Rose, by the way."

It was a charming display, and one not lost on Craig. He stood, and taking her proffered hand, actually bent over and kissed it.

"This is Craig Edgers, my darling. He was my roommate in college. I thought you might like meeting him," Selden said, thinking it was clever of him to position it that way, rather than telling her that Craig was only there because he wanted to meet a Victoria's Secret model.

"Craig Edgers?" Janey said, looking from Craig to Selden. "Selden," she scolded. "Why didn't you *tell* me you knew Craig Edgers?" And then, in a tone of blatant flattery that was almost embarrassing, she said to Craig, "*You* are a great writer. I've read all of your books, even before you became a best-seller. I think you're a genius . . ."

On the one hand, Selden thought, he had to hand it to her: This was the last reaction Craig Edgers had ever expected, and it showed. His aggression, always just under the surface, had shriveled like a cold penis, and Selden could suddenly see why he clung to it so fiercely—without it he was reduced to a fumbling nerd. He made a motion as if to push a pair of glasses up onto his nose, but remembering that he had replaced his glasses with contact lenses, rubbed the bridge of his nose instead. "Well," he said. "You're not in the minority there, at least not now!" And Janey said, "I'm so happy for you. It must be wonderful when everyone else finally realizes how talented you are!" And Selden added quickly: "Don't give him too much credit, Janey. If you'd known Craig for as long as I have, you'd probably just think he was annoying . . ." At which point both Janey and Craig looked at him like he was a stranger who had suddenly interrupted their tête-à-tête.

"Selden," Janey said sweetly, "would you mind getting me a drink?"

"Sure," he said. He wandered into the kitchen, thinking, *On the other hand . . .* But on the other hand, what? Was he envious? Of Craig Edgers? Was that what he was feeling? If he hadn't known better, he would have been under the impression that Janey was trying to seduce Craig. That intense way she had about her, of focusing all her energy on a person—he had thought that was reserved only for *him*. But maybe, he thought, pouring vodka into a glass and adding some orange juice, it *was* for him. Maybe this whole display was for his benefit—naturally, she *would* think that he wanted his old college roommate to like her; still, he didn't see that it was necessary for her to make Craig fall *in love* with her.

It was just such a surprise, he thought, to discover that his wife had been nursing a secret, ten-year obsession with the works of Craig Edgers. But even now, now that Craig was getting the popular attention he'd always craved, Selden still couldn't understand the hoopla over Craig's "lyrical" writing talents. Craig had sent him his first two books and several short stories over the years, hoping to interest Selden in purchasing them for the movies, but Selden had found his work pretentious and navel-gazing. He would never say that to Craig's face, but he had no problem telling other people on the few occasions when Craig's name had come up in conversation.

But maybe he was being too severe about Craig's talents. Maybe this harshness arose from jealousy. Picking up Janey's cocktail, he reminded himself that he had no reason to be jealous of Craig's work; after all, on the final scorecard—money—he was so far ahead, Craig would never be able to catch up. No, he was annoyed because the simple truth was that Craig wasn't a great writer, and he couldn't believe that his own wife didn't have the intellect or the discernment to realize it.

But that was vicious, he thought, forcing himself to smile as he handed Janey her cocktail. Janey wasn't educated; she'd barely finished high school. It wasn't fair to expect that kind of perspicuity from her. But as she took her drink, barely looking at him, he shuddered inwardly. She was perched on the edge of the couch, staring at Craig with adoring eyes. "But that's outrageous," she was saying. "Don't they understand the value of the writer? Who knows the work better? . . . Who knows more what it *should* be, understands its inherent meaning . . . ?"

He had to put an end to this conversation, he thought, taking a seat on the armchair across from them. He'd heard those very words from the mouths of his "intellectual" friends, and knew that she and Craig were having the usual conversation about the indignities suffered by the author in Hollywood. But somehow, hearing those words coming from her mouth devalued those opinions and made them seem trite. "Come on, darling," he said, sharply. "I'm sure Craig's had this discussion often enough . . ."

She turned to him with an expression of hurt pride, and he suddenly felt guilty. Who was he to control her conversation? And yet, it was just so disconcerting to hear these uninformed opinions coming out of her mouth and to see Craig greedily eating them up, for the sole reason that a pretty girl was finally paying attention to him. If only Janey would save her intellectual precociousness for him, he thought. At least that way he could guide her opinions . . .

Craig must have caught a whiff of his discomfort, because he leaned against the side of the couch and folded his arms in amusement, nodding at Selden. "So far, you're right about everything, Janey," he said. "But you should be directing your complaints to your husband. He's partly responsible for the state of entertainment today."

"You're giving me way too much credit," Selden snorted.

"But Selden," Janey said, her voice rising slightly in outrage, "you are in a position to do something. Did you know that one of the people who's bid on Craig's new book is Comstock Dibble?"

"He knows what he's doing."

"But Comstock Dibble?" Janey said. She turned to Craig. "Did you know that his father was a plumber? And he got his start by selling pornographic videotapes? I mean, what does he know about art?"

Selden laughed and idly stirred the ice in his glass. "That's just a rumor," he said, playing devil's advocate. "If Comstock Dibble wants to buy Craig's book, I'm sure he'll do a good job with it."

"But he doesn't want Craig to write the screenplay," Janey said.

"He's smart, then."

"Oh Selden," Janey sighed. "How can you not ask a brilliant writer to write the screenplay from his best-selling book?"

Selden stared angrily from Janey to Craig. He suddenly felt as if he might lose his temper, and knew if he did, he would certainly lose face. The reason why Comstock, indeed, why *no one*, would want Craig to write the screenplay was that Craig's work didn't contain any discernable plot, and as painful as that was for the artiste to comprehend, movies were all about plot. But if he entered into that kind of discussion with Craig now, Craig would never leave, and Selden suddenly wanted him gone. "Well," he said slowly, swirling the ice in his drink, "maybe Craig should be happy that someone wants to buy his book. They're hardly buying anything in Hollywood right now."

"That's a bunch of crap, Selden Rose, and you know it," Janey cried out. Glancing at Craig, she said, "That's what Hollywood people always say and you know it's a lie." She lowered her eyes and, completely changing her tack, stared up at Selden seductively. "You're *so* brilliant, darling . . . I told Craig that you should buy his book and turn it into an original movie for MovieTime!"

This was delivered with the confident presumption that here was an idea Selden was unlikely to think of himself, and Selden stared at her in surprise. She really was different tonight, he thought. Until that moment she had always been content to take a backseat when it came to his business discussions—she listened, and, he believed, learned, but she never made an actual suggestion herself.

"Well, what do you think, Rose?" Craig asked.

"I think I have to think about it," Selden said stiffly.

The two men locked eyes, like opponents about to engage in a fight, as Janey suddenly stood up, emitting a twittering laugh like that of a gay little bird. The effect, Selden noted with slight annoyance, was to immediately divert both his and Craig's attention back to her.

Conscious of their eyes on her, she crossed the room and slid into the armchair with Selden, so that she was practically sitting on his lap. He shifted his hips to the side to make room for her, thinking that it was about time she paid some real attention to him. He caught Craig's eye and, without betraying any emotion, smiled. Craig nodded slowly, his mouth turned down in a sour expression, as if he suddenly realized that he'd been cheated, although he wasn't sure why. But Selden understood: Craig had believed that Janey's intimate attentions had meant something; that she was actually interested in him, but now he saw that Selden was the only one she *really* cared about . . .

"Have your agent send me your book," Selden said, thinking that as order had been restored to his universe, he could afford to be generous.

Craig picked up the hint and stood up. "I guess I should be going. Lorraine will have the dogs out."

Janey rose languidly, as if her mind and her body were already occupied elsewhere, and held out her slim hand, leaning forward to kiss Craig on each cheek. "We will see you again, won't we? I'd love to have dinner, just the four of us, including your wife . . ."

As if reminded of the social gulf between the two couples, Craig said, "Oh, Lorraine hardly goes to the kinds of restaurants I'm sure Selden takes you to . . ." and Janey impulsively took his arm.

"Don't be silly," she said warmly, walking him toward the door while glancing back at Selden. "If we had our choice, we'd probably eat at hot dog stands. Isn't that right, Selden?"

And Selden, feeling a sense of relief, as if some unnamed danger had passed, said, "Sure . . ."

When the door had closed behind Craig, Selden turned to Janey and pulled her to him. "Sorry," he said, with a knowing laugh. "Craig is such a crashing bore. He hasn't changed a bit since we were at Harvard together." He expected her to agree with him, but instead she drew back and slipped out of his grasp, wandering toward the living room.

"Boring?" she said hesitantly. "I didn't think he was boring at all. In fact, I thought that was one of our more interesting evenings."

"Did you?" he said, genuinely surprised. He was again reminded of their difference of opinion regarding Craig's work, and he frowned. "Well, he certainly seemed to like you . . . and Craig doesn't like anybody."

"Well!" she said, with a little laugh. She crossed the living room to the window, looking down on Sixty-third Street. "I wish . . ."

"Yes?" he said.

She turned, leaning against the windowsill as if she were suddenly weary. "I just wish we spent more time with people like Craig. He's so smart . . . and has such a real understanding of life . . ."

"Ha," he said dismissively, suddenly bored with the topic of Craig Edgers. He picked up the manila envelope from the writing desk, and took a seat on the edge. "In any case, we've got much more important things to discuss. I hired a private detective . . ."

At the words "private detective" she looked at him in horror, and he wondered what was going through her mind to make her so frightened. He held up the manila envelope and shook it. "This contains some astounding information . . ."

"On what?" she cried.

He looked at her, not comprehending her reaction. "On Patty and Digger," he said. "You're going to be very pleased with me. It turns out that Marielle Dubrosey is married . . ."

Janey looked at him in astonishment, relief flooding her face. "She is?"

"It's great news," Selden said confidently. "It means that the baby probably isn't Digger's . . ."

He thought she would be thrilled with this information, but she suddenly frowned and turned back to the window. "Oh," she said. "But I thought . . ."

"Should we call Patty now and tell her?" he asked. "I thought we might do it together."

"Oh no," she said, taking a step toward him. "It'll be late in Europe . . . past midnight, and . . ." She bit her finger, as if to stop herself from crying.

Her gesture released his tender feelings for her, and he stood up, taking her in his arms. "What is it, my darling?" he asked. "I thought you'd be pleased. You should have seen this private detective, he was exactly like something out of central casting . . ."

"It's nothing," she said, turning her head away. "It's just that I told Mimi that Zizi had to move out so Patty could move in . . . I thought she and Digger weren't getting along, and now Mimi will be angry with me . . ."

"But why should Mimi care where Zizi lives?" he asked, turning her face toward him with his hand. "You're not saying . . ."

"Oh God, no!" Janey said vehemently. "They're just friends . . ." She took a step back, covering the pearls with her hand.

He laughed, thinking he suddenly understood the source of her behavior. "You're frightened, aren't you?" he asked, and she nodded. "Frightened that I'm going to be angry about the pearls . . ."

Her eyes suddenly grew wide and filled with tears. "I couldn't help myself," she cried. "Especially with Mimi buying a diamond necklace for a hundred and fifty thousand . . ."

"Can I at least see what I bought you?" he asked, pulling her hand away from her neck. She stood uncomfortably, tilting her head back slightly and arching her neck, like a little girl who knows she's about to be punished and is determined to maintain her dignity.

He touched the pearls with his finger and then drew her toward him. "I'll tell you what," he said, whispering in her ear. "I'll let you keep the pearls, if you promise to look at that house in Connecticut . . ."

For a moment, her eyes darkened as if she'd been unexpectedly thwarted. But then she sighed and nodded. And he would have been perfectly happy with her response, he thought, if it weren't for the completely blank expression on her face.

That Janey Wilcox could really be quite a bitch, Mimi thought angrily, pulling on a pair of short suede boots with beige mink cuffs. She heard the maid moving about in the bedroom, and she called out to her.

"Yes, Mrs. Paxton?" Gerda asked, sticking her head in the doorway of the dressing room.

"Are the boys settled for the night? I have to go out to meet Mr. Paxton."

"They're playing on the computer," Gerda said.

"Good," Mimi said. She picked up a multicolored snakeskin Fendi purse, checking to make sure it contained a tube of lipstick and a comb. "We probably won't be back for a couple of hours, so make sure the boys get to bed."

"Very good, Mrs. Paxton," Gerda said, wondering at Mimi's sharp tone.

Mimi strode down the hallway and through the living room to a foyer, which led to another hallway, at the end of which were the maids' rooms and two small bedrooms for George's children. She poked her head into one of the bedrooms: Georgie and Jack were huddled in front of a brand-new state-of-the-art computer, like two small (well, one small and one very large, she thought) animals crouched in front of a fire; they barely looked up when she entered. "Good night, boys," she said. "Your father and I will be home later, so don't wait up."

"G'night," Jack mumbled. For a second, Mimi wondered if she should make the motherly effort to kiss them good night, but Georgie's slightly hostile expression deterred her, and she closed the door with a small bang, suddenly reminded of how much the boys seemed to love Janey.

Goddamned Janey, she thought, removing a sable coat from the front hall closet and slipping it over her shoulders. On the surface of things, it wasn't her fault that her sister needed a place to stay, but Mimi suspected some kind of subterfuge. It wasn't *what* she had said but the *way* she had broached the topic—without warning and with a superior tone in her voice, as if she had wanted revenge for something Mimi had done. Mimi couldn't imagine what she was getting at, which potentially placed her in a position of weakness, and so she had backed off.

But it was all so damn inconvenient, she thought angrily, entering the elevator. The elevator man smiled at her, but instead of chatting with him, as she usually did, she merely nodded. In two weeks, she and George were leaving for Aspen, and she supposed she could try to put Zizi up in a hotel, but that would increase the possibility of getting caught. The beauty of Janey's apartment, even though it was absolutely rank (the first time she'd seen it, Mimi had been shocked that Janey had lived there and she imagined her as a phoenix who rose from the ashes of her dingy apartment every night), was that it was discreet: There were no doormen to take notice of her comings and goings, and the other residents of the building were too old or too poor to possibly know who she was. Well, she would figure something out, she thought fiercely, pulling on her gloves as she crossed the lobby. And in the meantime, she would punish Janey a little, by pretending to be too busy to see her, so she understood she wasn't ever to use that high-handed tone with her again . . .

The doorman held open the door, and she stepped outside. It was snowing quite hard now, but Fifth Avenue had a wonderfully hushed quality and the softened streetlights shining into the blackness of Central Park created the feeling of an enchanted forest. She started forward, meaning to get into her car, but she suddenly heard someone call out her name, and recognizing Zizi's voice, nearly jumped out of her skin.

For a second, she stood stock still, and then, realizing that she was completely visible in the bright light coming from the lobby, quickly moved to the side of the building, into the darkened area by the bushes. Zizi was covered with a heavy dusting of snow, as if he'd been waiting outside for a long time, and she immediately knew that something was terribly wrong.

"What's happened?" she asked in a stage whisper, longing to brush the snow off his head but knowing that any gesture she made might be observed and duly noted by the doormen.

"I have to talk to you," he said. The expression on his face was angry, as if he'd suffered a great insult and was holding her responsible.

"We can't talk here," she said, glancing around nervously. "Can't I see you tomorrow?" she pleaded. And then added, "I have to meet George . . ."

"That's always the problem," he said, disgustedly. And in that moment, she knew he was going to break up with her.

She took a few steps down the block, as if to lead him away from danger. "Please, darling," she said reasonably, knowing the only way to prevent the situation from exploding was to remain calm. "Let's talk about it tomorrow. I'll come to you after lunch. Around two perhaps . . ."

He shook his head stubbornly; she could see that his mind was made up. "We mustn't see each other anymore," he said, with devastating simplicity. She had known that this might happen eventually, but she took a step back, feeling like her insides were crumbling, aware that she mustn't make a scene, and that she wouldn't be able to sway his decision. Zizi was young and often confused about how to live his life, and when he made a choice he clung to it with fierce resolve, as if to beat his uncertainty into submission.

She wanted to scream, "*Why?*" like a wounded animal, but years of social training suddenly kicked in, and she managed to draw herself up and, with a completely neutral expression on her face, ask, "Where will you go then?"

He looked relieved that she wasn't going to make a fuss, and that hurt her more than anything, she thought sadly. "I'm going to Europe," he said. "I saw Harold Vane this afternoon, and I leave tomorrow."

She smiled at him as if he were a stranger at a cocktail party, feeling as if she were standing outside her body, watching two people in a play. She held out her hand. "This is good-bye, then," she said.

He took it, searching her face for some deeper response, but she was incapable of giving it to him. And then, in a moment of passion, he leaned forward and grabbed her awkwardly by the shoulders, kissing her on the cheek.

"Someday I'll be rich," he said fervently. "And then I will come and find you."

She was too shocked to respond. He let her go and took a step back. If he didn't turn away, if he approached her again or tried to speak further to her, she would collapse, she thought, she would fall to the sidewalk in a heap . . .

But he didn't approach her. After one last, longing glance, he abruptly turned away, and began rapidly walking up the sidewalk, making a sharp turn up the side street as if he didn't trust himself not to look back.

She stood looking after him for a few moments, and then took stock of herself. She was strangely okay, she thought; the trick now was to put the incident out of her mind, until she was alone and could analyze it and mourn in private. Somehow, her legs moved, carrying her to the car; Muhammad got out and opened the door.

"I hope that man wasn't bothering you," he said. She slid onto the backseat; the door closed behind her with a firm, metallic click.

"Not at all," she said evenly, as Muhammad got into the front seat. "He's an old friend of mine . . . He just told me that his mother died."

"That's terrible," Muhammad said. "I hope he is okay."

"I think . . . he's pretty upset about it," she said distractedly, wondering how she'd gotten into this absurd conversation.

The car went around the corner, and began a slow crawl up Madison Avenue. They finally reached the Carlyle Hotel, and Mimi got out. George was at a table with some out-of-town business associates; going through the round of introductions was agony. Would she have a drink? No, she would prefer not to, and she thought the snow was beautiful, but inconvenient. She doubted that anyone would be snowed in in the morning, the snow was supposed to end around midnight. George finally took his leave, and they exited through the revolving doors, with George following behind her. He never quite got the nuances of proper gentlemanly behavior, like the fact that a man was supposed to get into the backseat of a car first, so the woman didn't have to slide, or that a man always led through a revolving door, so the woman didn't have to push. Out on the sidewalk, he stopped, and looking up and down the street, asked, "Should we take Pike or Muhammad?"

She paused, struck by the absurdity of the question, and by the reality of having *two* cars and *two* drivers. When she was a child, everyone she knew had cars and drivers, but to have two would have been considered excessive and déclassé, and instead of finding the situation amusing, as she normally would have, she now saw that it was merely depressing . . .

"Let's take Muhammad," she said. Her knees suddenly felt weak, and she was afraid that they wouldn't support her if she tried to step up into the van.

"You're the boss," George said, holding the car door open for her.

As he settled onto the seat next to her, she saw that he was looking terribly pleased with himself—his expression was the same as if he'd just closed a huge deal. Earlier in the day, he'd asked her to meet him at the Carlyle, promising some kind of "surprise," and she'd been curious, but now she hardly felt up to it. "George," she asked, placing her hand over his, "can the surprise wait until tomorrow? I'm feeling a little . . . ill."

George instinctively moved his hand away from hers, and as he did so, she realized that she did, indeed, feel sick. She was overcome by a wave of nausea, but in a second, it passed, and she leaned back against the seat.

"It won't take more than a few minutes," George promised, dispassionately, and then he began a conversation with Muhammad about the stock market.

Mimi tuned him out, the way she often did these days, and tried to think about her bed, where, if she was lucky, she might be in half an hour or so. But it was of little comfort—George would be in the bed, too, and looking over at his bland, round face, she suddenly wished she could get away from him. She thought about shouting to Muhammad to stop, and running out of the car; she would go to a local bar and drown her sorrows in whiskey. But she couldn't do that . . . the car was pulling up in front of a building on Park and Sixty-ninth Street . . .

Mimi looked out the window, staring at the heavy wooden door in confusion. She recognized it immediately; she knew the apartment it led to intimately—one of her girlfriends had lived there as a child, and later, despite the fact that the apartment had changed hands several times, she'd attended dozens of parties there. "I don't understand," she said. "Are we going to a party? The Finchbergs haven't lived here for over a year . . ."

George took her arm and hustled her out of the car. "We're not *going* to a party," he said, raising his eyebrows in glee, "but I certainly hope we'll be *giving* a few of our own . . ."

She stopped and caught her breath, immediately comprehending his meaning. "Oh George," she gasped, noting that for some reason she seemed to be having a hard time breathing. "You didn't . . ."

"I did indeed," he said, ringing the bell. "I snapped it up before it even came on the market."

They walked through the lobby and got into the tiny elevator. Mimi suddenly had the distinctly unpleasant feeling that her bowels were going to loosen uncontrollably, and she felt the blood drain from her face. But George didn't appear to notice—he never noticed anything with her, not really, she thought hopelessly, and half the time he tried to treat her like an employee . . .

The elevator door opened and they stepped out into the magnificent foyer. Mimi tried to look around, but there was a buzzing in her head, and a shadow seemed to be creeping in from the periphery of her vision. The renovation and redecoration of the apartment would take months and months, she thought, putting her hand to her head to stop the growing blackness, and then George would expect her to entertain lavishly and extensively—that was the reason he had married her. But who was she fooling, she thought desperately, as the buzzing in her head seemed to grow louder. This was her life, she had chosen it, and now, with this apartment, there would never, ever, be any getting away from it . . .

And in one final, frantic gesture, she grabbed at George's coat sleeve, feeling the soft cashmere fabric slip out of her fingers just before she crumpled to the eighteenth-century inlaid marble floor.

ELEVEN

IT WAS THE middle of the month, and, so far, aside from the incident with Zizi, Janey was having a marvelous December.

While the rest of the country was fixated on the presidential election scandal, consumed with dimpled and dangling chads, a certain segment of New York society had more important things on their minds: Specifically, the Victoria's Secret Fashion Show. For the first time in history, the show was to be televised; in the week leading up to the show, every newspaper in town had carried photographs and stories about the models, and the *New York Times* had even done a feature piece about the advisability of showing nearly naked women on network TV. The result was that Janey was recognized nearly everywhere she went, and while her "fame" wasn't of the type that drove people to ask her for her autograph, it was glamorous enough to secure her the very best booth at Dingo's, the hot new restaurant that had opened at the end of November.

For reasons that could only be explained along the same lines as why bees suddenly decide to swarm and leave the nest, Dingo's had become *the* place for lunch, with a pecking order as regimented as a chicken coop. For two hours a day, between twelve-thirty and two-thirty, Dingo's was its own small fiefdom, full of intrigues and veiled threats and mini power plays, which were as thrilling to its denizens as they were horrifying to the few poor souls who occasionally wandered into Dingo's unawares, only to be told that a table was not available, or that the wait would be at least two hours.

The Victoria's Secret show was on Thursday; the Tuesday before the show found Janey lunching at Dingo's for the third time in a week: First with Selden, then with her sister, who had returned from Europe, full of stand-by-your-man sentiments that had nearly turned Janey's stomach, and now, on that Tuesday afternoon, with Craig Edgers. The maître d', a prematurely gray-haired Scotsman named Wesley, had signaled to her from the crush of fur and cashmere overcoats packed into the narrow foyer, and, holding two menus aloft, led her through the crowd to one of the five banquettes reserved for celebrities and the city's most important power brokers. The attention never failed to gratify her, reminding her that beauty was indeed its own reward—and during these titillating moments, it crossed Janey's mind that she hardly needed "real" accomplishments when she could command the best table at the most exclusive restaurant in Manhattan.

And the thrill was made doubly pleasurable by being seen in the company of Craig Edgers. He was now Manhattan's indisputable literary light, living proof that a writer could once again produce a novel that was both intellectual and commercial, at last laying to rest the argument that had plagued the publishing world for the past twenty-five years: Could a literary work sell as many copies as what was commonly considered "trash"? Craig had answered the question with his success, and nearly everywhere Janey went someone mentioned his book. Most people loved the book but admitted to only a grudging respect for its author, who was said to be arrogant and full of himself, as well as mean.

"Which is exactly what you would expect," Janey had said to him on the phone, when reporting back one of these conversations. "After all, you've changed the face of American publishing; naturally people are going to be jealous."

Nevertheless, jealousy had had no effect on Craig's new status, and Janey drew satisfaction from the surprised and curious glances they elicited when they crossed the room to their table. Craig was sporting a four-day growth of beard, which had been popular among certain actors five years ago, but Janey had no doubts that he'd be recognized. The crowd at Dingo's prided themselves not only on being newsmakers, but on knowing the news and the "in" people well before this information was filtered to the general public. Craig was an elusive new star, and the fact that Janey had caught him, and that *he*—a genuine intellectual—was hanging out with *her*, conferred on her an intellectual status never accorded her before. It was, she thought with some gratification, an even exchange: Her glamour for his brains.

They slid into the banquette and Craig regarded her with a malicious gleam, which Janey had learned by now was a defense he employed whenever he felt insecure or out of his element. He clumsily unfolded his napkin and placed it on his lap, looking around the room with undisguised curiosity. "So this," he said, "is what it's like to be Janey Wilcox. On a daily basis."

"Or *with* Janey Wilcox," she said. Her face held that particular intense animation that was second nature for her when she was in a public situation—it was designed to draw glances and yet appear unaware of them. In a teasing tone, she added, "Come on, Craig. Surely you've been here before? After all, you're only the most important New York writer to come along in the last twenty years."

For a man who prided himself on his intellect, Craig was ridiculously susceptible to easy flattery, and he immediately relaxed, leaning forward to reveal that, actually, he had been to Dingo's before, with his agent, but they'd been relegated to one of the small square tables in Siberia in the back room. Janey knew just what response to take: One of outraged indignation at the "false" way he'd been treated before he'd become successful. It was one of Craig's pet peeves—along with the superficiality and frivolity of New York society. Janey wasn't, by nature, particularly opposed to frivolity or superficiality, but she had immediately grasped that this was a topic over which they might bond, and she encouraged Craig's vitriol, even adding some of her own: She told him about the dreadful way she'd been treated before she'd become a Victoria's Secret model, and had even hinted at her troubles with Comstock Dibble—"things" she swore she hadn't even told Selden.

The result was that Craig Edgers was now madly in love with her.

The seduction had been perfectly calculated on her part, and was justified by her recent and unassailable belief that men like Craig Edgers—intellectual artists who "understand" the longings of the human soul—were her true soul mates, the sort of men who should be her companions. Her seduction of Craig fell under a completely different heading than, say, the seduction of a man like George. Men like George were interesting only because they had money, while men like Craig didn't need money to be interesting.

She'd subtly pursued a phone friendship with him at first, using as an excuse the possibility that Selden might produce his movie. That had led to lunch at a dingy Mexican restaurant on Second Avenue near his apartment, and, on another day, to an afternoon visit to the apartment itself. The apartment was a depressing two-bedroom in a white brick high-rise building, constructed for the middle classes in the late fifties; it was poorly kept up and furnished with cheap Scandinavian furniture that had probably been purchased in the eighties. Photographs of him and his wife, Lorraine, during various stages of their marriage decorated a sideboard, and one wall was filled with books. Janey examined the photographs, genuinely interested in the kind of woman Craig had married, and wasn't disappointed: Lorraine was an athletic, plainly pretty woman of about his age, who had maintained the same hairstyle for a number of years—a frizzy, shoulder-length bob that jutted from the sides of her head like wings. Janey had remarked, in a false voice designed to subtly convey disdain, that Lorraine looked "nice." It also amused her to see that most of the photographs were taken in glamorous vacation spots like Martha's Vineyard and Aspen, indicating that while Craig and his wife may not have had money, they weren't above befriending people who did.

The pretense for her visit was to examine Craig's collection of classic books, which, she had explained, were one of her secret passions, and the next hour had passed in a haze of sexual tension. Janey had no intention of actually having sex with Craig, but she wasn't going to rule it out if the moment was right and the situation worked to her gain. As she contemplated Craig's prized copy of *The Great Gatsby*—an early signed edition with the original cover depicting a woman's eyes floating in a night sky—she was reminded of how heady it was to wield power over a man, and a plan formed in her head. The little time she'd spent with Craig had been a kind of awakening, and she suddenly realized that the one thing that had been missing from her life, the one thing that had prevented her from being really happy, was intellectual prestige. Her plan would not only justify her actions, it would change everyone's opinion about her. She knew people thought she was beautiful, but now they would know she was smart, too.

The idea was simple: She would produce the movie version of *The Embarrassments*. It seemed an almost crazy idea at first, but the more she thought about it, the more it made sense. So far, Craig had resisted selling the book to Comstock Dibble, who was still refusing to let him write the screenplay, but Craig didn't necessarily need Comstock Dibble, or, indeed, any movie studio at all—not with so much money floating around. And she knew plenty of rich men who might be willing to put up the money, who might enjoy thwarting a man like Comstock Dibble. Why, she could probably get George Paxton to invest—and then Craig would write the screenplay, and she would find the actors and director, perhaps playing one of the female parts herself. And wouldn't that be a surprise for Selden!

And now, at lunch with Craig, she meant to subtly broach her plan. The waiters were hovering around their table like flies, the blasé crowd at Dingo's was sneaking looks—and, Janey imagined, speculating madly about the unusual pairing. Brushing her hair over her shoulder, Janey leaned in toward Craig, and with a little giggle, said, "No one would dare put you in Siberia now." Craig gave her a triumphant smile, and said, "Especially not now. Did I tell you that *Time* magazine wants to do a story about me?" And with a roll of his eyes, as if he'd always expected such approbation, added, "Finally."

"Oh, Craig!" Janey said, feeling a fresh surge of excitement. The general New York attitude was that the more famous your friends were, the better *you* looked, and she couldn't help but imagine how Craig's *Time* piece might impact her life. "Will they put you on the cover?"

"There's been talk of that. But naturally, I have concerns." He looked at her meaningfully. "You know how these things work, Janey. You have no control over what they write and the kind of angle they'll take, and I don't want to sully my literary reputation by appearing in a magazine aimed for the common populace."

"But you *have* to do it," Janey said, frowning. "You must see why it's so important."

"Tell me," he said. And Janey couldn't help but marvel afresh that Craig Edgers, *the* Craig Edgers, literary star, was asking her for advice!

"Think about all the people you'll reach," she said passionately, as if the topic had been of the utmost concern to her for most of her life. "People who have probably never read a great book in their lives, who think that 'literary' means boring!" She glanced down demurely at her plate. "My God, Craig," she said softly. "To be given the chance to affect so many people like that . . . Why, it's nothing less than an honor. It's the kind of thing I'd like to do someday. There's . . . there's real meaning in that. What's the expression? It's an unexamined life worth living . . ."

Craig gave her a patronizing smile. "That's not quite it, but the sentiment is right."

"Oh, naturally it's right," she said, boldly. "You'll have to give up some control over your image, but think about how much you'll gain."

He sat back and regarded her thoughtfully. "You're the only person I can talk to about this stuff. My wife doesn't want to hear it . . ."

"Only because she's threatened. By your success. Suddenly, *your* life has changed and she doesn't know what it's going to do to your relationship."

"But what is the point of having a wife if she deliberately refuses to understand?" Craig asked, playing with his fork.

Janey gave him a mysterious smile but said nothing. Most women would have taken Craig's remark about his wife as a chance to paint themselves as superior to Lorraine in understanding and sympathy. But Janey knew that more often than not, the technique failed—it made a man think you were desperate to be with him. And the way to control a man was to let him sell himself to you—not the other way around.

Indeed, within seconds, Craig leaned over and said, in what Janey imagined was an uncharacteristic revelation for him, "I've been thinking about you."

"I've been thinking about you, too," she said, noting that this was now the perfect opportunity to introduce her plan.

"This is going to sound crazy. But I've been musing . . . I'm going to make you a character in my next book." He sat back on the banquette and took a sip of water, regarding her thoughtfully.

"Oh, Craig," Janey said. She was caught slightly off balance, and taking a moment to regroup her strategy, she suddenly saw him as he might appear to someone who didn't know him and wasn't acquainted with his accomplishments. The overriding impression, besides the plaid, lumberjack shirt, was of a man who was not quite clean, who had doubtless at times gone for days without brushing his teeth, who had flecks of dandruff between his eyelashes and blackheads on his back.

And then, in a gesture that shocked her, given the environment, he sat forward and clumsily placed his hand over hers. For a moment, she froze, but quickly realized that if he thought she found him repulsive, he would retreat and she would lose him. Instead, she placed her other hand over his and said, in a voice that rang with flirtatious undertones, "I know I should be flattered, but honestly, Craig, I'm frightened. Why, the way you depict some of the people in your book . . . it's positively Machiavellian. You can be quite the cynic, you know, and I can't *imagine* how you'd depict *me*—probably as one of those man-eating bitches!" And Craig laughed and said, "It should be pretty obvious how I would depict *you,* Janey. You know I'm besotted with you!"

"Do I know that, Craig?" she asked—innocently enough, but with just a hint of warning in her voice.

Craig didn't pick up on the hint. "If you weren't married to my goddamned best friend," he went on, "I'd ask you to go away with me for the weekend."

"But Craig," she cried, feigning shock. "What about your wife?"

"I'd lie and tell her I was going to Chicago. To see old friends."

He was so quaint and yet dead serious, Janey thought. It was almost . . . sweet. "We could tell Selden you're writing a book about me," she said, wondering how far he would go. "We could tell him that we needed to spend time together, so you could . . . study me."

Now he was right where she wanted him. His eyes nearly crossed with desire as he managed to gasp out, "But I could never do that to Selden." He took a sip of his water, and added, "Besides, Selden wouldn't believe it for a second. He's not that stupid. He knows how I feel about you—the bastard is probably laughing behind his back at me!"

Janey pushed her lips out into a little pout. "You're right, of course," she said. "But if we could think of a way . . . to spend more time together legitimately . . ." She knew she had to be careful not to *specifically* promise him sex, while at the same time allowing him to think that, at some point, he *might* get it. "I've been having the craziest thoughts," she said, playing with her fork. "Too stupid to tell you, really. You'll laugh at me."

"Laugh at you is just about the last thing I'd do," he said.

She looked him full in the face, her expression suddenly serious. "What if . . . *I* were to produce the movie version of *The Embarrassments*?"

For a moment, he simply stared at her, his expression one of incomprehension.

Clearly, it was the last thing he was expecting, and before he could protest, she hurried on: "Oh, there it is. I've gone and blown it. I knew you'd laugh at me," and turned away.

"No, no. It's an . . . *interesting* idea."

"Well, it *would* be, if you bothered to give it some thought," she said silkily. "You want to write the screenplay and crack Hollywood, and I can help you. All it takes is money, really, someone to put up the cash for the project. And that's where I'd come in. George Paxton is one of Selden's best friends, and a great friend of mine, too. He's invested in movies before. George will . . . well, George will do pretty much whatever I ask him. He's even told me that if I could find a project for him . . . ," she lied smoothly.

Craig's eyes narrowed. "But what about Selden?" he asked.

"Oh, Selden!" Janey said, airily. "That's the beauty of it. Selden could buy your book . . . but we both know he won't—he doesn't have the sensitivity to understand it. Think of how surprised he'll be when he finds out. It'll be a good way of teaching him a lesson."

"Janey," Craig said patiently. "You're beautiful and I would never insinuate that you weren't smart. But you haven't any experience. These Hollywood people are killers. Everyone knows that. They might not . . . take you seriously."

"Because I'm a Victoria's Secret model?" Janey asked, biting her lip. "But there could be advantages. There isn't anyone I couldn't get a meeting with . . . And if the modeling is a problem . . . why, I'd give it all up for the chance to do something important!" she cried. "Especially if it was something, and some*one*, I really believed in."

She turned to him with shining eyes, knowing that there was nothing more attractive to a man than passion, and she cried out, "Oh, Craig! If you don't let me work with you, I don't know what I'll do!" And suddenly, he was right beside her, patting her hand and murmuring words of encouragement. "Well, sure, Janey. If you really want to . . . If you really feel that way . . . Of course you can."

The bustling backstage noises of a hundred frenzied human beings engaged in the task of putting together the Victoria's Secret Fashion Show was not enough to drown out a high, childish voice that rose above the din to declare: "And it isn't *enough* to be beautiful and have your own money these days. Now a girl has to be able to give a great blow job—on demand—and be kinky in bed. I asked him, Just what do you mean by kinky? And he said, anal sex, at least once a week, and then he said something about a dog collar . . ."

The voice was suddenly drowned out under a short burst of staccato music that came from the other side of the thin partition that hid the runway as Janey turned with a superior smile toward the speaker. Seraphina, a dark-haired beauty with only one name, was seated two chairs away from her in front of a long, makeshift makeup mirror, her soft brown eyes opened wide in outraged injury. Janey's brief assessment of the girl, formed in the space of two afternoon rehearsals, was that she was a dumb, silly thing. No more than twenty-one years old, she had little to talk about besides the men who had tried to sleep with her and the family she had left behind on a farm in South America. For a moment, Janey had wondered if she had appeared as ridiculous as Seraphina at that age, but deciding she hadn't, she'd dismissed Seraphina, although it was difficult to ignore her when she was in the same room. Silenced now by the motions of the makeup artist, who was attempting to draw a line around dark lips so full they were reminiscent of a vagina, Seraphina continued to gesticulate madly.

Behind Janey, her own makeup artist, Contadine, stood mixing a variety of liquid foundations on the surface of her hand. Their eyes met in the mirror as Contadine, who had an opinion about every topic under the sun and felt the constant need to share her wisdom, motioned with her head toward Seraphina. "Isn't it the truth though?" she said, stepping forward and gently dabbing Janey's face with the foundation. "The stories I could tell you," she continued. "No matter how much we demand from men, they always control the game. Every time we think we've got some freedom or independence, they up the stakes. Hell. It's all this Internet stuff, you know? This porn everywhere. At one time they would have been *lucky* to get a blow job. Now they want three girls and a monkey, and all of 'em worshipping at the altar of the cock . . ."

Contadine laughed loudly, taken with her own wit, as Janey pressed her lips into a cold smile. She'd had millions of these conversations over the years, and the presumed camaraderie coupled with the required false gaiety was always exhausting; Janey understood why movie stars demanded that makeup and hair people keep their mouths shut. But if she demanded quiet she would be labeled a prima donna. All she could do was remain silent and hope that Contadine would take the hint.

She closed her eyes for a moment, and Contadine asked, "You're not nervous, are you?" Janey gave her an incredulous look in the mirror and Contadine patted her shoulder. "I didn't think so. Not you, anyway." She leaned close, lowering her voice and glancing down the row of chairs where the eleven Victoria's Secret models were in various stages of hair and makeup. "Hell, you're one of the few real pros here. Half of these girls have hardly been on a runway before, and they're going to send them out with their butt cheeks hanging out? The whole thing's hysterical if you ask me."

As this didn't really require a response, Janey merely shrugged her shoulders, but there was no stopping Contadine. "Well," she said, "I've heard *you've* got it together at least. Didn't I read somewhere you got married?"

"That's right," Janey said. "To Selden Rose." She shifted in her chair and regarded herself appraisingly. Although she was the oldest of all the girls (only the German girl, Evie, who was thirty, came close to her age), her professional assessment was that she looked the best she ever had. There was a fullness to her beauty, and a confidence, and something else—an intelligence, as if she had an actual life away from the runway—unlike the half-formed, simplistic faces of the younger girls. And yet, after just fifteen minutes in this environment, she had begun to feel the same creeping dullness that threatened to slowly blot her out, until she was merely a husk of face, hair, and body, a shell that could walk and talk, but was dead inside . . .

"Oh right," Contadine said, snapping her fingers. "Selden Rose. That's his name." She nodded as if she finally understood the solution to a math problem. "He's that guy . . . a photographer, right?"

"No," Janey said, with momentary irritation. It was so typical of people in this world to always think that they knew everyone and everything, which was ironic since the borders of their world were so very small. "He's the CEO of MovieTime."

"Good for you. That's even better," Contadine said. "A businessman. My mother always said, marry a businessman. They're stable."

Janey stared at Contadine, wondering if she should let the inaccuracy about what Selden really did for a living pass. After all, what difference did it make?

" 'Course the problem with some of these business guys is they're boring," Contadine continued. "I had a girlfriend, she decided she'd had enough of the creative types who never paid for anything, so she met this investment banker . . ."

Janey had had enough, and gave Contadine a superior smile. "Selden isn't exactly a businessman. He used to be the president of Columbia Pictures."

Contadine paused and expertly flicked the tip of her makeup brush with a long, manicured finger, causing a fairy shower of sparkly pink powder. "Ahhhh," she said, nodding wisely. "That's why I know the name. I think I have a girlfriend who dated him."

Janey closed her eyes to allow Contadine to apply the pink powder to her lids, suppressing a jolt of surprise as she did so. The backstage scene at a fashion show was always a notorious hotbed of gossip and innuendo, both for the repetition of gossip, and for the creation of it; if she betrayed too much interest, Contadine would be repeating the story all over town tomorrow.

"I doubt it," Janey said, with a curt laugh meant to stifle speculation. "Selden's only been in New York for six months, and we've been married for three. And before that, he was married for twelve years. So it would be rather difficult . . ."

"I know I'm right about this," Contadine said mildly. "Now that you mention Columbia Pictures, it's all coming back to me. It was my friend Estie. She's a singer—or calls herself one, anyway," Contadine said, with a smirk. "But I'm being unfair. Estie *is* really talented. And she's a riot. It's just that her looks keep getting in the way."

"What a surprise," Janey said.

"Well, she's the type of girl men go crazy over." Contadine leaned in conspiratorially. "One of those English princes—I can't remember which—was after her. He took her to St. Barts. It was all totally hush-hush and no one was supposed to know anything. But she managed to call me from the bathroom, saying the guy had a really small penis." Contadine took in Janey's look of disdain, and went on airily, "Oh, you'd love her, I swear. And I'm ninety percent sure she told me that after that, she was going out with this guy, Selden Rose. I remembered it because Selden is such a funny name. I mean, no offense or anything, but it sort of sounds like a dentist."

Janey turned in her chair and let out a short, annoyed laugh. "That's proof that she doesn't know Selden. The last thing anyone would call him is a dentist . . ."

"Oh, I didn't say she *did* call him a dentist," Contadine went on, with irritating persistence. "Only that the name reminded me of one. She said he was really determined—she wasn't that interested though, you know the type, she wants to marry Tom Cruise—but she thought he was going to leave his wife and marry her, until there was some kind of trouble over a necklace . . ."

"A necklace!" Janey said.

"Sure. Estie's one of those girls . . . you can't believe the jewelry and presents men give her. One guy gave her a Ferrari just for going on a date with him. I'd hate her for it, but the truth is, Estie needs the money. She's too short to be a model, and even though she can sing, she can't act at all . . ."

"Well, she's not Selden's type, that's for sure," Janey said, with unassailable confidence. "I know my husband, and he can't stand those kinds of women. On the other hand, if this Estie were after *him* . . ."

"Oh, Estie's never gone after a man in her life," Contadine said smoothly, brushing a speck of brown powder from Janey's cheek. "In any case, I wouldn't worry about it. After all, *you're* married to him, not Estie."

Janey said nothing as she digested this information. It was likely that not a word of it was true, and that Contadine had Selden mixed up with someone else, but on the other hand, there could be some reality to the story. Janey had never talked to Selden about the reasons for his divorce: On the few occasions when she'd brought it up, he'd only smiled, as if he were embarrassed, and said it was the usual case of a couple growing apart.

But there was no time to think about it, because in the next moment, Contadine stepped back and said, "There you go, you look perfect," and Janey was immediately accosted by a dresser who wanted to check the fit of her first "outfit"—a blue
sequined bra. Janey followed her across the floor, weaving through a crowd of styl-
ists, models, press people, cameramen, publicists, and anyone else who had managed, through vague connections, to get their hands on a backstage pass. As she
made her way to a clothing rack, from which hung a large white piece of cardboard
with her name scrawled on it in black Magic Marker, a short man in a tartan suit ran
up to her. "Darling!" he screamed. "E! Entertainment Television wants to interview
you, now!"

"In a minute, Walter," she said calmly to the publicist. "Tell them to interview
Evie first. She's ready."

"She isn't," Walter said. "She just got into a fight with a makeup artist—he said
her face looked too fat. As if it's *his* fault. 'Course, I guess I'd be sensitive too if
someone called me the German sausage in the newspapers . . ."

Walter's attention was momentarily diverted by another young man's fresh
screams of joyful recognition, and Janey was suddenly amused by the sheer circus
atmosphere of it all. It was as if human beings were never more at their best than
when importantly involved in the most frivolous of pursuits—and she was suddenly
reminded of Craig Edgers. Despite his beliefs to the contrary, there couldn't be that
much harm in allowing your life to float on an occasional bit of superficial fun, and
if this was how all of New York society wished to amuse itself, why shouldn't she be
at the center, where she belonged? After all, while it might be true that no one
would take her "seriously" as long as she was "only" a Victoria's Secret model, the
reality was that people wouldn't necessarily give her the time of day if she wasn't . . .

She slipped her arms through the sequined straps of the blue bra and turned
toward a small mirror; her dresser, Marie, held up a pair of silicone breast
enhancers. "Oh no," Janey said. "I'm big enough as it is."

"Everyone is wearing them."

"I'm already a C cup," Janey said. "I don't need to be bigger."

"But all the other girls will be bigger. You don't want to be the smallest girl out
there."

"Marie," Janey said playfully, "do you think there's a direct correlation between
the rise in the stock market and the size of women's breasts?" It was a question
Craig had posed to her at lunch the other day, leading to a fifteen-minute discussion about men and women and money. While Janey expressed her opinions, Craig
had sat listening, rapt with attention, which was something that Selden never
seemed to do these days. But what did she expect? Craig was a true intellectual, and
true intellectuals understood that everybody was smart and that everyone had a valid

opinion, if only *someone* would listen. But Selden . . . well, as Craig pointed out, Selden was a bit of a sellout, although Janey still wasn't sure she completely agreed.

Marie threw her hands up in frustration. "What do I know about the stock market?" she asked. "You think I have money to throw around like that?" She approached with an enhancer in each hand, and Janey allowed her to slide the cool silicone underneath her breasts, pushing them up and out of the blue sequined bra at an alarming angle.

"Now I look like a cartoon character," Janey complained. She turned to Marie, and with a wicked smile, said, "I'm thinking about having my breast implants taken out. What do you think about that, Marie?"

Marie looked like she might expire. "You can't do that!" she scolded. "You will ruin your career. And what kind of inspiration will that be for other women?"

"Janey? Now?" Walter Speck asked, appearing from behind her rack of outfits. Janey looked toward Marie, who rolled her eyes and nodded.

"You know the drill," Walter said, handing her a silky pink robe. "You love Victoria's Secret, blah blah blah, Victoria's Secret makes women feel good about themselves . . ."

"They do?" Janey asked.

"You're not going to start making trouble now, too, are you?" Walter asked, hurrying her toward a corner of the room where a camera crew was stationed. "Evie is bad enough . . . It's always you older girls . . . You turn thirty and suddenly you think you've grown a brain."

"Maybe we have," Janey laughed. She sat down on the chair indicated and tilted her head back to allow a makeup artist to powder her face. "But you don't have to worry, Walter. I'm thinking about quitting anyway. To pursue other interests."

"Lord no," Walter muttered.

"Is that an official announcement?" someone asked.

"Certainly not," Walter snapped.

"Now Janey," the interviewer said. She was a blond-haired peppy girl of about twenty-five, whose ordinariness was relieved only by the fact that she worked for a television show. "In about fifteen minutes, you're going to walk out there in front of thousands of people . . . practically naked!"

"Yes. That's right," Janey said, as if she found the prospect slightly dull.

"Doesn't it . . . make you nervous?" the girl twittered. "I could never do it, no matter how much you paid me!"

Janey gave her a small, pitying smile, thinking that was the point: No one *would* ever pay her . . . Aloud, she said, "I think of my body as art. If you're a model, your art is your body, the way a painting is art for an artist."

"My goodness!" the girl exclaimed. "I've never thought of models as artists. From now on, I'll look at models with a new respect!"

Janey gave her a big, fake smile.

"Now here's a question we're asking all the girls," the girl continued. "Did you do anything special today to get ready for the show?"

"Not really," Janey shrugged. Certainly this twit didn't need to hear about the collagen injections she'd had two days ago in her lips and in the lines leading from her nose to the corners of her mouth, or about the high colonic and the bikini wax she'd had yesterday. "Frankly, I did what I usually do. I had some business meetings in the morning with my agent, and then I had lunch with my good friend Craig Edgers."

The name had its intended effect: "Craig Edgers?" the girl squealed. "The best-selling novelist? And what did you talk about?"

"Oh, the correlation between the stock market and how it affects our perception of the perfect woman's body," Janey said casually.

For a moment, the girl looked at her blankly, and then covered quickly by saying, "Well, we're certainly going to see some perfect bodies here! Thank you so much, Janey. And thank you for being a smart model and an inspiration to the women of today."

"Nice. Very nice," Walter said, taking Janey's arm and leading her away. "I loved that bit about lunch with Craig Edgers." Then he stopped and looked at her, frowning slightly. "You're not making it up, are you? It's just the kind of thing some gossip columnist will get a hold of and . . ."

"Don't be ridiculous," Janey said reassuringly. The inaccuracy as to the date didn't bother her a bit: After all, she *had* had lunch with Craig, and everyone knew that the press always got everything wrong.

"A friendship between you and Craig Edgers," Walter said eagerly. "That's good for at least a 'seen around town.' Where did you have lunch, anyway?"

"Dingo's," Janey said. "Where else?"

The after-party was held at the nightclub Lotus. With Selden holding her hand, and Mimi and George following in her wake, Janey entered the party in a blaze of flashbulbs, feeling as if all the threads of her life had finally come together to produce this moment of triumph. She was quite sure that none of the other girls had received as much applause as she had, and she basked in the idea that she'd been singled out for special approval. Once inside the party, she was quickly surrounded by an expanding circle of well-wishers; out of the corner of her eye she saw her sister and Digger, around whom the media frenzy appeared to have died down, probably because they hadn't split up; standing a few feet away was Comstock Dibble. She hadn't heard a peep from him or his lawyers since she'd spoken to George, and flush with the victories of the day, and knowing he wouldn't dare make a scene at a social event, especially one at which she was the star, she decided to confront him.

She found him at the bar, talking to an actress named Wendy Piccolo. Wendy was a tiny thing, no more than five feet tall, which made her, in Janey's mind, nearly invisible. Brushing past Wendy and raising her eyebrows with the innocent earnestness of a child, Janey cried out, "Comstock! I haven't seen you for ages! You never call me anymore!"

Comstock turned, his eyes flashing in fury, but, as she'd expected, he knew enough to keep his personal feelings in check. Recovering quickly from her unexpected sally, he growled lazily, "It's only because I can't reach you. You've become so famous you don't have time for any of your old friends."

"I always have time for you, Comstock. You know that."

He turned away to take a sip of his drink, perhaps in the hope that Janey would disappear, for when he turned back, it was with a look of disbelief that she was still standing there. She gave him a superior smile, as if to imply that she wasn't scared of him, and he acquiesced by asking her what she'd been up to recently.

"I have to say, I'm loving being married," Janey said, glancing at Wendy to include her in the conversation.

"Oh, I know exactly who you are now," Wendy drawled, as if before that moment Janey had been of no interest. "You're Selden Rose's wife."

"That's right," Janey said with false brightness. "But how do *you* know Selden?"

"Oh, from parties," she said, with a shrug of her skinny shoulder. "And we've had lunch a few times. He was always talking about his beautiful wife, Janey. But it wasn't until I saw you that I put it together."

Janey laughed, but instead of mollifying her as to the relationship between Wendy and Selden, Wendy's comment made her feel vaguely uncomfortable. On the surface, Wendy was perfectly charming, but underneath her words, Janey sensed the viciousness of a cat that will suddenly reach out and claw you for no reason, and she said coldly, "I'll be sure to tell Selden I saw you."

"Selden's trying to steal Wendy from me," Comstock said, narrowing his eyes over the rim of his glass.

"Is that so?" Janey said.

"He wants me to star in this new television series. But I keep telling him that I'm strictly a movie actress. On the other hand, Selden is soooo brilliant. And all of his work is so *intellectual*," Wendy said, pronouncing the word as if it were a delicious piece of candy. "But of course you know that. You're married to him." She smiled and cocked her head to the side, which had the unwonted effect of making

Janey want to squish her under her heel. "Is he here? I must go and say hi to him. I don't want him to think I'm ignoring him."

She scampered off, and Janey leaned toward Comstock with an indulgent smile of disdain. "My goodness," she said softly. "She certainly is tiny."

"She is tiny," Comstock agreed. "But she's one of the most talented actresses in America today."

"How funny," Janey said. "You'd never know."

"Oh, she's very modest. And her career hasn't been handled well in the past five years. That's one of the reasons I've been trying to help her."

"And after you help her . . . will you have your lawyers send her a letter demanding that she pay you back?"

The words were delivered with Janey's typical, soft-spoken innocence, and at first, Comstock had no reaction, other than hardening his face into a terrifying mask that nearly caused Janey to draw back in fear. His expression seemed to say, "I'll break your kneecaps," and she knew that if she backed down, he would do everything he could to destroy her. She had to make him know that he was in the wrong, and with haughty indignance, she demanded, "Well?"

He snorted in disgust. "I was wondering when you were going to have the guts to deal with this. You probably thought that if you did nothing, it would go away. And that trick of putting George Paxton's lawyers on me. Bad move. You should have come to me yourself."

Janey nearly laughed. A crazy sort of anger overtook her, blotting out the fear she'd felt moments before. "Excuse me, Comstock, but *you* are insane," she said daringly, not quite believing she had the guts to challenge him in this way. "You put your lawyers on *me*. How dare you? Besides, I earned that money, fair and square."

"Oh, I'm sure you think you did," Comstock said with an evil smile. "Your type always does. And I suppose it never crossed your mind that I *didn't* put my lawyers on you."

"So you're not even going to take responsibility?" she asked, knowing that this was one of the tricks employed by most of the rich, successful men she knew when they were up against the wall: They would simply claim not to know anything about it.

"As a matter of fact, I am."

"And I suppose you're going to say that you have no idea what I'm talking about."

"Oh, I know what you're talking about," he said heatedly. "And if you'd done the right thing . . . if you'd at least come to me first . . . Even George Paxton's lawyers aren't going to be able to help you with this one, and believe me, they don't want to be involved." He leaned toward her with a frightening smile and his tone changed completely. Speaking as if, to the casual observer, they were having a perfectly pleasant conversation, he said, "You've caused me a lot of trouble, Janey, and that's something I won't forget. I'll get out of it eventually, but I wonder if you will."

She gasped and felt her heart thumping with fear and rage. "How dare you threaten me?" she said.

"Don't take it as a threat," he said. "Consider it a warning."

She opened her mouth to reply, but at that moment Mimi materialized in front of them. "Hello, Comstock," she said pleasantly, lifting her face to receive a kiss on each cheek. "I'm sure you must have loved the show. Wasn't Janey wonderful?"

"Spectacular. Who would think that walking would pay so much?" he asked with a cruel laugh.

Janey responded with a cold smile; her only pleasure was in thinking how fantastically shocked and angry he would be when he found out that she was producing *The Embarrassments* and not he.

"And where's Mauve?" Mimi asked.

He looked at her with surprise. "I thought you girls kept closer tabs on each other than that," he said. "She's in Palm Beach."

"Oh, that's right," Mimi said. "Give her my love, will you?"

"I'm sure you'll talk to her before I will," he said. He picked up his drink and walked off.

"Well," Mimi said, giving Janey a cold smile. "What was that about?"

"Who knows?" Janey shrugged, wondering frantically how much of the conversation Mimi had overheard. "Comstock is just crazy . . ."

"So is half of New York," Mimi said. Janey looked at her. She hadn't seen Mimi for a few days—every time she called her Mimi said she was in the middle of something and had to get off the phone—and now she realized she was behaving strangely. With a jolt of panic, she wondered if Mimi suspected that something had happened between her and Zizi, but she quickly reassured herself that the problem was most likely the fact that she'd told Mimi Zizi had to move out—and Mimi had seen that her sister and Digger were still very much together.

"Listen, Mimi," she said. "I'm sorry about the thing with Zizi. I had no idea that Patty and Digger were going to reconcile . . ."

"Oh, I'm sure you didn't," Mimi said coldly. And then she walked off.

Janey thought about going after her—she didn't want to have a problem with Mimi, especially when she was about to involve George in her secret project—but her attention was diverted by the sight of Wendy Piccolo sitting wedged between Selden and George.

George sat with an untouched martini in front of him, staring into the room with an attitude that indicated he was merely tolerating the situation until he could escape for home. But Selden was bent toward Wendy, and they were giggling as if sharing a private joke. Their heads were so close together they were nearly touching; Wendy's large brown eyes were luminous and her short, dark hair gleamed like a helmet in the pinkish light of the club.

For a moment, Janey was struck with anger, her only thought being how could Selden do this to her on her big night, when she was the star, and in front of such a crowd of people. But she recovered herself; after all, on the face of it there was nothing unusual going on. Selden looked up at her and smiled, while at the same time Wendy's eyes slid up and registered her presence. Again, there was nothing particularly unusual in these gestures. But to Janey, they were like warning signposts at the start of a long, dark tunnel—a tunnel that sloped downward with an unpleasant surprise at its end. For immediately after acknowledging her, Selden and Wendy went back to their conversation as if she were nothing more than a nuisance.

Janey's immediate instinct was to find the most attractive man in the room and flirt outrageously with him, but at that moment George saw her and waved awkwardly, and with a sigh she slid into the banquette next to him. Mimi sat down next to Selden and immediately inserted herself into the conversation between Selden and Wendy, and with Selden's attention momentarily diverted, Janey studiously ignored him by sagging against George in an attitude of exhaustion, and went so far as to allow George the intimate gesture of kissing her on the forehead.

"Have some of my drink, Janey," he said, pushing his martini toward her. "You look beat."

"And you're not drinking at all."

"Can't on a weekday," he said. "I'll never understand why people in New York go out every night. Why are the biggest parties always on Monday nights, for instance? It ruins the rest of the week."

"You'd think they had better things to do with their time . . ."

"But they don't," he said, smiling at his joke. "Now take you, Janey," he said. "You're a supermodel, but I always think of you as being a serious person. I still think you can—and ought—to do more with your life."

For a moment, she brightened, and said quickly, "Actually George, there *is* a project that I've been thinking we might work on together . . ."

"That so?" he said.

"But I don't want to discuss it here." She looked at him meaningfully and said, "Maybe we could have dinner?"

"Anytime. Just so long as I check with Mimi to make sure she doesn't have anything else going on that night."

"Did you see Comstock?" she asked casually.

"I saw you talking to him. I thought he was our sworn enemy," George said.

His intimate tone filled her with pleasure, and she was instantly reminded of how attractive she'd found him that night, two months ago, when she'd gone to see him in the new apartment.

"Oh, he is," she said eagerly. "But in these circles he's unavoidable." Turning her head sideways, so that she was nearly whispering in his ear, she said, "He said things that frightened me, George. I'm scared. I was wondering if maybe I should give him that money back."

"Don't you do any such thing!" he said, in a vehement whisper. He pushed back from her a little and turned to face her squarely. "Don't you understand what that will say about *me*?"

"*You*, George?" she said with an incredulous laugh. "I'm sorry, but I hardly think it affects *you*."

"Oh, but it does, you see. Because you've gotten me involved now. I went to an awful lot of trouble with my lawyers to get them to make that call, and they did. And from what I hear they took care of it pretty well. So if you go and give Comstock the money now—well, it makes me and my lawyers look like fools. It's nothing short of an insult!"

Janey was instantly horrified; she usually never made these kinds of mistakes in judgment. She suddenly realized that she had absolutely no intention of paying Comstock back, and had only mentioned it to George in an attempt to remind him of their special bond. And George, of course, had taken her seriously. "My God, George," she said, putting her hand to her heart, thereby drawing his eyes to her breasts. "You're right, of course. I don't know anything about business and how these things are done. But I *did* come to you for advice first, before I did anything. So there's no harm done."

George regarded her through narrowed eyes, while Janey, panicked that she'd completely blown her chance of doing future business with him, looked at him pleadingly, biting her lip. "Don't be angry at me, George, please," she whispered. "I didn't mean it. I was just kidding . . . to see how you'd respond . . ."

George looked at her as if he didn't believe her, and then, as if he'd just heard a particularly amusing joke, laughed out loud.

"You're a wild card, Janey," he said, shaking his head.

Janey breathed a sigh of relief. The moment of danger had passed, and feeling her confidence return, she slipped her hand under the table and squeezed George's leg. "So are you," she said seductively.

But suddenly, Wendy broke into their conversation. Mimi had engaged Selden, leaving Wendy out in the cold, and now Wendy had turned to George as if she were determined to annex him next. She was, Janey thought angrily, one of those women who must always be the center of attention with men, although if you judged her solely on her looks, you wouldn't have thought she would have the audacity. "Did I hear you say business?" she asked, with an inappropriate sort of eagerness. "I love business. I read the *Wall Street Journal* every day."

The remark made Janey want to laugh out loud and at the same time filled her with a bilious jealousy. *She* read the *Wall Street Journal*, too—if not every day, then at least a couple of times a week—and somehow, the fact that this little creature read it as well seemed to demean her own efforts, revealing them to be a pathetic and obvious stab at appearing intelligent. Aloud Janey said smugly, "Of course, we're talking about business. George is a businessman," to which Wendy replied to George, "Oh, I *know*. I read about you in the papers all the time!"

But George, unlike Selden, wasn't the least bit interested, and could only be bothered to reply with a grunt and a dismissive, "Well, I hope not too often." Janey took the opportunity to lean over to Selden. "Darling," she said, "I'm so very tired. Do you mind if we go home?"

"I've been waiting to go home all night," he said. And then added, "I've told Wendy we'd give her a lift home. She's on the way."

It turned out that Wendy wasn't at all "on the way," as she lived in a shabby brownstone on the Lower East Side, and for much of the ride Janey had to endure Selden and Wendy's discussing the pros and cons of various obscure plays they'd seen in the last ten years. At last, sensing Janey's boredom, Wendy asked brightly, "Janey, have *you* ever thought about acting?" and Janey stared at her in shock for a moment, before replying coldly, "But I *am* an actress."

Wendy looked from Janey to Selden in a moment of confused embarrassment, which was so perfectly executed that Janey couldn't help but wonder if she'd made the remark deliberately. But Selden, completely unaware of Wendy's treacherous behavior, took Janey's hand and said proudly, "Janey was in that action-adventure movie. You remember . . ."

"Oh yes, I do," Wendy said. "I'm sorry, though. I never saw it. It's not the kind of movie I normally go to."

"Janey's got a huge following of pimply adolescent boys," Selden said.

"Oh, I'm sure," Wendy said, with an obvious stab at kindness. "And of balding adolescent men as well!"

They laughed as Janey fumed in silence, and when the limousine finally slid in front of Wendy's building and she had exited with gay promises of a future dinner, Janey turned to Selden and said coldly, "Well. She certainly is a funny little thing."

But Selden, whether through ignorance or a willful decision to ignore her true meaning, simply said, "Oh yes. She's got a great sense of humor. She really is a remarkable girl . . ."

"Remarkable?" Janey said. "I'd hardly call her that."

"Oh, but she is. She's bright as a whip and completely self-educated. She comes from the Appalachian Mountains in Kentucky . . . I think most of her family is illiterate. You'd never guess that she comes from a family of coal miners . . ."

"Coal miners!" Janey snorted. "Come on, Selden. Surely you don't believe that. It's just a little too good to be true . . ."

"Why shouldn't I believe it?" he asked.

"Well, in any case, she's madly in love with you. She just about admitted it at the bar."

In the brief silence that followed, Janey fumed that if there was nothing to this idea, Selden would have immediately laughed it off. Instead, he turned to her, and, with a confused look that indicated a struggle for comprehension, he said, "Janey, are you *jealous*?"

Janey was still prepared to be angry, but she suddenly saw how ridiculous she was being. Selden was the last person who would be unfaithful. But it might be useful for him to understand that he wasn't ever to toy with her affections, and so, with a toss of her head, she emitted an incredulous, "Me? Jealous of Wendy Piccolo? I think not."

"Well, how do you think *I* felt," he asked, squeezing her hand, "watching you up there on the runway, knowing that all those men were ogling you . . ."

"I would think it would make you feel very, very special," she said, warming up to him. Now that the topic had returned to her, where it belonged, she suddenly felt secure again.

He leaned forward and kissed her on the cheek, snuggling in next to her. "Are you excited about Christmas?" he asked eagerly.

"I guess so," she said, in the childish teasing tone they'd used with each other when they were first married. "But I do wish you would tell me where we're going, Selden Rose. Otherwise, how am I supposed to know what to pack?"

"I told you, summer clothes," Selden said proudly. Janey flinched slightly at the words, the proper term for vacation clothes being "resort wear." But she couldn't expect Selden to know *that*. "I just hope it's St. Barts . . . ," she said.

"It might be," he said with a playful shrug of his shoulders. "And then again, it might not. Remember, it's a surprise."

She giggled and slid down into the seat next to him, suddenly reminded of her own scheme—and thinking about how, if everything went according to plan, she'd soon have a nice little surprise for *him* as well.

TWELVE

THE FRIDAY MORNING after the Victoria's Secret Fashion Show found Mimi in her apartment, sitting at one end of the fourteen-foot mahogany dining room table. Bowing her head, she stared down at the lump of scrambled eggs on her plate in disgust. There was something quite wrong with her, she thought: She was ravenously hungry, but for the past several days, ever since Zizi had ended their affair, the sight, and in particular the *smell*, of food had been making her nauseous. She picked up her fork, scooping up a small bit of egg in the hope of getting it down, but the eggs were a sickening yellowish gray, and she gave up, wiping her mouth with the corner of a linen napkin instead. The eggs, no doubt, were a sign of the cook's displeasure in having to prepare this meal—it meant extra work and she had to come in early. But Mimi had been firm . . .

In the misguided notion that they were, indeed, a family, George insisted that he and Mimi have breakfast with his boys. And so, scrambled eggs, sausage, bacon, and toast sat on the sideboard on warming platters, accompanied by freshly squeezed orange and grapefruit juice, a variety of jams, and a dish of marmalade. Georgie Jr. stood in front of the sideboard, surreptitiously stuffing sausages nearly whole into his mouth. George looked up and caught him, and with a warning "Georgie" told him to sit down at the table.

"But I want another . . ." Georgie protested.

"You've had enough," George said, frowning as he unfolded his napkin. Lately, it seemed that George had finally come around to the realization that Georgie Jr. did, indeed, need to lose weight, and it was beginning to annoy him. Nevertheless, he persisted in believing in some kind of fantasy that once in Aspen, Georgie would miraculously shed pounds, thanks to all the exercise he'd be getting. But Mimi knew better: During the past two Christmases, they'd hired an all-day ski instructor for the boys each day, but somehow, Georgie had always managed to escape, and on more than one occasion had been run to ground in the local supermarket . . .

"If I can't eat, what am I supposed to do then?" Georgie demanded of his father.

"You can sit and watch us eat," George said.

That was cruel, Mimi thought, but she said nothing.

She glanced over at the sideboard, where Jack was meticulously cutting a slice of toast into six tiny pieces. Usually, the marmalade sat untouched, but on this particular morning, Jack apparently found it tempting, because he spread one of the pieces with the gooey orange jam.

"When are we going to Aspen?" Georgie asked, as if he couldn't wait to get away.

"You know when we're going, Georgie," George said. "Tomorrow morning."

"Are we taking the Lear?" Georgie asked.

"Yes," Mimi said.

"Why can't we take the G5?" Georgie demanded.

"Because it's too big to land in Aspen," George said. "You know that."

"I do?" Georgie asked.

I can't believe this is my life, Mimi nearly said aloud.

Jack sat down at the table, hoisting himself up onto an eighteenth-century Chippendale chair (worth about $15,000, Mimi thought, unable to help herself), and folded his legs under him. He took a bite of the toast spread with marmalade, chewed thoughtfully a few times, and then squinched up his face in horror and spat the half-chewed mess onto the Sevres china plate in front of him.

Mimi looked to George for help. "Jack!" George roared. Jack jumped as if shot out of a cannon and fell off his chair.

"Sit down, Jack," George insisted.

Jack looked at him defiantly. "No . . . ," he said.

"Then go to your room."

"Gerda," Mimi called. Gerda appeared in the doorway and Mimi motioned for her to take away Jack's plate.

"I hate my room!" Jack cried. "It's too small . . ."

He was really being a brat, Mimi thought, praying he wouldn't be like this in Aspen. If he was, she had a feeling that she was finally going to lose it . . .

"Well, the next time you come to New York, you'll have a new room," George said, as if this would solve everyone's problem. "Mommy and Daddy have bought a new apartment . . ."

"Are you and Mommy getting back together?" Georgie asked in surprise. He looked from George to Mimi with an evil expression on his face.

"This mommy," George said. "Mimi Mommy."

Jack began shaking his head, muttering to himself. "How many times do I have to tell you?" he said, in a strange voice that almost sounded as if he were attempting to imitate an adult. "How many times do I have to tell you . . . that she is *not* our mommy!"

Mimi looked at him in shock, and suddenly burst into tears.

Five hours later, at exactly one-thirty, Mimi was seated in the best booth in Dingo's, nervously waiting for Janey to arrive. The morning's events had thrown her off; it bothered her enormously to have appeared weak and vulnerable in front of George's children. Naturally, George had made both boys apologize, but in that vicious way that children had, they managed to do it without appearing the least bit contrite . . .

She took a sip of water, glancing about at the crowd. There was a famous fashion-magazine editor in the booth next to hers, eating a bloody steak; on the other side was a well-known local newscaster. But she must be getting jaded, she thought wearily, because the crowd already looked tired, like a second-string cast brought in to play the Wednesday matinee of a Broadway show. How much longer would she have to do this? she wondered. Would anything new ever happen to her again . . . or was it to be this way for the rest of her life, the same dreary rounds of parties and committees and socializing, the same faces getting older or more pulled . . . ?

She idly picked up the menu, trying to distract herself from these negative thoughts. Everything was fine, everything was normal, and she had a wonderful life, she reassured herself. It was just that ever since Zizi had broken up with her, she'd been so ridiculously *emotional*. Little things that had never bothered her before suddenly seemed hugely important, causing a completely inappropriate response—like the way she had yelled at Gerda the other day for leaving a dust cloth behind one of the curtains in the living room. Gerda had looked at her like she was insane, and, of course, she'd apologized, but then Gerda had had the temerity to suggest that perhaps it was "the change."

She put her hands over her face. Was it really possible, then, that she was beginning to go through *menopause*? She was only forty-two, but everyone knew these things could happen, and if it *was* true, it would certainly be a fitting ending to her affair with Zizi. She would be officially dried up, and then *no* man would want her for sex; the plus would be that she'd never have to worry about finding herself in a situation like the one she'd been in with Zizi . . .

A waiter asked her if she wanted anything to drink, and she ordered a glass of champagne. She reminded herself that she'd known all along the affair would have to end; it was just that she hadn't expected to feel such a loss when it did. Perhaps it was the fact that Zizi was gone so suddenly: If she hadn't fainted, she might have made up an excuse to get away from George to find him; and if George hadn't insisted on calling the doctor, who had given her a sedative so strong that she had slept until five the next day, she probably would have gone to his apartment. By the time she'd recovered, it was too late—she imagined he was already on the plane to Europe—and she was left feeling like her insides had been cut out . . .

Until that moment, she hadn't realized how much she'd relied on him to make her life better. He was a valve, an outlet that allowed her to blithely continue on with her marriage, allowing her to pretend that there was nothing missing from her life. Zizi had provided the kind of pure love and affection that's free of pretense and is such an astonishment to young people who experience it for the first time. And she *had* been in love with him—and at a time in her life when she thought she'd never be in love again, when she'd thought those feelings were gone forever.

The waiter placed a glass of champagne in front of her, and she took a sip, hoping that it would lift her spirits. But the bubbles felt harsh against the back of her throat, and she was suddenly hit with another wave of nausea. She put the glass down and held her napkin to her lips, praying that she wouldn't be sick. But so far, these waves of nausea hadn't actually made her throw up . . . She had to get a hold of herself, she thought angrily. Aspen would help—and hadn't her mother always said that a change of scenery was the best thing for a broken heart?

She sat back against the pink suede banquette, tempted to dip her napkin in her water glass and place the cool cloth on her forehead; but knowing the gesture was too obvious and too dramatic, she looked at her watch instead. Janey was ten minutes late—normally, she would have been slightly irritated to be kept waiting, but on this afternoon, she knew she had to let it pass. Her recent thoughts about Janey had been too harsh. After all, it wasn't *Janey's* fault that Zizi had broken up with her, and the issue about the apartment was simply coincidence—Patty had been on tour with Digger in Europe, so how was Janey to know they'd reconciled?

Mimi had come to these realizations that morning as she'd sat sobbing in her dressing room. She'd finally accepted that she desperately needed to talk to someone about her situation, and that person was probably Janey. Mimi began to remind herself of the good points of her friend's character: Although Janey could be arrogant and full of herself, and at times seemed to think she was entitled to everything, wasn't that simply the result of being young—of being thirty-three and feeling like you still had your whole life ahead of you? Mimi was quite sure she hadn't been much better at Janey's age, and she believed that Janey had a good heart . . . She could *trust* Janey: Janey had been there at the beginning of the affair; she'd been loyal and kept her mouth shut; and she *knew* Zizi—at least a little. And Janey had certainly had her share of man troubles . . . Janey would *understand* . . . And so she had called Janey to ask her to lunch, and frankly, she'd been relieved when Janey had accepted in her usual spirit of friendliness, as if Mimi hadn't snapped at her at all last night . . .

"Hi darling," Janey purred, leaning over to kiss her. Mimi was startled—she must have been so engrossed in her own thoughts, she hadn't seen her come in.

Janey looked particularly beautiful today, Mimi noted. Her face glowed with animation, as if she were lit from within. She always looked lovely, Mimi thought, but like most women, she was at her best when she was happy. "You're in a good mood," Mimi ventured.

"Oh, only because of the show," Janey said casually, sliding into the banquette. She'd been relieved to get Mimi's call as well that morning; she hadn't spoken to Mimi for days and suddenly realized that she missed her friend terribly. But Mimi looked so . . . *morose*, Janey thought, immediately wishing that Mimi would lighten up. Tomorrow was the Saturday of Christmas week and everyone was leaving town, so this lunch at Dingo's was the last opportunity to see and be seen, and she meant to make the most of it. "The show got tons of coverage," Janey drawled, in a voice that was just loud enough to draw attention to herself, "and it was a bit scandalous, so of course, everyone's talking about it . . ."

"Is it scandalous?" Mimi asked, raising her eyebrows.

"You know," Janey said. "It was on network TV, and the Republican right is in an uproar . . . They want to control the way everyone thinks . . ." She caught the expression on Mimi's face and added, "Not *your* father, of course . . ."

"Of course," Mimi said. Her father had just been appointed secretary of commerce under the new Republican regime.

"Oh, Mimi . . . How *are* you?" Janey asked, having decided that by now everyone in the restaurant knew she was there, and she could at last focus on her friend.

Mimi shrugged and played with her water glass. "Do you know where Selden's taking you for Christmas yet?"

Janey shook her head and ordered a vodka on the rocks with a twist of lemon. That little awkwardness between herself and Mimi was still there, but here was an opportunity to get the source of the rift out in the open. "Selden and his surprises!" she exclaimed, as if outraged. "It's beginning to drive me crazy . . . Do you know that he never even *told* me he was going to hire a private detective?"

"Selden hired a private detective?" Mimi asked.

"Didn't you *know*?" Janey said. "He hired a private detective to investigate Maribelle Dubrovsky or whatever her name is, and the detective found out that she's married. That's why Patty and Digger are back together . . ."

"But were they ever really apart?" Mimi asked.

"Patty *said* that they hadn't been getting along on tour, and that she was going to leave him when they got home," Janey said, brushing her long hair over her shoulder. Naturally, Patty had never said any such thing, but Janey knew Mimi would never question it. "And *then*," Janey went on dramatically, as if to add heft to the veracity of her story, "Patty got the phone call from Selden." This part, at least, *was* true, and Janey smiled innocently. "I'm really sorry I didn't let you know sooner, but every time I tried to call, you were busy with the boys . . ."

"I *know*," Mimi said emphatically, feeling slightly guilty. Having now heard the whole story, she realized how silly she'd been in thinking that Janey had somehow wanted to wound her. "It's just that the house is always in chaos when the boys are there . . ."

"Of course, now that Patty's with Digger, Zizi can stay . . . ," Janey said. Saying the name Zizi felt like eating a spoonful of dirt, and she hoped Mimi hadn't noticed . . .

"Oh, it doesn't matter anymore," Mimi said with a shrug. She took a sip of water, not daring to trust the champagne. "Zizi and I broke up," she said. And with a short, husky laugh, added, "Or, to put it more accurately, *he* dumped *me*."

Janey returned to the Lowell Hotel two hours later, still reeling from the news of the affair's demise. Naturally, as Mimi quietly relayed her sad tale, revealing how much she'd loved Zizi and how unbearable it was to be without him, Janey was a model of sympathy. She kindly pointed out that Zizi was bound to end it sooner or later, that she'd heard he was out with other (younger) women, that he'd obviously only been after her money and was probably trying to use her to get ahead, and, of course, the old standby: That it was better it should end *now*, while Mimi still had some shreds of dignity left, before she was *really* hurt . . .

But inside, her thoughts were far less charitable. She would hardly have been human if it didn't cross her mind just once or twice that maybe Mimi *deserved* this for having taken Zizi away from *her* last summer . . . and that she'd been right about Zizi all along. And who could blame her for thinking that, somehow, her encounter with Zizi had caused this, and how clever she was to have engineered it. For a moment, she thought about telling Mimi that Zizi had come on to her, but then she thought better of it. She couldn't help thinking that it was entirely possible that maybe Zizi had broken up with Mimi because he secretly wanted to be with *her* . . .

"Why, Selden darling, you're home," Janey exclaimed as she entered the suite and found Selden packing his things in the living room. "What are you doing home so early, darling?" she asked, kissing him on the lips.

"Packing," he said. She was in a good mood, he could tell, and that made him happy.

"But we're not leaving until tomorrow morning," she pointed out.

"At seven A.M.," he said. He went into the bedroom to look for some socks; she followed him.

"I hate getting up so *early*," she said, with the petulance of a child.

"But we'll be on the beach by noon," Selden said. "Won't that be nice?"

"I guess so," she said, in the little-girl voice he loved.

"You'd better start packing, too," he said. "Should I get down your suitcases for you?"

"Oh, yes, Selden. Please," she said. "I'll take the Louis Vuitton duffel and the hanging bag, and my makeup case, of course."

"Of course," he said, smiling. As he opened the closet and reached up to take her suitcases down from the shelf, she came up behind him and put her arms around his waist, nibbling at his ear.

"Where *are* we going, darling?" she asked. "You *have* to tell me. Tell me *now* . . ."

He laughed and took a few steps backward, pulling her down onto the bed. Maybe they'd start their vacation with a little prevacation sex, he thought happily. "Okay," he agreed, "if you promise not to tell anyone . . ."

"I promise," she said, matching her tone to his.

"We're going to Mustique!"

"Mustique?" she exclaimed. She sat up in alarm, biting her finger. Mustique was supposed to be glamorous, but part of its glamour was being there with the right crowd. And she didn't know of anyone who was going there this year. "But . . . what will we *do* the whole time? We won't know anyone . . ."

"Ah ha!" he said, still thinking she was going to be pleased with him. "That's where you're wrong. You *will* know people . . . We're spending Christmas with the entire Rose clan. Isn't that great?"

She gasped and jumped off the bed. "But I've never even met them," she cried.

"Exactly," he said. "And it's about time you did."

"Oh, Selden," she said with annoyance. She'd known she would have to meet his family at some point, but she'd assumed Selden would give her fair warning. And on the scale of things, spending Christmas vacation with his family was even less glamorous than spending it alone with Selden . . . She went into the bathroom, and with a small bang, firmly shut the door behind her. He heard the lock turn, and as he flopped back onto the bed, had the sinking feeling that they weren't going to be having prevacation sex after all.

The endless, rhythmic *thwack* of a tennis ball was nearly putting Janey to sleep and, making an effort to keep her eyes open, she forced herself to at least pretend to concentrate on the game below. From her vantage point under a tree on the little hill above the court, she could see most of the island spread out before her, with its manicured green fields crisscrossed by narrow, black asphalt roads and, in the near distance, the aqua blue Caribbean Sea. On the road that passed by the tennis court, two housemaids in starched gray uniforms chatted gaily as they slowly made their way up the hill, as if they had nothing more unpleasant to contemplate than an endless series of days that were exactly the same as this one . . .

On the court below, Selden was playing tennis with his father, Richard Rose; his brother, Wheaton, was umpiring. All three men were in whites, following one of the rules of the Mustique Corporation, which called for the upholding of traditional tennis garb. Standing at the end of the court near Selden, Wheaton made a crossing gesture with his arms. "That ball was out!" he shouted. "Out! Sorry, Dad."

"Don't worry. I'll still beat the bastard . . . ," Richard Rose gasped, throwing the ball up into the air and smashing his racket against it.

Seated on the grass next to her, Paula Rose, Selden's mother, cried out a warning *"Richard!,"* causing Selden, Wheaton, and Richard Rose to glance up the hill in their direction.

"I'm trouncing the old man and he's losing it!" Selden called excitedly to Janey. Janey gave him a wan smile, as Paula Rose called out sharply, "Just make sure you don't lose your *manners!*" She turned to Janey and, with a shake of her head, said, "The boys just love their tennis. I think the biggest mistake I ever made was allowing Richard to put in a court at our house in Chicago."

Janey scratched at a mosquito bite on her leg and, trying to appear interested, said, "Is that *so?*" The very first thing Selden had said to his father when they'd arrived, three days ago, was: "So, Dad. Have you found the courts yet?" She scratched harder and the bite began to bleed slightly, offering some relief. The island was full of mosquitoes; even sleeping under a mosquito tent was scant protection, because the insects buzzed around the netting with an angry viciousness that kept her awake half the night. Selden was fine, but *she* was exhausted. If she could only get a decent night's sleep, she thought desperately, she might be able to get through this week without going nuts . . .

"The temperature's perfect for tennis now, isn't it?" Isabelle said pleasantly. Isabelle was Wheaton's wife and a perfect example of good, midwestern values: She was friendly and kind—and utterly bland—with a personality that was free of sharp edges or interesting angles.

"Thank God it's not too hot now," Paula Rose agreed. "When you come to these Caribbean islands, you've got to play early in the morning or late at night. When we were in Round Hill six years ago . . . ," she said, and began a long story about the difficulties of securing court time in a climate in which there were only two or three comfortable hours in which to play. Janey quickly lost track of the story, becoming absorbed in the progress of an ant that was dragging a small leaf through the grass at her feet, which was a mistake, because suddenly Paula Rose turned to her and said, "Well, Janey? What do *you* think?"

"Oh," Janey said, looking up and attempting to smile. Her mouth hurt from three days of being forced to smile at all kinds of things that she wasn't the least bit happy about. "What do *I* think . . . ?"

"About Richard getting sunstroke . . . ," Paula said, exchanging a glance with Isabelle.

"Thank God he recovered," Janey said, trying to get into the spirit of the conversation.

"Well, *naturally*, he recovered," Paula said, looking at her like she was an idiot. "But for those two hours, when we had every doctor in Jamaica . . . I was sure he was having a heart attack. 'At least wait until we get back to Chicago to die,' I told him. So now, every time we're on vacation, he always promises that he won't let anything happen to him until we're back home . . ."

While Isabelle laughed gamely, Janey found herself unable to summon any response. She was trying to fit in, she really *was*, she reminded herself. But Selden's family was so foreign to her, it would have been easier if they literally were from another country, like *Sweden*, perhaps . . .

Oh, they were all perfectly *nice*, of course—on the surface. Take Mrs. Rose for example, she thought, glancing over at Paula. Having told her little story, she was now casually ignoring Janey, appearing to be completely absorbed in the game between Selden and Richard. She was what people called "well preserved"; she appeared every morning in a crisp white T-shirt and khaki shorts, an Hermès scarf tied around her neck, with carefully applied makeup and blown-dry hair. She was an attractive woman, and considered by the rest of her family to be endlessly interesting because she was still a journalist for the *Chicago Sun-Times*. At the beginning of the first evening, she'd been so gracious, showing Janey to her room and remarking over Janey's "lovely" clothes and shoes and handbags, that Janey had imagined that they actually *might* become friends, that Mrs. Rose might be the mother she'd never had . . . And then, at dinner, she'd sat next to Selden's father, Richard. Richard had a kindly cartoonish face; a retired lawyer from the Chicago firm where Wheaton still worked, Richard Rose now put all his energy into his diet and exercise program, which, he explained, was responsible for the fact that he had so far managed to ward off "the cancer." Janey, feeling insecure, had probably paid him a little *too* much attention, and the next morning, there was a decided chill in the air . . .

On the court below, Selden hit a forehand that whizzed by Richard and, throwing down his racket, declared himself the winner. In a moment, the three men came strolling up the hill, and Janey stood up, hoping that the day's tennis activities were finally over. Maybe she and Selden could get a drink somewhere—she'd heard there was a cool outdoor bar on the island where Mick Jagger supposedly hung out . . .

"We've got the court for another hour," Selden said breathlessly. "Who wants to play next? Janey?"

"You *know* I don't play tennis," Janey said, and before she could suggest that she and Selden go, Richard interrupted her. With a scolding "Never too late to learn," he said, "Selden, you've *got* to get her lessons."

"I'm not very athletic . . . ," Janey began helplessly.

"Isabelle didn't start until *she* was thirty-one," Wheaton pointed out. "She's pretty good now. Sometimes she even takes a game off me . . ."

"Only when you feel sorry for me," Isabelle said, with a laugh.

"Paula?" Richard asked.

"I've got to go back to the house and check on that cook," Paula said. "I want to make sure she got the roast beef for Christmas dinner . . . Does anybody know if the supermarket is open tomorrow?"

"Until noon," Selden said.

"That's a relief," Paula said.

Janey gave up. "You and Wheaton play," she said to Selden. "I think I'll go back to the house. I'm tired . . ."

"Tired!" Richard exclaimed. "You're the youngest one here."

"It's the mosquitoes. I can't sleep," Janey explained.

"We had a huge one buzzing around our heads last night, didn't we, Wheaton?" Isabelle said. "Somehow, it got through the mosquito net . . ."

"Those nets are no good," Richard said. "You've got to use the plug-in thing . . ."

"Really?" Isabelle said. "We couldn't figure out how to make ours work."

"I'll show you," Paula said. "First you have to take the repellent out of the little aluminum package . . ."

Selden took a step toward Janey and put his arm around her. He was sweaty and she recoiled slightly. "Are you sure you don't want to watch me whup Wheaton's ass?" he asked.

"Selden . . . ," Paula said warningly.

"I'll watch you tomorrow," Janey said wearily.

"Come on, girls," Paula said. "Richard, are you coming?"

"I'm going to stay here for a bit."

Janey started down the hill with Paula and Isabelle. "Selden's playing a lot of tennis . . . ," she ventured, in an attempt to make a joke. "I hope *he* doesn't have a heart attack or something . . ."

Naturally, Paula took the comment the wrong way. "Selden?" she asked, expiring a small puff of air as she looked at Janey incredulously. "Selden is in *great* shape . . ."

"Oh, I know, but . . . ," Janey said, weakly.

There was a white Jeep parked at the bottom of the hill and Isabelle got into the driver's seat. Janey struggled for a moment to push up the passenger seat, feeling Paula's impatience as she stood behind her. She finally moved the seat forward and got into the back. Paula heaved herself onto the passenger seat. "Are you sure you don't mind driving?" she asked Isabelle.

"Not at all. I love it," Isabelle said.

"These roads are so narrow and twisty, they make me nervous," Paula said with a laugh. And then, as if remembering that Janey was in the car as well, she looked over her shoulder. "Do you drive, Janey?" she asked pleasantly.

"Yes," Janey said. "I have a Porsche."

"A Porsche!" Paula exclaimed. "My goodness. Then *you* should be driving . . ."

"It was a gift from the Victoria's Secret people," Janey said, scratching her leg.

Paula glanced at her in the rearview mirror. "Do you have to give it back?"

"No," Janey said. "At least, I don't think so . . . I wouldn't give it back anyway."

"You wouldn't?" Isabelle asked. She and Paula exchanged a look.

"No," Janey said, her irritation bubbling to the surface. "Why should I?"

There was no polite answer to this question, so Paula changed the subject.

"Are your parents upset that you aren't spending Christmas with them?" she asked.

"No," Janey said. They were in the little town now, a picturesque village lined with small, brightly colored buildings that housed shops selling T-shirts, ice-cream cones, and sarongs.

"They're not?" Paula asked in surprise. "If my boys didn't spend Christmas with me, I don't know what I'd do . . ."

"I don't get along with my parents that well," Janey said primly. "My mother's never liked me . . ."

This must have stirred Mrs. Rose's heart, because she cried out, "Oh, Janey. That's awful!"

"It's okay, really," Janey said. "It's not such a big deal."

They got through the town and drove past the tiny harbor. There were two huge yachts anchored offshore, and Janey wondered who was on them. If only, she thought for the hundredth time, Selden had bothered to tell her where they were going *beforehand*. At least that way she would have been able to find someone who knew the island, who could have made introductions . . . There had to be *some* interesting people here . . . But instead, she was stuck with Selden and his family, and if Mrs. Rose had her way, every Christmas was going to be exactly like this one . . .

Isabelle drove the Jeep up a steep hill, and up an even steeper driveway to their villa, a white stucco affair with a large stone fireplace that was situated on a cliff overlooking the harbor. The villa, at least, was nice—supposedly one of the best on the island—but what was the point of having a great villa if no one important was there to *see* you in it?

"I guess I'll have to go back in a hour to pick up the boys," Isabelle said. Janey winced; they were really starting to get on her nerves now, with their quaint little colloquialisms, like calling the men "the boys" and the women "the girls" . . .

"Maybe we should rent another Jeep," Janey suggested. "That way . . ."

Paula Rose cut her off. "Selden was thinking the same thing, but I told him *not* to waste his money," she said firmly. "We've had dozens of family vacations with just one car . . . And besides," she added. "I think it's *fun*, being all cozy together. It's just like when the boys were young . . ."

I am now officially going crazy, Janey thought, as they went into the house.

She had scarcely lain down for ten minutes when Isabelle knocked on the door and came into the room.

"Are you sleeping?" Isabelle asked.

"Not really," Janey said.

"I was thinking about going into town to do a little shopping before I picked up the boys. Do you want to come?"

"Sure," Janey sighed, thinking that shopping might be just slightly preferable to staring at the ceiling.

"I'll meet you at the car in five minutes, then," Isabelle said.

Janey got up and looked at herself in the wicker mirror, positioned over a long, glass-topped white wicker dresser. She had a slight tan, giving her skin a golden glow, and she looked good, despite her exhaustion. But she always looked better in warmer weather, and, changing out of her shorts and into a sleeveless Pucci shift and flat gold sandals, she reminded herself that she had to make the best of it . . .

But it was all just so slightly disappointing. She'd brought all of her beautiful resort wear, which she now realized was completely wasted, especially given the fact that Isabelle's wardrobe seemed to consist solely of shapeless cotton print dresses and colorful nylon surfer sandals. Even if they *did* come across some chic people, she'd never be able to introduce them to Isabelle, and once again she wished she were anywhere but here—any place where she didn't have to be around Selden's family. Even Patty and Digger were in Aspen, Patty's excuse being that she and

Digger had had such a stressful year, they couldn't bear to be with anyone who was related to them . . .

Isabelle was standing by the Jeep, a worn leather knapsack slung over one shoulder, bouncing the keys in her hand. "God, you look great," she said, getting into the car. "I'd ask you where you got that dress, but it probably costs a million dollars . . ."

"No," Janey said. "It's Pucci. It was probably only two hundred dollars . . ."

"That's way more than I could afford to spend on a summer dress," Isabelle said with a laugh.

"But I thought Wheaton was a lawyer," Janey said. "And you work, don't you . . . ?"

"I'm a headhunter," Isabelle said, nodding. "That's how I met Wheaton. It's great, because every day is different. I'm the kind of person who doesn't like to be bored," she explained, "and Wheaton is the same way, so it works out."

Janey nodded, unsure of what to say. It seemed to her that Isabelle and Wheaton were exactly the sort of people who did like to be bored, as so far they'd been perfectly content to do nothing but play tennis and go to the beach. But feeling a response was required, she said, "Wheaton is *adorable*."

"Do you think so?" Isabelle asked, carefully steering the Jeep around a sharp corner. "Once you've been married for a while, you forget what your husband really looks like."

Janey didn't, in fact, think Wheaton *was* so adorable—his eyes were set close together over a slightly bulbous, crooked nose; like Selden, he had a slightly goofy quality that kept him just on the wrong side of handsome—but now that she'd said it, she couldn't go back. "Oh yes," she said emphatically. "He's so . . . *cute* . . ."

"He thinks so anyway," Isabelle said with a genial laugh, as she parked the car in front of the boardwalk that ran along the ocean side of town. In an automatic gesture, Janey pulled down the sun visor and checked out her appearance. As she reached for her lipstick, Isabelle said, "I'm just dying to know the name of that lipstick you wear. It's so pretty . . ."

"It is, isn't it?" Janey said, running the lipstick lightly over her lips. "It's not quite red and not quite pink . . ."

"It's a bit of both, isn't it?" Isabelle said.

"It's called Pussy Pink," Janey said, replacing the cap on the tube and slipping it into her purse. "I've been wearing it for years. I found it in Paris . . ."

"Did you live in Paris?" Isabelle asked.

"Oh yes," Janey said. "Most models do when they're first starting out."

"I've always wanted to live in Paris," Isabelle said. "It must have been fascinating."

"It was . . . interesting," Janey agreed cautiously. Paris was full of unpleasant memories, most of which she preferred to forget. Changing the subject, she asked, "Do you and Wheaton have children?"

"We don't," Isabelle said, fastening her long, frizzy dark hair to the back of her head with a plastic clip. She could probably still be pretty, Janey thought, if she would take care of herself a little—dye her hair to cover up the gray streaks and have those two deep lines between her brows injected with Botox. "But Wheaton does," she continued. "From his first marriage."

"I didn't know Wheaton was married before," Janey said, as they began walking toward the shops.

"It was a long time ago," Isabelle said. "I think Mandy—that's her name—was kind of the town slut and Wheaton felt sorry for her. Anyway, she got pregnant and Wheaton married her, and they have a little girl . . . Well, she's not so little anymore, she's fifteen."

"That's a difficult age," Janey said wisely.

"It is," Isabelle said. "And she's a wild girl—I keep telling Wheaton that if he's not careful, she's going to end up pregnant, but you know how men are. They just never see the things that women do, do they?" She stopped in front of a shop to admire a pair of flip-flops festooned with plastic flowers. "But I have to say, Paula is just amazing. She still sees that little girl every weekend, no matter what . . ."

"Do you want to have children?" Janey asked, as they went into the shop.

"We've been trying . . . ," Isabelle said, picking up the pair of flip-flops and turning them over to check the price. "My doctor says I'm going to have to do in vitro next. But you have to take shots, and I'm not sure how I feel about that, you know? And then sometimes I look at Wheaton, and I think, Wait a minute. I already *have* a child . . ."

Janey nodded. This was, she understood, the way most women felt about their husbands, and she knew Isabelle meant it as a source of camaraderie. But Janey only found it depressing. "You should buy those," she said, nodding at the flip-flops in Isabelle's hand.

"Should I?" Isabelle asked.

"Why not? . . . If you like them," Janey said.

"They're only eight dollars," Isabelle said, considering.

"Then you should definitely buy them," Janey said firmly.

Isabelle paid for the flip-flops and they left the store. On the sidewalk, Isabelle turned to her and smiled. "I'm sure this trip must have been a bit of a surprise," she said cautiously.

"Oh, it was," Janey said, nodding.

"Paula told Selden to tell you, but he wouldn't," she said, pushing the flip-flops into her knapsack. "I think Selden can be a bit stubborn. But maybe," she added, with frightening insight, "he was afraid if he told you, you wouldn't want to come."

· · ·

"Shall we open our presents now or later?" Paula asked excitedly. It was Christmas morning and they were having breakfast, seated at the dining room table located outdoors under a vine-covered trellis, where they took all their meals.

"Now," Wheaton demanded childishly.

"We have to wait until we at least finish eating," Paula said. And Janey, listening to this exchange as she scooped a wedge of grapefruit onto her spoon, imagined that Paula and Wheaton had probably had this conversation every Christmas morning for the past forty years.

"It's so weird, not having a tree at Christmas," Isabelle said.

"It's very LA," Wheaton agreed.

"That isn't true," Paula said. "Selden and Sheila always had a tree in Los Angeles."

"Just a small one," Richard said.

"Dad, when did you ever see our tree?" Selden asked.

"We were there one year. Don't you remember?"

"That was the year Sheila . . . ," Wheaton ventured.

"Let's not talk about it," Selden said quickly.

"Absolutely," Paula agreed.

"Where should we open our presents?" Isabelle asked. "In the living room?"

"There's no tree anyway," Richard said. "I say let's open them right here. Live a little, eh, Selden?" he asked.

They were still opening presents forty-five minutes later as Janey took a sip of orange juice and stared morosely down at the table. Next to her was a neat pile of wrapping paper, which Paula Rose had insisted on saving, carefully folding the pieces and handing them to Janey to "take care of." Next to the pile were the two presents Janey had received: A folding Totes umbrella from Wheaton and Isabelle, who explained that they hadn't known what to get her but that every woman needed an umbrella for her purse; and an Hermès scarf from Paula and Richard, which Janey had enthused over and then returned to its orange box. Janey had given Selden a pair of Prada sandals, a pressed leather Prada wallet, and a Prada shaving kit, which, she'd explained to Paula, she'd purchased at a thirty percent discount, but which Paula declared "excessive" nevertheless.

It was all just so awkward and embarrassing, Janey thought, as she watched Isabelle cooing over a pair of hand-knit heavy woolen socks—a gift to her from Paula. Selden hadn't told her they were going to be with his family, so naturally, she hadn't bought them any gifts, and every time someone opened a present, it was a reminder of how out of place she felt . . .

"Well, I guess you all know what our present is," Selden said, pushing back his chair and standing up. He had paid for the entire trip, including the villa rental and plane fare for the family. He walked over to Janey, and motioning for her to stand up as well, put his arm around her. He lifted his juice glass in a toast. "Here's to our family vacation, and to my new wife, Janey. And to many more Christmases just like this one."

"Hear, hear," Richard said.

"Thank you, Selden," Paula said, holding out her arms for a hug. "And thank you, too, Janey. You really shouldn't have."

"Oh, I . . . ," Janey said awkwardly.

"That reminds me," Selden said, snapping to attention. "I've got one more present. For Janey."

They all looked at Janey as Selden disappeared into the living room.

Paula Rose raised her eyebrows. "I hope he isn't spoiling you, Janey," she said, as if this "extra" gift were somehow Janey's fault.

"Oh, he's far too practical for that," Janey said.

Selden returned carrying a large white envelope. He handed it to Janey ceremoniously and sat down next to her.

She turned the envelope over. In the return address space was printed "Millionaire Real Estate, Greenwich, CT."

"What is this, Selden?" she asked, with a mixture of curiosity and dread.

"It's an envelope!" Wheaton exclaimed, taken with his own humor. "Get it? An envelope . . . ?"

"Is there anything *in* it?" Isabelle asked.

"Of course there is," Paula said sharply, silencing her.

"Open it!" Selden said eagerly.

She looked at him in fear, sliding her finger underneath the flap.

Inside was an eight-by-ten, six-page color brochure. On the cover was a photograph of a gnarled, sickly looking tree surrounded by scrub brush situated on a small hill. At the bottom of the hill was a dirty beach that ended in a point surrounded by greenish brown water. "Welcome to Pirate's Pointe!" the lettering declared.

"Oh . . . my . . . God," Janey said. She'd thought that Selden had understood that the matter of the house in Connecticut was closed, but apparently, she hadn't made her feelings clear, and he had simply taken her silence as acquiescence . . .

"Keep reading," Selden said, pulling his chair close to hers and turning the page as if he were reading a bedtime story to a child. On the next page was a map of Greenwich, Connecticut, with "Pirate's Pointe" shaded in red; it was a narrow spit of land, shaped like a crooked finger that jutted out into Long Island Sound. Unable to contain himself, Selden began reading aloud: "Pirate's Pointe is eight pristine untouched acres located in the best section of exclusive Greenwich, Connecticut, on Long Island Sound. Forty-five minutes from New York City and four hours from Boston, this is a millionaire's dream. Secluded and private, it's like owning your own island, and yet you're just steps away from a major metropolitan area . . ."

"Can you afford this, Selden?" Paula Rose interrupted.

"Of course, Mother," Selden said. He continued reading: "On offer for the first time in one hundred twenty-five years, Pirate's Pointe is a piece of living history. For only the most discriminating buyer . . ."

"I don't understand," Richard Rose said. He got up and stood behind Selden, peering over his shoulder at the brochure. "Have you *bought* this land?"

"I closed last week," Selden said proudly. He took Janey's hand and squeezed it. "We're going to build our dream house there. We'll have a pool and a dock, a couple of boats, and a tennis court . . ."

Wheaton emitted a long, low whistle.

"I think you're going to have lots of guests," Isabelle giggled.

"What do you think, baby?" Selden asked, gently pressing Janey's hand.

They were all looking at her again.

"I'm so happy . . . I think I'm going to *cry*," Janey said.

"Right," Richard said, after a brief pause, clapping Selden on the back. "What should we do next?"

"Oh, Richard," Paula sighed. "Let them *absorb*. This is a huge step, buying a house."

"They didn't buy a house, they bought land," Richard corrected her. "You mean let them *enjoy*. As soon as they start building, it's all over."

"We'll have contractors, Dad," Selden said.

"Pshaw," Richard said, with a dismissive wave. "Remember when we built our house?" he asked his wife.

"When *I* built it, dear," Paula said. "I couldn't get *you* to do a thing, remember?" She turned to Janey. "I couldn't even get his opinion on the kind of doorknobs he wanted."

"I wasn't exactly slacking off back then," Richard said to Selden. "I was only working fifteen-hour days . . ."

"Are you sure you're going to have time for this, Selden?" Paula asked.

"Janey will," Selden said, squeezing her hand again. "She's incredibly good at details. You should see what she goes through before she goes out at night . . ."

"Oh, I'm sure . . . ," Paula said mildly.

Janey pulled her hand away. "That isn't exactly true," she snapped.

"Huh?" Selden said, looking at her in confusion.

She got up and went into the bathroom. She stared at herself in the mirror, realizing that she'd suddenly become trapped in exactly the sort of existence she'd spent her whole life trying to avoid.

When she came out, they were watching a tape of the Victoria's Secret Fashion Show in the living room. The lyrics "Baby don't hurt me" were playing. "I hope you don't mind," Selden said, looking up and motioning for her to sit next to him on the couch. "I wanted my parents to see it."

"It was on TV," Janey whispered angrily into his ear.

"No one told us," Isabelle said.

The tension in the room was palpable. Richard Rose's face was frozen in an expression of indifference, as if he couldn't trust himself to reveal any interest in the spectacle on the screen. Paula looked disapproving; Wheaton amused. "Hold on, everyone," Selden said, completely clueless. "Here's where Janey comes out . . ."

Suddenly, Janey appeared at the top of the runway in the blue sequined bra and panty set. She paused, and sweeping the crowd with her eyes, began sashaying down the runway with a superior expression on her face. Watching herself, she cringed—her breasts looked enormous, and the men in the audience were whistling and making catcalls like adolescent boys at a seedy strip joint. Sensing her distress, Isabelle leaned over and patted her knee. "You look just great, Janey," she said kindly. "Doesn't she look great, Wheaton?"

"Sure," Wheaton muttered, looking down at the floor.

Suddenly Paula stood up and, striding to the television set, snapped it off.

"Hey!" Selden said.

"Janey looks absolutely beautiful, dear," Paula said firmly. "But I really don't think this is appropriate fare for Christmas Day. Do you?" And then, as if nothing at all had happened, she said brightly, "Should we have our usual afternoon? Beach and then tennis?"

They all stood up. Selden clapped Wheaton on the shoulder. "How about a quick game before the beach?"

"Sure," Wheaton said. They began filing out of the room. Janey turned away, acutely conscious of the fact that during the entire debacle, not one of them had had the guts to even look in her direction.

"Are you coming, Janey?" Paula called, without turning around.

"In a minute," Janey said.

She was suffocating. She had to get out of the house; she had to get away from them. It was obvious now: She didn't belong here and she didn't fit in. They knew it and she knew it, and there was no use pretending otherwise . . .

She went down the hallway to her bedroom. Selden already had his tennis shorts halfway up his legs, as if he couldn't wait to get out of the house. "Hey babe," he said, wriggling his bottom to help inch the tennis shorts over his hips.

"That was *incredibly* embarrassing," she spat.

"Oh, come on, babe," he said, fastening the shorts around his waist as he came toward her. He kissed her on the cheek. "You can't pay attention to Mother. She's very conservative. She knows what you do for a living . . . she just doesn't want to be reminded of it, that's all. Don't worry," he said, giving her a little shake. "I'm sure she still loves you . . ."

"She can't stand me," Janey said. She went to the closet and took down her Louis Vuitton duffel bag.

"Hey," Selden said. "What are you doing?"

"I'm leaving," Janey said. "I'm taking the next flight out of here."

"Come on, babe," Selden said. "You're kidding, right . . . ?"

"I've never been more serious in my life," she said, through gritted teeth.

He grabbed her arm. "Mother didn't mean it, I promise," he said soothingly. "I'll get her to apologize . . ."

"It's not just *that*!"

"What is it then?"

"It's *everything*," she said viciously. "This whole vacation *sucks*. We can't even go to a bar and have a drink . . ."

"Is that what you want to do?" he asked, taking a step away from her. "You want to go out partying . . . ?"

"Not *partying*," she faltered. "I'd just like to meet some interesting people . . ."

"This is a *family* vacation," Selden said coldly. "I get to see my family maybe once a year, so if you don't mind, I'd like to spend my time with *them*—as opposed to a bunch of strangers I'm never going to see again."

"It's fine for you," Janey snapped, "because they're *your* family . . ."

"They happen to be *your* family now, too," Selden said. He crossed the room and picked up his tennis racket. "So I'd appreciate it if you could refrain from making a scene. You're acting just like a child . . ."

"Oh. And you're not?" she accused.

"Maybe I am," he said harshly. "But I *paid* for this vacation. It cost me thirty thousand dollars. And I intend to have a good time."

"So what am *I* supposed to do?"

"Just go to the beach and work on your tan," he sniped. "I'll be there in less than an hour, okay?" And with that, he left the room.

Janey sat down on the bed in a huff. She looked at the duffel bag and suddenly realized she didn't have the energy to leave—to book a ticket and pack and order a taxi and get to the airport and then fly all the way back to New York, changing planes in Miami . . . Her eye fell on the white envelope, which lay on her pillow. Selden must have placed it there, as a reminder for her to start planning their house. In a fit of rage, she picked it up and flung it across the room, where it bounced off the mirror with a satisfying *thwack* and fell to the floor.

From the other side of the thin bedroom wall, she heard Paula call out: "Is everything okay in there?"

"It's fine," Janey called back. "I just dropped something." She put her head in her hands, wondering if this day could get any worse.

An hour later, Janey lay on her stomach on a striped towel, filtering sand through her fingers and thinking about how much she hated Selden and his family. Next to her sat Isabelle, a cheap local straw hat clapped on the top of her head. As if somehow aware of how badly things were going, Isabelle was silent, pretending to read a mystery novel she'd found in the house. Paula and Richard were at the other end of the beach, taking a walk.

The silence between the two women grew heavy, and finally Isabelle put down her book. As if she couldn't think of anything else to say, she commented, "You've got a great figure, Janey. Do you work out?"

"Hardly," Janey said.

"You're kidding," Isabelle said, staring at the ocean. "I'd have to work out all day every day to have a figure like yours."

And even then you never would, Janey thought, suddenly sick of this endless obsession that people had with her body. "I get that all the time," she snapped, no longer inclined to be polite. "And it's a huge bore. Everybody's body is what it is, you know? It's like intelligence—you can't change it that much."

"I'm *sorry*," Isabelle said. "I didn't mean to offend you . . ." She picked up her book and started to read again.

"Forget about it," Janey sighed. She rolled onto her back and closed her eyes, and immediately felt bad. Isabelle was the only person who'd been even remotely nice to her, and now she'd insulted her. "It's not your fault," she said apologetically. "It's just that Selden and I got into a fight . . ."

"About something stupid," Isabelle said, nodding.

"I . . . guess so," Janey said, hoping that she wasn't going to have to go into the particulars.

"That happens to me and Wheaton every time we go on vacation. There's always one day when we get into a huge fight . . . about *nothing* . . . and we're mad at each other for hours and then we realize how stupid we're being and we make up." Isabelle put her book down and turned to Janey. "I think that kind of thing is actually *good* for a relationship, don't you?" she asked. "I always think it's *cleansing* . . ."

Janey sat up on her elbows. "What was Selden's first wife like?" she asked casually. "He never talks about her . . ."

"Oh!" Isabelle said. She frowned. "Well, she was *very* smart, and *very* successful—she was an entertainment lawyer—I think she had lots of big movie stars as clients. But in the end . . ." She broke off, and, looking at Janey, said, "Do you promise not to tell Selden I told you? Because I know he really doesn't like to talk about it, and Wheaton will kill me . . ."

"I promise," Janey said. She rolled over onto her side and smiled.

"Well, in the *end* . . . I guess Selden just stopped paying attention to her or something, because she started getting all this plastic surgery. Not that there's anything *wrong* with plastic surgery," she added quickly, as if not wanting to offend Janey. "But it was just sort of like she was addicted. She got breast implants, and then she had a nose job, and that wasn't enough, so she had some kind of eye lift and I think she even had that operation where they suck out the fat . . ."

"Liposuction," Janey said.

"That's it," Isabelle said. "I mean, she looked good and everything, but she also looked kind of weird. And then there was some other stuff that happened . . . something about a necklace, and then it turned out that maybe Sheila was cheating . . . I'm not really sure, but apparently, it was one of those things that got really messy . . ."

"Is that so?" Janey said, encouragingly.

"Yeah," Isabelle said. "So I guess that's why it's so important to him to have a normal life. Even before he met you, all he talked about was how much he wanted to get married again and have kids . . ."

"Yeah," Janey said, sarcastically. "I *know* . . ."

"You don't seem that thrilled about the house," Isabelle said gently.

Janey sighed, picking up a handful of sand and letting it run through her fingers. "It's not that I'm not happy about it," she said, "it's just that I don't have any time to work on it. Selden doesn't know this, but I'm about to start producing a movie."

"You *are*?" Isabelle asked, impressed.

"That's right," Janey said, nodding her head. "I've bought the rights to a bestselling book—*The Embarrassments*, you've probably heard of it—and in the next couple of months I'll be raising the money and getting a director and lead actor on board . . ."

"That's interesting," Isabelle said. "What's it about?"

"You should read it," Janey said. "I was actually thinking that I might play one of the female parts. I've done quite a bit of acting . . ."

"Have you?" Isabelle remarked. "Selden didn't tell us you were so talented."

No, I'm sure he didn't, Janey thought ruefully, but at that moment their conversation was interrupted by the arrival of Paula.

She plunked herself down on the end of Isabelle's towel. "That was a lovely walk," she said breathlessly. "You girls should try it."

"Oh, we will," Isabelle nodded. "We were just sitting here talking."

"Were you?" Paula said. "Girl talk?"

Isabelle looked at Janey. "Janey was just telling me that she's going to produce a movie."

"Really?" Paula said, looking skeptical. "What movie?"

"It's still in development," Janey said quickly. "We're working on getting the money right now . . ."

Richard, who was a few steps behind Paula, suddenly appeared and stood above his wife. "Janey's going to produce a movie," Paula said to him.

"I thought Selden was a producer," Richard said.

"He is," Paula said. "But now Janey says she's going to be one, too." She raised her eyebrows, giving Richard a look.

"I'm curious about one thing," Richard said. "How long can a career as a model last?"

"Well, Lauren Hutton . . . ," Janey began.

"Oh, but she's an exception, isn't she?" Paula said, cutting her off. "I'm sure you want to have children soon . . ."

"I guess so," Janey said in frustration.

Selden came down the little dirt track leading to the beach. He was smiling and appeared to be in a triumphant mood. "Hello, Mother," he said, throwing a towel down onto the sand. "You'll be happy to know that I whupped his . . . butt."

"Thank you, dear," Paula said.

"Where's Wheaton?" Isabelle said, looking around.

"He dropped me off," Selden said. "He had to go back to the house. He forgot his bathing suit . . ."

"Typical," Isabelle said, with a laugh.

"I'm dying for a swim," Selden said. "Anyone want to come?"

"Go on, Janey . . . ," Paula said.

"I don't like . . ."

"The water's warm," Richard said. "Almost *too* warm . . ."

Selden held out his hand. "Come on, babe," he said.

Janey had no choice. She let him take her hand and pull her to her feet. They started down the sand toward the water. "I really don't want to go in," Janey said, with some irritation. "The waves are too big . . ."

"Come on," Selden said. "A little water never hurt anyone . . ."

He pulled her down to the water's edge. A wave crashed over her feet and she jumped back. "It's too cold!" she cried.

"It is not," he said. He waded in up to his knees and a wave crashed over his chest. "Come on!" he cried. He jumped out of the water, sputtering. "It's perfect . . . ," he said.

"Selden!" Paula shouted. Janey turned around; Paula was waving frantically. Selden saw her and pushed through the water like a bull, brushing past Janey in his haste to get to his mother. "What's the problem?"

"Something's happened," Wheaton said. He was standing by the towels. "I think you and Janey had better go back to the house . . ."

"What *is* it?" Selden asked, picking up the towel and drying his face.

"Something with Janey's sister . . ."

"Patty?" Janey screamed, running up the beach toward them.

"Take it easy," Selden snapped. "What's happened? Is she all right?"

"I couldn't really tell. A guy named Digger called . . ."

"That's Janey's brother-in-law . . ."

"He said to tell you to call him and that Patty was in jail."

"Oh my God," Paula said, clutching her heart.

"I'll take care of it, Mother," Selden said sharply, pulling his shirt over his head.

"We'd better all go back to the house," Paula said, gathering her things.

"You stay here," Selden commanded. "There's no reason to let this ruin *your* day . . . Come on," he said, motioning for Wheaton and Janey to follow him.

He raced up the dirt track. Janey followed him, stumbling over the little stones—in her haste she'd forgotten her shoes. Selden jumped into the front seat of the Jeep and Janey got in next to him. "Did he leave a phone number?" Selden demanded of Wheaton, who was in the back.

"No," Wheaton said. "I assumed you knew where to find him."

"Goddammit, Wheaton," Selden said, slamming his hand on the steering wheel. "Where are they staying?" he asked Janey.

"I'm not sure . . . ," Janey faltered. "The Four Seasons . . . The Ritz?"

"It's got to be the Ritz-Carlton," Selden said. "There isn't a Four Seasons in Aspen . . ."

Selden raced the Jeep up the driveway to the villa, scattering small stones in every direction. At the top of the driveway he stopped the Jeep with a jerk and ran into the house. *He's loving this,* Janey thought in horror. *He's loving every minute . . .*

By the time she got into the house, Selden was already on the phone, talking to Digger. "Let me speak to him," Janey said, holding out her hand. He shook his head and waved her away.

"It's my sister!" she hissed.

Selden gave her a dirty look to keep her at bay. "Uh-huh, uh-huh," he said, nodding. "I see. And did you get the name of the jail . . . Okay . . . And they took them both away. No, they're not going to let you see her . . . You need a lawyer . . . Don't worry about it. Just stay by the phone. I'm going to make a few phone calls and I'll call you back." He hung up the phone.

"What is it?" Janey cried.

He looked at her and sat down in a chair. "Okay, here's what happened, as far as I can tell. Patty and Digger were in the supermarket in the checkout line. Apparently Marielle Dubrosey found out they were going to Aspen and followed them there. She came up behind Patty . . ."

"In the *supermarket* . . . ?"

"In the supermarket," Selden nodded. "And she said something to Patty and Patty turned around and slapped her."

"Well, good for Patty," Janey said.

"Good for Patty, except that Marielle punched her in the stomach. And then Patty supposedly shoved her, and Marielle fell down. And then the police came and took them both to jail."

"It's going to be in all the papers," Janey said angrily.

"Yes, it probably will be," Selden said. "But right now, the most important thing is to get Patty out of jail."

"We'd better go back to New York," Janey said.

"There's nothing we can *do* in New York," Selden said.

"Well, there's nothing we can *do* here either," Janey snapped.

Selden held up his hands as if to ward her off. "Just let me take care of it, okay?" he said. "I'm going to call Jerry Grabaw."

"The PR man?" Janey scoffed. "It's *Christmas Day* . . ."

"That won't bother Jerry," Selden said. "He loves this kind of stuff."

Selden finally got off the phone three hours later. In the meantime, the rest of the party had returned from the beach and had demanded an explanation. There was no way to make sense of the situation without relating the whole sordid story from the beginning, and while Janey talked, Paula Rose kept glancing over at her husband, her lips pressed into a thin line of disapproval. At last Janey escaped to her room, where she lay on the bed, furiously biting her nails.

"Well, that's it for the moment," Selden said, coming into the room and flopping down on the bed next to her. He passed his hand over his eyes. "Jerry found someone who knows the judge and managed to get him to go to the courthouse so Patty could be bailed out. She'll have to appear at a hearing in a month, unless he can get them to drop the charges, which they probably will, considering it's Aspen and they're celebrities, and these kinds of things happen all the time . . ."

"That's nice," Janey said, coldly. She was pleased that Selden had been able to fix the problem, but annoyed at the way he had simply taken over without consulting her. After all, Patty was *her* sister, and Selden hadn't even let her talk to Digger . . . It was just like the Connecticut house—and this vacation—she thought angrily, the way he had gone ahead and made decisions without bothering to consult her . . .

"Damn," Selden said, sitting up. "I'd better go tell my mother. This kind of stuff makes her nervous . . ."

"Yes, you'd better do that," Janey agreed.

Selden got up and went into the bedroom next door. "Mother," Janey heard him say.

"Oh, Selden," she heard Paula answer.

"Don't worry. It's all taken care of," Selden said.

Janey got up, and tiptoed to the wall. The walls were so thin, she realized she could hear every word of their conversation as clearly as if they were in the same room.

"I'm not happy about this," Paula Rose said.

"It'll blow over," Selden said. "You have to realize that Digger is a rock star . . ."

"Exactly," Paula said. "Everybody knows that rock stars take drugs. And God knows what else . . ."

"Digger is actually a perfectly nice guy from Des Moines," Selden said reassuringly.

"But what about the sister?"

"She's a lovely girl," Selden said.

There was a pause, and then Selden said, "Mother, what's really bothering you?"

"I don't want to rain on your parade, darling," she began, "but this marriage you've entered into . . ."

"What's wrong with it?"

"Janey is probably a perfectly nice girl. But both she and her sister seem to have problems. The sister's in jail . . . And did you know that Janey hasn't talked to her mother in months? I'm only concerned about your welfare, darling. I don't want to see you hurt again . . ."

"Oh, Mother . . . ," Selden laughed. "You're being hysterical."

"I'm not," Paula protested. "And this modeling business. I'm just not sure that it's a proper job for your . . . wife. Girls like that want other things . . ."

"You're being old-fashioned," Selden laughed. "The modeling can't last forever—maybe another year at most. And then, chances are you'll have a grandchild . . ."

"But Selden, darling, I don't think that's what Janey wants. I have the feeling she's interested in a different kind of lifestyle . . ."

"Mother, she wants to settle down and have children," Selden said insistently. "Look at you. What woman wouldn't want to be like you?"

"That's very flattering, darling. But all afternoon she kept talking about this producing idea . . ."

"Oh, Mother," Selden said dismissively. "That's just talk. Janey gets these little ideas in her head and the next minute, they're gone. I promise you by next week she'll have forgotten *all* about it."

"I just hope you're right," Paula said ominously.

And on the other side of the wall, where Janey stood eavesdropping, her mouth opened in horror and she slid to the floor, clapping her hand over her mouth in shock. Selden suddenly appeared in the doorway and glanced around the room, looking for her. Spotting her on the floor, he said, "Darling, what's wrong?"

"Nothing!" Janey said quickly, scrambling around on her hands and knees. "I just lost an earring, that's all." She stood up, fiddling with her earlobe.

"I'm sorry," Selden said. "I don't think I've been very nice to you today. I'm in desperate need of a drink . . . What do you say we go to that local bar you were talking about? Maybe meet some interesting people . . ."

"Sure," she said sarcastically, the conversation with his mother still ringing in her ears. "But what about the car? We don't want to leave the rest of the family stranded . . ."

"They'll just have to get along without it for a couple of hours," Selden said with a grin. "After all, it *is* my car . . . I'm paying for it, remember?"

The rest of the holiday dragged on with interminable dullness. Janey made as much of an effort as possible to be pleasant: Now that she had hard evidence that Paula didn't like her, she was determined not to give her the satisfaction of being proved right. But that didn't mean she had to make it easy for Paula, and starting the evening after Christmas Day, she enticed Wheaton and Richard into a game of poker—and once they'd agreed, naturally Selden had to play as well. Paula didn't like it, but the boys shooed her away—as Janey suspected, once they got into the game, there was no stopping them. Paula fumed, while Janey cleverly took every third hand. They were only playing with change, but Janey beat them all three nights in a row, sweeping piles of pennies into her handbag afterward, and that made her feel a little better . . .

But inside, she was festering. Every time she looked at Selden, she recalled the conversation she'd overheard with his mother, and a little more salt was added to the wound. She would show him, she thought; she would make him eat his words. And then he'd be sorry . . .

They left for New York on December 31, arriving back at the hotel suite at just past nine o'clock. The flights had been packed and there were delays in Miami; all Janey wanted to do was sleep, as if sleep might erase the memory of the last awful week. But Selden wouldn't hear of it—it was New Year's Eve. The fire was laid with birch logs and he lit it, and then ordered up two bottles of Cristal Champagne with four ounces of beluga caviar from room service.

"I'm not really in the mood for champagne," she said irritated, thinking that, once again, Selden was doing what he wanted, with no regard for her feelings.

"You've got to drink champagne on New Year's Eve," he insisted. "It's bad luck not to."

He pulled her down onto the couch next to him and stretched contentedly, while Janey sat stiffly by his side. "I can't think of a better way to spend New Year's Eve than a romantic evening at home," he said.

Janey said nothing, glaring at the fire. She'd never understood the concept of the "romantic evening at home"; if she *had* to be home, she'd rather be watching TV and eating take-out food in bed rather than trying to summon up some fake feeling of romance . . .

"I've got a great idea," Selden said eagerly. "Let's drive out to Connecticut tomorrow and I'll show you the land. We'll make a day of it—we'll have brunch on the water somewhere, and then we'll visit the land . . . And maybe afterward, we can stop by the Macadus' . . ."

This, Janey thought, was the last straw. She stood up and walked to the writing desk and, turning around, she said coldly, "We really need to talk about that land, Selden."

"It's a great piece of property," he protested. "It's right on the water . . . You can't find land like that today . . ."

"I think you might as well sell it," she said firmly, narrowing her eyes.

"What are you talking about?" he said, beginning to get irritated. "I just bought it. I'm not going to turn around and sell it."

"Well, I'm not going to have time to work on the house. I'm going to be very busy for the next few months . . . maybe even for the next year or two."

"Are you?" he asked. The buzzer rang and he stood up, walking to the door. "Doing what, I might ask?"

A waiter came in carrying a tray with two buckets of champagne and four glasses. It seemed to take him forever to arrange them on the coffee table. "Should I open these for you, sir?" he asked.

"It's fine, I'll do it myself," Selden said.

The waiter left, and he popped the cork on one of the bottles, pouring out two glasses. The action seemed to soothe him, and he said in a reasonable tone of voice, "Look, if you're worried about being pregnant . . . of course, you'll have help. And a nanny when the baby is born."

She emitted a short, cruel laugh. "This isn't about children," she said.

"What *is* it about, then?" he demanded.

She smiled. "As a matter of fact, I'm going to be producing the movie of Craig's book, *The Embarrassments*. He's already agreed to let me do it . . ."

Selden had just taken a mouthful of champagne and he nearly spit it out in surprise. Then he threw back his head and laughed.

Janey stared at him, her face full of fury. "I can't imagine why you find that so funny."

Smiling, he took a step toward her and tried to put his arm around her, but she drew away. "Come on, babe," he said. "Producing a movie's a *huge* job. It takes *years* of experience. You'll never get it done . . ."

"How do you know that?"

"I *know*," he said. He turned away from her and prodded the fire with an iron poker. "Don't take it personally," he added casually, "but this is my business. I can't tell you how many people have come to me wanting to produce a movie, and the few who try almost always fail . . ."

"Fine," Janey said. "I'll try it, and if I fail, I fail. But I don't think I will."

He looked at her in surprise, and then took a step back, shocked by the blazing hatred in her eyes. "Janey!" he said.

"Fuck you," she said softly. She stormed out of the living room and into the bedroom, where she began to unpack. He followed her.

"Look, Janey," he said. "I don't think I'm making myself clear. I do not want you producing Craig's movie . . ."

"Why not?" she demanded, not looking at him. "Because you're afraid I might actually succeed?"

"No," he said, carefully balancing his glass on the bedside table. He folded his arms. "Because you're guaranteed to fail. Craig's book doesn't have the kind of story that translates into a film. In fact, it doesn't have any story at all . . ."

"You're just jealous!" she spat. "You're jealous because Craig is talented and you're *not* . . ."

She suddenly gasped and bit her lip, afraid that she'd gone too far. But it was *true*, she told herself, and maybe it was time Selden knew it . . .

She removed the Pucci dress from her hanging bag and hung it up in the closet, hardly daring to look at him. She bent back over the bag, and when she looked down, she saw his feet in front of her. She straightened up with a defiant look on her face, daring him to challenge her.

His face was impassive. Swirling the champagne in his glass, he said quietly, "If you want to be with a man like Craig Edgers, don't let *me* stand in your way."

"Don't worry," she snapped. "I won't."

She pushed past him and went into the bathroom, locking the door behind her.

"Janey," he said. "You come out of there and talk about this."

"There's nothing to talk about," Janey said coldly, from behind the door.

"Janey!" he said. Silence. He banged on the door. "Janey, come out of there!"

There was no response. And then he heard the sound of the taps turned on full blast.

"Goddammit, Janey!" he shouted. "This is a *hell* of a way to start the new year!"

Book three

THE G5 LANDED on the runway at Charles de Gaulle Airport, and then taxied to a private jet strip where it was met by a Mercedes limousine and two French customs agents. It was eleven-fifteen in the morning, sometime in the middle of February 2001, and Janey looked out the window at the drizzly gray French day and sighed. Sent to Paris with Mimi! It was so annoying, she thought, to have been packed off like a misbehaving child who'd been sent to her room . . .

She slipped on a pair of soft, dove-gray gloves, frowning as she did so. The trip couldn't have come at a worse time. She'd been so close to getting George to sign a letter of intent regarding their movie project, and then, just as it seemed he must commit to the project and write a check, along came this sudden invitation to accompany Mimi to Paris. Mimi had to go to Paris for a fitting of some haute couture dresses she'd ordered from Dior in October and she didn't want to go alone, and if Janey accompanied her, she would introduce her to Raumond, her French decorator. Apparently Raumond *never* took on new clients, but might consider working with Janey if she came to Paris in February when he had a tiny break in his schedule.

"It's all so silly," Janey had complained loudly to Selden. "Especially since we don't have anything to decorate!"

This was a touchy topic for both of them, and Selden gave her a measured look. "We will eventually," he said carefully. Janey stared back at him defiantly. He had not sold the land or dropped the idea of building a house. He'd simply stopped mentioning it—just as she didn't mention her meetings with George. "Really, Janey," he said, "this is a high-class problem"—and that had shut her up. Neverthe-

less, ever since Mimi had suggested the trip to Paris a week ago—"New York is so
awful in February; there's nothing going on," she pointed out—Janey couldn't help
feeling that there was some kind of conspiracy afoot to get her out of town. Selden
had come home one evening full of excitement about the trip, having heard about it
from George, he said. Janey was immediately nervous, especially as she'd just seen
George herself that afternoon, and their meeting hadn't been exactly all business.
Her first thought was that George had told Selden about it—but if he had, she
would deny it all, she thought quickly; she would say that George had come on to
her and she'd refused him, and in retaliation he had made the whole thing up . . .

But Selden had seemed relieved, not angry, and after a few moments she reassured herself that George wasn't a blabbermouth. Indeed, she realized, it was Selden
she had to worry about, not George. In the last month, ever since that terrible New
Year's Eve, Selden had developed a patronizing attitude toward her, as if she wasn't
intelligent or knowledgeable enough to understand his business. To the unsuspecting eye, they appeared to be a power couple on equal footing. But Janey was beginning to know better, to understand that Selden really only wanted her as a
showpiece—as the beautiful Victoria's Secret model who confirmed his status as an
alpha male—and she was beginning to resent it. When she gave her opinions on
show business or politics or fashion, she would catch him watching the faces of others, to make sure she wasn't boring or embarrassing them, and if he felt she was, he
would interrupt her, leaving her to finish her thoughts to an audience who had
turned away.

It came to a head one evening in mid-January during a dinner at Harold Vane's
house. There were two tables of ten and Janey was seated next to the Republican
senator from New York, Mike Matthews. He was a handsome man in his sixties,
powerful and charming, with a clawlike grip that he exercised when making a point
by grabbing her hand and not letting go, even when he was addressing the table. It
was just the sort of evening Janey loved, filled with important people and flowing
with what she considered significant conversation. Toward the end of dinner the
topic turned inevitably to the pros and cons (mostly cons—after all, this was New
York) of the Republican Party. Janey launched into a diatribe about the Republican
Party's biggest flaw—that they didn't support women and abortion. There were four
other women at the table, one a revered television journalist in her fifties, who cried
out, "Hear, hear," and suddenly there was one of those lulls in the room when conversation inexplicably stops, and Janey's voice carried clear across the room: "Really,
Senator! If you personally don't support abortion, then I say you're a hypocrite.
You've been a single man for thirty years, and in those thirty years you can't tell me
that you've never had a girlfriend who got pregnant."

For a moment, there was shocked silence, and Janey felt herself redden with embarrassment. Turning toward Selden, who was seated at the other table, she caught the rigid tension in the back of his neck, but a second later, the silence was broken by the warm laughter of approval that comes after a well-told joke, and Janey felt her esteem rising in the eyes of the room. Before, she had been a pretty girl of not much account; now she was one of them—attractive, yes, but with a brightly wicked sense of humor. The senator attached his claw to her arm and addressed the room. "Folks, this young lady is exactly what the Republican Party has been missing!" and the jovial crowd broke up for coffee in the living room.

The senator escorted her through the short foyer leading to the ornate living room, which Harold had decorated in the style of the American Empire period, during which the house was built. There were silk-covered settees with clawed feet and intricately inlaid marble tables, so that the whole effect was of stepping back in time; Janey wouldn't have been surprised to see horse-drawn carriages making their way up Park Avenue.

There was a grand piano in one corner of the room, and Harold had arranged for two young opera singers to perform. Janey took a seat on a long, blue upholstered bench and accepted a demitasse cup of coffee from a uniformed maid, smiling up at the senator as she did so. For a moment, Janey wondered what it would be like to be married to him—especially as everyone said he might run for president. It might be fun to be the First Lady, and she said, "Please sit down, Senator. I'm dying to know if the rumors are true."

He accepted her invitation and joked, "Most rumors do have some truth to them, but if you're wondering about whether or not I'm going to run . . ."

"Oh, I was talking about all those rumors about you and the ladies . . . ," Janey began. And at that moment, Selden appeared beside them.

Janey looked up at him, an invitation to join them in her eyes, but his mouth was frozen in a tight smile. "I'm sorry about my wife, Senator," he said. "She often says things without thinking about them." He sat on the edge of the couch and took Janey's hand, and in a voice meant to be joking, said, "She has a habit of talking about things she doesn't know anything about."

"Is that so?" the senator asked slowly. He gave Selden a cold smile and continued, "It seems to me she's at least as intelligent, if not more intelligent, than most of the people in this room. All she did was point out what most of them were thinking but didn't have the guts to say."

"As long as there's no offense . . . ," Selden faltered.

"There isn't, on my part," the senator said, giving Janey a sympathetic look. "But if you ever decide to lose this guy," he said, addressing her directly, "I'm available."

They all laughed, and at that moment the music began, putting an end to the conversation. Janey tilted her head in an attitude of appreciation, but inside she was fuming. It was as if all of her suspicions about Selden's behavior toward her were suddenly revealed in a bright light from which there was no turning away, and in the car on the way home, she exploded.

"Don't you ever do that again," she hissed. They both sat staring straight ahead, and for a few seconds he said nothing. Then he rubbed his chin with his gloved hand, and in an unemotional voice said, "It was an embarrassing remark."

"The only thing that was embarrassing was your behavior," Janey snapped.

"Can we discuss this at home, please?" he asked, indicating the driver.

Back at the hotel, the argument went around and around in circles, with Janey accusing him of being patronizing and disrespectful toward her, and Selden denying any knowledge of what she was talking about. The fact that he wouldn't acknowledge her feelings drove her to heights of fury she had rarely experienced, and she finally went at him with clenched fists. He threw her back onto the couch, and she sat shaking with tears and anger, but the dam had broken and he spun around in a rage. She had never seen him really angry before, and she was terrified.

"If you want to know the truth, you do embarrass me," he said with cold fury. "Night after night I have to listen to you spouting your mouth off about things you know nothing about, arguing with people who are worlds away from you in terms of experience. You've always gotten away with it because you're beautiful. But if you were half as attractive, believe me, no one would be listening to you!"

She gasped. No one had ever spoken to her that way, and at first she wasn't sure how to react. Was it possible that what he was saying was *true*? But to admit to such a flaw would be death, and she screamed back: "Didn't you hear what the senator said? That I was more intelligent than most of the people in that room?"

"Of course he tells you you're intelligent," he said, bending toward her with a sneer on his face. "He's a politician. An expert at telling people exactly what they want to hear—truth be damned. Didn't you see the way he was staring at your breasts and grabbing your hand? Because I did, and so did everyone else in the room. He wanted to fuck you and was willing to say anything to make it a possibility. And you wonder why I'm embarrassed? And you wonder why I don't respect you? When it comes right down to it, you're the one with no respect—for anybody but yourself." He began pacing the room, patting the top of his head in the comical gesture he adopted when he was nervous, his distress growing as if every motion of his hand wound him up further.

"I've heard you tell world-renowned movie directors how to direct their next picture," he continued. "I've heard you tell producers who they should cast, and businessmen how to run their businesses. And all this without an achievement or an accomplishment, not one, under your belt . . ."

"So you're saying that I'm not entitled to my opinions, just because I haven't had the same advantages as everyone else?"

"It's not about advantages," he said, spinning around and pointing his finger at her. "It's about hard fucking work and putting yourself on the line, risking failure, again and again." He paused, took a deep breath, and continued. "Oh, I don't care what you say to your silly friends or that coterie of men you've slept with who follow you around. But when you're dealing with my associates, people who have spent their entire lives trying to accomplish something . . ."

She gave a short laugh. "Really, Selden? You're saying that Mimi and George are silly? And I think this idea of yours of a coterie of men I've slept with . . ."

"All I'm saying is to take a backseat in some of these discussions. Why are you always pushing yourself forward? Try being an acolyte for a change. Shut up and you might find that you actually learn something!"

They stared at each other in mutual hatred, and Janey wondered bitterly how it was that she was able to be just that—an acolyte—to all of the other rich and powerful men she knew, and yet she was unable to be that way with her own husband. It was true, she thought suddenly—she didn't respect him. Had she ever? But this idea was so horrifying to her that she knew instinctually that she must turn it around so that she was the victim.

"I can see what this is about, Selden," she said, her lip trembling as if she were about to cry. "You don't want me to grow or change. It threatens you. But as a matter of fact, I've always been this way. I've always worked at improving myself and trying to do something with my life. If you think I'm going to sit by your side like some little mouse, you're sorely mistaken. And if my behavior makes you uncomfortable, then I'd like to suggest that it's *your* problem and *your* insecurity. How dare you lay it on me!" And with that she burst into tears and ran into the bedroom.

When he came to bed about an hour later, she pretended to be asleep. After a while, she heard his gentle snoring, but she lay awake for hours. Her pride battled her cynicism, with pride urging divorce and cynicism pointing out that no matter how awful Selden was, she didn't want to go back to the life she'd had. Eventually she fell asleep, and woke to the sound of the shower, feeling exhausted.

He came into the bedroom with a towel wrapped around his waist. He sat down on the edge of the bed, combing his hair back and twisting his body toward hers. "Listen," he said. She thought he was going to apologize, the way he usually did after a fight, but instead he said, "I just don't think we should ever . . . fight like that again, okay?"

It wasn't what she wanted to hear, but she smiled up at him resignedly. He leaned over and gave her a brief kiss on the lips. "I'll see you later, okay?" he asked.

"Okay," she said with a mournful sigh.

"Come on, Janey. Don't be ridiculous," Mimi said, two days later. "George is exactly the same way. Didn't anybody ever tell you that all husbands are alike?"

They were lunching at Dingo's in an atmosphere that seemed as weary as the long New York winter. "Oh yes," Mimi went on with a malicious gleam in her eyes. "It's one of the great disappointments in life, along with having children. You always think that you're marrying an individual, a man you've chosen above all the others. And when you finally get there, what you discover is that you've married a type. 'The marrying man.' And when it comes right down to it my dear, one husband is no better or worse than any other husband. In fact, there are times when I think they're completely interchangeable!"

Janey looked at Mimi and gave her a wan smile. Ever since Zizi had dumped her, Mimi had changed, Janey thought. She'd become bitter—one of those forty-something women who are angry because their lives didn't turn out the way they expected. She had everything, but her sour attitude implied that she'd somehow been cheated, and once again, Janey reminded herself that, no matter what happened, she mustn't turn out like Mimi . . .

"Really, Mimi," Janey said, nervously twisting her engagement ring as if it were a sign of bondage and not love, "I don't mind if Selden is like other husbands, it's the disrespect I can't stand. How dare he?"

"Disrespect is part of the package," Mimi said with a shrug. "The day a man marries you, a part of him loses respect for you because of the very fact that you *did* marry him—he knows his flaws and thinks his wife's a fool for putting up with them."

"But he's trying to break me down!" Janey cried.

"Is he?" Mimi asked. "He doesn't think so, in any case. He thinks he's asserting his rights as a husband. Which, my dear, unfortunately include telling you what to do."

"George doesn't tell you what to do," Janey pointed out slyly. Ever since she'd begun having meetings with George about *The Embarrassments* project, her admiration for him had grown. He was always in a good mood, and they seemed to spend half of their time together laughing . . .

"Of course he does," Mimi snapped, frowning. "George is terribly bossy, and I expect Selden is as well. But if they weren't bossy, they wouldn't be as successful as they are, and we never would have married them in the first place." Mimi fixed Janey with a gimlet eye and continued, "The difference is, when George gets to be too much, I gently correct him. It's a bad idea to go head-to-head with these types of men—you'll always lose. Once they start arguing, their egos demand that they win at any cost, and they'll say or do anything to achieve that end. Oh, I know you're tough, Janey," she said with a little laugh. "But believe me, you're not that tough. If you were, you wouldn't be married. You'd be the CEO of a corporation or running a movie studio."

"A woman ought to be able to be married *and* be a CEO!" Janey lashed out. But Mimi merely smiled and said, "Ought to, yes. But can you name one? The fact is, there aren't any—or not more than two or three, in any case. Most powerful men won't tolerate that kind of toughness in a woman. They marry to get away from it."

"But I'm not being tough," Janey insisted. "All I want is a little respect from Selden. There's no reason for him to act like I can't do anything . . ."

Mimi raised her eyebrows and laughed. "Janey," she said patiently. "You're thirty-three years old. I know you think that's old, but it's not. When I was thirty-three, I had huge fantasies about the way my life was going to turn out, too—about what I was going to do and who I was going to marry . . . Oh, I know you've got larger aspirations, Janey," she continued, "but my advice is to take another look at your life. I'd be doing you a disservice as a friend if I didn't tell you that you're messing up your marriage. This project you're trying to do with George, for instance—"

"Why shouldn't I have a project with George?" Janey asked, quickly cutting her off. She felt a touch of guilt about George, but had no intention of allowing Mimi to guess that there was anything more to their relationship than pure business. Her tone was light, but there was a challenge beneath it. "Mimi, if you're saying that I shouldn't have a project with George because he's your husband, why, you might as well say I shouldn't have a project with *any* man who's married. Yes, I am working on a project with George, but he only *happens* to be your husband."

Mimi laughed. "Darling," she said, touching Janey's hand, "you're still not getting it. It doesn't matter who you work with. The point is that you're trying to compete with Selden."

"How much does Selden *know*?" Janey asked, toying with her water glass.

Mimi sighed. "I haven't said a word and neither, I think, has George. But Selden *will* find out at some point, and when he does, I know he's going to be angry."

Janey laughed a little too loudly, as if the whole thing were completely ridiculous. "Why on earth should Selden be angry?" she asked innocently. "If anything, he should be proud."

Mimi regarded her thoughtfully. "But he won't be proud, Janey. Don't you see?

He'll feel like you're trying to undermine him. Trying to show him that you're just as good as he is, and you'll be attacking him in an area that really counts—his work."

"Well, maybe Selden needs to understand that there's more than one talented person in the marriage," Janey retorted.

Mimi sighed. "It's not that he doesn't think you're talented, Janey," she said. "But if he wanted to be married to someone who did the same thing he does, he would be. He was *already* married to someone in the business, and it didn't work for him. He wants someone *different*. I'm sure he loves the fact that you have personality and your own opinions, but he also married you because he thought you were a beautiful, sweet girl who was completely sympathetic . . . to *him*. He feels like he rescued you . . ."

"Rescued? *Me?* Did he actually say that . . . ?"

"Not in so many words, but . . . let's face it, Janey, you didn't always have the best reputation."

"And Selden believed that!"

"Of course not. If he did, he wouldn't have married you." Mimi turned her head away and sighed. "He felt that the things that people said about you . . . were wrong. And I did, too—I still do, of course. But he thought by marrying you, he was giving you the life you'd always wanted and deserved. And naturally, he thought you wanted to have children, to make a *family* . . ."

"We've only been married for six months," Janey protested.

"All he wants is a little understanding, Janey. Selden wants to feel like you're proud of his achievements. And if you insist on trying to get into his business, he'll feel like you don't think he's good enough at what he does."

"Of course I think he's good enough at what he does," Janey snapped. She threw her napkin down on the table, shaking with anger. Why was everyone always trying to put her down, to push her back into what they perceived was her "place"— and suddenly, all of her old insecurities about herself and her abilities came flooding back.

The feeling was both familiar and acutely uncomfortable, for it implied a lack of control that was intolerable to her. These feelings, she knew, could be dangerous; they might drive her to do foolish, hurtful things . . .

And Mimi, thinking about marriage, was reminded of her mother. "There are certain sacrifices, Janey . . . ," she said kindly. "If you're not willing to make them, it's very difficult to succeed at anything . . ."

Mimi was probably right, Janey thought, but she was too angry to admit it. "If you're talking about moving to Connecticut," she said, "there's no way I'll ever do that . . ."

Mimi gave Janey a look that Janey was convinced was pitying. "I was thinking more about Patty," she murmured.

Janey glared down at her napkin. Was Mimi deliberately trying to goad her? Patty was a bit of a sore point and Mimi knew it, simply because Patty had been proved right and Janey wrong. After the Aspen incident—which both Patty and Digger now regarded as one of the huge jokes of their relationship, especially the part about Patty's going to jail—Marielle Dubrosey had admitted that the baby wasn't Digger's. The story had immediately disappeared as if it had never occurred, and Patty and Digger had gone "underground," keeping mostly to themselves. However, they still saw Janey and Selden for dinner—Selden seemed to consider their relationship one of his "pet projects"—and Patty always thanked Selden for his help and reminded Janey that she and Digger were now closer than ever. It always set Janey's teeth on edge, especially as her own relationship wasn't everything it should have been . . .

But she wasn't the only one, Janey thought now, looking at Mimi. Recalling that afternoon with Zizi, she thought harshly that Mimi was a fool. She was looking particularly tired these days—it was as if her beauty had simply given up, and it was so sad . . . But maybe that was to be expected. After all, Janey thought, all Mimi *really* had in her life was George. And if George's recent behavior toward Janey was any indication, it was entirely possible that soon, Mimi might not even have George to comfort her . . .

Janey bit her lip and lifted her gloved hand, tracing a line of rain that was running down the window of the plane. In the two weeks following that lunch with Mimi, she had done some things. Not terrible things, exactly, but things that were best not thought of again, at least not for the moment.

In the spacious seat across the aisle, Mimi was unbuckling her seat belt. "Finally!" she cried. "It's wonderful having your own plane, but I do miss the Concorde." She stretched, and turning to Janey exclaimed, "Don't you just *love* Paris!"

Janey smiled indulgently. Unlike, it seemed, everyone else in the world, she didn't necessarily love Paris—it held too many disturbing memories. But she was glad to see Mimi happy: Ever since Mimi had mentioned the trip, her attitude had changed completely. She was like the old Mimi, Janey thought, full of energy and kindness, and she even looked like her old self. As if awakening from a brief hibernation, Mimi's beauty had returned in force: her face was smooth and glowing, and she'd cut her hair so that it formed soft waves around her face, giving her a look reminiscent of a fifties movie star.

"Come on," Mimi said excitedly, urging Janey out of the plane. "Don't worry about the luggage—the stewards will take care of it and send it on to the hotel. I'm going to tell the driver to go around the Eiffel Tower. It's a little tradition of mine," she said, taking Janey's arm as they walked to the Mercedes. "In any case, we're going to have fun. Won't it be nice to forget about our husbands for a week?"

Janey laughed and nodded, thinking that this would be easier said than done. She was perfectly willing to forget about Selden, she thought grimly, but she had no intention of allowing George to escape.

The dream began in the ocean under moonlight.

At first she could hear the splash of the foam on top of the huge gray-green waves and she felt the salty wind in her face. And then she saw that she was riding a huge dolphin, standing on its back and holding a dorsal fin that was taller than she was. She was slim and muscular and tanned, a Valkyrie from another world, the only one who could ride the magical dolphin. They were on a mission to rescue a man, but as they reached the man, they were hit by a towering wave that shot the man forward, throwing him to safety. And when the wave crashed to the shore, the girl and the dolphin were gone. With her heart breaking, Janey knew that she, the girl, was dead.

The man was carried to a tiny seaside village populated by locals and a motley yet beautiful band of young Americans. The man—he was hardly a man, really, not more than twenty-four years old—had a broken leg. Two days later, the dolphin was discovered. He was badly injured and the villagers had made a pen for him in the water, hoping he would recover. The next day, a young woman appeared in the village. It was Janey, but not the Janey who was the girl on the dolphin, but her younger sister. Not Janey's real sister, Patty, but some kind of sister to herself. She was beautiful as well, but wondered if she could ever live up to her older sister's heroic acts. But still, she had to try. The heroine was dead, and she had to find out what had *really* happened.

She stood on the beach, tracing a line in the sand with her toe. Her heart hurt over the injured dolphin and the dead heroine, but she had a mission to accomplish. The young man approached, looked at her, and they instantly fell deeply in love.

The young man led her to the Kon Tikki bar. She had lonely and dangerous adventures ahead, but she wondered if she might indulge in love one last time. Could she hold his interest? All the other young women on the island were beautiful, far more beautiful than she, but *he* wanted *her*.

She danced for him in the Kon Tikki bar. And then taking her hand, he led her away from the crowd. He was in love with her. They kissed and made love, melding together perfectly as one, losing themselves in each other and in the overwhelmingly delicious sensation of pure sex. It went on and on. He took her from every angle. She felt no fear, no anger, no insecurity, just that bright white love of complete acceptance . . .

And then she had to go. She had to complete her mission. She walked down the beach to the dolphin's pen. She reached out her hand and the dolphin looked at her with the saddest eyes she'd ever seen . . .

With a deep cry of anguish she slowly awoke, the dolphin materializing into the hard outlines of the armoire against the wall on the other side of the room, the sea fading into the heavy red silk curtains that blocked out the daylight. For a moment, she couldn't recall where she was or what she was doing there, but then, through a process of elimination, she remembered that she was in Paris, at the Plaza Athénée, and that she had arrived two days ago with Mimi. But emotionally, she was still in the dream. She longed to go back, to be in that place where she had a purpose, and to feel that love again . . . If only she could find that feeling in the waking world, she thought with frustration, leaning back against the down pillows. If she could experience it just *once* in real life . . . And turning over to gaze wearily at the clock—it was 10 A.M.—she remembered that there *was* one man who might have satisfied her longings, and that man was Zizi . . .

Why hadn't he wanted her? she wondered. And recalling the last moments of their awful encounter, it suddenly struck her that somewhere along the road of her life she might have made a wrong turn. That wrong turn was like a tree trunk, spawning a series of branches that had also become wrong paths, and yet she had trudged on, hoping that one of the paths would somehow lead her back to the right road. If only she had grabbed hold of her life at an earlier age, and taken the risks to do what she'd believed in for herself, she might never have ended up here, she thought angrily—in Paris, and married to a man who didn't love her, or who at least didn't love her in the way she wished to be loved. As she lay in bed, terrible memories of that embarrassing week in Mustique came flooding back, and she heard the words of Selden's conversation with his mother as clearly as if they were in the room mocking her:

"She and her sister have problems . . ."

"Janey gets these little ideas in her head . . ." And she put her hands over her ears, thinking she was going to scream. Somehow, she thought frantically, she would get back on the right road . . . She would get the respect she deserved . . . It was all possible, if only George would come through!

She glanced at the clock again—it read 10:10, meaning it was just past 4 A.M. in New York and far too early to call. She'd left three messages for George in the past two days, and each time his secretary had asked her to hold on for him, only to get back on the phone to inform her that, actually, George was out at a meeting and would have to call her back. So far, he had yet to do so, and now Janey was beginning to fear that he was *deliberately* avoiding her calls. If only she wasn't in Paris! she thought with frustration. If she'd stayed in New York, she would have been able to track him down, contriving to run into him at a restaurant or even on the street. George was a creature of habit, and she had unconsciously recorded his regular movements: Wednesdays found him lunching at Dingo's, Thursdays at Patroon, and at five-thirty sharp three evenings a week, he went to the New York Athletic Club on Central Park South.

She willed herself to get out of bed and into the shower, adjusting the temperature to produce a cool stream of water. Jet lag was always worse on the second and third days, and she needed to be sharp. George must be made to understand that in the matter of their project, he had but one move: to sign the contracts and write the checks. And he had to know that if he thought he could put it off by shipping her to Paris, he was seriously mistaken.

The cool water took the fuzziness out of her head and, drying herself with a thick towel, she objectively examined the "George situation." Was it possible that she had played her cards wrong? For the last month, ever since she'd broached the topic with him just after New Year's, she'd played her hand beautifully, resisting giving him the one thing—she imagined—he *really* wanted. Thanks to her relentless (yet gentle) cajoling, he had finally given in to the idea of her producing the movie based on Craig's book, and had even embraced its merits. Contracts were drawn up and reviewed several times by his lawyers. And then, convinced of her own desirability, and certain that sex would seal the deal, she had "given in" to him one afternoon in his office.

She had known when she'd begun pitching him the idea that ultimately it would probably come down to that, and in the beginning she'd made a cold, calculated decision that her success was more important than some false notion of virtue. Of course, it didn't hurt that she *did* find George attractive and amusing, and at times even entertained fantasies of what it would be like to be married to him. But it wasn't until the act was over, and he was zipping up his pants, that she had an inkling that something had changed. He'd kissed her warmly on the cheek, but it was what he'd said afterward that had disturbed her:

"Thank you," he'd commented, as if praising a waiter after a good meal. "That was very nice."

"Nice?" she said in surprise, slightly hurt by his assessment. Knowing that the act would have to be memorable, she'd given him her very best blow job, sticking her index finger up his anus as she twirled her tongue over the top of his penis.

"Okay," he relented, sensing her disappointment. "It was very good. Will that do?"

And then he had escorted her to the door with about as much interest as he would have shown his accountant, and for one moment, she'd felt horribly guilty about Mimi . . .

"What about the contracts?" she'd asked casually, trying to pretend that nothing had happened.

"Oh, the contracts," he said, rolling his eyes. "We'll talk about them tomorrow." He was holding open the door—she had no choice but to walk through. "Have a nice afternoon," he called after her.

But he hadn't been willing to discuss the contracts the next day, or the day after that. Oh, he still took her calls, but every time she tried to bring the subject up, he quickly changed it, and then, as if on cue, his secretary would cut in, telling him he had an important call on the other line. By the time the evening to leave for Paris had arrived, he still hadn't signed the contracts, nor had he told her when he *would* sign them. And by then, Craig was calling daily . . .

Craig had been promised $300,000 to write the script, and another $700,000 on the day the picture commenced shooting. Janey was to receive $100,000 up front, and an additional $400,000 on the completion of the shoot. They would have eighteen months to write the screenplay and sell the movie to a studio. Naturally, George was technically a producer as well (although, as the person who had put up the money, he didn't necessarily have to do anything) and would receive the biggest percentage of the profits. But it was all so frustrating, Janey thought, tossing the wet towel onto the bathroom floor and wrapping herself in a terry-cloth robe. Especially as all George had to do was write a check for $400,000—a pittance for him, and probably less than what Mimi was spending on her couture dresses . . .

And now, here she was, thousands of miles away from New York and George. If she could actually see George, she had no doubts about her ability to influence his hand. If only she hadn't played her last card, she thought, hadn't been so sure that the game was over. Suddenly, those last fatal minutes with George played in her head like a bad movie, and she threw herself onto the counterpane, pounding the pillow in aggravation.

But she mustn't think about it. She had to put those ten minutes out of her mind, and never think of them or speak of them ever. If she didn't think about them, it would be like they never happened; gradually "they" would go away and no one would be the wiser. Instead, she had to focus on the project; on getting George to take her call and sign the contracts, and afterward, everything would be okay.

She glanced around the room. The ornately furnished suite, which she'd found charming at first with its decorative eighteenth-century furnishings, suddenly seemed to be closing in on her, and it occurred to her that a walk and some fresh air might give her a better perspective. She brushed her hair and powdered her face, then slipped on a pair of Versace slacks with a silky wrap top. She threw a matching coat over her shoulders and picked up her purse, preparing to venture out into the city she detested.

"*Pardonnez-moi,*" she said, leaning toward the attractive balding Frenchman standing behind the concierge's desk. "*Est qu'il y a un message pour moi?*" she asked in her broken, badly accented French. Passing the desk, she'd decided to stop and inquire if she had any messages—after all, it was entirely possible that George had called her during the night but hadn't wanted to disturb her.

"*Oui,* madame," the concierge said smoothly, as Janey wondered why it was that in France, bald men always managed to look elegant, while in America they all looked like Bruce Willis. "I believe there *is* one for you."

It was all *fine* then, she thought with relief, eagerly tearing the envelope open in anticipation. But it was only a message from Mimi, asking Janey to meet her at Christian Dior at one.

Her first reaction was anger and disappointment, and seeing her expression, the concierge inquired, "Is everything all right, madame?"

No, it's not, Janey nearly snapped, but caught herself in time. She couldn't let her fear get the better of her, for if George sensed it, he would be certain to drag out the process of signing the contracts even longer . . .

"*C'est d'accord,*" Janey said to the concierge, smiling. George was a tough businessman, she reminded herself; he was probably playing a game with her to find out how tough *she* could be. Well, she thought, glancing at her watch, he was about to discover she could be very tough indeed . . .

She still had a good hour and a half before she had to meet Mimi; in the meantime, she would visit that cosmetics shop and pick up a few extra tubes of her favorite lipstick, Pussy Pink. Signaling to one of the taxis lined up in front of the hotel, she decided that she might not even call George that day, or the next, or the day after that. Knowing that she was with Mimi and not hearing from her for a few days was bound to make him at least a little nervous . . .

She took the taxi to the boulevard Saint-Germain on the Left Bank. The sights of the city were as familiar to her as if she'd never left fifteen years ago, from the mad traffic on the boulevard that ran from the Hotel Crillon, past the Tuileries and across the Seine, to the quaint little shops on the boulevard Saint-Germain. Spotting the place she was looking for, she motioned for the taxi driver to stop.

The door to the shop opened with the tinkling of bells, and Janey went inside. The shop was tiny, mostly taken up by a long counter that ran across its length—it was one of those places where you had to know what to ask for in order to get what you wanted. Approaching the shopgirl stationed behind the counter, Janey asked, *"Vous avez la rouges à lèvres,* Pussy Pink?" The shopgirl nodded, and went into the back room.

At the very least, coming to Paris would allow her to stock up on her favorite lip color, she thought wryly. But in a moment, the shopgirl returned from the back room, shaking her head. "I'm sorry, madame, but there is no more Pussy Pink."

"No more Pussy Pink?" Janey asked in consternation.

"No, madame . . ."

"Well . . . when will you have more?" Janey asked. And then, remembering she was in Paris, added, *"Encore . . . ?"*

"It is *finis,"* the shopgirl said with a shrug, as if she'd already lost interest in the conversation.

"What do you mean, *finis?"* Janey said.

"The line. It is finished. No more."

"But you can still buy it at Barneys," Janey said, as if this were proof the shopgirl was lying.

"Maybe they still have one or two, *oui,"* the girl said with another dismissive shrug of her shoulders. "But when they run out, it is gone."

"Do you mean . . . ?"

"That is right," the girl said. "The color . . . it is, how you say, discontinue?"

Janey left the shop in shock. Pussy Pink had *only* been her signature lip color for nearly fifteen years, ever since she'd first come to Paris . . . Her roommate, Estella, had told her that she should always wear the same lip color to help the photographers remember her. And it had helped, although maybe not in the way she'd intended . . .

And now . . . she couldn't *believe* it. For a moment, she stood outside, completely at a loss as to what to do. She bit off a tiny piece of nail and spit it out. The demise of Pussy Pink meant that some essential part of her identity was gone, and she wondered how she could ever replace it. It was a sign, she thought wildly . . . but of *what?* And then, as if on automatic pilot, her feet took her up a side street, and in a moment she found herself standing in front of a familiar wooden door.

Yes, she thought, the discreet red plaque with the gold lettering that spelled out ZOLLO MODELS was still on the wall, as was the brass handle on the heavy walnut door that opened onto a courtyard and, at the end, to worn stone steps that led to the Zollo International Modeling Agency. She would, she thought, never forget that first day when she had passed through the red door at the top of the stairs. It was 1985, and she was eighteen years old. "Why is New York still sending me the pretty girls?" Jacques Zollo, one of the proprietors, had cried out upon her entrance.

Janey hadn't known what to say as she'd silently handed him her book.

"Tall and skinny, *oui*," he'd said, nodding and flipping rapidly through the sparse pages. "But zee face, it is all wrong. Too American. If only you come to Paris two years ago," he said, pointing to a series of framed magazine covers on the wall featuring blond-haired girls with blue eyes. "Everybody want that look then. But now?" he shrugged.

"Please," Janey said desperately, tears filling her eyes. She'd just arrived in Paris from Milan, where she'd spent four miserable months trying to get modeling work without much success; her New York agency had decided that she might do better in Paris. She couldn't speak a word of French and every minute in Paris was an agony: She couldn't buy food in a shop, for it was always behind glass counters and had to be specifically requested, she couldn't figure out how to buy toothpaste at the pharmacy, and she didn't understand the money—not that there was much of it, anyway. She was tired and broke and hungry; if she couldn't find work in Paris, she'd be sent home, and then her mother would laugh at her and say, "I told you so . . . I knew you'd never be a success . . ."

"Please," she said again, in a whisper. "I'll do *anything* . . ."

Jacques Zollo regarded her quizzically. He was a handsome young man in his early thirties—almost too handsome, Janey thought—and finally, after what seemed like hours, he said, "You will do lingerie?"

"Lingerie?" Janey said fearfully. Lingerie was the one category of modeling her New York agency had warned her against, but she quickly made up her mind. She was standing here in front of Jacques Zollo, despondent and broke, and with a casual shrug of her shoulders, as if she weren't afraid at all, she said, "Sure, why not."

Jacques wasn't entirely convinced. "You haven't had the . . . ," he said, cupping his chest as if he were holding breasts.

"You mean breast implants?" Janey said. "No. No, I haven't even thought of that . . ."

"Good," he said. "In America, the big breast is very popular. But here in France, we do not like our women to look like cows."

"Oh, no," Janey said. "I would never . . . do anything like that to my body. Ever."

Janey turned away from the wooden door and looked down the street. Well that, she thought now, was a lie, because eventually she had gotten breast implants. But it was hardly surprising, since it seemed that she rarely kept her word to herself anyway. And shortly after that first meeting with Jacques, she'd found herself doing all kinds of things she never in a million years imagined she would . . .

You mustn't think about it, she scolded herself, especially not now. She turned away and began walking again, heading into the Latin Quarter, where there were all kinds of little galleries that might distract her. But her brain, it seemed, had a mind of its own, and now that one little piece of memory had broken through the barrier, others were rushing it as well, threatening to drown her in a flood of memories . . .

There were the go-sees where five hundred young women showed up from all over the world, desperate for work . . . the fashion executives who always seemed to have a "cousin" or a "friend" who needed a date . . . and the agents who would deduct a girl's wages if she refused to cooperate. Almost every girl's virtue was compromised to some extent, but the girls who fared best were the ones who just happened to have the right "look" for the moment: A buzz would develop around them and they'd usually manage to snag a photographer as a boyfriend, which ensured them *more* work—and protection from the sleazy men who seemed to be everywhere. Those girls were lucky—they'd end up back in New York in a year or two, and some of them would end up being supermodels . . .

But then there were the *other* girls, the girls no one ever heard from again: The girls who freaked out or slit their wrists or took too many drugs and ended up in the hospital. These types of incidents were well known, and a topic of conversation among the girls and the agents and the photographers, but they were always hushed up, and very soon thereafter, the New York agency would provide a first-class plane ticket back to the obscure town from which the girl had originally hailed.

Janey had been in Paris for just two weeks when one of these scandals erupted involving a girl named Donna Black. When Janey had first heard the news, she was in a photography studio in Le Marais, modeling lingerie for a company called LaBaby. It was the first real job she'd had, and the shoot was for an ad campaign, which meant she would finally make some actual money. The ad was to feature two blond girls wrapped in each other's arms—selling the fantasy that the two girls were about to remove their (expensive) LaBaby lingerie and have sex with each other. The other girl was named Estella; coincidentally, Estella's roommate was Donna Black.

Both Donna and Estella were from Indiana, but while Donna's father was a doctor, Estella's father was a petty drug dealer. Estella claimed her mother was a waitress, but there was something in the way she knowingly rolled her eyes every time she said "waitress" that made Janey think her mother was actually some kind of prostitute.

Estella herself was a girl who had nothing to lose. Through modeling, she'd risen much higher and faster than she ever could have expected growing up in Indiana, so that everything was a bonus. Tough-mouthed and funny, she was what Janey's mother would have called a bad influence. She made fun of the photographer, who spoke very little English, imitating his pantomimed movements when he attempted to show them what to do, and she asked the client how much he would pay them if they actually did have sex. The client wasn't upset by this; all he said was "It is a beautiful thing to pay a woman for sex," which sent Estella and Janey into paroxysms of laughter, and for the rest of the afternoon, they kept repeating the line over and over again, to the consternation of the photographer and his assistants.

Toward the end of the day, a call came in for Estella from Jacques, and Estella returned to the set in shock. "Donna Black just stabbed Antoine DuBourgey," she announced unceremoniously. Antoine DuBourgey was an executive at a cosmetics company; apparently Donna had been having an affair with him, until she walked into his apartment and found him in bed with another model. These kinds of things happened all the time in Paris, but chaos ensued in the studio; the shoot would have to be continued the next day, the photographer said, as no one could work in the face of such juicy gossip.

Janey and Estella grabbed their things and left, and as Janey followed Estella down the stairs, she thought, from the bobbing motion of Estella's head, that she was crying. But when they reached the street, she saw that it was just the opposite: Estella was laughing hysterically. "I always knew Donna was gonna blow—did you know that she saved jars?" she asked, clutching Janey's arm.

Janey's immediate reaction had been one of horror, but during her few months in Europe she'd discovered that her instinctual response to things was often wrong or considered bourgeois. And so, carefully watching Estella, she did what she'd learned to do in these situations, and copied Estella's response. Laughing along with her, Janey said that she couldn't think of anyone who deserved it more than Antoine, adding, "Do you think he's . . . dead?"

"Oh, I doubt it," Estella said with authority, as if she had firsthand knowledge of the topic. "It's not that easy to kill someone with a knife. You basically have to slit their throat or stab them about a dozen times." She paused to flip her long hair over her shoulder. "Donna wasn't that strong, you know," she said. "She hardly did any exercise—that was one of the reasons Jacques was going to send her back."

The two girls looked at each other and laughed; the reality was that models never did any exercise—they stayed slim on a diet of champagne and cigarettes.

"It's a big pain for me, though," Estella continued. "I'll have to find another roommate. Donna never worked but at least her father paid her rent."

And suddenly Janey, flush with the sharp sophistication of knowing and understanding such decadent, glamorous people, found herself volunteering to move in.

Estella lived on the Left Bank close to the Seine in a high-ceilinged apartment that one entered through a courtyard. The layout of the apartment made no sense to Janey—there were *chambres* that could be reached only by passing through other rooms—but it was a big step up from the apartment she'd been living in before. Estella's apartment, which was technically rented by a model who had lived in Paris five years before and had moved back to New York where she was now "the face" for a large cosmetics company, was furnished in what, to Janey's eye, looked like expensive French antiques, but were in reality pieces of furniture one could pick up at any Parisian flea market. But what was most astounding to Janey was the small *chambre* connected to Estella's bedroom. It was filled with a modern-day pirate's loot of shoes, handbags, Louis Vuitton luggage, jackets, dresses, sweaters, and jewelry—all of it designer and costing far more than Estella could ever afford. Janey's eyes widened at the sight of so many riches; she felt her world expand as if filled with air. She had been raised in a fairly modest, puritanical lifestyle in which excess was considered an unspoken sin, but seeing Estella's bounty shattered her childhood values as sharply as an object hurled at a mirror, and suddenly she found herself staring at the other side of the looking glass.

"Oh, borrow whatever you want," Estella said, seeing Janey's stunned expression. "Just ask me first, okay? I can't stand girls who just take things . . ."

"But how . . . ?"

"My boyfriend." Estella shrugged. "He's always giving me presents."

Janey stared at Estella in confusion; Frenchmen were known for being notoriously tight, thinking they could make up with words what they refused to spend in francs.

"He's Arab," Estella said, fingering a padded suede Chanel handbag that was "the accessory" to own that season, and which, Janey knew, cost upward of $2,000. "Some girls don't like Arab men. They're afraid of them because they're so rich. But they'll buy you whatever you want and take you on trips. Sayed has a yacht and we're going to cruise around the South of France this summer. It's the place to be and everyone's there. You *know*," she laughed, seeing Janey's confused expression. "Saint-Tropez and Cap d'Antibes and Monaco. Sayed's promised to introduce me to Prince Albert . . ."

This was delivered with such flippant sophistication that even though Janey *knew* Estella was putting on airs, she was speechless. She was completely unfamiliar with the world Estella was talking about, but she could see it, dangling just beyond her fingertips like a glittering diamond bracelet.

"The thing about Arabs," Estella said casually, "is that they always like to have a lot of beautiful women around. So maybe I could get Sayed to invite you on his boat. And if not, I'm sure someone else would . . ."

An alarm went off in Janey's head, but she squashed it. "Oh, we'll see," she said with a deliberate mysteriousness, as if she might have better things to do . . .

But when she went into her own room to unpack, she was confronted by her two hard-sided baby blue Samsonite suitcases. Her mother had "generously" bought them for her for her trip, but suddenly, the two suitcases seemed to sum up everything that was wrong and embarrassing about her: She was shabby and American and unsophisticated—and on top of it, there were girls who had come from less but had quickly gained more. While she was thinking this over, Estella appeared in her doorway. She was wearing a multicolored Chanel jacket over jeans, the Chanel bag slung casually over her shoulder, and looking, in Janey's mind, exactly how a glamorous young lady should appear.

"I'm going out for some *pain*," Estella said, pursing her lips around the French word for bread. "Do you want anything? Cigarettes?"

"I don't smoke," Janey said.

"You don't?" Estella asked, and then laughed. "Well, you'll have to start. Everybody smokes in Paris." She turned, and whistling the tune of a French disco hit, sashayed out of the apartment.

Janey silently returned to her unpacking. But as soon as she heard the heavy door to the apartment close, she found herself sneaking back into Estella's *chambre* of treasures. She reminded herself that she had been raised with good values, was a nice girl from a nice family who had been taught from an early age not to covet, but now she wondered what that really meant. Wasn't it just a way of preventing people who could never get what they wanted from feeling bad about their lives? For now she *did* covet in every way, and with a keen sense of purpose. Was it her fault that she'd been brought up not to expect much more from life than a vague kind of job and a vague sort of marriage with some shadowy children attached? What sort of deep meaning was she supposed to garner from *that*?

But here, she thought, touching the fabric of a fine silk dress, these things were *real*. No matter how many times she'd been warned about the dangers of wanting things, in her mind, they were *achievements*. They were like a magical duty of some kind, paid to those whom God or fate mysteriously chose to honor, and it seemed that one had hardly to do *anything* to receive them. Wandering through the room as if drugged, Janey pulled a long pinstriped jacket off its hanger; the collar was trimmed with golden fur that was softer and more luxurious than anything she'd ever felt before. Standing before the full-length mirror, Janey slipped the jacket over her T-shirt and pulled up the collar. With the fur close to her face, she no longer looked like the pretty American student studying abroad. She was suddenly transformed into a stunningly beautiful young woman for whom anything in the world seemed possible. Even, it seemed, marrying Prince Albert and becoming a real princess!

And as she turned from side to side, falling in love with her reflection, she thought, Yes, she coveted. But the difference was that now she saw that she could have. And somehow, she *would* have, very, very soon.

FOURTEEN

JANEY LOOKED UP with a start, realizing that she'd been so deep in thought, she'd crossed the Seine and was now back on the Right Bank, and dangerously close to the Place Vendôme. She halted for a moment, and then, like a moth drawn to a flame, she took a few steps forward and suddenly found herself in the square itself.

She supposed that after fifteen years away from Paris, it was inevitable that her walk would take her here, staring up at the elegantly imposing façade of the Hôtel Ritz. For wasn't it in this very spot that it had really begun, where she had taken that first wrong turn? Where she'd stood, fifteen years ago, staring up at this very hotel, about to make an irrevocable decision that would set the course of her life?

But maybe she was being overly dramatic. *She had been so young then,* a voice inside her reminded herself; how could she have known better? But people did know better, another voice told her, even when they *were* young. But in the end, wasn't it only an event? An event that had led to other events, and then those events had come to an end, and she had somehow managed to "get over" them. Or had she? Because, it seemed, she was still spending a lot of time "getting over" things. And if you were always spending your time getting over your past, how were you supposed to get on with your future?

She looked around and realized that the square was strangely deserted for a Wednesday afternoon, and spying an empty bench, she crossed the cobblestones and sat down. She put her head in her hands, remembering that day, long ago, when Estella had finally returned from getting *pain*—three days later. Janey had been so lonely, and so relieved when Estella had walked in the door at four in the afternoon that she'd hardly noticed that Estella's pupils were huge and her hands were shaking, or that she was smoking one cigarette after another and didn't seem to be able to sensibly answer any of Janey's questions. Finally, Estella swept into the kitchen and dramatically declared that she needed a drink; in her frenzy to open a bottle of wine the cork broke off, and Janey had to take the bottle from her and push the cork in with the butt end of a knife.

"I was worried about you," Janey said apologetically. "I thought maybe you'd died, or had an accident, or maybe something had happened with Donna . . ."

"She's gone for good and they'll never let her show her face in France again," Estella said, taking a swig of wine directly from the bottle. "And I say good riddance to bad rubbish. She was a fucking bore . . ."

"But where were you?"

"I just ran into Sayed is all and we had a party."

"A party? For three days?"

"Once we had a party for a week. Anyway, it isn't over, and I've come back to get you. Sayed's uncle is in town, and *he* wants to have a party. So what do you say?"

"Do they speak English?" Janey had asked. She'd been so miserable, she would have gone anyplace where there were people who conversed in her own language. Estella simply laughed and said, "Of course, dummy. They all went to like Cambridge or something." And then Janey had gone to change.

When she came out of her room, Estella shook her head and murmured, "Wrong, all wrong. Rasheed likes women to look like ladies," she explained. She led Janey into her room, selected a print dress, and thrust it upon her. "Rasheed?" Janey asked.

"Rasheed al . . . ," Estella replied, revealing his full name. Janey took a step back; she immediately recognized the name and didn't know whether to be excited or frightened.

"You know," Estella said, with a smile. "He's one of the richest men in the world . . ."

Janey had expected that the party would take place in a house or an apartment, but instead, she and Estella had taken a taxi to the Place Vendôme. As the car pulled up in front of the entrance to the Hôtel Ritz, Janey had looked up at the mustard-colored façade in awe. It was so big, she thought, and so elegant; nevertheless, a warning went off in her head. "A *hotel*?" she asked.

"It's where he *lives*, dummy," Estella said, paying the driver. "He *could* buy any house in Paris, but he lives in a hotel because it's more convenient. All rich people are like that."

And then, when they were standing on the cobblestones in front of the hotel,

Estella had suddenly grabbed her arm, and looking Janey square in the eye, she said, "Now listen."

"Yes?" Janey asked.

"You and I are friends," Estella said, "so I want you to know what the deal is. If Rasheed grabs you and pushes you down on the bed . . . well, you don't *have* to do anything. But if you *do*, it's two thousand dollars or a piece of jewelry."

For a moment, Janey stared in shock at the bustling, brightly lit hotel. Aha, she thought. So that's how it's done. But of course it was that way, she realized; she and Estella didn't really belong there in their own right, and what she should do—*must do*—was thank Estella and go home.

But it was such a *long* walk home. And she was wearing high heels. And there was nothing waiting for her at home anyway, except another lonely evening. With the dramatically short vision of youth, all she could see ahead of her was one long, empty, meaningless night stretching into another long, empty, meaningless night; with weeks and even months passing in which she would be no farther along in life than she was right now. She turned to Estella and, with far more bravado than she actually felt, said, "Okay."

Estella took her arm, laughing, and led her into the hotel lobby, smiling at the doormen as if she owned the place. They crossed the floor, their heels making grown-up clicking sounds on the inlaid marble, and then they entered the elevator. In the elevator, Estella checked her appearance in the mirror, and then turning casually to Janey said, "Remember, it's two thousand dollars or a piece of jewelry. But I think it's better to take the cash. You can always get some boyfriend to buy you clothes and jewelry, and that way, you don't have to ask *them* for money and they won't think you're a . . ."

"Right," Janey said. She glanced at her face in the mirror, reminding herself that so far, she was still okay: She hadn't accepted Rasheed's advances—*yet*. She would decide when she saw him, she thought, and if she didn't like him, she would leave . . .

The elevator door opened and they walked down a long, cream-colored hallway with a red carpet, stopping in the middle of the hall in front of a set of double doors. Estella rang the bell; in less than a second, as if he'd been waiting, the door was opened by a small, nondescript man wearing a djellaba. He bowed slightly as they entered; he seemed neither surprised to see them nor like he was particularly expecting them.

"Is Rasheed here?" Estella asked boldly.

"He is finishing a business meeting. You'll wait here, please?"

They entered the main salon in the suite. It was the grandest room Janey had ever seen—filled with antique chairs and settees in small groupings—and yet there was something depressing in its enormity. The room was empty save for the two of them, and with a sudden bolt of fear, Janey cried out, "But I thought it was going to be a party . . ."

"Don't worry," Estella said casually. "There probably will be, later." She flopped down onto a pink silk sofa, watching the manservant, and when he'd bowed and left the room, Estella grabbed Janey's hand and said in a stage whisper, "Come on!"

"But we can't just . . ."

"I do whatever I like. Rasheed knows that," she said proudly, pulling Janey out of the living room and into a smaller room furnished as a library, with a wet bar along one wall. She searched the shelves above the bar and turned, triumphantly holding a small silver tray. "Well, come on," she whispered. "Hurry up!"

"I don't . . ."

"Rasheed doesn't mind if people do cocaine, as long as they don't do it in front of him." She put the tray down on top of the bar and, using a silver razor blade, formed the small mound of white powder into four lines. Then she picked up a silver straw and inhaled two of the lines, turning to hand Janey the straw. Janey was momentarily shocked—she'd heard about cocaine, but she'd never done it; up to that point she'd been completely ignorant about the reason behind other girls' frequent trips to the bathroom on shoots, or the way they constantly wiped their noses and wanted to tell you everything about anything that had ever happened to them. They must have simply assumed that she was just like them, she thought, and no one had ever gotten close enough to her to find out . . .

"Don't tell me you've never done cocaine," Estella said, rolling her eyes. "Jeez. Do I have to teach you *everything*?"

"I don't . . . ," Janey repeated lamely.

"Well, you'd better try," Estella said. "It makes everything a lot easier. You'll see."

Janey took the straw from Estella's hand and cautiously inhaled a quarter of one of the lines as if she were sniffing poison. "For Christ's sake, do it all," Estella demanded. "Do you know how much that costs?" Her eyes darted back and forth nervously as she watched Janey, making sure she inhaled her full allotment of the cocaine, and when she finished, Estella quickly grabbed the tray from her and snorted directly from the pile.

From somewhere in the vast suite came the sound of two male voices, and Estella replaced the tray on the shelf and then casually extracted a bottle of pink champagne from a small refrigerator.

Two men passed by the door.

"Rasheed!" Estella called out. The two men stopped and came into the room.

One was young, in his early thirties; the other was older, maybe in his forties or early fifties. Janey stared at the older one, Rasheed, with curiosity: She'd never seen an Arab man before and had been half expecting a man in a turban and flowing robes like something out of *The Arabian Nights*. But this man was of medium height and dressed in an exquisitely tailored suit; his skin was a yellowy beige and he had a small, blackish gray mustache. He was more attractive than not, Janey thought, and yet his face displayed no emotion, as if he were used to keeping his thoughts and feelings entirely to himself.

He came halfway into the room and the corners of his mouth twitched into a cold smile. "Ah yes," he said in a voice with a slight English accent. "I see you have found refreshments."

"This is Janey Wilcox," Estella said, with far too much enthusiasm. There was an unpleasant dripping in the back of Janey's throat; her hands suddenly felt clammy and she had the distinct feeling that she was going to vomit. She stared at Rasheed wide-eyed, wondering if her distress was obvious, but all Rasheed did was nod at her, his eyes flickering over her from the top of her head down to her shoes. The man with him, the younger one, looked from Rasheed to the girls; he seemed unclear as to what was going on or what sort of protocol was expected of him. After an uncomfortable silence, he finally stepped forward and held out his hand. "Justin Marinelli," he said with an American accent.

The American was wearing gold wire-rimmed glasses and a yellow tie, and for some reason Janey noticed that he had a wedding ring. As they shook hands, she suddenly had the crazy idea of throwing herself on his mercy, of begging him to take her out of there and take care of her and get her home, but then Rasheed was saying, "I will escort Mr. Marinelli to the door and then will return for a tour," and the moment was gone.

"I think I'm going to be sick," Janey said vaguely, leaning against a chair.

"Don't be ridiculous," Estella said, removing the tray from the shelf and quickly chopping out four more lines. "That happens to me all the time when I first do a hit—as soon as you do another line, you'll feel better." Janey took the tray from her and inhaled two lines, and as she did so, Estella said, "He liked you, I could tell."

"He didn't even shake my hand," Janey said.

"He's the richest man in the world," Estella replied incredulously. "You can't expect him to bother with things like *that*. He's busy."

"Too busy to shake hands?"

"Listen," Estella said. "You can't let him intimidate you. You've got to treat these rich guys like they're ordinary. That's the trick, you see? They secretly love it, because . . ."

At that moment, Rasheed returned. His dark eyes flicked to the unopened bottle of champagne, and he turned and clapped his hands and called out, "Mohammed!" In a second, the man who had opened the door scurried into the room, but Estella was quicker, and with a great flourish she picked up the bottle of champagne and said, "Oh, don't be ridiculous, Rasheed, I'll do it. My mother used to work in a bar. You know? A place where people go and drink?"

"Yes, I know about bars," Rasheed said, watching her out of narrowed eyes.

"But you never go to them," Estella said, in the sort of joking tone one might use with a child. She turned to Janey as she wrenched the cork from the bottle. "He doesn't drink, you know?" The cork popped out of the bottle with a spray of white foam, and Estella stepped back, laughing and holding the bottle high in her hand, the consummate party girl. "Should we use glasses, Rasheed? Or drink straight from the bottle?"

"Glasses please," Rasheed said in a toneless voice.

Janey looked at Estella and saw with a pang of regret that she was probably the silliest girl she'd ever known. She wasn't even sure that she liked her much, but she realized that now was not the time to be making judgments about Estella's character, and on top of that she felt an almost insatiable craving for alcohol. She greedily took a glass of champagne from Estella's hand and downed half of it, then refilled her glass to the brim. Rasheed turned and led them out of the room.

The "tour" of the suite was probably nothing more than a pretext for the sex act that might follow, and yet Rasheed dragged it out, explaining the history of the hotel, the furnishings, and the paintings, and Janey was taken aback by how much he knew—if she lived to be a hundred, she would never know as much as this man. His knowledge only served to reinforce the realization that she'd barely been educated and probably never would be, and she wondered if she appeared as dumb as she felt. Estella wouldn't stop making silly comments, and an unspoken competition developed between them—for every dumb comment Estella made, Janey tried to distinguish herself by asking an intelligent question. If Rasheed thought that she was a smart girl, if he saw that she was different from Estella . . .

At last they reached a large, tiled room containing a pool. This was the only private pool in a hotel suite in all of France, he told them; the tiles had been imported from Italy two hundred years ago and depicted Poseidon on the bottom of the pool. Janey had no idea who Poseidon was, but she squinted intelligently at the merman holding a trident, as Rasheed excused himself and motioned Estella to the other side of the pool.

A brief conference took place and Estella nodded. She returned to Janey's side while Rasheed remained near the door.

"He likes you. He wants to show you his bedroom," Estella whispered.

Janey had been dreading this moment, but surprisingly, when it came she felt not fear but a strange boldness, as if the normal boundaries that stood between her and life had been removed, and she turned to Estella and smiled. She had thought that she would refuse, but now she felt an odd eagerness for it. She strode toward Rasheed and as she approached, he nodded; as they passed out of the tiled room and into the hallway, he made the courtly gesture of taking her arm.

They entered a large bedroom with a huge canopied bed. As he motioned that she was to remove her underpants, Janey remembered that she was practically a virgin. She'd had sex exactly three times, with an American student from Rutgers University whom she'd met in Milan. The experience had been painful and mostly uninteresting, and it had astonished her that she seemed to have no emotional connection to the event. Each time it had taken place, she'd felt completely divorced from her body, as if she were floating above herself, watching the action with bored detachment—a fact not lost on the American student. He'd been insulted and incensed at her lack of response, and had finally accused her of being frigid. This had occurred at an outdoor café, where they were drinking coffee, and Janey had nearly cried out with the shame of it; for, not knowing any better, she was sure he was right. Speechless with horror, she had simply gotten up and left, and when she saw that he wasn't going to follow her, she had cried. And then she'd thought about it a bit and decided that the problem was that she hadn't really been the least bit attracted to him. He'd had a persnicketiness about him that bordered on the pathological—he was always washing his hands—and when they were at cafés he insisted on wiping his utensils with a wet nap, a package of which he carried in his knapsack.

And now, sitting on the bed, without her underpants on and with her ankles crossed, Janey watched Rasheed unzip his pants and felt the same curious detachment. She idly wondered what he might do, wondered if he would tie her up and ravish her. It didn't strike her as an unpleasant idea, merely as something that was unlikely to happen, especially as Rasheed removed a pair of English boxer shorts and then carefully folded them on the bench at the end of the bed. He approached her and Janey saw that he had a hard-on and that his penis was bigger than the American student's, with a dark brown shaft and a coffee-colored tip. He raised his hands—for a second, Janey thought he was going to kiss her—but all he did was unbutton the top three buttons of her dress. Reaching inside, he pulled out her breasts. He regarded them thoughtfully, but didn't touch her. Then he pulled her skirt up and gently pushed open her legs. Janey let herself fall back on the bed.

She stared up at the canopy. It was minutely pleated and gathered in the middle, and Janey wondered how they managed to pleat such heavy fabric. She could feel his fingers exploring around down there and pushing into her vagina, and she heard him say, "Nice and tight—that is good," but it didn't seem to have anything to do with her. Then he hoisted himself up and pushed into her. It was unpleasant and slightly painful, and once again Janey wondered why everyone made such a big fuss about sex—surely he couldn't be enjoying this any more than she was. She concentrated on the pleats above her head, thinking about how many people must have labored to make this canopy, and wondering if they knew where it would end up—over the bed of one of the richest men in the world, who paid young women to let him put his penis in them—and in a minute or two, it was over.

She felt him pull out his penis and she sat up. He patted her leg and smiled—his smile seemed genuine but cold—and he said, "Very good. We are finished." For a moment, she felt outraged—was their interlude of no more significance to him than a coffee break?—and she wanted to cry out, "Was that *it*?" But there was something about him that made her hold her tongue, despite what Estella had told her.

She hopped off the bed and pulled on her underpants. He carefully put on his boxers and his pants, and, tucking in his shirt, walked to a desk on which sat a plain leather briefcase. He opened it, and Janey was startled to see that it was filled with money.

It was exactly the sort of thing one sees in movies but doesn't expect to ever see in real life. Janey couldn't see the denomination, but the money was in American dollars, bundled and neatly stacked. The experience of seeing a real briefcase filled with money *alone* was almost worth the price of entry, she thought, and she wanted to laugh with glee. For a second, she had a vision of herself knocking Rasheed over, grabbing the briefcase, and running out of there. There had to be at least $40,000 or $50,000—and surely the richest man in the world wouldn't miss a few thousand dollars. It would mean so little to him and so much to her . . .

His fingers fumbled slightly with a stack of bills, and then he turned and walked back to her, subtly extending his hand toward hers. Janey took the money. She didn't want to appear greedy, but she couldn't help glancing down at it—there were three one-thousand-dollar bills in her hand.

She had never held so much money, and for a moment, she thought she might faint. Rasheed took her by the shoulders and pulled her forward, kissing her on each cheek. And then he said the strangest thing: "I hope I pleased you."

Janey looked at him full in the face and her eyes widened. She wanted to laugh out loud, but knew it was bad enough that she was staring at him with what must be an incredulous expression on her face. How could a man this rich, this intelligent, be so stupid as to think that he might actually have pleased her? . . . And then it all came together in her mind as sharply as the point of a pencil: So this was what it was about, and it was all so unbelievably easy. She was suddenly overwhelmed with her own sense of power, and glancing down at the money again, she lied as easily as an amoral child, in words she would come to use over and over again . . .

"Oh yes, Rasheed," she said. "You were absolutely wonderful."

His face lit up with pride as he took her arm. Leaning in conspiratorially, he said, "Next time, maybe you will move around a little. To please me?"

So there *was* to be a next time. And why not? Giving his arm a little squeeze, she said, "Of course, Rasheed."

"And now I will return you to your friend."

As they entered the large salon, he said, "I hope you enjoyed your tour, Miss Wilcox." Turning, with a courtly nod of his head, he added, "Please excuse me. I have some business to attend to, but you must stay and enjoy some refreshments."

"Thank you," Janey said. She glanced up and saw Estella staring at her from the other side of the room, her eyes filled with curiosity. But thankfully, she said nothing, as there were now two young men in the room, drinking champagne and snorting coke.

Janey awoke the next day at seven in the evening. Her throat was so dry she could barely breathe, and one nostril was completely blocked. The other nostril made a watery, wheezing sound when she blew out of it, and her whole body felt weak, as if she had the flu and were suffering from a high fever. She managed to get out of bed and, stumbling down the hall, made her way to the bathroom. There was music coming from the living room, and when she looked in, she saw the two young men from the night before, bent over a coffee table. The room reeked of cigarette smoke and sweat; there were ashtrays and glasses filled with cigarette butts. She shuddered with disgust and went quickly into the bathroom and shut the door.

She blew her nose, expelling hard, yellowish chunks of snot—it looked like pieces of the inside of her nose were coming out—and then she greedily drank from the tap, even though everyone knew that was a bad idea, and splashed her face with water. The end of the evening was a complete blank; she had no idea how she'd gotten home or ended up in her bed, but she was still wearing her underpants and a T-shirt, so that was good. Then she remembered the incident with Rasheed, and clutching her stomach, she sank to the floor with shame. How could she have done such a thing? And even worse, she'd agreed to do it again!

But gradually, some sort of self-protective reasoning took over, and she acknowledged that it hadn't been all that bad, really, it hadn't done any damage to her physically, plus she had three crisp one-thousand-dollar bills tucked away in the zippered pocket of the cheap purse she'd had since high school—and now she'd be able to buy a new one, a glorious Chanel bag like Estella's. She picked herself up and drank from the tap again, then regarded herself closely in the mirror. She looked exactly the same as she had the day before.

She returned to her room, and as she got back into bed, Estella came in. She was wearing only her bra and panties, and she flopped down onto Janey's bed, giggling. "God, what a night!" she exclaimed. "That was fun, wasn't it?"

Janey laughed weakly. "What happened?" she asked.

"God, you were the life of the party," Estella said, with a note of jealousy in her voice. Janey stared at her wide-eyed—she'd never been called "the life of the party" before—and Estella said, "Oh yes. You were dancing on the table at Le Jardinese."

"Le Jardinese?" Janey said, and coughed. Slowly, it was all coming back to her: First there had been the party at Rasheed's, which had gradually grown and grown, filling up with lots of swarthy young men—all of whom had European accents and seemed to be very rich—and lots of beautiful young women, including two or three famous models whom she recognized. Then there had been an outing to a club— Le Jardinese, she supposed—where she seemed to spend hours and hours in the bathroom talking to some American girl who kept saying, "Don't let them steal your soul." But after that, the evening was a complete blank, and she said, "After Le Jardinese?"

"Oh, we came back here at about six in the morning," Estella said, and yawned. "But you have nothing to worry about. You were so high Sayed gave you a Halcion and you fell asleep on the floor. Then someone dragged you in here I suppose."

"Oh God. I'm never doing coke again . . ."

"Are you crazy? What we need right now is a little wake-up line," Estella said, and she uncurled her fist, revealing a small paper packet. She scooped up some powder with her fingernail and held it under Janey's nose.

"So," she said slyly. "How much did he give you?"

"What?" Janey asked. She sniffed.

"Rasheed. How much money did he give you?"

Janey looked at her. "I guess that's my business."

"Just curious, that's all," Estella said.

"Three thousand dollars."

Estella considered this for a moment, staring down at the packet and then carefully folding it up. "That's more than he usually gives a girl. He must have meant some of it for me."

"For *you*?" Janey exclaimed incredulously. "I was the one who . . ."

"Oh sure, but that's not the deal. The deal is, if you bring him a girl and he has sex with her, *you* get five hundred dollars."

For a moment, Janey just stared at her, unwilling to comprehend the enormity of the situation. How was it possible . . . *was* it possible that someone, a supposed friend, could be so coldly calculating, could set her up and sell her like . . . an ani-

mal? Turning away from Estella, she wiped her nose and said slowly, "I don't ever intend to bring him any girls, Estella."

Estella rolled over and regarded her with hard, glittering eyes. "Maybe *you* don't, but I do," she said. "I have to, you see? Obviously I can't be having sex with Rasheed when I'm with Sayed. Especially as I'm trying to get him to marry me. Besides, I don't see what the big deal is. I helped you out and you help me out. You should be thanking me."

"He gave me the money in thousand-dollar bills," Janey hissed. "So I can't exactly rip one in half, can I?"

Estella raised herself and sat cross-legged on the bed. "So give me a thousand, then."

"No!"

"Come on, Janey. Don't be crazy. You and I are girlfriends. We have to stick together in these things. Besides, you wouldn't want anyone to find out, would you?"

Janey felt herself whiten. How could she have allowed herself to get into this situation? She felt as if she'd fallen into a dark hole from which there was no escape, and pulling the covers over her shoulders, she gasped, "You wouldn't."

"Oh, I would do *anything*," Estella said casually. "That's the thing about me. Nobody gets the better of me." For a moment, the two women's eyes locked, and Janey saw that she was stuck with Estella, stuck with her and what she had done. She should never have trusted Estella; she wasn't the kind of girl she should have been friends with at all. But Estella was practically the only person she knew in Paris, and now that she'd had sex with Rasheed, it felt like the incident would bind them together for life. There would be no getting away from her ever; her only choice was to continue on as if they *were* friends. And with a steady arm that belied the trembling she felt inside, she reached out and grabbed her purse from the side of the bed.

She unzipped the pocket tucked into the side of the purse, and drew out one of the bills. She held it out to Estella, who plucked it from her fingers and folded it neatly, tucking it into her bra. "You can consider the other five hundred next month's rent if you want to," she said evenly.

"Jesus, Estella," Janey cried. "We're . . ."

Estella patted Janey's leg. "If you want to think about yourself that way, Janey, it's your problem," she said calmly. "*I* don't and never will. Christ, be reasonable," she added kindly. "These fucking Arabs have so much money, why *shouldn't* we get some of it? We're going to have sex with men anyway, so why not get something out it? Just because men are pigs . . . well, that's not our problem, is it? Besides, it's not like he hurt you or anything. It's not like he took something away from you, is it? 'Cause there are tons of guys like him you could sleep with and think you were in love with, and they'd treat you exactly the same way." She stood up and stretched. "Now, the good news is that Sayed really liked you. He said you can definitely come on the boat next week. Have you ever been to Saint-Tropez?"

Janey shook her head.

"You're going to love it!" Estella exclaimed. "It's the most fun place in the world. If you thought last night was fun, wait until we hit La Voile Rouge . . . ," and she went out of the room.

Janey sat staring after her. There was no way she was going to Saint-Tropez with Estella and Sayed. Tomorrow she would start looking for another apartment; she would lie to Estella and say that her brother was coming to Paris for the summer and she had to live with him; and when she ran into Estella she would be friendly but noncommittal, and eventually the whole thing would go away.

But the next day brought a fresh round of depressing go-sees, and it was the same the day after that, and on Wednesday she nearly cried when Jacques told her that even though she'd managed to get one ad campaign, if she didn't get more work soon, he'd have to send her back to New York. So by the time Thursday came around and Estella handed her a plane ticket to Nice with her name on it, she was too confused and exhausted to refuse.

It was the path of least resistance. The one she always took.

At first, Saint-Tropez was every bit as glamorous as Estella had promised: Each day "officially" began at 2 P.M. with a group lunch at the beach restaurant 55 (pronounced Cinquant-Cinq); this was followed by the consumption of endless bottles of champagne at La Voile Rouge, where women took their tops off and danced on the tables; then there was a nap back on the boat followed by an exhausting round of parties that concluded in some club or another. No one went to bed before six, and it was a given that the women never paid: The French Riviera was only about one pleasure after another, and Janey quickly discovered that there was nothing that gave more happiness than pretty young things. Intelligence was not a requirement—in fact, it was frowned upon—and all that was demanded was a shallow sophistication, easily obtained with designer fashions and a willingness to find everything and everyone amusing, to overlook indiscretions (or to make witty comments about them), and to never reveal one's true feelings.

But after a few days on Sayed's yacht with Estella and various other reprobates, Janey began to see that there were higher levels to aspire to: Although Sayed was considered rich, he and his hard-partying friends certainly weren't the richest, and everywhere she looked, she saw people who were more elegant and more sophisticated, and she began to wonder if there was some way she could ratchet herself up a social notch or two.

On the Saturday of the second weekend, an enormous yacht pulled into the

Saint-Tropez harbor around noon. Janey and Estella were sitting topless at the front of Sayed's yacht sunning themselves; at first, they were both too engrossed in their conversation to notice. Estella was applying nail polish to her toenails, and there was annoyance in every stroke of the brush—Janey, she said with irritation, was "fucking up."

Janey knew what the problem was: Ever since that night in Paris, she'd kept at least one of her vows—she had refused to do cocaine. By not doing the drug, however, she had turned herself into an outsider, and the atmosphere on the boat was becoming hostile.

"Why can't you try to be a little . . . *nicer?*" Estella asked.

By "nicer" Janey knew that she meant having sex with Sayed's friends.

"If I have to be high to have sex with someone, I'm not going to do it," Janey said stubbornly.

"That's completely pathetic," Estella said. "There's no reason to have sex unless you *are* high. Otherwise, it's totally boring. Besides," she added, "you had sex with Rasheed . . ."

"That was different," Janey said. She wasn't exactly sure *how* it was different, but she liked the sound of it.

"I don't know why I decided to help you," Estella said angrily, pushing the brush into the bottle of nail polish and screwing on the cap. "But if you don't shape up, I won't be able to help you at all. Men get tired of paying for women who won't put out, and frankly, I can't blame them."

Janey looked down at her fingernails and frowned. It wasn't that she *wasn't* willing to put out, but that Sayed's friends just didn't seem good enough.

"Well?" Estella demanded, wriggling her toes.

"I—" Janey began, but at that moment she was cut off by the long, low rumble of a stately horn.

Estella immediately jumped up and ran to the railing. The huge white yacht was slowly pulling into a space three slips away from their own—it had speedboats and Jet Skis in back, and a helicopter on the top, and was so large it made Sayed's ninety-foot "yacht" look like a rowboat.

"That's Rasheed's yacht," Estella said, her eyes narrowing in concentration. "I'm going to tell Sayed to go over there and let him know that we're here."

Estella disappeared down a narrow flight of steps as Janey leaned back against the cushions on the deck. She closed her eyes, but her whole body was tingling with excitement. She had a feeling that something was about to happen—that Rasheed would single her out. And sure enough, in about half an hour, Estella reappeared on the deck with an envelope in her hand. She didn't look happy as she held the envelope out to Janey with a terse *"Here."*

"What is it?" Janey asked innocently.

"You know what it is," Estella said, glaring. She sat down cross-legged next to Janey.

The envelope was nearly as heavy as cardboard, and Janey carefully undid the flap and removed a note card. The card was embossed with a gold replica of the yacht, with the name *Mamouda* underneath, and as Janey read the note, she felt an enormous sense of relief. She was practically out of money; in exchange for a brief sexual encounter she would at least be able to buy her own ticket back to Paris and to survive for another month.

"What does it say?" Estella demanded, attempting to read the note over her shoulder.

Janey slipped the note back into the envelope. "It's from Rasheed—he wants me to go to lunch on his yacht this afternoon at two."

"So you'll miss our lunch at Cinquant-Cinq."

"I guess so," Janey said.

"Well, just remember. Whatever he pays you, you owe me five hundred dollars," Estella said warningly.

"Right," Janey said sarcastically. She had absolutely no intention of giving Estella a penny of her money, and this time, she thought, she would find a way to make sure she didn't.

Janey assumed that Rasheed's use of the word "lunch" was a euphemism for sex, but as she stepped onto his yacht, she immediately saw that "lunch" meant exactly what it implied. On the aft deck, a large teak table was set with linens, crystal, and silver; a pretty young blond woman wearing white gloves was passing a silver tray with caviar while a handsome blond youth dressed in a white shirt and khaki pants was pouring pink champagne and mixing cocktails. There were several people standing or sitting stiffly on the banquettes that lined the deck, and the atmosphere was one of desperately studied elegance, as if these adults were really children playing at putting on an adults' tea party. The only one who seemed immune was Rasheed, who came forward as soon as he spotted Janey, and formally shook her hand. "Miss Wilcox," he said, nodding. "I'm so pleased you could come."

"Thank you so much for having me," she replied, glancing over Rasheed's shoulder at a middle-aged fat man who had followed Rasheed across the deck. The man had a great roll of sunburned lard around his neck that jutted out of the collar of a plaid, short-sleeved shirt, and as he stepped forward, he regarded Janey hungrily. With the briefest smirk on his lips, Rasheed turned and introduced them.

"This is Mr. Dougrey. He's from your native country, I believe."

"Paul Dougrey," the man said, holding out a beefy hand. He had watery blue eyes and graying blond hair that was combed over the top of his head from a low part that started just above his ear, and despite his obvious physical deficiencies, Janey could tell that he thought he was very attractive. "So you're American then," he asked, and without waiting for a response, continued, "Always damn nice to see another American. There are too many damned French people in France." As he laughed heartily at his own joke, a tall, stunningly handsome man with blond hair bleached white from the sun approached Rasheed and whispered something in his ear. Rasheed nodded and turned. "You'll excuse me for a moment," he said. "I'll leave you two Americans to discuss the midwest, which I understand holds a great fascination," and then he disappeared inside the yacht.

"So you're from the midwest?" Paul asked.

"No, Massachusetts," Janey said.

"I'm from Indianapolis myself. My fiancée insisted that we had to take a trip to France, said it was the thing to do," he said, nodding toward an aerobicized woman in her late thirties, who was sitting stiffly with a dark-haired young woman and Justin Marinelli—the same man she'd met at Rasheed's suite. He laughed. "I figured it was a good way to kill two birds with one stone," he said. "She gets in her socializing and I do some business with Mr. Al . . ."

Janey nodded, longing to move away. She had only been in Europe for six months, but she was shocked at the subtle change it must have wrought in her, for she suddenly understood the European penchant for viewing Americans as loud and boorish. She took a step to the side, but Paul stepped in front of her.

"So what are you doing here?" he demanded with a grin, exposing large, yellow teeth that reminded Janey of a golden retriever.

"I'm a . . . model."

He leaned toward her, and with a leering grin said, "Well, seeing as you're American and all and obviously gainfully employed, maybe you can explain what the deal is here."

"The deal?" Janey asked in alarm.

"Sure," Paul whispered. "These girls here," he said, glancing at three beautiful bored-looking young women who were grouped together on a banquette, silently drinking champagne. "Are they . . . you know . . . ?" he asked, making a gesture with his hand.

Janey took a step back. "I have no idea," she replied primly. "I've only met Rasheed once, and then he asked me to lunch . . ."

"Well, you hear rumors and all. And damned if not one of those girls speaks English, or if they can they can't be bothered . . ."

"And what's your business?" Janey asked quickly.

"Munitions," he said, folding his arms across his chest. "Rasheed and I are going to do a little business. I own a company that makes the casings on bullets. And Rasheed here, well, for all his fancy yachts and stuff, he's nothing more than a glorified gunrunner . . ."

Inwardly Janey gasped, but luckily Paul's attention was suddenly diverted by the arrival of a famous movie star in his sixties, accompanied by his famously elegant wife, who was wearing a blue silk turban. Rasheed suddenly materialized and greeted them with a reserved enthusiasm, as Paul leaned in to say, "Well, the man's got pull, you've got to give him that much. Although I know Kim was hoping to meet some kind of European royalty . . ."

Janey gave him a brief smile and slipped away to the other side of the deck. She leaned out over the railing, taking in the now familiar sight of the Saint-Tropez harbor, with its decorative yellow buildings and the row of blue awnings that shaded the cheap cafés. Although the exotic spectacle never failed to thrill her, reminding her that despite the trials of the past two weeks she'd still managed to get somewhere, this time gazing at the bustling harbor was merely a pretense to secretly study the other guests.

The three "models" were obviously Rasheed's girls and, despite their apparent charms, were of little interest to anyone. Janey immediately summed them up as no competition; and yet they also served as a warning as to how one might be treated. While she was willing to take money from Rasheed—as a gift, she reminded herself—she had no intention of becoming one of these faceless bodies that filled in spaces at a luncheon table and performed sexual acts on demand, and for the first time she took comfort in the fact that she was an American girl and all that might imply. Her eyes slid toward Kim, Paul's fiancée; the two were now engaged in conversation with the movie star and his wife, their facial expressions and gestures revealing the heightened animation that ordinary people take on when suddenly confronted with the famous. Janey had disliked Kim on sight, for everything about her was graceless—from her highlighted hair that showed dark chunks at the roots to her clothing, which was expensive but badly chosen—but now, watching Kim enmesh the movie star with the presumptive intimacy that comes so easily to Americans, Janey felt an outpouring of affection for her. Kim, who was in her mid- to late-thirties, was nothing more or less than she appeared to be: a woman trying to better herself in life, and if that meant putting up with Paul, so be it, especially as she probably genuinely loved him as well.

No, she needn't fear anything from Kim, but the same could not be said of the dark-haired beauty who, Janey presumed, was Justin's wife. Janey recognized her disdainful demeanor as the mark of someone from a good, respectable French family that was most likely in possession of an ancient aristocratic title . . . And Janey couldn't help being amused by the fact that she looked like she could barely tolerate being on a yacht with what she undoubtedly considered questionable company. Her black hair was drawn back into a tight bun, as if the severity of her hairstyle might shield her from any disreputable undercurrents, while Justin stood over her engaged in a hushed conference. His closed expression revealed the frustration of a man who has grown used to the fact that he'll never be able to please his wife and yet is still in love with her, and watching them Janey was suddenly filled with a nagging anxiety about her own situation.

She turned away for a moment, and down the long, hundred-foot teak walkway saw two white-coated figures slip into a sliding doorway as invisibly as if they were ghosts, but her eyes were drawn back to Justin and his wife. Her head was turned away from him as she delicately took a bite of toast smeared with tiny black eggs; although the company might not have been up to her standards, she wasn't above eating her host's caviar. Justin gave his wife a warning frown, and then, in obvious exasperation, looked away and his eye caught Janey's. For some reason, she blushed but held his gaze. Her eyes were as curious as his, and with a guilty look he turned back to his wife as Janey pretended to be very interested in a crewman who was scrubbing the deck of the boat next door.

When she turned back to the group, she saw Justin making his way over to Kim and the movie star and his wife. His manner was easy and confident; he possessed the unapologetic American air of a young man who is going places, coupled with a European passion for life. Janey saw immediately that he was just the sort of man a girl should marry. But she also saw, with a touch of anger, that he was just the sort of man who would *not* marry a girl like her. The same ambitions that had brought her to Rasheed's yacht drove him as well; the difference was that hers came out of desperation while his were piloted by entitlement. She was, she realized, far too common and ordinary to interest a man like Justin in marriage. And while he had obviously aspired to a match that could elevate him socially, however much one might criticize him for it, he had managed to pull it off. With a flash of disheartening insight she saw that no matter what anybody said, it was a man's world and the rules were designed to allow men to take what they wanted, while women were left to hope and wait, or to make their way as best they could . . .

In desperation she looked around for Rasheed and saw that he was talking quietly to Paul and two of the Arab men, who were obviously his henchmen. She didn't understand why she'd been invited to this lunch, which was apparently some kind of business affair disguised as a social event, unless it was to even out the numbers of men and women. Rasheed was taking small notice of her, and doubting he would have sex with her after all, she suddenly found herself desperately missing the $2,000 or $3,000 she would have collected. Looking around at the rest of the party, she felt more alone than she had in weeks. Her loneliness was like a gauzy white shroud separating her from the world, and for a moment she felt as if she had become invisible, while at the same time conscious that every small movement she made was being magnified and thrown into glaring relief. She jerkily brushed her hair over her shoulder, wishing that she'd taken Estella's advice and started smoking—at least that way she would have something to do with her hands. And then, with overwhelming relief, she looked up and found the handsome young man standing by her side.

"You look as though you need a drink, mate," he said with an easy jocularity that was in direct contrast to her unease. His accent was not quite English as he said, "Didn't anyone offer you champagne?"

"I . . . I don't know," she faltered, instantly aware of how stupid her remark sounded.

But he appeared to take it at face value. "As you don't have a glass in your hand, I assume they haven't," he said, and with a sharp look summoned one of the white-coated waiters to their side. In a few moments, Janey was gratefully sipping a glass of champagne and staring up at him with large blue eyes. "Aren't you having any?" she asked.

"Can't," he said. "I'm on duty."

"On duty?" she asked.

"Believe it or not, I'm the captain of this ship," he said, leaning in with a playful wink. "Ian Carmichael," he said, holding out his hand.

"Janey Wilcox," she said.

"And what brings you, Janey Wilcox, an obviously nice American girl, onto the *Mamouda*?" he asked. He was smiling, but there was a serious look in his eyes that hinted at kindly depths, and with desperate honesty Janey cried out, "I have no idea!"

He regarded her quizzically, as if judging the reality of her despair. Leaning toward her, he said conspiratorially, "No one knows why they're on this boat, with the exception of Mr. Rasheed. He knows all, and they"—he gestured at the guests—"know nothing. But I suppose they find it interesting enough to play along." He paused for a second, and then, reverting to his lighthearted tone, asked, "Do you know Robert Russell?"

"The movie star?" Janey asked, shaking her head. "No. I don't know anyone famous."

"He's a nice man, and so is his wife. You ought to go introduce yourself."

"I couldn't!"

"Ah, but you have to," he said. "You can't spend all afternoon talking to me, much as I'd like to."

She looked into his eyes. Was he warning her or merely giving her friendly advice? She felt a frisson of sexual attraction and wondered if he felt attracted to her as well, but his eyes were as calm as the blue waters in the harbor. And as she moved away from him toward the other guests, she had the disconcerting feeling that she was leaving reality and entering a movie set.

Observing her progress, Robert Russell called out, "Hello there, young lady," which, Janey thought, might have been motivated by his desire to relieve himself of Kim's company, but within seconds she was ensconced in the little group. And several minutes later, Robert's wife, Zara, who was as charming as her reputation implied, was promising to write down the name of the shop where she'd bought her turban . . .

The luncheon itself seemed to consist of two separate parties. There was Rasheed's end of the table, populated by his henchmen, the models, and Paul, and Janey's end of the table, which consisted of Russell and Zara, Kim, Justin, and his wife, who was called Chantal. The meal consisted of five courses with a prodigious amount of wine and silverware, and as soon as Janey sat down at the table, she remembered that although she'd been raised with no thought to the development of her brain or any marketable skills, she *had* been brought up with manners—at least to the extent that she knew which fork to use. This tiny bit of knowledge coupled with the champagne she'd drunk gave her the confidence to proceed in a situation for which she was socially ill-equipped, and she began to relax when she saw Kim use her salad fork for the first course of smoked trout, and caught Chantal's disgusted expression. But Chantal and Kim and Zara were united by the fact that they all had children, and Chantal, although she was but twenty-three, had just had a baby. It seemed to Janey that in polite society, there must be only two types of women, those who had children and those who did not, and no woman could hate another woman who had experienced the mysteries of childbirth.

Indeed, when asked about the birth (by Kim, before the first course was even finished), Chantal shook her head and glowered at her plate. "No man can understand, no matter what they say," she said, with a sharp look at Justin. Janey wondered if this was the cause of Chantal's hatred of her husband, or if it was merely one of a litany of complaints. And then the conversation mysteriously moved on to curtains—specifically $20,000 drapes Kim was considering buying for her and Paul's New York apartment.

Throughout this, Janey made appropriate facial gestures and little murmurs of assent, but her head was spinning. How was it possible that there was this much money in the world—enough to spend $20,000 on one window treatment? In the town where she'd grown up, everyone had played tennis and golf, but they'd also clipped coupons and bought steak when it was $1.50 a pound instead of $3. She was an interloper in this world, and yet, at the same time, it didn't feel impossible that she should be here. Studying Chantal, she decided that she was certainly as attractive as she was, although she had to admit that she lacked Chantal's elegance. But surely, elegance could be learned, and, almost unconsciously, she began to mimic the way Chantal held her fork and dabbed at the corners of her mouth with her napkin.

Justin was seated to her right. She felt that there was something between them, and yet he seemed to be making a studious effort to ignore her. The fact that he was married to Chantal piqued her interest, and she wondered how difficult it would be to get him to sleep with her. She was driven not by malice but by the simple desires of youth to spread its wings and see how far it could go, and with a little smile, she turned to Justin and asked, "Do you have a yacht as well?"

Justin gave her a startled look, as if he couldn't tell whether she was joking, and said, "No. Chantal's family has a villa in Mougins."

He glanced at the other end of the table where Rasheed was deep in conversation with Paul and one of the Arab men, and Janey, watching his eyes, said, "Do you work for Rasheed?"

"I'm an investment banker."

"I see," Janey said, nodding wisely. She had no idea where Mougins was or what an investment banker actually did, but decided it didn't really matter. She was a slate devoid of knowledge on which anything might be written and remembered, and she began asking him questions about his business. She'd had surprisingly little experience with men, but almost immediately Justin warmed up and began talking, and some part of her brain noted that this was the way to get a man's attention.

By the time the main course was finished, everyone at her end of the table was quite drunk, and Robert was telling ribald stories. Janey had found out that Justin came from Buffalo—"Buffalo!" she'd exclaimed. "That's not very glamorous!"—and that he was the youngest partner at his firm and had worked his way through Yale. Her knee just happened to brush against his, and when he didn't pull it away, she increased the pressure. She felt the heat and confusion of his sexual desire, and, as she had after the sexual encounter with Rasheed, was once again intoxicated with her power to attract men—it was almost like a drug.

As a large bowl of raspberries was served, Ian materialized at her side. He leaned down and whispered that she had a phone call and asked her to follow him; Janey looked up at him in drunken confusion. But as she was about to protest, a look in his eyes silenced her. She glanced toward Rasheed and saw his eyes flicker over her like a snake. Then he gave her a slight nod.

She stood up, steadying herself on the back of her chair. Was this to be the moment then, after all? If it was, she felt ready—she would service Rasheed and then return to the table with no one the wiser and $3,000 in her pocket, and she was surprised to find that she felt as though she were about to get away with something rather than commit some pathetic crime. She followed Ian into a large room that was furnished with long couches and coffee tables; there was a gold bar at one end and a parquet dance floor complete with a disco ball in the middle.

"Ian," she whispered, giggling. "Who would be calling me?"

"I don't ask questions. It's not my place," he replied, looking slightly embarrassed.

But instead of taking her into a bedroom, he led her through a hallway and down a spiral staircase into a room that was clearly some kind of office. He excused himself and closed the door.

Seated behind an ornate French desk was one of the Arab men from the lunch. He motioned for her to sit down.

"Mr. Rasheed has found that you please him," he began. "He would like to ask you to be a guest on his yacht."

Janey was shocked—this was the last thing she'd been expecting, although she'd heard that Rasheed did have girls on his yacht, and also that he gave them money. But she certainly hadn't imagined he was *that* interested in her; why, he'd hardly paid attention to her at lunch. With a laugh, she asked, "But why?"

"It is not for me to say," murmured the Arab. "But he offers you ten thousand dollars a week."

Janey nearly laughed out loud. The ridiculousness of the situation was overwhelming. How on earth had she ended up on some rich Arab's yacht, being offered $10,000 a week to have sex with him? The craziness of the situation nearly propelled her up from her chair and out of the room. Of course, she had to refuse, she had to return to Paris and try to get some modeling work, but then she remembered that she didn't have the money for her ticket back, and immediately her mind began making calculations. She lived on about $2,000 a month—$10,000 would buy her at least five months of peace. She could stay on the yacht for one week—and then she would take up her life again and maybe even find a real boyfriend, someone like Justin.

"Do you agree?" the Arab asked.

"Oh, sure," Janey said, feeling emboldened by the wine she'd drunk at lunch.

"Very good," the man said. "Then you will sign this." He slid a piece of paper toward her. "It is nothing. A confidentiality agreement. You will agree not to talk to the press about Mr. Rasheed. You will agree never to write about him. If you do . . ."

"What? Are you going to have me killed?" Janey asked. A sudden jolt of fear had inspired her to attempt a joke, but the man said nothing, staring back at her with black eyes.

In a second, she made her decision. The $10,000 was too tempting, and besides, she couldn't imagine a day when she'd ever be in a position to talk to the press or to write about Rasheed anyway. Accepting a silver pen from the Arab, she neatly signed her name in a schoolgirl script.

Sitting back in her chair, she attempted another joke. "So," she asked. "When do I start?"

"Oh, right now, Miss Wilcox."

"Then I guess I'd better get my stuff."

"There is no need. We have people who do these things."

"But . . . I've got to say good-bye to my friends. I have to tell them where I'm going," she said with rising panic.

The Arab smiled at her coldly, pushing his fingers together to form a tent. "I'm afraid there is no time for that," he said.

And then it felt like her heart was suddenly being squeezed by a giant claw as he added, "We leave for the Turkish islands in half an hour."

FIFTEEN

THE WHITE-HOT SUN beat down relentlessly on the multicolored buildings that lined the small harbor. It was three in the afternoon and at least ninety-five degrees, but neither the blazing sun nor the heat had prevented the small but determined crowd of tourists from wandering up and down the narrow cobbled street that ran from one end of the harbor to the other. Nestled into the side of a hill at the end of this street was a small café with outdoor tables shaded by a rickety wooden roof, and at one of these tables, Janey Wilcox sat drinking a Coke and fanning herself with an old issue of *Time* magazine.

Not two feet away from her, an orange and yellow tomcat sat on a wooden piling, staring at her with large hazel eyes. He had a torn ear and a scratch over one eye, and when he determined that she wasn't going to order food and feed it to him, he began licking his paw and slowly washing his face. Janey glared at the cat as she sipped her Coke through a straw. The whole place was overrun with cats; as soon as you sat down they would surround you, even being so bold as to sit on an empty chair at your table.

Janey sighed and leaned her head on her hand, looking out over the harbor. She supposed that it had its charms, but this was now the third day they'd spent anchored outside the harbor and the whole scene was wearing thin. The other girls didn't understand why they had to spend three days here, but they weren't bright enough to figure it out, even after the morning they'd anchored in the bay of a remote and seemingly uninhabited island, and had been told to stay in their staterooms with the curtains drawn.

Naturally, they'd complied—but Janey hadn't, and standing on her bed and cautiously lifting a corner of the curtain, she'd peeked out and seen three soldiers wearing camouflage outfits and carrying machine guns making their way down a rocky hill toward the boat. Then she'd fallen back onto the bed, covering her mouth with her hand and willing herself not to scream. Ever since that first afternoon, when she'd returned to the deck and found all the guests gone—with the exception of the three young women—and the crew running around and pulling up anchors, she'd been convinced that she was about to be sold into white slavery. And for the next three hours, huddled in her stateroom, which was about a thousand times nicer than the cabin she'd had on Sayed's boat—it had a marble tub in the bathroom and just about every kind of shampoo, soap, and body cream you could think of—she remained convinced that she was about to be sold into white slavery.

The lunch and the offer of $10,000 was all a con to get her on the boat and then sell her, she'd thought, as she lay moaning on her bed in the fetal position. After all, Rasheed was a gunrunner—Paul had said so himself—and if he was running guns, maybe he was running girls as well. And on top of that, not one person in the whole world knew she was on Rasheed's boat with the exception of Estella— and Estella wasn't exactly the sort of person who would send for help.

Naturally, nothing whatever of the kind had happened—yet, Janey thought, gazing out at the shallow water in the harbor. On the other side, children were playing on a dirty sand beach, while behind them, two workers hammered lazily at a board of wood on a sawhorse. But the initial sight of the soldiers had convinced Janey that she had been right all along—and that it all, finally, made sense: Where else would they have dared make the transaction but on a deserted island where no one would ever see? And then, she would disappear as completely as if she'd never existed, and God only *knew* what they would do to her. Well, she decided, they were going to be in for a little surprise: She'd already decided that they would have to kill her first before she went with them.

And now, sitting at the café with nothing at all to do, she replayed that time in her cabin, analyzing her reactions. It was interesting what panic could do to a person. For a good ten minutes, she'd been dizzy and confused, and had completely lost her bearings—if it weren't for gravity, she wouldn't have been able to tell up from down. And then, for some bizarre reason, she had climbed into the marble bathtub and covered herself with towels. And yet, as frightened as she was, she'd *still* noticed that the towels were exceptionally thick and fluffy. And then she had actually thought about taking a bath, but quickly rejected the idea because if they were going to come for her, she didn't want to make it easier for them by being naked. Finally, she got out of the bathtub and, thinking more clearly, decided that if they were going to sell her, she should be prepared in case she got the opportunity to escape. Putting on a pair of khaki shorts, she began stuffing the pockets with anything that might serve as a weapon—nail scissors, a sewing kit, even a tiny travel-size bottle of shaving cream. Then she snuck back to the bed and peeked out the window again.

Rasheed was standing on the shore talking to the three men. She couldn't see his face, but she knew it was him, because ever since they'd left the South of France, he'd taken to wearing the traditional Arab garb of long white flowing robes coupled with a pair of reflective Ray-Ban sunglasses. Rasheed's two henchmen were standing behind him, also carrying machine guns. There was quite a bit of gesturing, and then all the men turned and began walking along a narrow dirt track, passing out of her line of vision.

She had plopped back down on the bed, poking herself with the nail scissors. She was being crazy again—it was only some kind of arms deal after all. But that Rasheed was clever. When they were summoned from their rooms two hours later, the salon had been done up as a winter wonderland, complete with fake snow and wooden branches spray-painted white and strung with tiny Christmas lights. In the middle of the disco floor sat a large, white birthday cake on which was written *Bon Anniversaire Irina*. All twenty members of the crew stood in a semicircle and sang "Happy Birthday" to Irina, who was tall and dark, with large breasts and hips and a miraculously tiny waist, while Irina looked confused.

"But it is not my birthday," she protested, in heavily accented English.

"Mr. Carmichael," Rasheed said to Ian (he never called anyone by his first name). "Is this correct? Miss Stepova says it is *not* her birthday."

"I checked her passport, sir, and today's the day," Ian said firmly.

"Maybe *I* make mistake?" Irina asked. And then Rasheed had given them all diamond tennis bracelets.

"It wasn't her birthday, you know?" the girl named Sallie whispered later, when the four girls were sunning themselves on the deck. She was English and never tired of reminding them that she came from a good family with connections to the royals, acting as if it were the most natural thing in the world to be a guest on Rasheed's boat.

"Irina . . . make . . . mistake? No?" said the Brazilian girl named Conchita. She could barely speak a word of English, and cried at least once a day, invoking her "Mama." Ian said she was going to be put off the yacht when they got to Monaco.

"Janey?" Sallie asked. Her accent was hard, like two grating pieces of metal, and if Janey had known more about the English, she would have quickly understood that Sallie's claims to an aristocratic background were completely false. But all she knew was that she couldn't stand her, and rolling over onto her stomach, Janey said casually, "Who cares?"

"I get bracelet," Irina said, waving her wrist in the air.

"You know something, don't you, Janey?" Sallie said, crawling toward her. "You've probably talked to Ian about it."

"Ian?"

"Don't think we haven't seen you sucking up to him. You're probably shagging him on the sly. Remember, there are cameras in every room."

"Then all you have to do is watch the tape."

"What is *tape*?" Irina asked.

Ian! Janey thought. The sound of a helicopter brought her back to the present, and she looked up to see Rasheed's shiny black helicopter swoop low over the harbor and then rise into the air, disappearing over the mountain that rose steeply from the back of the town. With Rasheed gone, maybe Ian would come now. She had engineered the possibility by announcing at lunch that she wanted to go into town to look for newspapers. Rasheed raised his eyebrows, and with a hint of a smile said, "Miss Wilcox, I did not know you read Turkish. Perhaps you have hidden talents we do not know about?"

"Oh yes, Rasheed," she said mischievously. "Many."

"Do tell, Janey," Sallie said, her mouth half full of fish. "Are you planning to grow breasts?"

"What is *breasts*?" Irina asked.

And now, very faintly, Janey was sure that she heard the sound of the Lazer. Holding the magazine over her head to shield her eyes, a sleek gray dinghy rounded the point of the harbor, piloted by a tall blond man. From a distance, most of the crew, who were either Australian or English, looked exactly alike with their slim bodies and blond hair, but Ian was taller than the rest, and she was sure it was he. Her heart beat rapidly as the boat swung into the harbor and passed the café; jumping out of her seat she ran to the edge of the dock and waved. He acknowledged her with a large grin and steered the boat to the pier in the center of the town.

She returned to her seat, nervously fiddling with the diamond bracelet on her wrist. How had this happened? She was desperately in love with him—when she wasn't contriving ways to brush against him she spent her time fantasizing about having sex with him, about escaping the yacht and having a life together. And yet, in the seven days she'd been on the yacht, she hadn't had more than half a minute alone with him. But even in those brief thirty seconds, she was sure that she saw depths of great understanding in him, that he saw who she really was.

He tied up the Lazer and began making his way toward her. She had fallen in love with him that first night on the yacht, when, shaking with fear, she had run into him on the deck on her way to dinner. "They're going to sell us into white slavery," she hissed angrily. He was so taken aback by her comment that he'd laughed out loud. "Tell you what," he said. "If they do, I'll protect you. I promise to be the highest bidder." Then he had laughed again and shaken his head in amused disbelief. The incident had become a running joke with them—when Janey saw him, she'd say, "I hope you're saving your money." And he'd respond, "It's all in the mattress," and wink at her.

He was nearly at the café when he suddenly turned into a white building with an official-looking brass plaque on the door, which was the customs office.

She took another sip of her Coke and willed her heart to stop beating. He would come to her—he had to. He had seen her, and as she was a "guest" on the yacht he would have to at least acknowledge her and say hello. But immediately her mind began spinning fantasies. He would take her back to the yacht, and with Rasheed gone, maybe she could sneak into his cabin. Sallie had said there were cameras in every room, but perhaps that didn't extend to the crew; she couldn't imagine Ian tolerating a camera in his room. He was so beautiful and wise . . .

Fifteen minutes later he emerged from the customs office, and with a wave of his hand approached her table. "How were the Turkish newspapers?" he asked.

"Oh, I found I couldn't read Turkish after all," she said airily.

"Well, the good news is that we leave for Monaco this afternoon. You ever been to Monaco?"

"No, but maybe Rasheed will want to put me off the yacht."

"I don't think so," Ian said, cocking his head to one side. "He seems to really like you."

"It's probably my poker playing . . . Do we have to go back to the yacht right away?"

"I'll let you finish your Coke," he said.

"Then I'm going to finish it very slowly," she said, looking up at him and smiling. She loved it when he took a commanding tone of voice with her. It made her feel like a child who has just been assured that everything is going to be all right. "Why don't you have one, too?" she asked innocently.

"Because," he said, leaning over the table, "it wouldn't do for us to be seen together."

"We can go in the back."

"Now that would be even worse. They'd think we were hiding."

"Are they watching us?"

"'Course," he said, in a tone of voice that might or might not have been joking. "See that man over there?" he asked, indicating a heavy-set man with a shaved head. "You ever seen him before?"

"No-o-o-o-o."

"He's on the yacht. He's one of Rasheed's bodyguards."

"I don't care!"

"Oh Lord, Janey," Ian sighed. "Don't you know what they do to women who commit adultery in their country? They toss them into an empty swimming pool and throw stones at them until they're dead."

Janey gasped and looked in horror at the man with the shaved head, who was busy trying to kick a cat that had wandered too close.

"I don't believe you," she said.

He shrugged. "Maybe I'll have a Coke after all." He went to the bar and returned with a bottle and an empty glass, and sat down across from her, carefully moving his chair back from the table. "We'll talk about Monaco," he said.

"I don't want to talk about Monaco."

"You'll love it," he said, taking a sip of Coke from the bottle. "Great shopping. And then there's the casinos."

Janey rested her elbows on the table and leaned toward him. "I don't care about shopping. I could care less about clothes. Or this bracelet!" she said, shaking her wrist.

His eyes narrowed as he took another sip from the bottle. "All of you girls care about clothes. And money."

"Ian," she said softly. "I'm in love with you."

She had never told a man she was in love with him and had never expected to. But the situation was so unreal that the words had simply slipped out of her mouth. It was a relief to say them. If they were in love, it made the reality of her position romantic as opposed to sordid. It would become nothing more than a funny incident they would tell their children . . .

He looked away, and when he turned back he said, "What are you doing on the yacht, Janey?"

"I don't *know* . . ."

"From the minute I saw you, I asked myself, 'What the hell is *she* doing here?' Which isn't to say that I don't understand why most of these women come on board. But you, Janey," he said, shaking his head. "You don't need to do this. Sure, you're beautiful. But you're smart. You've got something going on in your head. Why don't you go back to the States and become a doctor . . ."

"A *doctor?*"

"Does anybody know where you are?"

"I told you, I was practically kidnapped . . ."

"Would anyone care?"

"Of course. My family . . ."

"Most of the girls who come on the yacht don't have anyone who would care or notice that they were gone."

"Ian," she said, nervously fiddling with the bracelet. "What are *you* doing on the yacht?"

"You ought to get off in Monaco," he said. "It'll be easy to leave there. Go back to your family."

"I saw him doing an arms deal."

Ian carefully put the near-empty bottle of Coke on the table. He stood up slowly. "I'm going to pretend that I never heard that. And you're going to pretend that you never said it."

"Ian," she whispered. "If I get off the yacht in Monaco, will you come with me? Can we be together?"

He laughed, breaking the tension. "We'd better get back to the yacht."

"But could we?" she demanded. "I know you're crazy about me. I've seen the way you look at me . . ."

"Have you?" he said with a funny, perplexed air. "Then I suppose I'd best make sure I don't look at you that way again."

But she didn't get off the yacht in Monaco.

Instead, she became consumed with the idea of playing a dangerous game—of being the center of her own drama—and with the foolishness of a schoolgirl, she convinced herself that she couldn't bear to be away from Ian. She was sure he secretly wanted her, especially as he hadn't denied it, and she did her best to make him jealous: Day after day, she'd return to the boat laden with bags from Dior and Christian Lacroix, making sure to catch his eye from where he was stationed on the poop deck. "What are you doing, Janey?" he'd ask, brushing past her.

"It's not so bad," she'd shrug.

"Not so bad on the outside, maybe, but we both know what it's really about, don't we?"

"I'm in love with you, Ian," she'd whisper and sigh.

Of course, she had to hide her true feelings from Rasheed. But wasn't that part of the fun? The deception made her feel alive; it heightened her senses so that every moment felt like a particularly rich scene in a film. In Monte Carlo, she dressed up in long gowns to accompany Rasheed to the casino. There were always men watching her, staring at her, attempting to speak with her, and with the arrogance of youth she finally *knew* that she was beautiful, and thanked God for having been made so, unable to imagine a worse fate than being ugly.

But one night she got a little shock.

She was with Rasheed and a group of women at the nightclub Jimmy's; making her way to the ladies' room, a man suddenly came up to her and pushed her against the wall. Breathing alcoholic fumes into her face, he sneered, "You must be awfully good if you're with Rasheed. I hear he has only the *best* . . ."

She pushed him away in disgust, and ran into the powder room. With a shaking hand, she opened her Chanel bag and took out her Pussy Pink lipstick, applying a comforting daub. She was shocked; the South of France was filled with women like her, beautiful young women with no visible means of support, and it being France, no one questioned their presence. It couldn't be that obvious, she thought, glancing over at two attractive young women who were clearly American. Their clothing, she noted, wasn't nearly as expensive as hers, and out of the corner of her eye, she saw the two girls take in her appearance and then whisper something.

She turned in fury, daring them to question her. "Well?" she demanded. "What is it?"

"Nothing," one of the girls shrugged. But as they passed by, she heard the other one whisper, "*Puta,*" the Italian word for whore, under her breath.

For a moment, she couldn't breathe. She took a step back and stared at herself in the mirror in horror. So it was obvious then, what she had become. She was wearing an expensive Thierry Mugler gown with a gold Chanel cuff at her wrist. She had thought she looked elegant, but she now saw that she was clad in the finery of a prostitute, and she wanted to rip the dress from her body. But then reason took over. Beautiful clothes and jewelry were so expensive, and she wanted beautiful things to decorate her body . . . And there was no other way to get them except to use her body and her beauty in exchange. And how was that so different from women like Kim, she wondered defiantly, who married a rich man to pay for their houses and $20,000 window treatments? The only real difference was that they were married and she wasn't . . .

And she went back to the yacht in a huff.

She ran into Ian in the salon—he was straightening up in anticipation of the party that would undoubtedly take place there later.

"Oh, Ian," she cried. "Some awful girls . . ."

And Ian, seeing her face and guessing at what had happened, shook his head. "There's an old saying, Janey," he said. "Beware what you consume, lest your appetite grow by what it feeds on."

And then somehow, July turned into August. And in August, it all came crashing down.

She was with Rasheed and two other girls (there were always other women coming and going on the yacht, and Janey had learned to do her best to ignore them, making it a point to not even remember their names) and they were in Cannes, walking along the boulevard de la Croisette on their way to the beach restaurant at the Carlton. Janey was wearing a sleeveless Ungaro dress with high, padded shoulders; her hair was pulled back into a bun and she had a heavy Chanel pearl necklace around her neck. The group was talking about a party they'd been to

the night before at a wealthy American widow's villa, when suddenly she felt someone grab her arm, and a disturbingly familiar male voice cried out, "Janey?"

She stopped. And then, almost in slow motion, the rest of the little group came
to a halt and turned, staring in curiosity at the bearded young man in the khaki
shorts and rough suede Birkenstock sandals with a heavy backpack slung over his
shoulders.

It was her brother, Pete.

A pretty young woman with long dark hair and a distinct resemblance to Ali
MacGraw stood open-mouthed a few feet away. She was Pete's girlfriend, Anna,
the girl he'd been dating through high school and college. She took a step forward.
"Janey?" she asked.

Pete looked from Janey to the girls to Rasheed. A look of shocked disgust
crossed his face as his fingers dug into her arm and he shouted, "What the *hell* . . . ?"

A soft rain had begun to fall on the Place Vendôme. Janey looked up; she ought to
get going, find a taxi and meet Mimi at Dior. The rain would ruin her hair and her
expensive clothing; Mimi would be wondering what had happened to her. But she
didn't care. The pain of remembering made her insides feel as if she were filled with
broken glass, and the cool, light rain came almost as a relief.

It had taken two days to get off the yacht. Ian had told her that she had to wait,
let Rasheed come around to the idea himself. Propriety dictated that it should be
his suggestion, and besides, she wanted her money.

Finally, on the third morning she was once again summoned into the office.
Just as before, the Arab man was seated behind the desk. "Mr. Rasheed thanks you
for your company, but thinks it best if you now leave. You will find your bags packed
and waiting for you at the end of the gangplank. A car will take you wherever you
wish to go." And then he had handed her a small, hard-sided Louis Vuitton case.
"Mr. Rasheed wishes you to have this as a token of his appreciation. It is suggested
that you leave immediately."

She left the office clutching the case in her hands. She passed through the
salon and out onto the deck, where she'd had that first fateful lunch six weeks
before. She could see her bags neatly stacked next to the trunk of a black Mercedes
with tinted windows; the driver, another Arab, stood outside. She looked around
wildly for Ian. He had to know she was leaving. Was he going to let her go without
saying good-bye?

As she reached the gangplank, she held back for a moment. The August sun
was already unbearably hot and for a moment she felt dizzy. And then he was by her
side, gently taking her arm. "Do you need help, Miss Wilcox?" he asked.

"Oh yes!" she cried, looking meaningfully into his eyes.

"Be careful," he said, glancing toward the Arab.

There were so many things she wanted to say to him, and no time. She felt tears welling up in her eyes, and suddenly, she was exhausted. How had she ever become so tired? "Ian . . . ," she said.

"I'm glad you're going, Janey. It's about time."

They reached the end of the gangplank and stepped onto the cement dock. "Are these all your bags?" he asked, in an official-sounding voice. Janey looked at her bags in confusion. She had no idea . . . There were four Louis Vuitton suitcases in all, stacked one on top of the other like the luggage of some very glamorous movie star.

She thought she was going to cry again, so she opened her purse and took out a pair of dark glasses. The Arab man put the suitcases in the trunk.

"Ian . . ."

"Yes, Miss Wilcox?"

She didn't know what she wanted to say. He took a step back from the car as the Arab opened the door. She looked back at him, and then, taking three quick steps toward him, said, "Why *are* you on the yacht?"

He looked at her and sadly shook his head. "The same reason you were, Janey. Money."

"But . . ."

"I've got an ex-wife and a child to support in Australia."

She breathed a sigh of relief. Why, he might have been married. "Will I ever see you again?"

"I don't know."

"Say you love me, Ian. Please. Because I still love you."

His smile was filled with sorrow, and for a second, he reached out and pushed the sunglasses up on her nose. "You'd better go now. And don't cry. Remember, big girls don't cry." Then he reached out and shook her hand. "Good-bye, Miss Wilcox. Have a pleasant trip."

As soon as she got into the car and it slowly pulled away, she started crying for real, the tears running down her cheeks underneath her sunglasses. And then, after a few minutes, she remembered the small Louis Vuitton case, sitting on the seat next to her. Glancing at the driver, she quickly placed the case on her lap and gingerly sprung the lock.

She cautiously opened the lid, and then, viewing the contents, sat back against the seat, her heart pounding. She immediately forgot all about Ian, forgot all about everything in fact, except for the bundles and bundles of thousand-dollar bills stacked inside. All she could think over and over again was that she had done it— somehow she had done *it*. And while she wasn't exactly sure what "it" was, she knew that it certainly felt good . . .

As the car moved slowly through the traffic on the boulevard, and then turned up into the hills, she surreptitiously counted the money. It was all there, every penny—her "fee" plus her poker winnings . . . Why, with this money, she didn't *have* to go back. She was free! She could go anywhere she wanted in the world, do anything she wanted—she could live in Tahiti and write a book. Yes, and why not? She'd always had a vague idea of writing a book, of becoming a famous novelist . . . People would come up to her and tell her that she'd changed their lives with her words . . .

She must tell the driver to turn around right now and go to the airport. At the airport, she would choose a destination that suited her fancy, get on the plane, and disappear, completely free from everything . . . But for some reason, due to fear and guilt perhaps, she didn't. And so the car drove up into the hills, past gas stations and supermarkets and furniture stores, and finally stopped in front of the youth hostel, a run-down building with peeling blue paint that she imagined was crawling with lice . . .

Her brother and his girlfriend were seated at the café next door, drinking coffee. As the car pulled up, Pete stood up and frowned. The driver opened the door and Janey got out. She was wearing an expensive Lacroix outfit with high heels, and was suddenly conscious of how ridiculous she looked. As the driver unloaded the bags, Pete said, "Jesus. Do you think you have enough luggage?"

"I'm not backpacking," Janey snapped.

"I spoke to Mom. She says she wants us to come home right away. She wants us to leave from Nice airport and not go into Paris. She wired me the money for the tickets."

"I have my own money," Janey said.

Jesus! The money. She was going to have to hide it in her suitcases. Wasn't there something on the customs form that said you couldn't bring more than $20,000 in currency into the country? What if she got caught and went to jail? She felt dizzy.

"The plane leaves at three o'clock. So we'd better get going."

"Can I go to the bathroom?"

Pete rolled his eyes as Janey dragged her suitcases, one by one, into the toilette. It was a typical French toilet—basically a hole in a cement floor over which you were supposed to squat, but at least it was empty. With shaking hands, she split up the bundles and transferred the money to the bottom of each suitcase, counting it again just to make sure. It was all still there—$100,000 in brand-new thousand-dollar bills.

They took a taxi to the airport. Crammed into the backseat of the cheap car,

Pete turned to her, and in a low voice that threatened to boil over into fury, said, "You could have been killed, you know? Nobody knew *where* you were—Mom was about to call the French police."

"I was fine," Janey said wearily. "I *look* fine, don't I?"

"You look like a . . ."

"What!"

"Take it easy on her, hon. She's just a kid," Anna said kindly.

"She *was* just a kid! She isn't anymore . . ."

"What do you care?" Janey said. "It doesn't affect *your* precious life."

"It's going to kill Mom. Kill her. Does that mean anything to you? Do you ever think about anybody besides yourself?"

"So don't tell her."

"I think we're beyond that now," Pete snarled.

Janey paid for the taxi, and after that, they hardly spoke again.

Both her parents picked them up at Logan Airport. Her mother took in her clothing and her suitcases, her mouth disappearing into a tight line. The next day she took her to the doctor.

The diagnosis was mononucleosis. Her mother said she was lucky she didn't have syphilis. In the car on the way back to the house, her mother suddenly pulled over to the side of the road. "I must know, Janey," she said. Janey looked at her mother and felt all her old fears from her childhood bubbling to the surface. She knew her mother had never liked her; every conversation they'd ever had seemed to consist of her mother's making disparaging comments about her, and her trying to defend herself. Her mother flipped down the visor of her red Oldsmobile and began applying lipstick. "Did you sleep with him?" she asked.

"Who?" Janey said.

"You're such a stupid girl."

"Who, Mother? Say his name."

"That . . . Rasheed person." She turned to Janey and hissed, "He's a criminal."

"How do you know?"

"You are so stupid. How did I get such a stupid daughter? What did I do wrong?"

She started up the car and pulled back onto the street, but she wasn't finished. "Did you ever think about me and your father? Everyone at the club . . ."

"Fine!" Janey shouted. "I'll leave. I'll go somewhere and disappear. You never have to see me again. You can pretend I don't exist."

"And now you're sick."

"I'll kill myself."

"Don't be an idiot!" her mother screamed. Jerkily steering the car into their driveway, she said, "I always knew this would happen. I warned you. Men take advantage of girls who are not beautiful . . ."

"I was with him because I *am* beautiful," she screamed, jumping out of the car and slamming the door. "And you can't stand it, Mother. You just can't stand it that you're not the prettiest anymore!"

Janey spent the next two months lying in the single bed in her old room. She felt like Alice in Wonderland, where everything had mysteriously shrunk and she'd grown larger; at times she felt like she was going to blow up and the whole house would explode around her. Her mother signed her up for community college, and Janey, made mute by shame, didn't even protest.

But eventually, she gained strength, bolstered, perhaps, by the fact that she had $100,000 hidden behind an old dollhouse in her closet. As she lay in her childhood bedroom that fall, she thought that she could erase the past and start over—after all, she was young, and when you were nineteen years old, you didn't need to be scarred by anything. But somehow, the seed had been planted and taken hold—or perhaps the seed had always been there, waiting for the right combination of elements to germinate, and somehow the seed had had a life of its own and had driven her on and on.

Four months later, she saw Ian again. She was back in New York, living in the apartment she still rented, and one night she got a phone call.

She picked up the phone, and an unfamiliar male voice said, "Janey! I can't believe it. I've been trying to track you down for days!"

"Who is this?" she asked coldly.

"Don't you recognize my voice? Guess."

"I can't."

"It's Ian. Ian Carmichael. I'm in New York . . ."

They agreed to meet at a bar around the corner from her apartment. She hadn't stopped thinking about him, but when he walked in, she wondered why. Her heart turned cold: Taken out of his natural environment she suddenly saw that everything about him was wrong. In the glaring, unforgiving light of New York he seemed about as sophisticated as a midwestern tourist—his sweater was acrylic, and his black leather boots, which he proudly displayed, having just purchased them on Third Avenue, were unbearably ugly. They each drank three shots of tequila as Janey desperately tried to summon up the feelings she'd had for him that summer, but it was no use. She'd thought his teeth a dazzling white—now she saw that they were yellow and chipped. His eyes—those blue eyes that she'd gazed into so long-ingly—were too close together and he'd cropped his luxurious blond hair so that attention was drawn to his nose. He explained that he was in New York for two weeks ordering some equipment for the *Mamouda*, and he kept commenting over and over again that he couldn't believe he was actually seeing her. When he took her hand, her instinct was to draw it away.

The inevitable moment arrived and she took him back to her apartment. He kissed her standing in front of the fireplace, but his probing tongue made her want to scream. She had waited so long for this moment—what was wrong with her? They began to make love, and Janey prayed that the passion from the summer before would come back to her, but it didn't. When he licked her between her legs she only found it annoying, and she prayed that he would fuck her so it would end. Finally, he did, but she felt so passionless she kept her eyes open, and at last he said, "I'm going to come. Is that okay?"

"Yes," she sighed. "Please do."

He finished and lay on top of her. Then with a little sigh and a shake of his head, he pushed himself off the bed and began putting on his clothes.

"Where are you going?" Janey asked.

"I'm going. That's all."

"But I don't understand."

"You understand okay."

"But I . . ."

"Look, Janey," he said, pulling his sweater over his head. "Don't say you love me, because you don't."

"How do you *know*?"

He sat down on the edge of the bed. "You were never in love with me, Janey. Can't you see that?"

She opened her mouth to protest but he silenced her with his hand. "It was just some fantasy you made up in your head. To keep yourself from going insane. 'Cause if you ever bothered to think about what you were *really* doing . . ."

"I *did* love you!" Janey insisted. She sat up and gathered the sheet around her.

He stood up. "You're a cold girl. You're too cold to love anyone."

The words struck her like a blow. She gasped and fell back against the wall, but he turned and walked out of the room. Forgoing the sheet, she ran after him. "How *dare* you say that? It's not true!" But he wasn't having it. He opened the door, and turning back to her, she saw that his face was filled with hatred. "You're like a black widow," he said. He walked out and started down the stairs.

"Ian, *wait* . . ."

"A black widow spider," he muttered to himself, going down the stairs.

She shut the door and fell against it, sobbing. Why was this always happening to her? Why didn't anyone understand . . . ?

But in a few minutes, her tears had dried up, and she went to the mirror. She stared at herself for a long time, and then began laughing hysterically. It was a joke, really, to be so beautiful—a miracle. People stopped her on the street to tell her she was beautiful; men craned their necks out of passing cars. Two months before, at the beginning of October, fate had intervened and the Eileen Ford agency had called her. A catalog company wanted to book her for a month, and within two days she'd moved back to New York. There was no more talk from her mother about community college; indeed, her mother had driven her to the Amtrak station in Boston and, giving her a reluctant smile, had kissed her on each cheek. "Try to call once in a while," she'd said.

Janey took a step back from the mirror and covered her mouth with glee. Her beauty—her precious, glorious beauty—had saved her.

The light drizzle had turned into a cool, persistent mist, and, sitting in the Place Vendôme, Janey wiped the moisture from her face. Had her beauty *really* saved her—or had it led her down a false path? Even from the very beginning, with Rasheed . . . if she had really tried to do something with her life, instead of always relying on fate and her beauty to intervene, she might really have something in her life. For what was the point of beauty if there was something missing inside? Everyone else seemed to have some essential piece except her, and that piece was the part that connected actions to an emotional core. Despite all the men she'd slept with in the past fifteen years, she'd had only six orgasms in her entire life. And as for love— well, that was something she couldn't begin to fathom. Of course, she thought she loved Selden, but really, her feelings for him weren't any different from the feelings she had for every other man—meaning that she felt something that could be defined as affection as long as she was getting something tangible out of the relationship. Even Ian had seen it fifteen years before. And as for Rasheed . . . it must have been as obvious to him as a red light glowing on the façade of a house of prostitution.

But was she born that way, or had she become that way by the wrong choices? No one could be born with such an emptiness inside; at least there was still some part of her that believed *that*. For now she could see that she would never know true love or find it until she didn't require anything from a man, and money was the least of it . . .

She raised her head, and a voice inside her cried out that it wasn't too late. All she had to do was to live every day of the rest of her life in a different manner. There was still time to fix things up with George, and instead of coming on to him, she would lay her cards on the table in a businesslike manner. She would tell Selden about her plans. After all, it was possible that Selden really *did* love her . . .

Her internal clock told her that too much time had passed and, looking at her watch, she saw that it was nearly one o'clock. She must go to meet Mimi. And it suddenly occurred to her that if she told Mimi the entire story (leaving out the part where she'd given George the blow job, of course), she might be able to get Mimi to influence George. The important thing now was to *do* something with her life, to take action so that she would never be in this situation again . . .

And then, as if by magic, a tall blond man appeared in the mist, walking rapidly toward her. At first, she could barely believe her eyes, thinking for a second that the ghost of Ian had somehow come back to haunt her. But as the man drew closer, she saw that it was Zizi, and suddenly everything made sense: Mimi had insisted on this trip because she'd *known* Zizi would be in Paris, and she'd used Janey as a beard . . .

But maybe that wasn't true, Janey thought in bewilderment, as he came to a halt in front of her. For in the next second, he began speaking the words she'd been longing to hear . . .

"You must come with me," he said firmly.

She stood up and followed him as if in a dream, through the lobby of the Hôtel Ritz and into the elevator. It was like she'd stepped back in time to that fateful moment when she'd passed through this lobby for the first time, and now, she thought wildly, destiny was giving her a chance to go back in time, to right what she had done wrong. The elevator stopped on the third floor, and Zizi pulled her along the hallway like a child. But she was a child, she thought; she was new, and now, with Zizi by her side, she would start everything in her life afresh . . .

And then the dream turned into a nightmare.

They entered a one-bedroom suite. The minute they walked through the door her crazy idea that she and Zizi were going to be together was quickly dispelled by the realization that Harold Vane was in the room. What was *he* doing there? she thought with irritation. And then he turned around. And she saw by the expression on his face that something was terribly, terribly wrong.

"I saw you from the window," Harold said. "I sent Zizi down to get you . . ."

"But why? What's happened?" Janey asked cautiously.

"Everyone is looking for you," Zizi said.

"For me?" Janey cried. She frowned in annoyance. "I don't understand."

Harold came toward her with outstretched hands. "Janey," he said. "You and I have been friends for a long time. So I think I should be the one to tell you this . . ." And then she gasped. "Has someone died? Is it *Selden* . . . ?" And as soon as the words were out of her mouth, a nasty little voice in her head pointed out that if it *was* Selden, if he *was* dead, then it would solve all her problems: She'd be rich and free; she could do whatever she liked . . .

"It's *not* Selden," Harold said.

"Well then," she said, slightly disappointed. "What am I doing here?" Harold opened his mouth to speak, but no words came out, and she looked from Harold to Zizi with a rising sense of panic. For the first time, she noticed that there was a strange mark on Zizi's forehead, like a large spot of black soot, and suddenly she realized that she'd been seeing that same spot on other people's foreheads all morning. An illogical terror gripped her: The end of the world had come, and she had been singled out for elimination . . . She gasped, pointing at the spot on his face . . .

"It's Ash Wednesday," Zizi said gently, taking her hand.

It was just past 7 A.M. in New York, and Selden Rose was in the shower.

He ran a bar of soap over his body, thinking, as usual, about his wife. She had been gone for three days now, and it was exactly as people always said: Absence *did* make the heart grow fonder. In the last day or two, he'd come to the conclusion that maybe he *had* been too hard on her. He still didn't want her pursuing this ridiculous idea of producing Craig's movie, but he certainly could have been a little gentler about letting her down . . . And with a pang of guilt, he realized that what she'd said about his being jealous of Craig's talent wasn't entirely wrong. He turned off the water and stepped out of the shower, thinking that if she really did want to become a producer, he should give her a little help . . . He knew plenty of people in the business—maybe he could find someone who would give her a job as an assistant.

He rubbed a towel over his hair, and as he did so, the phone began ringing.

It must be her, he thought, pleased that she was thinking of him as well. He would tell her that he missed her and ask her to come back early, and wrapping the towel around his waist he went into the bedroom and picked up the phone.

"Hello darling," he said in anticipation.

"Rose?" a startled male voice said.

"George!" Selden said, slightly disappointed. He knew that George was an early riser, but he couldn't imagine what would compel George to call this early in the morning.

"Selden," George said. His voice sounded grim, and Selden immediately wondered if something had happened to Mimi. "There's been some trouble, Selden," he said. "And I'm afraid it involves your wife."

After a few more moments of this disturbing conversation, Selden hastily threw on some clothes and raced down to the lobby. "The *Post*," he demanded of the concierge. "Give me the *Post*."

With an embarrassed look on his face, as if he had hoped never to be in this position, the concierge reached under the desk and reluctantly handed him the newspaper.

The headline nearly caused his knees to buckle beneath him, and he quickly folded the paper in half, hoping that he had not seen what he thought he had.

With his heart pounding in fear, he walked back to the elevator (he wanted to run, but the concierge was watching him) and punched the button. At last the elevator arrived; when he got in and saw that it was empty, he unfolded the paper. The three terrible words hit him like three sharp blows to the head, and he stumbled back, reeling, banging his shoulder on the wall. But still the words were there, mocking him in huge black type over a color photograph of Janey from the Victoria's Secret Fashion Show. She was wearing the blue sequined bra and panty set, and she was leaning toward the camera with her hands on her hips, her lips pursed together in a kiss.

"MODEL?/WRITER?/WHORE?" the headline demanded, like a jeering crowd calling for an execution.

He lowered the paper in shock. He couldn't comprehend . . . He didn't understand . . . But the words marched by in his head like a child's taunting schoolyard rhyme: Model-slash-writer-slash-whore—*ha ha*—model-slash-writer-slash-whore—*ha ha* . . . As he lifted the paper again, he felt torn in two: His brain screamed that it simply wasn't possible, while the tremors in his body told him that it was . . .

And there, at the bottom of the page, were the smaller words: "Comstock Dibble Caught in Screenplay for Sex Scandal."

What? he thought. And then, *How . . . ?*

The elevator door opened as he turned the page and read, "Comstock Dibble is a . . ." *Bastard!* he thought, filling in the rest of the sentence as the door to the elevator began to close. Fumbling with the paper, he stabbed at the DOOR OPEN button, causing the newspaper to slip out of his hands, the pages scattering across the floor of the elevator and into the hallway. The door started to close again and he jabbed it open with his elbows. Wrestling with the pages, he managed to gather up the whole mess in his arms, and trembling with hurt and rage, he carried the hateful pages to his door.

He could not get his key in the lock. He turned and leaned against the door in frustration, rolling his eyes at the ceiling in a cry for help. Then he looked at the number and saw that he was at the wrong suite—he had gone left when he should have walked right.

He had to take control of himself, he thought, hurrying down the hall and entering his suite. He reminded himself that his specialty was solving problems.

However terrible this appeared to be, it probably wasn't as bad as it looked. Whatever it was, he could handle it . . .

But could he? he thought, with a sickening lurch. He dropped the pages onto the couch and began pawing through them to find the story. There was page after page of sports—who knew New Yorkers cared about sports so much—and then business and then three pages about food and restaurants . . . and finally, toward the bottom of the pile, he found the pages he was dreading. There was yet another photograph of Janey from the Victoria's Secret Fashion Show and—horribly—one of Comstock Dibble, seated in the front row. He had a sly look on his face, and the caption referred to him as "The Diminutive Dibble Dog." And indeed, Comstock did look like some kind of short-legged beast: He seemed to consist largely of a barrel-shaped body, to which four small appendages had been attached as if by pins. His arms stuck out from his sides, and his feet barely touched the floor.

Selden had to turn away.

But then he turned back to it. Life demanded such things; he had to read it sooner or later, and not reading it wouldn't make it go away. "Comstock Dibble is a movie genius who likes to have his fun, and likes to use his company's money to pay for it," the story began.

In a bizarre twist yesterday, the Diminutive Dibble Dog was caught writing company checks to various women, including the supermodel Janey Wilcox, in exchange for sex, claiming that the money had been paid to the women for their "screenplay-writing services." Problem is, not one of the women is a writer.

While the company has paid big-name writers, like Jay McInerney, hundreds of thousands of dollars to pen hit movies, apparently, not all of Dibble's commissions were legit. In the past three years, Dibble paid fifteen women $30,000 to write screenplays that were never delivered. A company spokesperson claimed to be shocked that Dibble, a well-known fixture on the Manhattan party circuit, who was honored by the mayor this September for his humanitarian efforts in fashion, would have paid women for sex. "He's always done well with the ladies," he said. "Maybe he was just being nice?"

Dibble's taste ran from call girls to party girls, from aspiring actresses to supermodels. Two summers ago, Janey Wilcox, 33, the stunning supermodel who walked the runway in the Victoria's Secret Fashion Show this December, boasted to pals that she was writing a screenplay for the Diminutive Dibble Dog while secretly entertaining him in a Hamptons love nest that he paid for. Last summer, Wilcox, who friends call "ambitious," snagged millionaire movie mogul Selden Rose, 45, the CEO of the cable channel MovieTime and married him in a rush ceremony in September. Dibble, meanwhile, is engaged to . . .

Selden Rose took a step back. He could not go on, he thought, *he could not go on* . . . So she *had* slept with him, he thought, frantically pounding the top of his head as if to hammer in the facts. She had *sex* with him. What did she do with him? he thought wildly. Did she suck his cock? Had he put his cock . . . inside her, where *he* had been? The thought was sickening—that and the fact that she'd lied to him. She'd specifically told him she hadn't, and she'd been *lying* . . . That was the part that was perhaps the most *unbearable* . . . she lied and she did it deliberately with a perfectly innocent expression on her face, as if he were some stupid kind of patsy!

Oh God, he thought. His mother was right . . .

He didn't know where to turn, what to do, who to call. He walked to the window and opened it; a blast of cold air hit him like a slap. Across the street were two men dressed as if for combat, in camouflage pants and heavy jackets with bulging pockets; in a second he saw that they had large black cameras slung over their shoulders like machine guns. So the jackals were gathering already: The story must be circulating all over New York by now, everyone would be reading it and laughing at him; his mother would find out and his ex-wife and someday, if he ever had children, they would unearth the story from some vast electronic wasteland . . . And as he stood staring down at the street in horror, a taxi pulled up and another photographer got out. He turned away. He went into the kitchen and stared at the coffeemaker.

What was he supposed to do now? he wondered.

And then, a small, hopeful voice whispered that maybe it wasn't true—that maybe it was *all* a lie. The media got things wrong all the time; everyone knew that they made things up. Or maybe they'd just made a mistake, and Janey's name didn't belong there at all. If it *was* true, he thought, there would have to be some evidence of it, and hurrying into the living room, he looked at the small French writing desk and remembered the drawer stuffed with her papers . . .

He yanked it open. Plato's *Republic* was still on top. Did that mean she hadn't touched her papers since that evening with Craig Edgers—or that she'd simply decided to keep the book there for safekeeping? He took it out and tossed it onto the chair, then he pulled the drawer off its runners and dumped the contents onto the floor. Dropping to his knees, he began riffling through the mess. If it was true and she *was* guilty, would she be stupid enough to keep the evidence? But guilty people usually did, out of some misguided idea of being clever enough to outsmart the truth. And then his eye spied the official-looking letter he'd seen in the drawer that evening when Craig was there. Picking it up, he looked at the return address, and with a sinking heart saw that it read "Parador Pictures."

He withdrew the letter. The date at the top was October 15, 2000. With his face set in a rigid mask, he began reading:

Dear Ms. Wilcox,

As of June 15, 2000, we have been attempting to speak with you regarding the matter of Comstock Dibble. This is our fourth attempt . . .

So it *was* true then—every word of it, and she'd known about it all along, even before they were married. She had deliberately deceived him from the very beginning, and looking again at the amount she owed, he was stunned. Why hadn't she come to him for help, or at least paid off the amount without telling him? He knew she was cheap, but it astounded him that she was so miserly that she would risk ruining her own life . . . and his.

And now she had.

But *maybe,* he thought wildly . . . maybe she didn't *have* the money. What if she sent money home to a . . . sick grandmother . . . or was paying for some niece's or nephew's private-school education. Maybe she was *broke,* and she was too embarrassed to tell *him* about it . . .

In a blind frenzy, he began pawing through the papers, looking for a bank statement. Pouncing on a computerized printout, he held the sheet away from him and looked at the balance.

She had $400,000 socked away in a savings account.

She had the money! he thought, shaking his fists in the air. She had had the money *all along* . . .

But suddenly his anger was spent, and he was overcome by despair. He put his head in his hands, and then, as he could not remember doing in years, he sobbed.

SIXTEEN

"SCREWPLAYS!" THE HEADLINE on the *New York Post* declared gleefully.

Mimi Paxton shifted uncomfortably on the tissue paper, feeling it crinkle beneath her naked bottom.

From the hard, molded plastic chair where the previous patient had thoughtfully left it behind, the *Post* seemed to be calling to her, begging to be picked up and read. So far, she had managed to resist . . . but if only the doctor would come, she thought impatiently. If there was one rule in New York it was this: No matter how rich you were, you *still* had to wait for the doctor . . .

She lifted one of her buttocks, trying to tuck the gown underneath, and in the process her eye fell on the *Post* again. Two weeks had passed since the story first broke with that chilling and now infamous headline: "MODEL?/WRITER?/ WHORE?" Some people said that it rivaled the *Post*'s most famous headline: "Headless Body Found in Topless Bar." But this story had what reporters called "legs"—it was about money, sex, power, and movies, and in the middle of it, like a character right out of central casting, was a beautiful lingerie model. The papers were still running something about the scandal every day like an ongoing soap opera, and apparently the public couldn't get enough, as if no one had anything better to worry about. But that was another rule of New York: One man's misery was another man's triumph (even if it only meant getting a taxi on a rainy day at rush hour); and another man's shame could provide entertainment for millions.

Usually the cover included a photograph of Janey—there seemed to be a never-ending supply, and one day they'd done a whole inside page of photographs of her from her early modeling days, which was, Mimi thought, probably even more embarrassing for her—but today, the cover showed a rather goofy-looking young black man sporting trendy glasses. She squinted at the name, thinking, *that was it*— Scooter Mendelsohn.

She didn't need to read the *Post* to know what that story was about, she thought, transferring her weight from one buttock to the other. George had merrily told her all about it, claiming it was "one of the great moments in business." Well, Mimi thought, it was certainly one of *his* great moments in business. The real hero was that little Scooter Mendelsohn from Brooklyn, and George had already promoted him to a junior executive at Parador Pictures, which was quite a coup for Scooter, considering that he was only twenty-one. But George had big plans for him; he said that Scooter exemplified exactly the sort of morality that had been missing from Parador before . . .

It wasn't, George explained, the fact that Comstock had paid women to write screenplays that never existed that had brought him down, but the way he'd gone about trying to cover it up. Oddly enough, George said, if Comstock had paid the women more—if he'd given them $100,000 or $200,000 or even *$300,000*— he probably would have gotten away with it. Anywhere from $100,000 to $300,000 was the standard industry amount for a screenplay; and it wasn't out of the ordinary for a movie company to pay a writer and then get burned when the writer simply didn't deliver. But when Comstock decided to sell part of his company and the accountants began preparing the books, they were struck by the unusual number ($30,000 instead of $300,000), and they panicked. The legal department began sending out letters—and naturally, none of the women complied—and why should they? George asked. After all, they thought they were being paid for *sex* . . .

And then, George explained, puffing himself up like a blowfish, Janey had come to him with her letter, and this was what had put the idea in his head to buy Comstock's company *himself*—after all, the very best deals were struck when the buyer had secret information that the seller didn't want to get out. However, George reassured Mimi, this was one part of the story that would never become public—George certainly didn't want people thinking that he would take advantage of a poor little twit like Janey Wilcox, who actually seemed to have some public sympathy on her side. And so, the only people who knew that Janey had come to him for help were Janey and himself, of course, and now Mimi . . .

And the fact that the "screwplays" had become public knowledge didn't have anything to do with George at all. The burden of that proof rested entirely on Comstock Dibble himself; if he had admitted to his transgression instead of thinking he could outwit George Paxton, the whole thing never would have come out in the press.

According to Scooter Mendelsohn, who had told all this to George, who had told Mimi (and, by now, various other personages as well), two days before the big buyout meeting, Comstock Dibble called Scooter, who was then a sort of assistant's assistant, into his office.

Apparently, Comstock Dibble was in such a sweat that he basically had an entire box of Kleenex tissues stuck to his head. Comstock was always a terror in the office, but in the past two weeks, he'd been especially fearful, and had even made his tough-guy publicist cry—and he was a fifty-five-year-old man who everyone suspected had once been in the syndicate! Scooter knew this, because he'd gone into the men's room to take a leak, and he'd heard the guy crying from inside one of the stalls, and he knew it was him because he looked under the stall and saw the wing-tipped shoes the guy always wore. So it was with a great deal of trepidation that Scooter entered Comstock's office.

"What's your name again?" Comstock demanded.

Scooter had only worked there for six months, but he was too frightened to be insulted. "Scooter," he said.

"Can you make a cover page for a screenplay?" Comstock barked.

"Sure . . . ," Scooter said, wondering what he was getting at.

"Good. I want you to take these names with these titles," Comstock said, handing him a list with a bunch of women's names on it, "and then I want you to take these screenplays," he said, pointing to a pile on his desk, "and I want you to rip off the real covers and put the new covers on them. Got it?"

Scooter naturally hadn't, but he was too afraid to say so.

"And I want the new covers to be different colors, too!" Comstock barked at him as Scooter grabbed the pile of screenplays and quickly left the office.

Back at his desk, Scooter had done exactly what Comstock wanted, and at first he didn't think that much about it, especially as everyone in the office had now come to the conclusion that Comstock Dibble was officially insane. But then he got to the last name, Janey Wilcox, followed by the title *A Model's Story*. He was about to put this new cover page on the screenplay *Chinatown*, when he began putting two and two together. He knew that name, he thought. Wasn't Janey Wilcox that Victoria's Secret model? She certainly was no writer—that was for sure. It was a mockery of the movie business, putting the name of a screenplay she obviously hadn't written on the cover of such a great movie. That was the thing that *really* got him, he said. If he'd been putting the fake title on *Showgirls*, for instance, he might not have even cared . . .

Scooter left the doctored screenplays on Comstock's assistant's desk at the end of the day and went home. *Chinatown* was in his head, so he rented it and then ate a bunch of frozen mini pizzas. And then he started thinking again. His whole life had been shaped by movies—movies were *everything* to him. Movies were sacred; they were what made people's lives worth living. All he'd ever wanted to do, ever since he was a little boy and his mother had taken him to see *Wall Street,* was to be in the movie business. And now he was, and he couldn't shake the feeling that somehow, he'd done something wrong . . . that Comstock had asked him to do something . . . *illegal.*

He'd seen enough movies to know that he had to make some kind of decision. In movies, when people didn't do *the right thing,* something bad always happened to them. He might get fired . . . or worse, he might *never work in the movie business again.* And so, he decided, he had to tell someone . . . but *who?*

Sitting there watching *Chinatown,* he suddenly remembered that Parador Pictures was being sold; it was supposed to be a secret, but everyone in the office knew about it because they were all afraid for their jobs. He couldn't remember the name of the man who was buying it, but he did remember the name of the company—Smagma. He remembered it because it sounded so ominous, like something out of a James Bond movie . . .

He couldn't sleep all night, and the next morning he got up early and, at about 7:30 A.M., called information. There *was* a Smagma Enterprises in New York City, and he took down the number. He didn't think there would be anyone in the office that early, but he decided to call anyway, for practice.

And then, to his surprise, the phone was actually answered by a very nice lady who said, "Smagma Enterprises."

"I . . . I'd like to speak to the head of Smagma," he said nervously.

"That would be Mr. George Paxton," the lady said. "Who's calling, please?"

"You don't know me," Scooter began, "but I work for Parador Pictures . . ."

"Hold on, please," the lady said pleasantly, as if it weren't the least bit surprising that *he,* Scooter Mendelsohn, would be calling George Paxton . . .

And then the great man, George Paxton himself, had gotten on the phone. And Scooter had told him the whole story . . .

The big moment arrived the very next morning, when George Paxton and six very serious-looking men in suits showed up at the Parador offices and went into the conference room with Comstock Dibble and his men.

At around four in the afternoon, Comstock's assistant appeared at Scooter's desk carrying a pile of screenplays—the fake ones and the real ones that the company had commissioned in the past couple of years—and plopped them down. "You did it," she hissed. "You take them in. I'm too scared."

And so Scooter picked up the pile of screenplays and knocked on the door of the conference room.

And then, what happened next was exactly like a big scene in a movie, except that it was better because it was *real*.

"Thank you, ah . . . *Scooter*," Comstock said, as Scooter placed the screenplays on the conference table in front of him. He knew that Comstock was trying to be on his best behavior, because he actually remembered his name for once. He was just turning to walk out the door when the man at the other end of the conference table stopped him. Scooter knew instantly that it was George Paxton by the way he was sitting—with his legs apart as if he already owned the place. "Hold on, Scooter," George said. "Why don't you stick around for a minute? I think you might enjoy this."

Scooter looked at Comstock, who had that crazy look in his eyes that everyone in the office knew meant you should run in the other direction, but as George Paxton was clearly running the meeting, there was nothing he could do.

"Now then," George said, nodding at Comstock.

"Right," Comstock said. He pointed to a piece of paper. "Here's a list of the screenplays we've commissioned in the past three years, and here," he said, patting the pile of screenplays, "are the screenplays that have come in . . ."

"Is that so," George Paxton said. He looked over the list (everybody had the same list in front of them), and then he said, "I'd like to see the screenplay by Janey Wilcox, if I may."

"It's not one of our best," Comstock Dibble said. He had his requisite box of Kleenex tissues in front of him; he pulled out a hunk and began mopping his face. "In fact," he said, "you could say it's a complete disaster. But we decided to take a chance on a woman who possibly had more talents than her, ah, very obvious ones . . ."

Everybody laughed, and Comstock tried to divert George's attention. "Scooter?" he said. "Why don't you make yourself useful and show Mr. Paxton the screenplay by Darren Star. Now, this, George," he said, "is absolute *genius* . . ."

"I'm sure it is," George said genially, pressing his palms together. "But I'd still like to see the screenplay by Janey Wilcox."

"Darren's is . . ." Comstock faltered.

"Janey Wilcox . . . ?" George said, raising his eyebrows.

And then, of course, according to the now legendary tale, George had stood up and flipped open the Janey Wilcox screenplay, and had read aloud the famous line from *Chinatown*: "My daughter, my sister, my daughter, my sister . . ."

It was all such a *farce*, Mimi thought, shaking her head as she glanced back at the newspaper. What nobody could understand now was how Comstock could have been so stupid. But George explained—over and over again at the intimate dinner parties they'd been attending instead of following their usual social calendar—that it wasn't unusual for seemingly successful people to suddenly crack. Especially if they were doing something illegal. They kept pushing the envelope farther and farther, taking bigger and bigger risks, and the longer they got away with it, the less they bothered to cover up their mistakes—as if they were subconsciously trying to get caught. History was littered with hundreds of characters like Comstock Dibble, George said, and with the stock market beginning to slide, he suspected that they'd be seeing a lot more "Dibble Dog" behavior in the future . . .

Mimi sighed and looked at her watch again, wondering how much longer she was going to have to sit there. It was now going on half an hour . . .

Gingerly opening the robe, she looked down at her belly. She was beginning to show, and pretty soon she'd have to start telling people. She was finally three months pregnant, and even though, at her age, you weren't supposed to tell anyone until after your first sonogram (in case there was something wrong with the baby and you had to have an abortion, which she couldn't even begin to contemplate), Janey had somehow known two weeks ago, when they'd had that final showdown at Christian Dior.

Mimi stared at the door, painted a clinical gray, willing it to open. It didn't, of course, and she examined her fingernails instead. She hadn't seen Janey since that afternoon in Paris, but she'd heard she was still in the city. That was typical Janey, she thought: Any sensible person would have immediately left town, like Mauve Binchely, for instance. Mauve had gone to Palm Beach, where she was holed up at her mother's house, and both she and her mother were hysterical. The mother had grown up with the old-fashioned edict that a lady is in the papers only three times in her life—on her birth, her marriage, and her death—and in a scant two weeks, Mauve had surpassed that quota by ten. As Comstock Dibble's (now former) fiancée, she'd been mentioned in nearly every story, and the *Post* had dubbed her "the Slinky Socialite." That was making Mauve crazy, too—she kept asking people exactly what "they" meant by it. But actually, Mimi thought, it was quite kind, considering what Mauve *really* looked like.

She leaned back against the examining table and closed her eyes. The person who had fared the worst was Janey Wilcox—the paper had dubbed her "the Model Prostitute"—and even if it wasn't entirely true and Janey wasn't technically a hooker (except, maybe, for that one summer with Comstock), there wasn't a thing either she or Selden could do about it. Janey was a public figure now and she pretty much had to take whatever they dished out.

But *still*—Mimi couldn't help feeling a little bit sorry for her. No one deserved to be called a prostitute in the press every day, unless it was a profession that they had willingly chosen, like that Sydney Biddle Barrows woman, who was known as the Mayflower Madam. But "madam" was much better than being called a plain-old prostitute, because it at least implied that you had some business sense, and the *real* problem with Janey, it seemed, was that she had no sense at all . . .

This, anyway, was what Mimi explained to people when they asked her what Janey Wilcox was really like.

And knowing Janey, Mimi thought, she probably didn't care. Janey had probably already turned it around in her head, and had convinced herself that it was actually some kind of compliment . . .

In any case, during those few minutes at Christian Dior, she certainly hadn't behaved the way a normal person would have, Mimi thought, glancing at her watch again. Not that, given the circumstances, there probably was a "normal" way to act. But still, if *she'd* been in that situation, if she'd just found out from Harold Vane that she'd been called a whore on the cover of the *New York Post,* the last thing she would have done was to get into a taxi and go to Christian Dior. She would have been too hysterical. And at first, Janey had looked terrified. But then she'd gotten that weird blank look in her eyes, as if she'd disappeared into another world and some kind of cyborg had taken over her body . . .

"Mimi," Janey had said in that musical voice as she came into the fitting room. But her accent was too heightened, as if she were playing at being herself, and her eyes were wild. Mimi had jumped in terror, causing the fitter—a small uniformed French woman named Colette—to prick her finger with a pin.

And Mimi, who was shocked to see her there, looked at her watch and cried, "Janey . . . !"

And then they had stared at each other, both wondering how much the other one knew . . .

It was a hideous scene, and Mimi shuddered at the memory. She could have forgiven Janey *anything,* Mimi thought, touching her belly—anything but that incident with Zizi. She would have excused the screenplay scandal, she would even have forgiven Janey for having sex with *George,* which, she suspected, if Janey hadn't already, she would soon. But Zizi was an entirely different story. Zizi was her *love* . . .

The night before the scandal broke, Mimi had secretly seen Zizi in her hotel room at the Plaza Athénée. Despite what Janey thought, she hadn't known that Zizi was in Paris until she'd run into Harold Vane at Hermès that afternoon, where he was buying a new saddle. Janey was in the hotel, having given the excuse that she needed to make some important business calls, so Mimi had gone out alone. Harold told her that he and Zizi were at the Ritz—and that they were leaving in two days for Deauville to look at some horses.

She had sworn that she wouldn't pursue Zizi, but given her condition, a sense of honor demanded that she tell him that he might be the father. She didn't want anything from him, nor did she intend to leave George. But the news caused something in Zizi to break, and he had finally explained why he had left her. *"Whore,"* Janey Wilcox had called him. And all he could think was that he didn't want to end up like *her* . . .

And then the story of how Janey engineered her way into his apartment and tried to seduce him came spilling out. Mimi was terrified. Not by the fact that Janey had wanted to sleep with Zizi, but in the way she'd been so calculating about it—concocting that story about being freaked out about her sister (especially since it was painfully obvious to almost everyone that Janey didn't really care about her sister at all, except to use her), and then making up that story about how her sister needed the apartment.

Mimi was astonished that Janey could be so vindictive. At first, she couldn't accept it. There must be some mistake, she thought. But her womanly instincts told her that it was true, and her thoughts ran the gamut from pure hatred of Janey— thinking that she was capable of nearly anything, including murder—to her own error in having taken Janey under her wing. Despite the fact that people kept warning her that Janey had taken money from men, and that she'd broken up a few marriages, that she even had sex with men in bathrooms, Mimi had stubbornly insisted that Janey was actually a nice girl who was no more than the unfortunate victim of vicious rumors, her only real crime being her beauty. And Mimi had fallen right into the trap: Ever since she was a child, she'd always chosen the slightly broken-down girl to be her best friend. There was Mauve Binchely, whom the other girls had made fun of, and Pippi Maus, who had drinking and drug and sex problems, and now there was Janey Wilcox, who came saddled with an unsavory reputation. Mimi even remembered hearing something long ago about how Janey had spent time on the yacht of a very rich Arab . . . But who knew if that was true? Mimi's flaw was pride and stubbornness: It was almost as if, in choosing these women as her friends, she wanted to prove to everyone else that they were wrong and she was right, that these women did, indeed, have value.

Well, Mauve and Pippi had been her friends for years, and despite their apparent quirks, they were steadfast companions. But Janey had deliberately tried to hurt her, and Mimi felt as wounded as if she'd been betrayed by a lover. No, indeed, what Janey had done was *worse,* because one never expected that kind of behavior from a girlfriend—whereas with a man it was always a possibility. But one *knew* that going in . . .

And so Mimi had decided she would have it out with Janey and be finished with her. Oh, she would still have to see her from time to time—with Janey married to Selden now, she was unavoidable. But she would make it very clear that they could no longer be friends, at least not for a while . . .

And then the interview had not gone *at all* the way she'd expected.

It was drizzling when she left the hotel at 12:30 P.M. The air was sharp—as cold and damp as her heart. As she hurried down the boulevard, she inwardly railed against Janey Wilcox. Did she think that Mimi was so weak and so vulnerable that she would let her get away with it? For certainly, she had to know that Zizi might tell her eventually—and with a small cry of recognition, she suddenly realized that *that* was why Janey had tried to get Zizi out of her apartment! It was such a clumsy maneuver it was nearly pathetic. And for the fifth or sixth time that morning, she questioned what she was about to do. Perhaps it would be better to say nothing— after all, the deed was done and more than two months had passed; it had no bearing on her life now. She had silently forgiven other friends for transgressions, but then she remembered that no friend had committed a crime quite so egregious. And as she hurried across the boulevard to Christian Dior, she realized it wasn't necessarily what Janey had done in the past that was a problem, but what she might do in the future . . .

"*Bonjour Madame Paxton*," the receptionist said brightly. "You are here for your fitting?"

"*Oui*," Mimi replied. "And I have a friend coming at one. Her name is Janey Wilcox. Be sure to let her up?"

"Very good, madame," the receptionist said, standing up to push open a door behind her. "The fitting is in the Saint Laurent showroom . . ."

"Yes, thank you. I know where it is," Mimi said.

And then she had hurried along the subtle pinkish beige corridor to the room where Yves Saint Laurent had shown his first collection. Although she naturally hadn't realized it at the time, it was somewhat of an irony that the fitting had taken place in that room. For after Yves Saint Laurent had shown his first collection as a fashion designer, the boulevard outside had been filled with paparazzi and fans. It had been one of those great moments in history, when a man makes his name . . .

But the room, in particular, was nothing special to look at. It was long and narrow with high ceilings and louvered French windows and a mirror along one wall, painted and carpeted in that same soothing pinkish beige that whispered money and class.

A clothes rack stood to one side, filled with the beautiful dresses she'd ordered last fall. In the middle of the room was a wooden block with two steps. Mimi stripped down to a strapless bra and a pair of nylons, as Colette, the fitter, took a blue chiffon gown from the rack and put her arms through the skirt, holding it above her head so Mimi could slip it on.

She was nervous. The clothes were bound to be a little tight and she was uncertain about what to do. Should she have the seams let out—or save everything for next year? Colette yanked gently on the zipper, trying to pull together the sides of the bodice. At last the zipper went up, and they both breathed a sigh of relief.

Colette looked slightly disapproving. "Madame has . . . ?"

"Oh no," Mimi said, shaking her head. She put her hands on her belly and Colette's face lit up in understanding. "Ahhhh," she said, nodding wisely. "That is *très bien, n'est-ce pas?*"

"*Oui,*" Mimi said. "*Je suis très heureuse.*"

And then, at about five minutes before one, François, the charming Frenchman who was the corporate head of Christian Dior, came into the fitting room. "I think you might like to see this," he said, holding a fax out to her. Mimi had looked at the fax, with that terrible laughing headline, and had let out a little scream. "*Excusez-moi,*" François said. "I did not mean to upset you—but I thought perhaps she was a friend of yours?"

"She is—or rather, she was," Mimi said in confusion. "She's supposed to be on her way over here . . ."

"I do not think she will come today," François said. "The whole fashion world is talking about it—apparently she was a model in Paris a very long time ago."

"Yes, I suppose she might have been," Mimi said vaguely. She didn't want to give François any information that he would immediately pass on . . .

François had left the room, and Mimi's first thought was, Poor, poor Janey! Naturally, she'd wanted Janey to be punished for her behavior, but she certainly wouldn't have wished anything like this upon her! But then she looked at the fax again, and she realized that she wasn't very surprised—no, she wasn't surprised at all. All of New York would be waking up to the story now; faxes were already being circulated in Paris, and probably London and Milan as well . . . And, of course, it would be all over the Internet. Janey must know by now, she thought, and in that case, she certainly wouldn't keep their appointment. And given this recent development, it was entirely possible that Mimi wouldn't have to confront her at all . . .

And she had felt a weight lifted.

And then, about fifteen minutes later, Janey had walked in.

Mimi's first thought was that Janey somehow didn't know—and that she was going to have to tell her.

"Janey . . . !" she cried.

Janey looked at her wildly, circling around the pedestal like a tiger about to eat her. "Where are you going to wear that dress?" she asked.

"To the New York City Ballet Gala," Mimi said. Janey mustn't know about it, then, she thought, otherwise, why would she be asking about the dress? "I was going to ask you to be on the committee . . ."

"Were you?" Janey said, lifting her eyebrows in surprise. "That's strange, considering the circumstances . . ."

So she *did* know, Mimi thought nervously. And, as if in confirmation of this fact, Janey said, "Oh yes. I know all about it." But her next comment nearly knocked Mimi over.

"Somehow," Janey said, in a weird, eerily calm voice, "you've engineered this whole thing to get me out of Paris . . ."

"Janey!" Mimi cried in shock.

"So you can have Zizi all to yourself!" Janey added triumphantly.

Mimi took a step back in surprise, nearly falling off the pedestal. As she righted herself, she found her whole body was shaking with fear and disgust . . .

"I just saw Zizi," Janey said. "And he told me the whole story."

Mimi raised a trembling hand to her chest, wondering if she had somehow gone insane. How was it that Janey was speaking the very words she had intended to say to *her*?

"And I thought you were my *friend*," Janey continued. "Oh, everyone told me that you were spoiled and selfish, that you always had to have your way; that you'd do anything to get what you wanted. But I didn't believe them." She turned on Mimi, her eyes glittering like black sapphires. "Do you know how many times I've had to defend you? How many times I've had to tell people that you were actually okay . . ."

"Janey!" Mimi cried in terror. "What are you talking about?"

"I can't believe you would do this to me," Janey said, taking a few steps toward her. "First you force me to come to Paris with you—to cover up the fact that you're trying to get Zizi back—and then, when you see him and he rejects you—when he refuses to have sex with you—you call George and tell him to make up this story . . ."

Mimi put her hands over her mouth as if she were going to scream. In that moment, she knew without a doubt that every word Zizi had spoken was true. Janey had simply taken the plot and rearranged the characters, casting herself as the victim. But she couldn't *truly* believe that what she was saying was real . . . ?

Mimi looked at her. Janey's eyes were shining but blank, as if the high beams were on but no one was driving. She took another step closer, and Mimi shrank back in fear. "But it's not going to work, Mimi," Janey said. "I'm surprised that even you would do something that stupid . . . Accusing me of taking money from Comstock Dibble. Because the fact is that I *did* write a screenplay. And once the press gets wind of it, they're going to turn around and come after *you* . . ."

Mimi sank to her knees. Little gasps of fear that sounded like coughs were coming out of her mouth. Colette ran to her—naturally, her English wasn't anywhere near good enough to know what was going on, but she did recognize physical distress. "Madame Paxton!" she cried. *"Vous êtes . . ."*

"De l'eau, s'il vous plait . . . ," Mimi gasped.

Colette hurried out of the room as Janey watched her go. And then Janey took another step forward. She was carrying gloves and she began slapping them against her thigh, as if she might use them to hit Mimi . . .

"Janey," Mimi panted. "You have to know that not a word of this is true. I only found out about the scandal five minutes ago—five minutes before you walked in. And as for Zizi, I saw him last night, and he told me . . ."

"What?" Janey asked dangerously. "That I had come on to him?" She turned her head and laughed. "Of course he was going to say that. It's what every man claims when you reject them . . ."

"You called him a whore," Mimi gasped.

"And why shouldn't I?" Janey said. "After all, that's what he is, isn't he? A male whore? A man who took money for sex?"

Mimi rose shakily to her feet. Her only thought was that she must somehow get Janey out of the room and away from her. She walked slowly to the rack of clothes, holding on to the metal rod for support, and forcing herself to appear calm, she said evenly, "Maybe you're right, Janey. Maybe everything you're saying is true . . ."

"Of course it's true," Janey snapped. But the fact that Mimi was agreeing with her seemed to pacify her somewhat. "I know this can't be easy for you, Mimi; I know how you felt about him," she said. "But when I saw him half an hour ago, at the Ritz, he told me that you'd been stalking him, that you'd followed him to Paris, and that he'd had to reject you. The fact is, he wants *me* . . . He told me he would be with me in a minute, if I weren't already married to Selden."

Mimi nearly laughed. That, she thought, was the last thing Zizi would ever say. But Janey was pulling on her gloves—if Mimi handled her carefully, in a moment or two she would be gone. "I see," Mimi said, nodding thoughtfully. "And what about Selden?" she asked, as if they were having a perfectly normal conversation about men and relationships.

"Oh, Selden," Janey shrugged. "He would be devastated if I left him . . . and that's what I had to tell Zizi."

"Naturally," Mimi said, swallowing her revulsion. The worst thing about it, she thought, was that if you didn't *know* Janey, you might actually believe her.

"I only came to warn you," Janey said, beginning to walk toward the door. And then, with a triumphant look of disdain, Janey's eyes traveled to Mimi's belly. "But I see that I'm too late."

Mimi nodded silently.

Janey's gloved hand touched the brass knob on the door. "I really am your friend, Mimi. I've always loved you, ever since I was a kid and I used to see your picture in magazines. I always wanted to be just like you when I grew up. And I hope that after all this is over, we can still be friends . . ."

Mimi's smile was tight. "Of course, Janey," she said cautiously. "We'll always be friends. You know that."

Janey started out the door. And then she turned back. With a malicious gleam in her eyes, she asked innocently, "By the way. Who's the father?"

"Madame!" Colette said, hurrying into the room with a cup of water before Mimi could answer. She gave Janey a dirty look and shook her head; Janey shrugged her shoulders and started off down the hallway. Colette handed Mimi the cup. *"C'est tout d'accord?"*

"Non, Colette," Mimi said wearily, taking a few sips. *"Je suis très fatigué. Je prenderais un' autre appointement demain . . ."*

"Mais oui, bien sûr," Colette declared. *"C'est naturallement. C'est le bébé."*

"Oui," Mimi nodded. *"Le bébé . . ."*

"Le bébé," Mimi said aloud, touching her stomach. She glanced at her watch again. Where *was* that doctor? She closed her eyes in annoyance, and as she did so, she could still see Janey's terrifying visage as she uttered that last devastating pronouncement . . . It was like Janey's beautiful head had split in two, and a long-necked serpent had emerged and swooped toward her, laughing and snapping its jaws at her. She could still see its shiny, scaly, black skin and those teeth and that long red tongue . . .

Exactly what was it, she wondered, that had caused Janey to snap like that—to completely rewrite the truth about her and Zizi? Was it the shock of seeing herself on the cover of the *Post,* or was it something else, something deeper? At first, she had thought about warning George and possibly Selden about how dangerous Janey might be, but then she'd have to reveal her own actions. And it wasn't like Janey hadn't been punished enough. Mimi imagined she'd have to move to Connecticut with Selden, where she would be forced to keep a low profile . . . But Selden would probably divorce her, and then what man would be stupid enough to want her? *Plenty,* she answered, with a wry laugh. But Janey would have to disappear, at least for a while . . .

But a little voice inside her warned that Janey would never do that and, opening her eyes, she pounded on the examining table with her fist. *She must stop think-ing about that Janey Wilcox,* she scolded herself. Janey was not important now . . . The only thing that *really* mattered was the baby . . .

It was amazing to be given such a gift, she thought, placing her hands on her stomach; even one that came at such a price. For in having this baby, she was faced with an age-old predicament: She wasn't completely sure who the father was. It was an untenable situation—on the outside she went about her business as if George *were* the father, but inside she guessed it was Zizi's. The result was that every wak-ing moment she felt like a fraud—the terrible secret burdening her more heavily than carrying the actual child. She was no better than Janey Wilcox, she thought, and she deserved to be punished as well. And if the child was Zizi's, she would be: Although the child would be released from her body, the *secret* never would—and she would carry that burden for the rest of her life . . .

But what was she to do? Perhaps the honorable thing would have been to have an abortion, for that would be apt punishment for her sin, and then George would not have to be deceived. But why should the child be killed for *her* crime?

"Good morning!" the doctor said cheerily, coming into the room at last. "Are you ready for your sonogram?"

Mimi nodded, and the doctor continued, "There's just one thing we need to know first. Do you want to know the sex of the child . . . ?"

"Yes, I do," Mimi said cautiously. She leaned back against the examining table and suddenly felt guilty again, reminding herself that she was a sinner. Could the doctor tell? she wondered. But of course she couldn't . . . And after all, the child could still be George's . . .

But she hoped not! she thought, with an inner cry. After all, she was a woman who had been in love, and naturally she wished that the child had been conceived in love as well. So who could blame her if she prayed fervently that the child would be a boy—and that he would look just like Zizi?

Janey Wilcox stood in the suite at the Lowell Hotel, carefully straightening the pages of that morning's *New York Post.* The phone was wedged between her shoul-der and her ear; nodding and emitting an occasional "Uh-huh," she added the paper to the large pile of press clippings stacked up in a corner of the living room.

She was talking on the phone to Wendy Piccolo. In one of life's weird twists, Janey and Wendy had become phone friends, speaking to each other once and sometimes even twice a day, chatting for hours until Wendy had to leave for the theater, where she was playing Blanche DuBois in *A Streetcar Named Desire.*

The unlikely friendship had begun nearly two weeks ago, on the day the *Post* headline had screamed, "MODEL PROSTITUTE" above a slightly grainy photograph of Janey taken from the Victoria's Secret catalog, in which she was wearing a filmy peignoir and mules with pink ostrich feathers. It was the time of year when it feels like winter will never end, and that winter, the winter of 2001, had been particularly snowy. Dirty piles of snow lined the streets, and slushy puddles the size of small ponds formed in the crosswalks. One's feet were always damp and everyone, it seemed, was cranky.

In truth, the friendship started because Wendy was bored, and Janey couldn't leave the suite.

And so, nearly two weeks ago, at three o'clock on the afternoon of the "MODEL PROSTITUTE" headline, the phone rang. On Janey's first day back from Paris, the phone had rung incessantly with calls from reporters, and Janey had been expressly forbidden to answer it. But the hotel was well-versed in the special needs of celebrities, and the next day they switched the number. And then the phone hadn't rung at all, except for Selden, who had called about six times to make sure that she was still in the suite, and her new publicist, Jerry Grabaw, who wanted to see if she needed anything and kept reassuring her that everything was going to be okay . . . eventually.

Well, she knew *that*, she thought in annoyance. After all, wasn't the whole thing really just one . . . big . . . huge . . . *mistake*?

She'd picked up the phone expecting it to be Selden, but instead it was Wendy Piccolo.

"May I speak to Selden, please?" Wendy's deceptively sweet voice had inquired, and Janey recognized it immediately.

"Selden is in his . . . office," Janey said, as if any intelligent person would know this. Wendy was not put off. "Janey?" she asked.

"Yes," Janey replied stiffly, wondering how Wendy might think it could possibly be anyone else.

"Actually," Wendy said, her voice betraying a touch of guilt, "I called to talk to you. I was wondering how *you* were doing."

Janey seized on this gambit like an eagle snatching a rabbit from a field—so far no one, it seemed, had been the least bit concerned about how *she* felt; they were all too busy worrying about how her problem affected *them*. "It's a total *nightmare*," she cried. "There are something like a hundred photographers outside and I can't leave the suite . . . I'm going insane. And then all this publicity and people calling . . . And the worst thing about it," Janey said, walking to the window and, for probably the thirtieth time that day, peeking through the closed curtains at the crowd of photographers standing across the street, "is that not a word of it is true. What nobody seems to understand is that I *did* write a screenplay . . ."

"Of course you did," Wendy said, her voice trembling with outrage in the traditional female manner of always championing the woman's cause over the man's. After all, it wasn't the facts that mattered necessarily, but the moral fairness of the situation, she thought, and she continued: "Even if you *didn't,* it wouldn't matter. It's Comstock who's committed the crime, not you or those other girls."

Oh yes. The "other" girls. Janey had nearly forgotten about them. But who *were* they? Call girls, waitresses, and aspiring actresses. No one had ever heard of them before. They weren't famous . . . and it wasn't their pictures on the cover of the *New York Post* day after day. "The problem is that none of *them* wrote screenplays," Janey said. "So the press lumps *me* in . . ."

"Because you're beautiful and well known," Wendy explained. "Face it, Janey, without you, they wouldn't *have* a story."

She was just so *right,* Janey thought, and told her so . . .

And then, to her slight surprise, Wendy called again the *next* afternoon. She'd talked to the other actors in the cast of *Streetcar,* she said, and they'd all decided that Janey was this incredibly tragic figure, just like Hester Prynne in *The Scarlet Letter.* Janey hadn't read the book, but she had seen the movie with Demi Moore, and, she had to admit, it *was* just like that. Then Wendy said that someone suggested they should all get T-shirts made with "THE MODEL PROSTITUTE" printed across the front to wear in sympathy. Janey had laughed uncomfortably at the idea, but she liked the fact that people were thinking about her, and she had even liked the way Wendy had said the word *Streetcar,* as if Janey were an insider in the theater, too.

And now, Janey sat on the arm of the flowered chintz couch, swinging her leg in boredom. In the great female tradition of friendship, she and Wendy were having nearly the same conversation they had every day.

"It's just so dull to have to stay in all the time," Janey moaned.

"I know, Janey," Wendy said sympathetically. "But I keep telling you: You're going to have to leave that suite one of these days . . ."

"Oh, but I *can't,*" Janey sighed in irritation. "Selden will kill me. He won't even let me go near the window."

"What's *Selden* going to do?" Wendy asked, for about the fifteenth time. "Divorce you? If he was, he would have done it *already* . . ."

"I suppose you're right," Janey sighed.

"Why shouldn't you?" Wendy asked craftily. "Go out, I mean." She, too, was getting slightly tired of the same old conversation—she wanted something to happen so Janey would at least have something new and entertaining to tell her about, which she would then be able to share with the rest of the cast of *Streetcar*—not to mention all her other friends.

"Maybe *we* should go out—together," Janey said, expelling a large, slow breath of air, as if it weren't really something she expected to be able to do. She, naturally, was being equally as crafty—she knew that if she was seen with Wendy Piccolo, whom the press, apparently, "adored," it would go a long way in shoring up her own shaky social position . . .

"Oh, we will. *Soon*," Wendy promised, without any intention of making this a reality—or certainly not in the near future. Talking on the phone with the Model Prostitute (which was how she and all her friends referred to Janey behind her back) was one thing, but being seen out with her? She wasn't that dumb, and besides, her agent would kill her . . .

But as she didn't want to insult Janey (not just yet anyway, someone would probably make a movie out of Janey's life, and Wendy had half a mind to play her), she added, "You *know* I really want to, but I can't—at least not for six weeks, not until I finish the play . . ."

"I should come and see you in it," Janey said.

"Oh do!" Wendy said. "You and Selden should both come."

"If only I could make people understand that I *did* write a screenplay . . . ," Janey cried, returning to her favorite topic.

And then, as she always did when the subject of the mysterious screenplay came up, Wendy said pleadingly, "Janey, why don't you just go and get it?"

"But I *can't*," Janey said. "I told you, it's in my old apartment and I can't leave the hotel . . ."

"But you could give me the keys," Wendy said, "and *I* could go and get it . . ."

"You'd never find it," Janey said with a deep sigh. "That place is such a mess—I had a tenant, you know, that polo player Zizi, and apparently he was a pig . . . I'm not sure even I could find it, or that it's even there. My worst fear is that maybe I left it in that cottage I rented in the Hamptons two years ago . . ."

"Oh, I *know*," Wendy said, "but even so . . ."

"And I never turned it in," Janey said mournfully. "So there's no date on it. There's nothing to prevent people from thinking I wrote it after the fact . . . after I'd been accused." And, of course, there were *other* reasons as well, she thought . . .

"I suppose there is that," Wendy said, a touch of annoyance creeping into her voice.

The moment passed, however, and the two women hung up with promises to speak later.

Janey kicked at the leg of the coffee table. Maybe, she thought, she *should* give Wendy the key to her apartment to go look for the screenplay. Of course, there was no screenplay, only thirty pages, but the fact that she'd sent Wendy to find it would shore up the reality that there was one. She could just imagine Wendy defending her to the rest of the cast of *Streetcar*: "She sent me to look for it," Wendy would say, "and if there wasn't a screenplay, why would she do that?"

But it was too risky to send Wendy to her apartment, Janey decided. If she did happen to find the screenplay . . . *No,* she decided. She couldn't be too careful these days . . . She stood up and went to the window again, peeking carefully through the curtains. There were only three photographers now—a motley little crew who were stamping their feet in the cold. They looked like the dregs of the paparazzi; the kind of guys no one would have talked to in high school. Every day, their numbers had dwindled by three or four, and the scene was now a far cry from the day she'd returned, and walked in to find at least fifty photographers stationed across the street. There was such pandemonium that the police had finally erected blue barriers, but even *that* was nothing in comparison to the scene at the airport . . .

She'd had no idea that the story was so big until she had gone through customs and passed through the swinging doors into the corridor that led to the exit. Oh, she'd known that she was "in trouble" and that Selden would be furious with her, and might even be angry enough to threaten to divorce her. But she was quite sure that she would be able to convince him otherwise—if she felt like it.

So when she saw that the corridor was filled with a mob of photographers instead of the usual limousine drivers in search of their passengers, it still didn't register that they were there for her. And then one of them had screamed out, "There she is!" And there she was indeed, pushing her own unwieldy luggage cart filled with her Louis Vuitton suitcases like some schlub from New Jersey, and she hadn't even had time to put on her sunglasses . . .

And then they were all screaming her name and shouting things at her, like, *What was the most amount of money she'd ever been paid for sex?* There were so many of them, and the flashes from their cameras were literally blinding . . . Naturally, it was frightening, but there was something that was just a little bit heady about it, and she remembered thinking that this was how Princess Di must have felt . . . And then they were all around her—in her face and in front of the cart—and finally, she just couldn't move and she threw her arm over her eyes and opened her mouth to scream . . .

And then a man's hand emerged from the sleeve of a pinstriped suit and grabbed her arm, pulling her away, and some other man was pushing her cart like a lawn cutter through the mass of photographers, mowing them down, and suddenly they were on the curb and there were five policemen standing outside and the man in the pinstriped suit was urging her into a long black limousine with tinted windows. The man followed her into the car and slammed the door behind him, while the photographers surrounded the car, still shouting and snapping pictures. The man—he was older and attractive in a conservative, dull kind of way that is the sign of people with no imagination—crawled forward to the partition. "Go, Chester, go!" he shouted to the driver.

"What about the luggage, sir?"

"Ronald will take care of it. Just get out of here before they start breaking windows . . ."

The car had taken off with a lurch, and Janey fell back against the seat. And then there was silence. The man turned to her and held out his hand. "I'm Jerry Grabaw, by the way," he said with a slight Brooklyn accent. "Your husband hired me. I'm your new publicist." His mouth stretched into an ironic smile. "Congratulations," he added. "Now you're really famous."

Janey had just looked at him in shock.

Janey peeked through the curtains again. In the last five minutes, one of the photographers had left—but maybe he'd only gone to get something to eat. Well, she certainly *was* famous now, Janey thought, letting the curtains fall back together as she glanced at the pile of newspapers stacked in the corner, with no thanks to Jerry Grabaw.

She knew Selden was paying Jerry Grabaw a lot of money, but so far, he hadn't taken any of her "theories" seriously—like, for instance, the fact that George Paxton was the one who was responsible for bringing her down. "An interesting idea," Jerry had said smoothly—in his pinstriped suits, he looked, and acted, Janey thought with annoyance, more like a conservative businessman than a celebrity publicist— "but in light of the facts, I think we have to let Comstock Dibble take the blame."

"George is a *friend* of mine, Janey," Selden fumed, as if to remind her of this obvious fact. "Why would George do anything . . ."

She was about to open her mouth to speak, but the expression on Selden's face made her think better of it. On top of everything else, it probably wasn't a good idea for Selden to know that she'd gone behind his back right from the very beginning to ask George for help . . . or that she'd then gone to him for money . . . And she certainly didn't want him to ever suspect how far she'd gone to try to get it . . .

She spied through the curtains again. Jerry had told her to keep the curtains closed and to stay away from the windows, because the paparazzi had telephoto lenses that could take a picture from a hundred yards away through glass—not that she'd want them to get a shot of her looking like this, anyway. She'd hardly changed her clothes in the past two weeks, thinking that there was no point if no one was going to see her. But how many photographers would be there tomorrow? she wondered. Two . . . one . . . maybe they would all be gone. They were giving up, she realized, and considering today's *Post*, which had hardly mentioned her at all, they were possibly even losing *interest* . . .

Turning away from the window, and unable to think of any other way to amuse herself, she sat down on the couch and picked up a fashion magazine. She'd read this one at least three times by now; she'd been so bored she'd even read the ads. She threw the magazine back on the coffee table in disgust, wondering how she was going to fill her time until Selden got home at six. She could call Jerry and ask him to get her some new magazines; she might even ask him for a book. But she was too distracted to read anything that might require as much concentration as a book . . . and she was sick of TV.

Oh! she thought in frustration. She was sick to death of *everything* . . .

She stood up and began pacing the short length of the living room. She'd *wanted* to get away—maybe to Europe or to one of those horse ranches in Montana—but Selden said he couldn't. Despite their troubles, he still had to be in his office every day, and he didn't trust her on her own. How much longer was she going to be trapped in this suite then? she wondered. Two *more* weeks? A month? *Six* months . . . ?

Peering through the curtains yet again, she thought: Why *shouldn't* she go out? The photographers were nearly gone anyway . . . And Wendy was right—she was going to have to leave the suite sooner or later. Why shouldn't it be *today*?

But where—and with whom? She glanced at the clock—it was just before noon. Normally at this time she would be getting ready to go out to lunch at Dingo's . . . and she suddenly realized that that was *exactly* what she should do.

Dingo's, she decided, was perfect: There would be just enough important people there—enough so that her entrance would have an impact, but not so many that it would appear that she was trying to make some kind of statement. Of course, it was also a bit of a risk. What if they didn't give her her usual table . . . What if they wouldn't even let her in. But they would have to—and Wesley loved her anyway. Why, she had practically made that place . . .

But who could she go with? she wondered, nibbling at a scab on her index finger.

There was only one person, really—her sister. Patty wouldn't want to go, but Janey would make her.

But there was a more important question that concerned her, and that was specifically: *What to wear?*

She had to look perfect for her reentrance into society, she thought, hurrying to her closet. There was the Luca Luca red tweed suit with the beautiful fur collar . . . She could wear the suit with the black pearls. And with her six-karat diamond engagement ring and pavé Tiffany diamond wedding band sparkling on her left finger, she would look the very opposite of anybody's idea of a prostitute . . .

No, *white*! she thought, suddenly. She *must* wear *white*. White was the color of purity. It signified innocence and virtue . . . But most of her white clothes were for summer—except for the vintage Kors dress she'd worn to that dinner in Connecticut . . . She gasped at her boldness—did she *dare* wear *that*? She did, she thought with excitement, hurrying to her closet to pull out the dress. It would be shocking, it would be audacious even; it would show them *all* that she didn't care *what* they thought of her. And she had a white wool coat she could wear over it. And she would wrap her head in a white pashmina and put on a pair of dark glasses . . .

She went into the bathroom and began preparing her face. She hadn't worn her makeup in so long, the maid had wedged her makeup kit onto the top shelf of the medicine cabinet. She yanked on it, and as she did so, her last tube of Pussy Pink lipstick fell out and dropped into the marble tub. Its pink cap snapped and broke off on impact, and she cried out in horror.

What did it mean? she wondered, sadly picking up the broken pink plastic pieces and holding them in her hand. The lipstick was ruined—she couldn't carry it in her purse without a top, because it would somehow twist out and stain everything else in her bag. But maybe, she thought, touching the pieces and then dropping them into the small wastepaper basket, it wasn't such a bad omen after all. Maybe it was simply a sign that her old life had ended, and somehow, a new, better one had begun.

Selden Rose sat at his desk, staring at the contract in front of him.

He'd been working on getting the contract for months—it commissioned a well-known playwright to create a series about a family who ran an underground gambling casino in the basement of a town house on the Upper East Side—and although the writer hadn't officially written a word, there was already some good buzz about the project. Now that this contract was nearly finished, he intended to go after Wendy Piccolo to play the beautiful, wild, never-married daughter. But as usual these days, he found he could barely concentrate on the words right in front of his face . . . The very fact that he had to read a contract for a screenplay was a constant reminder of the situation with Janey. With a sigh, he pushed the contract to the side, and then got up and looked out the window at the downtown view. It was another overcast day, and he could barely make out the silver outline of the twin towers . . .

He looked at his watch—it was past eleven-thirty. He hadn't gotten nearly enough work done that morning, and now he had to have a private lunch with Victor Matrick in the executive-executive dining room. He wished he could put it off—indeed, he would have given anything to be able to get out of it altogether—but that, of course, was impossible. Victor's secretary had called his secretary a week before to set up the lunch, and then she had called this morning to confirm.

He'd had only two lunches alone with Victor since coming to the company: One, when Victor had been thinking about making him the CEO of MovieTime, and the other, two weeks after he'd taken the job. But he wasn't surprised that Victor wanted to have lunch with him. Not really. In fact, he'd been expecting it, given all the unwanted publicity Splatch Verner had received lately.

He had no idea what Victor was going to say, but he imagined it wouldn't be pleasant.

He'd been worrying about it all morning, considering every angle that the Old Man might take, but finally he had come to the conclusion that—once again—he was at a loss. Which was exactly what he told his mother when she called every third day at 5 P.M. like clockwork—just to see if there were any terrible "new developments" that she should brace herself for beforehand.

At ten minutes to noon, he went up in the elevator to the forty-second floor, then walked down the hallway to the private elevator that was the only means of access to the forty-third floor and Victor's lair. The elevator had an intercom instead of a regular UP button, and he pressed the tiny silver knob at the bottom.

"Yes?" one of Victor's three secretaries inquired.

"It's Selden Rose. For lunch with Victor . . . ?"

"Of course, Selden," the woman said cheerily. "Come right up."

The elevator door opened and he got in.

In three seconds, he arrived on the forty-third floor. One of the secretaries was waiting by the elevator to greet him.

"Hello, Selden," she said pleasantly. "Mr. Matrick is just finishing up a call; he'll be through in about five minutes. In the meantime, I can take you into the dining room."

They walked down a long, narrow corridor that was painted blue and hung with paintings in gilt frames. There were several doors on either side, painted a deeper blue, with molded trim that matched the blue on the walls. In the middle of the hallway, the secretary stopped and opened one of the doors, holding it open as she stepped aside for him to enter.

"I hope you have a lovely lunch," she said; and then added, "Oh, I nearly forgot," and handed him a small white card edged with the same blue as the doors. "Your menu," she nodded.

"Thank you," he said. He stepped into the room and looked down at the card. "Iceberg lettuce and California tomatoes *with* Maytag blue cheese dressing," it read, "*followed by* . . . fresh pan-fried Dover sole *with* asparagus and new potatoes . . . *followed by* . . . walnut brownie topped *with* homemade vanilla ice cream."

Sounds delicious, Selden thought grimly. And absentmindedly folding up the card and shoving it into his pocket, he looked around.

Every attempt had been made to make the diner think that he was possibly in Europe and not in a still-unfinished building on Columbus Circle—from the row of French doors that led out onto a terrace, through which were visible shapes of topiary now covered by snow, to the paneled walls, to the carved wooden dining room chairs placed around a long table laid with two place settings. The exception was the large flat plasma screen set into the wall at one end of the room—presumably so the diners could watch the latest offerings from Splatch Verner while they consumed the cuisine prepared by the private, five-star chef.

One place was set at the end of the table facing the screen; the other was just to the right. Selden sat down in front of the latter.

He looked up at the screen and sighed.

As if by magic, the screen flickered and a program appeared featuring a not unpleasant-looking middle-aged man. It was *The Jerry Springer Show,* and Selden sighed again. The Old Man was notorious for singling out executives to show them episodes of the show, after which he would pontificate about the significance of the show in American culture. It appeared that today he was to be the victim, and, despite his abhorrence of the show, he began watching, knowing that there would be some kind of quiz later.

Onscreen, a hideously unattractive young man with pimples and a rat tail of hair sprouting from the back of his head came out from behind a partition. After a few seconds of looking confused, he was joined by a prettyish blond girl (who was, Selden immediately decided, far too attractive for Rat Tail); in a moment, she began screaming in his face. Then another young woman in a pink tube top came out and started screaming at the blond woman. It was nearly impossible to understand what was going on or what they were upset about or indeed, what they were even *saying,* because the two women kept using expletives, which the censors had to constantly bleep out.

Then Blondie shoved Tube Top, and two burly security types, who looked as if they'd seen this far too often, pulled them apart. Blondie starting attacking Rat Tail again; meanwhile, Tube Top turned to the audience and, "shaking her booty," pulled down her top, exposing her breasts. These delights were quickly covered by a black band. Selden sighed again, and began patting the top of his head.

Then he caught himself and stopped. The irony, no doubt, was that the net result of this debacle would be that all his hair would fall out from abuse.

On top of everything else.

The door opened and Victor Matrick came into the room.

Selden stood up.

Victor Matrick was a tall man of medium build; despite his age, which some insisted was over eighty, he looked the picture of health, with a headful of thick white hair and ruddy cheeks to go with it. He was notoriously hearty—or could be, anyway—and coming into the room with the slight slouch that tall men learn to adapt so they don't hit their heads, he patted Selden on the back and then clasped both Selden's hands in his and shook them up and down.

"Selden," he said, nodding. "Selden Rose. It was so good of you to accept my invitation to lunch," as if, Selden thought bitterly, he had had any choice in the matter. "Shall we sit down?" he asked, taking the seat at the head of the table. "The first course will be along in a minute; the staff here is pretty good at timing things . . ."

"Of course," Selden murmured, sitting down after him.

Victor Matrick unfolded the linen napkin that had been placed in the middle of his plate. "So what do you think of the show?" he asked, nodding at the screen.

"Well. I . . ."

"I'm sure, like a lot of people, you find it fairly horrifying," Victor Matrick said, giving Selden a smile that revealed perfectly white, evenly spaced teeth—obviously all fake. "I used to myself, so I understand . . .

"But then," he continued—it was apparent that this was a speech he had given many times before—"I really began to think about it," he said, nodding his great, white head. "I always like to spend a lot of time thinking about anything that really bothers me, because if you can figure out why something's bothering you, chances are that you might discover something pretty amazing. And then I came to this conclusion." Victor put his elbows on the table and pointed up at the ceiling with his two index fingers. "Do you want to know what it is?"

Do I have any choice? Selden thought sarcastically; but, naturally, all he did was nod eagerly.

"It's *bawdy,*" Victor said.

"Bawdy, sir?" Selden asked.

"Bawdy," Victor nodded. "It's the most basic form of entertainment, and it's been around for a million years—probably since people first got the idea to entertain themselves. Look at that audience, Selden," Victor said, causing Selden to look back at the screen. "It's no different than it was four hundred years ago, when the peasants used to sit in the stalls and throw tomatoes at the performers onstage, right before the French Revolution . . ."

"I *think,* Mr. Matrick," Selden ventured, "that the French Revolution took place about *two* hundred . . ."

"I was never good at history, Selden," Victor Matrick said. "Most modern men aren't—and it doesn't make a bit of difference. Look at those guests, Selden," he commanded. "The freaks, the geeks, the peasants . . . society has always found a use for them, and they've always been a part of society. Look at those *faces,*" Victor urged. "Do you see any intelligence there . . . any glimmer of a larger understanding of moral values?"

Selden had to agree that, in general, he did not.

"And that's okay," Victor Matrick said, giving Selden an encouraging slap on the back, like a kind father who has just found out that his son has been cut from the football team. "God makes all different kinds of human beings, and it's not our place to judge them." And then, just when Selden was beginning to hope that he was going to get away with nothing more unpleasant than a lecture about *The Jerry Springer Show,* Victor suddenly became serious.

He leaned back in his chair and folded his arms. Now it's coming, Selden thought; Victor was going to bring up his recent job performance . . . But instead, Victor still seemed to be obsessed with *Jerry Springer.* "Do you know the difference between those folks up there on the screen and us folks down here who are about to eat a delicious lunch in the executive-executive dining room at Splatch Verner?"

Selden had a feeling that he probably shouldn't answer that question, so he fudged it with an "Uhhhhh . . ."

"The difference," Victor stated, "is not that we're better than they are, but that *they can't help themselves* . . . and . . . *we can.* They don't possess the intelligence to know better . . . but . . . *we do.* And so, while it's perfectly acceptable for them to provide a—shall we say—more *basic* form of entertainment to the general public . . . for *us,* for those of us who work here in this company and represent Splatch Verner, it is not." He paused, and added, "I think you understand *exactly* what I'm saying?"

Selden gulped. "Yes, Mr. Matrick, I do."

Even though, he thought, he didn't. Not exactly.

"I thought you would," Victor said. A door opened, and a young man in a uniform came in, bearing their salads.

"Ah, Michael," Victor said. "Just in time."

The waiter, Michael, set the salads down in front of them. Selden looked at his in despair. There was no way he was going to be able to eat all this food—he wouldn't be able to get down half . . . Picking up his napkin, he pressed it to his mouth. "But are they happy, Victor?" he asked, feeling like he ought to say something.

"What?" Victor asked, looking at him. "Who?"

Now he was in the shit, Selden thought. "Those people," he said. "Those people on *The Jerry Springer Show.*"

"Oh, Selden," Victor said. He sighed perplexedly, and then, in a completely unexpected gesture, he gave Selden a look of such infinite sadness that Selden felt his stomach drop to the floor. "What do *you* think?" he asked.

Selden said nothing, watching as Victor opened his mouth wide, shoved in a forkful of iceberg lettuce and began chewing thoughtfully, looking at Selden all the while. Selden considered trying to eat something himself, but he had the distinctly unpleasant feeling that Victor wasn't through with him.

And he wasn't.

Victor swallowed, took a sip of water, and, without preamble, said: "You have to do something about your wife."

"My *wife*, sir?" Selden squeaked.

"Your wife," Victor nodded. He shoved more lettuce in his mouth. Selden could see gooey bits of blue cheese dressing stuck to his gums where the dressing had mixed with Victor's saliva. He thought he was going to throw up.

For a few moments, neither one of them spoke. Selden wished that the floor would open up and swallow him, or, better yet, that Victor would swallow him. Whole. Like a lion. Or rather, more like an alligator. Lions only ripped their victims from limb to limb. Alligators drowned their victims first and *then* ate them.

And then Victor went back to watching the show *again*, forcing Selden to do the same. It was, Selden thought, like the very worst form of torture. The bleeps were like jolts of electricity, underscoring his lack of initiative. Had he fallen so far and sunk so low that he was just going to *sit there*, without the guts to defend either himself or Janey—his *wife*?

"Sir," he said, clearing his throat.

"Yes?" Victor asked. His face was all kindliness, the visage of a modern-day Santa Claus.

"My wife—Janey—has maintained that she's the victim in all this," Selden said hesitantly. And she had maintained it, he thought; although whether it was the truth or a calculated attempt to rework the facts or an instinctual defense mechanism, he couldn't tell. "She says she *did* write a screenplay . . ."

"If she's telling the truth, and she *is* innocent," Victor asked, getting right to the point, "then where *is* the screenplay?"

Selden couldn't answer that question.

"You see, Selden," Victor went on, "the problem is simple. You can't *handle* a woman like Janey Wilcox . . ." And seeing Selden's face, he held up his hand for him to wait until he'd finished. "That's not a criticism," he said bluntly. "Because the truth is, Splatch Verner can't *handle* her either." He paused. "Bad choice, Selden," Victor said. "You're going to have to get rid of her."

Selden said nothing. His mouth was dry and he lifted his water glass to his lips. Victor picked up his fork and began eating again. But after a moment, he put his fork down and wiped his mouth. And then, as if he were giving Selden a Christmas present, he said, "Naturally, I'll give you two weeks to decide," and smiled.

And at that moment, Selden finally understood exactly what Victor was saying: He was going to have to choose between his wife and his job.

• • •

Janey Wilcox's situation was, of course, but one little story in the city's own never-ending saga of ambition and endeavor, of striving and dealing, of triumph and failure that kept it wonderfully and disturbingly always the same, that made New York the most exciting city in the world, and, at times, the most depressing. And so, entering Dingo's at 1:30 that day, Janey had the sudden comforting feeling that nothing had changed, that everything was the same, that maybe the scandal had barely happened at all.

There was the usual crush at the door: The ebullient greetings of recognition between people who had but seen each other the night before, the not-so-subtle scanning of the crowd, and even the requisite out-of-town couple who had read about the place in *Zagat's* and thought that they had accidentally stumbled into hell. With her dark glasses and a pashmina covering her famous shining blond hair, Janey elicited nothing more than a few curious glances, reminding her of how right she'd been to come.

Her sister, on the other hand, had required quite a bit of convincing. Patty did not think it was a good idea, and had told her so—and Janey had been forced to resort to threats of suicide if she didn't get out of the suite. Naturally, Patty hadn't believed her, but she said if Janey was that desperate . . .

"This is pathetic," Patty said, emerging from the crowd.

"It's fun," Janey said firmly. "It's always fun at Dingo's."

They shed their coats as Janey peered through the paned glass that separated the vestibule from the first of two dining rooms. The front room was *the* place to sit, and was separated from the second dining room by a bar. Day after day, eager patrons would wait at the bar in anticipation, only to be shown to the disappointing back room, where they would find only other diners such as themselves. The front room was strictly reserved for the crème de la crème of New York society: the visiting celebrities, the socialites, the business and media moguls, the magazine editors, the showbiz people, and anybody else who happened to be in the news. But even within this heaven was a smaller circle of desirability: one of the three booths on either side of the room. The booths on the left side were considered slightly better than the booths on the right, which were closer to the door, and of the left-side booths, the middle one was the most prestigious. Janey had sat in that booth a couple of times, but most often she was shown to the booth on its left, closest to the window, which she considered not only "her" booth, but also more advantageous: It afforded not only a view of the sidewalk, but also the opportunity to display oneself to the passersby outside as well as to the patrons inside the restaurant.

Today, she noted, handing her coat and scarf to the coat-check girl, the mayor was sitting at the middle booth with the police commissioner and Mike Matthews, the senator. Her booth, she saw happily, was empty, and her mind was immediately filled with visions of success: She knew Mike well enough to say hello—and he would undoubtedly introduce her to the mayor, and wouldn't that be something for the gossip columns. And then there was the sheer pleasure of being seen in her old booth, and what fun it would be when she told Selden and that annoying Jerry Grabaw that they were both wrong, that her life could go on exactly as before . . .

And then Wesley, the maître d', was hurrying toward her.

"Janey!" he said. He was frowning slightly and rubbing his hands together in consternation—not exactly the greeting she'd been expecting. But he did give her the usual kiss on each cheek, and taking advantage of the moment, Janey said gaily, "I bet you're surprised to see me!"

"Actually, I am, love," he said with a slight grimace. "I wish you'd called and told me you were coming. We're awfully booked up today . . ."

"Janey, let's go," Patty whispered. "We'll come back tomorrow . . ."

"Don't be ridiculous," Janey said with a forced smile. People had begun to notice she was there; she could tell by the sudden frisson of energy in the air. It would be impossible to walk out now—it would look like she'd been deliberately slighted—and then people might think it was acceptable to cut her, and she might not be invited anywhere again . . .

Adopting a bantering tone, she said teasingly, "Darling, my booth is free . . ."

"That's just the problem, love," Wesley said in dismay. "It's been specially reserved. But I do have a nice table in the back . . ."

"Janey, come on," Patty whispered more insistently.

This was, Janey knew, nothing less than a showdown, and if she was to succeed, she had to stand her ground. "There are no nice tables in the back, Wesley. You know that," she said firmly.

Wesley laughed reluctantly, and Janey sighed inwardly with relief. "Wait here and I'll see what I can do," he said.

He made a show of consulting with his second-in-command, a pretty young woman who then made a show of consulting the reservation book. In a moment, he returned with two menus and led them into the first room. "It's not your usual table, but I think it will do for today," Wesley said with, Janey noted, the proper amount of obsequiousness.

While she'd been standing by the door, Janey had noticed little glances from the other diners, but now, as she walked into the room, she felt them staring openly. The expressions, she noted, registered excitement, amusement, and disdain—it was like being on a stage, she thought. But wasn't that what people always said about New York City restaurants? That they were like theater? If they wanted a show, she would give them one, she thought, defensively. And as she strolled behind Wesley (she assumed that Patty was following behind, but she couldn't exactly worry about *her* at the moment), she reminded herself that she had beauty, and something more than that as well. There were plenty of beautiful women in the city, but few who had captured the spotlight, and though she wished the light were a little more flattering, hadn't she always known it was inevitable that one day she would be the center of attention?

Wesley, she saw, was leading them toward a small table that was meekly stationed at the foot of her treasured booth, and, arranging her features into a casual smile, as if she were unaware of the buzz around her, Janey made a beeline for the center booth where the mayor and Mike Matthews were sitting. Her table was close enough to the booth to justify this detour, she decided, and she was not going to pass up the opportunity to redeem herself in front of the potentially vicious crowd at Dingo's. She had seen the mayor glance at her curiously once or twice, and had seen Mike stare at her in shock, and then quickly look away. As she approached the booth, she saw the three men stiffen and resume their conversation with renewed vigor, as if to pretend that they were completely unaware of her presence. But Mike had been so kind to her at Harold's party, she thought, certainly he wouldn't snub her.

"Mike!" she said. Her expression was perfect: a subtle combination of surprise mixed with pleasure.

And then Mike went on with his story, as if she weren't there.

"Mike," she said, adding a touch of impatience to her voice.

The mayor looked up at her, forcing Mike to do so as well.

She expected his face to register at least recognition, but instead he frowned, as if annoyed at being interrupted, and in a voice that said he had no idea why she was talking to him, he asked, "Yes?"

"Mike," Janey said, shaking her head as if to scold him for not remembering her, "it's Janey. Janey Wilcox. We've met a couple of times. At Harold Vane's . . ."

"Oh yes. Of course," Mike said, nodding his head coldly. There was an uncomfortable silence, and finally, giving her the ultimate New York dismissal, he added, "Nice to see you again."

And went back to his conversation.

"Nice to see you," Janey said, as if nothing were out of the ordinary.

Patty was already seated at the table. She couldn't bring herself to look at Janey; when Janey sat down, Patty stared at her napkin.

"So," Janey said, making a show of flipping open her napkin and placing it on her lap. "What's new?"

"Oh, Janey . . . ," Patty said, shaking her head.

The waiter came to the table.

"Would you like something to drink?"

"Yes," Janey said firmly, as if she'd eagerly been awaiting this question. "I'll have a vodka on the rocks with a twist of lemon, and Patty . . ."

Patty looked up in despair. "I'll have a water."

"Bottled or tap?" the waiter asked.

"Bottled. Fizzy," Janey said.

"Well," she said, sitting back in her chair. "It certainly is nice to get out of the hotel for a change. Mike was happy to see me. Did you see that?" Janey asked.

"No," Patty said, quietly.

"I'm just pissed that they wouldn't give me my booth," Janey said.

"The table is fine," Patty said.

"It's horrible," Janey said. "It's practically in the middle of the room . . ."

The waiter came back to the table with their drinks. "How are you?" Janey asked him pleasantly.

"I'm okay," he said evenly.

"It's so funny that Wesley didn't give me my regular booth," Janey said.

"I think it's specially reserved today."

"Oh, it's always specially reserved," Janey said airily, "but usually for me!"

The waiter nodded his head, and Patty said, "Janey, *please* . . ."

"What, Patty?" Janey asked. There was a challenge in her voice. "Do you think I'm going to sit here like a meek little mouse . . . like *you*? I haven't done anything wrong, Patty; that's what you need to remember . . ."

"Okay. I *know*," Patty said, looking nervously around the room.

"For God's sake," Janey said to her sister. "You of all people know I'm innocent. You know I wrote a screenplay—I told you all about it that summer . . ."

"But that doesn't mean . . ."

"It's all George Paxton's fault anyway," Janey continued, cutting Patty off. "He used me. He got the idea to buy the company from me, and then he sold me out." She sat back, looking at Patty for confirmation. Her only mistake was in going to George for help, she thought angrily. If she hadn't showed him the letter, he would never have had the idea to go after Comstock's company, and the stuff about the money would have passed unnoticed, even if she never paid it back. She'd been such a fool to trust him, she thought, glancing at the empty booth behind her. And if she'd known better, she would be sitting there right now and everything would be fine . . .

"Oh, *Janey*," Patty sighed. "I don't even know what you're talking about. But in any case, does it really matter?"

"Of course it matters," Janey snapped.

A different waiter came to their table. Janey thought he was going to take their order, but instead, he said, "I'm sorry, ladies, but I have to move the table." And then he inched the table forward, away from the booth, as if they were somehow contaminated . . .

Janey and Patty exchanged a look. "I'm going to speak to Wesley," Janey said.

She made a motion as if to stand up, expecting that everyone's eye would be upon her. But not a face was turned in her direction, and suddenly, the conversations became louder and more amusing, and everyone became a little more important, as they do when someone truly famous enters a room. And looking toward the entrance, Janey saw the cause of the commotion: The movie star Jenny Cadine was in the restaurant.

Her real name, it was rumored, was Jennifer Carrey, but she had changed it to Cadine when she was sixteen, apparently in honor of Balzac's character in *Cousin Bette*. She was barely thirty years old, but she'd won the Oscar for best actress two years ago, and she was as tall and golden as the statuette itself. She was dressed beautifully, in the ruffled Yves Saint Laurent shirt that was supposed to be all the rage that spring, and Janey immediately wished that she'd worn the tweed suit instead of the revealing white plastic dress. The dress would have been perfect for a nightclub, but now, in the light of day, she was conscious of appearing cheap, of trying too hard. Everything about her suddenly felt wrong: from her long, straight, blond hair (Jenny's hair was always different, and today it was colored a golden-red and hung in perfect ringlets down her back) to the red lipstick she put on in lieu of the damaged Pussy Pink.

And as Wesley triumphantly led Jenny to the empty booth, studiously ignoring Janey on the way, Janey saw that Jenny was wearing pink lipstick—and it was nearly the same shade as her own beloved signature color. *I must ask her what it's called and where she got it,* Janey thought irrationally, for she suddenly felt a sense of relief. So that was the reason for Wesley's cool reception, she thought. It had nothing to do with her, nothing to do with the scandal at all. It was only that Wesley had promised her table to a movie star . . .

Following in Jenny's wake was a short, middle-aged woman with a mouth like a fish. Probably Jenny's publicist, Janey thought. The two sat down in the booth, and the conversation in the room reached a fevered pitch as everyone tried to ignore the fact that they were in the same restaurant with the beautiful Jenny Cadine, the movie star and Academy Award winner . . .

And oh, what glory it was, Janey thought happily. The world suddenly seemed to have righted itself, and tomorrow, the gossip columns would probably carry the story that Jenny Cadine had been spotted lunching at Dingo's, and then would go on to list who else was in the restaurant. There was the mayor and Senator Mike Matthews, and certainly, Janey thought, smiling at Patty, they would mention her . . .

Wesley himself went to Jenny's table to take her order, and suddenly, Janey's mood swung 180 degrees in the opposite direction. Watching him leaning over Jenny's shoulder to point out something on the menu, she realized that Wesley had never treated her that way—even though she'd been a regular celebrity customer for months. And she began to fume: Why should she be asked to step aside for the Jenny Cadines of the world? She was as beautiful as Jenny Cadine, she thought, sneaking a look at her out of the corner of her eye—probably, in most people's opinion, more so. Because while Jenny made a great first impression, when you really looked at her, you saw that her face was actually a bit uneven, and that her nose was crooked and a tiny bit long . . . And then, glancing back at Jenny again, as she unfolded her napkin and briefly surveyed the crowd like she was some kind of queen, Janey wondered: Why shouldn't she become a movie star herself! How silly she'd been, she thought, trying to be a producer. Where was the glory in that? Because, if she asked herself what she really wanted, she would have to say that she always wanted respect . . . She always wanted to be shown to the best booth at every restaurant . . . And she wanted to be the undisputed star no matter where she was . . .

And then, something terrible happened.

Jenny Cadine's publicist was looking around the room—her small pursed mouth opening and closing like a guppy in search of food—when her eye fell on Janey. And her face froze.

Leaning toward Jenny, the publicist began whispering in her ear. Jenny Cadine glanced briefly at Janey, her eyes opening in sudden understanding. She lowered her head and nodded several times, and then Jenny and the publicist stood up, gathered their things, and walked out.

There was a shocked hush in the restaurant, but as is usual in these kinds of situations, someone went on talking. The person happened to be a woman sitting at the next table, and while not everyone in the restaurant heard her, there was no pain spared Patty and Janey.

As clearly as if she'd been sitting at their table, they both heard: "It's because of those scandal sisters—Janey and Patty Wilcox. One's called the Model Prostitute and the other was married to a rock star. He got some singer pregnant and the younger one, Patty, was in *jail* . . ."

"Let's go," Patty said, placing her napkin on the table.

Janey felt the room spinning around her. Until Jenny Cadine walked out, the attitude toward her had been mildly tolerant, but now it was decidedly hostile, and no one was bothering to hide their looks of disdain. Janey stared down at the table, willing herself not to cry. She would get through this, she thought with determination. Somehow, she *would* . . . and other people had probably survived worse.

"Janey . . . ," Patty said gently.

"If you leave me here, I'll die," Janey said.

The waiter brought two salads to the table. His manner was unmistakably chilly.

"We're going to cancel our main courses," Patty said softly. "If you could just bring the check . . ."

"Of course," the waiter said, without looking at them.

"Janey," Patty said. "Why do you do this? Don't you see that it's over?"

Janey said nothing. She picked up her fork, chasing a piece of lettuce around on her plate.

"Why do you want to be here anyway?" Patty asked. "Why do you even want to be in this world?"

"Patty," Janey sighed.

"It's finished," Patty said. "New York is finished for both of us. I don't know what you're going to do, but Digger and I are moving to Malibu. We bought a house, and Digger is going to take a year off from the band."

"That's nice . . . ," Janey said listlessly, as if she hadn't heard a word Patty had spoken.

"Janey . . . ," Patty said. She touched Janey's arm and shook it slightly. "You have to listen to me. You have to leave New York. There's nothing here for you—maybe there never was. You need to find something real. You're living in a fantasy world . . . You've *been* living in a fantasy world ever since you got back from Europe that summer."

Janey said nothing. The waiter brought the check, and Patty opened her purse, fumbled with her wallet, and managed to extract five twenty-dollar bills. She put the money down on the table and stood up.

"That's too much," Janey whispered.

Patty just looked at her.

But the sight of money seemed to revive her a little, and somehow, Janey managed to rise, and with her head held high, walk all the way through the restaurant and out into the vestibule. The coat-check girl silently handed them their coats, as if she knew they would be leaving, and as they were putting them on, Wesley came out.

"Janey," he said.

Janey turned. Her eyes narrowed. "Yes, Wesley?" she asked coldly.

"Listen, love," he said, taking her arm and leading her toward the door. "You and I are old friends, so I know that you're going to understand what I have to tell you."

Janey said nothing. Her mouth felt full of sawdust.

"You know how these things work," Wesley said in a perfectly pleasant tone of voice. "We survive on our clientele . . . on being able to attract the right sort of people. If something happens to affect that . . . my boss will kill me and *I'll* lose my job . . ."

Janey ran her tongue over her teeth and swallowed. "Excuse me," she said, pushing past him.

"Janey," he said, following her out of the restaurant and onto the street. "Don't blame me. If I had my choice, I wouldn't care if you ate here every day. But Jenny Cadine's publicist is in a snit—she doesn't want the name of her precious client to appear in the same paragraph as 'the Model Prostitute.'"

"Well, now she's guaranteed it."

"Janey!" Wesley called after her. He was rubbing his arms and jumping up and down in an attempt to stay warm. "I don't want to be in this situation any more than you do. But I can't afford to lose my job."

"I understand," Janey said.

She turned. She wasn't sure where she was or which direction was home; all she knew was that she had to keep her head high and her eyes wide open. Staring straight in front of her, she began walking, and in a moment Patty came running up from behind and caught up with her.

"Oh Janey!" she cried breathlessly.

Janey turned her head. She looked at Patty as if she'd completely forgotten that she was there, and Patty saw that her eyes were glistening with tears. Her heart went out to her only sister; she wanted to hug her and comfort her, and reassure her that somehow, everything was going to be okay. But Janey didn't even pause. She just kept walking stiffly on and on, as if she'd been walking for a long time across an endless desert, and had forgotten how to stop. And then she said: "You see, Patty? It's what I was trying to explain to you at lunch. I won't *let* them stop me. I won't *let* them bring me down."

"But *Janey* . . . ," Patty said in despair.

"*Especially* not now," Janey said.

"I went out today," Janey said to Selden.

She was naked in the tub under a pile of soap bubbles. A row of small scented candles was lined up neatly along the edge.

"Yes, I know," Selden said blandly. He was trying to keep the creeping anger out of his voice, but he wondered how much more he could take. He'd had plenty of bad days, but this one just might qualify as the worst: First there was the lunch with Victor Matrick, and now this. Jerry Grabaw had called him at three o'clock that afternoon—he'd had a call from one of the columnists at Page Six, who'd already heard about the incident at Dingo's, he explained. And now they were going to run the story on the front page of the *Post* tomorrow.

"You know?" Janey asked. She could barely, Selden thought, even bother to register surprise anymore.

"Jerry called me," he said.

"Oh."

He left the bathroom and went into the bedroom to change his clothes. Every night was the same now, and, in an ironic way, he supposed he'd finally gotten what he wanted: They stayed at home and ordered in take-out food or room service and watched TV. "What do you think you want for dinner tonight?" he called out to her.

"I don't know," she called back. "Chinese?"

"We had that last night."

"Indian?"

"I think I feel like a steak," he said. "We'll order from room service." In truth, he hardly felt hungry. But good midwestern homilies reminded him that he had to eat to keep his strength up.

He removed his suit and pulled on a cashmere crewneck sweater and a pair of jeans. There was no point, he thought, in even talking about this latest incident. Nothing could be done; it was too late.

He went into the living room and sat down on the couch. In a minute, Janey joined him. He switched on the TV. The news was on. There was a water-main break in the Bronx; a fire in the basement of a restaurant in Chinatown. A commercial for Prozac came on, followed by a spot for *Entertainment Tonight*. "Who will take home the golden statue?" the blond announcer asked cheerily, as if there were nothing more pressing in the world to think about. "Oscar preview tonight . . ."

Janey turned to him. "Are you going to the Oscars this year?" she asked.

He shook his head, not taking his eyes off the television. "Victor Matrick doesn't think it's a good idea."

"Oh," she said blandly.

The exchange brought the lunch with Victor Matrick to the foremost part of his mind. It wasn't that he ever forgot any element of the debacle; it was just that the pieces kept shifting, like apples floating in a bucket, one thought momentarily submerged while another one took its place.

He stood up and went into the tiny kitchen, and began fixing himself a vodka. "Do you want anything?" he asked politely.

"Are you having a vodka?" she asked.

"Yes," he said.

"Then I'll have one, too."

So this was how their lives were to be now, he thought, taking another glass out of the cabinet and filling it with ice. They were going to be like two old people who tiptoed around each other and drank steadily to dull the pain.

Except, he thought, pouring vodka into her glass, now he had to make a decision.

The task that Victor had demanded of him was completely unfair, he thought angrily. It was biblical, like Abraham's being asked to sacrifice his son, or King Solomon, who offered to cut a child in half to solve an argument. Until today he had somehow assumed that he would be allowed to skate along unsteadily, in the assumption that eventually, everything would return to normal. And he had done his best to *behave* normally, he thought, his deep irritation growing. He was at his desk every day at nine, just as he had always been—he took meetings and went to lunches and supervised programming. But despite his efforts, everything was *not* the same, and everybody knew it. There were whispers in the hallway, and half the time, when some writer was pitching an idea or his secretary was telling him about her children or Gordon was banging on about his sexual exploits, his mind would begin wandering, and he would start going over every element of the disaster, thinking that if only she'd told him, if only she hadn't been so cheap, if only she hadn't been so easily taken in . . . and then his mind would come back to that unanswerable question: *Why?*

And then he would look up, and everyone would be staring at him.

And he would panic, wondering what he'd missed.

He went back into the living room and handed her her drink. She took it with a terse, "Thanks," not bothering to take her eyes off the television.

He looked at her. She was wearing the same designer jeans and sweatshirt—VIXEN it said across the front, in fuzzy, dirty, light blue letters—that she'd been wearing practically every day since she'd come home from France. As if sensing his eye upon her, she shifted on the couch and pulled up the waistband of her jeans. She bathed regularly, he knew that (all too well), but the jeans and sweatshirt were misshapen and appeared distinctly unclean, and he was reminded of that George Bernard Shaw line: "Beauty is all very well at first sight; but who ever looks at it when it has been in the house for three days?" And in his rising fury, he bitterly thought, *No, who ever does?* and even though they still slept in the same bed every night, he couldn't bear the thought of making love to her. Every time he contemplated it, he saw the hideous face of Comstock Dibble—with that sparse red hair and the gap between his teeth—laughing at him.

He sat down on the couch. "Why did you do it?" he asked.

"Do what?" she said, not bothering to look at him.

He took another sip of vodka. "Go out today."

"Oh," she said coldly. "Wendy Piccolo told me to."

"What?" he said, immediately not believing her.

She turned to him. In a tone of voice that implied that somewhere along the line she'd explained all of this to him before, she said, "I was talking to Wendy Piccolo. She told me that I had to go out sooner or later, and I agreed."

He put his glass down on the coffee table. His eyes narrowed in confusion. "I don't understand. When did you see Wendy Piccolo?"

"I didn't *see* her," Janey said patiently, as if she were dealing with a small child. "I *spoke* to her on the *phone*."

"She called you," Selden said incredulously.

"Yes," Janey said. "She *did*. She calls me every day and we talk."

"So you and Wendy are friends."

"That's right," Janey said, sipping her vodka. And then she turned back to him accusingly. "Don't act so surprised, Selden. What do you think? That I'm so awful I can't have friends anymore?"

"I'm just surprised, that's all," Selden said meekly. That was what he always had to do with her now, he had to push himself down and make himself meek in order not to . . .

"Well, don't be," she said. She stood up as if she were about to get something from the kitchen, and the moment might have passed if she hadn't said, "Anyway, I didn't think you'd mind. Especially since she's *such* a good friend of yours . . ."

He looked at her blank, slightly truculent expression, and with a sickening insight, he wondered: *Would she* ever *begin to understand what she had done?* And then his anger broke free; it tore out of him like a wild animal. Until that moment, he'd been able to keep his anger tamped down; he had not once lost his temper in front of her, he hadn't screamed at her or shaken her or laid a finger on her (although it had crossed his mind, once or twice), and he hadn't cried in front of her, although he'd longed to do *that*, too. But now he could no longer control himself.

"You leave her alone!" he shouted.

She took a step back from him—more out of surprise, he thought, than fear, and suddenly, it all came boiling to the surface.

"Don't you see how people feel about you now?" he screamed. "You're like a virus . . . a deadly evil virus that harms everyone you come into contact with. You've practically ruined my career . . . made me the laughingstock of the entire industry . . . And look what you've done to poor Craig Edgers. Your stupid scheme prevented him from selling his book to Comstock Dibble, and now Dibble's out of the picture and you've probably only cost Craig what could be millions of dollars." He was red in the face and his voice was nearly hoarse as he continued, "And does Craig deserve that? The poor guy only worked his *entire life* to get where he is today, and with one stroke of your evil wand you destroy all his chances. So if you think I'm going to let you get to Wendy . . ."

And through it all, she just stood there, taking it. He couldn't believe it. She didn't fight back, she didn't defend herself—she just let him spew on and on, almost as if she enjoyed seeing the spectacle of him losing control . . .

And then she turned on her heel and walked out of the room.

He knew exactly what would happen next. She would go into the bathroom and turn on the taps full blast, and then, knowing that he was frightened and contrite on the other side of the door, she would ignore him, bathing herself like a precious piece of china, and when she came out, she would act as if nothing had happened at all . . .

He would wait, he thought, fuming. He would just wait . . .

After about ten minutes, he heard the water stop, and sneaking into the bedroom and putting his ear to the bathroom door, he heard the splashing sound of her entering the water. "Janey!" he said firmly. "This is not something you can just wash away. Do you understand? It can't be cleaned with your fancy perfumed soap bubbles . . ."

There was no response.

With a sigh, he went back into the living room.

As usual, his anger was short-lived and he was suddenly exhausted. He simply didn't have the constitution for rage. Although he could be tough in business, Victor Matrick was right: He couldn't handle a woman like Janey Wilcox, he thought, sinking onto the couch. He put his head in his hands. Despite everything that had happened, he had remained in love with her, he thought. And he clung to the idea that he loved her still. It would be impossible for him not to do so, for if he found that he didn't love her, he would have to shine that same cold bright light on every aspect of his life, and then he might discover it was *all* a sham . . .

Men can be notoriously simple in matters of the heart, and Selden Rose, unfortunately, was one of those men. He had fallen in love with Janey Wilcox the moment she'd sat down next to him at Mimi's party, and in the single-minded way of men, he loved her simply because she *was*—because she *existed*—and because he could never quite possess her. He hadn't really wanted much from her—only that she love him a little and give way to his wishes now and then and stand by him. And with the irrational blindness of a man misguided by what he is convinced *is* love, he still hoped that she loved him, too. For he honestly believed that if she did, despite the odds against them, they would manage to get through this together. When a man falls in love like this, a woman may abuse him terribly, and while he might eventually hate her or call her crazy, it's nearly impossible to convince him that this isn't true love.

But women are more complicated when it comes to their affections: They rarely love simply for what is—but for what might be, and more importantly, for how it might affect them. This is why a woman will endure a great deal of abuse in love—as long as she believes there is something to be gained. But when a woman sees that a man can no longer help her, when his actions become detrimental to her lifestyle, she can fall out of love as suddenly and as firmly as an apple falling from a tree. There is no putting the apple back on the tree, just as there is no going back in love. Her heart closes against the man as resolutely as if he had never existed. And so, as Janey Wilcox sat in the bath, coldly turning her relationship with Selden Rose over and over again in her mind, she saw that it was finished.

Selden was of no use to her anymore. His outburst had told her everything she needed to hear. He was a wimp and a coward—if he'd had any guts, he would have accompanied her to Dingo's long ago, for no one would have dared to tell the CEO of MovieTime that *he* wasn't welcome back. But Selden couldn't even do that much for her: He had not made an effort to defend her and he wouldn't in the future; and he hadn't even believed in her innocence. The tiny bit of affection she had felt for him left her body like water running down a drain.

She didn't even feel sad, she thought wearily. She would never cry again for any man—not for the Selden Roses of the world, and not even for the Zizis. Now, she thought, it was only a matter of waiting. Despite everything that had happened, she still had her beauty. And she knew as long as she had her beauty, something interesting could still occur . . . and at the very least, there would always be some man who would pursue her . . .

But next time she would be more careful. And angrily sweeping the bubbles away from her body, she was once again reminded of George Paxton. If only, if *only*, she thought furiously. George had tried to ruin her, but she wasn't finished yet . . . He must be made to see that he owed her . . . and somehow, she would make him *pay* . . .

Back in the living room, Selden sat woodenly on the couch, thinking about what he was going to do about his relationship with Janey. As he realized once again that he was at a loss, his eye fell on the pile of newspapers Janey had stacked in the corner. And as Janey sat scheming in the bath while Selden sat ruminating on the couch, they both came to the same bitter conclusion: The only person who had come out well in this whole debacle was George Paxton.

SEVENTEEN

SELDEN ROSE SAT in his office, staring at the small Tiffany clock on his desk.

A minute passed, and 10:03 turned into 10:04.

He felt like Dorothy in *The Wizard of Oz*, locked in the castle of the Wicked Witch, staring at the hourglass as grains of sand rushed to the bottom.

He had exactly six hours, fifty-five minutes, and forty-three seconds to live.

Two weeks had passed. Two weeks exactly from that fateful day when he'd had lunch with Victor Matrick. His time was nearly up; in a few hours it would be over.

And he still hadn't made a decision.

That morning, he had woken up and, for several minutes, had stared at his sleeping wife, willing himself to memorize her face. Her skin was smooth, without a line, the color of ivory. There was a blush of pink across her cheeks, and her lips were the shade of ripening cherries. He'd never understood why she always wore that pinkish red lipstick when her own natural lip color was so beautiful—but then, there were so many things that he hadn't understood about her. Her eyes were closed tightly, as if she didn't want to wake up, and her hands were loosely clenched in childish fists beneath her chin.

"I love you," he whispered. "Oh, I love you . . ."

He'd wanted to smooth back her fine blond hair from her forehead, but he didn't want to wake her. Did she have any idea of what might happen to her . . . ?

No, he thought, sitting in his office. He would not do it. He would not sacrifice his wife for his job.

He had to draw the line. The man who could do what Victor Matrick wanted was a man without a soul. He had seen such men and women all his working life, first in Los Angeles and now in New York, and he had always thought of them as "Pod People"—people who on the outside looked like human beings, but on the inside were devoid of real human emotions. So often, these were the people who rose to the top of their fields, but Selden had always laughed at them, with the scorn and relief of someone who believes that *he* will never have to become like that to get ahead, and is therefore by definition superior.

And he had believed, just ten months ago when he'd arrived in New York, that he would be able to rise to the very top of Splatch Verner, that he might, through hard work and an innate desire to do good, someday take over Victor Matrick's job.

But now his eyes had been opened. He knew it was never going to happen that way.

On the other hand, if he did what Victor asked, if he "got rid" of Janey, it would be perceived as a statement that he was a man who would take no prisoners. He would be someone to reckon with; he would be feared. He would be promoted, of that he had no doubt. And then he would choose a third wife, someone more "appropriate" to the company's image, someone, he imagined, like Dodo Blanchette.

And if he didn't take Victor's "advice," what then? They wouldn't fire him out-right—it would be far too risky, and it might even open them up to a lawsuit for some kind of discrimination (discrimination against one's spouse—that would be a new one, he thought). Instead, he would be placed in one of those untenable positions in which more and more responsibilities were taken away from him, until at last all he would have left would be his desk and his secretary. And then his secretary would be transferred to another department, and he would be moved to a smaller office, where he would have to share a secretary with someone else. And then, finally, he would have to quit. In other circumstances, he might have been able to find another job. He could go back to Los Angeles and take a job as an executive at one of the big movie companies—a job that would easily pay a million dollars a year. But at the moment, he knew he was considered a joke—the guy who had married the prostitute instead of just paying her like everybody else.

And he had worked so hard all his life! he thought, resting his head in his hands. His work had been his joy and his salvation. Every time he put together a movie and stepped onto the set on that first day of production, each time a movie opened and he saw the great box-office numbers, every time one of his movies had won an award, and then, each time he'd been promoted, he'd felt an indescribable high, like the universe was opening up to him, like it was *his* . . . His first wife claimed that his addiction to work and achievement had ruined their marriage; she had bitterly pointed out that if he had paid more attention to her, then maybe she wouldn't have started an affair with that associate who worked in her office. That news had stung; it had momentarily crippled him, especially when he found out that the affair had been going on for the last two years of his marriage, and that she was so brazen that she had even arranged for her paramour to spend Christmas in Aspen, when they were there. Selden had even had lunch with the guy, and still, he'd had no clue. But he'd never loved Sheila the way he loved Janey, and he had only married Sheila out of guilt—after they'd been dating for five years she'd given him an ultimatum. At the time, it had simply seemed easier to give in than to have to go through the hassle of finding someone else.

If the choice had been Sheila or his job, it would have been easy, he thought harshly. But Sheila never would have put him in this position—she didn't have the imagination to do so. Janey, he thought, had an odd way of managing to pull everyone else into her disasters, and in the process, they all got hurt. She was like a siren, he thought, luring sailors onto the rocks . . .

He looked at the clock again. It was 10:43.

The only person who hadn't been smashed to bits was George. And George had bought Comstock's company. It would seem that George should have suffered at least a broken leg . . .

The clock now read 10:45. He picked up the phone and called George.

While George Paxton enjoyed beauty in his home, his office, he felt, should reflect the idea that it was a place of business, and one of the tenets of business was that money should not be wasted. And so his office, while large, was strictly utilitarian; the only two concessions were a massive oriental Indian silk rug, which Mimi had had specially made, and a five-by-ten-foot slightly jumbled-looking portrait of George, which Mimi had commissioned to be painted by the contemporary artist Damien Hirst for half a million dollars as a wedding gift.

There was a long row of glass windows, covered by plastic louvered shades, which provided a view into the towers of several other midtown office buildings, and in the center of the room was a grouping of hard, black Le Corbusier couches and armchairs. It was on these chairs that George and Selden now sat.

They were drinking coffee from blue paper cups, decorated with the logo of the local Greek deli.

The meeting, Selden felt, was not going well.

"You've got no choice, Selden," George was saying. "You've got to look at it logically. You've only known her for maybe eight or nine months. Meanwhile, you've been working for over twenty years . . ."

George took a sip of his coffee. Selden was being so obstinate, he thought. Couldn't the man see what he had to do? It was all ego, he thought, and ego had brought him down. And if he continued to let his ego get in the way, it would really be the end.

Selden looked out the window. He could see straight into the offices across the street, where a man sat in front of a computer while he talked on the phone. Should he tell George that he was still in love with Janey? he wondered. But that would probably make him sound weak. He picked up his coffee cup from the glass table. "What if the whole thing is a mistake?" he asked. "It's like executing the wrong man . . ."

George sighed. "Nobody is going to die here," he said, slightly irritated. "It's not a good situation, but maybe you've got to face the facts. Grow up. Do you want to be a player, or do you want to keep playing the fool?"

"If there was some way . . . ," Selden said.

"Jesus Christ, Selden," George said in disgust. "You know as well as anyone that this is part of the business of being a CEO in the first place. You've got to be able to make the hard decisions. No one gives a fuck about the easy ones—we've got assistants to do that."

"She thinks that somehow you're to blame, George," Selden said, allowing a slight edge to come into his voice.

George rolled his eyes and smiled. "What else do you expect her to say? Did you think that she was going to take personal responsibility for her actions?"

"If she hasn't, she won't be the first one," Selden said.

George stared at Selden over the rim of his cup. The man, he thought, was not handling the situation well. He looked exhausted and slightly hungover, and he guessed that Selden was still in love with her. Janey, he guessed, would take Selden right down with her, which was what Victor Matrick must have seen as well. The only solution was to separate Selden from Janey—and to that end (and for other reasons as well), he certainly would never tell Selden about seeing the letter from Comstock. He sighed. Of course, there were other things he could have revealed about Janey, things that would have made the situation very clear. But he couldn't do that to Selden either. There was no point in kicking a man when he was already down, and Selden, he felt, couldn't sink any lower.

"Selden," George said. "You're looking for something that doesn't exist."

"I'm not sure about that, George."

"Girls like Janey Wilcox don't make good wives," George said.

Selden placed his cup on the glass table. "What do you mean by 'girls like Janey Wilcox'?" he asked tersely.

"Come on, Selden," George said gently. "You and I both know that there are women you marry . . . and women you don't. Janey Wilcox is one of the women you don't."

"Give me a good reason why," Selden said, pressing him. His voice, George noticed, was beginning to sound desperate. "I'm not trying to be an asshole," he said. "I'm just trying to understand."

"She wants something," George said. "That's apparent to everyone. She wants something, but nobody can figure out what it is. And I doubt she knows herself. And people who don't know what they want, don't make good partners. In business or anything else."

"Thanks, George," Selden said despondently.

Selden rose and George stood up as well. He felt sorry for the man, he thought, but he would get over it; people always did. Putting his arm around Selden's shoulder, he said encouragingly, "It's like cutting off your little finger. You want to do it quickly—don't keep sawing away at it with a steak knife. And once the finger's gone, you notice that you hardly needed it after all . . ."

"Right," Selden said. The two men shook hands.

"Come by the apartment next week for dinner," George said. "I'll have Mimi arrange it. Her assistant will give you a call . . ." And then Selden was gone.

George breathed a sigh of relief.

He walked to the window and looked out—at the same man Selden had seen. That guy had no life, George thought. He was in front of that computer all day every day, and George wondered idly what it was that he did.

He turned away and went back to his desk. He thought about Selden and felt slightly guilty.

But what was he to do? Tell the man that his wife had come to him for money for her crazy little "project," which was undoubtedly a scheme along the same lines as what she'd tried to pull off with Comstock Dibble? And then tell him what she'd done to try to get the money? He thought back to the pathetic show she'd put on that day in his office, when she had knelt down and given him a blow job. Naturally, he had accepted it—what man wouldn't?—after all, everyone knew a blow job wasn't *really* sex. But she was like so many of those women who tried to use sex to get what they thought they wanted. They actually believed that men were so stupid and so horny that they'd agree to just about anything—for the sole reason that a woman had the man's dick in her mouth.

He had done his bit, he thought: He had very properly thanked her afterward.

And that was all she was going to get from him.

Of course, he'd known that that afternoon wouldn't be the end of it; that eventually, she would come back for more. Women like her always did; they always thought that you owed them and that they could somehow threaten to make you pay.

And so he hadn't been surprised when she had suddenly appeared in his office about a week ago.

"George," she said, sitting down in the black Le Corbusier chair. She slid her fur coat off her shoulders, as if she intended to stay for a while. "I think you understand why I'm here."

"I think I do," he said, raising his eyebrows in a smirk. "Let me guess. You couldn't get enough of me."

"Don't even think about being an asshole, George," she snapped. "You may be able to get away with that with Mimi, but you can't with me."

"So Mimi has something to do with this."

"She has something to do with something," she said, mysteriously.

"I suppose you two aren't talking?" George asked.

"I'm not talking to *her*," Janey said, swinging her leg. Her leg, George noticed, was bare, although it couldn't have been more than thirty degrees out, and looked particularly attractive in its open-toed sandal.

"If you want me to put in a word . . ."

"I want money," she said bluntly, standing up.

"Everyone wants money," George said genially. "Can you tell me what you intend to do to earn it?"

"I've already earned it, George, you know that," she said, walking toward him. She reached his desk and put her palms on the surface, leaning toward him so that her entire breasts were nearly visible under the scoop neck of her sweater. "You got the idea to buy Comstock's company from me. Which means, in standard business practices, that you at least owe me a finder's fee."

He sat back in his chair and looked at her. Once again he was struck by the fact that she wasn't as stupid as she appeared—not by half. It was a shame, really: If she spent as much time applying herself to doing something worthwhile as she did to her scheming machinations, she might actually be able to get somewhere in life.

"You would be right about that, of course," he said, folding his hands under his chin. "If it had been a standard business deal. Meaning," he continued, raising his eyebrows, "that instead of coming to me for help with Comstock, you had shown me the letter and told me that you thought it might be a good opportunity for me to buy Comstock's company . . ."

"That doesn't make a bit of difference!"

"Oh, but it does," George said, nodding thoughtfully. "Our deal was of a very different nature. You asked me to do you a little favor—which I did. And in return, you did me a little favor. And that, my dear, is where our relationship begins . . . and ends."

"So you don't intend to do anything at all," Janey demanded.

"No," he said definitively. "I do not."

She had huffed and she'd puffed, muttering something about how he owed her, but he was finished with her. No, he'd thought, he wasn't inclined to do anything for her. She'd served her purpose, she'd been momentarily amusing, but now he must sever all connections with her. If he didn't, she would be back—again and again and again.

He had picked up his phone and asked his secretary to put his next call through, and he had spun his chair around and begun talking. And when he had spun it back again, she was gone.

And now, sitting at his desk and thinking about poor Selden, he hoped she was gone for good.

The elevator door opened on the floor of George's office, and Mimi Kilroy Paxton gasped in shock, completely taken aback by the sight of Selden Rose.

Her first thought was that she'd never seen a more desolate man. His face was shaven in uneven patches, as if he hadn't the concentration or the desire left to perform the most basic ablutions, and his physical attitude was that of a man who has slowly been beaten down in defeat, and aware that the death blow is about to be dealt, knows he no longer has the strength to ward it off. But it was his eyes that shocked her. His once lively brown eyes, which had always twinkled in boyish delight as if life held all kinds of pleasures, were now as dull as an old piece of cardboard that had been left outside and exposed to the elements.

He was staring straight at her, but his eyes were unseeing, and as the door opened, he made no move to get in, as if he were paralyzed.

"Selden!" she exclaimed.

At the sound of his name, her presence suddenly registered, and he took a step forward in greeting. "Hello, Mimi," he said.

She came out of the elevator and took his arm, drawing him down the hallway. "Selden," she said, in a voice full of concern. "Are you all right?"

"I'm as fine as a man can be in my circumstances, I suppose," he said resignedly.

"You must tell me about it," she said firmly. "After all, I feel like I'm at least partly responsible for your situation . . ."

"You, Mimi?" he asked, shaking his head. "You haven't done anything . . ."

"Oh, but I did," she insisted. "I introduced Janey to you in the first place . . . I told her to marry you . . ."

"You were only doing me a favor," Selden said. "I asked you to introduce me. Remember?"

"But what will you do?" Mimi said gently. She knew something of Selden's predicament from George, who had heard about it from some of the other executives at Splatch Verner; at this point, nearly every executive in the upper echelons of business had heard the rumor about Selden being asked to give up Janey, which was now being circulated as a morality tale as to the pitfalls of dangerous women . . .

"I'm at a loss," Selden said, shaking his head. "Everyone thinks she's guilty and she claims she's innocent."

"What does she say—exactly?" Mimi asked.

"She says she wrote a screenplay . . . and that somehow George is responsible. She says he ruined her . . ."

"Does she say why?" Mimi asked.

"Of course not. Nor can she explain the whereabouts of the missing screenplay. Probably because it's all a lie . . ." He looked pleadingly into Mimi's eyes. "And now everyone agrees that I should divorce her."

"Oh no, Selden, you can't do that," Mimi cried.

"Then I will lose my job," Selden said. "At this point, I'm beginning to think it's the only solution. I'm still in love with her, you know."

Mimi bit her lip. "Have you talked to George?" she asked.

"I've just been to see him. He was no help at all—but why should he be?" Selden said. "It's not his problem."

"Oh Selden," she cried. And in that moment, she made a decision. Despite her resolve not to, she had been thinking about Janey Wilcox almost constantly, and she had read about her terrible humiliation at Dingo's with a fearful heart. Janey, she felt, had been punished enough; if the punishment continued, it would be like putting someone in jail for a petty crime, from which they came out a hardened criminal, determined to have revenge on the system. She knew from experience how vengeful Janey could be, and she understood that the more people tried to squelch her, the more her resentments would grow. She might be forced to disappear for a while, but eventually she would reemerge—like some alien life form that has been frozen in the snow—only bigger and more powerful than before. And then, who knew what kind of havoc she might wreak?

No, Mimi decided, the very best thing for everyone concerned would be if life continued on as normally as possible. It would be a disaster if Selden divorced Janey, for what would she do then? She'd be desperate and angry . . . and Mimi suddenly saw that Selden and Janey had to stay together, and that they should buy a house in the suburbs of Connecticut. Away from the temptations of glamour, money, and fame, it was probable that Janey would become no threat to anyone; she would safely shrivel like an apple one leaves out in the sun for months and months and then paints a little face on.

"Selden," Mimi said, drawing him closer. "I don't know if Janey wrote a screenplay, but I do know that she was right about George. She went to him months ago, when she first started getting the letters, and asked for his help . . ."

Selden's face suddenly came to life; he looked like a dog that might bite. "So I've been deceived then," he said. "All this time, by my best friend . . ."

"Now, Selden," Mimi scolded. "You know it isn't like that. I'm sure George didn't tell you because he didn't want to upset you . . ."

"Thank you, Mimi," Selden said angrily. "I'm glad you finally had the decency to speak the truth."

Selden strode to the elevators with Mimi hurrying after him. "Selden, you needn't abandon us, you know," she said. And then, as the doors opened and he got in, she called after him encouragingly, "You're a good man, Selden. No matter what happens, always remember that you tried to do the noble and honorable thing . . ."

And then she went into George's office. She didn't mention her encounter with Selden, nor did she ever plan to. There were some things women knew that were best kept quiet, and so she patted George on the cheek and laughed at all his jokes and told him, once again, how wonderful he was. For she had already decided that if she had to deceive him, the very least she could do was to love him, and to be the best wife and mother she possibly could be.

So, she had told the truth, Selden Rose said to himself, as he looked up at the small black brick building before him. About one thing, anyway. And as that had turned out to be true, it was even possible that this screenplay she kept talking about existed as well.

He frowned, checking the number again on the painted black door. Could this possibly be the right address? he wondered. He might have gotten it wrong, but he had a good memory for numbers, and he was quite sure that this was the address he'd seen on the mail forwarded from her apartment.

124 East Sixty-seventh Street, Apartment 3A.

He looked back up at the building.

It was barely even a town house, with the entrance right at street level and next to a Chinese take-out place. It might have once been a town house, he supposed, but someone had long ago replaced the original façade with a flat front, from which two small windows peeped sadly from the narrow width of each of its four stories.

124 East Sixty-seventh Street was one of those New York addresses that sounds perfectly acceptable, but isn't. The building was located in a normally good block—between Park and Lexington Avenues—but Sixty-seventh Street fed into a thoroughfare that led through Central Park; it was notoriously noisy and filled with trucks. Looking up and down the block, Selden saw that the other buildings weren't much better—as if the landlords knew there was no point in improvement.

On the wall next to the door was a small metal box with eight buzzers. Next to 3A was a tiny piece of paper that read WILCOX in faded black Magic Marker. That wouldn't help him, he thought, as there was no one there. He searched for a buzzer marked SUPER, but not finding one began pressing all the buzzers, in the hope that someone would let him in. In a just a few seconds he heard the lock click in the door, and he pulled it open and went inside.

Directly ahead of him was a dark, narrow staircase, and to his left, a depressingly lit hall with squares of old black-and-white Formica on the floor. A middle-aged woman with a face dotted with mysterious-looking growths stuck her head out a door. "Yeah?" she demanded suspiciously.

"I'm looking for the super," Selden said, shifting his expensive black gloves from one hand to the other.

"Down the hall," the woman said, with a nod of her head. "If he's not there, he's probably in the Irish bar across the street."

The super, however, was home, and Selden explained that he was Janey Wilcox's husband, and needed to get into her apartment.

"Oh yeah," the super said. He was an old-looking man in a sagging undershirt who probably wasn't as aged as he appeared. "I remember your name from the papers. How is she doing anyway?"

"As well as can be expected," Selden said evenly.

"Well, tell her that she's got to make a decision about her apartment," the super said, handing him the keys. "She had that blond fellow living here, and he used to have some woman who came to visit him . . ."

"Janey?" Selden asked, startled.

"Noooo," the super said slowly. "She was an older gal. Maybe around forty. Anyway, he moved out and now the apartment's been sitting empty for months. The owner doesn't like empty apartments, even if they are still paying the rent . . ."

"I'll tell her," Selden said, taking the keys.

He started up the narrow staircase. Had she, Janey Wilcox, the beautiful Victoria's Secret model, really hiked up and down these dirty stairs several times a day? he wondered. Why on earth had she lived here? On the second-floor landing, he smelled the inevitable odor of bad cooking, and he wrinkled his nose in distaste, and then, on the final hike up to the third story, he saw that he was being accompanied by a large cockroach. He considered squishing it, but decided against it given its size: It would only leave a large gooey mess on the bottom of his shoe.

Her door had three locks on it, and as he fitted each key into the slot, he wondered again how she could have lived here.

And then, with a little laugh, he remembered why: She was cheap.

The door pushed open with an eerie squeak, and for a moment he hesitated, uncertain as to whether or not he really wanted to go in. The apartment smelled of garbage or of something left rotting in the refrigerator, and peering into the half-lit interior, "squalor" was the first word that came to mind.

But he had to enter, he reminded himself. He had to at least try to save her.

He stepped inside. Immediately to his left was a tiny kitchen with rusted appliances and a cabinet door hanging off its hinges. From the look of it, it appeared to have been in that condition for a while, as if she couldn't be bothered to fix it. To his right was a room about ten by fifteen feet, with a shallow fireplace, and at the opposite end was one window. To the right of the window was another door that opened into what could, roughly, be called a bedroom. It too contained one window, as well as a dresser, a bed on a small platform raised on stilts, and underneath, two rods for hanging clothes.

He had made it inside her apartment, but now, where to possibly begin?

Looking up, he spied a Burberry bag on top of the bed. It appeared new; curious, he reached up and took it down. Inside was a box, and inside the box was a pair of boots in the Burberry plaid. He looked back inside the bag and saw the receipt, and studying it, he found that the boots had been charged to his credit card and that Janey had signed his name, and that she had received a thirty percent discount. The date on the slip was December 8—the same day, he remembered, that she had bought the black pearls. He wondered at the significance of this—the date, the boots, and the fact that she had left them here—but he couldn't work it out, and so he moved on.

He went back into the living room. A small wooden desk of the type that students usually purchased at a place like the Door Store stood in front of the window. The top of the desk was mysteriously bare, but peering underneath, he found an almost brand-new Apple laptop computer sitting on top of a small pile of pink paper.

And he suddenly knew that he had found it.

He knelt down and lifted up the computer, extracting the papers from beneath. She was secretive, but not really one for hiding things well, he thought, remembering how easily he'd found Comstock's letter.

And then he thought, pink? Pink paper? For a screenplay? It was so innocently girlish.

And indeed, there, on the top page, were the words "TRADING UP?"; and underneath, "A Screenplay by Janey Wilcox."

He had found it! he thought, shaking with excitement. And then he remembered the time. Hastily pushing up his sleeve, he consulted his watch and saw that it was already 12:30. He had less than five hours . . .

But *no,* he thought joyfully, that wasn't true. Not anymore. Why, with this in his hands, he now had all the time in the world . . .

And plunking himself down on the faded red velvet couch, he turned over the title page and began reading . . .

Twenty minutes later he stopped, and leaning against the back of the couch, he put his hands over his face.

Oh, the darling, the absolute darling, he thought wildly. She was a wonder and a mystery—and yet so patently obvious. The "screenplay" was only thirty-three pages long and barely resembled the standard form—it was more a hodgepodge of notes for scenes with the occasional line or two of dialogue thrown in for good measure. But feeling as if he finally understood his wife, and remembering her high standards for "art," he wasn't surprised that she'd refused to show it to anyone: Nearly everything in her attempt was a pathetic cliché.

He turned back to the first page. The main character didn't even have a name— she was referred to only as The Girl. In the beginning of the story, The Girl was four years old and was in a ballet recital, playing a birthday candle on a cake, spinning around and around. Afterward, her father (whom The Girl loved more than anyone in the world) came up to her and hugged her, and then The Mother (she had no name either) grabbed The Girl's arm and pulled her away and yelled at her for getting her tutu dirty. Then it skipped ahead to when The Girl was ten. She was in the bathroom, trying on The Mother's lipstick, when The Mother burst in. She "snatched" the lipstick out of The Girl's hand.

THE MOTHER *(snarling)*

I just want you to know one thing! If your father and I get divorced, it's all your fault!

THE GIRL

No, Mama, please.

THE MOTHER

I'm going to lock you in your room. Until you learn to behave. Look at yourself. You look like a slut!

THE GIRL

I'll run away, Mama.

THE MOTHER

I wish you would. Do you know how much trouble you've caused in this family?

Selden smiled indulgently and skipped ahead.

Now this part, he thought, was slightly more interesting. The Girl was on an Arab's yacht—she'd been tricked into becoming some kind of sex slave by another girl, who she referred to as The So-called Girlfriend. Night after night, The Girl huddled in her cabin in terror, hearing the screams of The Russian Girl shouting "Nyet! Nyet!" as she was gang-raped by The Arab's henchmen. "It was then," he read, "that The Girl decided she had to survive. She *would* survive. She would figure out a way."

This was followed by a scene in which The Girl was sitting at a table, playing poker with the three Arab henchmen:

ARAB NUMBER ONE

I raise you a hundred.

THE GIRL

I'll double you. Two hundred to show.

ARAB NUMBER ONE

How did that happen!

THE GIRL

I win. Again.

Now where on earth had she come up with that? Selden wondered. Again, it was the kind of clichéd story that people liked to think was true—but nobody really believed. Although the part about The Girl playing poker to survive was a nice, original touch—a sort of new twist on Bluebeard—and it showed some real imagination . . .

But what difference did it make *what* she had written? he asked himself, gathering up the pages in glee. The only thing that mattered was that she'd tried—that she'd had the right intentions all along. And that she'd been telling the truth. She kept telling him that she'd written a screenplay, and he hadn't believed her . . .

He suddenly felt a crushing guilt.

But . . . he would make it up to her, he thought quickly. He would give her anything she wanted. Now that he had the pages in his hand everything was clear. She'd been right all along: She *had* been framed. Why had he doubted her? And rolling the pages into a tube, he slipped them into the breast pocket of his coat for safekeeping.

He hurried out of the apartment, the keys rattling in his hand. Thank God neither one of them would ever have to come back here, he thought. He would tell her to give up the apartment . . . Why, he would tell everybody everything. He would call Jerry Grabaw and let him know that *he had the screenplay* . . .

And then he would tell Victor Matrick. Turning the key in the lock, he thought about how good that would feel. He was suddenly reminded of Victor's terrible words—that Splatch Verner couldn't handle a girl like Janey Wilcox—and for once, Victor would have to admit that he was wrong. He would see that the opposite was true: Splatch Verner needed wives like Janey Wilcox, wives who were beautiful, smart, and talented. Under his tutelage, Janey would finish the screenplay—and hadn't he helped dozens of writers through the process before? And how much better it would make him look, when people understood that his wife was much more than a pretty face. Even his mother would be impressed . . .

But as he shoved the keys into his pocket, he paused. What if people still didn't believe him? What if they said that she had written the pages *after*—after the scandal broke in order to try to appear innocent?

It wasn't important, he thought firmly. And as he rushed down the stairs, he realized all that mattered was that *he* knew the truth, and knowing the truth, he didn't give a damn what other people thought.

Janey Wilcox stared at her reflection in the bathroom mirror.

She was both excited and nervous, and it always soothed her to see that she was still lovely, that her beauty was in full bloom and showed no signs of fading, despite the hardships of the past month.

But those hardships, she reassured herself, were finished—or would be, very soon. In twenty minutes, a car was arriving to take her to JFK, and then she would get on a plane, and a new life would begin . . .

Tearing herself away from the mirror, she reminded herself that she still had one or two little things to take care of before she left, and she hurried into the bedroom.

Four Louis Vuitton suitcases lay open and neatly packed on the bed, awaiting her final inspection. All that remained was the blue velvet box in which she stored the black pearl necklace she'd purchased in that brief time when she and Selden were in love—to which she'd now added her second most treasured possession: an invitation to the *Vanity Fair* Oscar party.

She went to the bureau and snapped open the lid on the blue velvet box. There it was, right on the very top—the most coveted invitation in the world. She took it out and lovingly ran her finger over the raised gold lettering that read *"Vanity Fair"* in the same famous typeface that appeared on the cover of the magazine every month, and then opened it up. On the top left-hand corner, her name, *"Janey Wilcox,"* was written in gold calligraphy, followed by a summons to join *Vanity Fair* for a seated dinner after the Academy Awards Ceremony at 9 P.M. sharp. Several hundred people were invited to the party afterward, but the invitation to the dinner was notoriously exclusive—strictly A-list movie stars, directors, and studio heads, with no press allowed until later, so the stars could fearlessly let down their hair.

Of course, she'd immediately seen that she must keep the invitation a secret and not tell anyone—especially not Selden or Jerry Grabaw or even Wendy Piccolo. And so she'd quietly made a few arrangements—and luckily, she'd remembered that she had the perfect dress to wear for the occasion: a long seventies-style halter-top gown by Roberto Cavalli that she'd bought in Milan on her honeymoon. She'd been saving the dress for some big spring party, but there wasn't anything bigger than the Oscars, and she would part her hair in the middle and wear it straight down her back. And naturally, she would wear the pearls as well . . .

Setting the invitation aside, she lifted the pearls out of the box. Why shouldn't she wear them now? she thought giddily. As a sort of celebration gesture . . . for good luck? As she lifted the pearls to her neck, her elbow brushed against the invitation and it fell to the floor.

She was about to bend over to pick it up when she heard the key turn in the lock. She froze. *What was Selden doing home?* she thought, in a sudden panic. Her plane left for Los Angeles at three, and she hadn't expected him before the usual hour of five or six, by which time she'd be airborne and probably over Chicago. But there was literally no time to think about it, because in the next second, he was bounding into the bedroom, grabbing her in his arms and kissing her face, and exclaiming, "My love, *my love,*" over and over again, like some two-bit actor in a cheesy film.

What the hell was she going to do *now?* she thought in horror.

"Selden. Selden darling," she said, struggling to match her tone to his while pushing him away. "What is it? What are you doing home?" In a moment, she thought, her heart thumping out of her chest in fear, he would see the suitcases, and then he would probably try to stop her . . .

"Don't you see?" he said, taking her by both shoulders and staring her in the face. His expression was ecstatic. "Everything is going to be okay now. It's all going to work out for us . . ."

"It is?" Janey asked nervously.

"I found the screenplay!" he shouted.

Her eyes opened wide in shock. She took a step back from him. "You did?"

"In your apartment," he said, fumbling with his coat. He withdrew a curl of pink pages and unfurled them on the bed. "It's barely a screenplay, but it proves that you tried—that you never for a minute thought you were taking that money for sex. Look, baby," he said, pointing to the top page. "You even made a title page . . . you called it *Trading Up?*; of course, you can't have a question mark in a title and you'd have to change it, but then you wrote all these little scenes, and sort of outlined what was going to happen between them . . ."

Janey felt faint. After she had written those pages two summers ago, she had closed her computer, unable to go on. It wasn't just that she'd felt the screenplay wasn't very good (which was embarrassing), but that she'd inevitably revealed the truth about her past . . .

"Selden," she gasped.

And then he looked up and noticed the suitcases on the bed.

"What are you doing?" he cried in consternation.

She suddenly found she could barely speak. "I'm . . . ," she faltered.

"But my darling, no!" he said, grasping her hands in comprehension. "You don't *have* to leave. Now that we have the screenplay, everything is going to be all right." He dropped her hands and began pacing the room. "I've been in this business for over twenty years, and I know when I spot talent. Oh, sure, it's full of clichés, but first drafts always are, and the stuff about the girl on the yacht is very inventive . . ."

"Selden, I *can't* . . . ," she cried.

"But you can, my darling," he said, holding out his hands. "Don't you understand? I'll help you. You'll write the first draft, and then we'll get someone to rewrite it. Naturally, Parador still has the rights, but now that George is in charge, it's easy. I'll get him to sign the rights over to MovieTime—and he owes me at least that much, the bastard . . ."

Janey took a step back in confusion, and Selden, seeing her expression, searched her face for an answer. "Ah, I understand," he said knowingly. "You're still angry at me because I didn't believe you. But it wasn't like that at all, my darling," he said plaintively. "I wanted to believe you about the screenplay, but I was so afraid that it wasn't true. I can understand how you must have felt, though . . . How you must have hated me. Just don't tell me that you've stopped loving me. Not now, now that we have a second chance . . ."

This couldn't be happening to her, Janey thought wildly. Not when she finally had a chance to *escape* . . .

"Baby, don't you see?" he asked. "We'd even give you a producer credit . . ."

She steadied herself against the dresser. If only he would go away . . . She couldn't *think* with him hovering over her. He was finally offering her everything she'd always wanted, but she was afraid . . . If she did finish the screenplay, what would happen if he figured out that it was all true? Would he subject her to the same hateful indignities she'd suffered in the last month? And in a subconscious cry of defense, she said, "No . . ."

He stiffened. "What do you mean?" he asked.

"I'm not sure," she said, grasping at the pearls in despair. If only she could tell him the truth, if only she could trust him . . . And then, the next words he spoke made everything horribly clear.

"I'm afraid there isn't a choice," he said coldly. "Two weeks ago, Victor Matrick told me I had to choose between you and my job . . . Naturally, I defended you—I told him that you *had* written a screenplay—but unless we go forward with this, the choice still stands. And I know you wouldn't want me to give up my job. Not when I've been working for over twenty years to get where I am today . . ."

Janey sucked in her breath. She felt the blood drain from her body; she thought she might vomit. And then her only thought was that she had to get away—she had to flee from this despicable creature who called himself her husband. She must force herself to move and to speak, she had to remain calm. She didn't know who this Selden Rose was (and, truthfully, had she ever really known?) and she wasn't sure of how far he might go.

In an unsteady voice, she said, "There's no need for you to make a choice. It's just that I have other plans . . ." She took a few steps to the bureau and rested her arm on top. She suddenly remembered that the invitation to the *Vanity Fair* party was at her feet—if only she could pick it up and put it in the velvet case without his noticing.

"Other plans," he said, pulling his head back in surprise like a turtle that senses danger. "What other plans?"

Janey brushed her hair back from her forehead. If she could keep him quiet, maybe even promise to return . . . "I just got the good news," she said evenly, unclasping the string of pearls from her neck and placing them in the box as if nothing were out of the ordinary. "My sister, Patty, is finally pregnant. She and Digger have taken a house in Malibu, and she wants me to join them right away." It was one of her typical half-lies, but she just might get away with it if Selden didn't get all excited and call her sister to congratulate her. And looking at his face, she saw that he did, indeed, appear to believe her . . .

"But that's ridiculous," he said, smiling tolerantly as he took a step toward her. "She's got months and months to be pregnant . . . You can go out there anytime. We'll *both* go . . . After we finish up this business . . ."

Her face hardened in frustration and he must have caught her expression, because his eyes suddenly narrowed and he said: "Unless . . ."

"Unless, what?" she asked, keeping her attention on the pearls.

"Unless you've got something else in mind?"

"What on earth else could I have in mind?" she asked, frowning at him in anger. And then, unable to help herself, her glance automatically went to the invitation at her feet.

He saw it as well, and before she could get to it, he leapt forward and snatched it up in his hand.

Without saying a word, he looked at the cover and then opened it.

At first, the expression on his face registered incomprehension, and he stared back and forth from the invitation to Janey in confusion. Her only thought was that she must get that invitation, for at the bottom was written, *"Please present this invitation at the door. No exceptions"*; and if he ripped it up or threw it out the window, she wouldn't have time to get another one, and then her whole life would be ruined. Her entire future lay in that invitation, and looking at him she suddenly hated him with the fury of a small child toward a bigger, bullying sibling. She wished he were dead—she would have liked to kill him . . .

"Give it back!" she screamed.

He took a step away from her, holding the invitation aloft between his thumb and forefinger as if he were exhibiting the murder weapon before a jury. "An invitation?" he said roughly.

"What do you care?"

"You'd choose a party over our marriage?" he shouted threateningly.

"Why not?" Janey cried. "You were ready to choose your job over me . . ."

For a moment, his eyes were wild with rage, and Janey let out a cry of fear, afraid of what he might do next. But then, as if he suddenly saw the truth in her words, his anger disappeared and he let out a heartbreaking moan of despair. He collapsed onto the edge of the bed like a puppet whose strings have suddenly been cut, his head sinking into his hands.

"An invitation," he groaned mournfully, shaking his head. "An invitation to a party. It was only ever about that . . ."

Janey just looked at him.

He raised his head and stared at her with damp eyes. "Everyone told me I should end it with you. But I didn't want to. I still loved you . . ."

"Liar," she hissed. And walking toward him, she held out her hand.

For a moment, he was confused. Was she making a conciliatory gesture? But then he saw that her eyes were on the invitation, that it was all she wanted from him now, and with a great, heaving sigh, he handed it to her.

She took it.

And with that gesture, he saw that he'd been completely wrong about her from the very beginning. She didn't love him; she probably never had. It was always about the next best thing for her, and he'd been but a stepping-stone on her journey. If she had loved him, she would have stayed with him . . . She would have helped him and done what he'd asked and finished the screenplay. It was a test and she had failed . . .

And something inside him began to fight back. His pride rose up from the depths of his despair—and his proud male vanity finally kicked in. It was true what everybody said about her then, he thought—she was a whore—and he was lucky to be rid of her. And at last, with the understanding and relief that his own self-respect was bigger than hers was, he said: "It's really over now, isn't it."

His words were a statement rather than a question, and there was something so definitive in his tone that Janey turned back. No matter how terrible a marriage might be, no matter what egregious acts two people might perform upon each other, the fact remains that they once declared publicly that they loved each other. Janey suddenly had a feeling of misgiving—as if now that he'd said it was over, she wasn't sure that was exactly what she wanted. For a second, she hesitated. Was it really too late? Should she go to him and rip up the invitation herself, throw her arms around him and tell him she was wrong?

But as her eyes traveled over his face, she was consumed by a feeling of suffocation. If she went to him, he would be all she had, and she knew that just he, alone, would never be enough. She would never be able to be her real self with him; he would always be judging her under the surface. He was pathetic and weak, he had nearly sold her out once, and certainly, he would do it again . . .

And in a voice that was so cold it chilled even herself, she said, "It was over a long time ago, Selden."

She carefully placed the invitation in her jewel case. Looking over her shoulder, she saw that he was still sitting there, staring into space, and she gave him a look of annoyed disgust. Now that it was really over, she wished he would leave so that she could finish her packing—couldn't he see that he was in the way?

She snapped the velvet box closed and walked to the bed, placing it inside her small, hard-sided Louis Vuitton carry-on. And as she did so, her eyes fell on the pink pages of her screenplay. In a moment of fury, she snatched them up, thinking that she might rip them in half.

But something stopped her. And pressing the pages flat, she placed them in the suitcase as well.

EIGHTEEN

"WHAT CAN I get you?" the stewardess asked, leaning across the seat. "Champagne? Orange juice? Or something else?"

Janey was about to say "champagne," but stopped herself. "Water please," she said.

Instead of scurrying off to fetch her drink, however, the stewardess leaned in conspiratorially. Lowering her voice to a whisper, she said, "I recognized you as soon as you came on board. And you don't have to worry . . . ," she said, glancing around as if photographers were about to jump out of the overhead compartments. "I'll make sure no one bothers you during the flight."

"Thank you," Janey said dismissively.

She buckled her seat belt and leaned her head back against the seat, exhaling a long sigh of relief.

She had just made the flight—the stewardess said she was the last one to board—and as she'd raced down the concourse, her big fear was that they might have given away her seat. But they hadn't, and first class wasn't nearly as full as she'd imagined it would be—she had the two seats next to the window to herself. The explanation must be that most of the people who were going to the Academy Awards were already in Los Angeles, in order to attend the pre-Oscar parties. But that was okay, she thought, she'd be there next year, when she had more time to plan. And this way, her arrival at the *Vanity Fair* party would be a complete surprise, and wouldn't jaws drop back in New York when they read the papers the next day . . .

"Here's your water," the stewardess said pleasantly, handing her a glass (and it was a real glass, too, she thought, because she was in first class) with the comforting logo of American Airlines etched on the side.

"Thank you," Janey said politely.

She took a sip of water and carefully placed the glass on the little tray in the armrest. She would have preferred champagne, but she couldn't take the chance of having her face swell up due to the combination of airtime and alcohol. She had to look absolutely stunning tomorrow night; she had to be a perfect beauty. Tomorrow night was her only chance now . . .

She took another sip of water and looked out the window at the men in orange uniforms loading the last pieces of luggage onto the plane. She should have had the champagne after all, she thought, especially as it was free. Or rather, she corrected herself, *especially* as she was paying for it.

She frowned and looked at her ticket, struck once again by the exorbitant fee for a one-way flight to Los Angeles: $5,000!

She would have flown business class to save $2,500, but she was too famous now. If someone on the plane reported back to the newspapers that she'd been seen in business, they would twitter with scorn.

Still, the cost of the ticket made her feel almost physically sick. Had she ever paid for her own plane ticket before? she wondered. This time she'd had no choice—while *Vanity Fair* had agreed to put her up at the Chateau Marmont for two nights, providing transportation to and from the airport and the party, they had refused to spring for airfare. She wouldn't have minded so much if it weren't for the fact that a week ago her Victoria's Secret contract had been cancelled . . .

"Ladies and gentlemen," the stewardess's voice said over the loudspeaker. "Captain has informed us that we've been cleared for departure. Please fasten your seat belts and turn your attention to the screen above you for some safety announcements."

Janey glanced briefly at the flickering screen and yawned involuntarily. As if, she thought, anyone didn't know how to fasten a seat belt . . .

And then she must have fallen asleep, because the next thing she knew, she suddenly jolted awake. And for a moment, she was uncertain as to her location . . .

And then she remembered: plane, Los Angeles, *Vanity Fair* Oscar party. She looked at her watch—four hours had passed! How had that happened? She usually could never sleep on a plane, but the last few weeks must have completely exhausted her.

Her throat was parched, and leaning across the aisle seat, she waved to the stewardess.

"Ah, you're awake now," the stewardess said, clucking over her like a mother hen. "You've missed the meal . . . I thought about waking you but I didn't want to disturb you. Would you like something now? Cheese and biscuits perhaps, and maybe some red wine?"

"Just water, please," Janey croaked.

And then, as the stewardess was handing her a bottle of Evian water and a glass, she heard the sound of a familiar male voice, coming from a few seats in front of her. "I want *Erin Brockovich*," the voice demanded childishly—and Janey was suddenly struck by the incongruity of a man's voice coupled with a child's petulance. It was really, she thought, incredibly unattractive.

"I'm sorry, sir," the stewardess was saying, leaning over him. "But we only have three videocassettes and I'm afraid they're all taken."

"Well, search the plane!" the voice scolded, as if unable to comprehend why she hadn't done this yet.

"I'm sorry, sir, but other passengers . . ."

"Tell one of them to give it back. Tell them it's for *me*."

The stewardess sighed, and walked briskly to the back of first class, rolling her eyes in a huff. When she'd passed by, Janey rose slightly and peered over the top of her seat to the second row in front of her. Yes, she thought, she was right. She would recognize the top of that head with the three red hairs poking out anywhere: It was Comstock Dibble.

She sat back in her seat with a plop. Well! she thought. That was interesting. He must be on his way to the Oscars, and undoubtedly he'd be at the *Vanity Fair* party afterward. It would take a lot more than paying women for sex and doctoring a few screenplays for him to be excluded from the party. He was a man, after all, and men in Hollywood could get away with anything . . .

He was even, she guessed, demanding *Erin Brockovich* to refresh his memory so that he would have something to talk about with Julia Roberts!

"Ladies and gentlemen," the captain's voice came over the loudspeaker. "We're now flying over the Grand Canyon. And if you look to your right, you'll see an amazing sunset . . ."

Janey was on the left side of the plane, so naturally, she couldn't see it, she thought with some annoyance. She looked out the window anyway, but all she saw was a long stretch of red sand.

And then she heard, "Janey? Janey Wilcox?"

Oh Lord. What now? Janey thought. She turned and looked at the woman standing in the aisle next to her. The woman had somewhat the appearance of a transvestite, with a square mannish jaw and broad shoulders, coupled with excessively bleached hair and unnecessarily long red acrylic nails. "Don't you remember me?" the woman rasped. Her voice sounded like she'd been up all night, drinking whiskey and smoking cigarettes.

"Ah, Dodo," Janey said, nodding coolly.

"Well!" Dodo exclaimed. "I have to say that I never expected to see you on this plane!"

Janey lifted her glass to her lips and gave Dodo a stiff smile. "Why shouldn't I be on this plane?" she asked.

"I'm not saying you shouldn't be," Dodo said quickly, as if to cover up the implied insult. "Are you going to the Oscars?"

"Of course," Janey said evenly. "Are you?"

"I'm covering it," Dodo said, rolling her eyes. "But it's such a pain—the network is making cutbacks, and they've eliminated first class from the budget. Which means that everyone, including the talking heads, has to fly business . . ."

"What a shame," Janey said. Dodo, she thought, was such a bore. And in an effort to get rid of her, she said, "Well, I suppose I might see you at the *Vanity Fair* party then . . ."

"Oh!" Dodo said, raising her eyebrows. "Are you going to that, too?"

"Naturally," Janey said. "I've been invited to the dinner."

"Have you?" Dodo gasped. And then, as if this was too much to bear, she excused herself to go to the bathroom.

Business class passengers were expressly forbidden to use the first class toilets, and for a second, Janey thought about tattling to the stewardess about Dodo. But the fact that *she* was going to the *Vanity Fair* dinner and Dodo wasn't, combined with the reality that Dodo now knew about it, was, she felt, penalty enough.

In the first class bathroom, Dodo squatted over the toilet while she dissected this information. How was it, she wondered, that that little tart Janey Wilcox was invited to the *Vanity Fair* Oscar dinner and not she? For years, she'd been trying to get into that dinner, only to be told each time that it was "not a possibility this year," but that perhaps she should "try again next year," the implication being "when she was more famous."

Life was so unfair! Dodo thought, extracting a long length of toilet paper with which to blow her continually runny nose. It just went to show you that hard work really didn't pay off . . .

And then Dodo suddenly figured out the answer and nearly laughed out loud with glee. She had a friend who had worked at *Vanity Fair*—a reporter named Toby Young—who had once told her that every year the editors invited the woman they'd dubbed "Bimbo of the Year" to the party. And obviously, this year Janey was "it."

She couldn't wait to get off the plane and call Mark, she thought, dropping the hunk of toilet paper into the tank. Mark would think it was hilarious, and what a good laugh they'd have about it with all of their friends. Janey Wilcox, the Model Prostitute . . . and now Bimbo of the Year . . .

But then she had another thought: Even if Janey *was* the Bimbo of the Year, the very fact that she was at the *Vanity Fair* dinner would give her a kind of reverse cachet. It might, indeed, become very chic to "know her." And it was possible that it would be cooler and more interesting to remark, "Janey Wilcox is a good friend of mine, and actually, she's a nice girl," when people mentioned her name instead of rolling your eyes in disgust.

And with this in mind, Dodo left the bathroom, determined to "make friends."

"Janey . . . ," she rasped.

Janey looked up in annoyance, as if she couldn't believe that Dodo was back.

"Do you mind if I sit down?" Dodo asked, giving the Louis Vuitton carry-on, which Janey had placed on the seat next to her in order to avoid this possibility, a meaningful look.

"I'm a bit tired, but . . . ," Janey said, removing the suitcase and placing it under the seat in front of her. Dodo, she could see, was determined.

"Thanks," Dodo said, sitting down. "Anyway," Dodo continued, as if they'd been in the middle of a long conversation, "I have to tell you that I *really* admire you. I thought I was strong, but you must have the constitution of a horse. If people were saying those things about me . . . ," she laughed. "Well, they probably do say those things about me, just not in public. I mean," she said, leaning so close that Janey could smell her boozy breath, "if they're going to make a big deal out of it every time a girl gives a guy a blow job . . . they're won't be any room for real news, will there?"

Dodo laughed uproariously at her own joke, as two other first class passengers turned around and stared.

"Oh, mind your own business!" Dodo snapped, sotto voce.

Janey winced. It was a mistake to have allowed Dodo to sit down. Dodo wasn't at all the sort of person she should be seen talking to, especially not now . . .

And then Dodo said something that caught her attention.

"I say it's a travesty, what Selden Rose did to you."

"Excuse me?" Janey said.

"You know," Dodo said, frowning in outrage. "It's despicable, really."

Janey gasped—did the whole world know everything about her?

"You're certainly being brave," Dodo said, shaking her head in wonder. "I told Mark that if he ever considered doing something like that to me, I would literally kill him. Or I would hire someone else to kill him . . ."

Janey felt an unpleasant tingling sensation course through her body. "Mark?" she asked.

"Well, Mark did tell me," Dodo said with chagrin. "Although there was no reason why he shouldn't—I mean, practically everyone at Splatch Verner knows about it . . ."

Janey heard alarm bells going off in her head.

"It's disgusting that a company should be allowed to force a man to make a decision like that," Dodo said. "It certainly says something about the state of American business these days . . . I say you're well rid of him, and that's exactly what I told Mark," Dodo concluded with a sympathetic smile.

Janey sat back in her seat, stunned. "Really, Dodo," she said. "It didn't happen that way at all. He begged me to stay . . ."

"Well, however it happened, I hope you take the bastard for everything he's worth!" Dodo said fiercely.

"Oh, yes," Janey said, nodding. If only Dodo would go away . . . She had to get her thoughts together . . .

The stewardess passed by and Janey gave her an imploring look. She nodded in understanding and leaned over to Dodo. "Excuse me, ma'am," she said, "but unless you're in first class, I'll have to ask you to go back to your seat. We'll be landing soon . . ."

Dodo got up, and, giving the stewardess a dirty look, disappeared behind the blue curtain that separated business from first class.

Goddammit! Janey thought angrily. Why had she let Dodo sit down? As soon as they landed, Dodo would start spreading the story all over New York *and* Los Angeles, with the added fillip that she had actually talked to Janey on the plane. And once again, the story wouldn't be accurate—as far as she was concerned, she had rejected Selden, not vice versa. But now that she had left New York, naturally, everyone would think Selden had dumped her for his job, and how would that make her look? There were people who treated their dogs with more respect . . .

It was only, she thought bitterly, yet *another* misperception she was going to have to correct . . .

At least she was in a position to do something about it, she thought—she would start right away, tomorrow night, at the *Vanity Fair* party. And pulling her suitcase out, she placed it on the seat next to her and snapped open the lock.

There, on the very top, was the blue velvet box, and as if to reassure herself that it was all going to be fine, she opened the case and took out the invitation.

The edges were as sharp as ever; it was still in perfect condition. When the party was over, she would hang on to it, she thought, she would keep it forever and ever. For wasn't it her lucky charm?

The invitation had arrived, as if by divine intervention, at the end of that day when she'd been in the depths of despair. That morning, the headline in the *New*

York Post had screamed: "MODEL PROSTITUTE GETS DUMPED," and had gone on to outline the fact that her Victoria's Secret contract was not going to be renewed; she'd been traded in for a younger (and presumably less controversial) prototype: a wholesome, twenty-two-year-old girl from the midwest. But what had been particularly irritating was the line from her spokesperson, Jerry Grabaw.

"Janey loved working with Victoria's Secret, but feels like it's time to move on to other projects," he'd said. Adding, "Janey Wilcox is a survivor."

She'd guessed all along that her contract wouldn't be renewed, and she was almost fine with it until she had come up against that one word: "Survivor." How she hated that word! "Survivor" implied someone who had to claw and dig her way to the top, someone who could barely make it. And that was completely different from the way she had always percieved herself, ever since she'd made it off Rasheed's yacht. She was a winner, not a survivor, and they were two entirely different things.

A winner implied a person to whom things came naturally. There was a reason, she thought, why everybody wanted to know a winner, while on the other hand, nobody necessarily wanted to know a survivor . . .

And the word had put her in such a snit that she'd actually gone down to George's office to have it out with him.

The meeting hadn't gone exactly as she'd planned, but what else had she been expecting? George liked to pretend that he was all-powerful, but when it came right down to it, he was useless—as completely useless as Selden. She should have figured that out on the day she'd given him the blow job. Why, he was practically impotent; it had taken her a good ten minutes to bring his flaccid penis to something even resembling an erection . . .

And then, in total dejection, she'd returned home. And as she'd sat, drinking vodka, she'd been so low that she'd actually thought maybe she should consider suicide . . . And then the buzzer had rung from downstairs . . .

The invitation was hand-delivered by special courier straight from the offices of the editor in chief of *Vanity Fair* himself, and while it had arrived somewhat out of the blue, she hadn't really been surprised. She'd known all along that something big would happen, that something would come along to jettison her out of this mess— after all, hadn't her life always worked that way? Although for one brief moment, after she ripped open the envelope and saw the contents, she *had* wondered why she'd been singled out for this particular honor when half of New York, it seemed, was ashamed to be seen with her. And then, of course, she'd immediately understood: The editors at *Vanity Fair* knew she was a star; they were probably even planning a big story about her, and there was a very good chance that they'd put her on the cover. And why not? she'd thought. By now it should be obvious to *everyone* that people were dying to read about her . . .

And suddenly that afternoon, the world had righted itself again. And every-thing would have been fine, she thought, leaning back against the seat, if it weren't for the debacle with Selden.

She knew that the pain of the breakup would at some point hit her full force, but in the meantime, she couldn't be weak and give in to her feelings. There would be plenty of time to cry later (wasn't there always), but now, somehow, she had to spin the story about Selden to her advantage.

She sighed and stared out the window. A host of possibilities raced through her head, but suddenly, she realized that *maybe she didn't have to lie at all.* Hadn't she just seen the effect of the story on Dodo Blanchette? Dodo had been outraged at Selden's treachery, and if *she* was, chances were others would be as well. She would tell people that Selden Rose was the only man she had ever loved, and she couldn't believe what he had done to her. She would claim to be completely distraught, and why not? she thought smugly. After all, there was nothing men fell harder for than that old story of a beautiful woman who'd been wrongly accused . . .

And on top of it, she thought, glancing at her suitcase, she now had the screen-play to prove it. Well, sort of, anyway. The contents made it too explosive to show anyone—every time she thought about it she cringed with shame. Which was too bad, especially since Selden had genuinely seemed to think it had merit. But wasn't it just her luck, she thought bitterly, that the one thing she had that could save her she couldn't use . . .

In front of her she heard Comstock Dibble complaining to the stewardess that his champagne was flat, and suddenly she had a frightening thought. Did she dare? she thought wildly, her heart thumping in her chest. But why not? Wasn't it exactly what she'd thought in Paris that day, before she'd found out about the story in the *Post*? That if you spent your whole life trying to get over your past, you couldn't have a future?

She bit her finger. Was she really going to spend the rest of her life trying to cover up a youthful mistake? It wasn't like pretending it hadn't happened had helped: After all, she didn't have everything she wanted, and if she was really hon-est with herself, she didn't have anything at all. Once again, she was back in the same place she always seemed to end up—with no job, no money (except for what she'd saved in the bank), and no man—and having to defend her reputation with only her beauty to save her . . .

She shuddered. In three months, she'd be thirty-four, in a few years, forty. What if her life continued on and on in the same pattern? What if she ended up being one of those women who never really get anywhere, who end up at forty with no relationship and no career? She had seen those women at parties, laughing too hard and wearing clothing only twenty-five-year-olds should wear, and meanwhile, even a pustule like Comstock Dibble wouldn't give them a second glance . . .

No! she nearly cried aloud. She wouldn't end up like that—she must take a chance. For wasn't that what she'd really denied herself—a chance? Hadn't she always taken the easy route because she was frightened—scared that she wouldn't be good enough or wasn't what she believed she really was? Fear had led her to Selden; fear had led her to George and the mess she was in. Did it really matter if people knew about her past? She'd already been publicly labeled a prostitute—what else could life do to her? And hadn't she survived . . . ?

Ugh, she thought. There it was again, that word "survivor." But maybe it wasn't so bad. Maybe, in order to become a winner, you had to be a survivor first . . .

And standing up, she walked to the front of the plane.

"Hello, Comstock," she said smoothly, as if nothing at all had happened between them.

He looked up and frowned, disturbed by the interruption, and then, when he saw who it was, his eyes hardened like two cold stones.

"What do you want?" he asked.

She leaned across the seat. "Don't you think it would be better for both of us if we were seen talking?"

He was about to protest, but then a lascivious gleam came into his eyes. He patted the seat next to him. "What do you want to talk about?" he asked.

"My screenplay," she said, handing him the pages.

NINETEEN

ON THE NIGHT of the Academy Awards, a huge orange moon hung over the city of Los Angeles like a gold medallion, and as usual, the press faithfully reported that its luminescence was no competition for the human stars below. To the public, Oscar night is a glamorous swirl of seemingly heroic achievements accomplished by humans more beautiful and blessed, but to the denizens of the tight little world that composes Hollywood, it's also an evening of a hundred little intrigues and slights, petty connivances and novelettish manipulations. At 9 P.M. West Coast time, the last golden statuette has been handed out, but the fun is just beginning.

Tanner Cole, the movie star, looked out of the tinted window of his limousine and frowned. Ahead of his car was a line of at least twelve other stretch limos, all angling to deposit their famous passengers in front of the narrow awning that had been set up in the parking lot of Morton's restaurant, the site of the annual *Vanity Fair* Oscar party. "Oh man," he said out loud. As he'd told dozens of reporters over the years, he loved everything about being a movie star, he loved everything about this night, he even loved everything about this party. Except for the line of limousines. He hated waiting. It really was possible to have too many famous people in one place.

He extracted a chaw of tobacco from a silver pill box and placed it between his gum and lip. The problem, he thought, was the goddamned press line. Every star had to get their picture taken, and if there was another big star in front of them, they would wait in their car so as not to have their thunder stolen. It was all such a goddamned bore, he thought with annoyance, and to him, a sign that these "stars" weren't real actors. Real actors didn't care about press lines. Real actors knew that press lines weren't part of "the work," and for real actors "the work" was the only thing that mattered.

He pressed the button to open the window, and spat out a large, gooey green mass of tobacco. Tanner Cole, who had attended the Yale School of Drama twenty years ago, considered himself an intellectual, and, although he would only admit it to his closest friends, far above the grasping, petty, vulgar machinations of Hollywood. However, he wasn't above pointing out to reporters that his friends included real people, like Craig Edgers, who was, at that moment, staying with him in his mansion high in the Hollywood Hills. Four hours earlier, he had left Craig in the hot tub, sipping a glass of iced green tea.

Every year, Tanner Cole hosted what had now become a famous after-party following the *Vanity Fair* Oscar party, and this year, Tanner had managed to lure Craig Edgers out for it. He didn't know the whole story, but apparently Craig was having some trouble with the screenplay for *The Embarrassments*, and Tanner had promised to help him by introducing him to some people. Naturally, Tanner loved the book (hell, he thought, he "loved" everything), so who could blame him for wanting to play the lead . . .

The limousine came to a stop, and he squinted out the window again. There were still at least six cars ahead . . . What the fuck, he thought. He didn't have to wait. He could get out and walk. He wasn't one of those pansy celebrities who was so lame they needed someone to wipe their ass . . . And touching the intercom button that connected him with the driver, he said, "Yo, Kemosabe, stop the car. I'm gonna walk."

The driver frowned into the rearview mirror. "Are you sure, Mr. Cole?" he asked. "It might not be safe."

"I spent the last year shooting a movie in northern China," Tanner snapped. "I think I can handle the entrance to a fucking restaurant in Los Angeles . . ."

The car pulled over and Tanner got out, slamming the door behind him.

About four cars ahead, the actress Jenny Cadine sat enveloped in a haze of thick putrid smoke from Comstock Dibble's cigar. "Comstock, please," she said, coughing pointedly and waving her hand in front of her face. "If I'd known you were going to smoke, I never would have agreed to come with you . . ."

Comstock Dibble laughed meanly. His tuxedo was stretched tightly across his barrel chest, while, as usual, his pants felt like they were hanging below his belly. He'd squandered $5,000 on a custom-made tuxedo, but there didn't seem to be a tailor in the world who could get his proportions right, no matter how much money he spent. He unbuttoned the front of his jacket, and, to satisfy Jenny Cadine while making it clear that she wasn't more important than his cigar, he opened his window a crack.

Jenny Cadine sighed. "Thank you," she said, with an edgy smile. She wasn't in the best of moods, having just lost the Oscar to Julia Roberts. She shifted in her seat, feeling the full taffeta skirt of her dress crinkle beneath her. Why on earth had she allowed her stylist to convince her to wear a new, young designer? she wondered furiously. On top of missing out on the Oscar, her dress, which resembled a ball gown from the 1950s, was all wrong and tomorrow the papers would probably claim that she looked like a big, pink marshmallow . . .

She glared at Comstock's cigar, which he had somehow managed to position in front of her face, and expelled an annoyed breath of air. "About that part . . . ," she began.

Comstock smiled and tapped the ash from his cigar onto the floor. "It's a good one," he said. He might have been out of place on Park Avenue in New York City, but in Hollywood, he was completely at home. "It's potential Oscar material . . ."

"If you're talking to me about it, it had better be," Jenny said crossly.

Comstock laughed again. "I'm not sure that I am," he said. "Talking to you, that is."

Jenny rolled her eyes. She hated this part of her job, but there was no way around it. Even as a former Oscar-winning movie star, she had to fight to get the very best parts—she had seen too many actors' careers go down the drain when they'd made the wrong choices. And so, when her agent had called her that afternoon to inform her that the whole town was abuzz with this new Comstock Dibble project, they'd agreed that she should try to get Comstock alone. So after the Oscar ceremony, she had simply pretended that she couldn't find her car.

"Come on, Comstock," she said, changing her tone. "You know you're going to talk to me about it sooner or later."

"Am I?" Comstock asked, exhaling a large puff of cigar smoke. For the first time in weeks, he was enjoying himself. There was nothing he loved more than torturing actresses—especially one as full of herself as Jenny Cadine—and on top of it, he had the hottest property in town. He was, as he liked to say to himself, "back," and there wasn't a thing Jenny Cadine or anyone else could do about it.

Early that morning, drinking coffee and dressed in a tiny pair of red silk boxer shorts, Comstock had sat in his suite at the Four Seasons Hotel, reading Janey Wilcox's "script." When he had finished, his immediate thought was what a dummy she was not to have given it to him in the first place. But his second thought was that he knew exactly what to do with the material—it was the kind of story at which he excelled. It would be a modern-day classic—a tale of excess, of how a beautiful young woman lost her innocence through her greed. Naturally, she would have to fall, but then she would be redeemed—and wasn't that the great human story? Sin and salvation, over and over again, and it was his story as well . . .

And now, sitting in the limousine with Jenny Cadine, he congratulated himself on having saved himself once again. The trick was to simply throw another golden ball into the air, to distract everyone's attention. And then, taken with his own genius, he applauded himself for having signed Janey Wilcox up to do the screenplay in the first place. Hadn't he known that she had something "special" all along? He would be sure to let everyone know, so they'd understand the depth of his brilliance in having taken a chance on an unknown . . .

But he mustn't get ahead of himself, he thought, and taking a puff on his cigar, he stared at Jenny Cadine (who was certainly not looking her best that night) and asked casually, "How much do you know about the project?"

Jenny Cadine wasn't a particularly intelligent person (nearly every thought in her head had been placed there by her clever agents and managers), but this, she knew, was a cue to make an attempt at flattery. "Only that it's supposed to be genius," she said sulkily.

"It's the Janey Wilcox story," Comstock said, wondering what her reaction would be given that incident at Dingo's. As he expected, Jenny lived in such a tiny, insular world that the name hardly rang a bell. She frowned and bit her lip. "Wasn't she some kind of feminist?"

"You could say that," Comstock laughed, patting her leg. Jenny Cadine would make a perfect Janey Wilcox, he thought, if only she were ten years younger. It was such a shame that people had to get old . . .

"Comstock, really," Jenny gasped, as if she were about to expire from the smoke. "Could you please put out that cigar? You're killing us both . . ."

Comstock smiled and deliberately exhaled a noxious puff in her direction. "On the contrary, my dear," he chortled. "Smoke is a preservative . . ."

And in a limousine two cars ahead, Janey Wilcox looked down at her left hand and let out a little cry of horror.

She was still wearing her wedding and engagement rings.

Quickly twisting them off, she was about to slip them into her small silver Prada evening bag when she hesitated, holding the rings in the palm of her right hand. She was suddenly hit with a terrifying wave of remorse. If only Selden were there to see her, she thought, to see her in her big moment of triumph . . .

Looking down at her rings inevitably brought back that moment, just seven months ago, when she had stood under the hot white Tuscan sun, staring into the eyes of the man who was about to become her husband. She had been convinced that she was in love, but once again, love had let her down, and instead, she was alone . . .

Life wasn't supposed to be this way, she thought wildly. When something good finally happened, weren't you supposed to share it with someone? And she had no one, not even a friend . . . And sitting by herself in the vast black leather interior of the limousine, she very nearly felt like . . . *crying*.

But she mustn't do that, she scolded herself. Not when the makeup artist had spent two hours doing her face (and Janey had had to pay for that herself too, $500 because it was Oscar night), and she was about to attend the most important party of her life. Staring down at the rings in her hand, she felt regret mingle with excitement. New beginnings were always painful, and she was quite sure that this evening would change her life . . .

And what were those rings anyway, but a sign of bondage? She should fling them out the window, she thought dramatically, but the thought of possible future penury stopped her. The engagement ring alone had cost $40,000; what she should do was sell it . . .

And coldly dropping the rings into her bag, she removed her compact and studied her face.

It was one of those evenings when Janey was looking her very best. She was always technically beautiful, but on this particular night it was as if her beauty had a life of its own. Knowing that it was going to be called on to work its magic, it had made that extra effort, and this evening, she glowed as if lit from within. Her hair was sleek and shiny, and her teeth, set off against a new red lipstick she had found, appeared startlingly white.

She looked at her face with satisfaction, and then, snapping her compact shut, reminded herself that her beauty was not her only asset.

At about eleven o'clock that morning, she'd received a phone call from Comstock Dibble informing her that he wanted to turn her "script" into a movie. Two summers ago, when she'd started writing the screenplay, a phone call like that would have made her scream with joy, for that summer, when she'd had no money and no job, selling a screenplay was nearly more bounty than she could have imagined. But quite a bit had happened to her since then, and she'd certainly learned not to set her sights so low. Even a year ago, she would have been thrilled to have her movie made and would have allowed Comstock to do whatever he wanted with the project. But she was a little smarter now, and she didn't think she'd give up control that easily. She intended to get as much as possible for herself out of the project, and at the very least, she intended to become a producer . . .

But naturally, she hadn't told Comstock that, she thought smugly. His very first question was why hadn't she shown it to him before, and while she hadn't been able to give him an answer—the thought of explaining her feelings about those two months on Rasheed's boat nearly rendered her speechless—a flash of insight told her that if she *had* given it to him earlier, she wouldn't have been in the position she was in now. Even last summer she would have been nothing more than a pretty girl with a few scribblings on pink paper, but now, she was famous and everybody knew about her. And instinct told her that if Comstock Dibble was interested in her project, chances were, others might be as well . . .

The car moved forward to the entrance, and the driver opened his window, handing her invitation to a burly security guard. The guard shone a flashlight into the window and then the driver got out and opened her door.

She took a deep breath and stepped out.

And suddenly, starting up the red carpet under a flowered awning that led into the restaurant, she was barraged by a screaming, sweating, pulsating mass of humanity, shouting at her to look this way or that, to stop, to turn, to look over her shoulder, and elbowing one another to get a better angle, the photographers broke out from behind their barricades as several security guards rushed in to restrain them. At these kinds of events, there is always one person the photographers desperately want to photograph, because they know they can sell the picture to newspapers and magazines all over the world. That night, Julia Roberts, having won the Oscar, was number one, but Janey Wilcox was a close second. In the minds of the paparazzi, Janey Wilcox might not have been an actual movie star, but she was just as famous and more notorious, and all afternoon rumors had been flying that she had written an explosive screenplay and that Comstock Dibble was going to produce it, and that everything that had been written about her in the press was untrue.

Tanner Cole arrived at the entrance just as the commotion reached its peak. He frowned in consternation, wondering who could possibly be causing such a fuss. It was too early for Julia Roberts, and even the arrival of Pamela Anderson with Elizabeth Hurley the year before hadn't spawned this kind of frenzy. Was there some new actress in Hollywood that he didn't know about? As he stood there wondering, a security guard dragged the photographer from *People* magazine past him. "We love you, Janey," the photographer, who was a blond woman in her thirties, cried out.

"Who's that girl?" Tanner asked her.

"Tanner! Let me get a picture," the photographer shouted.

The guard put his hand up to stop her. "I told you. You're through for the night."

Tanner shrugged like it couldn't be helped.

The guards broke up the crowd and Tanner went inside.

"Who's that girl?" he asked Rupert Jackson several minutes later. The mystery girl was now in a cluster of Hollywood heavy-hitters, including the editor in chief of *Vanity Fair* magazine and the head of American Pictures. She was, Tanner thought, absolutely dazzling, with that long, straight, blond hair and those perfectly shaped breasts (obviously fake, but so what), outlined under that seventies-style halter dress. She was old enough to appear interesting and young enough to still be enticing, and Tanner Cole considered her the most beautiful woman in the room.

But it was her eyes that were really remarkable, he thought. In that moment before, when he had handed her her purse and their eyes had met, they had glittered like sapphires under long dark lashes, but it was their expression he found most arresting. Being an actor, he liked to think that he could see into the souls of his fellow human beings, and he was convinced he saw genuine sadness there . . .

"You really have been away for too long," Rupert Jackson giggled. "That's Janey Wilcox, the famous model-prostitute."

"What?" Tanner asked in shock. For a second, he felt like punching Rupert. "A real prostitute?" he asked.

"You're as dumb as a stick," Rupert scolded. "Obviously you ate too many chicken feet from craft services while you were in China. I daresay she's no more real prostitute than either you or I."

"Speak for yourself, Kemosabe," Tanner snapped. "How come no one told me about this chick before?"

"You're disgusting," Rupert said.

"Bring her to the after-party, will you?" Tanner asked. He wanted to make a play for the stunning Janey Wilcox, but he had no intention of doing it here, in front of this crowd. He was vigilant about maintaining his privacy.

Rupert scurried off to do Tanner's bidding. He always did everything Tanner wanted. He was in love with him—and as a reward, Tanner occasionally allowed Rupert to give him a blow job.

Janey Wilcox stood in the middle of the small crowd, nodding.

To the casual observer, she appeared perfectly in control, with her lips relaxed into a pleasant smile and her attention focused on the head of American Pictures—a woman in her mid-forties named Candi Clemens—who was in the middle of telling a story about her three-year-old child's last birthday party. But inside, a dozen thoughts and emotions were tumbling through her brain like dice in a cup . . .

She'd known she would be photographed, but she hadn't been prepared for such a frenzy, nor for the outpouring of affection. Just two weeks ago, she'd been a pariah and an object of ridicule to the photographers, but now, it seemed, everyone somehow knew that she had written a screenplay, and how satisfying it was to see that what she'd guessed would happen all along was finally coming true. She'd had to be escorted into the party by two security guards, and in the commotion she had somehow dropped her purse . . .

For a moment, it lay on the floor forgotten as she stared around the room in awe. The restaurant had been transformed into a glittering silver palace, the effect being that of having stepped through a mirror into a fantasy world on the other side. The floor was strewn with silver sequins; sprayed silver roses adorned Greek columns and silver cherubs decorated the ceiling and walls. And then a man mate-rialized at her side. He picked up her bag, and as he handed it to her, she swore she heard him mutter the word "charming," under his breath. Their eyes met and she nearly swooned when she saw who it was—Tanner Cole, the movie star.

"Thank you," she whispered.

"No problem," he said with a cool smile. He moved away, and as she watched him walk to the bar, she decided that if this were high school, he would be the star quarterback, and that somehow, by the end of the evening, she would have him . . . But then she saw him join Rupert Jackson at the bar. With a little smile, she was reminded of that first party at Mimi's, and wondering if Tanner Cole was secretly gay as well, she vowed not to make the same mistake. If only Bill Westacott were there to guide her, she thought wryly. Bill! She hadn't thought about him for months and months, and it was entirely possible that he might be in Los Angeles. She made a mental note to track Bill down tomorrow—if she was going to stay in Los Angeles (and she was beginning to think she might), she would need allies . . .

But she didn't have another second to think about it, because as soon as she took a step forward into the room, she was practically surrounded by a small cluster of well-wishers. Included in the group was the editor in chief of *Vanity Fair* himself, as well as Candi Clemens, the head of American Pictures. Janey didn't know much about Hollywood (yet), but she immediately sensed that Candi Clemens was one of the most important people in the room, and that her acknowledgment was quite an honor. And as she stood listening to Candi's description of the birthday party (it had a Japanese theme, complete with koi pond and sushi chef for the children), she was determined to make as much of the moment as possible.

"You see, Janey," Candi was saying, in a sharp, East Coast drawl, as if she were used to people hanging on her every word, "we had fifty children at the party, but everyone in Hollywood is rice free, so the children learn to eat sashimi before they can walk . . ."

Janey nodded wisely; she had no idea there were so many children in Holly-wood and imagined them running over the soundstages like little mice . . .

"And then we had a real geisha do the traditional Japanese tea," Candi contin-ued, with a glance at the man next to her. "But that was mostly for the husbands . . ."

Janey laughed at the joke, her voice pealing like a hundred tiny bells. Candi Clemens, who was about 5'6" and no more than 105 pounds, wasn't at all the sort of person Janey would have bothered with in New York. Her blond hair was cut into a precise bob just below her chin, and while it was apparent that she had certainly once been pretty, her looks had deteriorated into the vague attractiveness of a mid-dle-aged woman who knows she no longer needs to use them. In New York, Janey thought, Candi would probably have been one of those faceless Park Avenue women who is married to a banker and is on the parents' committee of her children's private school. But this wasn't New York, Janey reminded herself gleefully, and here, in Los Angeles, Candi Clemens ran a movie studio. Janey could see that people were a little bit afraid of her, and while she wasn't exactly sure what Candi *did* at American Pictures, she was already beginning to think the tag line "head of a movie studio" was the most glamorous-sounding job in the world . . .

And as Janey nodded, Candi launched into one of her favorite topics—the dangers of rice. Hollywood was an almost impossible place for women (although everyone seemed to think it was getting better), and one of her offensive maneuvers was to give business associates the deliberate impression that while she was capable of being an unadulterated bitch, she was, first and foremost, a mother concerned about her children. She was, indeed, concerned ("overly" would not be too strong a word to describe any aspect of Candi's personality), but she was equally interested in trying to wrest this Janey Wilcox project from Comstock Dibble. That morning, her assistant had run into her office with the news that Comstock had a screenplay by the Model Prostitute and was going to produce it, and Candi had immediately decided that she wanted it as well.

And so, as Candi went on about the horrors of refined carbohydrates on developing nervous systems, she was secretly assessing Janey Wilcox's character. She'd originally heard that Janey Wilcox was slated to be the Bimbo of the Year at the party, and under normal circumstances, she would never have bothered with her. To Candi, bimbos were like plankton—a necessary part of the food chain and little else—but Janey Wilcox wasn't your average beautiful airhead. For weeks, she'd been following Janey's story, wondering what kind of woman could survive such a public assault on her reputation. And now, glancing surreptitiously into Janey's eyes, Candi thought she saw the answer. Unlike Tanner Cole, who had perceived the sad eyes of a weary angel, Candi Clemens looked at Janey Wilcox and saw the perpetually turning wheels of ambition.

And she liked what she saw.

She would get Janey's project, she decided. But bringing the topic up now, at the *Vanity Fair* party, would be too easy, and besides, that wasn't the way one did business in Hollywood. The negotiations would have to be conducted with a sort of underhanded secrecy that could rival the CIA's, and so instead, Candi asked Janey if she had children.

Janey, of course, knew nothing of these maneuvers, but sensing that there was an opportunity afoot, she sighed regretfully. "I wish I did," she said mournfully. "I planned to, but then my husband . . ."

"Ah yes," Candi said sympathetically, remembering that Janey was married to Selden Rose. Sheila Rose, Selden's ex-wife, was one of her best friends, and suddenly, the fact of Janey's screenplay and the interconnections involved were simply too irresistible.

"You must come to my house for lunch on Sunday," Candi said firmly, as if there could be no doubt as to Janey's acceptance. "Just a little gathering—we do it every weekend. I'll have my assistant call you tomorrow with the address."

"I'd love to," Janey said, her eyes narrowing in canny delight at how she'd been in Los Angeles for less than twenty-four hours, but already the head of a movie studio had invited her to lunch. And to her house, no less, which was certainly several steps up from going to a restaurant . . .

But she barely had time to gloat, because as soon as Candi turned away (to greet Robert Redford), Rupert Jackson rushed up. He'd been watching and waiting for this moment, being well-versed enough in Hollywood politics to know that interrupting Candi Clemens would constitute a faux pas that might someday lose him a part.

But Rupert Jackson wasn't the only person who had been observing Janey. On the other side of the room, Comstock Dibble wiped the sweat from his face while pretending to be interested in the actor Russell Crowe's story about his lousy band in Australia. But out of the corner of his eye, he'd been secretly scrutinizing the exchange between Candi Clemens and Janey Wilcox, and he wasn't at all pleased. If Candi Clemens thought she could hone in on his new star, she was sorely mistaken. Janey Wilcox was his discovery, and he meant to keep her for himself. He wasn't yet sure what he intended to do with Janey (at some point, he would undoubtedly cut her out of the project), but in the meantime, he could keep her busy with enough pointless meetings to make her feel important, and if he had to put her up at a hotel, he would. And that, in itself, would be satisfying, especially as he'd be doing it with George Paxton's money . . .

And a few feet away, a tall, thin man resembling a dried vanilla bean took a glass of champagne from a proffered tray, and lifting the glass to his bloodless lips, observed Janey's progress as she crossed the room with Rupert Jackson. He noted that she was beautiful, but instead of seeing the shapely contour of a woman, he saw the more pleasing outline of a dollar sign. At forty-two years of age, Magwich Barone was the most powerful agent in Hollywood, as well known for his sexual escapades as for his ability to intimidate studio heads into giving his already undeserving (in his mind) clients even more money, and Janey Wilcox, he thought, was a perfect mark. She was already a star, and if he couldn't make money out of that, he should turn in his membership to the Agents Guild of America. He already saw her as a potential brand name . . . He might even start her off selling her own line of lingerie on QVC. But in the meantime, there was her project with Comstock Dibble, and he meant to insert himself right in the middle . . .

. . .

Two hours later, at about midnight, several long black limousines were snaking their way up Sunset Plaza Drive to Tanner Cole's mansion. In the back of one of these limousines sat the unlikely trio of Janey Wilcox, Jenny Cadine, and Magwich Barone.

Magwich popped open a bottle of champagne, and removing a small glass from a row set into a polished wooden rack, he looked at Jenny Cadine and asked, "Champagne, darling?"

"You know I don't drink," Jenny Cadine snapped, as if she couldn't believe Magwich wasn't acquainted with this information. She was seated next to Janey, and ever since Comstock Dibble had introduced them at the *Vanity Fair* party, she'd been fuming that this Janey Wilcox, who wasn't even a real actress, looked better than she did—especially as Jenny had been imagining that Janey Wilcox would be short, dark, and one of those feminist types who didn't shave her legs or armpits . . .

"Yeah, right," Magwich said, with a sarcastic grin, handing her the glass. "And you've never smoked a cigarette in your life, and," he said, rolling his eyes to the ceiling as if looking for the answer there, "you're only twenty-eight years old. Or have you decided to become twenty-nine now, just to throw off suspicion?"

"Magwich!" Jenny admonished him, taking the glass. She turned to Janey with a cozy familiarity and said, "Do you see what we have to put up with in Hollywood?"

"Oh yes," Janey said, with a calculating smile. "It must be awful for you." She sat back against the seat and looked from Jenny Cadine to Magwich Barone. A part of her could barely believe she was in a limousine going to an Academy Awards after-party with one of Hollywood's biggest agents and movie stars, but given the surreal nature of the entire evening, she wasn't really surprised. It was one of those rare nights when it seemed that anything (and everything) could happen, and she had decided to go with it, to see how far the ride would take her. Like so many of the people she'd met, Magwich and Jenny were as different from New Yorkers as aliens, but she'd been in foreign cultures before, and she was a quick study . . .

"Tell me, Janey Wilcox," Magwich said, passing her a glass of champagne. "Best-case scenario. If a genie jumped out of a bottle and was willing to grant you any job in Hollywood, what would it be? Think big, now. This is dream time. Wish fulfillment . . ."

Janey looked at him and nearly laughed. She had already discovered Magwich's propensity for speaking lines that sounded like they came out of a bizarre movie script. Despite his resemblance to a stick insect, he carried himself as if he were a combination of Cary Grant and Walter Matthau, and in the middle of the party, when Comstock was introducing her to Jenny Cadine (and that, in itself, was practically worth the price of her plane ticket, seeing Jenny Cadine sputtering in confusion as she realized that Janey Wilcox was the girl at Dingo's), Magwich Barone had suddenly materialized at her side. Raising his eyebrows at Comstock Dibble, like Comstock was a small boy about to do something naughty, he had turned to Janey, and practically making a bow, had said, "Magwich Barone, at your service." And before Janey could speak, Magwich had taken her arm and, leading her off, said, "I'm your new agent, by the way."

"Are you?" Janey had asked. Naturally, she had heard of the legendary Magwich Barone—a few years before, there was a big rumor that he had kept a well-known model locked in a closet for a day, letting her out only to have sex with him and to pee—and she wasn't at all sure that a man like that should be her agent. But she could already see that Hollywood was a place where a girl needed allies, and so she hadn't protested, especially when he'd said, "That Comstock Dibble is as wily as a coyote and more indestructible than a cockroach, and you're not to make another move until I've examined your contract." And when she told him that she didn't, technically, have a contract, he had snapped to attention like a rottweiler on the scent of a convict . . .

And then, it had seemed perfectly natural that he should accompany her to Tanner Cole's party, and that Jenny Cadine should come with them . . .

"Magwich," Jenny Cadine sighed in annoyance. "Janey already has a job. She's a feminist!"

Janey smiled at Magwich over the rim of her champagne glass, and Magwich answered her with a conspiratorial wink. Janey couldn't understand where Jenny Cadine had come up with this idea, and though she'd declared herself a feminist enough times to the various men who had dated her, she had a feeling that in Hollywood, "feminist" was a slightly dirty word. It was enough that behind their smiles, most of Hollywood probably still thought she was some kind of prostitute; she didn't need Jenny Cadine going around declaring her a feminist as well. Removing her compact from her bag and staring into it, she pursed her lips seductively. "Do you really want to know what my dream is?" she asked. And when Magwich nodded eagerly, she snapped the compact shut and stared at him boldly.

"I want to be just like Candi Clemens," she declared. "I won't be happy until I'm the head of my own movie studio . . ."

Magwich let out a low whistle. For a moment, he looked taken aback, but Janey wasn't concerned. Looking up at him through lowered lashes, she smiled. "If you're going to be my agent, darling, you need to understand what I'm really about," she said. She didn't care whether he believed her or not. After all, she'd told everyone in New York that she was going to be a producer, and even though they'd scoffed, look at where she was *now* . . .

Turning to glance out the window, she saw that the car was passing through a wooden gate at the top of a steep hill. On a bluff below, overlooking Los Angeles, stood a large Spanish-style house, with yellow stuccoed walls and a red-tiled roof. The car pulled up to the entrance and stopped.

The three passengers got out. Magwich slid his hand under Janey's arm. "You've got to remember one thing, Janey," he said smoothly. "I'm an agent. I never met an ambitious person I didn't like." He paused. "But for the moment, sweetheart," he said, giving her a meaningful look, "keep those thoughts to yourself. You'll find in this town, there are only two ways to get ahead—people think you're stupid, or they're scared of you. My plan is, we let them think you're stupid. Then we kill them."

Janey opened her mouth to protest, but suddenly thought better of it. She was the new girl in town, and she was determined not to blow it. At the very least, she would understand the rules before she broke them . . . "Of course, darling," she cooed.

Her acquiescence was rewarded with a squeeze from Magwich. "For tonight, sweetheart," he said, whispering in her ear, "all I want you to do is act like a star."

Now that she could do, she thought, entering the house. Wasn't that how she'd always thought of herself anyway, as a star?

The door was opened by a uniformed English butler, and passing through a green foyer with antlers on the walls, they entered a large living room. Along one wall, French doors opened onto a large tiled balcony; at the other end was a stone fireplace. The room was scattered with overstuffed leather couches and armchairs, but Janey hardly noticed the furnishings, because her eye was immediately drawn to Tanner Cole.

He was standing near the fireplace, resting his arm on the mantelpiece, and he had changed out of his tux into striped seersucker pants, which on anyone else would have looked stupid. On Tanner Cole, however, they created the impression of the classic American male—the guy who always wins all the prizes by birthright as opposed to effort—and somehow, compared to him every other man looked inferior. He had the kind of electric presence that draws every eye in the room, and all through the *Vanity Fair* party, Janey had found it impossible not to sneak looks at him. On several occasions throughout the night, she'd caught him staring at her, too, and judging from the hungry look in his eyes, she had decided that he couldn't be gay after all.

Once again, he looked up and spotted her, his eyes widening in recognition. But as he didn't make a move to approach her, she merely gave him the briefest of smiles. She could see that he was a man who liked to do things his own way, and so, for the moment, she would wait. She would let him come to her, and she was quite confident he would come . . .

And as she turned away, she nearly tripped over Craig Edgers.

He was slumped at the end of a long brown suede couch, his legs stuck out in front of him, staring morosely into a martini. Craig had been in Los Angeles for three days, but already he was beginning to understand that being a famous novelist in New York was quite a different matter from being one in LA. In New York, everyone seemed to know him—just the other day, a pretty young clerk at the bank had recognized him from the photograph on the back of his book, which was pretty amazing as that picture *was* ten years old—but in Los Angeles, he was invisible. A year ago, he wouldn't have minded, but six months of success had taught him to expect adulation, and in Los Angeles, he'd had none. Sure, people had "heard" of his book, and they'd "heard" it was great. But so far it seemed no one had actually read it, and that morning, in a meeting with a young executive at Fox Searchlight, the kid had actually had the temerity to suggest changing the main character to a twenty-five-year-old woman . . .

And now his old pal Tanner Cole was insisting he stay up for this party. He was becoming truly middle-aged, he thought; it was after midnight and he had the distinct feeling that it was way past his bedtime. But if he went to his room, Tanner would be disappointed—and tomorrow morning he would give Craig those mournful brown eyes and Craig would feel like a loser. Tanner Cole was unlike other men, Craig thought; he had an uncanny sensitivity that at first appeared to be put on, but that, after nearly twenty years of friendship, Craig was quite sure was real. He could change the atmosphere in the room with a mere look—if Tanner was happy, everyone felt that life was wonderful as well, whereas if he was morose, he could make you think you were in hell . . .

He raised his head, wanting to catch Tanner's eye, but instead he looked up and saw Janey Wilcox standing before him. The shock was so great, he nearly spilled his drink. It was like seeing someone who had returned from the dead, and judging from the expression on her face, she was equally surprised.

"Craig," she gasped. She couldn't imagine what he was doing at Tanner Cole's party, and she immediately recalled Selden's admonishment—that she had "ruined" Craig's life. Would he speak to her? she wondered, and before he had a chance to snub her, she sat down.

Craig *was* angry with Janey Wilcox, but while he told himself it was only because she'd messed up with his screenplay, the truth was he was miffed because she'd suddenly dropped out of his life. Sure, she had an excuse, but he still felt that she could have called him—indeed, she *should* have called him and explained the situation herself. In the past weeks, he had grown to hate her, thinking that she had tried to use him in some way (although he wasn't exactly sure how), and his resentment was that of a spurned lover, who can't understand why he has suddenly been dropped. During January and part of February, when she'd come to his apartment in the afternoons ostensibly to discuss his screenplay, he'd begun to believe that she was falling in love with him. It never crossed his mind that the possibility was unlikely; after all, she had told him again and again what a genius he was. The two of them, he thought, were like Arthur Miller and Marilyn Monroe . . .

Craig wasn't sophisticated enough to hide his feelings, and so, while he was secretly pleased that Janey had sat down next to him (if she had ignored him or passed on, his hatred would have been renewed afresh), he meant her to know that she had let him down.

"Hello, Janey," he said stiffly, taking a sip of his cocktail and staring fiercely into the middle distance.

"Craig," she said softly. She moved a little closer. "I'm so happy to see you." And she was, she realized suddenly. Hollywood was wonderful, but . . . "It's so nice to see a familiar face," she said aloud.

"Is it?" Craig asked petulantly. "You mean to say that all these people aren't your friends?"

As usual, Craig was no match for her. "Certainly not," Janey exclaimed. "I don't know *anyone* really . . . I just got here yesterday. And now I've come from the *Vanity Fair* party"—she couldn't resist slipping that in—"and, of course, everyone's really nice, but they're not like *us*, you know?"

Craig did know this all too well, and had to agree.

He took another sip of his drink. He felt himself beginning to fall under her spell again, but he didn't want to give in so easily. She had hurt him—she deserved to be punished. He thought about getting up, but the truth was, she was really the only person he knew as well, and he *wanted* to talk to her . . .

"You *could* have called," he said.

"I wanted to," she cried, indignant. And lowering her eyes she said, "But I couldn't. Selden . . ." She put her fingers to her lips, as if she were unsure if she should go on.

"Selden?" Craig asked. His tone was dismissive—in the weeks when he'd found himself smitten with Janey, he'd begun to imagine Selden as the enemy—he wasn't good enough for Janey, he'd decided; he had no sensitivity . . .

Janey took his tone as an opening. "I know you're one of Selden's best friends," she began, deliberately overstating the situation to gain Craig's sympathy, "and I probably shouldn't be telling you this. But for the past month, I was practically a prisoner in my own home—Selden wouldn't let me go out . . . He wouldn't even let me use the phone." She paused, judging the effect of her words, and pleased by the look of outrage on Craig's face, she went on: "I'm sure you've heard already, but Selden and I split up."

Craig hadn't heard, but the words were like music to his middle-aged ears. It wasn't, he thought, like he could do anything in particular about it (he was too afraid of Lorraine for that), but simply the *possibility* that revived him . . .

"That's too bad," he said smugly, not sorry at all.

"It is and it isn't," Janey said, with a shrug of her shoulders, indicating that life went on. "How long are you staying? I'll be here for at least a week," she said, thinking about the lunch at Candi Clemens's house. "We should get together . . ."

Craig had considered leaving the next day, but he reminded himself that he didn't have anything pressing in New York, and Tanner had told him to stay as long as he liked—a month if he felt like it. And why shouldn't he? he thought. It was fun being away from his wife, the weather was beautiful, and now that Janey was here . . .

"I might be around for a few days," he said, not wanting her to know that he had changed his mind in order to see her. "As long as Tanner doesn't kick me out . . ."

"Tanner?" Janey asked in surprise.

"Tanner Cole," Craig confirmed. And unable to prevent himself from taking the opportunity to impress her, he added: "I'm staying with him."

"Are you?" Janey said, trying not to appear too excited. But her mind was a whirlwind of possibilities . . . As Craig's "good friend" from New York, she'd have every excuse for coming around, and how much better it would be for Tanner Cole to see that she wasn't just some beautiful bimbo, but a woman who had weight, a woman who kept company with important intellectuals, like Craig Edgers . . . And now that she had Comstock Dibble in her back pocket (and, hopefully, Candi Clemens as well), there was no reason why she shouldn't revive their project. It would be the perfect pretext under which to see Craig, and if they met at Tanner's house, she was sure to run into him, and it would all appear perfectly innocent . . .

Glancing across the room at Tanner, she decided that the more she saw of him, the better she liked him. If she was going to have him, however, she would have him completely, and to do that, she mustn't give in too easily. She reached over and touched Craig's arm. "I know this is probably a sore subject," she began sympathetically, "but Comstock and I have worked out our differences, and he even says he's going to produce the screenplay I wrote." Craig looked confused at this information, but she decided to ignore his bewilderment, and quickly went on: "I'm going to see him this week, and I'd like to bring up the project again." She smiled mysteriously, and reminded of her brief conversation with Magwich, and his glee at the fact that she hadn't signed a contract, added, "I have some leverage over him. And if he's not interested," she continued, "I know the head of a big studio who might be."

She sat back on the couch, satisfied with her own hubris. It wasn't all entirely accurate, but instinct told her that this was the way one did business in Hollywood, and she was determined to succeed. But before Craig could congratulate her on her plan, Magwich appeared and handed her a drink.

"I thought you might be thirsty," he said, eyeing Craig with curiosity. Janey motioned for him to sit down. "This is Craig Edgers," she said smoothly. "Craig and I were just discussing a movie project we've been working on in New York . . ."

And suddenly, as if Janey Wilcox were both his guardian angel and his muse, Craig Edgers got lucky. Magwich Barone, who considered himself superior to Hollywood riffraff as well, was one of the few people who had actually read Craig's book in its entirety—all 532 pages. With the appropriate amount of awe in his voice that is so satisfying to an author, especially one like Craig Edgers, he gasped, "*The Embarrassments,* right?"

"That's correct," Craig said, obviously pleased.

Magwich leaned across Janey in his eagerness to talk to Craig. "Your portrayal of a middle-aged man in search of his inner youth was just devastating," he said. "I could barely leave my house for three days . . ."

Craig emitted an appreciative laugh as Janey sat back and smiled. Looking from one man to the other, she thought about how gratifying it was to put people together, bringing pleasure—and potentially business—to both parties. And if, in the meantime, the result was that they were both impressed with her for having such connections, that didn't hurt either . . .

She looked across the room, hoping to catch Tanner Cole's eye (and it wouldn't hurt if he saw her in the midst of such company, either), but instead, she was nearly taken aback by a startlingly familiar face. Standing by one of the French doors leading out onto the balcony was none other than Bill Westacott . . .

Bill! she thought. Bill was just the man she was longing to see, and now, as if in fulfillment of her earlier desire, he was here. Had he sensed that she'd been thinking about him? she wondered. And then, hearing her siren song, had he come running?

She looked from Magwich to Craig. Magwich was in the middle of comparing Craig's writing to that of the French author Flaubert, while Craig sat swilling his drink, nearly bursting the seams of his plaid flannel shirt with self-importance. They had all the signs of two inebriated men who think they've found a kindred spirit, and wouldn't miss her at all. "Excuse me," she murmured, and stood up.

Bill's eyes crinkled with amusement as he watched her make her way over to him. "Bill!" she cried with genuine delight.

"Hello, Wilcox," he said, leaning over to kiss her on the cheek. He turned his back to the room, shielding her body from the crowd, as if he wanted her all to himself.

"So I see that you've already taken over Hollywood," he said, taking a sip of his drink as his eyes bored into hers. "Magwich Barone seems pretty keen, and he doesn't give everyone the time of day . . ."

Bill sounded slightly envious, Janey noted—a sign that Magwich must be an agent worth having. "He says he wants to be my agent," Janey said coyly, remembering how much fun it was to bait Bill, "but I'm not sure. What do you think?"

But Bill only laughed. "Come on, Wilcox," he said. "You know me too well to try to get away with that trick. You've never taken advice from me or anyone else . . ."

"I told him," Janey said, with one of her conceited little whispers, "that I wanted to be the head of a movie studio someday . . ."

Bill laughed with glee. That must have really flummoxed old Magwich, he thought; he was probably guessing that Janey had no more ambition than being a game show host. "And what did he say?" Bill asked.

"He told me that I should act dumb at first," Janey said, frowning. "But really, I'm not sure I can . . ."

She was already getting the act down, Bill thought, and then realized this wasn't entirely accurate. She had always had the act, he thought; the problem was she'd lacked the stage on which to play it . . .

Until now.

"Janey," he said, unable to suppress a grin. "I'm sure you can do anything you want, including play dumb . . . By the way," he said, casually changing the subject. "How's the screenplay? I heard Comstock Dibble's going to produce it. Did you finish it after all?"

"Oh God!" she exclaimed, feigning displeasure. "Does everybody in Hollywood know about it?" She wriggled uncomfortably, and Bill was suddenly reminded of those languid afternoons they'd spent on the beach two and three summers ago, making love. She was so beautiful then, and so full of life (and misperceptions, of course, which at the time had driven him nuts), he had genuinely been crazy about her. What a fool he was for letting her go, he thought. He should have divorced his wife and married her, for back then, he'd known that she was in love with him, too . . .

"Okay, Bill," she said, sighing in resignation. She sounded slightly annoyed, but he saw that there was a mischievous glint in her eyes. "You were right." And when he raised his eyebrows at her, she bit her lip. "I didn't exactly finish the screenplay," she continued with an impish shrug. She leaned closer, to whisper in his ear. "I only wrote thirty-three pages. But the crazy thing is that it doesn't seem to matter. Everyone thinks I wrote a screenplay. And now I'm not sure what to do . . ."

"You'll figure it out," he said hoarsely, taking a step back to stare into her eyes.

The sight nearly broke his heart. Maybe it was all the trouble she'd had, but suddenly, he saw that she had grown. She was a woman now . . .

He had to turn away.

As he did so, however, he saw Tanner Cole's eyes sweep the room in search of her, and out of the corner of his eye, he spied her answering gaze . . .

And suddenly he knew their conversation was over.

"Oh Bill," she said. She reached out and touched his face, and he leaned his head into her palm, holding her eyes with his. In that instant, all their knowledge of each other—all their rivalries and resentments, their desires and aspirations—seemed to pass silently between them, and all was forgiven.

And at last, as if finally allowing herself to bask in the glory of the evening, she said, "Isn't it wonderful?"

She moved away, slipping out the French doors and onto the balcony. He had seen her do this trick a dozen times at parties, separating herself from the crowd in order to attract a man. At one time, he might have made fun of her, he thought, but he suddenly found he no longer had the desire to fault her.

He turned back and looked around the room. The crowd—movie stars and producers, screenwriters and agents, with a couple of makeup artists and personal trainers thrown in for good measure—had reached that frenzied moment when everyone knows the party will end soon and they have yet to accomplish what they came for. Hollywood, Bill thought sardonically, was American enterprise at its best—at its greediest and most ambitious, at its pettiest and most unkind. But that wasn't entirely true, he corrected himself. For there was legitimate talent—brilliance even—and the real reason why Hollywood still existed, why it kept grinding away, was that underneath the glitter was a genuine desire to do good. No one really set out to make a bad movie or a bad TV show; most people, he thought, longed only to be great. And if they didn't always succeed, if they fell short of the mark, wasn't that simply the penalty for being human? And as he glanced over his shoulder, watching Janey as she made her way out to the balcony to stand alone, he was filled with both fear for her and pride—pride in the way that she'd picked herself up and had taken a few baby steps to get ahead. She could be ridiculously stupid, he thought, but like most people, her only real flaw was being her own worst enemy. A trait that, he reminded himself, he might be accused of having . . .

And for a second, he thought about following her.

But then he stopped himself. Let her be, he thought. Let her enjoy the moment. Her success that evening was big, but it was a Hollywood success—sudden, magical, and overwhelming—designed to eventually destroy the soul of the unsuspecting recipient. In the future, there would be plenty of time for disappointments, for the discovery that you'd been betrayed, for the sinking realization that while one day you were "hot," the next day you were frozen, and no one would take your phone calls . . .

And out of the corner of his eye, he saw Tanner Cole heading out to the balcony. He wasn't going to compete with a movie star, he thought wryly. Not now, anyway. Janey had a new journey now, and one, he thought with sudden relief, that didn't include him. And as Tanner Cole passed by, he felt like saying, "Good luck, man . . ."

But naturally, he kept these thoughts to himself. And as he glanced back at Janey, poised on the balcony, he had a feeling that Hollywood would soon discover she couldn't be broken so easily. She seemed to have a spirit and hope in her that just wouldn't die . . .

And standing with one hand on the railing, Janey arranged her body in a three-quarter position, facing the panorama of lights below. She closed her eyes, breathing in the scented night air, knowing that she was creating the image of a lovely young woman who was lost in thought . . .

But this time, she really was lost in thought, she realized. She belonged here . . . Everything about the evening told her that she'd finally found her place. And opening her eyes to take in the view, she suddenly gasped and took a step back in joy. From her vantage point high in the Hollywood hills, the twinkling lights of Los Angeles lay spread out beneath her like a golden carpet, welcoming her.